Frances Anne Bond was born, brought up and still lives in Scarborough, North Yorkshire. She has worked in shops, as secretary to a headmaster in a private preparatory school and in the social services. She is married and has two grown-up daughters. She has been writing since she was a child, and has previously had articles and sho[illegible]ries published. Her four earlier novels ar[illegible] *[illegible]arks*, *Darling Lady*, *Return of th[illegible]* [illegible] *[illegible]nce Without Music*.

Also by Frances Anne Bond

Catching Larks
Darling Lady
Return of the Swallow
Dance Without Music

A Different Tune

Frances Anne Bond

KNIGHT

First published in 1994
by HEADLINE BOOK PUBLISHING PLC

First published in paperback in 1995
by HEADLINE BOOK PUBLISHING PLC

This edition published 2000 by
Knight an imprint of Caxton Publishing Group

10 9 8 7 6 5 4 3 2 1

ISBN 1 84067 250 1

Typeset by
Letterpart Limited, Reigate, Surrey

Printed and bound in Great Britain by
J. H. Haynes & Co. Ltd., Sparkford, Somerset

Caxton Publishing Group
20 Bloomsbury Street
London
WC1B 3QA

This book is dedicated to the memory of
John Callender Bond

'Dream a little dream of me.'

AUTHOR'S NOTE

About a year ago I chanced upon a book entitled *A Candle On The Hill: Images of Camphill Life*. In words and photographs it told the story of the Camphill Movement which was started in Scotland in 1939 by a man called Karl König.

Nowadays, the Camphill Movement has grown: seventy-two centres spread over four continents. The establishments vary according to the needs of the region but the underlying message incorporated in all the different schools, homes and villages is a message of love for one's fellow man. The communities are made up of the able-bodied and other people with varying degrees of physical and mental handicaps. Together they work and play, teaching each other and learning from each other.

I was thinking of the Camphill Movement when I created my fictional Greenwater Village.

I hope if any of you come across a copy of *A Candle On The Hill* you will spare the time to read it. I found the effort well worthwhile.

F.A. Bond

Chapter One

It was going to be a good day, Rosie just knew it. The morning had started so well. Her freshly washed hair was behaving itself, the radio was playing her favourite tune and now, after a week of rain, a pallid sun was brightening the grey November sky. She gave a decisive little nod as she took down a box of eggs from the kitchen cupboard. She must nurture the warm happy feeling inside her. It would help her when she presented herself for the interview. She paused in the task of preparing breakfast to anticipate her thrill of expectation. She wanted this job so much.

Only job wasn't the right word. During the last eight years she had worked in a laundry, as a shop assistant and as a waitress. They had been jobs. Nothing wrong with them, of course. In fact, she was proud of the way she had earned money after Howard's sudden death. Not once had she drawn dole, but today she was setting her sights higher. Today she was hoping to be appointed to a post that carried certain responsibilities. If she was successful, she would be working full-time, making decisions that affected other people and, at the end of the month, she would receive a salary, paid into a bank account.

She hummed along with the radio as she cracked one of the eggs into a saucepan of boiling water and then she glanced across at her son who was sitting by the kitchen table.

'No more cooked breakfasts, Mum,' he had said. 'I'm getting fat.'

Silly lad. There wasn't an ounce of spare fat on him. She studied his broad shoulders, his tall frame. It was probably Jill's idea that he should watch his weight. Jill was very weight conscious.

When Jill came round to the house to have a meal with them, Rosie always tried to tempt her appetite by cooking something especially nice, but Jill never ate much. None of the young women nowadays seemed to enjoy their food. Rosie sighed and went back to watching the egg. In her humble opinion the whole lot of them would look bonnier with a bit more meat on their bones. Cuddling Jill must be like cuddling a coat-hanger.

When Rosie had been twenty-one years old she had been a size fourteen and she'd collected plenty of whistles as she walked down the street. She had enjoyed the admiration but had never encouraged any of the young men. She had already been married for two years. Howard had been the only man for her.

Her wedding dress had been a size twelve though. Lovely it had been, midi-length with a tiny bolero jacket with long sleeves that came down to a point over her wrists. No one would have dreamed it was second-hand. She had bought it through the ads in the evening paper for twenty-five pounds.

Oh, she and Howard had been happy, a couple of kids. It was happiness and contentment that had made her gain weight. Mind, after Paula's birth she had gone up to a size sixteen. That had been too much, but the weight had dropped off again after Steve's arrival.

Buttering toast and thinking of her two children, Rosie

couldn't believe how the years had flown. It seemed only yesterday that Steve and Paula had been small. She glanced again at her son. He used to sit on that self-same chair when he was a schoolboy, chuckling his head off at the daft antics of the the cartoon characters in the *Beano*. Now he was six foot tall and studying the business section of the daily newspaper and his face was serious.

Her inward glow of cheerful optimism dimmed. Steve had become a lot more serious lately. Of course, his father's unexpected death had changed him. He had just celebrated his twelfth birthday two weeks before that dreadful day, and overnight, it seemed, he changed from being a child into an adolescent, terribly conscious that he was now the only man in the house. But beneath all the grief, bravely concealed at the time, he had still retained his boyish sense of humour and she had rejoiced when once again his laughter had rung out.

But recently he had been acting like a man in his late-thirties rather than a young man of twenty-one. She stifled a sigh. Of course, he was engaged now. He had the future to think about. He had responsibilities.

Staring down into the saucepan, she saw the egg white had solidified around the yolk, so she took down the plate which was warming on top of the over grill and slid the poached egg from the pan on to the slice of thick, buttered toast. She carried the plate over to Steve.

'Here you are. Eat it while it's hot.'

'Thanks, Mum.' He put down his newspaper and picked up his knife and fork, raising his eyebrows at her. 'It's still a cooked breakfast, you know.'

'Oh, get it down you. You'll only be having a sandwich for lunch.'

She poured herself a cup of tea and sat down. As she buttered a piece of toast for herself she thought, If I get the job, things will have to change. For a start, Steve will have to get his own breakfast. She picked up her teacup in both hands and took a sip of tea.

There would be no problem. Steve was capable of looking after himself. When she worked night shifts he often saw to household tasks. He put clothes in the washer, got his own tea and ironed his own shirts, although he never ironed them as well as she did. And he was always telling her she spoilt him. She did, too. She admitted it. She enjoyed looking after her son. It gave her pleasure. People didn't seem to understand that any more. The sheer pleasure of looking after people, because you loved them.

She still wasn't sure that Jill, Steve's fiancee, understood that, although she had once tried to explain to her. Jill had strong views of modern marriage.

'When husband and wife both work full-time, it's only fair they should share all the housework. Steve thinks that, too.'

Rosie had no quarrel with that opinion, but perhaps Jill thought she had, because her voice had sounded strident suddenly, and her cheeks had flushed. Both the stridency and the flushed cheeks had saddened Rosie.

'Yes, of course, Jill. I wouldn't have expected anything else. You'll find Steve is quite handy around the house.' She had hesitated, unsure how to proceed. 'But, you see, my generation were brought up with different ideas and it's hard to break the habits of a lifetime.'

She had smiled into Jill's tense face. 'As soon as I became pregnant with Paula I left work and became a full-time wife and mother. And I was fully occupied, believe me. In those days there were no automatic washing machines, or if there were, no one I knew had one. Howard got me a second-hand twin-tub after Steve's birth and I thought it was wonderful.'

She laughed. 'And there were hardly any convenience foods and no disposable nappies. Why, I remember, every Friday afternoon I baked my own bread. Can you believe that?'

Jill may have believed but she hadn't approved.

'Well, all I can say is, thank goodness things have changed. Who wants to be tied to the home all day?'

Rosie had wanted to reply, 'I did.' But of course, she didn't. That's another thing that had altered in recent years. Young people didn't take criticism from their elders any more. Sometimes Rosie felt her generation had had a raw deal. They had been brought up to respect and obey their elders, but just at the time they were becoming elders themselves, they were considered out-of-date and their views of little consequence.

Actually, the first ten years of her marriage, staying at home and being a housewife, had been the happiest time of her life. She had loved being indoors on a cold, rainy day, loved playing with her toddlers, loved listening to *Woman's Hour* on the radio and savouring the smell of freshly ironed clothes as she busied herself with household tasks when Paula and Steve had their afternoon nap.

She had loved it when Howard came home from work, cold and tired, and she saw his face light up at the warmth of the house and the sight of her and the little ones – they were always freshly bathed and ready for bed when he came in. He would kiss and cuddle them for a little while while she dished up the meal and then she would put them down to sleep and the two of them would sit down in front of the leaping flames of a coal fire and eat their meal.

In winter, she cooked a lot of casseroles, Howard enjoyed those. Nowadays, the young couples she knew seemed to live on Marks and Spencers ready-to-serve meals, if they could afford them, or take-away pizzas if they could not. Rosie shook her head. The way things changed, she didn't envy the young. Things had been natural and simple in her days. Your man went out and worked for the family and your job was to provide a happy home for him to come back to.

Some of the young women she saw in the High Street now, they were smartly dressed and carried briefcases, but you could tell from their faces they were tired out. Poor lasses. It was all right talking about sharing domestic tasks, but she bet most of the husbands didn't do their share of cleaning or tackled the nasty jobs, like cleaning the toilet.

Still, she mustn't be old-fashioned. Times changed, they always did. What was the phrase she had read in a magazine last week? 'Personal fulfilment', that was it. A buzz phrase, they called it. Well, mustn't smile, because although she was a widow with two grown-up children, that's what she was aiming for, personal fulfilment. If she was lucky today, she'd be a career woman. She set down her teacup with a bang.

'You're quiet this morning.' Steve's grin was cheeky. 'Things on your mind?'

'What do you think?' She reached across the kitchen table and picked up the newspaper.

He studied her face. 'Don't tell me. Let me guess.'

Rosie hunched her shoulders, a defensive gesture. 'I always read my horoscope. And today of all days . . .'

'Oh, Mum.' Steve ran his fingers through his thick fair hair.

'Horoscopes are useless. Think for a minute. Hundreds of thousands of other Sagittarians will be reading the same rubbish you're looking at now. How can the same prediction apply to everyone?'

'I know that.' Rosie found her star sign and pored over

it. 'But it shows general trends. It tells you whether the day will be good or bad.'

Stephen sighed. 'Go on, then. Read it out.'

Rosie frowned. 'It's a bit ambiguous.'

Avoiding his sceptical gaze, she read: ' "There is no doubting your professional drive today but do not expect a dramatic breakthrough. Some skilful juggling is required to keep on top of all the demands made on you." ' She pulled a face. 'Not too promising.'

'Ignore it. From what you said, you don't need the stars on your side. Your Officer in Charge is backing your application, isn't she? And you know you're popular with the residents. Surely that will count for something?'

Rosie shrugged. 'I hope so. But two people from the personnel department are conducting the interview. Mrs Horton is merely sitting in. And there's four of us on the short list.'

'I've every faith in you, Mum.' Steve glanced at his watch. 'I'll have to dash.' He came round the table and hugged her. 'What time's the interview?'

'Two o'clock.'

'I'll cross my fingers.' At the door, he paused. 'Does Paula know you've applied?'

Rosie looked down at her plate. 'No. When I get it, *if* I get it, I'll tell her then.'

'She hasn't been in touch, since that call last week?'

'No. I tried to ring her on Monday, but she wasn't in.'

Steve hesitated. 'Try not to worry.'

'I'm not worrying.' She gave a valiant smile.

He sighed. 'See you tonight then.'

Five minutes later, she heard the sound of his car driving away.

She stood up and carried the breakfast pots to the sink. As she washed them she tried to put her son and daughter's affairs out of her mind. Today was about *her*. She finished the pots, hung up the tea-towel and glanced out of the window. The sun was still shining but there were clouds massing in the sky. November weather could be changeable, particularly in this part of Yorkshire. She'd better take an umbrella with her. She wanted her hair to stay tidy for the interview.

She went upstairs to decide what to wear and as she did so, she tried to coax back to life the little glow of confidence she had felt earlier. She wished now that she had not read her horoscope after all.

Damn Stella Starshine and her predictions. What did she know?

Walking up the driveway to The Firs, Rosie saw Mr Dowsland sitting inside the porticoed entrance to the home. He wasn't wearing his overcoat. Rosie shook her head. She liked Mr Dowsland and she had a few moments to spare. She came to a halt in front of him.

'A better day, isn't it, Mr Dowsland? A bit cold, though. Shall I fetch your overcoat for you?'

The old man folded his hands across the ebony handle of his walking stick.

'Don't fuss me, young woman. I'll be going back into the sitting room soon. I just wanted a rest from Ida Greenhall. My goodness, that woman gets worse by the day. Her tongue's loose at both ends, I reckon.'

Rosie laughed. 'She's a nice lady and she's fond of you.'

'Aye, that's the trouble.' Mr Dowsland scowled and then studied Rosie's appearance. 'You're looking very nice. You've got make-up on, haven't you? You should use it more often. My goodness, if I were a younger man . . .' He stopped talking and his thin shoulders shivered.

'I couldn't cope with you if you were any younger.' Rosie put her hand under his elbow and helped him lever himself from the bench. 'Come on, I'll help you back to the sitting room.' She winked at him. 'I won't sit you next to Mrs Greenhall.'

She settled him in his favourite chair near the bay window and then slipped away quickly, before any of the old people could ask her what she was doing at The Firs. The residents were quick to pick up on any change of routine.

There were fifty old people living there and their ages ranged between late sixties and mid-nineties. The oldest resident was Miss Henchard and she was over a hundred. Although some of the older people were physically and mentally frail, many of them had minds as sharp as needles. Because, by necessity, they spent most of their lives indoors, they liked nothing better than to pounce on any item of interest in the lives of members of staff.

Their curiosity was usually of a kindly nature. Rosie remembered how they had bought and signed a congratulations card for Cook when her son had been awarded a place at university and how much they had sympathised with Joan Ackers when her daughter had given birth to a stillborn child.

And today Mr Dowsland had noticed she was wearing make-up. Rosie touched her cheek. Perhaps she'd overdone it? She'd better check. Running up the shallow-stepped staircase which led to the first floor of the building, she hurried into the empty staff room. There, she examined her face in a mirror. Was there too much blusher on her left cheek? Perhaps not, but just in case, she took a tissue from her pocket and rubbed first her left cheek and then her right. She was hopeless at applying make-up. If Paula had been at home, she would have done it for her.

Paula was a dab hand at arranging hair, putting on make-up, knowing what clothes to wear. Paula was a dab hand at everything.

The thought of her daughter stilled Rosie's hand and she gazed at her own reflection for a moment, unseeing. Then her eyes blinked and her head came up. Oh, for goodness' sakes, forget about Paula. The telephone call last week was nothing. Everything would be sorted out by now. Paula was like that. One minute everything was in crisis, the next minute life was wonderful. Anyway, things must be all right because she hadn't rung back. When there was no word from her daughter, Rosie knew everything was all right. Whenever she rang home, she was in trouble.

The funny thing was, when Paula did telephone, she never said anything important. She would ask after her mother and Steve, she would relate some story about Alison, her little daughter, but she never mentioned what was worrying her. And Rosie would listen for a certain flat note in her daughter's voice and when she heard it, the alarm bells would start ringing. Then she would enquire carefully about Paula herself.

'Are you all right, love?'

'Oh, yes. Everything's fine.'

And Paula would ring off, and that night Rosie would be unable to sleep. After two or three days she would ring Manchester and when she heard Paula's bubbly voice on the other end of the phone: 'I can't stop and talk, Mum. I'm taking Alison to nursery. Was it anything important?' she knew she could relax. 'No, love. Just wanted to hear your voice.'

But she had rung Paula twice this time and she hadn't been able to reach her.

Think about the job! Think about Mrs Horton's advice. Rosie straightened her back and went for her interview.

★ ★ ★

She thought she had done well, at first. The two men were polite and smiling and soon put her at her ease. As she answered their questions, mostly about the care of the residents, her confidence rose, particularly when she saw Mrs Horton begin to smile. But then the interviewers followed a different line of enquiry.

'Suppose you're in charge one night, Mrs Scott, and the fire alarm goes off. There are fifty residents in your care. What would you do?'

She gaped at the man asking the question. He was tall, slim and balding. His face held a kindly expression but his eyes were sharp and he was watching her closely.

'I'd . . . I'd contact the rest of the staff on duty immediately and evacuate the residents as quickly as possible.'

'I see. But what instructions would you give the staff? Would you tell them to concentrate on the stronger, more alert clients, or would you ask them to concentrate on helping the frail and confused out of the building first?'

'I . . .' She hesitated, too long.

The questioner made a note on his pad and consulted his notes.

'I see that on several occasions you have agreed to alter your hours regarding night cover, usually to help other members of staff. Is that right?'

'Yes. I'm a widow, my children are grown-up and I don't mind sleeping in. It's more difficult for the younger women working here. The ones with young children.'

The other man spoke. 'On checking the duty reports, it appears that rarely do you call for assistance during the night shifts. You must be extremely competent at managing on your own?'

Rosie flushed. 'I can usually cope. It seems a shame to wake someone, unless it's absolutely necessary.'

'A commendable attitude but,' the man steepled his fingers together, 'an attitude that could create problems.'

Her brow creased. 'I'm sorry, I don't follow you.'

The man looked at her solemnly. 'Say you go to attend an old gentleman who has fallen out of bed. He's a big, heavily-built man. You would do your best to get him back into bed again and reassure him. Is that right?'

Rosie considered. 'Yes.'

The man shook his head. 'Then I'm afraid you would be contravening the rules, Mrs Scott. The guidelines clearly state *two* members of staff should assist in lifting a resident from the floor.'

He must have seen Rosie's eyebrows draw together in a frown because he paused for a moment, then continued. 'I know rules are broken and I know why, but rules make sense, Mrs Scott. They should be followed.

'Lifting heavy weights on your own can easily lead to injuries. Having to be on sick leave for a considerable amount of time would be of no help to yourself or to the residents of this home. But there are other negative factors in trying to do everything yourself.

'Presumably it would take time to settle the old gentleman down again. And while you are busy with him, what about the other residents? Perhaps another light is flashing, perhaps more than one.'

He shrugged. 'Usually nothing too important. Someone has had a bad dream, perhaps, or someone needs help to get to a toilet. But suppose it's a real emergency, something that couldn't wait?' He studied her reddening face and his voice softened. 'We do appreciate your motives for not disturbing the Officer in Charge, but one must always think of the wider issues involved.' He wrote something down in his notebook.

She knew then that she had failed. A few more questions

and then the interview was over. In the reception lounge she sat and drank coffee with the other applicants. She tried hard to conceal her feelings and listened with rapt attention to the conversation, but secretly she was watching the other faces and wondering who would be successful, who would be her immediate superior.

Forty-five minutes later, the four candidates were summoned, one by one, to face the appointment panel again. Rosie went in first.

'We were impressed by the knowledge and understanding you show in respect of caring for the elderly, Mrs Scott. Mrs Horton provided you with a magnificant reference, but I am afraid, on this occasion, you have been unsuccessful.'

Rosie's face must have mirrored her disappointment, for the tall man hesitated.

'You're doing a marvellous job at the moment, you know. Good care assistants are the backbone of the community's health care programme for the elderly. Without people like you, the service would grind to a halt.

'But an Officer in Charge needs a wide variety of skills. You must know, from working at The Firs, that officers must attend meetings where the physiological problems of the residents are discussed. They must be prepared to deliver reasoned and informed input.

'Then there are quota forms to deal with, staff rotas to draw up, and all kinds of supervisory tasks.' He tapped his pencil on the blotter. 'You are also a popular member of the workforce here, Mrs Scott. That's good. But it's a sad fact that when a popular member of staff is suddenly promoted to a position where they have oversight of their former friends, then that very popularity can work against them.' He stopped speaking and waited for Rosie to reply but, for the life of her, she couldn't.

The disappointment she felt was tangible. A voice inside her taunted her. What did you expect, Rosemary? Surely, you didn't really think you could cope? The lump in her throat prevented speech. She nodded and stood up. Mrs Horton, regret showing clearly on her face, also stood up. She came round the desk and went to open the door for Rosie.

Upstairs, in the staff washroom, the tears came. Deep down, she had felt she had a chance. Mrs Horton had wanted her, and she ran the place. And, despite what that man had said, the other care assistants had encouraged her. They had all believed she would be successful. The other assistants . . . Rosie splashed her face with cold water and combed her hair. Her friends must not see how upset she was.

She left The Firs by a back door and went into town to do some shopping. She didn't feel like returning to an empty house. After buying groceries, she treated herself to a coffee. When she did finally catch her bus home it was almost dark. A cold, dark November evening, in tune with her mood. As she walked towards her home, she saw Steve's car parked outside. It was after five, she realised. She quickened her step only to slow down again. Steve would be waiting to hear how she got on.

She opened the front door and walked through into the kitchen. Steve was filling the kettle at the sink. He turned towards her and his face looked stern and remote. He didn't mention the job. Instead he said, 'Paula's here, Mum. With Alison. They arrived ten minutes ago.'

'Oh.' Rosie looked around. 'Where are they now?'

'In the bathroom. Alison looked tired out, poor kid, probably the train journey. Paula said she would bath her and put her straight to bed.'

Rosie slipped off her coat. 'Did Paula mention Dave?'

She bit her lip. 'It looks as though they're still battling. Perhaps she's come to spend a few days with us in order to bring him to his senses?'

'No.' Steve was spooning tea into the teapot. He did not look at his mother. 'I think things have gone too far this time.'

'Oh, Lord.' She slung her coat over the back of a kitchen chair. 'Mind you, I'm not surprised. I know she's been besotted with Dave for a long time, but eventually she's faced the truth. She's left him, hasn't she?'

'Not exactly.' Face expressionless, Steve put the tea caddy back in the cupboard. 'I gather he's left her.'

Chapter Two

'May I come in?' Rosie tapped on the door, opened it and squeezed into the small bathroom which was steamy warm and fragrant with the smell of her favourite moisturising bath lotion.

Her glance fell first upon her granddaughter. Alison was sitting in the bath scooping up handfuls of foam and spreading it, with fierce concentration, upon the tummy of a pink plastic doll. The doll's blue-painted eyes stared upwards towards the ceiling and its plump celluloid limbs floated aimlessly on the surface of the water. It looked, Rosie suppressed a shudder, like a tiny drowned baby. She put the thought from her and shaped her lips into a welcoming smile.

'Hello, darling. How's my favourite girl?'

Alison looked up, and for a brief moment her expression was wary, then her brow cleared and pleasure flooded her face. She lifted the doll from the bathwater, held it by one leg and presented it for inspection. 'Look, Granny, my baby.'

'She's lovely, and very clean.' Rosie reached out her hand and caressed her granddaughter's fine, damp hair. 'Just like you.'

'She's not finished yet.' Paula was kneeling down by the side of the bath, a bottle of shampoo in her hand. 'Her hair needs washing.' Unscrewing the top of the bottle, she commanded, 'Stop wriggling about, Alison, and put your head back.'

Rosie looked down. Paula's thick hair, which she was presently wearing in a chin-length bob, had fallen forward, veiling her face, but Rosie knew a little of what she was feeling. The tone of her voice and the screwed-up tension of her body betrayed her.

'Paula,' she said, 'I . . .'

'No, no, no!' A surge of water slopped over the rim of the bath as Alison threw her doll from her and began to scream. 'No hair wash, no hair wash.' Fat tears squeezed from her large brown eyes and she held up her arms imploringly towards Rosie. 'Out, Granny. Out.'

Rosie bit her lip. Alison's delicate pointed face was rosy from the heat of the bath water but her grandmother saw the dark smudges beneath her eyes and heard the quaver in her voice. She wavered.

'Do you have to wash her hair tonight, Paula? She does look tired. Won't it wait until tomorrow?'

Totally ignoring her mother, Paula put one hand beneath Alison's chin and tilted her head backwards. Ignoring Alison's wails, she poured a spot of shampoo on to her hair. 'Keep still or it will go into your eyes.' She massaged the lotion into a lather and it wasn't until she was ready to rinse her daughter's hair and when Alison's wails had subsided into sobs that she replied. 'This young miss has got far too full of herself lately, Mum, and I'm not having it. She's forever stamping her feet and refusing to behave. I swore I'd never have a spoilt kid and I'm making damn' sure she's not going to become one.'

'Oh, Paula, she's not spoilt, she's growing up, that's all. Remember the old saying, "the terrible twos"? Children do play up at her age. It's natural. They test you out. And, you know . . .' Rosie was staring down at her kneeling daughter, wishing she could see her face '. . . if things are bad between you and Dave, it's bound to have an effect on Alison.'

At the mention of her husband's name, Paula finally looked up.

Pretty children often grow up to be plain adults. Paula had been a pretty child but in her case, growing up she had simply grown more beautiful. Staring down at her, Rosie felt a constricting pain in her chest. Friends often told her that Paula had inherited her looks, but she knew that was untrue. There was a superficial resemblance between mother and daughter, but that was all.

In her youth, Rosie had been what was then called a handsome lass. She had a shapely figure, blue eyes, dark, glossy hair and a fine high colour. Her mouth was generous, her chin square and, when she smiled, which was often, a dimple showed in her right cheek.

Paula was five feet four, exactly the same height as Rosie, but she was slightly built with fine bones. Apart from the height, the only other thing she had inherited from her mother was her thick, dark hair; otherwise she was the image of her grandmother. She had Minna's fine delicacy of features and her heart-shaped face. Her dark brown eyes her father had given her, and her complexion was her own, peaches and cream.

Once Paula had attained her mother's height and when they stood next to each other, Rosie had always felt over-blown and florid, like a gipsy standing next to a princess, but she had been proud of her child.

And it had always been like that, even through Paula's teenage years, when she had experimented with bizarre make-up, cropped her hair and coloured it red or green; when she had walked about in ripped jeans and clumpy boots, she had still looked like a princess. But she didn't look like one now.

The soft dark wings of her hair had fallen back to reveal a huge, ugly bruise spreading across the right side of her face. Her nose was swollen, her right eye was partly closed and her lip was split.

Rosie's hand flew to her mouth. 'Oh, my God!' she gasped. 'Paula, what happened?' But she knew, and bile filled her mouth at the thought of her son-in-law.

And Paula wasn't about to confide in her. She merely pulled her hair forward to hide her damaged cheek and said, 'Get me another towel, would you, Mum? This one's wet. Steve must have used it.'

Her message was clear and Rosie, her cheeks flushing, understood.

'Yes, of course.' She left the bathroom and blundered her way to the airing cupboard on the landing. Her heart was thumping. Dave and Paula argued, she knew that. But for him to hit Paula, and with his fist by the look of it, that was unbelievable.

With trembling fingers she took down a large soft bath towel and buried her face in it. Her daughter's marriage had always confused her. On the few occasions she had visited the couple, she had never felt comfortable in their company, particularly during the first year, because their marriage was altogether too public.

Even from the very beginning it was as if they delighted in tormenting each other. There would be sly little digs, disparaging remarks, and they were both as bad as each other. Paula had a better job than Dave, a job she enjoyed, and seeing the couple together, Rosie thought that Dave resented the fact. He would sulk when she worked late or, alternatively, be over-solicitous to her when she came home.

'You look worn-out. You'd better have an early night. And tell your boss to go to hell next time he puts on you. My wife's not turning into a drudge to make more money for that fat bastard.'

And Paula, who had returned home happy and lively, would turn to the mirror and examine her face anxiously. 'I look all right, don't I, Mum?'

But at other times, it was Paula's turn to provoke Dave. Over their meal, she would laugh and mention some man she worked with at the office. She would say how often he stopped by her desk, how he made excuses to talk to her and how he had recently bought himself a new BMW and suggested he should take her out for lunch one day.

She would chatter away so innocently and Rosie would shift uncomfortably in her seat, listen to her little drops of poison, and watch Dave's face, waiting for him to explode. And, of course, inevitably, he did.

And then all hell would be let loose. They would scream and yell at each other. Paula would throw things and then dissolve into tears and Dave would slam from the flat and go and get drunk. But when he came home again, they would make up. They always made up.

They rowed and made up again after Dave wrecked their old Ford Escort and was done for drink-driving and when Paula stayed out all night after an office party. She said she had drunk too much and stayed with a girlfriend and Rosie, who was staying that weekend, believed her. Paula was wild and she enjoyed flirting, but after meeting Dave she had never looked at another man seriously.

But it was all too much for Rosie and she stopped travelling through to Manchester to visit her daughter. If Paula wanted to see her and Steve, it was better she came through to see them. It wasn't so much the quarrelling, Rosie uncomfortably acknowledged, it was the aftermath; for when Paula and Dave made up, they behaved as though there was only the two of them in the whole wide world. They would smile into each other's eyes, laugh at secret jokes, and they couldn't keep their hands off each other.

Rosie was no prude and during her married life she and Howard had enjoyed a healthy sex life but their loving had been conducted in private. It was never a show, for other people's entertainment. Not that she thought her daughter and her husband were deliberately putting on an act, it was just that half the time they didn't seem aware of her presence. And so she was always relieved when it was time for her to pack her bag and catch the train home.

She had been terribly worried when Paula had told her she was pregnant. She had pretended to be pleased, of course, and later, when Alison was born, she had made all the right noises when friends and neighbours had congratulated her on becoming a grandmother, but inwardly she had been full of apprehension. How would two such self-obsessed people cope with a baby? But they had, at least for the first year. They had seemed happy, even though Paula had given up her job and Dave's work as a messenger could hardly support them. And then the rows had started again.

But this was the first time he had hit her. Or was it? Maybe this was the first time she had been allowed to know about it. Rosie closed her burning eyes, remembering what she had heard and read about wife-beaters. Paula must make a clean break. If he had hit her once, he would do it again, and there was Alison to consider. She took a deep breath and returned to the bathroom. Avoiding looking directly at her daughter, she shook open the towel and said: 'Come and get dried, Alison.' And then, quickly, 'If you've finished, Paula?'

'Yes.' Paula stood up. 'Thanks, Mum. I'll go down and fix her some supper. She must be hungry. She wouldn't eat anything on the train.'

Paula went downstairs and Rosie helped Alison to climb out of the bath. Then she began to towel her granddaughter dry. How small and frail her body felt. She dried between her toes and smiled when the child began to giggle. Then her smile faded. Had Alison been there when the blow was struck?

Her concern for Paula transmuted into a greater anxiety as she pulled Alison's flowered nightdress over her damp hair. What else had the child seen? What horrendous arguments followed by equally tempestuous reconcilliations had occurred before her uncomprehending eyes? As she fastened the buttons on the nightgown, her fingers trembled and a spurt of anger mingled with the sympathy she felt for her daughter. She was sorry for her, of course she was, but Paula was an adult now, and what's more she had always courted danger.

Her fingers stilled. No, that wasn't really fair. Paula had been a headstrong child but it was only after Howard's death that her wild streak had surfaced. Before that dreadful day, Paula had been happy. They all had.

She and Howard had enjoyed a good marriage and a good relationship with their children. Perhaps the only imbalance was the way Paula always turned to her father for help and advice and Steve always turned to her. It worried Rosie sometimes, but she understood why.

Exactly sixteen months after Paula's birth, Steve had arrived. Rosie remembered how her mother had taken the news of the expected second baby.

'My God, Rosemary, so soon! Have you never heard of self-control not to speak of birth control?'

She remembered she had turned red and mumbled some

reply. She had been a fool to imagine her mother might have been glad for her.

But Howard had taken it in his stride.

'Not to worry, love. We wanted a brother or a sister for Paula, didn't we? And this way, we get through the nappy stage all at once. Anyway, I'll give you a hand.'

He had kept his word. He had been besotted with Paula from the first moment he had laid eyes on her, and so he had cheerfully taken over many of the tasks of caring for her in order that Rosie might concentrate on the new arrival. And it had continued that way.

Howard had loved both his children, but Paula had a special place in his heart. Boys ran in Howard's family. He had four uncles and two brothers. Paula was the first girl in three generations and she had grown so pretty and so smart. One day, when she was about four, Howard had taken her with him to visit a friend who worked in some riding stables. He came home chuckling.

'My God, you should have seen her. Turned my back for two minutes and there she was, trying to climb up on to a horse's back. No fear at all.'

He had swung Paula high in the air and she had screamed with delight.

'You mustn't spoil her, Howard.'

'I won't. When I go again, I'll take our Steve.'

And so he did, but Steve didn't like horses much. Steve looked like his father and the rest of the Scott clan. He had fair hair, brown eyes and big hands and feet. He had their sweet nature, too. He knew he couldn't captivate his father as Paula did, but he didn't seem to mind. Just so long as everyone was happy, that's all Steve wanted.

And they had been happy. The children had grown and started school. They both did well. Steve slogged away at his lessons and was always in the upper half of his class.

Paula idled away most of the time then worked like fury for a couple of days before exams and was always in the top five. However, in a social sense, Steve was more highly regarded by the teaching staff. There were times when Paula found herself in trouble. On several occasions, Rosie was asked to the school to discuss her daughter's behaviour.

Back home, she tackled Paula about her attitude. 'Miss Jennings said you were insolent to her. It won't do, Paula. You should respect your teachers.'

Paula's lips had pressed into an obstinate line. 'She's a rotten teacher. She lets the bullies and the cheats get away with murder but if anyone halfway decent does the tiniest little thing, she jumps on them. It's not fair.'

Paula had a great sense of fairness.

Rosie tried to explain the need for discipline, but she wouldn't listen. Only her father could get through to her.

'There's good teachers and bad, Paula, like everything else in life, but there's no point building up trouble for yourself. I reckon you'll just have to keep quiet and make the best of it. You'll be moving up to another class soon and, anyway, no one ever said life is always fair.'

And then she looked thoughtful and pulled at her lip, before smiling at him and nodding her head.

Did she remember his comment about fairness, Rosie wondered, when three years later she came home to the news her father had died suddenly at work from a massive heart attack?

She had really freaked out then. And Rosie herself had been paralysed by shock and misery. If it hadn't been for Steve . . . Rosie straightened her back.

He was meeting Jill tonight. She must speak to him before he went out. There were arrangements to make. Where would Alison sleep, for instance?

Her brows drew together and then, observing Alison's anxious expression, she smiled at her. 'Let's get your hair dried, before supper.' She led the little girl through into her own bedroom and picked up her silver-backed hairbrush, the one Alison always enjoyed playing with.

Howard had bought her the dressing table set on their seventh wedding anniversary. Brushing the toddler's hair, Rosie thought it was no wonder she couldn't understand her daughter's marriage when her own had been so different. Howard had been a quiet steady man. He had never whisked her off to dine out or brought her unexpected gifts, but he had never forgotten her birthday or their anniversary and they had never gone to sleep on a quarrel.

She smoothed a lock of Alison's hair over her fingers, trying to coax a curl, but it remained stubbornly straight. It was a good hairbrush, she thought, it had stood the test of time. If Howard had lived their marriage would have been like that. Such a long time since his death and yet she was still lonely for him.

Over the years, there had been a few occasions when she had been asked out. The men had been known to her, decent sorts, but she had never been tempted. She still felt married. The handle of the hairbrush felt good in her hand. The matching comb had been lost years ago and the mirror she had been forced to throw away when the glass cracked, but the brush she used most days.

Alison's hair was almost dry. Rosie had been crooning to her granddaughter as she brushed but now she saw Alison's thumb had crept into her mouth and her eyelids were closing and so she stopped her wordless song. She put down the hairbrush.

'There, all done. Your hair does look pretty.'

It didn't really. Alison's hair was fine and a mousy colour. It's just like your father's, thought Rosie, and felt a stab of hatred flash through her.

As she carried the child downstairs, she heard a mumble of soft voices coming from behind the closed kitchen door. Good. Steve hadn't left yet and brother and sister were talking. She set Alison on her feet and opened the door.

Steve had an old newspaper spread out on the floor and was crouched down cleaning his shoes. Paula was spooning something from a pan into a bowl. It looked like porridge. She looked up, came over, and taking hold of Alison, lifted her into a chair. Then she pushed it up to the table and put the bowl and a spoon in front of her daughter. 'Go on, eat it up.'

Alison's sparse eyebrows drew together in a frown. She shook her head.

'Don't start, Alison. Eat it up.'

'No. Want alpha spaghetti.'

'Granny hasn't got any. Eat your supper.'

Rosie, watching the scene with foreboding, felt a guilty pang. Why hadn't she kept a tin of alphabetti spaghetti in the cupboard? She knew Alison liked it

'No.' Alison pushed the bowl away.

Paula's voice went thin. 'Mummy's taken the trouble to make you something to eat and you'll *eat* it, Alison. Do you hear?'

Rosie took a step forward but before she had time to say anything, Steve intervened.

Wiping his hands on a duster, he shuffled across on his knees towards the table and, reaching Alison, grinned at her. His head was on an exact level with hers. 'Porridge is my favourite, Alison. May I have some, please?'

As she turned her head towards him, he showed her his hands. 'But I'm very dirty, so you'll have to feed me.'

She grinned and spooned porridge into his mouth.

'Umm.' He swallowed manfully. 'Lovely. Now it's your

turn. Hurry up and have some, before I eat it all.'

She thrust a full spoon into her mouth then fed him again. 'Now you.'

Rosie relaxed and grinned at her daughter, who turned away, saying: 'Make a playtime of meals and they expect the same treatment every time.' She began to run cold water into the pan. 'Anyway, I don't suppose she'll eat it all. Kids don't eat stuff like that any more.'

'Really?' Rosie felt aggrieved. 'Well, that's a pity. I'm sure there's more goodness in porridge than in tinned spaghetti.' She waited, and when Paula remained silent looked back at Alison and Steve and, quite unforgivably, turned her irritation upon her son. 'Is that your best shirt, Steve?'

Unable to speak, Alison's spoon in his mouth, he nodded.

'Then why on earth wear it to clean your shoes?'

He swallowed. 'I'm running late. I thought I'd get away without having to clean them but when I realised how dirty they are . . .'

'You don't expect Steve to go out with dirty shoes, Mum? Not when he's meeting Jill?'

There was a moment of quiet when Rosie and Steve stared at Paula and then he rose from his knees. 'She's eaten most of it,' he said, his face expressionless. Without looking at his sister, he went back to where his shoes lay, brushed away vigorously for a moment and then stowed away the shoe box and disposed of the newspaper. 'I've got ten minutes to spare. I'd better shift a few things out of my room before I go.'

'Don't put yourself out on my account.' Paula's back was towards them as she washed out the dishcloth. 'Alison and I can manage in the little back bedroom.'

'You can't, Paula. The bed's too small for two people

and it needs airing.' Rosie ran her fingers through her hair. 'I'll go up in a minute and change the sheets on Steve's bed. The sofa will be all right, love?' She looked apologetically at him.

'Sure.'

'The sofa?' Paula turned and faced them. There was a little mocking smile on her face. 'He's much too big a boy for the sofa, Mum. Why don't you stay over with Jill for the night, Steve?' She paused. 'After all, you are engaged now.'

'Paula . . .'

'It's all right, Mum. Just leave it.' Steve went out and slammed the door behind him.

Through narrowed eyes, Rosie studied her daughter's face.

'Why do you do it, Paula? He's only trying to help.'

She picked up a teatowel and dried her hands. Her face was a picture of innocence. 'Do what?'

'Get at Steve all the time? God knows, he's been a good brother to you. And yet, all the time, you pick, pick, pick at him. You're enough to try the patience of a saint.'

Paula tossed her head and once again Rosie saw the ugly bruise, but this time she suppressed her feeling of pity. 'Why do you do it?' she asked again.

'Why? I don't know. He irritates me.' Paula pondered the question. 'Maybe that's it, Mum – what you just said.' She laughed at Rosie's look of incomprehension. 'Steve, my sainted brother. He's just too damn' good to be true.'

'That's nonsense. Just because he thinks differently from you . . .'

'You can say that again! You should have seen his face when I turned up on the doorstep today. He was horrified.'

'That's nonsense. Steve's fond of you. If he looked

horrifed it was probably because of the state of your face . . . Oh, I'm sorry.'

Rosie crossed to where her daughter stood and touched her arm.

Paula shrugged. 'So am I.' She looked across at Alison. 'Look, she's falling asleep. Will you go and see to the bed, and then I can take her up? And Mum . . .'

Rosie had started to walk towards the door. She paused. 'What?'

'I'm sorry. I'm all strung up at the moment. We'll talk tomorrow, eh?'

'Yes.'

Steve was coming downstairs as Rosie went up.

'I'm going now.'

'All right, love. Have a nice evening.'

'I'll try.' He put his head on one side. 'Don't worry.'

'No.' She forced a smile. 'Things always work out, don't they?'

'Sure.'

She stood to one side to allow him to pass. 'That little bedroom's awfully cramped. But I don't suppose you'll be in it long.'

He hesitated. 'Do you think she'll go back to him?'

'I don't know. I can't see it ever working.' She sighed again. 'All I really want is for both of you to be happy, but happiness seems hard to come by nowadays. Still,' she patted his cheek, 'you're a good lad, Steve. I don't have any worries about you.'

'No.' He cleared his throat. 'Just now, I remembered about the job. How did it go?' He hesitated. 'With all the upset with Paula, we haven't had time to talk. Did you . . . ?'

She shook her head. 'No. I didn't get it. Apparently,'

she forced a smile, 'I'm a great care assistant but I haven't the brains or the professional know-how to go any further up the ladder.'

'Oh, Mum.' His strong young arms came round her in a hug. 'I am sorry.'

'It's all right. I'm over the disappointment now.' She felt her tension dissolve in the warmth of his affection. 'I suppose I *was* aiming too high.'

'Nonsense, they don't know a good thing when they see it. They want their heads examining.' Steve hugged her again and then released her.

She managed to laugh. 'Get away with you. You're just prejudiced. Anyway,' her face sobered, 'under the circumstances, with Paula turning up and everything, perhaps now isn't the right time. Perhaps next year.'

'That's the spirit.'

She stood on the stairs until the door slammed behind him. Then she collected fresh linen and carried it into his bedroom. As usual, it was in complete chaos. There were cassette tapes on the floor which she picked up. He wouldn't appreciate Alison delving into his music collection. But where would he keep them? There was no room in the back bedroom.

Behind the door lay a crumpled track suit. She picked that up, too, held it at arm's length and wrinkled her nose. Definitely one for the washing basket. As she carried it through to the bathroom, she heard a thin, tired wail from downstairs. It reminded her that her first priority was to remake the bed.

But as she smoothed sheets and put fresh pillowcases on the pillows her movements remained slow and heavy. Maybe next year, she had told Steve. This year, next year, sometime, never. Steve had sympathised with her, but he didn't fully understand. No one did.

She didn't understand herself. When had she started to change? Was it when she had started work at The Firs and realised she was good at her job? When she knew she was doing something worthwhile and doing it well?

She shook out the counterpane she had fetched from the airing cupboard and spread it upon the freshly made bed. It was cream-coloured with a border of tiny forget-me-nots. Alison would like that. She gave it a final pat and switched off the bedside lamp before going towards the door. It was dark now but the landing light shone a beam of brightness through into the bedroom. It glanced off a mirror on the far wall.

She turned, paused, and curiously studied her own reflection. The darkness surrounding her stripped her face of all colour. Through the mirror, her hair was merely a blur, her eyes were dark pits and her face was pale, ghostly.

She shivered, suddenly aware of her own mortality. Maybe it was that? After all, her children were grown and Howard had gone and she now spent her days looking after people who were drawing to the end of their lives. Maybe that's why she felt the urgency to do something with the remainder of her life?

Well, what if it was? Her chin lifted defiantly. Why shouldn't she make plans? By today's standards, she wasn't even late middle-aged. She would change her life for the better. She'd help Paula as much as she could and she'd be a good granny to Alison, but she'd think about herself too.

She hurried from the dark bedroom and closed the door behind her. Not this year, maybe not even next year, but sometime . . . definitely sometime.

Chapter Three

Steve arrived outside Jill's home with two minutes to spare, which was good because Jill hated him to be late. He turned into the gravelled driveway, cut the car engine but delayed for a moment before getting out. Sometime during their date – he stared into space – he would have to tell Jill of Paula's precipitate return home. But when? When would be the right time?

It was fair that Jill knew about the bad as well as the good things that happened within his family, she was going to be his wife, after all. And she already knew that Paula and her husband had a volatile relationship, but this latest episode . . . Steve found himself strangely reluctant to discuss it with her. I'll tell her after the meal, he decided. She'll be relaxed then and in a more sympathetic mood.

Vaguely uncomfortable at the direction his thoughts were taking him, he got out of the car and closed the door. He glanced up at the night sky. The North Star winked at him benignly and he felt comforted. Jill, he reminded himself, was not only intelligent and lovely, she was an exceptionally well-balanced individual. That was why she found it difficult to understand how some people's lives simply slid into an unholy mess. Without realising it, he gave a little sigh.

Steve could anticipate Jill's reaction to his news about

Paula because they had been a couple for a long time. Their first date had been one month after his sixteenth birthday, and they had gone bowling.

'Don't worry, I'll show you what to do.'

At the age of twenty-one, Steve could now smile, remembering his nervousness that night. He had, he remembered, hidden behind bravado. Hadn't his two previous visits to the bowling alley made him an expert?

Jill had listened to his instructions with a faint smile on her face and then she had bowled five strikes in a row.

'I've been coming here for nearly a year.' She had tossed her thick hair back from her flushed face and grinned at him.

'Why didn't you tell me?'

'You never asked.'

An uncompromising girl, was Jill, and most of the time he liked that.

By the time Steve had reached his fourteenth birthday he had grown into a tall, good-looking boy, and without conceit, he knew it. So did the groups of thirteen- and fourteen-year-old girls at his school who congregated together at breaktime and scared him half to death with their sideways glances, their whispers when he had to walk past them, and their whoops of cackling laughter when he blushed at their earthy comments.

Of course, when they weren't directing their attention at him, he looked at them, especially those who wore skirts up their bottoms and too-tight school jerseys, but that was all he did. Sport was less complicated. He spent his spare time and energy on football and cricket and made first team at both sports. He still enjoyed playing cricket.

Jill had been different. She had sat next to him on the bus one day during a school outing and chattered away naturally, no pouting of lips or gales of silly laughter which always made him feel he was being laughed at. He had relaxed and begun to enjoy her company and by the time they were heading back to the school, he knew he wanted to ask her out, and more, he knew she would accept. She made decisions quickly, did Jill, and he knew her well enough to predict her reactions to his news about Paula.

Her eyes would open wide.

'My God – you're saying he *hit* her, really hit her? That's terrible. She should go to the police, file a complaint against him, and she must never, never go back to him.'

Of course, Jill had never met Dave and she had never seen the couple together. She didn't really know Paula all that well. Throughout their long association, Steve's girl-friend and his sister had met . . . What? Maybe four or five times. That was because, since childhood, he and Paula had led such different lives. Unconsciously, Steve lifted his hand and scratched his head. And yet, until Paula married and moved to Manchester, he had lived in the same house, in daily contact with her.

What a pity they had never been close, but he supposed their relationship was much the same as experienced by other brothers and sisters. When they were little, even though the age gap between them had been slight, Paula had bossed him about. She had given him orders and when he sometimes rebelled and refused to do what she asked, she had nipped and pinched him, then put on an innocent expression when one of their parents had come to see what was happening. He had hated her then, particularly when their father had explained to him that boys should never hit girls. But Dad had always favoured Paula.

But then things changed. Steve put on a spurt of growth and came to tower over her small frame even though he was still a schoolboy. He realised how pretty she was and how all the boys fancied her and he had come to admire her spirit and her vivacity and to wish, inwardly, that he possessed her boldness and self-confidence.

At times, his brotherly concern had involved him in her escapades. One evening when he had been near his fifteenth birthday, he had seen her arguing with a hulking leather-clad youth outside a take-away kiosk.

Paula was shooting her mouth off as usual and the guy with her had suddenly turned nasty. He had grabbed her by the shoulders and shaken her like a rat. But when Steve had rushed over from the other side of the road to intervene, she had exploded.

'Keep your nose out of my affairs, little brother. Go and do your homework or something. I can look after myself.'

And when the little group of onlookers had laughed, Steve had, he remembered, felt a strong desire to slap her himself.

That's why he wasn't prepared to jump to any conclusion about what had happened between his sister and her husband. Of course, it was a horrible thing to hit a woman, but what had she done to provoke Dave? He shrugged his shoulders. Standing outside in the cold wasn't going to do any good. And Jill was waiting.

He put his sister from his mind and moved away from the car. As he walked towards Jill's home he reflected, not for the first time, that the red-brick Victorian villa before him, although well-maintained and substantial, was not an attractive building. He looked at the large bay window jutting out from the front of the house and realised it reminded him of Terence Catley's large Roman nose. And the overhanging ivy running along the top of the window was reminiscent of Jill's father's bushy eyebrows, which grew in a straight line above his deep-set eyes. The thought amused him and he was still smiling when he rang the doorbell.

Delicate chimes sounded within the house and a moment later Jill opened the door to him. As he expected, she was ready for their night out, dressed in a soft blue jersey wool dress which was belted tightly around her slim waist, her hair freshly washed and set.

She stood to one side to allow him to enter and then she stood on tiptoes and dropped a swift, light kiss on his cheek. 'I won't be a minute. I just have to go upstairs to get my black handbag. Why don't you go in and say hello to Mum and Dad?'

'I will.' He watched her run upstairs first, admiring the swirl of her skirt around her slim legs, and then he turned to the door on his right, tapped and entered.

He just had time to register Mrs Catley was seated by a table near the window when Terence Catley turned his massive head away from the twenty-six-inch television set and boomed a welcome.

'Come in, my boy. Take a seat.' He winked at Steve. 'Keeping you waiting, is she?'

'No. She'll be down in a moment.' Replying, Steve made a conscious effort not to use the word 'sir'. He was positive Catley expected him to, and so, stubbornly, he did not.

Terence Catley always greeted him in a genial manner but Steve was pretty certain he had not been happy about their engagement. Oh, he had made the right noises and the right gestures. He had kissed Jill, he had smiled and shaken Steve's hand. He had brought out a bottle of sparkling wine to celebrate, but Steve had seen the extra colour flood into his face at their announcement and the sudden coldness in his eyes. His reaction had surprised Steve. Good Lord, Jill and he had been going out together for ages, surely her old man knew they were serious about each other?

That night, Steve had gone home and thought about it

and decided it was because of his job. Terence Catley was a self-made man, a supplier of agricultural machinery, and although he was by no means a millionaire, he was comfortably placed. Jill was his only child. Maybe he thought she could do better. Steve decided to talk to his future father-in-law, explain his plans. Without telling Jill, he had arranged to meet him.

'I love Jill very much, sir.' He had called Terence Catley 'sir' then. 'We're young, I know, but we're so happy together, I'm sure we'll make a go of it. And we're not intending to get married immediately. I've got plans. I've already spoken to the Manager at the bank about possible advancement and he's been most encouraging. You don't have to worry.'

And Catley, his face as smooth and bland as a billiard ball, had replied: 'I'm pleased to hear you're planning for the future, Stephen.' He had then glanced at his watch. 'But we must talk later. I have an important appointment in a few minutes.' Stephen had been dismissed.

Neither man referred to the conversation again and, as time went by, Steve's relationship with Terence Catley appeared cordial. When Steve called at the house, he received a clap on the back, an invitation to sit down and have a drink, but in reality, the two had little in common. If a conversation between them lasted more than a few minutes, they began to disagree. Then a note of condescension crept into the older man's voice, he would cut through something Steve was saying, change the subject entirely, or yawn and switch on the television set.

'There's a race I want to watch at three-thirty.'

Steve resented the rudeness and the condescension, but mostly he managed to ignore it. If Terence Catley didn't want him as a son-in-law, he decided, it was just too bad. He would marry Jill whatever her father thought.

And so, secure in that knowledge, he smiled now at his future father-in-law before sitting down.

'She's just gone upstairs to collect her handbag,' he said, raising his voice so it could be heard over the noise from the television.

Terence Catley nodded, stared at him for a moment, and then turned his attention back to the TV screen.

Steve looked towards Mrs Catley. 'How's it going?'

Jill's mother had her chin in her hands and her elbows on the table. At the sound of Steve's voice she started, then raised her head and looked across at him. There was a look of surprise on her face, as if she had only that moment realised he was in the room.

Which was probably true, thought Steve. Evelyn Catley was a strange, fey woman but he liked her more than he liked her husband. He stood up and crossed the room to stand by her side.

'Why, you've nearly finished.'

'Yes,' she nodded. 'Beautiful, don't you think?'

'Yes.' He looked down at the work that lay on the table.

Evelyn Catley had a long, pale face and fine light brown hair which she wore in an untidy bun at the nape of her neck. Her dress was plain and a dark purple colour. It was obvious she was a woman who cared nothing for clothes. She wore no jewellery and her fingernails were close-clipped and innocent of varnish but there was an indefinable air of grace and good breeding about her. She looked a lady. The kind of lady, moreover, who would spend her leisure time in artistic pursuits, writing poetry perhaps, painting or fine needlework.

Nothing was further from the truth. Over the years Steve had learned from Jill that her mother was the daughter of an uneducated mill worker. She herself had only been saved from mill work because, as a child, she had passed a scholarship examination which had taken her to a grammar school. At twenty-five years old she had married Terence Catley. Just where and how they had met, Steve didn't know, but he often thought he had never seen such an ill-matched couple.

However, the union had been commercially successful. Jill had said that ever since she could remember, her mother had been involved in the financial side of her husband's business.

'Originally she did all the ordering and all the book work. She saw prospective clients, too. She was at the office all day every day until I came along. But then Dad put his foot down. The business was prospering and he said she must stay at home more, look after me. She still did all the accounts though, only she did them here, at the house.'

Jill had laughed. 'Actually, my mother was never cut out to be the Mother Earth kind of woman. She loved me, I'm sure, but she's so vague about everyday things. By the time I was five years old, I was looking after her: reminding her about the shopping, and when to start cooking the evening meal. That was important. Dad's always liked the meal on the table as soon as he came through the door.' Her smile had widened. 'He's still like that. A bit of a chauvinist, really, but he's too old to change now.'

Listening to her, Steve had thought, with a touch of asperity, that Jill had different rules as far as her father was concerned. She was very keen on equal division of labour for everyone else. Still, he reminded himself, she was intending to work full-time after their marriage.

Mrs Catley had no connection with her husband's work any more. The business had continued to expand and nowadays Terence employed a team of accountants to work for him.

He wondered how she passed her time. Terence still

worked long hours and when he wasn't working he was at the golf club. Evelyn had no interest in sport but she wasn't a committee type of lady either. No large hat and white gloves for her. She didn't entertain. She didn't go out much. The only thing that seemed to engage her enthusiasm was her one hobby.

Evelyn Catley had become a devotee of jigsaw puzzles. Steve thought it a joke when Jill had told him about it. An intelligent woman spending hours doing jigsaw puzzles! But when next he visited the house and saw the one she was working on, he realised it was no ordinary jigsaw. She bought the puzzles through a specialist catalogue and they were always fiendishly difficult, with thousands of pieces and complex designs. Often they were two-sided or a strange shape.

The one on the table in front of her had grown since he had last visited the house. He saw it was practically completed. He bent forward to study the picture more closely. It depicted a dense jungle, the colouring a subtle shading of differing greens and blues. Hiding away behind the tangled foliage, glimpses of mythical beasts could be *almost* observed . . . There were serpents, a possible unicorn and strange birds.

Steve admired the puzzle but still he wondered why she did them? All that work, just to break the thing into pieces again once it was completed. What satisfaction was there in doing that? This particular puzzle must have been even more difficult than usual. He knew she had been working on it for almost a month.

He cleared his throat. 'A wonderful picture, Mrs Catley, are you thinking of framing it?'

'Oh, no.' She tapped her thin fingers on the bottom of the puzzle. 'I never do that.'

Something in the puzzle caught his eye and he studied it

more closely. In the top left-hand corner was a sort of yellow and black blur. It looked as though something was actually moving, quickly, stealthily. He blinked. Was the shape supposed to be a tiger?

' "Tyger! Tyger! burning bright." '

The soft chant and her laugh made him jump. He jerked and straightened up. When he looked at her she stared back at him, straight into his eyes. Her usual air of amiable vagueness had vanished and he saw how bright and sharp were her eyes. He swallowed.

When the door opened and Jill came hurrying into the room he went to greet her with a feeling of relief. Thank goodness, he thought, as he slipped his arm around her shoulders – thank goodness she didn't resemble either of her parents.

The Sheesh Mahal restaurant was crowded but Steve had booked and so they had a good table. It was set back in a corner and shielded by a large potted palm which meant they could watch the other diners but preserve their own privacy.

Jill was in good form, chattering away throughout the meal, and Steve was happy to sit back and listen to her. I'll tell her about Paula when they bring the coffee, he thought. That would be a good time.

But as the dark-skinned smiling waiter placed coffee cups before them, Jill suddenly introduced another topic of conversation.

'I drove past the new bungalows they're building in East Crescent Road today, you know the ones I mean?' She smiled her thanks at the waiter who withdrew.

Steve nodded. 'Of course. We looked at the plans, remember?'

'Yes.' She stirred her coffee, looking down at the spoon

and not at him. 'They're so attractive, Steve. Much better than they looked in the drawings.'

He sighed. 'They're way out of our league, Jill.'

She leaned forward in her chair. 'Yes, I know we *said* that, but honestly, Steve, we'll never find anything so good again. And remember, house prices are tipped to rise during the next two years.'

He reached forward and laid his hand over hers. 'I agree with everything you say. I'd love to go over to the estate office and put down a deposit tomorrow, but we can't, Jill. We can't afford it. Anyway,' he shrugged, 'the bank will probably move me around during the next three or four years.'

'I know that, but we could always rent it out. It could make money for us. Then later, when we want to start a family,' she flashed him a grin, 'we could decide what to do, sell for a profit or come back here to settle. We'd be near our families then, and just think, the bungalows are near the schools and the shops.'

He moved his hand away. 'Too many ifs and buts. It's a pipe dream, love.'

'It isn't. I'm sure Dad would help.'

'Thanks, but no thanks.' A slight edge sharpened his voice. 'We'll do things our way, Jill, without help from your dad.'

Momentarily, her face showed disappointment but then she sighed and nodded. 'Yes, you're right, of course. I'm sorry. I guess I got carried away, thinking of us living in one of those lovely homes.' She drained her coffee cup, replaced it on the saucer and raised her eyebrows at him. 'So, what's happened to you today?'

She really was a smashing girl. She was disappointed, obviously, but she wasn't going to sulk or turn sarcastic. He imagined what Paula's reaction would have been in a similar situation and then, as if on cue, Jill said: 'Something's on your mind, I can tell. You've been distracted all evening.'

'Well . . .' He told her of his sister's sudden arrival and the reason why.

'Oh Lord, poor Paula.' Her eyes were round with concern. 'And that poor little girl, too. Your mother must be upset. What does she say about it?'

'Not a lot, as yet. We're still recovering from the shock.'

'Yes, I suppose so. He's the one that left the family home, you say?'

When Steve nodded, she continued her train of thought, her mouth setting into a straight line. 'Well, that's good riddance to bad rubbish, I would have thought. And if he comes sneaking round again, she mustn't go back to him. A man who starts knocking his wife about is beneath contempt.'

'It's too early for decisions.' Steve jumped back into the conversation, obscurely anxious not to be right about Jill's reaction to his news.

'Anyway, Paula will sort it all out. If you remember, she's no shrinking violet.' He attempted, not wholly successfully, to smile.

Jill shook her head. 'They did rush into marriage, didn't they? I remember you telling me how crazily in love they were. They should have waited a bit, found out more about each other. Sexual attraction is all very well but . . .'

Steve decided they had pursued the subject long enough. He'd had enough of Paula and her troubles and Jill looked very sweet with that little frown creasing her forehead.

'More like us, you mean?'

She paused. 'What?'

'We took our time before engaging in sexual attraction

stuff, but it was worth waiting for, wasn't it?'

He reached for her hand again and nibbled at her fingertips.

She blushed. 'Steve! People are looking.'

'No, they're not. And what if they are?' He kissed the palm of her hand before releasing her. 'Do you want me to order you a brandy?

'No, thank you.' Her cheeks were rose pink now and there was a half smile on her lips. Paula and her troubles were forgotten.

They left the restaurant and drove out of the town centre, through the main residential area and up a leafy, winding road that took them to a high point on the outskirts of the town.

Here, set amongst well-kept lawns and shrubberies, stood the town's impressive War Memorial. Nearby was the only building, a small cafe, now boarded up and silent. In the summer, the cafe was a little goldmine, catering for the many visitors to the area. People would come up to see the view and then go there for morning coffee or afternoon tea.

On sunny weekends, Steve and Jill had often sat in the garden behind the cafe, eating cream buns and admiring the roses. Tonight there were no roses and no other visitors, just the lights of the town twinkling below them in the darkness and the sloughing of the wind in the trees.

Steve switched off the car engine and slid his arm around Jill's shoulders. She snuggled closer to him. They sat quietly, admiring the view.

They were both Yorkshire-bred, being born in the town which lay below them. They had grown up used to fine views and plenty of space. They had hung over the rails at the cattle markets and heard farmers discuss the finer points of their beasts. They had picnicked on the moors on hot sunny days when even the insects had drowsed in the fierce heat. When they grew older, they had tackled some of the famous long-distance walks, swearing under their breath as unexpected hail showers had nipped their noses and turned their fingers to ice.

They were adults now, and they knew their life might take them away from this place of their birth, but they knew it would always be somewhere in their hearts.

'Look,' Jill pointed. 'You can just see our house.' She chuckled. 'The lights are still on, Dad must be waiting up for me.'

Steve pulled a face. He searched the mass of pin-prick lights for his home but it was impossible; he gave up. A small terraced house did not show in such an impressive scene.

He could see St Mary's easily enough. The slender spire rose from the floodlit area in the centre of the town. The parish church was fourteenth-century and therefore worthy of the expense. Around the church was a jumble of quaint streets which blended residential and commercial properties in equal proportions. They had risen upon the remains of the original medieval settlement which brought many visitors to the area. When Jill and he married, the cars would drive through those streets as both of them were entitled to be married in the parish church.

He smiled as Jill snuggled up closer to him.

'Are you cold?'

'No.' She shook her head. 'It's warm enough with the heater on. I wish we could go home though.'

'I know.'

As they both lived at home it was rare they had a place where they could be alone. When his mother was working nights it was possible but she was on days at the moment and, anyway, Paula and Alison were staying now.

Steve sighed. 'Maybe we should have tried to rent somewhere?'

'My dad would have *loved* that.' Jill pulled a face. 'Anyway, we manage, don't we?'

She had undone the buttons on his shirt and now she was scratching her fingernails lightly across his chest.

He closed his eyes. 'Umm.'

'Nice?'

'You know it is.'

He turned to face her and unbuttoned her dress. The material was soft to his touch but her silky bra and then her naked breasts were softer still. He trailed his fingertips down and round her rib cage then gently touched her nipples, smiling when she gasped. He loved to please Jill and he knew what she liked. He brought his lips down on hers for a long kiss.

Their friendship had remained innocent boy and girl stuff for a long time. By mutual consent, they had waited until it felt right for both of them before they made love. On Jill's seventeenth birthday they had decided the time was right. Steve was eighteen. The first time their loving had been self-conscious and more than a little clumsy, but ultimately highly satisfying. It was even better now.

However, Steve shifted his position. A car was not the most comfortable place in which to make love.

'Steve.'

Jill was leaning back on her elbows. A ray of moonlight had dappled her bared breasts and shadowed her features. A surge of wanting flowed through him.

He swallowed. 'What?'

'Try putting the seats back.'

He did, blessing their luck that no one ever visited the War Memorial site this late at night.

Jill lay crossways across the seats and he eased himself

on top of her. He felt her hands pressing on the base of his spine and her tongue delicately exploring his half-open mouth and he groaned softly and entered her body. They moved slowly, and then more quickly as they moved together towards fulfilment and both gave a little cry when the moment arrived.

For a few seconds afterwards they clung together and then Jill tried to wriggle out from beneath him.

'You'll have to move.'

'Why?'

'Because my left leg's gone to sleep.'

'Sorry.' He disentangled himself. 'Is that better?'

'Yes.' She gave a little giggle.

He regarded her moonlit profile indulgently. 'What is it?'

'I was just thinking, what a good job your manager can't see you now.'

'Oh, I don't know.' Steve shrugged back into his shirt and did up the buttons. 'The bank want thrusting young men, full of enthusiasm.'

She gurgled with laughter and sat up. 'That's true.' She pulled her dress over her bare breasts and shoulders and put her discarded bra into her coat pocket. Then she sighed. 'We'll have to go soon.'

But neither of them felt inclined to move. Outside, a light wind ruffled the branches of a group of nearby oak trees. A few brown, withered, tenacious leaves fluttered down to the ground in a soft whisper. Down in the town a dog barked.

Steve rubbed at the misted-up window and looked out. Nothing moved. They could have been the last two people in the world. He glanced up at the nearby War Memorial. The moonlight was silvering the lists of names engraved in black on the stone. The tall granite column had been there all his life, he had seen it in the distance from his bedroom window, but suddenly, with a sense of shock, he truly comprehended the enormity of the long lists of names.

Most of those commemorated had been men in their twenties. They had been young and ardent. They had met their friends in the pubs, played football, made plans for their future and loved their girls, just as he had made love to Jill. A lump grew in his throat. The poor buggers. How unfair life was.

He looked down at Jill, yawning now and resting her head on his shoulder. He had known her forever, it seemed. Some of his friends teased him about the long relationship.

'There's plenty more fish in the sea, Stevie boy.'

'You want to try a few more samples before you tie yourself down for life.'

He'd just laughed and shrugged his shoulders. He and Jill were made for each other, he didn't need to sleep around.

He studied her face and, as if feeling his gaze, she tilted her head back and looked at him.

'You're quiet.'

'I'm fine.'

'Good.' She sat upright and ran her fingers through her hair.

'You'd better take me home.'

'Yes. Pity, eh?'

They both laughed.

And ten minutes later, as he drove carefully down the winding road back to town, Steve was still smiling.

Chapter Four

Next morning, Rosie overslept. If it hadn't been for Steve tapping on her bedroom door just before he left the house she might still be asleep. She'd had a terrible night, sleeping only fitfully. Worry over Paula and her marriage had been the main cause of her sleeplessness, but interspersed with her daughter's troubles had been thoughts of her own disappointment.

She still couldn't believe the job had gone to someone else. Despite all her modest talk to Steve she had inwardly believed she would be successful. She *should* have been successful. Ever since Mrs Tyler had left she had filled in for her and done a good job, too. It wasn't fair.

She felt rebellious, a strange feeling for her. At two in the morning, sick of tossing and turning, she crept downstairs and made herself a drink of tea. Huddled up in her dressing-gown, it was freezing in the kitchen, she took her cup of tea through into the living room. She switched on the electric fire, wishing the house had central heating.

They had never been able to afford it. A no frills life, that's what I've had, she thought. The image of Howard's strong, serious-looking face flashed across her mind and made her feel ashamed. She had never thought about their lack of central heating when he was alive. She had never minded saving carefully to pay quarterly bills and occasional treats for the children because she knew she had a loving husband who worked the hardest he could to provide for them.

She remembered how her mother had tried to dissuade her from marrying Howard.

'A pleasant enough young man, Rosemary, but with nothing particular to recommend him. And you're so young. Wait a little. You're a pretty girl, I'm sure you'll meet someone who can offer you a better standard of living.'

Pretty but not intelligent. Remembering, Rosie grimaced. And what a ridiculous remark for Minna to make because that was exactly what *she* had done. She had married beneath her and spent the better part of her life living in a drab little house in the middle of Halifax.

Of course, Rosie hadn't been able to mention that because her father had been in the room when the conversation had taken place. He was in his chair reading the newspaper, listening to their conversation but taking no part in it. He was on her side though. Rosie knew he was when he had smiled at her after her mother had thrown up her hands and left the room.

Rosie, loving her father, had smiled back at him. At least Dad had understood. Quietly, he had supported her in her determination to marry Howard and he had walked down the aisle with her and delivered her into her sweetheart's safe-keeping.

When her father had died, it had been a terrible blow to Rosie, but she told herself that at least he had known she was happy and had lived to see his grandchildren born. And then, not too long afterwards, Howard had died too and her grief had been terrible.

Crouched over the electric fire, nursing her cup in her folded hands, Rosie mused on the different levels of individuals' grief. Howard's sudden death had shattered her. She had wanted to die, too; but she had two children to care for and so she had fitted together the pieces of herself and carried on as best she could.

When her father had been rushed into hospital, her mother had travelled with him in the ambulance and Rosie had stayed at home. Three hours later, Minna had returned. She told Rosie of her father's death and then she had gone and shut herself in her bedroom. After half an hour, she had come into the sitting room. Taking a writing pad from the bureau and sitting down at the table, she had begun to write out a list of things to do. After the funeral service, she had continued her life as if nothing particular had happened.

Watching the red bars of the fire, Rosie found herself yawning. She put her cup on the coffee table and rubbed her eyes. She must go back to bed. In a few hours, she was due at work and then when she came home again, Paula and Alison would need her loving attention. She didn't relish the thought of work. The news would be out in the morning. Everyone would know she had failed the interview.

She grimaced. She'd have to play the part of a good sport. Shrug off her real feelings and appear bright and cheerful. She'd try and wake up fifteen minutes early. That way she could wash her hair and use a little make-up and present a brave face to the world. Full of good intentions, she went back to bed . . . and she had slept in.

Dashing through the swing doors at The Firs, the first person Rosie saw was Mrs Fountain, a favourite of hers. The smiling delicate-featured old lady stepped out of the lift and headed towards Rosie clutching an umbrella in her hand.

'Is it warm outside? I thought I might take a walk in the garden before breakfast.'

'Actually, it's rather cold, Mrs Fountain. You'll need your coat if you're going . . .' Rosie's voice faded away.

Mrs Fountain had dressed carefully for her walk. She was wearing purple earrings which exactly matched her purple-coloured dress. However, the bra she was wearing on top of her dress was white.

Rosie drew in her breath and went to stand next to the old lady. She slipped her hand beneath Mrs Fountain's elbow. 'I think we'd better go back upstairs and get your coat, and while we're up there, perhaps a slight adjustment . . .'

She corrected Mrs Fountain's dress and escorted her back to the lift and then she hurried into the staff room to don her overall.

It's just another day, she told herself.

She glanced at her watch and rushed to the second floor to give Mrs Garmonsey her bath. Mrs Garmonsey had to be put into a Parker bath because she could do so little for herself, but she had a cheery disposition and chatted away happily as Rosie bathed her. Because her patient was relaxed, Rosie relaxed, too. After dressing her, Rosie took her down to breakfast.

The dining room at The Firs was an attractive, low-ceilinged room. It was constructed in the shape of a letter L, the tables being set out in the longer part and the short section at the end being the sun lounge.

Positioning Mrs Garmonsey at the end of one table, Rosie thought what a fine sunny day it was turning out to be. The sunlight was streaming in through the picture window and the lawns outside were green after the overnight rain. If there had been leaves on the trees outside, she thought, it would have been easy to believe it was summer, except for the low temperature.

Walking into the sun lounge, she smiled. Why, even the resident cat, Boswell, was contributing to the illusion of summer. During the winter months Boswell always snoozed the morning away in the boiler room, but today he was here, sprawled out, peaceably asleep in the multi-coloured lozenges of colour cast on the carpet by the sun penetrating the leaded lights along the top of the window. She bent to stroke his head and he opened one almond-shaped eye and blinked at her.

As she straightened up one of the kitchen staff passed her. He looked at her sorrowfully. 'Tough about the job, Rosie. Better luck next time, eh?'

She tensed, then relaxed. 'Yes, thanks.'

She went to check the list for breakfast trays.

Throughout the morning, she received similar messages of sympathy. The words varied, depending on who was delivering them. The glum-faced union representative growled: 'Might have known they'd bring in an outsider. Management don't approve of a rank and file member moving out of their range.'

Privately, Rosie agreed with him but she thought it best to remain neutral.

'I had a fair interview, Mr Topham. I hadn't realised the amount of responsibility the job entailed.'

'If you say so.' Mr Topham wandered off, looking depressed, but as the hours passed by, Rosie found she was feeling better about herself. She still had friends and a job she enjoyed doing.

But during her afternoon tea break, a woman sitting next to her mentioned it would soon be Christmas and immediately Rosie's spirits plummeted. Christmas was not her favourite season. Despite all her efforts, she felt the loss of Howard more deeply at Christmas and preparing for the big day brought back memories. Putting up the holly, dressing the tree, she remembered how excited Steve and Paula had become when they were children. They had followed Howard everywhere, demanding to be allowed to put the fairy on top of the tree, help him with the paper chains and switch on the coloured tree lights.

He had always let them, smiling indulgently but keeping a careful eye on them in case they hurt themselves. Rosie sighed. She had looked forward to Christmas in those days.

But things were different now, and if Paula and Alison were still with her, and if Minna came for the day, then things would be difficult. But maybe Minna would decide to spend Christmas on her own this year.

Rosie wished she could go away for Christmas, all by herself.

The so-called festive season had developed into its present pattern after the death of Rosie's father. Minna had sold the house in Halifax and moved to be closer to her only daughter. Her action had surprised Rosie.

The relationship between herself and her mother had been cordial but not particularly strong. However, on reflection, Rosie realised Minna did not have a particularly strong relationship with anyone, therefore it made sense for her to be in closer touch with Rosie.

Accepting that, Rosie helped her mother settle in her new home, and thereafter invited her, each year, to join them at Christmas time. After Howard's death it seemed more important than ever that Minna spend Christmas with them. Their little family was diminishing, it behoved them to stick together.

Perhaps Minna didn't see it that way because sometimes she accepted Rosie's invitation and sometimes she declined it. Whichever way, the day itself was never a success.

If Minna said no, then Rosie spent the two days before the holiday dashing backwards and forwards to her mother's flat with groceries, provisions and little treats and presents. Then, on Christmas Day, she felt guilty, thinking of Minna spending the most important day of the year all on her own in that dreadful building.

If Minna agreed to join the family for Christmas Day then the complications began. First, Steve would pull a face about collecting her.

'You come with me, Mum,' he would ask, his voice plaintive.

He hated being alone with his grandmother. He never knew what to say to her. And then, whatever time they arranged, it would turn out to be inconvenient.

'There's a carol service on the radio at eleven. I particularly wanted to listen to it. Can't you come for me later?'

Rosie would explain that they were used to eating Christmas dinner at one o'clock.

Minna's eyes would round. 'You mean, we're eating at *lunchtime*?'

More apologetic explanations.

'It's better that way, Mother. Steve likes to go round to Jill's house on Christmas afternoon and I must admit, I enjoy putting my feet up and watching TV.'

'Oh, I see.' Minna's mouth would thin. 'Well, don't alter things on my account. But don't buy in any extra food for me. I shall eat very little. I'm not used to a big meal at lunchtime.'

Rosie propped her elbows on the table, rested her chin on her hands and sighed. Last Christmas had been an edgy and uncomfortable day, but this year anything could happen. She closed her eyes and imagined her son-in-law turning up on the doorstep and creating a scene.

'Rosie?'

She opened her eyes. 'Yes.'

'Are you all right?' The woman standing by her chair looked at her curiously.

'Yes.' She scrunched up her face, a half-humorous, half-apologetic expression. 'I was thinking about Christmas.'

'Oh.' The other woman's face cleared. 'Are you off for the holiday?'

'Yes.'

'Oh, you lucky thing.'

'Yes.' Rosie nodded. That's an idea, she thought. Perhaps I could swop with someone, come into work. Immediately, she was ashamed at her thoughts. If Paula and Alison were to share Christmas with her she must put on an especially good show, particularly for her granddaughter.

'I'm working.' The woman paused. 'Mrs Horton's sent down a message for you. Will you go and see her, after your break?'

'Right, I'll go now.' Rosie stood up.

The woman lingered. 'Sorry you didn't get the job. We thought you would.'

Rosie smiled. 'Thanks.'

Mrs Horton's office door was open. Rosie tapped and went in.

'Ah, Rosie.' Mrs Horton looked up from her desk and smiled. 'I won't keep you long. Just wanted a word about the way your interview went.'

'There's no need.' Rosie shrugged her shoulders. 'I *was* disappointed, but everyone's been so nice about it, I feel better now.' She paused. 'I should never have applied. I aimed too high.'

'Nonsense.' Mrs Horton frowned. 'Or if you did, it was

partly my fault.' She saw the puzzled look on Rosie's face and explained. 'I was keen to have you as my back-up and so I encouraged you to put in for the job. I should have thought more deeply about the implications before I opened my mouth.' She sighed. 'I tend to forget how things have changed since I first started out. Nowadays, there's so much emphasis on exam results and paper qualifications.'

Rosie nodded and said, a trace of bitterness showing in her voice, 'That lets me out, then. I've no qualifications at all.'

'But you're a natural for the job, Rosie.' Mrs Horton stared at her. 'I know that academic achievements are important because everything is so technical these days but sometimes I feel the basic necessities are being overlooked.' She frowned. 'I get quite cross, Rosie, with the way things are run now.'

She sighed. 'I attend endless meetings where I have to sit and listen to County officials and grey-suited accountants spouting their bureaucratic gobbledegook.'

She threw out her hands in an extravagant gesture. 'Everyone is an expert nowadays on money matters and they act accordingly. We hardly ever discuss individuals any more. No, we discuss cost-effectiveness and dates for yet more meetings. We don't concentrate on *why* people develop disruptive behaviour, we discuss whether The Firs is "logistically able to continue to fund a place for them".'

She swung her chair around and frowned out of the window and then she looked back at Rosie and smiled at her startled expression.

'Oh, Lord. I'm sorry. Forgive me my little outburst. Put it down to my having a bad week.' She looked back at her desk, shuffled some papers. 'And I called you in to talk about your next move.'

'What next move?'

Mrs Horton left the papers and said quietly, 'It's not too late, you know.'

'Not too late for what?' Forgetting her employer's surprising outburst, Rosie collected her thoughts together. 'Do you mean the post of Second Officer's still vacant? Has Miss Benson changed her mind?'

A ray of hope warmed her heart.

'Oh, no. She's looking forward to starting here. I think she'll be very good.' Mrs Horton was watching Rosie closely. She saw her look of disappointment.

'But, consider, there's plenty of other County homes for the elderly in this area.'

Rosie shook her head. 'I know, but you heard what the man said. I haven't got the necessary qualifications.'

'You could get them.'

Mrs Horton paused to let her words sink in to Rosie's mind and then said softly, 'You already possess the basic skills, Rosie. And you have a natural flair for this kind of work. You get on with the old folk and also with the staff. All you need, really, is the necessary paperwork. You need a diploma certifying you as competent to care for the elderly.'

'You're not suggesting I go to college?'

'No, that's not necessary.' Ignoring Rosie's frown, her employer continued: 'As it happens, our own Local Authority runs a course that would offer you what you need. You'd have to study, of course, go on day releases, work at home, but you could do it, I'm sure of it. And if I recommend you, I think you would be offered a place.'

'Oh, I don't think so.' Rosie shifted uncomfortably. 'I'm not academically clever, I never was. I couldn't even help the children with their homework. I'd just make a fool of myself. Besides, I have family commitments.' She thought briefly of Paula and Alison, waiting for her at home.

Mrs Horton scowled at her. 'You disappoint me. I thought you were keen to get on.'

'I am, but I thought my work here spoke for me. I didn't think I would have to study.'

'Well, now you know differently.' Mrs Horton picked up a pencil and tapped it on her desk. 'So you're just going to give up?'

Rosie, blushing scarlet, did not answer.

But Mrs Horton hadn't finished with her.

'Your children don't need you, Rosie. You've told me about them. They're adults now and leading their own lives. And why do you think you've no brains? You seem bright enough to me. You don't have to study things like Greek or Latin, you know.'

She leant forward over her desk. 'The course is based on mostly practical subjects. It covers staff management and quantity control but you know a little bit about that because you've been helping me. Then there's psychology.' She laughed. 'We use it every day here.' She studied Rosie's face. 'You *could* do it, you know. Why not give it a try?'

Rosie felt trapped. She wanted to say yes because she wanted to please Mrs Horton, but she dare not. Something inside her was telling her she was bound to fail and if she failed, she would disappoint her employer as well as herself. She clenched her hands by her side and muttered: 'I need to think about it.'

Mrs Horton sat back in her chair and sighed. 'Well, it's up to you.' She looked at her watch. 'I have rather sprung the idea on you, haven't I? Think about it and come and give me your final decision later, but don't take too long deciding.' She stood up. 'I'm out of time. I must go and see Cook about something.'

Rosie walked towards the door with her. Just before leaving the room, Mrs Horton stopped and rested her hand on Rosie's shoulder. She said, her voice serious, 'I'm not just trying to help you, my dear. We do need to recruit truly caring people in this profession, particularly nowadays, so please don't dismiss my suggestion out of hand.

'And just in case,' she smiled, 'I'll find out a few details.'

Reacting to the warmth of her friendship, Rosie smiled back.

'Thank you.'

They walked down the corrider. Just before she left Mrs Horton, Rosie asked, 'Cook's not been on the rampage again, has she?'

The question was only half joking. The new cook at The Firs was quite a character. Strong-willed and famous for her sudden changes of mood, she was nevertheless an important member of staff. Food was of prime importance to the elderly residents.

'No.' Mrs Horton chuckled. 'But you might say she's suffered from a sudden rush of blood to the head. For some reason, she wrote down "quiche" on the dinner menu. Since the menu was posted up, about forty per cent of our residents have come to me and complained. They've even threatened to go on strike. As Mr Partridge said: "If you start serving us foreign muck, we'll complain to the County Council." '

Rosie was puzzled. 'Cook always serves bacon and egg pie and chips on a Friday.'

'Exactly.' Mrs Horton nodded.

'Oh, I see.' Rosie started to laugh.

Mrs Horton grinned. 'I wish the residents did.' She shook her head. 'Now do you understand why the course includes psychology?'

Chapter Five

'I've made a chicken casserole for us, is that all right?'

'All right – it's marvellous!'

The bus had been crowded and Rosie had been forced to stand during her journey home. She flopped into a chair and kicked off her shoes, wriggling her toes with satisfaction. It was lovely to come into a warm house. She looked across at Paula and saw, with greater satisfaction, that the bruise on her face was fading.

'I don't have to go in to work again until Monday, thank goodness. I'll have time to play with you, my pet.' The last few words were directed at Alison who had appeared in the kitchen doorway and was smiling at her from behind the thumb she had firmly anchored in her mouth. Rosie held out her arms. 'Do I get a cuddle?'

Alison came running. She was wearing red overalls with Mickey Mouse emblazoned on the bib and was clutching the same naked doll that had shared the bath with her.

'Ow!' The rigid limbs of the doll struck Rosie's chest as she hugged the toddler. She pulled back. 'Your dolly's hard, Alison. Haven't you got a nice teddy to cuddle?'

'For some reason she prefers that thing.' Paula was straining the vegetables. She tipped the boiled potatoes into a Pyrex bowl and put it in the oven. Then she headed for her daughter.

'Come here, Alison. Let Mummy wipe your hands.'

Rosie stood up. 'I'll just nip upstairs.' She paused. 'I suppose Steve is eating with us?'

'Yes. He's in the bath.'

Paula scrubbed Alison's grubby paws with a flannel. 'Quite particular now, isn't he? I don't remember him being like that when I lived at home.'

'He was in his teens then.' Rosie shuddered. 'Thank God he did change. I hope he won't be long, though. I would like to clean up before we eat our meal.'

'Oh, I'm sorry.' Paula's voice was cool. 'I should have timed things better. I thought you would both be hungry when you got in.'

'No, no. It's a wonderful surprise to come home and find the meal already cooked.' Rosie hesitated. 'I'll be down in a minute, honestly.'

Oh dear! As she hurried upstairs Rosie felt despondent. She'd forgotten how touchy Paula could be. Was she going to have to watch her every word to her daughter? She sighed. And it appeared the old animosity was surfacing between brother and sister. If only the house was bigger.

She stared round the small landing and through the open door into Steve's bedroom which Paula and Alison were now using. Crowded together as they were, there was simply no space for antagonism. She sighed again, remembering how easily she and Steve co-existed.

He had vacated the bathroom and was in the little box room, the door firmly closed. Rosie went to wash her hands and face. Inside the bathroom it was warm and steamy. Before washing her face, she rubbed the clouded mirror and studied her reflection. She looked as she felt, tired and anxious.

Perhaps this evening, when Alison was in bed, she and Paula would get a chance to talk. Perhaps her daughter would tell her what had happened to make Dave hit her in the face. But then again, perhaps not. Rosie ran hot water into the sink and picked up the soap.

She rinsed her face with cold water and glanced back at the mirror. Already it was clouding again and trickles of condensation were sliding down the glass. Her reflection was not true, it was fragmented and indistinct.

She turned away feeling angry with herself. She was like her reflection, blurred and indeterminate.

Why couldn't she be like her mother, strong-willed and resolute? Minna, in her position, would not lurk in the bathroom wondering how to approach her daughter. She would have tackled Paula as soon as she had returned home, demanding the facts. She wouldn't have considered hurt feelings or privacy. She would have listened to what her granddaughter chose to tell her and then she would have advised her as to the best course of action; and if Paula had chosen not to follow her advice, Minna would have shrugged her shoulders and dismissed the whole business from her mind.

If the headstrong child wouldn't listen to her elders and betters, well then, let her go her own way.

But she mustn't skulk about in the bathroom. Rosie opened the window to dispel some of the condensation and then went back downstairs.

She was about to go into the kitchen when Steve came hurtling down the staircase behind her.

'Hi, Mum. What a long face. Cheer up, it's not that bad.'

At least he was in good spirits. She smiled at him and thought: It will be if we're not sitting down to eat within the next few minutes.

It hadn't occurred to Paula that her mother and brother

were finding her present behaviour difficult for the simple reason she had not thought about them. The only person she thought about was Dave, and when he would telephone her to make up. Indeed, because she had thought of nothing else, the whole day had passed like a dream.

In the morning she had tidied up and played with Alison. She didn't expect her husband to phone until after lunch but he might, so she didn't go out. She didn't want to go outside the house anyway, she looked such a sight.

Dave, she reasoned, would arrive back at the flat about midday. He would be feeling terrible because last night he was certain to have got drunk and finally crashed out on someone's sofa. He would be worse than usual, because their fight had been so horrendous.

Paula stared into space. Dave had been looking for trouble when he came home and she had been in the mood to dish it out. He had been moody and bad-tempered for days and when he had refused to answer her when she asked him something, she had hit the roof. She had said things that should have remained unsaid and, worse than that, she had used sarcasm as a weapon.

Dave couldn't cope with sarcasm and it was then that he had hit her and told her to get out.

'I'm sick of you mouthing off. I'm sick of your demands. What the hell do you want of me? For Christ's sake get out and take the kid with you.'

Paula's hand went up to her damaged cheek.

She remembered her feeling of shock and she also remembered that Dave's face had mirrored the same shock.

Oh, he had slapped her a couple of times before, as she had slapped him, but this was different. He had hit her with his fist.

She had staggered back against the wall and stared at

him. He had stared back and then said the words that had been even more chilling, because this time he did not shout.

'I think we ought to split up, Paula. We're destroying each other.'

And he had walked out.

But he hadn't meant it. He couldn't mean it. He would ring soon and ask her to come home.

But he hadn't yet, and her panic was rising. Throughout the rest of the day, she kept busy. She had prepared the evening meal and hoovered and dusted the house. She was glad Steve and her mother were not there. Without their presence, she could pretend nothing had happened. She could pretend she was back at the flat, doing normal, everyday things.

Fortunately, Alison had behaved herself. She had slept late, appearing downstairs just after eleven, drowsy and quiet. Paula had washed and fed her and then dumped her in front of the television set where she had been quite content to sit and watch a variety of cartoons followed by a black and white film made in the thirties or forties. Cary Grant starred along with a blonde woman and a chimpanzee.

Alison liked animals, particularly dogs and monkeys. A couple of months ago, Dave had taken them to a zoo. He had lifted Alison up to see the camels and he had said . . . Paula raised her fist to her mouth. Please God, let him ring.

Ever since her mother and Steve arrived home she had been on edge. They had both eaten heartily and over-praised her cooking. She had swallowed a couple of mouthfuls and tasted nothing. If Dave telephoned now, she thought, they would be straining their ears to hear her conversation. Why had he waited so long? He should have known how difficult it would be for her. But a difficult call was better than none at all.

After the meal, later in the evening, she sat by the bed and watched Alison sleep. Her daughter's face was serene and relaxed and, without warning, Paula began to cry. She cried for a few minutes and then stubbornly fought back her tears. She whispered aloud: 'Dave, you bastard, you *have* to call me. Don't you realise, we're no good without each other?'

She mopped the tears off her face with her sleeve. Her mother mustn't know she'd been crying.

Rosie was downstairs watching the television but Paula knew, the moment she walked through the door, her mother would spot any tell-tale signs. She didn't miss a thing, her mother. Paula glanced back at her daughter and doubted that she would ever be so perceptive about her. She loved Alison but Dave was more important to her, always would be.

She supposed Rosie was what was called a 'natural born mother', which was lovely when you were little, but not so hot when you grew up because whenever you were miserable, a motherly sort of mother began immediately to probe into your private life. And because their interference was so loving and gentle, you couldn't turn round and tell them to go to hell.

Mum had been like that after Dad had died so suddenly and now she was itching to get involved again. Why couldn't she realise there was nothing she could do? You can't mend a grown-up problem with a kiss and a sticking plaster.

Paula sighed. Only she and Dave could sort this problem out, and they would, because ever since the day they'd met they'd known they belonged together.

★ ★ ★

Five years ago. The room Paula was sitting in faded for her as she remembered. There had been a rave in an empty warehouse on the outskirts of Manchester and she had gone there with two mates. The place had been packed and the atmosphere had been electric. It was just what she needed. She'd finished with her latest boyfriend the week before. No big deal that. She hadn't even liked him much but he had been better than nothing. But after the split she had felt depressed.

Four months earlier she had left home and gone to share a flat with a girl she knew called Tracey Hall. Tracey was living in Manchester. Paula had been fed up with all the rules, rows and hassles at home so travelling to Manchester had been exciting. She had been full of hope and full of plans.

'I'll be fine,' she told her worried mother. 'I've got a place to stay and a job promised. There's absolutely nothing to worry about.'

On the train she had been bubbling with excitement. She was striking out on her own. She was free. But on arrival, her dreams had turned sour. Her flatmate Tracey was a slut. The flat was dirty and Paula couldn't bear it. She spent her first weekend in Manchester cleaning up and Tracey had found her need for cleanliness both annoying and hilarious.

'Don't expect me to turn into a fusspot like you. If you don't like living here you'd better find somewhere else.'

So after that, she was cleaning up for both of them. Paying half the gas and electricity bills was more expensive than she had realised and the offered job didn't pay too well. The work, in a cut-price music shop, wasn't too bad but after a week it bored her, and the spotty, shambling boys who hung around all day listening to tapes were just the same as the ones back home.

Of course, her rare phone calls home told a different story.

'Everything's smashing, Mum. Yes, I'm eating enough and the work I'm doing is really interesting.'

How could she admit that her mother and brother had been right about everything? When she applied for better jobs and was turned down, she realised, yes, she *should* have stayed on at school. She *should* have thought more about her future. Then she looked at the smug airheads who turned her down and her mouth set. Maybe it wasn't too late. She was as bright, if not brighter, than they were. To the great amusement of Tracey, in the autumn she signed on at night school for a course in business studies. The first evening, she covered her nerves by spraying blue colouring on her dark hair and wearing green and yellow leggings, a lurex top and black boots. She certainly stood out in the class of young women wearing sensible low heels, plain white blouses and dark skirts. She saw their sidewards glances and ignored the faces they pulled. Three months later the smiles had disappeared because she consistently scored the highest marks in the class.

By then she had finally accepted that, for some reason unknown to her, she was an oddity. She just didn't fit. She hadn't fitted in at home, nor at school, and she didn't fit in with Tracey and her mates. So be it. She'd get by. She worked hard at her studies and went out with the most attractive boys who ogled her at the record shop. A couple of times, when she was feeling particularly lonely, she slept with one of them, but it didn't mean anything. Every Thursday she wrote a short letter to her mum. She didn't want to go home – God, no – but it was nice to know someone was thinking of her.

Once a week she went out with Tracey and her friends

and got drunk with them. The world seemed a warmer place on those nights. She was offered hard drugs but wouldn't touch them. Drugs were for airheads. A joint now and again didn't do any harm, but nothing else . . . ever. As she already knew, she was an oddity.

There were drugs circulating at the rave but it didn't bother her. She often wondered why the 'oldies' made such a song and dance about the drug scene. It was a waste of money advertising against drug taking, stuff like that. It was up to the individual, wasn't it? If people were thick enough to blow their minds, let them. Different with the youngsters, of course.

If she'd caught anyone handing stuff to Steve when he'd been a kid, she'd have shopped them. Not that Steve would have been tempted. Her brother was so straight, he might as well be in his coffin already.

Well, it was a great rave, one of the best she had ever been to. Flashing strobe lights, hysterical music, and a seething mass of gyrating bodies, sweaty with heat and excitement. She'd plunged into the thickest part of the mob and thumbed her nose to the guy offering her a handful of pills. On nights like this, she didn't even drink – only water to stop dehydrating. The atmosphere was enough to give her a high.

She had danced for hours, her hair was wet and her jeans and top were soaked with perspiration, and then someone dancing next to her flaked out, just slumped on the floor, and she caught his prone body with her foot and stumbled. She would have fallen, but a hand snaked out of the crowd and caught and held her. She looked up and there he was. She remembered how her stomach had started a funny, jittery little dance.

'You all right, little lady?' He had a soft, sweet, sexy voice.

When she didn't reply, he had taken her hand. 'Let's get out, take a breath of air.'

Outside – she had never forgotten – the air had smelt as clean and sweet as if cars had never been invented. The stars above them had glittered as if they'd been taking grade A speed and even the noise from inside faded.

They were in the darkness, alone. Four miles away lay a motorway but a distant car horn and the moving specks of lights merely emphasised their aloneness . . . two expectant bodies, waiting for something to happen.

'My name's Dave. What's yours?'

She told him.

He smiled. He had fair hair, straight brows above eyes which were an unusual pale green colour, and sensual, well-shaped lips. 'Paula, that's nice.'

Her heart turned over. She couldn't stop staring at him.

His smile faded as he studied her face. 'You're really beautiful, Paula, do you know that?'

Normally, she would have made a wisecrack. 'Can't you think of a better opening line?'

Now, wordlessly, she shook her head.

'I've been watching you all night. Are you with someone? I didn't see . . .'

'No.' She whispered, then almost shouted, 'No . . . I came with some girlfriends.'

'I came alone. I wasn't going to, and then I did.' He touched her arm. 'I must have known.' He laughed when she shivered and then he put his hands on her shoulders and pulled her close to him. She shut her eyes and he kissed her closed eyelids and then her mouth. He's confident, she thought, and very sure of his power. She smiled to herself.

He was quite small, maybe five foot six or seven, but his

slim body was muscular. She felt his lean hips pressing against her.

'Do you want to go back inside?'

'What?' She opened her eyes and then shook her head.

'Neither do I. We'll go to my place then.' It was a statement, not a question. He took her hand and they walked towards the car park. 'Got a jacket?'

'No.'

He whistled softly through his teeth. 'You'll be cold. You'd better wear mine.'

He helped her on with his leather jacket and she wrapped it around her and smelt the smell of him and then sat behind him on the powerful 500 cc motorbike and they roared off, away from the lights and music. Head down, protected from the whipping wind by his back, Paula felt so alive she thought she might die of it. She tightened her grasp around his waist and wanted them to go on and on . . . never to stop, to travel to the ends of the earth together.

But he did, of course. Dawn was breaking when he cut the power and turned the bike into a crescent of houses named Bingham Road. They stopped outside a block of flats on the corner. A milk wagon was rattling along the road and it terrified Paula because, suddenly, the real world was intruding into the magic.

But ten minutes later, when they had hurriedly shucked off their clothes and were together on his bed, the magic was there again, only stronger. He stared at her and then his hands and lips moved over her body and she felt like a flower opening for the first time. This was what she had yearned for, she thought, and this was the end of loneliness. She made a small sound and put her hands upon his fair hair and he raised his head and smiled at her. 'You're even more beautiful than I imagined.'

'So are you.'

For a long moment they didn't move but the silence between them was full of words, and then he pulled her closer. She wound herself around him and their bodies melded into one. There was a joining and a loving, a giving and a receiving, and it was almost too wonderful.

And so afterwards, when it was over, they said little. They lay in bed, drank Coke and studied each other's faces, and then they nibbled at each other, like puppies playing. Then they slept, tangled in each other's arms, and upon waking, they knew without words that they were an item.

Downstairs, the phone trilled. Paula stumbled to her feet, hurried to the door and rushed down, her heart beating wildly.

'Sorry, it's for me.' Steve looked up from the hallway and gave an apologetic smile. 'It's Jill.'

She nodded. The smile on her face felt as though it had been stitched on with a red hot needle. 'That's all right.'

Damn Jill, she thought. Damn her to hell. She turned and went into the sitting room.

Rosie looked up. 'You've been a long time, love?'

She nodded. 'Alison took a long time to go to sleep.'

'Oh dear. I suppose the strange bed . . .' Rosie's voice trailed away. She looked back at the television set and then stood up and turned it off.

Paula groaned inwardly.

'Paula, I do think you should tell me about this upset with Dave. Perhaps I can help in some way?'

'It's not that serious, Mum. We had one of our rows and . . .'

'But your face.'

'It looks worse than it is. I was being a perfect bitch, Mum. Alison had been off-colour and I was stuck in the flat with her and then Dave came home and I started on at him. There was an overdue electricity bill and Dave's pay packet was short and, well, things just got out of hand.'

Rosie shook her head. 'There's absolutely no excuse for a man to hit his wife. Your father . . .'

Paula's hands began to tremble. 'Dad was a patient man, Mum, and let's face it, I'm a totally different person from you.'

Steve stuck his head around the door. 'I'm off round to Jill's, Mum. Won't be late.'

The two women looked at him.

Paula was glad of his intervention, Rosie annoyed.

'All right, Steve.' She frowned. 'You don't have to tell me every time you go out, you know.'

He blinked. 'Sorry.'

The front door closed behind him with the suspicion of a bang.

'Jill likes to keep tabs on him.' Paula raised her eyebrows. 'Doesn't he meet his friends any more? Go running or out for a few drinks?'

'Sometimes.' Rosie's brow creased. 'He's talking of resigning from the cricket club. Too time-consuming, he says. Too many away matches.'

'Oh dear.' Paul looked slantwise at her mother. 'Who helped him reach that decision?'

'Well . . .' Sensing a trap, Rosie paused. 'We were talking about your problems, Paula, not your brother's. Look, if money worries are causing the rows, perhaps I can help out? I have a bit put by.'

'I wouldn't hear of it.' Paula shook her head. 'I've never taken a penny from you since I went to Manchester and I'm not starting now. Anyway, it isn't the real problem.' She chewed on her lip and decided to reveal the tip of the iceberg.

'Now I'm doing temping work, I sometimes earn more money than Dave. I think that hurts his pride. He can't get any higher in the firm he's working for and there's no other jobs around at the moment. He gets moody and bad-tempered. And then Alison is still a devil about sleeping. She wakes up and shouts for me most nights and then next day we're all tired.'

'But other young couples have similar problems and the man doesn't hit his wife.' Rosie shook her head. 'I'm worried for you, Paula. What if he hits you again? Are you telling me that you'll just put up with it?'

'He won't, Mum. He was dreadfully upset. I know he won't do it again.'

Rosie's face was stern. 'I hope you're right. Anyway, Steve seemed to think that Dave has left you. Is that right?'

Concern flowered on her face at Paula's sudden change of expression.

'I'm sorry. But maybe it would be best if he did stay away. You're young and you're a lovely girl, Paula. You could manage without him.'

She didn't understand, not one tiny bit. She would never understand. Her mother thought she understood people but they had to be people like her. Steve, for example, or the old buffers she cared for at The Firs. People whose fires had burnt low or never caught alight to start with.

Paula clenched her hands. 'I don't want anyone else, Mum. I only want Dave. And despite everything, he wants and needs me. He'll ring me tomorrow, for sure. And then I'll go home and you can stop worrying about me and you and Steve can settle down to your quiet, boring little life again . . .'

For one long moment Paula stared unflinchingly at her mother and then, with a toss of her head, she was gone, the door slamming shut behind her.

Chapter Six

The frontage to the tower block of flats in which Minna Norwood lived was bleak in the extreme, being a large, bare concrete area fringed by vague grass borders. Across the middle of the square a path was marked out which led up to the main entrance to the building. Someone in the past, perhaps a council official long-since forgotten and maybe depressed by the grimness of the area, had arranged for wooden benches to be placed at intervals alongside the long, straight path, and between the benches stood green-painted flower tubs. Because it was now winter the tubs were empty, but Rosie thought they were actually less depressing that way. As she walked past them she remembered last spring.

It had been a day in late April and she was with her mother when the council lorry had arrived. From Minna's seventh-floor window Rosie had watched the gardeners as they took trays of plants from the lorry, diligently filled the tubs with compost and then planted out the small flowers, blue forget-me-nots and velvety gold and purple pansies.

'Come and see.' She had looked over her shoulder. 'They look lovely, Mother. Come and see the difference they make.'

Minna had stayed in her chair. 'Waste of time and money. They won't last five minutes.'

They certainly hadn't lasted a week. On Rosie's next visit, half of the cuttings were dead or dying through lack of water and the other half, having been wrenched from the tubs by persons unknown, were brittle brown skeletons lying on the concrete.

It had been a fine day, Rosie remembered, and she had stood in the sunlight and bent her head, mourning them, and her depression had deepened when she looked up again and watched the little children shouting and playing on the hard grey concrete and the young mothers sitting on the benches rocking a pram with one hand and drawing on a cigarette with the other. Poor, poor children, she had thought, deprived of the pleasures of rolling in grass, picking daisies and staring up at the blue sky through branches of cherry and apple blossoms.

She had been sniffing when she arrived on the seventh floor of Talbot Towers.

'Hay fever, I expect,' said her mother.

Rosie had nodded and blown her nose. She couldn't possibly explain her thoughts to Minna. Her mother had no interest in the natural world. A freshly cleaned oven or a beautifully ironed blouse was a thing of beauty to Minna, not a river with swans or a horse chestnut tree in full bloom. The depressing view from her window didn't bother Minna because she never looked out.

But what about the other tenants, how did they cope? Rosie looked up at the building she was approaching and felt cheered when she spotted, among the rows of anonymously shrouded, net-curtained windows, brief signs of individuality. On one windowsill she saw a row of flowering cactus plants; on the floor above a large poster of Spider Man had been pasted to the window, and on the top floor, like a flag of defiance, the bottom of a bright poppy red curtain had escaped through a partly opened window and was flapping enthusiastically in the gusting wind.

She had arrived at the entrance. She shifted her shopping bag into her left hand, pushed open one of the heavy doors and went into the building. Her footsteps clattered on the tiled floor as she walked over to the lifts. She pressed the call button, which should have been illuminated but wasn't, and stood back to wait, looking around her.

The hallway was gloomy. The windows either side of the entrance doors were protected by wire meshing which cut down on the daylight but there was still enough to observe the plaster flaking off the distempered walls and Rosie was sure the large patch of damp on the lofty ceiling had grown since last week.

She wondered, not for the first time, why her mother resisted all the attempts she had made to find a more suitable home for her. Attractive housing for single elderly people was hard to find but since Minna had moved to Talbot Towers there had been two good possibilities of a change of residence. However, her mother had shown no interest.

The last time Rosie had broached the subject was fifteen months ago when she had heard about a rented flat which was shortly to become available in a housing trust development. The flats were attractive, in a decent area, and much closer to Rosie's own home and so she had rushed straight round to Minna to tell her about it.

Her mother's reaction had been disappointing. 'I'm not up to the hassle of moving. I'm all right here.'

'But we would help you move, Mother. Steve could move most of your stuff using his car. It's not as if you have masses of furniture, you have never been a hoarder.' Rosie had glanced round her mother's spotlessly clean but sparsely furnished home. 'Why don't you come and see it?

It's very nice and only twenty minutes' walking distance from my place.

'There's five flats, set back from the road which has very little traffic. There's a lovely communal garden that you could sit in. Please, Mother, come with me to see it. I can order a taxi. We can't waste time because several other people are interested in it.'

'Well, let one of them have it. I've no desire to sit around in a garden with a group of senile old people, and you know I have a bad reaction to wasp stings.' Minna had sniffed. 'Of course, I understand *your* enthusiasm. If I moved, it would be easier for you.'

Rosie had flushed but met her mother's eye. 'Yes, it would be. I have to catch two buses to come here, you know. If you moved to the place I'm telling you about, I could visit more often.'

Minna had turned her face away then and Rosie hadn't been able to see the effect of her words. None, probably. She had sighed and given up.

'Very well, I won't mention the subject again, only this place is so dreary. I know you had to find somewhere to live in a hurry after Dad died and you sold the house. I expect the fact that your friend Mrs Laws lived here swayed your judgement, but she's been dead these past three years and . . .'

Minna interrupted her. 'We both know why I came here to live. I found I couldn't afford to live anywhere else. The house in Halifax sold for next to nothing. It was old property. Your father never gave a thought to the future. I had to find somewhere to live and I couldn't come to you, could I?'

Rosie bent her head. 'There wasn't the room, Mother.'

'I know that.' Minna sounded irritated. 'Don't look so hangdog, child. You know I would have hated living at your place with two children running around.

'Anyway, I'm getting sick of this conversation. I'm settled now and perfectly content. This flat's snug enough and the old man who lives next-door is as quiet as a mouse. If I move, who knows who I might find living next to me?

'At least the other residents on this floor are white-skinned and reasonably sane! What if I moved and found revolting curry smells drifting through to my place or even a couple of mentally disturbed people living next-door to me? They do that, you know. The council's closing all the mental homes and letting these people back into the community.' She sniffed again.

And then, as Rosie looked at her, speechless, she poured out another cup of tea and continued.

'I'm surprised you thought Mrs Laws was a friend of mine. She was a very *silly* woman.' She handed the silent Rosie her cup and saucer. 'She had a wonderful stamp collection though. Her husband started it, I believe, in the thirties. There was one particular stamp from British Honduras.' Minna sipped her tea. 'I really thought she might have left it to me. We used to talk about philately, you know. She knew I was interested. But that nephew of hers got everything, even though he never visited her.' She sighed and then asked: 'Did you bring me the packet of ginger biscuits I asked for?'

Rosie had handed her the packet of biscuits and her mother had stood up and put them into the biscuit barrel. She hadn't noticed her daughter's sudden lack of conversation but Rosie had been shocked. Her mother was, she knew, a self-centred and selfish woman, but Rosie had always told herself that at least she had had one close friend.

Now it appeared the only reason for that long friendship was the possible gain of an extremely valuable stamp.

★ ★ ★

She blinked when the lift jolted to a halt and the doors slid open. Busy with her thoughts, she had reached the seventh floor without noticing. She stepped out and walked along the corridor towards her mother's flat, rang the doorbell and waited, wiping her feet on the coconut matting doormat. It usually took a little time for Minna to answer.

Rosie heard her mother's footsteps and then the rattle of the safety chain being released.

'Rosemary?'

'Yes, it's me, Mother.'

Who else? she thought. To her knowledge her mother seldom had a visitor. Why, even Steve had to be bribed to visit his grandmother.

The door opened. 'Come in.'

Rosie entered the flat. She watched Minna replace the doorchain and then followed her as she walked through the tiny hallway into the sitting room. Minna walked slowly and Rosie, studying her back, suddenly realised how thin her mother was. She also noticed that Minna's shoulders were beginning to hunch and she felt a sense of shock. She had thought nothing would ever get the better of her difficult, imperious mother but she had been wrong because old age, the final adversary, was never defeated.

Minna crossed to her favourite, high-backed chair with the wooden arm-rests and Rosie, seeing how carefully she lowered herself into it, remembered the beautiful but remote mother of her childhood and discovered she had a lump in her throat. She swallowed hard.

Minna's full name was Wilhelmina. Her father, Pieter Van Heerden, had come to England from Holland sometime just before the turn of the century. A handsome and virile young man, from all accounts, he was soon married to an English girl and the couple had hoped for a large family. Their hopes had not been realised. Wilhelmina was their only child. She was christened with the name of her paternal grandmother.

So much Rosie knew, but very little besides. There were many such gaps in her knowledge of her family history. Her parents' marriage had been a peculiarly silent union and there had been just the three of them. Like her mother, Rosie was an only child and as an adult, thinking back to her childhood, she had realised that in all her memories, there had been a strange lack of wider family links.

Indeed, even the relationship within the immediate family had been strange. In her memory, she was always with one or the other parent. The only time she could remember being in the company of her mother and her father was at family mealtimes.

But, on the whole, she preferred not to try and remember too much. It was better to forget her childhood with the unexplained silences and tension and concentrate on her marriage to Howard, which was when her real happiness started.

There were, of course, a few happy childhood memories. There had been the Saturday afternoons spent helping her father in the garden, she remembered those. She had planted seeds and waited impatiently for them to grow. She had held the heavy sweet-pea plants as high as she could while he fastened them to canes to support the weight of the flowers. She had loved sweet-pea blossoms which she thought resembled a flock of brightly coloured butterflies flirting their wings in the warmth of the sun.

Her father had been a great vegetable grower. Rosie remembered picking garden peas and broad beans with him and then the two of them would sit on the back step of their terraced house to shell them. She could clearly recall the sound of the peas plopping into a cream enamel saucepan and remembered the feel of the earth between her fingers as she searched for new potatoes when her father forked them from the rich loamy soil.

He had smoked a pipe, but only in the garden. Years later, one whiff of pipe tobacco would tumble her back into childhood and she remembered how he had looked then, wearing his shabby gardening trousers and big boots, his blue eyes crinkling as he smiled down at her.

'You're a grand help, Rosie. Now you run to the top of the garden and fetch us a sprig of mint to go with the spuds.'

When he was gardening he would tell her things and smile but in the house her father was quiet and solemn. Indoors, he didn't exactly ignore her, but he was more distant, spending most of his time reading and listening to the radio.

Her mother was quiet too, but her quietness had been different. Rosie had been uneasy at Minna's quietness, she had shrunk from it. On the bad days, when the silence was a dark cloud over the house, she lost her own voice and spoke in whispers. Somehow she knew that her mother's quietness held despair and that one day, the despair might break through and overwhelm all of them. She knew, but she didn't know what to do about it.

Sometimes, in bed at night, she thought that perhaps it was all her fault. Perhaps her mother and father had been happy together until she came along to spoil things. But she tried not to think like that. After all, she hadn't asked to be born and she did try and be good.

And then later, when she had started school, anger became mixed up with her guilt. Why couldn't her mother and father be ordinary, more like the parents of her schoolfriends? Why didn't they joke and laugh a little, even have a row now and again?

But nevertheless, she loved them, her father for his kindness and her mother for her beauty. Minna was far more beautiful than any of the other mothers. Her hair was so dark and shiny and all her movements were quick and neat. Everything Minna did, she did well, and she transformed everything she touched into a thing of beauty.

Unlike their neighbours, their front step was always spotless, their windows shone with much polishing, and their net curtains were immaculate. Rosie and her parents lived in a terraced house in a grey area in the middle of the industrial town of Halifax and when Minna hung out her sheets in the back garden, they shocked the eye of the beholder with their whiteness.

Before she started school, Rosie had taken for granted her mother's industry. In the same way, she accepted that tables and sideboards were polished with beeswax regularly and covered with delicately crocheted mats. She took for granted that chairs were covered with hand-embroidered arm and head covers to keep them clean and her father always changed his clothes when he came home from work.

But after starting school and being invited to tea from time to time – she was a popular girl because she was so obliging – Rosie began to realise that her schoolfriends' homes were different.

Their houses were not dirty but they were unkempt. The kitchen floors were usually linoleum-covered, as was hers at home, but in her friends' houses, the lino often looked as though it needed a scrubbing and once she had felt her shoes actually stick to the floor.

Many a time there was no tablecloth on the kitchen table and jars of jam were dumped on it and not transferred into jam dishes as at home. On one never-to-be-forgotten day, she had asked leave to go to the toilet and the privy in the backyard had horrified her. Their own toilet was outside but it was sweet-smelling and clean. This one was awful. There were mouse droppings on the floor and cut-up newspaper hanging from a nail which which to clean yourself.

After that experience, Rosie always made sure she went to the lavatory *before* she went anywhere, but she still accepted invitations to tea.

What did jam jars and sticky floors matter when there was life and noise in a place; where there were kittens in a basket by the fire and it wasn't a crime to drop crumbs on the carpet? And her friends were tactful. They never held it against her that her dresses all had hand-embroidered collars and she wore clean socks to school every day.

Fortunately, Minna had never been interested enough to ask questions about Rosie's visits to her schoolfriends. It was a close-knit community, the girls all lived in the same area and she knew her daughter would be safe. The only rule was that Rosie must tell her mother where she was going and she must be back in the house for seven-thirty.

She was never late. She would go in by the back door and Minna would raise her head from her sewing and ask: 'Enjoy yourself?'

And Rosie would nod and her mother would put down her stitching and go and run a bath for her. Whenever Rosie went anywhere her mother lit the ancient gas boiler, which creaked and groaned but worked quite well, so that there was enough hot water for a bath when she returned home.

Minna did not go out much apart from shopping, she didn't seem to need company. She read and she enjoyed listening to music on the radio. Occasionally, she went alone to attend a concert. The rest of her life, it seemed to her daughter, was spent in a constant battle to keep her home, her husband and her daughter clean and tidy.

She had her work cut out for her with her husband. Thomas worked for a firm called Dean Clough's. They owned a large textile mill and he serviced all the machines. He came home filthy. Nevertheless, every morning a clean working shirt was laid out for him, his overalls were boiled three times a week and his boots were cleaned daily.

Rosie had assumed her father cleaned his own shoes and boots and the first time she saw her mother polishing away at them she had gaped, open-mouthed. Why was her beautiful mother, with her fine, long-fingered hands and tiny wrists, cleaning Dad's filthy working boots?

She had turned and glared at her father who was seated at the kitchen table reading a book. How *could* he sit there and let her do such menial work?

Maybe the depth of her outrage reached him for he had glanced up from his book and looked at her. She had never forgotten the expression that flitted across his face; it became one of the memories she would have preferred to forget.

Clearly, he had seen her disgust and accepted it. He had held her gaze and his eyes had pleaded with her, as though he wanted her to understand but there was no way to explain. She had scowled at him and he had looked away and then a moment later had picked up his book and left the room, closing the door quietly behind him.

And when the door had clicked shut, Minna had looked up from her work. She had glanced at the door and then at her daughter and a strange, bleak smile had played about her lips.

Very similar to the smile she was smiling now. Rosie jumped as her mother said: 'For goodness' sake, Rosemary, where have your wits flown to? Take that vacant look off your face and sit down.' The smile faded away. 'There's nothing wrong, is there?'

'No, everything's fine.' Rosie thought guiltily of Paula. Was she going to be brave enough to recount the story of her daughter's woes? 'I'm just a bit tired, that's all.'

'That's not like you.' Minna studied her daughter. 'I hope you're not getting 'flu. There was a report on the radio this morning about a new strain which is affecting the whole of Yorkshire and Lancashire. If you feel ill you shouldn't have come. I could have managed for a few more days. At my age, one has to be careful about infection.'

'No, really, it's nothing like that. I'm fine.' Rosie sat down in the nearest chair. 'Actually, I was just remembering something.'

'You've not forgotten to pay my electricity bill? I particularly asked . . .'

'No, Mother.' Rosie extracted the receipted bill from her handbag and placed it on the nearby occasional table. 'There's the receipt and,' she rummaged in her shopping bag, 'I changed your library book, too.'

'Umph!' Minna reached forward, picked up the book and scrutinised the cover. 'I don't think I've read it, although it's hard to tell nowadays, they all seem much the same.'

'The woman at the library's read it and she said it was good.'

Rosie leaned back in her chair and wiggled her toes within her shoes. At home she would have kicked them off, but she dared not here.

'That means it's probably full of sex scenes.' Minna shook her head and replaced the book on the table. 'If men and women actually behaved like the characters on TV and in books nowadays they would drop dead of exhaustion before their fortieth birthdays.' The bleak smile reappeared. 'Of course, people always have to have some obsession. When I was a young girl, the obsession was with death, not sex.'

'Perhaps it's a change for the better then,' murmured Rosie, thinking longingly of a warm, caring body in her bed at night, not necessarily for sex, just a loving cuddle.

'So tell me, how how are the children?' Minna sat back in her chair. She always demanded a progress report, more on the lines of their social advancement rather than their state of minds. 'Has Steve heard anything about the training course? And what about Paula? She wrote to me, you know. Last month, did I tell you?' A note of satisfaction sounded in her voice.

Paula was her grandmother's favourite which was strange, thought Rosie, considering how often Minna condemned her granddaughter's streak of wildness and her lack of consideration for others.

'That handsome young man she married, I hope she's keeping a tight rein on him?'

'I suppose so.' Rosie forced herself to meet Minna's gaze. I can't tell her, she thought with a sinking heart. I'm too much of a coward. 'Didn't she mention him in her letter?'

'No. She said she was working as a secretary to the managing director of a large chain of supermarkets.' Minna frowned. 'If only she'd settle into a proper job. Temping work is so unreliable.'

'I think it suits her for now. Alison's only two. Perhaps when she starts school Paula will go for a more settled job.'

'It was stupid of her, having a child so soon. In this modern day and age there are ways to prevent pregnancy.'

'Yes, I know.' Rosie shifted in her seat. 'But sometimes people in love get carried away, forget to take precautions.'

'Well, they shouldn't. They don't know how lucky they are. In my day . . .' Minna stopped talking and pressed her lips firmly together.

So she hadn't wanted me! The thought wasn't a new one, but for Rosie it still had the power to hurt. She shrank further back in her chair. After a pause, she said: 'You've not seen Alison since she was a baby. You'd be amazed at the change in her. Perhaps Paula could come over, bring her to see you?'

Let Paula explain to Minna how she got her black eye, she thought with uncharacteristic bitterness, since Minna had such regard for her.

'Perhaps.' Minna sounded non-commital. She stood up and moved, a little stiffly, towards the kitchen. 'I'll make the tea.'

Rosie nodded. She had stopped offering to make the tea a long time ago. Minna liked to do things her way.

Rosie had slipped off her coat before sitting down but now she put it round her shoulders again. The flat felt cold. The gas fire was turned on but she noted it was on the lowest possible setting. She wondered if her mother was truly able to manage financially.

Minna would never discuss her financial affairs with her daughter. 'I have enough to manage on, so long as I'm careful,' was all she would say. But perhaps the rate of inflation . . .?

Dare she ask her mother? And would Minna tell her, even if she asked? And how would it help? There was little she could do. Since Howard's death she had been forced to draw upon her own savings more and more. She sighed. Perhaps she was imagining a problem where there wasn't one. Minna's financial affairs couldn't be too bad, her treasures were all around the flat and some of them were valuable.

Rosie looked up at the two old Italian prints on the wall, she remembered those from her childhood, and the grandmother clock ticking softly in the corner of the room. On the sideboard stood two photograph frames. She stood up and went over to look at them.

The modern beechwood frame held a photograph of Rosie taken with her father when she was twelve years old. Dressed in their best, they stood stiffly side by side, smiling self-consciously. The other photograph was in a large, round, heavy silver frame, a frame that was certainly worth a lot of money. The photograph was old, the likeness of a dapper, good-looking man in his late forties. He was, Rosie knew, Pieter Van Heerden, Minna's father and her grandfather.

As she had done so often before, she stared at the figure. She had always been fascinated by the photograph. Her grandfather had obviously been posed by the photographer. In front of a backcloth of sky and trees he smiled out at the world. He wore a curly-brimmed bowler hat perched at a rakish angle on his head, and his right hand was clenched on the lapel of his jacket, obviously a ploy to show off the heavy gold watch chain draped across his broad chest. His other hand, at a slight angle from his body, rested on the top of a slender walking cane.

He had died long years before Rosie's birth and she wished she knew more about him. Minna never spoke about him and she had never asked.

'I bet *you* weren't obsessed by death,' she whispered aloud and her lips curved into a smile involuntarily at her grandfather's still potent insouciance and charm.

'Did you say something?' Minna came back into the room carrying a tray containing teapot, milk jug, sugar basin and two cups and saucers. She looked at her daughter with curiosity and Rosie coloured.

'No.'

'I thought you did.' Minna set down the tray and poured out two cups of tea, using a silver tea-strainer.

'Didn't you like the teabags I brought you last week?' Rosie accepted her cup of tea and changed the subject.

'No, not much. The tea was too strong. You can take the remainder back with you when you go.'

'I will.' Rosie sipped at her tea with relish. 'I always use teabags now, I can't be bothered with loose tea any more.'

'Well, you were always a little careless about the niceties of life, Rosemary, and now that you have to work . . .' She paused. 'I must confess, I do wish that your father and I had given more thought to your future when you were young.' She frowned. 'I doubt whether you would have managed a place at grammar school, but perhaps we could have got you into a technical college. You could have studied catering perhaps?' She shrugged her shoulders. 'Of course, you married so young, there was really no time to consider a career.'

Rosie's cheeks reddened. She took a deep breath. 'Marrying Howard was the best thing I ever did, Mother. We were very happy together. Of course it was difficult after he died, but the job I have now suits me fine. As a matter of fact,' she swallowed nervously, 'the Officer in Charge, the woman I work for, thinks I should aim for promotion. She's put my name forward for a course the Local Authority runs. If I'm successful, I'll be given a diploma and I could get a much better job.'

'Good gracious.' Minna put down her cup. 'You do surprise me.' She looked at Rosie thoughtfully. 'Are you sure you're up to it, though? I mean, it sounds interesting, but consider the disappointment if you fail. You know you've never been any good at academic subjects. Anyway, you have enough to do without taking on difficult study work.'

Oh, why hadn't she kept her mouth shut? Rosie's hand shook a little as she replaced her cup and saucer on the teatray. 'Well, nothing's actually settled yet, but Mrs Horton thinks I can do it. Anyway, the work is not purely academic. There's practical work, and we study behaviour patterns and look at ways to make old people feel more secure and happy.'

'Oh, one of those new-fangled courses? I've read about them.' Minna's voice was dismissive. 'Apparently people sit on the floor in circles and discuss their innermost feelings. They hug each other, too.' She picked up the teapot. 'You'd probably cope with that. Do you want another cup of tea?'

Rosie shook her head.

Three-quarters of an hour later, she caught the bus back home. She walked into the house and took off her coat.

'Mum?'

The kitchen door flew open and a radiant-faced Paula appeared.

'Dave's here. That's his car, outside. Well, it's not his car, he borrowed it off his friend. He's come to take us home.' She laughed, a loud, joyous sound. 'I'm getting our stuff together. I'm glad I've caught you because we'll have to leave soon. I was going to write you a note if you didn't get back in time. Good job I didn't go with you to Grandma's, eh? If we leave almost immediately we can be home by nine-thirty. Isn't that great? You don't mind if we rush away?'

Rosie thought that it wouldn't matter whether she minded or not – Paula glowed like a flame. It would be useless, and unkind, to attempt to dampen down the happiness. And, anyway, she didn't want to. Her mind returned briefly to her mother's remarks about the course. She smiled at her daughter.

'I'm so pleased for you, love.' She looked round. 'Where's Dave?'

'Upstairs, playing with Alison. Mum, you won't—'

'I won't say a word.' Rosie put her arms around her daughter and hugged her. 'Ring me when you get home.'

'I will, Mum.'

She wouldn't, they both knew.

Paula hurried upstairs again and a minute later Dave came down. He glanced at Rosie, a guarded expression on his face. He left it to her to open the conversation.

She stared at him. 'Paula seems delighted to see you.'

'Yes.'

'You're going straight back?'

He shifted his feet. 'Well, I thought it would be best. Joe wants his car back for work tomorrow.'

She nodded and wondered what to say next.

Dave didn't look like a man who would hit his wife. He looked like a young poet with his soft fair hair falling forwards over his youthful face. The memory of Paula's bruised cheek flashed into Rosie's mind and, despite her promise to her daughter, she heard herself saying: 'How could you hit her, Dave? I thought you loved her.'

He blinked his eyes rapidly. 'I do, Mrs Scott. I do love her.'

'Then why?'

He dropped his head. 'She gets me so mad, sometimes.'

'That's no excuse.' Rosie's voice hardened. 'All couples have rows, but the man doesn't bruise his wife's face.'

'It will never happen again, I promise you.' Dave took a step towards her. 'Paula's my life. What's happened has scared the hell out of me.' He looked at her with pleading in his eyes. 'We've always rowed, that's the way we are, but I think we've learned our lesson.'

He saw Rosie's outrage at his use of the word 'we' and

smiled a little bitterly. 'You must know your daughter can be hard to take sometimes, but I realise there's no excuse for my action. I guess we'll have our moments in the future, but there'll be no more violence. Please believe me.'

She studied his face. 'I hope so, Dave. I truly hope so.'

With a whirlwind of slamming doors and carrying of cases they departed. Rosie's last glimpse of them was the car speeding off and Alison's bewildered little face staring out at her from the rear window. She was clasping the bare, pink dolly to her meagre chest.

Then the house was quiet and Rosie, too tired to eat, went to bed. She left Steve a note, informing him of events. Of course, once in bed her mind began racing.

Would Paula and Dave ever live peaceably together? How would their volatile relationship affect Alison? Then her thoughts flipped to Minna and her finances. Could her mother afford the ever-increasing expenses of running her flat?

She heard Steve come in, bang about in the kitchen and then tiptoe upstairs so as not to disturb her. She was in such a state by then that she even worried about her son. He was too young to be contemplating marriage. Yet, she remembered, she and Howard had been just as young.

Finally, she twisted and turned in the suddenly too-hot bed and worried about herself. What a fool she was, imagining she could pass examinations at her age. She was a housewife, plain and simple. She couldn't be anything else, even though her husband was dead and her children no longer needed her. All she could do was care for old people and worry about everyone.

She remembered back to when she was a teenager living in Halifax in the fifties. In the area where she lived, the women didn't worry about bettering themselves. They were happy to stay at home. The women who did work did so out of necessity not choice. She had been like them, but suddenly she was not. She wanted more.

Remembering her mother's cruel comments, she sighed and tried to stop her brain racing. At last she slept and in her dreams her grandfather appeared. He raised his stick in a jaunty wave and she smiled at him. Then her sleep deepened and she let go, drifting away into tranquillity.

Chapter Seven

Minna Norwood frowned as she stood by her window and watched the figure of her daughter walk along the pathway towards the road. Rosemary's posture, she thought, had become very sloppy. All those years of reminding her to hold her head high and keep her shoulders down, and yet look at her now. Why, she resembled a worn-out, middle-aged woman.

The thought so annoyed Minna, she put out her hand to open the window, meaning to call out to Rosemary, tell her to straighten up and walk tall, but, of course, she didn't. One should never shout out of windows, whatever the provocation. Anyway, Rosemary was too far away now, she wouldn't be able to hear. Minna stood and watched the ever-diminishing figure of her daughter and her frown deepened for, quite suddenly, the awful truth struck her – Rosemary *was* middle-aged.

The dismay she felt made her angry. She was not a fool, she was aware of Rosemary's age, but somehow she had never before thought of her child as being middle-aged. Whenever she thought of Rosemary, it was memories she thought of: the chubby solemn-faced toddler, a thinner and more cheerful schoolgirl. She remembered how Rosemary had looked on her wedding day, an unexpectedly radiant bride, and then, when her children had been born . . . Minna shook her head, realising that was the last time she had really *looked* at her daughter.

This sudden uninvited glimpse of reality, therefore, was a shock. The tired-looking woman below, walking slowly and weighed down with a heavy shopping basket, was her daughter, and definitely middle-aged. And if Rosemary was middle-aged, then what was she?

She was old. Facing the bitter self-knowledge, Minna let drop the net curtain she had been holding and went back to her favourite chair near the gas fire. She sat down, held out her hands before her and studied them. Yes, they were an old woman's hands, wrinkled and marked with brown age spots. She marvelled at how blind she had been. And yet, she thought for a moment and then nodded her head slowly, was it so strange, how the years had slipped away unnoticed? Wasn't it true that her thoughts turned more and more to the past and less to the present?

'I'm a stupid old woman,' she said aloud.

She realised she was shivering, so she broke her own rules and turned up the fire, deciding to allow herself half an hour of luxury. The expense of heating the flat was becoming frightening but for once she refused to let the thought of the bills worry her. She always scraped up the money somehow. She rested her head against the wing of the chair and closed her eyes. The warmth was comforting and she relaxed as the peace and quiet of her room wrapped itself around her. She began to feel better. Did it matter that she was old? After all, there was no one to really care.

Even that thought did not distress her. She could hardly complain of loneliness because, through all her life, she had loved places rather than people. With one exception, of course. Her father she had loved more than the truly magnificent house in which she had spent her growing years and it was memories of him and of that house which had become her secret talisman against life's adversities. She pulled a face, remembering some of her other homes – the rented accommodation and some particularly squalid lodgings. However would she have coped without her memories?

Whenever life had become too awful, whenever she was in despair, she retreated into the past and re-created the time she had lived in her beautiful house, and through her memories she was somehow strengthened and given the will to carry on.

But she was not in despair now. In fact, now she was over the first shock of surprise, she realised she was quite content. How ridiculous of her, to feel upset about being old when a moment's thought revealed the compensations that age brought.

She thought about her early life, the times she had burned with useless passion and longing; the energy she had wasted trying to change things that couldn't be changed. What a fool she had been. No, it was youth that should be distrusted. Old age was a sanctuary.

She opened her eyes and looked around the room. This flat was a sanctuary. Rosemary couldn't understand why she wanted to stay here and there was no way she could explain, because she knew her daughter would never understand.

Poor Rosemary. Minna's smile disappeared. She had been unkind to her today. She should have encouraged, not belittled, her ridiculous scheme to study for a better job. But really, it was all nonsense. Rosemary would never be able to cope with the studying and she wasn't single-minded enough to make a success of anything. She was always too busy fussing over other people, her children, the old, the ill and the feeble.

And *you*, an inner voice whispered.

Minna sighed and sat upright in her chair. She hated feeling guilty and she felt guilt every time Rosemary visited her but couldn't change her behaviour towards her daughter. As a child and as an adult, Rosemary had irritated. She was so meek, she had no spirit.

If only she'd stand up for herself sometimes, answer back, defend herself, or even fling out of the flat in a temper. But she never did. No, all she did was shrink back inside herself and smile nervously.

Her timidity brought out the worse in Minna, she acknowledged it. She had never used physical force against her daughter, thank God, but she had been cruel to her in other ways. She sighed, remembering her barbed remarks which had grown sharper throughout the years. She had been dreadfully unhappy herself, of course, but that was no excuse for taking it out on the child.

And yet it wasn't just her own frustration that had prompted the harsh words, it was because she'd loved her daughter. At an early age she had learned that the world was a cruel place and had desperately tried to equip her only child for survival in it. She had wanted Rosemary to grow up with confidence in herself, to develop boldness to face her enemies, but Rosemary had no confidence, no boldness, she had humility.

And much good it had done her. A childhood of ingratiating herself to find friends who weren't worth having, a mediocre job for a couple of years and then marriage. Minna rubbed the base of her thumb where rheumatism was reminding her of its presence.

The day Rosemary and Howard married was the only time she had held her tongue. She hadn't approved, of course, but the happiness in the young couple's faces had silenced her. And they had continued happy for a time, until Howard's unexpected death. Then it was back on the treadmill for Rosemary, menial jobs, worrying over money, and looking after her grown-up children and spiteful old mother. Minna sighed again. Poor Rosemary, what a life.

She thought back to their conversation, when Rosemary had mentioned the possibility of studying for a diploma course and she had said her piece. There had been one brief moment then when she thought the worm would turn. She had waited in anticipation. But, no, her daughter had paused, breathed hard for a moment and then changed the subject, looking at her with her father's guileless blue eyes.

With an impatient movement, Minna leaned forward and turned down the fire. She didn't want to think about Thomas today; feeling guilty over the way she treated his child was enough. Trying to change the direction of her thoughts, she glanced around the room.

Rosemary was always trying to persuade her to move, but she wouldn't. She was content to stay here. Because she was on the seventh floor, she couldn't hear the outside noises and when she looked out of her windows, she saw only the sky. That pleased her because, with a little imagination, it was easy to pretend she was living somewhere else.

The flat itself was boxlike, comprising three medium-sized square rooms, a tiny hall, and an even smaller combined bathroom and toilet. It was easy to clean and Minna kept it immaculate. When she moved in, she'd had the walls painted a pale mushroom colour. It was a good neutral shade which showed off to advantage her two decent paintings.

She had bought dark blue curtains for the windows, and when the doors and skirting boards had been painted white, she had carefully positioned her treasures. Her grandmother clock stood where she could see it from her chair, the lacquered vase was on a small shelf facing the windows and her Regency figured mahogany sewing box was in the corner of the room. And, lastly, she had found the right place for her photograph.

She went and retrieved the silver photograph frame from the sideboard. She carried it back to the chair and sat down. A stab of rheumatism pierced her left hip as she did so. She flinched; one part of old age she could do without. She settled herself into a more comfortable position and stared down at the likeness of her father and then she lightly traced his features with the forefinger of her right hand. How handsome he was. Dear Papa.

His little princess, he had called her when she was small. She grimaced. It was a good job he couldn't see her now. She laid the photograph frame gently on her lap and retreated, as she did so often, into her memories.

Her tenth birthday, that was worth remembering. It was lovely weather, she recalled, which was appropriate for a June birthday, but it was extra special because her papa, who was an extremely busy man, had promised to devote the whole day to her. He had promised to take her somewhere she had never been before and somewhere she would never forget. And she never *had* forgotten that June day in the year 1920. She closed her eyes.

She could hear him shouting.

'Hurry up, Minna. We'll be late.'

'I'm coming, Papa.'

She ran out of her room and along the corridor, past the Edwardian mahogany display cabinet inlaid with ebony and satin wood, and the Victorian three-fold silk screen, the panels of which depicted exotic birds in foliate garlands.

Sometimes, waiting for Papa to come home, she sat behind the screen, tracing the outline of the birds with her fingers and imagining them alive and screeching in some exotic country across the seas, but she hadn't time for them today.

She skipped down the winding staircase, catching a glimpse of herself in the bevelled mirror which hung in the hall. She was wearing one of her birthday presents, a pretty white voile dress, and she looked, she thought complacently, very nice indeed.

Her mother had given in to her pleadings and the dress had been made in the adult style, narrow in line, with an unshaped bodice and long waist. She was wearing knee-length white stockings and white shoes, which were a bit babyish, but the brief skirt of her dress flared out as she moved and drew attention to her slender legs and that pleased her.

Betty, the little maid, had helped her brush her hair and then polished it with a silk scarf. It bounced halfway down her back in a dark cloud. Her father had refused her pleadings to have it cut and today, as she tossed back a curl, she was glad he had done so.

He was standing at the bottom of the staircase waiting for her and his eyes were alight with laughter.

'The only woman in the world who would dare keep me waiting.' He held out his hand and smiled. 'But now I see why. My little princess has turned into a fine lady overnight.'

'Oh, Papa!' She jumped from the fifth step from the bottom and he caught her and swung her round.

'For goodness' sake, Pieter, put her down, she's not a baby any more. Anyway, you know what a vain little minx she is. If she thinks her outfit's disarranged she'll be back upstairs prinking for another half hour.'

'I won't. You know I won't.' Minna's eyes felt hot with anger as she stared over her father's shoulder at her mother, who was slowly descending the staircase behind her. How plain she looks, thought Minna viciously. How old, with her hair pulled back in a bun and those dark clothes she always wears. And she's so thin . . . apart from that horrible bump, of course.

She averted her eyes and wrapped her arms tightly around her father's neck. 'Tell me where we're going?'

She could smell the lotion he had recently splashed on his smoothly shaven cheeks and the fainter smell of tobacco which permeated his clothes.

He hugged her to him and then set her down upon her feet. 'Not yet,' he murmured. He turned and held out his hand to his wife. 'We must go, Edith, we're running late already.' He put his hand on Minna's shoulder. 'Say goodbye to your mother.'

'Goodbye, Mother.' Minna shrugged loose and was already dashing towards the door.

'Perhaps you ought to take a coat.' Her mother had now reached the bottom of the staircase. She paused for breath, one hand pressed against her side. 'One never knows what the weather . . .'

'The child's fine as she is, and it's going to be an absolutely beautiful day.' Minna's father bent and brushed his cheek against that of his wife.

Minna glanced at them and then flung open the front door. It already was a beautiful day. She blinked in the brightness and then ran down the steps leading to the house and hurried towards her papa's most recent acquisition, a large, white automobile, gleaming in the sunlight.

'Hurry, Papa.' She hopped up and down waiting for her father.

He laughed as he followed her to the car and opened the door for her.

'Where are we going?' she asked again, as he started up the engine. Twisting round, she spotted a picnic hamper in the back of the car. 'Oh, a picnic. Are we going to the country?'

'Yes, and no.' Pieter Van Heerden sounded the horn and drove off with a flourish. 'We're going to the races.'

'Oh.' Her face fell.

He looked at her and laughed. 'Don't worry, I know you don't care for horses, but believe me, my dear, betting on the gee-gees is a different matter altogether from riding them.' He turned the car out of the crescent of houses in which they lived and swore under his breath as a strange contraption appeared directly in front of them and then swerved out of the way.

Minna was interested and sat forward in her seat. 'What on earth was that, Papa?

'A death-trap, Minna, otherwise known as a motorcycle and sidecar.'

Papa was cross. He was scowling and suddenly slammed down his hand on top of the dashboard, making her jump. 'What the hell is motoring coming to?' he demanded. 'When everywhere you look, scruffy little clerks and shop assistants who don't know how to drive are careering around the country in things like that?'

Minna considered. 'If they're dangerous,' she said, 'why don't they buy a car instead?'

Her father gave a short laugh. 'Give them time, my sweet, and they will. When you're grown-up, I wager the roads will be choked with working-class louts driving their piddling little Austin 7s and Morrises through England's green and pleasant land.'

Looking at the heightened colour in his face, Minna

decided to change the conversation, although personally she didn't see why working-class people shouldn't have a car, if they wanted one. After all, Papa had been working-class when he was young and had come to England from Holland. She had even heard him boasting about it once when there had been guests for dinner and several bottles of claret had been consumed. She had been listening outside the door of the dining room.

'. . . arrived without a penny to my name and not ashamed to admit it.' It was her father's voice, a little slurred. 'By God, England's a wonderful country. If you've brains and you're prepared to work hard, there's nothing you cannot do.'

Maybe most of the working-class people didn't work hard enough, that's why Papa thought they shouldn't have cars. Minna chewed on a fingernail and then, realising, folded her hands in her lap. The maid Betty, her friend, worked hard. She was on the go from morning to night but it was doubtful her family would ever have a car. Maybe they didn't have brains.

She dismissed the problem as being too complex and sat quietly, admiring the polished brass fittings on the car and then the scenery as they progressed into more rural surroundings.

'I don't really want to go to the races, Papa,' she suddenly announced. 'Can't we go somewhere else?'

'No, I'm afraid not.' Her father was calm again. His voice sounded amused. 'All the arrangements have been made and we are meeting friends.'

'Oh.' She relapsed into silence, feeling aggrieved. They would be Papa's friends, not hers, and she wasn't interested in racing and it was *her* birthday, not his.

Obviously sensing her thoughts, he looked down at her. 'You'll have a good time, princess. I promise you.'

Unappeased, she scowled and said nastily, 'Did you tell Mother we were going to the races?'

The note of amusement in his voice departed. 'No, I didn't.' He concentrated on his driving for a moment then said, 'Your mother has other things on her mind at the moment, without bothering about our day out.'

Minna studied the back of her hands. 'She's thinking about the baby, you mean?'

'Yes, the baby.'

They drove on and then he said, in a conciliatory tone of voice, 'You must try and be more civil to your mother, Wilhelmina. I know that lately she has been somewhat remote, but she's not feeling well and she's worrying. You know she has suffered a great deal during the last three years.'

She clenched her hands. He meant the two dead babies. He shouldn't talk about them on my birthday, she thought. He shouldn't talk about sad things and he shouldn't call her Wilhelmina either. He only did that when he was vexed with her. To her annoyance, her eyes filled with tears. How could he be so cruel, making her cry on her birthday? But then she remembered – it wasn't only her mother who had suffered.

The day the second baby had died, she had been in the hallway when her father had rushed into the house, summoned from his office by the family doctor.

He had looked dreadful, ashen in colour with his hair wild and disarrayed. She had shrunk back against the wall as he hurried upstairs and for the first time in her life she had been glad he had not noticed her.

Thinking about that day and the days that followed, when Papa had shut himself away in his study for two days and then the day the two tiny coffins had been put into the ground, she felt tenderness for him. She put her hand on his arm.

'Very well, Papa, I'll try, and I'm quite happy to go to the races.'

He laughed and took his hand off the wheel to caress her cheek. 'You'll have a lovely time, princess, I promise. We're to have a wonderful picnic and I'll let you have some champagne with your strawberries. It must be a secret from your mother, though.' He winked at her. 'You can help me pick the winners and we'll stroll down to the ring and see the horses and the jockeys. I'm looking forward to showing off my beautiful daughter and you'll be able to see all the fashionable clothes worn by the ladies.' He grimaced. 'It will make a change from those dowdy things your mother insists on wearing.'

She nodded but felt unsure. His friends might be nice, but she would have preferred to have him all to herself on her birthday, and as for the beautiful ladies . . . surprisingly, a wave of sympathy for her mother flowed through her. Mama was often stern with her but she was fair and she couldn't dress in fashionable clothes, not when she was expecting a baby.

'Which racecourse are we going to?' she asked in a small voice.

He threw back his head and laughed. 'There's only one place to go racing in June, Minna, and that's Ascot!'

Papa's friends, when they joined them, were very fine indeed. Some of the gentlemen wore top hats and frock-coats but they were mostly oldish. The younger men, of whom her father was one, wore more informal three-piece suits, but their clothes were very fine and made of the best materials.

Minna thought her father would have looked much more handsome wearing a top hat. She challenged him. 'Why haven't you got dressed up, Papa?'

'Today isn't one of the big race days, Minna. It's more of

a fun day, more appropriate for your birthday. Anyway,' his voice dropped, 'your mother would have known our destination then, wouldn't she?'

As her father had predicted, it was the ladies who fascinated Minna. She had never seen such beautiful creatures. Their clothes were so pretty and made of such light materials, silk and crêpe-de-chine. Minna thought of the horrid serge gym-slip she had to wear at school and decided she couldn't grow up fast enough.

Their hats were silly, though. They were so deep-crowned and wide-brimmed it was difficult for her to see their faces or for them to see anything at all. They all made a great fuss of her, crowding around her like a flock of butterflies. It was nice but she didn't like it when they patted her face as though she was a baby.

'I'm ten years old,' she kept telling them, but they just laughed.

The picnic was fun. Some of Papa's friends had been driven to Ascot and it was their chauffeurs who spread out the large white linen tablecloths on the grass and unpacked the picnic hampers. Watching them carving slices of tender pink ham and tumbling strawberries into cut glass bowls, Minna wondered why Papa hadn't used Randell, their chauffeur. He wanted today to be a secret, she thought, remembering his earlier comment – a special secret to be shared by just him and me. She thrilled with pleasure.

Whilst eating the picnic food, some of the ladies removed their hats and Minna was even more fascinated, though a little shocked by them. They produced long cigarette holders and smoked, even though people were eating, and she thought all of them painted their faces. They had such cupid-bow red mouths and such pink cheeks. They were still being kind to her. They picked out the largest strawberries for her and chatted to her in their high, breathless voices.

'Your father's told us so much about you, darling.'

'You must help me pick a winner. It's your birthday, so I guess you'll be lucky.'

'Oh, to be young again, young and innocent.'

The last remark was from a willowy brunette wearing a dress with a very short skirt and flesh-coloured stockings who sat next to Minna and her father during the picnic and drank, Minna noticed with disapproval, a vast quantity of champagne.

'Is she a friend?' she whispered to her father.

'She'd like to be.' Pieter raised one eyebrow and smiled at his daugher. 'Why?'

'I don't like her.'

He spluttered over his champagne glass. 'Oh, my princess, spoken like a true woman.' He looked round the group of people and said, in a low voice, 'Who *do* you like, then?'

Minna looked round the group surrounding them and considered. 'Her.' She pointed to a lady who had chatted with her earlier. 'That lady, in the blue dress.'

He looked in the direction in which she pointed. 'Ah, yes. Cicily Chesterton.' He looked again and then, turning to Minna, saluted her. 'I admire your judgement.'

She smiled at him and ate more strawberries and cream. He had been right, as always . . . she was enjoying herself.

When everyone had finished eating, the racegoers left the servants to clear away and turned to the serious business of the day.

'Coming to check out the odds, Van Heerden?'

Minna saw her father shake his head and smile. 'Not just yet, Grafton. I promised to show my daughter around.'

Bursting with pride, Minna took the arm he so gallantly offered to her.

They strolled round admiring the horses and the jockeys in their colourful clothes. She saw more ladies in beautiful clothes and then her father took her to see a line of men who were standing on boxes and shouting and making funny gestures to the crowds that surrounded them.

'They're bookies, Minna.' Pieter laughed. 'They're the only chaps who *know* they'll end the day winning.' He explained Tic-Tac to her, the bookies' sign language to telegraph the latest news from one betting ring to another. 'The white gloves are used for visibility.'

She clung to him, enjoying every minute. She didn't care about the betting or the bookies, but she was woman enough to appreciate the sideward glances her father attracted from ladies passing by, and exulted in the fact that all his attention was focused upon her.

'Now, Minna.' He was studying his little book. 'It's time for some serious thought. What are we going to back in the first race? You pick.' She did so and shouted as the horse galloped round the track and came in second.

But as the afternoon wore on and the sunshine turned hazy, her pleasure dulled. Her father became more interested in comparing prices and talking with his friends and she became bored with watching the horses. In truth, she found them frightening when they pounded towards the winning post, their eyes rolling wildly and foam flecking their muzzles.

Just before the fifth race her father left her in the charge of one of the ladies and went to the bar for a drink. Minna decided her feet hurt from standing too much and so, without telling anyone, she made her way back to the cars.

'Hello, miss.' One of the chauffeurs was sitting on the grass reading a newspaper. He had unbuttoned the high collar of his uniform and his face was a reddish-brown from the effects of the sun. He looked nice and she smiled at him.

'Are there any strawberries left?'

'No.' He scrambled to his feet. 'But there's some fruit, apples and pears.' He took a box from the back of the car.

She selected a pear, sat down on the grass and took off her shoes. A shadow fell on her and she looked up to see the lady in the blue dress standing over her.

'That looks good. I think I'll join you.'

She said something to the chauffeur and waited as he took a rug from the car and placed it on the grass and then she also took a pear and sat down next to Minna.

'Have you enjoyed your birthday?'

'Oh, yes.'

'Really?' She looked amused. 'I would have thought you'd have preferred a party with your friends.'

'I don't care for parties, and I'd rather be with Papa than with anyone.'

The lady looked thoughtful and bit into her pear. 'Yes, I can see that.'

'At last, a winner.' The deep voice made them both jump. 'Ten to one, too.' Pieter Van Heerden seated himself on the grass and slung his arm around Minna's shoulder. 'You shouldn't have sneaked off like that, Minna. Lydia was worried.'

'I was all right, Papa.'

'Yes. You found yourself some good company, I see.' Her father didn't mean the chauffeur. He was smiling at the lady in blue and she was smiling back.

The banging on her door aroused Minna from her half dream, half sleep. She blinked and passed a hand over her eyes. The sounds and sights of Ascot racecourse sixty-five years ago receded, and she was once more back in her flat in Talbot Towers. The banging came again. She sighed and hoisted herself to her feet.

It was the little man from next-door, peering apologetically through his thick glasses.

'I'm so sorry, but the meter's run out, see, and I've no ten-pence pieces. I wouldn't worry you but I don't want to go out in the dark.'

Was it dark outside? She blinked again and went to find her purse.

No good telling him to pay his bills quarterly, he would never manage to save the money. She exchanged money with him and closed the door.

Rosie, she thought, would be astounded to see how gracious she was to a dithery old man, but she had a fellow sympathy for him. He too was old enough to remember the days when cars were few on the road and the sight of ladies smoking in public provoked a feeling of shock. She smiled faintly, although she doubted he ever went to Ascot.

She turned off the fire, tidied up and then prepared for bed. Perhaps it was as well Mr Jones had disturbed her when he did, she mused. After all, she had relived the happiest part of her tenth birthday.

She and Papa had left the racecourse after the last race, laughing and shouting goodbye to their companions. Papa had been in high spirits, singing aloud as they sped homewards. Only as they had approached home had his face sobered.

'No need to make a big thing about today, Minna. Between you and me, your mother doesn't approve of betting. If she asks, of course you must tell her, but if she doesn't, well – just say we were in the country and had a smashing picnic.'

Her mother didn't ask, not that day or ever. They

reached home to find Edith Van Heerden had been take ill two hours after they had left the house. The doctor had been called but he couldn't save the child, a boy. Edith Van Heerden was ill but would recover.

'I saw 'im,' Betty told Minna in a hushed whisper that night. 'Poor mite. Perfect he was, with a milky white face and a wisp of hair. He even had nails on his poor little fingers.'

And the sixteen-year-old maid and the ten-year-old girl wept for the poor little baby and his parents.

But later, in bed, Minna had cried for herself, because the baby had died on her birthday which meant Papa would never want to celebrate it again.

Chapter Eight

'It's from Head Office.' Steve flourished the letter he had been reading in the air. 'They've accepted me for the Management Training course. I'm to go to London in two weeks' time and then I'll be starting the real thing next April.'

'That's great, Steve.' Rosie put down her piece of toast. 'But London. I didn't think you'd have to go there!'

He laughed. 'It's not so far. There *is* life outside Yorkshire, you know.'

Rosie bristled. 'There's nothing wrong with Yorkshire, my lad. It's a beautiful place and you'd be hard put to improve on it.'

He smiled, refolded his letter and put it back into the envelope. 'Spoken like a true "tyke". But, you see, Mum,' he sat back in his chair and explained, 'the trip to London is to attend a three-day preliminary seminar. They hold it there because people will be coming from all over the country. The actual course will be based somewhere nearer home, I expect. I'll find out more when I attend the seminar.'

Rosie studied his face. 'You're looking forward to going, then? You're not feeling nervous?'

Steve flushed. 'A bit. But obviously I'm delighted I've been accepted for the course. As for London,' he ran his fingers through his hair, 'I'm looking forward to seeing the place.' A tinge of embarrassment coloured his voice. 'What an admission, eh? Twenty-one years old and never been to London.'

Rosie had resumed her breakfast. She swallowed and then said, tartly, 'You've been to plenty of other places. Norway, Germany, Spain.'

'Yes, I know. But holidays abroad don't count.'

She raised her eyebrows. 'Don't they? I wish I'd been abroad. Do you know, the most faraway place I have been to is Scotland.'

He laughed. 'A mate of mine visited Glasgow last year and had difficulty understanding the language, so perhaps you can class Scotland as a foreign country, Mum. Anyway,' he looked at her with affection, 'wait until you pass your exams and you're swanning around in charge of your own nursing home. You'll be holidaying in foreign parts then.'

'I doubt it. You need someone to go with.' Realising the comment sounded pathetic, Rosie hurried on, 'Anyway, I've been thinking, I might not do the diploma course after all.'

'Oh, Mum . . .'

She saw his frown and wished she had never told him about her conversation with Mrs Horton. Hunching her shoulders defensively, she said, 'Well, I can't help wondering whether it's worth the bother. I'm happy in the job I have now.'

He shook his head. 'I can't believe this conversation. You were so enthusiastic when you told me about it. You said you wanted to do something with your life, Mum. And look how you've encouraged me to try for promotion at the bank.'

She stared at him, started to reply, but he was already on his feet.

'Hey, look at the clock. I'll be late.' He stopped in the doorway. 'We'll talk about this tonight, Mum. Okay?'

Left alone, Rosie stared down at the remains of her breakfast and wondered. Now why had he said she'd encouraged him to try for promotion? She'd done nothing of the sort. She had assumed he was happily settled in his present job. It was Jill who had first put the idea of promotion in his mind and Jill who had pushed him to do something about it. He had just said what he did to make her feel guilty, she thought, but the feeling of unease lingered.

Rosie refilled her teacup and brought her commonsense to bear. Don't go looking for trouble where there is none, she told herself. Jill was the ideal wife for Steve, of course she was. She was pretty and bright and had a bit of go about her. Steve was a lovely lad but there was no denying he was a bit too easy-going and casual. He needed a partner who would push him. And they did love each other, that was plain for all to see.

Only . . . Rosie's brow remained furrowed as she finished her breakfast, stood up and cleared away the pots . . . only she wished he would express a few opinions of his own occasionally. Jill, it seemed to her, was always the one who led and Steve followed behind, which didn't make for an equal partnership.

She sighed. There was nothing she could do about it. The children were grown now and her days of usefulness had passed. Paula was away living her own life, no matter how erratic, and Steve must live his. He would go on his course and then after that he would get married and move away and she would be alone, just as Minna was alone in that horrid flat of hers.

Trying to lighten the cloud of depression that had descended upon her, Rosie decided to do some cleaning.

She was on the afternoon shift at The Firs, so she had time on her hands. She collected her dusters and polish from the cupboard beneath the sink and then went to the understairs cupboard to extract the vacuum cleaner.

It was a heavy, old-fashioned machine. She was breathing hard when she finally removed it from the cupboard and bent down to push the plug into the wall socket.

When young, the children had christened the cleaner 'Mrs Noah's monster', saying it must have been used in the Ark. The corners of Rosie's lips tilted upwards into a smile as she remembered. She had bought the cleaner from a neighbour shortly after her marriage and it had been old then.

'Soon as it breaks down, I'll buy you a new one, love,' Howard had promised, but it never had broken down. Now, Rosie braced herself and flicked the starter switch. An ear-splitting roar shattered the silence. The ancient vacuum cleaner was not only heavy, it was noisy. Rosie could never hoover at night for fear of upsetting the neighbours. Also, it had a habit of gobbling up anything and everything left on the floor.

She pushed the machine over the fitted carpet being careful not to catch the furniture and remembered some of the things it had consumed. The pieces of Lego, the toy soldiers, the table tennis balls and Paula's french knitting. It had coughed a little, she recalled, over the cotton reel with the four nails driven in the top but then had digested it quite easily.

One day, all hell had been let loose when Paula had returned from school to find her pet hamster had disappeared. She had flown at Steve, accusing him of leaving the door of the cage open, wailing, 'The monster has eaten Hammy!'

Fortunately Howard had been at home. He had calmed

Paula and then detached the dust bag from the cleaner and they had gathered round him in silence and watched as he sorted through the contents. There had been no mangled corpse. Hammy had been found the following day in a cupboard, nicely settled in a nest he had made out of Paula's socks and knickers.

Rosie's thoughts were distracted momentarily when the motor of the cleaner paused for a moment and then made a gurgling noise. She waited apprehensively and then relaxed when it resumed its normal roar. For all its faults, she dreaded the thought of the monster's eventual demise. A modern, lightweight vaccum cleaner would be easier to use but it could never bring back her memories of happier days.

With the dust banished, together with a pencil and a misplaced clothes peg, Rosie manhandled the monster back into the cupboard and then, without enthusiasm, she began to polish. Housework held no charms for her. It was just a task that had to be done.

Unlike Minna, she took no pleasure in a shining house. She didn't like dirt, but crumbs on the carpet and a few light cobwebs drifting in corners did not bother her. She had no heirlooms to care for, her pieces of furniture were strictly utilitarian. She never told Alison not to touch or admonished for kicking at the legs of chairs whilst wearing her shoes. No, her wealth was her memories.

She sprayed more Windolene on the windows and as she polished, she thought about the old ladies living at The Firs. So many of them cherished one particular object; a cracked china teacup, a string of beads, an apostle spoon. Yes, she decided, women were good at memories. Maybe that's why they survived longer than the men. She knew from the accommodation lists they received from the

Council offices that women residents outnumbered men by three to one.

She pondered on this fact as she rubbed away at the windows. Working men had laboured long hours during the twenties and early-thirties, perhaps that's why they died at an earlier age. They were worn out. But surely, life for the women had been equally hard? They had worked too, in addition to looking after the home and bearing many children, some of whom they buried. Men and women had shared equally bad living conditions, poor medical care and lack of money, and yet the majority of women had survived their menfolk. Rosie shook her head. Were women therefore the stronger sex?

Mentally perhaps, but not physically. Whenever she read the newspapers nowadays, there were cases of sex attacks on women, rape and physical abuse. Paula's bruised face came into Rosie's mind and she shivered and decided she had done enough housework. As she put away the cleaning things, she thought she would ring her daughter later in the day. The last time she had telephoned, Paula had said everything was fine but Rosie needed to hear her voice again, to make sure she was telling the truth.

In the flat in Manchester, Paula was also tidying up. She had made the beds and emptied the bins but now she realised it was time to get ready for work. The temping agency had found her a new job at a firm of solicitors and she was due there at ten. Fortunately, the nursery had a place for Alison.

Paula went through into the bedroom to get ready. The drone of the television from the sitting room signified Alison was watching one of the endless cartoons that occupied the early-morning hours. The kid watched too much TV but what else was there for her to do? There were no other children living on this floor of the flats for her to play with and there was no way Alison could play outside in the corridor.

Paula sat down before the mirror and applied a little eyeliner to define the shape of her eyes and blusher to emphasise her high cheekbones. She didn't use lipstick or foundation cream. She brushed her hair, removed her dressing gown and dressed swiftly in a white blouse, slim dark skirt and a matching jacket. She grinned as she checked her appearance. Yes, that would do. She looked the part.

She relished the idea of a new job. Temping was great because you were never at one place long enough to get bored and each new post was a new experience. The woman at the agency had told her that this company had never before employed a temp.

'It's an old established firm, Paula, the sort of place where loyal employees stay until they retire. But two staff members have taken winter holidays this year and now one of their top secretaries has been rushed into hospital for an emergency operation. The old boy who rang me to ask for assistance was in quite a state.'

'Where's the office?' Paula had noted down the address.

'Very traditional, remember.' The agency boss had emphasised the words but Paula, seeing the twinkle in her eyes, had merely grinned.

'Okay. When do I start?'

She had left the agency smiling. They knew she was one of their best temps, that's why they paid her the top rate of pay, and goodness only knew, her smile faltered, she needed the money.

Dave's wage packet had been down again last week. She'd asked him why and he had mumbled something about 'cuts all round', but she hadn't believed him. However, she hadn't pressed the matter. The last thing she wanted was another full-scale row. They'd managed to avoid rowing since she returned home, but they had come close to it once or twice. And yet, at other times, it had been great. Not last night though. She erased that memory and thought about her work again.

Her last job she had loved. A successful advertising company had asked the agency for someone to help with the completion of a particularly rushed presentation. Her role had been a humble one, of course, but she had still been required to think on her feet and she was good at that.

The offices had been modern with bold decorations in primary colours, and first names were used, regardless of rank. There had been no regulations with regard to dress. Paula had worn her favourite clothes, brightly coloured leggings and loose tops. She had been sad when the job came to an end.

This new place was going to be a million miles away from Harris, Templeton and Dean. Paula slipped her feet into plain court shoes, stood up and took a last look in the mirror. The skirt and jacket looked fine. No one would think they came from an Oxfam shop. Lucky for her she had spotted them, because no way would she have paid out good money for the frumpy things. Still, it was important that she gave a good impression.

Being a temp was rather like being an actress: look the part and you were half-way there. And the other half should be no problem.

Paula was quick-witted and sharp. She picked up on things fast and the agency knew it. That's why they always came up with work for her when she needed it. And she needed it now more than ever. If the nursery had space to take Alison every day, she would work full-time.

But she was working today and mustn't be late. Hurrying into Alison's tiny bedroom, Paula snatched her daughter's coat from the Mickey Mouse hook on the wall. It wasn't much of a room for the kid, she thought, glancing round, but she had done her best with it.

She had painted the walls white to compensate for the tiny window set too high up to see out of, and affixed a frieze of cartoon characters around the room to give Alison something to look at when she was in bed.

Paula liked to peep in on Alison before she went to bed herself. The kid looked so cute snuggled down beneath her quilt clutching that awful doll. She had a shabby old rabbit, too, which was one of her favourite toys. She always took it to bed with her, but invariably it was on the floor when Paula looked in. Picking up the flop-eared, glassy-eyed toy and tucking it into her daughter's bed always made Paula feel maternal. Alison could drive her mad during the day, but it was different at night. Kids were easy to love when they were asleep.

She was just about to call Alison when she heard the sound of a key turning in the lock. She looked round in surprise as the door to the flat opened and her husband walked in.

'Dave. What are you doing home?'

He shut the door and slumped into the wicker chair which stood in the hallway.

'I feel lousy. I told them I couldn't work. I was sick and had to come home.'

She looked at him in silence and without sympathy although he did look ill. He was wearing his messenger's uniform and against the background of black leather his face had an unhealthy pallor. There was a fine sheen of perspiration on his forehead and she saw that his hair lay flat and limp against the contours of his skull.

Her eyes narrowed. 'Well, we know *why* you feel ill, don't we?'

He wiped his hand wearily over his mouth. 'For Christ's sake, don't start on me, Paula. I'm entitled to a night out once in a while. And I hadn't seen the lads for ages.'

'So you celebrated.' She made a gesture of distaste. 'You were sick in the loo last night. I don't suppose you even remember that. I cleaned it up this morning.' Her mouth hardened into a straight line. 'I'd have left it for you to do, but I couldn't. It stank to high heaven. And you were so drunk last night, you couldn't even find the bed.'

She waited for him to reply but he didn't. After a moment, she said, more quietly, 'I can't believe you, Dave, I really can't. You know you can't keep up with that crowd, so why go out with them? Surely you can find better friends?'

He had dropped his head as she spoke but now he looked up at her and there was anger showing in his eyes. 'Of course it escapes you, sweetheart. That's because you've changed so much. When we first got together, people like Andy and Mac were your friends as well as mine, but they don't rate in your world any more, do they?'

He rubbed the heel of his hand against his forehead, a frustrated gesture. 'No, you prefer city types now, blokes with three-piece suits and gold credit cards.'

She interrupted him. 'That's stupid nonsense, and you know it. I don't even *know* any city types.'

'Oh, no?' His gaze flickered over her. 'Where are you off to today then? I mean, just look at you.' He slumped back in the chair. 'Remember when we first met and you came back here with me, on the bike? You couldn't do that now, Paula. In that skirt, you couldn't even climb on the bloody thing!' He grinned mirthlessly. 'Perhaps I'd better sell it and buy a BMW.'

'What the hell are you babbling about?' She shook her head in disbelief. 'I can't stand here listening to all this rot. I'm going to work, Dave. *Work*, remember?' She took a deep breath. 'The agency contacted me last night. Four days working for a firm of solicitors. Nothing special about it. I wish there was.' Her voice rose. 'If it was specialised work, I'd get more money.'

He stared at her. 'Money, that's all you ever think about.'

'Someone has to.' She was practically screaming now. She heard herself but couldn't stop. 'Someone has to pay the bills.'

'I can pay the bills.'

'Can you? You keep taking time off and you won't get paid for today. If you keep on like this, they'll sack you for sure.'

'You'd like that, wouldn't you? You'd like me to get the sack. Then you could go swanning off every morning and I'd be stuck at home,' he grimaced, 'one of those stupid house husbands.'

She clenched her fists. 'Now we're getting to it, Dave. Hurt male pride, that's all this is. You don't like me earning more money than you do. You don't . . .'

'I don't give a fuck about the money!' He was on his feet and staring at her, his face a mask of pain. 'It's you, Paula. You've changed.'

She turned her face away. 'Of course I've changed. People do. Maybe you should try it. We've Alison to think about now and . . . hell!' Remembering, she glanced at her watch. 'I've got to take her to the nursery.' She glanced at him, a brief, almost pitying glance. 'You'd better get to bed, sleep it off.'

'Damn you! I've told you once, I wasn't drunk last night.' A strange expression appeared on his face. He looked at her intently. 'I was ill.'

'Oh, yeah.'

'I was. I was fine when we left the pub but we bought a Chinese takeaway. Perhaps it was . . .'

She wasn't listening. She turned away, towards the sitting room.

'Listen to me!'

She didn't see him move towards her, but she heard the crash as the chair hit the floor.

'Listen to me, you bitch!'

She felt his fingers biting into her shoulder.

'You stupid bitch!' He swung her round to face him then drove his clenched fist into her stomach.

She groaned and doubled up. Her arms curved round her body in an instinctive attempt to protect herself.

His motor cycle helmet had been on the floor next to the chair. Now it was rolling across the boards. It clattered against the skirting and came to a halt near her feet. She blinked down at it through eyes half-blinded with tears of pain. He must have caught it with his foot, she thought dully, when he sprang at her. What a pity he didn't trip over it. She felt a hysterical desire to laugh. She mustn't laugh, she mustn't. If she laughed, he would kill her. She closed her eyes and thought she might be sick.

'You don't *listen* to me. You don't *believe* me. You're so bloody *clever*.'

She half-opened her eyes as his fingers gripped her chin. He forced her head up. His expression was malevolent. There were beads of sweat on his forehead and she saw the arteries in his neck had swelled and were throbbing. I'm going to die, she thought. But I can't die, there's Alison! She forced the muscles of her throat to move.

'Dave, please.'

She heard the fear in her voice and he heard it too.

He raised his fist to strike her again.

'Mummy?'

The small voice, quavering with terror, stopped him. His arm fell to his side. He stepped away.

'Mummy?'

Somehow, she smiled. Somehow she straightened up and spoke normally.

'Yes, love.'

Alison had opened the sitting-room door, but just a little. Through the narrow crack her anxious face peered out, closed-up and pale as a sealed envelope.

Paula's heart twisted within her. Ignoring the pain in the centre of her body, she stooped down and patted her daughter's cheek.

'Has the cartoon finished?' Her voice sounded husky.

Alison put her thumb in her mouth and nodded. Her eyes wavered from Paula towards her father and then back again.

Say something, for Christ's sake! Paula wanted to scream the words at him. She wanted him to put things right. She wanted him to take that look off Alison's face but he did nothing. He stood with his back to the wall like a block of wood. His gaze was turned inwards.

One swift look at him and then Paula turned her attention back to her daughter.

'Is there another cartoon on, pet?'

Alison nodded.

'Well, you watch that one and then Mummy will take you to nursery.'

'Nuther one.' Alison considered and then she nodded. She went back to the television set.

Paula closed the door and turned back to Dave. She was

beginning to feel, not better, but steadier. Her stomach still hurt but the sick feeling had passed. She put her hand out and rested it against the wall, a sort of comfort, and she wondered what she could say.

But Dave broke the silence.

'I'm sorry. I don't know what came over me. I'm sorry.' He took a step towards her and then, seeing her flinch, covered his face with his hands and burst into tears.

She rested her hand gently on her stomach. If only it would stop hurting.

'Can you forgive me? Say you'll forgive me.'

His pleading voice made her look at him. His colour was ghastly and his green eyes were sunken pools in his head.

He looks worse than I feel, she thought, and despite herself she felt the first stirrings of sympathy.

He held out his hand towards her. 'I love you, Paula. Jesus, don't you know I love you?'

She took her hand away from the wall and stood up straighter. The pain was going now, subsiding into a dull ache. She felt weak and very sad.

'I'm going to take Alison to the nursery and then I'm going to work.'

'You can't. You should rest.' Dave's voice was humble. 'I'll take her. You go back to bed. You're the one who's hurt.'

She shook her head. 'I'll be all right. Anyway, I . . .' Her voice trailed away. She was going to say that she was going to work because they needed the money, but she dare not. She was still unsure of him.

'You go to bed,' she told him. 'You look lousy. We'll talk tonight.'

Talk, she thought drearily. What good will that do?

'If you're sure.' He nodded. He turned towards the bedroom then paused. 'You will come back?'

'Yes.'

She went to get her daughter.

Thankfully, Alison seemed to have forgotten her fright. She was laughing at the TV antics of Tom and Jerry. As Paula put her coat on, she twisted round to see what was happening on the screen. 'Look, Mummy. Look.'

But Paula didn't look. Today, of all days, she had no wish to watch the famous cat and mouse team, locked together in their love-hate relationship and doing their best to hurt each other.

Chapter Nine

Despite the energetic burst of housework, Rosie arrived early for work. The smell of the residents' lunch lingered in the hall and furious clattering noises from the kitchen signified crockery was being stored away in the cupboards. She had plenty of time and so she paused by the public phone booth in the entrance hall. She decided she would see if Paula was at home. She went into the phone box and dialled her daughter's telephone number.

After a few moments, Rosie heard her son-in-law's voice.

'Hello. Who is it?'

'Dave?' She was surprised. Her son-in-law was rarely at home during the day. She cleared her throat. 'It's me, Rosie. Is Paula there?'

After a pause which lasted a moment too long, Dave replied, 'No, she's working today.'

'Oh? I didn't think she had anything lined up with the temping agency right now?'

'She was fed up of being in the flat all day. She went to see them. You know Paula, she can always wheedle what she wants out of people.'

Rosie frowned at the edge to his voice. She hesitated and then asked, 'Everything going all right, Dave?'

'Sure, everything's fine.' His voice changed, became

almost hearty. 'Look, I'll get her to call you back this evening if you like.'

'Yes, but remind her I won't be in until late. I've just come . . .'

He hung up on her.

Rosie stepped out of the phone booth and studied the toes of her shoes. She mustn't over-react. Perhaps Dave was doing something that needed attention or maybe he was in a hurry to go back to work. Whatever it was, it didn't matter. She was working until ten p.m. and would be home about a quarter to eleven but Paula often rang her late at night, and if she didn't, they could always have a chat tomorrow.

She crossed the hall and went up the main staircase.

'Mrs Horton wants you, Rosie.' One of her fellow care assistants came staggering along the corridor carrying an armful of books.

'Thanks.' Rosie paused. 'Can you manage all those?'

'Yep. I'm taking them to the library. Someone donated them.' The woman grinned. 'Some Mills and Boon and a few Jackie Collins, should keep the old dears happy.'

Mrs Horton was at her desk, rifling through the contents of a folder with one hand and holding the telephone to her ear with the other. She nodded to Rosie.

'Yes, that's right. It's St Luke's Hospital, on Shafton Road. You're sure you can find the way? Well, go and get a pen and a piece of paper and I'll give you directions.' She covered the mouthpiece of the phone and said to Rosie, 'Mr Jennings has suffered a heart attack. The doctor's with him now. Says he has a chance, if we can get him into intensive care immediately. We're waiting for the ambulance and I'm breaking the news to his family.'

She turned her attention back to the telephone. 'Yes, Mrs Harland, I'll accompany him to hospital.' Her forehead wrinkled. 'Please don't cry. Your father's getting the best possible attention.

'Now, have you got something to write on? Well, if you come in on the . . .' Rapidly she dictated the route. 'Yes, that's right. I'll see you at the hospital.'

She put down the phone with a sigh. 'Poor woman, she's very upset.' She stared into space for a moment and then roused herself. 'Will you keep an eye on things here, Rosie? As you know, the new Second in Charge isn't here yet and Jenny Brownridge is out. She's taken two of our residents to the dentist.' She picked up a pencil and tapped it on the desk. 'Can you cope? I don't think Jenny will be long.'

'Yes, of course.' Rosie nodded. 'Anything special you want me to do?'

'I don't think so.' Mrs Horton had grabbed her shoulder bag and was stuffing various papers into it. 'Mrs Harland's coming over from Harrogate. She's Mr Jennings' daughter. Unfortunately, I haven't been able to contact the son. You could keep ringing the two telephone numbers on my pad. He lives in London. If you get in touch, ask him to contact the hospital. You know the number.'

'I will. Anything else?'

'Keep things ticking over.' Mrs Horton picked up her car keys and then paused. 'Oh Lord, I've just remembered. I promised Mrs Kingston I'd see her today at three-thirty. You'll have to deal with her, Rosie.'

'Mrs Kingston?' Rosie pulled a face. The one resident she never felt comfortable with. 'What about?'

'It's all in her file.' Mrs Horton pulled open a desk drawer, snatched out a file and handed it to Rosie. 'You know she shares a room with Dora Hills.'

'Yes.'

Mrs Kingston and Dora Hills were in a double occupancy

room on the second floor of the building. Unfortunately Dora, a lovely little woman who had lived at The Firs for years, was now suffering from senile dementia and Rosie knew there was constant friction between the two women.

'When Mrs Kingston arrived a year ago, she had a room of her own.' Mrs Horton was putting on her coat. 'But now, with the waiting list we have, there's no way I can give her a single. She's been badgering me to move Dora somewhere else.'

Rosie sniffed. 'She's no sympathy, that woman.'

'Oh, I wouldn't say that.' Mrs Horton gathered up her things. 'It can't be pleasant sharing with Dora. She's deteriorating badly.'

Rosie frowned. 'You're not getting rid of her, are you?'

'Of course not, we can cope, but I have to think of Mrs Kingston's feelings. I think I've found a workable solution. The details are in the file.' Mrs Horton strode towards the door. 'Read them carefully and then explain the plan to Mrs Kingston. I think she'll agree to my suggestion. However,' Mrs Horton paused and raised a warning finger, 'she must realise that someone new will be moving in with her.'

Rosie nodded, her face serious. She did not relish the thought of explaining anything to Mrs Kingston. She asked, 'Who *will* you put in with her?'

'A new resident.'

'Poor thing.'

Mrs Horton looked over the top of her spectacles.

'You don't like her?'

'No.' Rosie compressed her lips. 'I think she's one of the most selfish people I have ever met.' She thought, fleetingly, of her mother.

'Well, try and be tactful.' But her employer's tone of

voice was absent and Rosie knew her thoughts were with the old gentleman upstairs.

At three-thirty precisely, Rosie tapped on the door of number thirty-two. She felt nervous. As in any community, there were a handful of awkward people living at The Firs. Rosie could deal with all of them, except the woman she had now to talk to.

A heavily built old lady, Mrs Kingston always dressed in unrelieved black and went about with a grim expression on her face. With the other residents, Rosie enjoyed a laugh, but she had never dared tell Mrs Kingston a joke.

She thinks I'm common, she won't be pleased to see me when she was expecting Mrs Horton, she thought, sighed and then braced herself as she heard the old woman call: 'Come in.'

She stepped inside the room. Mrs Kingston was seated in her armchair. She stared at Rosie.

'There's been an emergency, I'm afraid.' The words came out in a rush. Rosie took a deep breath. 'Mrs Horton can't keep her appointment with you but she's asked me to see you instead.'

Mrs Kingston stared at her. 'What emergency?' With an impatient gesture, she motioned to Rosie to sit down.

Rosie did so and explained the situation.

'I see.' Mrs Kingston was silent, then she said, 'Well, I would have preferred to talk to Mrs Horton but, as her deputy, please tell me her decision. But before you do,' she raised her hand, 'I must tell you, I flatly refuse to share with Mrs Hills a moment longer. If the woman's not moved immediately, I shall write to the Director of Social Services himself, and ask him to intervene.'

'Dora will be moved within the next two days, Mrs Kingston.'

Rosie's voice was cool. She never even asked about Mr Jennings, she thought. And he's one of the few people she condescends to speak to.

'She's going to a room on the ground floor. The old gentleman who's in that room's leaving tomorrow, going to a nursing home nearer to where his family live.'

'You're giving her a single room!'

'Yes, but it wouldn't suit you, or many other people,' Rosie spoke hastily. 'It's next to the boiler house and it's very noisy. The old man's totally deaf. It didn't bother him. Dora's not deaf, but Mrs Horton thinks the noise won't disturb her.'

'Of course it won't disturb her. She lives in cloud cuckoo land most of the time.' A wintry smile creased Mrs Kingston's leathery features. 'Well, well. What good news. Please tell Mrs Horton I'm much obliged.'

'The move's for Dora's benefit, too.' Rosie's reply was quick. 'There's more staff around on the ground floor. We shall be able to look after her better.'

'I see.'

Was there a glint of amusement in the hooded, dark eyes?

'Well, whatever the reason, I'm delighted. The last months have been ghastly, but now . . .' Mrs Kingston turned her head and surveyed the room. 'Please remove the second bed as soon as possible. There's some of my belongings in the store room. Will you see they are brought up?'

'Mrs Kingston,' Rosie broke in, desperately trying to halt the old lady's flights of fancy, 'just because Dora's moving out, it doesn't mean you can keep this room for yourself. Another lady, a new resident, will be moving in next week.'

'What!'

Before Rosie's surprised gaze, the stalwart figure of Mrs Kingston appeared to dwindle. Her upright frame sagged, her cheeks hollowed and the hand she raised to her face trembled.

'But that can't be. Mrs Horton implied . . .'

'No, she didn't. I'm sorry, but she would never have said that you could have a double room to yourself. There's enormous pressure for beds, Mrs Kingston. People are waiting for months for admittance to homes like this one.' Rosie's voice died away. She was shocked to see tears sliding down the old lady's face. It was like seeing a stone statue weeping.

Forgetting her earlier misgivings, she went to clasp Mrs Kingston's cold hands within her own warm ones. 'Please don't get upset. The new lady's nothing like Dora. I've seen her file. She sounds nice. Mrs Horton has tried very hard to find someone you would like.

'Mrs Thorne's the widow of a headmaster of a private school. She's rather like you, well-educated, a lady.' Rosie paused. 'Normally she wouldn't come to a place like this, but her husband lost his money through some company crash and . . .' She stopped, discomfited.

A gleam which could have been amusement flickered in Mrs Kingston's dark eyes. She sniffed and felt in the pocket of her skirt for a handkerchief and said drily: 'You mean, like me, this woman is upper-class but impoverished?'

'I . . . I . . .' Seeing Mrs Kingston had not found a handkerchief, Rosie went over to the bedside cabinet and brought a box of tissues to her.

'Thank you.' The old lady was becoming more composed. She took a tissue, blew her nose loudly and then turned towards Rosie and studied her face.

'You really care, don't you?'

'What do you mean?' She was puzzled.

'You wouldn't do this kind of job if you didn't care.'

'Oh, I don't know.'

Mrs Kingston extracted another tissue from the box. 'There are people who enjoy working in homes and institutions because it gives them power. They control the people in their care, you see; the very old, the very young and the people who are,' she paused, 'mentally disadvantaged.'

'Oh, but surely, those kind of people are rare? The staff here are not like that, they do a good job.'

'On the whole, yes. The standard of care at The Firs is high because Mrs Horton is an excellent officer, but even here there's a . . . how can I put it . . .' Mrs Kingston frowned. 'An "us and you" situation.'

She looked at Rosie's unconvinced face and nodded. 'It's true. We residents are expected to knuckle down and do as we are told.' She sighed. 'It's most irksome.'

'But we try to make this a happy place. And when there are so many residents, there have to be rules.'

'Yes, yes. Like children, we must be happy.' Mrs Kingston abandoned her rigid position and sat back more comfortably in her chair. 'But, you see, I don't feel the need to be collectively happy with my little band of comrades.' Her mouth twisted. 'I like my privacy, and sometimes I show my irritation. That's why some of the staff, including you, consider me to be a troublemaker. Now don't shake your head.' She stared at Rosie. 'Put yourself in my place for a moment.

'Have you any *idea* how annoying it is to be told by a chit of a girl to "eat up your greens"?' She snorted. 'And badgered to "go and sit with the others in the TV room"? I *hate* TV. It's the refuge of morons. I don't wish to be sociable. What I want to do is to stay in my room and listen to music. But,' her lip began to tremble, 'if I am to share . . .'

'No, no. It's all right.' Rosie reassured her. 'Mrs Thorne, the new lady, is a great music lover. She was once a member of a famous choir.'

'Is that so?' Mrs Kingston had smoothed her hand over her face and was wearing her sardonic look again. 'You *have* done your best for me. Well,' she sighed, 'if there's absolutely no chance of my keeping this room for myself' – she watched Rosie shake her head – 'then there's no more to be said.'

She heaved herself from her chair and reached for her walking stick. 'Tell Mrs Horton I will do my best to be civil to my new companion.' She went and opened the door. 'Whatever happens, she has to be better than Dora Hills.'

Rosie looked down. 'I remember, when I first came to work here, Dora was a lovely little woman. But then she became ill . . .'

'Senile, you mean?'

'Yes.'

There was a small silence and then Mrs Kingston sighed. 'You have succeeded in humbling me, Rosemary. I was unkind to Dora, wasn't I?'

Rosie stood up and walked towards the door. 'Yes, you were.'

'Hmm. And *I* was lecturing you.' The old woman hesitated and then she stepped closer to Rosie and peered into her face. 'But it *was* terrible, you know. She used to moan and sob in her sleep. Some nights, she climbed into bed with me. I would wake in the night and feel her arm around me and her breath on the back of my neck.' She shuddered. 'I couldn't bear it. I couldn't!' She bowed her head.

Rosie's face softened. 'I'm sorry it's been so hard for

you. I'm sure you will be much happier, sharing with Mrs Thorne.'

'I hope you're right.' Mrs Kingston straightened her back. 'If not, I shall be down to see Mrs Horton again, complaining as usual.'

Rosie peeped at her, under her eyelashes, and then laughed when she saw the expression on the old lady's face. 'I'm sure you will,' she replied, and then added impulsively, 'I'm glad we've talked. You've made me think about things. Tell me,' she hesitated, 'have I ever . . .' Her voice faded away.

Mrs Kingston looked at her. 'Used your power to control people, do you mean?'

'Yes.'

'Hardly ever, only . . .'

'What?' Rosie tensed. 'Please tell me.'

'Last month, remember. You and another care assistant persuaded Mrs Johnson to let you cut and home perm her hair.'

'Yes. She had such long hair and it was difficult to wash and dry.' Rosie frowned. 'She was happy to let us do it. She said she was pleased. Surely we did nothing wrong there?'

'Mrs Johnson's not like me, Rosemary. She's a timid lady who likes to please. A couple of days after you'd permed her hair I found her crying. She told me that her late husband had always been so proud of her long, waving hair.' Mrs Kingston paused and stared at Rosie. 'There's no need to look so stricken. You can't get everything right.'

'No, but perhaps I ought to try harder.' Rosie took a deep breath. 'Thanks for telling me.'

It was past nine o'clock when Mrs Horton finished her

telephone calls. She sighed, stretched and stood up, meaning to make herself a cup of coffee, then someone tapped at the door.

She rubbed her hands over her tired eyes before calling out, 'Come in.'

'Can you spare me a moment?' A serious-faced Rosie put her head round the door.

'Two – at least.'

'Thanks.' Rosie came into the room. 'Mr Jennings still holding on?'

'Yes. I've just phoned the hospital. He's as well as can be expected. His son's arriving tomorrow.' Karen Horton turned towards the door. 'I'm going to make a coffee. Want one?'

'Yes. Thanks.'

The two women walked along the corridor.

'How did you get on with Mrs Kingston?'

'Bit sticky at first, but she's reconciled to the idea of sharing. I told her Mrs Thorne's a music lover and that pleased her.'

'Good.' Mrs Horton ran her fingers through her hair. 'We shall have to hope for the best. Let's hope Mrs Thorne's an easy-going lady. She'll need to be, sharing with Mrs Kingston.'

They turned into the staff kitchen.

'Oh, she's not that bad.'

Mrs Horton was surprised. 'Am I hearing aright?'

'Yes.' Rosie picked up the kettle, shook it and plugged it into the wall socket. 'About the diploma course . . .'

'Yes?'

'I've decided to do it. That is,' she glanced shyly at her superior, 'if you really think I can?'

Mrs Horton smiled. 'I do, and I'm delighted. I'll get things moving as quickly as I can. You'll probably be able to start the course immediately after the Christmas holiday.'

'That's fine.' Rosie made the coffee and handed a mug to Mrs Horton who accepted it gratefully.

'Thanks.' She sipped gingerly at the steaming hot liquid. 'When did you make up your mind, Rosie? You hadn't mentioned it and I was beginning to think you were going to say no.'

'I almost did.' Rosie stared down into her mug. 'But I'm realising that there's still a lot about this job I don't know. Perhaps the course will help me to sort out my own problems *and* become a better carer.'

Karen Horton looked at her over her glasses. 'You're a pretty good one already.'

Rosie shrugged, then grinned. 'There's always room for improvement.' She glanced at her watch. 'I'd better take this coffee with me and go and see to Mr Anderson. He's past his bedtime.'

'Oh, God!' Dave sat bolt upright in bed. 'I forgot. Your mum rang this afternoon. You're supposed to ring back.'

'Well, I can't ring now, can I?' Paula reached out her hand and picked up the alarm clock which stood on the small table near their bed. She squinted at the dial. 'It's nearly one.'

'Really?' Dave slipped his arm around her and cupped her naked breast. 'That late?'

At the hint of smugness in his voice, Paula stiffened and he reacted to her involuntary movement, sitting up in bed and anxiously searching her face for a look of pain. Moonlight was flooding in through the bedroom window enabling him to see her clearly.

'What is it? Is your stomach hurting? Oh God, I shouldn't have expected you to make love. I . . .'

'No. I'm all right.' Hearing the concern in his voice, Paula smiled. She reached over and touched his bare chest.

'I've told you, Dave. I'm fine. So no more recriminations, eh? We're sorting ourselves out, we've talked honestly and we know what we must do. Now, let's get some sleep. We're both up early in the morning.'

'All right, love.' He kissed her shoulder, slid down beneath the bedclothes, and within ten minutes he was asleep. Paula lay next to him and listened to his gentle breathing.

After a prolonged, successful bout of lovemaking, they usually both fell asleep quickly, but tonight sleep eluded her. She tried to relax, tried to quieten her mind, but it was no good, so she sat up in bed, doubled up her pillow and then leaned against it, moving cautiously so as not to disturb her husband. She stared out through the bedroom window, towards the moon, as it silently moved through the night clouds.

Strange how things turned out. This morning, taking Alison to nursery, she had decided to leave Dave. She couldn't stay with a man who hit her, even if she still loved him. She had kissed Alison goodbye and gone to find her new work-place in a trance-like state and her stomach had ached like hell. She was in a state of shock, she supposed.

Thank God, the atmosphere in the solicitor's office had been calm and peaceful. There had been none of the hustle and bustle which had typified the advertising agency at which she had worked previously.

At Jameson, Wyatt and Green there were quiet voices, bundles of dusty documents tied up with red tape piled on desks and spilling out of filing cabinets, and mercifully few telephone calls.

Slowly, as she typed out a long, boring conveyance, Paula's jittering nerves had steadied and the ache in her stomach had subsided, but then her emptiness had been filled with anger. How dare he! How dare Dave treat her and his little daughter so badly? He'll never do it again, she vowed.

All day she husbanded her anger carefully and by the time she and Alison went home, Paula had prepared herself mentally for one almighty row. He would sulk or bawl back at her, she thought, and she wouldn't care.

But it hadn't worked out like that. As she opened the door of the flat, smells of cooking wafted around her and Dave had appeared, wearing a blue and white butcher's apron, his face wreathed in smiles.

'Hi, sweetie.' He had swept Alison up in his arms and given her a smacking kiss. Then, placing her gently back on her feet, he had smiled shyly at Paula.

'Give me your coat, love. The meal's almost ready.'

Speechless, she had handed it over.

He had cooked steak, medium rare as she liked it, and baked potatoes. There was a mixed salad, garden peas and a bottle of red wine. He had even bought French bread from the delicatessen two streets away and a trifle in a little plastic pot for Alison.

All this, from a man who thrived on pizzas or Chinese takeaway. Paula had eaten her meal in silence but Dave chatted away as if nothing had happened. She kept glancing at him, not believing the scene.

After they had eaten, Dave washed up and, even more unusually, played with Alison for an hour before helping Paula put her to bed. He stayed with her to read her a story, finally coming out of her bedroom all smiles. Paula did not smile back. When he sat next to her and put his hand on her knee she pushed it away.

'Aw, come on, Paula.' The gaze he turned on her was uncomprehending. 'You'll forgive me, won't you?'

She tried to find the right words. She didn't want to antagonise him again. 'It's not that easy, Dave. Can't you see that?'

He hunched his shoulders like a schoolboy. 'I was way out of line, I admit it, but I've made amends, haven't I? I've a quick temper but . . .'

'You hit me in the stomach, Dave, with your fist. It's a wonder I wasn't seriously hurt. And Alison saw you do it.'

He studied the back of his hands. 'I know, and I've said I'm sorry. It won't happen again.'

'It's happened twice already.' She took a deep breath. 'I don't think I want to hang around to see if it happens again.' She stared at him. 'I'm not cut out to be a battered wife. I'm leaving you, Dave, and taking Alison with me.'

His head snapped up and she could see the shock in his eyes.

'You can't leave me. We love each other.'

'I know, but I'm still going.' Her voice was dull.

'But you can't. Please, love, don't say such things. I'd be no good without you.' His voice broke and his face mirrored despair.

She looked at him and knew he spoke the truth. He needed her more than she needed him. *He* was the fragile one. The knowledge confused her and she felt her resolve weaken. How could she leave him, when he needed her so much?

Perhaps he sensed her hesitation, for he took her hand in his.

'Please, darling, let's put all this behind us and start again.' He shook his head. 'I can't believe I hit you. I always swore I would never hit a woman, any woman. When I was little and saw what my mother went through, I swore I would never hurt anyone I loved.'

Paula pulled her hand free. 'What are you saying? Are

you telling me your father used to hit your mother?'

'Oh, yes. He put her in hospital twice. I hated him. I wanted to kill him, but I was too small.' Dave's green eyes were as ingenuous as the child he was describing.

Paula swallowed. 'What did your mother do?'

'Nothing. She was weak, she wasn't like you.' Dave sprang up and walked around the room. 'I've always admired your spirit, Paula. But look,' he came to a halt in the middle of the room, 'I can't go on apologising, love. Give me another chance and I won't let you down. This has been a rough patch, but we'll get over it, I promise.' He smiled at her. 'You still love me, don't you?'

Paula looked at him, at the way his hair fell over his forehead, at the lines of his body, the shape of his face, and she felt her heart beating high in her throat and knew she couldn't leave him. She told him so.

They made love there on the couch – hectic, feverish love – and then they showered and went to bed. There they talked.

Paula told Dave they must visit a marriage guidance counsellor.

'We have to, Dave. We have to understand these sudden rages you have. And now that I know your father hit your mother . . .'

'That's nothing to do with us.'

'It has.' She caught hold of his hand, made him look at her. 'Did you love your parents?'

'Of course I did.' He stirred restlessly. 'But then I began to . . .' He was silent, and then quietly: 'I couldn't do anything, you see. If I said anything to Dad, he hit me, and Mum never tried to fight him off. And I . . .' His shoulders began to shake.

'Hush, it's all right.' She put her arms around him and they made love again. This time there was no urgency, just love and gentleness and a wonderful feeling of release when they climaxed together. And then, a few minutes later, Dave had remembered her mother's telephone call.

Paula rubbed her eyes. It was almost dawn and outside a blackbird practised his song. Now she *did* feel tired. She plumped up her pillow and snuggled down in bed. In a couple of hours she would have to get up. She looked at Davc's sleeping figure. Surely she was right to feel optimistic? Last night they had talked as never before. She smiled. And then she yawned, and slept.

Chapter Ten

'I grew up in London, you know. In the twenties it was a wonderfully exciting place, but I suppose it's vastly different now, all tower blocks and offices and commuters packing on to the Underground.' Minna shook her head. 'I've no desire to return. I'd rather remember it as it was, remember the fun we had.' She pursed her lips and looked at Steve. 'Young people nowadays rarely seem to have fun, they have so little energy.'

Lost in her thoughts and seemingly unaware of her grandson's startled expression – Steve had never known Minna talk so much – she continued: 'When I was seventeen and eighteen, I was never home. There was so much going on, so much to do.' A reminiscent smile curved her pale lips. 'There were picnics and garden parties, and lawn tennis matches during the summer – I was a very good tennis player – and in the evenings we went out to dinner, or dancing. There were nightclubs everywhere. And the shows, of course. I saw Noël Coward once, in a Cochran review. He was just becoming famous in those days.

'And when the nightclubs shut we went on to bottle-parties. I remember they became the "thing" in the late-twenties. We'd pile into cars and drive to someone's house after midnight and we'd party and dance until seven or eight in the morning. Whoever hosted the party always provided breakfast, bacon and eggs and all that.'

She gazed into space for a moment then sighed, turned to her grandson and said: 'I hope you're staying in a decent area?' Her voice had regained its usual sharpness. 'What's the name of your hotel?'

It took Steve a moment to readjust. For the life of him, he couldn't visualise Minna as a young woman at a bottle party.

'Er, I'm not in a hotel. I've residential accommodation in St Hilary's Hall, where the seminar's being held. It's somewhere in the South Kensington area.'

'Oh, that should be well enough. That's the museum area, if my memory serves me right. Dull but respectable.' Minna cast a critical eye over her grandson's clothing. 'You're taking a suit with you?'

'Yes. The one I wear at the bank. These,' he gestured at his blue slacks and sports jacket, 'will do for travelling in.' He grinned and ruffled up his hair. 'You know I'm not all that interested in clothes, Grandma.'

'Maybe not, but it pays to look smart.' Minna placed her hands on the arms of her chair and levered herself upright. 'What time are you leaving tomorrow?'

'Early, by the first train.'

'Well, you needn't stay with me any longer then. I'm glad you called in to see me, Stephen, but I'm sure you'd rather spend the rest of the evening with that girl of yours.'

'Oh, there's no rush.' Stimulated by his grandmother's revelations and observing her painful progress across the room, Steve felt a pang of remorse. He had only come to see Minna because his mother had reminded him it was a month since his last visit.

'Still, I'm pleased you did come because I've something for you.' Minna had moved to the sideboard. She opened one of the drawers, took out a small packet and held it towards him. 'It's something for you to wear in London. It belonged to my father.'

She watched him as, blushing, he rose from his chair and came towards her. 'You know, as you get older,' she put her head on one side and studied him, 'I begin to see a slight family resemblance.'

'Do you?' Steve accepted his totally unexpected gift and gave her an embarrassed smile. 'But you shouldn't – I mean, I never expected . . .'

'Don't make a fuss about it, and don't bother to open it now. Keep it for later.' Minna stepped away from him. She went to the occasional table and began collecting up the used cups and saucers and stacking them on the teatray.

'I'll do that.' Steve stuffed his present into his pocket and rushed to take over. 'You sit down.'

'No, thank you. I already spend most of my day resting.' The sharpness in Minna's voice intensified and she put the milk jug down on the tray with the suspicion of a bang. 'By the way, Stephen,' she glanced at him, 'don't build your hopes up about the present. It isn't valuable. It's nothing, really, a mere trifle.'

His blush, which had been fading, deepened again. 'I know, I mean, that's okay.'

She picked up the teatray and turned, meaning to carry it through into the kitchen, but before doing so, she fired off one last shot.

'And, of course, when I said you resembled my father, I meant there was a *superficial* resemblance. You'll never be the man he was because you're a Scott, through and through.'

Arriving at King's Cross, Steve could have gone straight down to the Underground and travelled on to Kensington, but he didn't. His luggage was light and he was eager to catch his first glimpse of London, what the guide books called the 'illustrious heritage of glorious pageantry'.

In the event, he was disappointed. During the train journey, sudden bursts of winter sunshine had brightened the dismal passing landscape but as he left the station Steve realised a fine rain was falling from the sulky grey sky above him. The rain damped his jacket in seconds and he shivered suddenly, feeling the cold after the over-heated atmosphere of the train.

He turned up the collar of his jacket and looked around him, at the ceaseless lines of traffic clogging the roads and the people, so many of them of different nationalities, he noticed, hurrying to or from the trains.

There was a large, strange bundle propped up against a wall, not six feet away from him. The bundle moved, and Steve realised it was a man, an old man, a tramp. Steve had never seen a proper tramp before and he couldn't help staring.

Long yellowy-white hair sprayed wildly over the old man's shoulders, so much hair it was difficult to catch a glimpse of his face, but Steve saw the old newspapers stuffed inside his ragged coat and the black plastic bin liners shrouding his figure. The tramp wore shredding sandals and his feet were filthy. His toe nails, Steve saw, were revolting, long and hooked and a strange yellowy colour, but his ankles were thin, white and vulnerable, like those of a child.

Steve shivered again, but this time not from cold. He felt an urge to do something, offer the old man money, but he looked so wild. He was mumbling to himself, scratching at his head and face, and then he began singing. His voice was cracked and high, his words inaudible. Steve looked away.

A woman, rushing into the station, bumped into him

and knocked his hip with the corner of her briefcase. He smiled an apology and moved further away from the station entrance.

It was so busy. Blasts from taxi cabs filled the air and everyone was in a hurry. Steve went over to stand by a newsagent's kiosk to get his bearings. He saw a pedestrian crossing and decided to use it. As he waited for the lights to change he saw that directly opposite him a very young-looking policeman was in conversation with a woman.

Steve noticed the woman particularly because, despite the weather, she was dressed in a pair of tight black flimsy shorts and a low-cut, glitzy blouse. High-heeled, slingback shoes and a chain around one of her slim ankles completed her outfit. When the policeman looked stern, an expression which sat oddly on his plump youthful face, and took out a notebook from his jacket pocket, Steve suddenly realised he was seeing his first real prostitute.

His cheeks burned. But she's old, was his first thought, and ugly, who would pay to go with her? But he kept on looking. The rain had plastered her blouse to her skin. He could see clearly the shape of her large breasts. The woman's face was lined and her features coarse, but her legs were those of a young woman, supple, long and shapely. Steve looked at the silver chain around her left ankle and experienced a feeling inside which was vastly different from the emotions Jill aroused in him.

The lights had changed but Steve hadn't noticed. He stood still. A couple, their arms entwined, glanced at him as they pushed past and crossed the road.

The policeman had finished questioning the woman. He shook his head, almost playfully, put away his notebook and then laughed at something she said to him. The woman also laughed. She put her head on one side and grinned up at him and he gave her a mock salute as he moved away down the street.

Standing at the other side of the road, watching them, Steve felt an odd stab of envy. The policeman looked little older than himself and yet there was an easy familiarity in his movements. He was clearly at home in this place which was, for Steve, strange and unfamiliar. Shuffling his feet, for the first time in his life Steve realised how small and safe was the world he knew. Oh, sure, as his mother had pointed out, he'd had holidays abroad. He'd visited tourist resorts and drank and socialised with other holidaymakers, and then he had returned home, to the town and county into which he had been born.

The coastline, the moors and the Wolds of Yorkshire he loved, and his home town was a good place in which to live. It was a market town, solid, prosperous, and an important centre for shopping and services in the area. Steve had always considered it just the right size, being small enough to walk around and meet people you knew and yet large enough for you to pursue your life without interference or gossip.

Steve grinned, remembering how, during his schooldays, other boys had envied him. They had lived in the outlying villages, brought to school by bus.

'Thoo's a lucky sod, Steve Scott,' he remembered one of the lads saying. 'Things 'appen 'ere. Nowt 'appens where I live.'

Yes, there were always things happening. Fêtes and shows, a cinema and a posh hall where the Young Farmers' Association held their social bashes.

And, as everywhere else in the world, there were things that caused talk. There were unmarried girls who became pregnant and clandestine love affairs, but in an area where generations of the same family still lived and worked, where young people usually married childhood friends, there was even a cosy feeling about extra-marital sex.

The unmarried girls eventually found husbands, and if occasional whispers surfaced about certain married couples throwing their car keys into a circle at parties, well . . . that was all right. Everything was all right, so long as the things that happened took place in private.

Steve rubbed his chin. Life was certainly lived in his home town but there were no old tramps lying about to offend the eye and certainly no scantily dressed females strutting along the pavements, stopping cars and offering certain specialities in return for money.

Oh no! He froze. She had noticed him staring at her. She was smiling at him and glancing from side to side, looking for a break in the traffic. Good God, she was coming over. Steve panicked. He swung round, trampling on someone's feet in his panic to get away. Without glancing back, he raced down the stairs leading to the Underground and bought a ticket to Kensington.

Hilary Hall was another surprise. It was not the ancient stone-built seat of learning he had imagined, but a vast five-storied, redbrick complex with car parking facilities on one side and a neat lawn fringed by plane trees on the other. Inside, a huge electronic board flickered instructions to in-coming delegates.

Steve found his delegated reception area where the man behind a desk ticked his name off a list and handed him a badge for his lapel, a key and a large brown envelope.

'All the details in there. Your group has the run of the whole of the third floor. Welcoming sherry party scheduled for six-thirty this evening in the small lecture hall. Your room number is on the key. *Please* don't lose the key and don't take it home with you when you leave. Sleeping accommodation's round the back, in the Annex. Anything else you want to know?'

'No, thanks.' Steve picked up his bag and looked at the crowds milling around him. 'I wasn't expecting so many people.'

The man attending to him smiled faintly. 'They're not all your lot, Mr Scott. We've three different groups in at the moment and another twenty-five people are expected tomorrow. But each group has specific areas of operation. The bars are the only places you'll get to mix with people attending different courses. There's a small bar on the first floor, if you're interested, and the main one's down in the basement. They are always crowded, as you might imagine. Drinks are cheaper here than in the local hotels.'

'Thanks, I'll remember that.' Steve went off to find his room.

The sherry party was the usual sort of thing. A speech of welcome after which everyone eyed everyone else, made desultory conversation and wolfed down the finely cut sandwiches, looking round hopefully for something more substantial to eat. After exchanging a few polite words with his immediate neighbours, Steve looked round and realised he was one of the youngest men in the room.

The realisation both pleased and alarmed him. I must have made quite an impression, he mused, thinking back to his initial interview with the Manager at his branch and his subsequent meeting with a visiting Inspector from Head Office. On the other hand . . . His gaze wandered from face to face. He guessed the average age of the men attending the sherry party (there were only a handful of women present and they all looked middle-aged to him) was about twenty-seven or twenty-eight. Collectively, though, they gave the impression of being much older.

It wasn't the array of horn-rimmed spectacles or even the general uniform of dark suits and plain white shirts. Steve had expected those. It was the overall expression of seriousness on the faces and the solid air hovering over the little groups which had clustered together.

Steve nodded to the man standing next to him, took another glass of sherry from the tray the waitress offered to him and wandered about, listening to snatches of conversation.

'Obviously, the answer is rising share prices to make corporate activity in rights issues easier to promote.'

'Emerging markets in the Philippines suggest . . .'

'I heard a two per cent launch discount's a possibility.'

Steve put a hand over his mouth and burped discreetly. Sherry wasn't his tipple. He put the half-filled glass on a table and felt depression pressing down on him.

Everyone here sounded as though they knew a great deal more about banking than he did. So why had he been awarded a place? What was he doing here? And even more importantly, why had he tried so hard to come? Did he really *want* to become like the rest of the men in this room?

He leaned against a convenient wall and watched them all. Yes, of course he did. He wanted to be a success, he wanted to advance in his career, he wanted to give Jill the kind of lifestyle she deserved, but for Christ's sake . . . this was the welcoming party? Once again, he studied his companions. Couldn't they loosen up, just a little?

Fortunately, he was rescued from his mood of introspection by a black-haired man he had exchanged a few words with earlier. The man came up to him and spoke out of the side of his mouth.

'Hey, Steve, I'm starving and those sandwiches were diabolical. Let's go out and find somewhere to eat.'

A couple of streets away they discovered an Italian

restaurant and after eating a plateful of fettuccine and sharing a bottle of Chianti with his companion, Steve felt much more optimistic. They returned to St Hilary's. After bidding the other man good-night, Steve found his bedroom without difficulty, went to bed and slept like a log.

Next morning he attended a lecture on the increasing importance of investments from Latin-American countries on the world markets. The title had alarmed him, but to his relief he both understood and enjoyed the lecturer's message. But after the coffee break another lecturer addressed the question of the Monopolies Commission report on write-offs by certain individual banks.

The delivery of the second lecturer was poor. The man's voice was monotonous and Steve found he had no interest in the subject of the lecture. After ten minutes, his attention wandered so much so that when he suddenly heard the phrase, 'keeping abreast of full-term profits', a mental picture of the prostitute at King's Cross flashed across his mind. He shifted in his seat and was relieved when the meeting broke up at twelve-thirty.

Studying his copy of the day's programme, he saw that lunch was to be served at one o'clock after which two hours' free time had been scheduled. He'd skip lunch, he decided. It was time he went out and saw something of the city.

Using the Underground, he went to Covent Garden. Today, the weather was kinder and a watery sun shone from a pale blue sky. In the piazza, street entertainers performed a mime. Steve watched the show and then wandered around the colourful stalls in the central market area marvelling at the bewildering variety of goods for sale and taking the opportunity to buy a few Christmas presents for his family.

From an antiques stall he purchased a pair of delicate

pearl-drop earrings for Jill and a turquoise brooch for his grandmother. He hadn't opened her present to him yet, he remembered. As he waited for his gifts to be wrapped, he watched the people passing by on the crowded pavements.

American tourists were out in force. The men all seemed to wear brightly patterned trousers and checked caps and were in awe of their wives. They snapped endless photographs. Some of their subjects were the Indian and Oriental women who glided along silently, their eyes down, dressed in gracefully draped clothing, despite the cold weather.

Then there were groups of Japanese, also with cameras, and tall, sharply dressed West Africans who walked as though they had springs in their heels. Again Steve thought, I'm a long way from home. He went back to the Underground and caught a train to Westminster. He had just enough time to take a look at the outside of the Abbey and the Parliament Buildings.

He hung over the bridge for five minutes and watched the river sliding silently by and then walked around the grass lawns at the centre of Westminster staring upward at the statues of famous men – Palmerston, Disraeli and Churchill. They did something with their lives, he thought. Still, we can't all be famous.

Back at Hilary Hall, he hurried to wash and brush up before presenting himself for his interview. He felt he had acquitted himself satisfactorily when the man who interviewed him gave him a friendly smile as he left the room. A tea break, and then into the small cinema to watch a film about economic growth. Afterwards, in company with his fellows, he wrote up his notes and submitted them to the man at the door.

In the evening, after a shower and change of clothes, he decided to go down and see what was happening in the basement bar. He was physically tired but his brain was racing. What he needed, he decided, was to sit down, relax, and hopefully find someone to talk to who didn't want to discuss bank rates.

He was about to leave his room when he remembered his grandmother's gift to him. Taking his travel bag down from the top of the wardrobe, he found the package, opened it and then laughed. Inside the wrapping paper was a wide silk tie. It was a beautiful tie, but colourful – on a dark blue background, an olive green vine twisted and turned and on the vine, in splashes of glorious colour, scarlet flowers bloomed.

Steve lifted the tie up, examined it more closely, and then whistled through his teeth.

'Great-grandfather,' he said, aloud, 'if you wore this, you must have been some "goer". It's too rich for me, though.'

But in the act of replacing the tie in the paper, he reconsidered. In Covent Garden he had bought himself a present. It had been an impulse buy, a memento of his trip to London. Now he found his parcel, unwrapped his gift to himself, laid it on the bed and placed the tie on top. The shirt was in heavy cotton, long-sleeved and dark green in colour. Steve studied the effect. Yes, they went well together.

He stripped off his white shirt, donned the new one and then put on the tie. Not bad, he decided, looking at himself through the wardrobe mirror. Good job his slacks were dark-coloured, otherwise he would never have dared to wear the colour combination. He'd never wear it at home, that was for sure.

He went to the door, switched the light off and then paused and put it on again. He went back to the mirror. Could he *really* walk into a bar wearing a tie like that? He studied his appearance and then, remembering the soberly dressed company at the sherry party, he grinned and ran his hand over his springy fair hair. Yes, he could. Actually, he felt pretty good. He left the room, closing the door behind him with a bang.

The basement bar, as he had been warned, was packed. Steve eased his way into the crowd, fought his way to the bar and bought a drink, then he looked around him. The bar was low-ceilinged and full of hazy tobacco smoke. There were no unoccupied seats. Nevertheless, he was glad to be there.

A Tina Turner tape was playing and there was that animated buzz which came from people laughing and talking and enjoying themselves. Steve smiled down into his glass of lager. It was nice to be in a crowd, even though he was alone.

'Shove up, you lot.' A voice sounded to the right of him. 'Let the man sit down.'

Steve glanced over at the long table, already crowded with young people of both sexes. The girl sitting at the end of the bench raised her hand to wave at him. She was plump without being fat, with long, wild, reddish-brown curling hair and a friendly smile. 'Over here. We can manage one more.'

He hesitated, then nodded. 'All right. Thanks.'

The other occupants of the bench, although grumbling good-naturedly, had squeezed up and a few inches of wooden seat showed. Steve perched himself next to the girl.

She offered him her open bag of crisps. 'Want one? They're smoky bacon flavour. I shouldn't be eating them really, but oh, what the hell? Who wants to be a size twelve anyway?'

'Thanks.' He took one.

'Which lot are you with?'

'Sorry?' He bent towards her, trying to hear her amidst all the noise. Her skin was the lovely creamy colour that often went with red hair and he noticed a trail of freckles ran across the bridge of her nose.

'I guessed you're with the agricultural convention.'

'Er, no.' His brow creased and then cleared as he followed her line of reasoning. 'I'm with the bankers.'

She frowned. 'I don't believe it. A banker doesn't wear a tie like that one.'

He laughed. ''Fraid so.'

'Oh.' She looked disappointed, then leaned forward and shouted to a man further down the bench: 'You win, Pete. I owe you a pound.' She looked back at Steve. 'We're playing a game, see, trying to sort people out into their various groups.'

'Why did you think I was into agriculture?'

The girl wrinkled her nose. 'I didn't, not really, but you're not with us and I couldn't imagine you counting money.'

'There's more to banking that counting money . . .' Steve broke off the conversation because a large group of people standing in front of them suddenly decided to leave.

The volume of noise increased as goodbyes were called out. There was a lot of pushing and shoving as the remaining people regrouped and then – at last – there was more space. The group squeezed on the benches gave sighs of relief and spread out, taking over the nearest two tables. Steve, the girl and four other people stayed where they were.

He drained his glass. 'Can I get you a drink?'

'No. At least . . .' The girl was undecided. 'You don't have to, you know.'

'My pleasure. What would you like?'

'Same as you, please. A lager.'

'And your friends?'

'Oh, no. There's too many of them for you to get involved. Thanks all the same.' She smiled and Steve saw her teeth were large and white and incredibly even. He smiled back at her. 'And maybe we should exchange names, if we're drinking together.' He paused. 'I'm Steve Scott.'

'I'm Liz Morrison.'

'Now you know why I came to London, you must tell me what you're doing here?'

They were halfway through their second drinks. Steve had learned that Liz had a younger sister at university and her parents lived in Exeter.

'I haven't seen my folks for nearly a year so I'll have to go home and see them before I set off on my travels.'

'*Have* to go home.' It seemed a strange way to describe a visit to your parents. Steve looked down into his glass and made no comment.

'Anyway' – Liz was replying to his qucstion – 'you should know which seminar I'm attending. If I'm not involved in banking or agriculture, there's only one left. Remember the electronic board in reception?'

Steve frowned and concentrated. 'Wait a moment.' He paused, then his eyes opened wide. 'Are you one of the VSO people?'

'That's right.' Liz waved her hand to her companions. 'We all are.'

'You mean, you're going to work abroad, with starving babies and things like that?' Steve eyed his companion with increased respect.

'I wouldn't be allowed near starving babies.' Liz grinned at him. 'I'm not qualified enough to work on the medical side. I'm off to India next month to help build a well in a village that has no running water.'

'Good God.' Steve swallowed a mouthful of lager and looked around at the other people sitting near them. 'And the rest of them?'

'Two other people in the group are going to India but to different regions.' Liz pointed towards a tall, thin man with thick glasses and a beard. 'Richard's a surveyor, he's going to supervise building a bridge, and Annie, the woman next to him, is a nurse. She *will* be looking after malnourished babies. As for me, I have no particular qualifications.' She pulled a face. 'I'll just be a foot soldier.'

'When are you going?'

'In three weeks' time. This is our last briefing session.' Liz stopped talking when the man she had just pointed to stood up and pulled on his jacket. She picked up her shoulder bag from the floor and also stood up. 'Sorry, we have to split now.'

'Oh, don't go, not yet.' Steve wanted to know more.

'Have to. Duty calls. Late night discussion with our group leaders.'

'Well, perhaps we can meet tomorrow?'

She shook her head. 'Don't think so. Thanks all the same.'

'Oh.' He was disappointed. He stood up and grasped her hand. 'Well, thanks for making room for me.' He gestured to the bench.

She grinned. 'A pleasure. To tell the truth, I simply couldn't resist that tie.' She pulled her hand free from his grasp and followed her companions from the room.

Chapter Eleven

Steve thought he would never see Liz Morrison again but fate had different plans. The following afternoon, when he was shopping in Oxford Street, he spotted her again. He had finished his course at St Hilary's Hall earlier than he had expected and had decided to try and buy the rest of his Christmas presents for the family before catching a train back home. He bought a beautiful rag doll for Alison, he was fond of his little niece, a large jazzy scarf for Paula and slippers and perfume for his mother. Finally, he went into Selfridges and spent far morc than he could afford on a pure silk nightgown for Jill.

His fiancee was very much on his mind as he jostled his way through the crowds of shoppers, for he was harbouring a sense of guilt. When Jill had learned he had been accepted for the seminar, she had ımmediately made plans to come up to London to join him.

'I've a few days' holiday owing to me,' she had said. 'I can buy a cheap day return on your last day there, Steve. You could meet me somewhere for a late lunch and then we could do some shopping and travel home together. It would be fun.'

'No.' He had said the word sharply. Too sharply, for he had seen her face cloud over. Nevertheless, he repeated the word, although in a softer tone of voice.

'No, love, I don't think that's a good idea. I've no idea what time I'll be leaving St Hilary's, you could be waiting for me for ages. The shops will be seething with people and it's one hell of a journey, London and back in one day.'

She had been disappointed, but for once he had insisted and he had got his own way. The funny thing was, he didn't know *why* he had been so against her coming up to join him. He knew only that he wanted to be in London on his own.

Steve normally hated the frantic build-up to Christmas but for once, by the time he had finished his shopping, he had forgotten his inner reservations about the hype and commercialism of the festive season. The gorgeously dressed windows, the faces of the children with their noses pressed up to them, the wonderful street decorations, impressed and delighted him. The only trouble was, his feet were killing him.

Clutching his bag and his parcels, he forced his way through the throng of people and turned into a side street leading away from Oxford Circus. He might spy a coffee shop, he reasoned, somewhere he could sit down and rest. He looked about him hopefully, and there she was.

Liz was a few yards away from him. She was standing in the doorway of a ladies' hairdresser's putting her purse back into her shoulder bag. As he started towards her, she picked up the couple of carrier bags she had placed by her feet and set off, walking quickly down the street away from him.

'Liz. Liz Morrison.' He quickened his steps and then paused. Was he mistaken? He could have sworn it was her, but the girl in front of him had short hair.

She heard his shout. She turned and looked back, and it was her.

'Oh, it's you, Steve.'

He walked up to her. She looked different without her mass of red hair. She looked ordinary. The expression on her face was serious and he felt awkward and a little shy but then she smiled at him and he relaxed.

'I thought it was you, but then I wasn't sure.'

She touched her shorn head, a self-conscious gesture. 'I've just left the hairdresser's. What do you think?'

He hesitated. 'I'm not the kind of man to make snap decisions. Look, I'm dying for a sit-down and a cup of coffee. Will you join me?'

She nodded. 'All right. If we can find a cafe with any spare seats.' Ten minutes and three streets later, they found one, although they had to share the table with an exhausted-looking young mother with a pile of shopping and her baby, a little boy in a high chair busily smothering his face with chocolate ice-cream. Steve smiled his apologies to the child's mother as he squeezed past her and put two mugs of coffee down on the cafe table.

To Liz he said, 'Sorry about the wait. There was a queue at the till.'

She shrugged. 'Only to be expected at this time of year.'

Liz had also been Christmas shopping. Her carrier bags had a Father Christmas emblazoned on the side. She squashed them down by the side of her chair before picking up her mug of coffee and drinking from it. 'That's good.' She smiled at him over the rim of her mug. 'Thanks.'

He smiled back. 'I'm pleased I spotted you. Tell me,' he gestured towards her carrier bags, 'have you finished now?'

'Yes, I've got all the presents I need.' She took another sip of coffee. 'I'm off to Exeter tomorrow. Back home for a traditional family Christmas.'

There was that odd note in her voice again. Steve heard

it but decided it was none of his business. He sat back in his chair and studied her appearance.

'Yes, the new hair style suits you. I like it.'

A tide of colour rushed into her pale face. 'Honestly?'

'Yes.'

He wasn't being honest at all. He regretted the loss of her wild mop of hair. It had been her main claim to beauty. Still, his words did the trick. She looked much happier now.

'It seemed the sensible thing to do. Where I'm going, there'll be no hairdressers, no chemists selling shampoos and conditioners, and precious little hot water. Besides, I started thinking about the creepie-crawlies.' She shuddered.

Steve stirred his coffee and watched the froth disappear off the top.

'Didn't you think of them before you signed up for this trip?'

'Of course I did.'

There was a tinge of anger in her reply and Steve cautioned himself not to be stupid. He liked Liz and didn't want to upset her. It was none of his business what she did with her life. But, somehow, it was important to him to understand *why* she was going to India. Two years' hard work in a village where English was rarely spoken, and she hadn't even met the other workers on the scheme. What on earth motivated her to do it?

'Have you lived abroad before, Liz?' He shook his head when he saw her frown. 'I'm sorry, but I can't help being curious. I've never met anyone who's been brave enough to do what you're doing.'

She hunched her shoulders. 'It's not brave, and it's not unusual. Lots of people do it.'

'I've never met any of them.' Steve was quiet for a

moment reflecting upon the enormity of the differences between them. He knew he would never, ever, have the guts to do what she was doing.

'Where I live,' he said, 'people get excited about their annual holiday in Spain or even a weekend in London.' He grimaced. 'Hell, I was excited about coming here.' A tinge of red crept into his cheeks. 'Talk about a country bumpkin.'

'Don't say that.' Liz shook her head. 'There's a lot to be said for a settled way of life.'

When she saw the sceptical look on his face she spoke more quickly. 'Have you ever considered that people who flit from place to place, people who are always doing different things and changing their lives are actually cowards?'

He frowned. 'How do you make that out?'

'They're prepared to keep on the move rather than make a firm commitment, either to a place or to a particular person.'

He thought about her comment and then argued. 'You may be right but you're not like that. You've committed two years of your life to helping other people, strangers.'

She gave him a searching look and then, obviously deciding he was sincere, settled back in her chair and said. 'Don't give me a halo, Steve. I'm not a saintly do-gooder. What I'm doing, I'm doing for *me*.' She shrugged. 'Oh, I hope I'll be some use over there, but really, I'm being selfish. I need to sort myself out, you see.'

She twisted her hands round her coffee cup and sighed when she saw the puzzled frown on his face. 'You don't see, do you?'

For the moment, they had the table to themselves. The mother had collected her shopping and her chocolate-covered baby and departed. Liz studied the bottom of her mug for a moment and then put it down.

'Do you really want the story of my life?'

He nodded.

'Okay. In brief, since I left school I haven't been able to settle to anything. Six months in a job is about my limit so, as you can imagine, I've been a bit of a disappointment to my parents. They've just about given up on me and I can't say I blame them. I've bummed about quite a bit.

'Last year I was with the New Age travellers for nine months. I liked it at first but,' she shook her head, 'total freedom's a myth. And why should taxpayers fork out hard-earned money to people who refuse to take any responsibilty for their own lives?

'Anyway, I'd read about the voluntary service scheme and one day I suddenly decided to find out more about it. I discovered you don't have to be a genius to apply. So,' she paused, 'I applied.

'For the last eight months I've held down a horrible, boring job and I've managed to save a little money.' She pulled a face. 'The family think I've got my act together at last and they're welcoming me back into the fold.' She laughed and drank the last of her coffee. 'They don't know about India, yet. It's going to be a pretty lively Christmas.'

She looked across at Steve. 'There, now you have the story of my life. Satisfied?'

'Thanks for telling me.' His voice was non-committal. He, too, finished his coffee and then he put his hands palm down on the table and leaned forward, closer to her. 'But I still don't understand. You say you don't like routine work, but digging a well's going to be hard, boring, routine work, isn't it? So why do it? And in India, for God's sake.' He stared at her. 'How long will you be there?'

'The contract I signed is for two years.'

He was silent.

'Don't worry about it. It's me that going there, not you.' Liz tossed back her head. 'When the well's built, I'll be moved somewhere else. I won't be in the same village for the term of my contract.'

'But . . .'

'Steve, it's none of your business.' She paused, frowning. 'And I don't know why I'm even telling you this but I'm twenty-five years old and I still don't have a clue what I want to do with my life.' She gave a little shake of her head. 'It's not good enough. I'm sick of drifting from one situation to another. I suppose,' she paused again, 'I've had it too easy.

'Mum and Dad always sent me money when I was really on my uppers, and whenever I've got bored I've just packed up and moved on to something else. Now, it's time to stop. It's time I grew up. Maybe India will help me do that. I won't be able to cop out there. I realise I shall probably be miserable a lot of the time. But, hey,' she shrugged and managed a faint grin, 'suffering's good for the soul, they say.'

There was a short silence and then Steve put out his hand and covered hers, which were folded tightly on the table in front of her.

'Thanks for explaining.' He paused. 'And I still think you're brave.'

She grinned and he felt her hands relax beneath his.

'Well, you're entitled to your own opinion. Actually, it's not all heroic sacrifice. Part of me can't wait. After all, India!' She closed her eyes for a moment. 'Land of mystics and fable. Hell, it's an adventure, and just maybe I'll get to know the meaning of life.'

Steve laughed. 'Maybe you will. You're following in the footsteps of the Beatles, you know.'

She laughed with him. 'On the other hand, it could be

bloody awful.' She arched her eyebrows and the expression in her eyes became serious. 'I wonder, we get on so well . . . if I gave you my contact address, would you be prepared to write to me sometimes?'

Perhaps he delayed answering for a fraction too long for she added, quickly: 'Only if you want to, of course, and only out of friendship – one mate to another.'

He smiled and patted her hand. 'I'd be glad to.'

'Great.' She pulled her hands free, took an envelope from her bag and scribbled an address on the back of it.

Steve watched her. What a strange girl she was. She didn't look twenty-five years old. Her skin was so smooth and pale. She'd have to be careful about protecting herself against the sun, he thought. Sitting in the steamed-up, muggy atmosphere of the busy cafe he tried to visualise her in India, digging a well in the searing heat, and failed utterly.

She looked up and caught him staring at her. The colour flowered in her face and she lowered her eyes as she handed him the envelope.

'Thanks.' Their fingers brushed as he took it from her and placed it safely in the inside fold of his wallet.

'We'd better go,' she said.

Outside, they stood awkwardly, facing each other.

'I guess this is farewell then.' Steve put down his bag, moved his parcels into his left hand and held out his right. He tried to smile.

'Good luck, Liz.'

She didn't take his hand. She looked down at the pavement and said, in a small voice, 'Are you going back to Yorkshire now?'

'Soon. On the seven o'clock train.'

'Oh. Booked your seat, I suppose?'

'No, although I should have done. I'll end up standing

all the . . .' His voice faded away when he saw her intent expression. He felt an uneasy feeling in the pit of his stomach. Something was happening here, and he wasn't sure how to handle it.

'I hear the train service to the North's pretty good nowadays?'

He cleared his throat. 'Yes. It is.'

She took her gaze away from the pavement and looked at him. 'It's lousy at St Hilary's now. Practically everyone's checked out. All my gang's left. I've got my room booked until the morning. You wouldn't . . .' a quiver sounded in her voice '. . . you couldn't catch a later train, could you?'

'Well, I . . .' Steve's refusal died before utterance. She was scared, he realised. Scared of going home to face her parents, scared of going to India, scared of being alone with her thoughts. He smiled down at her. 'Why not? There's a late train, about eleven.'

They bought pâté, cheese and bread sticks from a delicatessen, and two bottles of red wine and a tiny novelty Christmas cake from a chain store. After all, as Liz said, she wouldn't have a proper Christmas for a long time so she might as well celebrate twice this year.

Her room at St Hilary's was identical to the one he had occupied. It was clean, functional and totally anonymous. Steve looked around and pulled a face. 'Not very Christmassy, is it?'

Liz laughed at his wry expression. 'Why should it be? There'll be no one here on Christmas Day.'

'But we're having a mini-Christmas this evening.' He held up the bag containing the wine.

'So, we'll have to use our imagination. For instance,' Liz waved her arm in the direction of the wardrobe, 'can't you see that absolutely wonderful Christmas tree they've moved in? Isn't it pretty? I love the little red silk bows. Proper candles, too, so much better than modern day fairy lights.'

The girl was mad. Steve looked at her indulgently. Mad, but fun. He entered into her game and cast his eyes at the ceiling. 'I wonder where they got the old-fashioned paper chains? Is that gold-wrapped parcel for me or you? And the plates for the party better be bone china.'

He laid the bags containing their purchases on the end of the bed and searched for the box holding the Christmas cake. He found it and held it up in the air, the small box resting on the palm of his right hand.

'We'll have to invite more guests, Liz,' he said firmly. 'We'll never manage to eat all this on our own.'

She hooted with laughter and collapsed on the bed. 'Idiot!' And then her face stilled. 'No more guests, Steve. I'm happy with the one I've got.'

His heart began to thump in his chest. He put the cake down and took a bottle of wine from the bag.

'Have you a bottle opener?'

'Never travel without one.' She turned away from him and searched in her capacious shoulder bag.

The light-hearted note was back in her voice. Steve heard it and relaxed but, at the same time, felt a little stab of regret.

They ate the food, drank the wine and talked non-stop. Afterwards, Steve could never remember what they talked about but he knew they had talked honestly and like old friends and they had laughed a lot. At some stage, they opened the second bottle and he forgot all about catching a train. When he remembered, it didn't seem to matter.

There'd be plenty of trains tomorrow. Tomorrow he would go home and Liz would go to Exeter and they would never meet again, but tonight they were together in this bare little room their imagination had furnished, and something magical had happened between them.

And then, when the second bottle was empty and Liz, sitting beside him on the bed, turned to him and took his face between her hands and kissed him, that seemed right, too.

'Thank you, Steve,' she whispered.

He flushed. 'What for?'

'Holding out your hand to a drowning woman. Oh, God!' She groaned and put up her hands up to her own face. 'What a terrible thing to say. It sounds like the opening line of a totally tasteless song.'

'It doesn't.'

'It does.' She lowered her hands and looked at him. 'But it's the truth. When I thought of coming back here, on my own, I felt terrified. I knew I'd collapse into a shivering heap on the bed once the door closed behind me.'

She chewed on her lip. 'I'm dreading tomorrow, you know. I'll have to tell my parents. God, they'll go mad, and then they'll look hurt and sad and blame themselves for my wayward behaviour. And my superior sister will be there, smirking and thinking: Liz has really done it this time. And I have, haven't I?'

'You've done something good, Liz. They should be proud of you. I am.' Steve paused, then continued slowly, 'And I think I envy you, too.'

Her eyes widened. 'You do, honestly?'

He nodded.

'You mean you'd like to spend two years grubbing about in the mud in a primitive village in India?'

There was a twinkle showing in her eyes and Steve was glad to hear the hint of humour in her voice. He laughed and put his arm around her. 'You know what I mean, Liz. You realised your life needed a change of direction and so you've done something about it. You've changed your life.'

She moved her shoulders restlessly. 'And what if it's a change for the worse?'

'Then you'll go down another road, won't you? After all, you've taken the first step. The rest of the journey will be easier.'

She blinked her eyes, nodded and then took his hand and grasped it firmly. 'You're right. If I don't like India, I can always come home. I'll get a steady job and settle down. On the other hand,' she smiled, 'I might stay there. Maybe an Indian prince will fall in love with me. I'll marry him, wear glorious clothes, and we'll ride on elephants and go looking for tigers.'

Her words brought a little jolt of memory. Tigers. Ah, yes. He remembered the jigsaw Jill's mother had been working on. The jungle background and the mysterious blurred figure that could, or could not, have been a tiger. He felt uneasy, remembering home and everything there, but the feeling faded when he stared into Liz's greeny-brown eyes. He thought of her hair as it had been when he first saw her, a wonderful mass of reddish-brown curls.

'You're a bit like a tiger yourself, Liz – brave and strong and beautiful.' He bent towards her and kissed her lightly on the tip of her nose. 'Whatever happens, I wish you luck.'

She raised her face to him and then, somehow, her arms were around his neck and he was kissing her on her lips. He felt the pressure of her breasts against his chest and the feel of her body made him feel dizzy.

He knew he should stop this, move away from her, but he couldn't because she was kissing him back, her mouth opening slightly as she responded to him. And then he was kissing her cheeks and her forehead, smoothing back her hair and regretting once again her lost beauty. How he would have gloried in plunging his hands into that mane of hair, lifting strands of it up to his lips, drinking in the scent of it.

He sighed and pulled away slightly, taking hold of her hands and turning them so he could kiss the delicate white skin of her wrists. It wasn't wrong what he was doing, it was the most natural thing in the world.

When he saw she was smiling, he returned his attention to her face. He brushed his lips softly along the angle of her jaw and then he kissed her throat and watched as his fingers, which had acquired a life of their own, unbuttoned the collar of her blouse, revealing a vee of smooth bare skin underneath.

'Wait,' she breathed. She moved away from him so she could undo the buttons of his shirt. She kissed his shoulders as she eased the garment away from him. Then she leaned back and pulled off her own shirt and unfastened her bra.

'That's better,' she murmured.

He caught his breath as she came to him again and her full, creamy breasts tumbled into his waiting hands. She was wonderful, gorgeous. Desire and arousal stirred in his body.

Jill's breasts are not like this. They are small and round and firm as apples.

The thought stayed in his mind and his hands stilled.

Immediately she sensed the change in him and drew back. 'What's the matter?'

'Nothing. Nothing's the matter.'

She knew there was. She sat quietly with her hands cupped in her lap like a small child, and her eyes were remote. She made no effort to cover herself.

'You don't really want me, do you? I guess I forced the

pace. I know I'm not anything special but . . .'

'That's not it. I think you're very special. But,' the words came out in a rush, 'I'm engaged, Liz, and I've never . . .'

'Oh.' Her voice was low. 'What's her name?'

'Jill.'

'Do you love her very much?'

He scrubbed his forehead with the heel of his hand and nodded. His eyes felt scratchy and sore.

'Well, then.' She swung her legs over the bed and stood up. 'I'm sorry if I came on too heavy. I must have embarrassed you.' She turned away from him and reached for her clothing.

He sat and watched her and a tight anger began to build in him. Anger at himself. Everything had gone wrong and he wished to God he had kept his mouth shut. Heaven knows, he didn't want to do anything to hurt Jill, but she was back at home and he was here. He was here with Liz and he had hurt *her*.

He had known her for such a short time, but somehow he could feel the depth of her hurt. Every line of her body, the way her face was averted from him, the futile fumbling with her clothes, all betrayed her desolation.

He didn't know what to do or say. He watched her as she moved to pull on her shirt and, as he saw the nape of her neck as she bent her head and the sweet curve of her breasts, he knew something else . . . it was wrong, but he still wanted her.

'No, please Liz, don't get dressed.'

He went to stand in front of her. He saw the tears on her averted face and brushed them away.

And then he said, 'Liz, I can't explain. I do love Jill, I can't lie, but being with you has been fantastic and you're so beautiful . . . I can't help wanting you. Knowing what you know, do you still want me?'

She smiled and put her arms around him.

Afterwards, he knew he would never be able to describe their lovemaking. There was physical passion, of course, the kind of passion he shared with Jill, but there were other emotions, too.

Before they made love, he had asked Liz about protection. 'Sorry, but . . .' he had felt the heat coming into his face '. . . I haven't anything on me.'

'I can see that.' She had chuckled. They were on the bed then, and naked.

'It's okay, Steve.' She waved towards the bedside cabinet. 'Look in the drawer.' She paused. 'But thanks for thinking about it, not many guys do.'

He felt a flicker of jealousy. She was experienced, far more experienced than he was. But then, looking into her smiling eyes, he had let the jealousy go. Whatever had happened and would happen was unimportant in this room. They were together now.

He pulled her closer to him and ran his hand gently over her ribcage. 'I would hate to cause you grief, Liz.'

She was silent for a moment and then she said softly, 'I think you already have. She raised her head from the pillow and laid her cheek against his. 'After tomorrow, we'll never, ever meet again, will we?'

His hand rested between her breasts. He could feel the slow beat of her heart.

'Perhaps not.' He shook his head restlessly. 'But let's not think about tomorrow.'

'You're right. Let's not think at all.' She moved closer to him and now it was her hands that wandered. Lightly she ran her fingers over his arms, his chest, his stomach, and then lower down his body.

He groaned. 'Stop that. What are you trying to do, finish the job before we've started?'

'Of course not.' She stopped touching him. She rolled over and lay on her back. 'Do with me what you will, master.'

He raised himself on one elbow and grinned at her. 'I want to get to know you, every bit of you.'

She put her arms behind her head and nodded, her expression serious. 'All right. Do it.'

Fifteen minutes later, he leaned over her and kissed her mouth gently. 'As I expected,' he said, 'you're a perfect example of womanhood.'

There were beads of moisture on her brow and her breathing was jerky but still she grinned back. 'Pretty solid specimen, eh?'

He frowned and shook his head. 'No, I meant what I said. You're perfect, Liz.'

Her features softened and he thought he saw her eyes moisten but he wasn't sure because she dashed her arm across her face and sat up.

'Thank you, Steve.' Her smile flashed out. 'Now it's my turn.'

For over an hour they brought pleasure to each other and delayed the final delight. They stroked and caressed each other's bodies until spirals of fire raced through them and they gasped and clung together and then moved apart, torn between their mutal desire for consummation and their longing for their lovemaking to continue.

Steve was amazed at his self-control, for Liz was incredibly sensual. She shuddered and moaned beneath him and her own tongue and fingers flitted over his body and drove him crazy. But what was even more special was the loving and willing way she offered herself to him, holding nothing back.

And so he concentrated on making the moments last. He stroked her body, teasing her and driving her crazy until, finally, she cried out aloud and he realised he could delay no longer. He wrapped his arms around her and his movements became stronger and more urgent. He groaned as the waves of passion overwhelmed him, and beneath him Liz cried out again and her back arched with the intensity of her pleasure, and then it was over.

They lay in each other's arms and spoke little. But they tried to stay awake, for both of them dreaded the morning.

Chapter Twelve

Christmas was almost upon them and Rosie had no idea what anyone was doing. Minna wouldn't say whether or not she intended spending Christmas Day with them and when Rosie had pushed her to make a decision, she had become sarcastic.

'Really, Rosemary, you do *fuss* so. I'll make up my mind and tell you later.'

Any later, thought Rosie, and it will be Boxing Day!

Paula was as bad. She had promised to reply to Rosie's invitation for Christmas over two weeks ago, but still her mother was waiting to hear from her. Rosie had tried to ring the flat but no one ever seemed to be in. That worried her more than the arrangements for Christmas. Where were they, if not at home?

And now Steve was acting out of character. He was quiet and moody and when she tried to speak to him, he made some excuse and went out. He hadn't told her a thing about his trip to London, even though he knew she was dying to hear all about it, and tonight he hadn't come in for his tea. Well, enough was enough.

It was rare for Rosie to lose her temper, but now she was spoiling for a fight. When she heard the front door close and Steve's footsteps in the hall, she went and stood in the middle of the kitchen. There was a glint of anger sparking her blue eyes and her hands clenched into fists as she held her arms rigidly by her sides.

She waited until he appeared in the doorway.

'What time do you call this?'

Steve halted. 'I don't know – about seven, I suppose.'

'It's twenty-five minutes past.'

Steve looked preoccupied. 'So?'

'What do you mean, "so"?' Looking up at the blank-faced stranger who had once been her sunny, chubby-faced son, Rosie resisted a strong urge to slap his face. 'Your tea's ruined, that's all. Couldn't you have told me that you were going to be late?'

He flushed. 'What would you like me to do, Mum, ring in and report to you every two hours?'

She frowned. 'Of course not, but I think I'm entitled to some consideration. You know I always cook for you and today's meal was particularly nice.' She paused and added, a little self-righteously, 'I gave it to next-door's dog, half an hour ago.'

She waited for his apology but he simply stared at her and then said slowly, 'And you know, Mum, that I've asked you several times not to get a meal ready for me every night. I don't expect it. You're at work and sometimes,' he paused, 'sometimes, it would be nice not to have to hurry home to eat. I might want to do something different.'

'What would you do?' Rosie was bewildered. 'It's winter. There's no cricket practice. And anyway, you always go over to see Jill after you've had your meal.'

He did not reply and the silence hung heavy between them. Rosie bit her lip. Her words had hurt him; because she loved him, she sensed it but she didn't know why. The tension added to her already overwrought emotions and she burst into tears.

'It was best steak. I thought you deserved a treat. You've seemed a bit down lately and I wanted to cheer you up. I did roast potatoes and your favourite parsnips, too.' Her shoulders shook and she hid her face in her hands.

'Aw, Mum.' His voice softened. In two strides he was next to her, patting her heaving shoulders. 'I'm sorry.'

His apology should have made her feel better, but it didn't. She felt worse. She felt guilty. She cried even more and heard him sigh.

'Come on, love, this isn't like you. Tell me what's really bothering you?'

So she told him the bit she understood. She told him about Minna and about Paula and of her frustration over Christmas, and then she felt better. She moved away from his comforting grasp, took a handkerchief from her apron pocket and blew her nose. 'I'm being ridiculous.'

He shook his head. 'No, you're not. You're lumbered with a family of selfish pigs.'

'No, no.' Her forehead creased. 'It's me. I've been in a funny mood for days. I don't know why. Perhaps it's the thought of the course coming nearer. I'll be starting after Christmas, you know.'

'Well, I can't help with that, but I *can* help with the Christmas preparations.' Steve put his hands on her shoulders, turned her round and gave her a little push towards the door. 'Go and put your coat on.'

First, he drove her to his grandmother's flat. Minna, taken unawares by the surprise visit, and perhaps disarmed by Steve's resolute manner, was quickly persuaded to come to a decision. Yes, she would spend Christmas Day with them.

'That's fine.' Steve stood up and helped his mother on with her coat.

'If I don't hear from you in the meantime, Grandma, I'll

come and collect you at a quarter to ten. I'll bring you back about nine-thirty p.m., if that's all right?'

He waited for her nod of agreement and then continued: 'We can't stay any longer. We're off to the supermarket before it closes. We've shopping to do.' He looked at his mother. 'They're open until nine every night this week, aren't they?'

Rosie nodded.

Minna went to her window to watch them leave. It was dark outside but the front of the block of flats was well-lit. She watched her grandson open the car door for his mother, close it after her and then walk quickly round to the driving seat. He glanced up at her window before getting into the car and raised his hand in a brief gesture of farewell. His face was a white blur, she couldn't see if he was smiling. She rather thought he was not.

His trip to London had altered him, she thought. Whether for good or ill remained to be seen, but it had firmed him up in some indefinable way. She watched the red rear lights of his car disappear from view and felt glad she had decided to spend Christmas with them. Perhaps, at long last, she might derive some interest from observing her grandson.

Minna had been a reluctant grandmother. Babies and toddlers bored her to tears. She had never collected photographs of Paula and Stephen when they were babies and found they had become even less appealing as they had grown.

Steve had become larger and remained boring and Paula had blossomed into a beauty but had become untrustworthy and rude.

When she had visited her grandmother in her fourteenth year dressed in what looked like men's working boots, a see-through vest-like top and ripped jeans, Minna had spoken her mind. So had Paula, then she had stormed out of the flat, slamming the door behind her.

'I will not entertain your child again,' Minna had informed Rosemary, her mouth so pinched in with disapproval it looked as though she had no lips. And she hadn't for almost a year, and came to regret her decision. She guessed, correctly, that she missed Paula more than Paula missed her.

And so she had relented. Paula recommenced her occasional visits to her grandmother, turning up after a row at home or when she wanted something, and Minna exuded disapproval but fed the child fruit cake and coffee. She never gave her money.

For her part, Paula entertained the old lady by recounting carefully doctored accounts of her activities to which her grandmother listened avidly.

Minna had missed Paula when she went away to live in Manchester. She thought, spitefully, that Steve should have been the one to leave home. A boy shouldn't live with his mother once he left his teens; a girl should.

Ah, well. She turned away from the window. Perhaps there was hope for Stephen after all, and perhaps Paula also would be home for Christmas. She'd like to see her granddaughter. She was older now, no longer wanting to shock by wearing outlandish clothes and peculiar hairstyles. It would be interesting to see if she had inherited her grandmother's flair for dressing.

Minna thought of her daughter and shuddered. Tonight she had looked quite unkempt. The next time Rosemary visited she must remember to suggest her daughter pay a visit to the hairdresser. She may not be going anywhere exciting for Christmas but she owed it to herself to smarten up a little.

* * *

With only half an hour to closing time, the large supermarket was unusually quiet. To the accompanying, repeated tune of 'Sleigh Bells', Steve whizzed his mother around the displays, placing into the trolley all the things she said they needed.

'We can't buy them all tonight,' she protested. 'I haven't got enough money on me.'

'I'll use my credit card.' He hushed her protests. 'It's all right, we can sort it out later. We'll go fifty-fifty, shall we?'

Back at home, he helped put the shopping away and then made a plateful of ham sandwiches and a pot of tea. They ate in a companionable, easy silence. When Steve stood up and started to clear away the pots, Rosie jumped up and stopped him.

'No, I'm doing the dishes. I insist.' She looked up into his face and smiled her apology. 'I'm sorry I worked my frustration off on you, Steve. Out of all the family, you're the one who causes the least trouble. You're a good lad.'

'Am I?'

His voice was even, kindly, but once again she saw his face change and in that split second, Rosie realised her son was no longer a boy. She must stop fussing, she mustn't refer to him as a lad. Steve had become a man and she must treat him accordingly.

She stepped away from him. 'I'll go and wash up.'

Two days before Christmas Eve, Paula got in touch. It was a short telephone call and she started with a string of excuses. She had rung home, several times, but no one had been home. The agency had kept her busy. She had taken Alison to a couple of Christmas parties.

Dave sent his love. Yes, things, were fine, honestly they were. Alison was growing so tall. She had painted a Christmas card for her grandma, it was in the post. She paused: they had decided to keep Christmas at home this year. They'd visit in the New Year. Yes, honestly they would. Love to everyone. Have a happy Christmas.

Rosie decided to believe her. Paula sounded rushed but happy enough. Anyway, it was too near Christmas to suggest alternative plans.

It would have been nice to see little Alison opening her gifts on Christmas morning, but perhaps, now that Minna was coming for the day, it would be better for them to visit in the New Year. If they came.

She replaced the telephone and went to bake some mince pies.

The church bells woke her early on Christmas morning. Warm beneath her quilt, Rosie listened to the joyous peals and felt her spirits rise. Perhaps today would be an exception, perhaps this year their little family gathering would celebrate Christmas in the appropriate, loving way; if only Minna behaved herself.

She behaved perfectly at first. She was ready for Steve when he called for her, she opened her presents and expressed herself delighted with them, and even ate some of her Christmas dinner. It was almost three o'clock before the milk of her human kindness dried up.

Rosie had suggested a cup of tea and a mince pie.

Steve had refused. 'Not for me, Mum. I'll be going over to Jill's in ten minutes and I'd better leave some space for my tea.' He winked at his mother as he left the room.

'He's actually going to eat tea, after that enormous meal?' Minna moved restlessly in her chair. 'And please don't mention mince pies, Rosemary, and don't produce yet more food.'

A peevish note sounded in her voice. 'I'm developing the most terrible indigestion. I knew I shouldn't have eaten my lunch, but rather than upset you, I forced it down. Now

I'm suffering for it.' She pressed her hand to her midriff. 'Have you any bicarbonate of soda?'

'I think there's some Rennies. I'll go and get them.'

'They're no use, and they taste of chalk.' Minna's mouth turned downwards. 'I would have thought aids to the digestion would be one thing you always kept in this house. Steve does love his chips, doesn't he?'

Head down, Rosie escaped into the kitchen.

'She's starting,' she muttered to Steve, and then, seeing him grin, added morosely: 'It's all right for you, you're going out. I'm stuck with her until this evening.'

Steve slipped on his jacket. 'What are you looking for?'

'Bicarbonate of soda. She says she's got indigestion.'

'We haven't got any, have we?'

Rosie was searching through her kitchen cupboards. She slammed shut the door she was holding. 'No,' she said hopelessly.

'I've an idea.' Steve took a bottle of mineral water from the refrigerator, poured some into a tumbler and then reached for another bottle.

Rosie's eyes rounded. 'No, Steve. You can't give my mother vodka. She doesn't drink'

'She used to. She told me that when she was young, she used to go to bottle-parties.' Steve poured a generous dollop of vodka into the glass, swirled it round and held it out to his mother. 'There we are, bubbles and all. Go on, take it in to her. She won't know. You can't taste vodka.'

'No, Steve, I can't. It might make her ill.'

'A drop of vodka won't hurt her, Mum. She'll think it's bicarb. It might even do the trick and steady her stomach. And if it doesn't, well, it will either cheer her up or put her to sleep for a bit.'

'I don't know . . .' Rosie wavered.

'It's up to you.' Steve slipped his car keys into his

pocket. 'But if you want to retain any kind of Christmas spirit, I say give her the vodka; it's obvious she's building up to one of her tirades.'

'Are you sure it won't hurt her?'

'Of course it won't. Why don't you have one yourself?'

Steve left and Rosie smelt and then studied the glass in her hand. It did look extremely innocent. She carried it through to Minna feeling like Lady Macbeth.

'So you found some? Good.' Minna took the glass from Rosie and drank deeply. She looked up at her daughter. 'Well, sit down then, don't hover over me.'

Rosie sat down and Minna took another drink.

'I'm disappointed Paula didn't come home for the holiday. It's such a long time since I've seen her. How's that husband of hers? Good-looking, if I remember, but vain. Still,' she sighed, 'they make a handsome couple.'

'They're all right, I think.' Rosie watched the last of the vodka and water disappear down her mother's throat. She bit her lip nervously and stood up again. 'I think I'll make myself a cup of tea. Would you like one?'

'No.' Minna leaned back in her chair. 'What a fidget you are, Rosemary, always bobbing up and down. I'm surprised you never lose weight.'

Rosie clenched her teeth. 'I'll only be a minute.'

When she carried her tea back in the sitting room Minna was not asleep but she was nodding and her eyes were half-closed.

Cautiously, Rosie picked up the *TV Times* and studied the programmes. As she turned a page, her mother's head jerked and her eyes opened.

Rosie looked across at her. 'Do you want to watch something on TV?'

'Good Lord, no. Christmas television's even worse than everyday television.' Minna yawned, stretched out her hands, studied the backs of them and then said, in a conversational tone of voice, 'Do you know, Rosemary, it's only lately I've realised I'm an old woman. Isn't that silly of me?'

Did she want an answer? Rosie studied her mother's face. She was looking decidedly dreamy and Rosie decided she did not. She was right, for a moment later Minna continued.

'When you're old, Christmas is just another day to get through.' She rested her hands in her lap. 'When I was young, Christmas was a magical time. No sitting around watching a stupid box when I was young.' She rested her head against the back of the chair. 'Of course, we had money. It's easy to make things appear magical when you have money.'

Rosie watched her transfixed. Was her mother actually going to reveal something of her past? Television forgotten, she crouched in her chair, hardly daring to move a muscle.

'Papa always bought me wonderful presents.' Minna smiled, remembering. 'Then, on Boxing Day, when I was small, he used to take me out to tea and then on to a pantomime. Pantomines in the twenties were absolutely gorgeous, the sets and costumes were out of this world, and of course, we all dressed up in our finery to attend the performances.

'Mother never came with us. She disapproved of what she called frippery. She sometimes suggested I had a party instead of going to see a pantomine, but I didn't like parties. The boys were always so big and rough, I was terrified they'd break my lovely things, and sometimes they did.'

A frown flickered across her tightly drawn features. 'I was given a beautiful Chinese ivory musical box when I was seven and on my eighth birthday a stupid oaf of a boy called Simon Batchelor broke it. I hated him.

'I threw a terrible temper tantrum, so bad all the children had to be sent home before tea. I was naughty, I suppose, but I did so love my Chinese music box. Anyway, after that Mother never tried to persuade me to have another party. Poor Mother. She loved me, I think, but she never understood me, not like Papa did.'

Minna fell silent, her drowsy face soft with memories, and Rosie, staring at her, wondered whether she dared ask a question. She took a chance and whispered, 'Your mother, what was her name?'

'For goodness' sake, Rosie, what a thing to ask. You know your own grandmother's name.' Minna sat up straight in her chair.

Her musings over the past had vanished, she was definitely back in the present.

Rosie's mouth dropped open in dismay and frustration. Oh, why had she spoken? But there was so much she wanted to know. More sharply than usual, she replied, '*I don't* know, Mother. You've never told me anything about your early life. You never told me Grandmother's name.'

Minna looked shocked. 'Did I not? Oh, dear, how remiss of me.' She stared into the fire for a moment and then back at Rosie. 'My mother's name was Edith. Before her marriage she was Edith Conlon. She was a plain-looking woman with little to say for herself. She could be stern but she was always fair. I must have been a sore trial to her.' She stared again into the heart of the fire. 'She was not a physically strong woman and she died when I was thirteen years old, Nevertheless, she was a good mother to me and I should have told you about her.'

'And your Papa?' Rosie asked, feeling greatly daring.

'He was called Pieter, but you know that. I've told you about him.'

'Yes. He came from Holland, he was successful in his career and he was handsome. But why . . .' Rosie paused.

There were so many 'whys'. If he was so rich, why had Minna married a factory worker and gone to live in a mean little house in Halifax? She had been beautiful, so why hadn't she married a rich suitor and lived in London?

Rosie examined the thought that Minna had fallen madly in love with her father and had eloped, but dismissed the idea as ridiculous. Her mother and father couldn't *ever* have been madly in love.

So what had happened to make Minna leave the beautiful house and lovely things? When and where had Rosie's grandfather died, and in what circumstances?

From being a little girl she had wondered about her mother's early life but never more fervently than now because Steve had told her about his strange conversation with Minna the night before his trip to London. He had recounted his grandmother's recollections and then asked: 'Do you think she's imagining it all, Mum? I mean, she's getting on now.'

Rosie had shaken her head. 'Whatever she is, Steve, your grandmother is definitely not senile.'

He had nodded and gone about his business and Rosie had gone about hers, but Minna's reminiscences had stayed in the forefront of her mind.

The photograph of her grandfather had fascinated her since she was a small child but as she grew older, she came to understand that being well-dressed didn't necessarily mean the wearer of the clothes was particularly rich. Pieter van Heerden, Rosie had decided, had probably owned a shop or a small business.

But from what Minna had told Steve and from what she

had just said, it appeared her mother had enjoyed an extremely wealthy lifestyle as a girl. Rosie was afire with curiosity, but knew she must tread carefully.

'You once told me that your papa was a self-made man, Mother.' Rosie paused. 'How did he manage to become so wealthy?'

'It's true he arrived in London with very little.' Minna smiled proudly. 'But he had such charm, such presence. Within a month he had obtained a post with Beecham's, the pill and patent medicine manufacturers, and very soon he was given promotion. After four years he took charge of the sales department, again with great success. He saved money and moved to Dunlop's, the rubber tyre firm, and invested the money he had earned in the business.

'He married my mother. She had some money, left to her by some distant relative. That, too, my father invested. In two years it had trebled in value.' She sighed happily. 'Papa had such business acumen, his friends called him "the lucky Dutchman". By the time I was born, he was heading up Dunlop's Board of Directors and was a well-known figure on the Stock Exchange.'

'He *must* have been special.' Rosie paused. 'Is that when he bought the beautiful house?'

'Yes. I was a baby when we moved there and I grew up in those wonderful surroundings. You can't imagine how beautiful, Rosemary.' Minna turned and smiled at her daughter and, fascinated, Rosie smiled back.

Outside, the daylight had ebbed away. The curtains at the window had not yet been drawn and the only illumination was the light from the flickering flames of the fire. In the firelight, Rosie thought Minna looked almost young again; her cheeks were pink and her eyes sparkled.

She had leaned forward in her chair and now she clasped her hands round her knees and stared into the fire. Rosie sat quietly. She knew that for Minna the room in which she was sitting had faded away and she was back in the scenes of her greatest happiness.

'There were eight bedrooms in the house and two bathrooms. All the rooms had a different colour theme. My room was the blue room.' Minna's voice was light and dreamy.

'It had a long window with a window seat. I used to sit there to write my letters and to read. There was a white marble fireplace and when it was cold, Betty would come up and light a fire for me.

'The main staircase was very grand, there was a balustraded gallery leading round to the top of the stairs. I remember the feel of the curving walnut hand rail.' Minna rubbed the the thumb of her right hand against the palm of her left.

'Papa's paintings hung on the walls of the staircase, mostly Italian pictures and a few Dutch seascapes. I used to make up stories about the ladies in the Italian paintings. They wore such wonderfully coloured clothes and carried little pug dogs or pretty little cages with songbirds in them.

'Papa knew about paintings. He bought them before they reached their full potential moneywise and then, whenever he decided to sell one, he always made a profit. Painting and cars, they were his passions.

'When I was fifteen, he bought the newest Rolls-Royce and two weeks later, Randell, our chauffeur, had one drink too many and crashed it when he was bringing Papa back from the office. I thought Papa was going to kill him.'

'What did he do?' Rosie whispered the words, totally caught up in her mother's reminiscences.

'Sacked him on the spot, of course, without references. He bought another car and advertised for another chauffeur. He was determined he wouldn't employ anyone who drank – not an easy task. In the event, Betty solved the problem for him. Her brother came up to visit her and he was . . .' She stopped abruptly.

Rosie waited, but her mother remained silent. She also drew back, away from the light of the fire, and Rosie could no longer see her face.

She couldn't bear for Minna to stop. 'Who was Betty?' she prompted. 'You mentioned her before.'

'She was a maid.' Minna's voice was a whisper. She had retreated so far back in her chair, her face was a white patch in the increasing darkness of the room.

'Did you . . .?'

'That's enough, Rosemary.' The voice was harsh. 'You're tiring me with your incessant questions.'

'But . . . you were enjoying telling me.' Rosie sat upright. 'Why suddenly stop?'

'Why not? The past has nothing to do with your life. It's dead and gone.'

'But Pieter and Edith, they were my grandfather and grandmother. Surely you can tell me about them?'

'I've talked enough.' Minna's voice brooked no further argument. She took a handkerchief from the pocket of her dress, blew her nose and demanded: 'Why isn't the light on? Christmas Day's dismal enough without sitting in shadows.' She stood up and walked towards the door. Rosie blinked when the room filled with brightness.

Her mother returned to her chair. She walked slowly, she was an old woman again. But Rosie, watching her with a tinge of sadness, was heartened when Minna smiled at her.

'Do you know, Rosie, all those memories have made me feel hungry. I think I'd enjoy a cup of tea now, and a mince pie.' She paused. 'The bicarbonate of soda you gave me did the trick, I knew it would.'

Chapter Thirteen

The moment Rosie stepped off the bus, the wind ripped through her new hairstyle and blew the skirt of her coat up above her knees.

'Oh, shit!' Although annoyed, she said the word softly, being one of a generation of women who had been taught it was rude to swear, and she put her hands up to her hair, leaving her knees to take care of themselves.

The bus conductor, standing on the platform and looking down at her, eyed her legs appreciatively. 'Rough old day, eh?'

'Yes.' She smoothed back her hair and glanced down the road. 'You're sure this is the right stop?'

'Positive. Woldview's just round the corner.' He pointed. 'About a quarter of a mile from here, maybe less.'

'Right. Thanks.'

Rosie stepped back. The conductor pinged the bell and blew her a kiss as the bus went on its way. She smiled her pleasure. Maybe her mother had been right in telling her to smarten up.

Minna's Christmas present to Rosie had been an envelope containing money and a note demanding that she take herself off to a decent hairdresser. And this morning, 11 January, she had done just that.

After the Christmas rush, the salon had been quiet and

so the owner had attended to her personally. He had sat her down and studied her appearance in the mirror before saying: 'You've fine, healthy hair, madam. I would not recommend a permanent wave, merely a good cut and a variation in style. If you will allow me . . .'

He had lifted the heavy wings of hair framing her face and held them high and loose above her ears and Rosie had been amazed at the transformation.

'Oh yes, please do what you think best.'

He had, and now the blasted wind was spoiling his careful, and expensive, handiwork.

Rosie pulled the collar of her coat up around her throat and walked. There was not another soul in sight although, as she passed by a clipped yew hedge, what sounded like a large breed of dog barked menacingly at her from the other side. The houses lining the wide road were large, private residences. They were set well back, fortresses of privacy, and afforded her no refuge from the biting wind.

She neared the bend in the road hoping the conductor's directions were accurate. She was already regretting her response to Mrs Horton's request. The prospect of a long, cold walk every day for the next couple of months made her feel resentful.

'There's a bit of a flap on at Woldview House,' she had said. 'Two care assistants have left suddenly and the place is dangerously short-staffed. I gather the new Officer in Charge, who took up his post last November, has been making a few waves.' She had smiled an ambiguous smile. 'Not before time, in my opinion.

'Anyway, I've been told to send someone over there, just temporarily, of course.' She had looked at Rosie hopefully.

'Woldview?' Rosie had frowned. That's way out of town – on the Beverley Road, isn't it?'

'Yes. Quite a long bus journey.' Mrs Horton shook her head. 'What a pity you don't drive.'

With a sinking heart, Rosie had realised the matter was already resolved. 'Couldn't someone else go? Someone who *can* drive?'

'I'm sorry, Rosie,' Mrs Horton had sighed, 'but really, you're the best person to send. They need someone experienced and now that the Second Officer has started work here, I can spare you. Besides,' she had smiled encouragingly, 'you've started your course and if you're serious about seeking promotion, this could be a good thing for you. It will go down on your record and could help when you apply for a higher grade.'

Rosie was dubious. 'It doesn't sound too good over there. Why did the two care assistants leave so suddenly, and what if I don't get on with the new man?'

'Oh, I think you will. I've met him twice and I think he's just what Woldview needs. His methods are somewhat unorthodox but I'm sure he'll get results, given time.' Mrs Horton paused. 'I promised you'd start there next week.'

The bus conductor was right. Rosie turned the corner and found herself standing outside an impressive set of wrought-iron gates, one of which bore a large, white-painted notice: Woldview House. The only thing was, the gates were not only closed, they were locked. Rosie fiddled with the lock and pushed at the gates but they wouldn't move. She broke one of her fingernails and, muttering under her breath, stepped back and stared upwards, trying to locate a bell or an intercom system which would allow her to make contact with the house. There was nothing.

This was ridiculous. She blew on her fingers which were cold and peered through the gates. There was no one in sight. What was she to do now?

A brick wall, about six feet high, led away from the gate. She followed it and after walking for about five minutes, came across a blue-painted wooden door set into the wall. Without hesitation, she pushed at the door and when, with a squeal of rusty hinges, it opened, she went through it.

She was standing in a bare patch of woodland and before her stretched the remains of a dilapidated garden. She saw neglected herbaceous borders choked by the mouldy debris of years of neglect and light-starved spindly shrubs dwarfed by the dark overgrown evergreens towering over them. She bit her lip and wondered where on earth she was. Surely this land was nothing to do with Woldview House?

She listened, it was deathly quiet . . . Even the fractious wind was subdued in this place. She could just hear it, sloughing resentfully through the bare branches of the trees above her head.

She took an uncertain step forwards, and then another one. The trailing branch from a barren, unpruned rose tree caught at her leg and snagged her tights and she jumped and then retreated towards the blue-painted door. But then, she heard a sound, a dull, thudding sound. She didn't recognise the noise but it spoke of human habitation. She stopped and faced the garden again.

There *was* a path, almost obliterated by undergrowth. She moved carefully towards it, stepping over a pile of decayed leaves which blocked her way. She went towards the sound. The path opened out, became easier to walk along. It led Rosie towards a lawned area, but still she could see no signs of a house. As she drew closer to the lawn she saw it was long-grassed and unkempt but she noticed the shrubbery facing it showed signs of someone's care. The thudding noise was closer now.

She stared around, noting the mossed-over sundial standing in the centre of the lawn. It was made of grey stone and looked very old. She thought, for the first time, how beautiful the garden must have been before the years of neglect.

She jumped when a voice called out.

'Where the hell have you come from?'

Across the lawn, facing her, was a man. He was balancing an armful of logs and she thought, That was the sound. He must have been chopping up a fallen tree trunk.

She cleared her throat. 'Excuse me. I'm not sure if I'm in the right place. I'm looking for Woldview House? It's a home for the elderly.'

The man, who was wearing a red-checked shirt and jeans, grinned and deposited the logs on the ground. 'You're in the right place but you've certainly taken the scenic route to get here.' He gestured to her to join him and when she did, albeit rather reluctantly, he pointed towards a nearby straggly hedge. 'See, through there. That's Woldview.'

Rosie looked through a gap in the hedge and saw the roofs and part of the top floor of a large Victorian mansion. She heaved a sigh of relief.

'Thank goodness.' Feeling more confident, now that she was near her destination, she turned to her companion. 'I didn't want to trek through this wilderness, but I had to.' Her eyes widened in indignation as she remembered. 'Do you know, the main gates to the property are locked?'

'You must be mistaken.' The man began to pick up the logs and stack them into a wheelbarrow standing nearby.

'I'm not mistaken.' She looked at him sharply. 'They're locked and I intend to complain to someone. It's disgraceful. Suppose someone comes to visit a relative. What will they think?'

'I've no idea.' He looked up and grinned at her and she wondered if he was part gypsy, for his hair, long and curling on his shirt collar, was so dark and his eyes so brown.

She felt flustered and very aware she was alone with him. The colour rose in her cheeks. 'They'd be distressed as well as cross. It's bad enough having aged relatives in a home, without being made to feel they're locked up like prisoners.'

He studied her face. 'Are you visiting someone?'

'No, I'm here to work.' She frowned and looked at her wristwatch. 'And I'm going to be so late. I must go.' She brushed passed him and went towards the house.

'Hang on a minute, I'll come with you. I'll show you a short cut.' The man reached for his jacket which was dangling from the branch of a nearby tree and shrugged it on.

'It's all right, I can manage. You have work to do.'

'The logs, you mean? I'll see to them later.' He fell in beside her.

Rosie felt small next to him. Her first impression had been that he was of medium height for he was strongly built with wide shoulders, but now she realised he was as tall, if not taller, than her son. She did not feel intimidated, however.

She sneaked a sidewards glance. His face was interesting, handsome in an unconventional way and full of character. She took a longer look, marvelling at her own interest. She saw he had a firm chin, strong cheekbones and a thin humorous mouth. His nose was a little crooked. Perhaps it had been broken in an accident or a fight?

Perhaps he sensed her gaze for he turned his head and grinned at her.

'Are you coming to help out?'

She nodded. 'Yes. I work for Mrs Horton at The Firs, but she asked me to . . .' Her voice faded. She shouldn't be telling her business to a gardener, she thought. Changing the subject she said, 'This place must keep you busy?'

'Yes.' He made no further comment.

'I mean,' she hurried on, 'there's an awful lot of land for one man to look after.'

They were almost at the house now. Rosie saw the drive was neatly raked and wallflower plants stood in tidy ranks in the flowerbeds near the entrance. 'I thought maintenance and garden work were contracted out nowadays. Have you worked here long?'

'No.' He rubbed his chin. 'I gather the original aim of the Council was to sell off most of the land to the rear of the property, but somehow it never happened. I guess the gardens must have been a sight to see forty or fifty years ago, but now they're just a mess.' He shrugged. 'I do what I can.'

'I'm sure you do.' She stopped walking and held out her hand. 'Thanks for showing me the way. I'll be all right now.'

He did not take her hand but said, 'I'm sure you will.'

She heard the note of amusement in his voice and wondered what caused it, but she was not offended. Close up, his eyes were more black than brown. She flushed. 'I hope they won't be cross. My first day, and I'm late. What will they think?'

He shrugged. 'Don't let it bother you. I'll come with you. I have a message to give to someone.'

'Oh, yes, of course.'

Her first impression of Woldview was that it was much grander than The Firs. Although all the trappings of a County Council home for the aged were to be seen – the notices pinned to the notice board, the stair lift affixed to the small staircase to the rear of the hall, the doors marked

'Reception' and 'Toilets' – the house retained an echo of its previous splendour.

There were portraits in oil on the panelled walls, fancy carving around the central light fitting and a large leaded-light window set in the wall of the first-floor landing. It beamed down fragments of refracted coloured lights on to the plain wood-sanded floor.

A woman of about twenty-two, dressed in a plain blue overall, was crossing the hall. She stopped when she saw Rosie and her companion

The gardener spoke. 'Barbara, this is Mrs Scott. She's the lady from The Firs who has kindly offered to come and work here for a while, until we get ourselves sorted out. Unfortunately, she's a little late, but that's our fault not hers. Will you show her round and introduce her to everyone? I'm going to change out of these clothes.'

As Rosie, her brow creased, stared at him, he walked towards the bottom of the main staircase. 'Oh, and find McCloud, will you? He swore faithfully that the gates were working properly again, but it seems they aren't. Tell him if they're still faulty at teatime, he'll be looking for a job. Okay?'

He nodded at the two women and then hurried up the stairs, taking two steps at once.

Feeling incredibly foolish, Rosie stared after him until she heard the young woman say, 'Will you come with me, please?'

'Yes.' She followed her.

'Excuse me, was that the new Officer in Charge?'

'Yes, that's Mr Goodman.' Her companion paused. 'Why?'

Rosie head drooped. 'I thought he was the gardener.'

'You did?' The woman laughed delightedly. 'Oh, my, I bet he enjoyed that joke.'

Rosie hoped she was right. She followed Barbara and was shown the downstairs of the building and introduced to several members of staff. Barbara was friendly and a chatterbox, interspersing facts with titbits of gossip and advice.

'This is the laundry room. The woman who does the laundry is a real grouch, you want to avoid her if you can. Both downstairs lounges have TV and the larger one also has a video machine. You have to watch an old man called Mr Vine when he's had visitors. He gets his nephews to tape saucy films for him and he sneaks them on when we're not about and scandalises all the old ladies. By the way, the chiropodist visits every six weeks and the physiotherapist twice a week.'

'Right, I'll remember that. Thanks.'

'We'll go upstairs now.'

Barbara chattered on and Rosie tried to concentrate on what she was saying, but her mind kept wandering back to the man in the garden. When Barbara pointed out Mr Goodman's office, she couldn't help commenting: 'He doesn't seem like an Officer in Charge, does he?'

Barbara looked serious. 'Oh, he can be a devil when he gets going.'

'But he seems so approachable.'

'He is, when things are going right. But woe betide you if you get on his wrong side.'

'Is that why,' Rosie paused, aware of the delicacy of her question, 'some of the staff walked out, shortly after his appointment?'

'They were no loss.' Barbara shrugged her slim shoulders. 'A lot of old fuddy-duddies, they were.' She dropped her voice. 'The woman who was boss before he came had been here for ever. It was rumoured the people over in Admin had been trying to get rid of her for years, but she wouldn't go. She was like the matrons used to be in the hospitals, very strict about rules.

'Anyway, she finally retired and Mr Goodman took over. He's exactly the opposite and things are much more free and easy now. For instance, he's introduced a pet, a lovely springer spaniel called Clarence.' Barbara laughed. 'The old folks love that dog, save titbits for him, things like that, but a few of the older care assistants thought it was disgraceful. They muttered about fleas and dirty pawprints on the carpets and one of them resigned because she disapproved so much. Another one left after a row with him. Good riddance, I say.'

'So you approve of Mr Goodman's changes?'

'Oh, yes. Although,' Barbara grinned, 'maybe the fact that he's so dishy helped in my decision. After working for prune-faced Mrs Webster, Mark Goodman's quite a bonus, even if he does have a temper.' She put her head on one side. 'He looks a bit Italian, don't you think? I wonder where he was born?'

'I don't think it's any of our business.' Rosie felt uncomfortable, discussing her superior with Barbara.

'I know it isn't, but you can't help thinking, can you?' Barbara refused to be diverted from the interesting subject of the First Officer.

'He's not married, you know, and I've never seen him with a woman.' She reflected. 'Do you think he might be gay?'

'No.' Rosie looked around for rescue. 'How many bedrooms on this floor?'

'Sixteen.' Barbara remained abstracted. 'Pity he's so old. If he were ten years younger, I could really fancy him.'

'He's not old!'

'He's pushing forty.' Barbara studied Rosie's expression. 'Why are you looking like that?'

★ ★ ★

'There's fifty-five bedrooms, five more than at The Firs, and less staff so I shall be busy, but I think I'll enjoy working there.'

Steve studied his mother's face as she chattered on. At the end of her first day at the new place he had expected her to be tired but she was remarkably vivacious. It surprised him. He knew she hadn't looked forward to working at Woldview.

'Was the bus journey awful?'

'No, not bad at all.'

'Good.' He pushed his plate away and looked at her again. 'I knew there was something different, you've changed your hairstyle.'

'Yes, this morning.' She touched her hair, an endearing, feminine gesture. 'Do you like it?'

He felt a rush of affection for her. 'You look lovely,' he said sincerely.

She blushed.

'What about the new man, the chap who's running the place? Is he difficult? You said . . .'

'He's,' she paused, 'very interesting. He has modern ideas, that's all, and some of the older staff don't approve. Barbara, the girl who showed me round, told me he has all kinds of trips planned for the residents. She says he's taking some of them to the Lake District for a weekend later in the year.'

She chattered on and Steve listened until, eventually, he had to stop her.

'Sorry, Mum, but I'll have to scoot. I promised Jill we'd go out tonight.'

'That's all right. I have to do some studying.' She watched Steve as he stood up. 'Since Christmas, you haven't seen Jill very often, have you?'

'No, but it's only the beginning of January.' He slipped his hands into his pockets, a defensive gesture of his since early boyhood. 'And it's year end at the bank, remember. I've been busy.'

'I'm sure you have.' She smiled at him. 'Well, give her my love.'

He nodded.

Steve took his time driving over to Jill's home. Deep in thought, he frowned at the direction his thoughts were taking him. Christmas had been passable but their last two meetings had ended badly. He sighed. He must be extra careful tonight not to upset her.

The hairline cracks in their relationship had started during the Christmas holidays. There had been no rows, no strong disagreements, but a series of tiny misunderstandings that had imperceptibly changed things between them. There started to be an inability to communicate with each other, and they both knew, no matter what their efforts, they were growing apart. They knew it, but didn't know what to do about it.

It was his fault. Steve accepted that. Jill had not changed and he had. If only I'd stayed at home, not gone to London, he thought, but he knew he was glad he had gone. And it wasn't just that he had met Liz and slept with her, it was a lot of things. In London he had realised it was a big world out there, and he had only one life. The knowledge had exhilarated but also unsettled him, and it had brought problems. He didn't know what he wanted any more.

But he still wanted Jill because she was part of him, and one evening, he had stumblingly tried to explain how he had changed. She had stared at him, totally uncomprehending, and he had hugged her and laughed and told her not to worry. She had smiled and kissed him and they had never referred to the subject again, but neither had they regained their former closeness.

The Catley residence came into view and he pressed his lips together firmly. He would try harder. He would stop being preoccupied with his feelings and think of Jill's happiness. He owed her that.

She was waiting for him, hair shining, pretty in a new dress. He took her to one of the picturesque country pubs, just outside town. There were horse brasses gleaming on the oak beam above the bar, soft-shaded lights in the alcoves and the smell of roast beef in the air.

'Do you want to eat?' he asked her.

She shook her head.

He brought the drinks to their table, white wine for her, half a pint of bitter for himself.

'Thanks.' She took the wine glass from him.

He sat down. 'What have you been doing with yourself this week?'

She stared at him. 'Waiting for you to ring.'

Straight away, he felt a niggle of irritation. 'You know I've been working late, Jill.'

'You could still have phoned me.'

'And you could have got in touch with me.'

'It's not the woman's place.'

He exploded. 'That's ridiculous.'

'Is it?' She sipped at her wine. There was a sulky look on her face. 'You've always phoned me before.'

Wearily, he nodded. 'All right, I'm sorry.' He drank the rest of his beer quickly and stood up to fetch another one. 'Shall I get you another glass of wine?'

'Good grief, not yet.' Her eyes were smoky with disapproval. 'And you should slow down a bit, Steve. It's early yet and you have to drive home.'

'For God's sake, I've only had half a pint. Anyway, I

thought you could drive home tonight.'

'So you can get drunk?' She shrugged. 'No thanks. I don't like driving in the dark.'

He went for another drink anyway, and came back argumentative. 'You're so careful about my drinking habits and yet your father's always driving his car when he's over the limit.'

'Daddy says he drives better after a drink.'

'That's bollocks! He'd been drinking when he crushed the right hand bumper of his car, just before Christmas.' Steve took a huge swallow of beer.

'Oh, stop it, stop it!' She stared at him, her eyes looking huge in her pale face. 'What's the matter with us? Why are we being like this? I don't understand.'

She reached out to him, caught hold of his hand and hung on.

He shut his eyes and remembered, with surprising clarity, their first date. She had been so lovely in her sports shirt and little swinging skirt and her hair had bounced on her shoulders when she had bowled. He had swelled with pride that he was with her. He thought of a phrase he had read or heard, 'Love is a rare commodity', and nodded his head, agreeing. He opened his eyes and smiled at her.

'It's all right, Jill. It's all right.' He pulled his chair closer to her and put his arm around her.

When it was late enough, they went back to her house. They both wanted to make love and tonight was an ideal opportunity. Her parents were in York. Terence Catley was speaking at a business convention and his wife had accompanied him. They had the house to themselves.

They didn't use her bedroom, the sitting room seemed more romantic with the lamps scattered around casting a rosy glow and the flames from the fire. They undressed and lay down on the thick hearthrug. Steve paced himself.

He always tried to make loving special for Jill because he knew it took her time to be ready for him.

He stroked her bare shoulders and kissed her throat and breasts. His fingers made feathery strokes over her thighs and hips. He did other things and she groaned softly and ran her fingers through his hair.

'I love you,' she whispered. 'I want you.'

But he delayed the final act because something inside him rebelled. He wanted her to do something for him.

Without words, and for the first time, he tried to encourage Jill to participate more in the act of love. He rolled over until he was lying on his back next to her and put his hand on her hair, gently indictating for her to bend towards his lower body.

She pulled away from him, her body stiffening. 'No, Steve. I know what you want me to do and I won't.' She sat up, frowning and pushing her hair out of her eyes. She looked lovely with the light from the fire painting rosy pictures on her creamy bare skin.

He stared up at her. 'Why not?'

'Because it's dirty. I would feel sick.'

His sensuous feelings vanished and he too sat up. 'Don't say that, Jill. It's not dirty. It's natural, another way of showing love.'

She shook her head, her face flushed and stubborn. 'I can't. I'd throw up.'

He felt shocked. 'I'm sorry. I didn't mean to upset you. I'll never ask you again.'

He leaned forward and kissed her cheek and then he reached for his clothes. She frowned. Her expression showed she was close to tears. 'Don't sulk. It needn't spoil things. We can still . . .'

'No, we can't.' He pulled his shirt over his head, stood up and put on the rest of his clothes.

She watched him silently. 'You're not staying? Mum and Dad won't be back until tomorrow.'

'No.'

Dawn was streaking the sky when he reached home. A January dawn, all high empty sky and broad red streaks of colour. Steve watched the sun come up from his bedroom window and then he took a writing pad from a drawer.

Sitting on his bed, he wrote his first letter to Liz, but when he finished it, he tore it up.

Chapter Fourteen

Rosie, waiting by the bus stop, put up her umbrella and shrugged philosophically. The old woman she'd been talking to before leaving work had got it right, it was true 'February fill dyke' weather. She glanced up at the dark grey sky. What a pity it was her day for visiting Minna.

After eight hours attending to the needs of the residents of Woldview, what she felt like doing was going straight home and wallowing in the bath for an hour. A bath full to the brim with hot water made scented and fluffy with the remainders of her Christmas gifts of creams and lotions.

But, she sighed, duty called. She comforted herself with the knowledge that there was plenty of food in at home, at least she didn't have to shop today. There was one call she wanted to make though. The book she had ordered from the library had arrived. She had received a postcard that morning.

A trickle of rain coursed down the back of her neck and she repositioned her umbrella and thought about her next appointment with her tutor in two days' time. She must get her essay finished this evening, she mused. The thought did not depress her. Indeed, the corners of her mouth turned up in a smile, it delighted her. She, Rosemary Scott, was writing about the Physiology of Senior Citizens and not only was she coping, she was beginning to get good marks. Her last essay had gained her a B+ and this time she was hoping for an A−.

A belligerent chirping noise from the hedge behind her distracted her from her thoughts. She turned and then laughed.

'Oh, it's you.'

Rosie had made the acquaintance of the robin who lived in the hedge near the bus stop some weeks before. Normally, he was a cheerful, jaunty little bird but today he looked decidedly bedraggled. He blinked at her and cheeped again.

She nodded. 'I know,' she said. 'Not fair, is it? The swallows should have taken you with them earlier in the year and I should be on a beach in Spain or Greece, not waiting for the bus.'

'I sympathise with your desire for Spain or Greece, but *who* should have gone with the swallows?'

The unexpected male voice made the robin flip his tail and disappear into the hedge of sopping wet evergreens.

Rosie swung round and a red stain of embarrassment spread across her face when she saw Mark Goodman's grey Sierra car parked by the bus stop. He had wound down the window and was leaning out to speak to her.

'I'll run you into town, if you like?'

'Oh, yes, please.'

She closed her umbrella and ran round to get into the seat next to him. 'I never saw you coming.'

'No. Your umbrella obstructed the view I suppose.' He put the car into gear and they moved away. 'And you were in the middle of a conversation. Who *were* you talking to?'

She hung her head, feeling foolish. 'A robin,' she mumbled, then hastened on, 'I see him quite often when I'm waiting for the bus and today the poor thing looked so bedraggled, I just found myself talking to him.'

His face relaxed into a grin. 'I'm pleased to hear it.'

'You are?' She frowned.

'Oh, yes. I was quite worried when I thought you were talking to yourself, but talking to a robin's feasible enough.'

He turned on the windscreen wipers. 'When I'm gardening, there's a particular blackbird who follows me around. He's really bossy. Just because I've turned up a few worms for him from time to time, he thinks he's in charge. He sits on the handle of the garden fork and chatters and whistles at me. I know he's telling me to pack in the boring stuff and dig him up something for his dinner and I get annoyed. I have been known to use strong words.'

She laughed, conscious of a warm feeling for him somewhere inside her. 'You enjoy gardening, don't you? I've seen you outside in pretty awful weather.'

He raised his shoulders in a small shrug. 'I suppose so, although I'm no expert. I think . . .' He paused. 'I think it's more that I like to work physically at something when I'm trying to sort out a problem in my head.' He smiled at her. 'I'm not used to sitting behind a desk all day. I'd always worked at physical jobs until I changed direction eight years ago. I love the work I do now but I get restless, staying in the office, so every so often I let off steam, chop logs or tackle that wilderness behind the house.'

Feeling the glow in her cheeks, the effects of his smile, Rosie looked out of the car window. 'You've enough scope in that garden to work off the problems of everyone in the country, I should think.'

He laughed. 'I know, it's an impossible task for one man, but I am making progress and by concentrating my efforts on one small area, I think I'm beginning to see results.

'I cleared an area around two pyracanthas when I first

arrived at the home and I noticed recently they're putting out new shoots. It would be great if they flowered again. They're lovely shrubs, you know.'

She shook her head. 'Sorry, I don't know them. I've only a tiny patch of lawn in front of my house and two ancient rose bushes. I don't really know anything about plants.'

He glanced at her. 'But you appreciate them, surely?'

She laughed and admitted, 'I like watching the gardening programmes on the television.'

'There you are then. I knew it. You've a warm personality, you *must* like gardens.'

Rosie felt a spurt of pleasure at his words but warned herself not to over-react. Mark's voice was light and conversational and his remark could equally well have been made to one of the old ladies who lived in Woldview. He was chattering on.

'Pyracantha's often called Firethorn. The shrubs can grow to ten feet, then they're really spectacular. The berries are red, orange or golden yellow, and the foliage's brilliant too. Fortunately, the birds tend to leave the berries alone, I don't know why.' He laughed. 'You'll have to ask your robin. Anyway, I'm trying to rescue some of the other perennials and restore a touch of former glory to at least part of the garden.'

He was quiet for a moment and then he said, 'My favourite place is where the sundial is. Can you imagine how it must have looked all those years ago, when it was properly cared for?'

She nodded. 'I'm sure it was magnificent.'

'Yes.'

With a speed which confused her, he changed the subject.

'You use the bus regularly?'

'Er, yes.'

'Don't you have a car?'

'No.' Rosie tensed. If only she had taken up Howard's offer to teach her how to drive, but the children had been tiny then, they had taken up all her time. Besides, she had been too nervous.

Their car had been old and sometimes unpredictable in its behaviour. Howard looked after it well but she had always been afraid that something may go wrong when she was behind the wheel. What if she ran someone over? And then later, after Howard's death, the question of a car never arose because she couldn't afford one. She waited for Mark to make one of the half-pitying comments her admission invariably drew forth.

'How on *earth* do you manage without one?'

'Oh, you poor thing. I thought everyone had a car?'

'I'd die without mine.'

It was always a woman who said that.

But Mark Goodman merely said, 'You should have told me. Woldview's isolated and getting to and from work without a car must be a terrific hassle. What do you do when you're working nights?'

'I manage. Sometimes my son brings me to work and Mr Cross gives me a lift back in the morning. If Steve can't bring me and the weather's horrible, I treat myself to a taxi.'

He pursed his lips. 'And today's weather isn't horrible?'

She shrugged. 'I've seen worse.'

He laughed. 'Karen Horton said you were an independent lady.'

They were approaching a busy junction and Mark was silent as he negotiated the turn. Then he said, 'Look, I'll try and arrange something to cover at least fifty per cent of your travelling. I come in to town most days and if I'm busy, someone else comes in. There are always small errands and commissions for the residents to sort out. We'll try and co-ordinate our trips to fit with the times your duty ends.'

She frowned. 'What would the other members of staff think?'

'Nothing at all. Most of the employees have cars and I think I'm right in saying that the four women who haven't live on the nearby housing estate. They can walk home in just over five minutes. None of them needs to use the antiquated bus service.'

She stirred in her seat. 'It's kind of you but I don't want to be singled out for special attention. I can manage.'

He turned in his seat to look at her. 'You're being rather silly, don't you think? And a little ungracious?'

She looked back, into his dark eyes, and the battle was lost before being fought.

'Well, I . . .'

'Look, Rosie.' He had glanced away from her and was checking the traffic. She tried to relax as she listened to him. 'I'm impressed with your work. You're just the kind of person I want at Woldview *and* you've fitted in well with the permanent staff. That doesn't happen often, as I can testify from my own experience. I was hoping to persuade you to consider working for me on a permanent basis, if Mrs Horton agrees, of course.

'But if you're slogging backwards and forwards to work on a country bus which stops every five minutes and puts an hour and a half on your working day, well, you won't be interested, will you?' He smiled again, a coaxing smile. 'So, you see, I have my own motives for making your travelling arrangements more agreeable. Please, allow me to arrange something?'

She dropped her head and nodded, more concerned with

her inner confusion than with thinking about transport arrangements. Good God, if only he knew! She'd willingly stay at Woldview. She'd walk there and back every day if she had to. Because she wanted to keep seeing him.

What was it about him, she marvelled, that made her pulse race, the palms of her hands sweat and her stomach lurch whenever she was near him? She knew nothing about him, he was a stranger to her and, she suppressed a sigh, he had no interest in her, apart from the fact that she was his employee. But these facts did not alter her wayward emotions. She sighed again. Coming alive again emotionally was proving painful.

When Howard died, Rosie's emotional life had continued through her children. It wasn't a deliberate decision she made, it just happened that way. Occasionally, through the years, she had struck up friendships with a few men. They had taken her out and and she had enjoyed their company but, inevitably, the moment had come when they demanded more from her, and she could never give it.

She explained: 'You're very kind, but I really don't want to get involved in a serious relationship. Let's just stay friends, shall we?'

But they hadn't. The men had stopped ringing her, drifted out of her life, and she had missed them for a few weeks and then forgotten them.

That first day, when she had made a fool of herself by thinking Mark Goodman was the gardener, she had told herself she hoped he would forgive her. She had hoped they might become good workmates and possibly friends. But even on that first day, she had been deluding herself because, right from the beginning, she knew what she felt was more than a stirring of friendship.

Now, sitting next to him, she thought that he had

become a friend, but that wasn't enough for her. She wanted more. But why now, and why him? She closed her eyes and wondered. Why was he the one to remind her of how devastating sexual attraction could be?

'Where shall I drop you off?'

'Sorry?' She sat upright, saw they had reached the centre of the town. 'Oh, anywhere round here will be fine.'

He drew the car to a halt and leaned over her to open the car door. His closeness scorched her. He was wearing jeans and boots and a navy blue teeshirt beneath his beaten-up old leather jacket. His lack of interest in clothes, his disregard for his personal image, was patently obvious. Oh, she thought, he's just lovely.

Smiling, she risked a close-up look at his face.

The dampness had curled his hair close to his head. His skin was still brown from last year's sunshine and when he smiled she saw the half moon fans of tiny wrinkles appear at the corners of his eyes.

'You won't need your umbrella,' he said. 'It's stopped raining.' His dark eyes regarded her thoughtfully and with interest.

He likes me, she thought, and a fountain of bubbles sprang up inside her. And he wants me to stay on at Woldview.

'Thanks for the lift.' She climbed out of the car and he drove away while she went to pick up her library book.

'My, you're looking well today, Mrs Scott.' The woman behind the library counter had known her for years. 'Your complexion's glowing. Must be all that rain, eh?'

'Maybe so.' Rosie handed her the postcard.

The woman took a heavy book from beneath the counter and handed it to her. 'Looks like you're going to be kept busy with this one.' She tapped the front cover.

She knew all about Rosie's course.

'Thanks.' Rosie slotted the textbook into her shopping bag.

'How's the studying going?'

'Very well.'

'I'm glad, but don't work too hard now.'

'I won't.' Rosie paused and smiled at the librarian. 'Actually, I enjoy studying.'

She left the library walking on air. She was looking good, even the library assistant noticed, and she had got to know Mark a little better and there was the promise of more car rides with him. She liked her work at Woldview and, as she had said to the librarian, she enjoyed studying.

She was busy, and she was enjoying life. She didn't knit, she didn't watch TV any more, she hadn't time. I feel, she thought, that my life has completely changed.

It hadn't, of course. There was still housework, and shopping, and Minna and the children, and she was still forty-three years old, but somehow she was different, and part of the difference was because she had started the diploma course.

She had been so nervous when she went along to the first session. She had sat at the back of the room and heard not a word of what was said. During the second session, she had listened but had not dared to contribute anything to the discussion which followed the lecture. But by the third session she was so engrossed in what the tutor was saying, she forgot her nerves and had stood up and put her point of view.

Now she couldn't wait for the next class. She had made new friends, the lecturer often complimented her on her insight, and her ambition was soaring. Even Minna's snide enquiries as to her 'late schooling' did not dent her confidence.

Minna. Oh dear, she was late for her visit! Rosie stored away her delicious thoughts until she could find time for them and ran to catch her next bus, the bag with the textbook in it banging against her hip as she hurried along.

It was a little after four when she arrived at Minna's. In contrast to her wide-awake expression and flushed face, Minna's movements were slow and fumbling as she opened her door. Her face looked so pale and her expression was so drowsy, Rosie's high spirits quite ebbed away. She looked at Minna and wondered how much of the day she slept away.

'Everything all right, Mother?'

'I wish you wouldn't always ask that.' Minna brushed a stray wisp of hair back from her face. 'I'm here, aren't I? I suppose that's all I can ask for at this stage in my life. Leave your shoes and coat in the hall. They're wet through.'

Reassured by her mother's acid tone of voice, Rosie did as instructed and then followed Minna into the sitting room.

'It's pouring down outside, that's why I'm so wet.'

'Is it?' Minna looked vaguely towards the window. 'I didn't notice.' She blinked. 'Sit down. I'll make the tea.'

Rosie sat down. Her mother was ageing. Her movements were less sure and the trembling in her hands was increasing. It was an inevitable process, but one Rosie hadn't expected to happen so soon. Minna had always been so strong. Rosie had been sure her mother would stay fit and well until late into her eighties and possibly defy death for another ten years after that. But Minna, it appeared, was not invincible.

Rosie considered what would happen when her mother couldn't manage on her own. She would resist going into a residential home with the last breath of her body, Rosie knew. Without realising, she clenched her hands until her nails bit into the palms of her hands. Steve would be moving out before too long. There would be room for her at home. The despair she felt was compounded by a feeling of guilt.

She couldn't bear to have her mother living with her, she couldn't! She was just starting to live her own life. It wasn't fair. But when was life fair? a little voice whispered.

Her newfound sense of balance steadied her. It was too early to panic. Her mother might perk up again. Perhaps it was the time of year that was getting Minna down? When the spring arrived, she might take on a new lease of life. Old people did that.

She accepted a cup of tea from her mother and drank it.

'Have you heard anything from her?'

She looked up, puzzled. 'Who?'

'Paula, of course. Who else?' Minna looked exasperated.

'No.'

'But haven't you rung?'

'Not for a little while, no. I've been busy.'

Minna brooded. 'She wrote to me. Did I tell you?'

Rosie nodded.

'She said she'd come and see me.' Minna's lips trembled. 'I've been waiting.'

She turned on Rosie. 'You must contact her. Something must have happened to the girl. I can't understand you at all, Rosemary. You used to worry about your children but now, when you come here, you hardly mention Paula or Steve. It's me, me, me. You've become totally self-centred since you took on that that stupid course of yours.'

'That's not true, Mother.' Rosie's voice was level and with inner delight she realised Minna's words had not hurt her as they used to. She sat forward in her chair. 'You know what's Paula's like. She's always breaking promises. That's the way she is.' She shrugged. 'I don't think she's in any kind of trouble, why should she be? She's just too busy living her own life to think about us.'

Minna crumbled up a biscuit on her plate. 'But she said she would come.'

'And so she will. She's probably waiting until the weather gets better.' Rosie looked at her mother's thin, bent shoulders and felt a pang of pity. 'Look, I'll try and get hold of her tonight. I'll tell her how much you are looking forward to a vist and try and tie her down to a date. Will that do?'

Minna nodded and Rosie thought perhaps that was another manifestation of Minna's becoming frail and more vunerable, the desire to see Paula. She certainly wanted to see her granddaughter more than she wanted to see her daughter.

It had also rained in Manchester. By the time Paula had picked up Alison from nursery school and taken her home, both of them were cold and wet.

Paula switched on the central heating, stripped Alison of her clothes and put her into the bath. Then, checking the time, she took off her own clothes, put them in the washing machine with Alison's things, switched on and then went and got into the bath with her daughter.

'There, that's better, isn't it?' Recklessly, she poured a dollop of bath foam into the bath, gave Alison her plastic duck and lay back in the water with a sigh of pleasure.

They were playing with handfuls of bubbles when she heard the door of the flat open. She frowned. Surely it was too early for Dave to be home? She held up a soapy forefinger in an effort to quieten Alison's shouts and called out: 'Is that you, Dave?'

He opened the door to the bathroom, walked in and lounged against the wall. 'Of course it is. Who else were you expecting?' His gaze travelled over her naked breasts and he smiled.

From the fatuous expression on his face she knew immediately that he had been drinking. Being without clothes made her feel vulnerable and uneasy. She leaned forward and pulled out the bath plug and immediately water began to gurgle down the drain.

'No, Mummy. No.' Alison hurled her slippery little body down to the bottom of the tub and tried to find the plug, hoping to stop the water escaping.

'Leave it, Alison. We're getting out now.' Avoiding looking at her husband, Paula stood up and reached for a towel off the rail. Dave beat her to it. He held the towel in one hand and eyed her body for a moment before handing it to her.

'Don't spoil your fun just because I've come home early.' His eyes narrowed as she turned away from him. 'I can wait for my meal. After all, I've only been working.'

Paula wrapped the towel around her. 'Why are you home so early?'

He yawned. 'I'm home early, my sweet, because there's been a walk-out. The management have been up to their usual tricks, trying to screw the workforce out of their hard-earned money, and the lads decided they've had enough.' He grinned. 'As they say on the telly, "Strike action is contemplated".'

'Oh, God.' Forgetting her initial unease at Dave's presence in the bathroom, Paula stepped out of the bath, hauled Alison out and began to dry her with fast, furious movements. 'Just as we're getting ourselves straightened out.'

'I knew that would be your reaction, so I said to them,

"We must discuss this. We've our families to consider." ' Dave turned and walked unsteadily to the door. 'So we all went to the pub.'

Paula's eyebrows drew together in a frown. 'And what decision did you reach?'

'We didn't.' He yawned. 'We're meeting there tomorrow.'

He went out and Paula lifted up Alison, took her through to her bedroom and dressed her in her pyjamas, then hurriedly dressed herself. Wearing workmanlike jeans and sweatshirt made her feel more in control of the situation. She ushered her daughter into the sitting room, turned on the television, then went through to the kitchen.

Dave ignored her. He was leaning against the sink and watching the clothes revolve through the glass door of the washing machine.

She eyed him warily. 'I'll start the meal, Dave. Do you want to go and have your bath?'

He did not reply, simply stared at the revolving washing.

She shrugged, turned her back on him and took down a pan from the cupboard. She half-filled it with water, put it on the gas burner and began chopping vegetables.

Since that awful day that Dave had hit her in the stomach there had been no more violence but their marriage could not be described as normal. Dave's behaviour had become erratic in the extreme.

Some days he overwhelmed Paula with attention, bringing her flowers, catching hold of her hand, kissing it and telling her how much he loved her, how he couldn't survive if she ever left him.

Other days, he came in from work sullen and uncommunicative. He would drink can after can of beer and slump in his chair watching the television until the programmes closed down, and then he would go to bed and sleep restlessly, twitching and calling out in his sleep.

When he did that, Paula would hold him close to her, tell him everything would be all right, and eventually he would quieten and sleep and she would lie awake and worry.

Her nerves were beginning to fray. Two days ago she had gone back to see the woman she and Dave had visited shortly after his attack on her. She had been a sensible, middle-aged woman and Dave had listened to what she had to say. He had promised to return for more counselling, but he never had.

'I don't need her, love. I've learned my lesson. I've promised I'll never hit you again and I never will.'

And he had kept his promise but, Paula shook her head, the strange way he was behaving was almost as bad as the sudden, shocking violence.

She told the counsellor about his sudden inexplicable behaviour and asked: 'Why is he being like this?'

The woman had tried to explain.

'I think your husband cares for you a great deal and in his own way he's trying to control his emotions but,' she sighed, 'he needs professional help.' With her fingernails she had tapped a tattoo on her desk. 'I'm afraid you must expect extreme mood changes. He's having an inward battle coming to terms with the violence he experienced in his childhood. Please, whatever you do, keep calm and avoid arguing with him, and try again to persuade him to come and see me.'

Paula's hands slowed at her work as she remembered the counsellor's further comments.

'If he won't accept help, then I'm sorry, but I think you must face up to the fact that there may be more outbursts of violence.'

At Paula's small sound of distress, the woman had

looked at her, a serious expression on her face. 'I hope I'm wrong, but I doubt it. And if I'm right, then only you can make the decision as to whether to stay with him or whether you should leave.

'If you decide to leave, then I can help with practical details, but, of course, I prefer to view the more positive option.' She had reached across and touched Paula's arm. 'Do your best to persuade Dave to come back and see me, with or without you.'

And Paula had promised. 'I'll try.'

She glanced across at him. He was still watching that damned washing machine. His fixed stare was getting on her nerves. She reached for a packet of pasta and said, 'Put the kettle on, love.'

He didn't appear to hear. He watched the washing for another minute and then he said in a quiet voice, 'There's a whole lot of my washing in the bin, Paula. Why didn't you put that in the wash, too?'

She froze. There was the silky edge to his voice she had learned to beware.

'I didn't think. Alison and I were so wet when we got in home, I just put all our clothes in the washer and turned it on.' She heard her words tumbling over each other and forced herself to slow down.

'I'll put your clothes in next. Is there something you particularly need?'

He came and stood behind her and she concentrated, very carefully, on the mushrooms she was slicing up.

'I need my wife to look after me properly, Paula. Are you sure you forgot my washing?'

She put down the knife, turned and faced him. 'Of course. What other reason could there be?'

'Perhaps you thought my dirty old working clothes were too scruffy to go in with yours and Alison's? I mean, you're getting to be such a snob these days, Paula, perhaps you thought your stuff would be contaminated by my gear?'

He put out his hand and, tenderly, brushed back a straying lock of hair from her forehead. 'Do you think that, love?'

She almost flinched, but didn't. Instead, she forced a smile. 'Your clothes are cleaner than Alison's, Dave. Honestly, I don't know what she does at that nursery school. You should see the state of her when I get her home.'

Paula was pleased with how normal her voice sounded. She saw him frown, as though he was puzzling things out, so she slipped her arms around his neck and said, 'For God's sake put the kettle on, Dave. I'm dying for a cup of tea. We'll both have one and then you can go for your bath. I'll dish up the meal when you get out.'

He touched her cheek, stared at her and then stepped away and picked up the kettle. 'All right.'

He made the tea, poured out two cups and took his cup into the bathroom with him. Paula took a sip of tea and, with fingers that shook slightly, scattered the pasta shells into the boiling water.

Chapter Fifteen

At the end of February, Paula and Alison came home for a weekend visit. Paula's first words, on walking through the door were: 'Sorry, but I can only stay until Monday morning, Mum. The agency want me to start another job on Tuesday.'

'Oh.' Rosie pulled a disappointed face. 'I thought you'd be staying for the week. Can't you put them off? You've been working so hard lately and being at different places every week must be awfully tiring.'

Paula laughed at her mother. 'Come off it, Mum. You know I enjoy the challenge.'

Rosie had looked at her daughter and felt reassured. Paula was her usual vivacious self. A little too thin, perhaps, but that's because she never stopped rushing around. She felt Alison tugging at her skirt and bent down and hugged her. 'And look at you. You've grown into a big girl since Grandma last saw you.' She took her hand. 'Come and see what I've made you.' She whispered: 'There's some gingerbread men in the kitchen.'

As she left the room with Alison she said, over her shoulder, 'I thought Dave was coming with you?'

She didn't see Paula's frown. 'He was going to come, but a friend of his managed to get him a ticket for the big match. He's really keen on his football, you know.' She paused. 'You don't mind, do you?'

'Of course I don't.' Rosie reappeared, leading Alison by the hand. The little girl was tucking into a large gingerbread man and her grandmother was smiling down at her with a look of total indulgence. 'So long as I've got you and Alison.'

Steve took his sister's sudden arrival coolly. He came in, brother and sister brushed cheeks, exchanged a few words, and then Steve announced he had to go straight out again.

'Oh, Steve.' Rosie was dismayed. 'I wanted us to have a family meal together.'

He shrugged his shoulders apologetically. 'Sorry, Mum, but I've already arranged something. It doesn't matter, does it? You and Paula will want to natter about women's things and we'll be having our usual slap-up dinner on Sunday, won't we? We can catch up on the news then.'

'Yes, but . . .'

'That's all right then.' He left the room.

'Still at Jill's beck and call?' Paula raised an ironic eyebrow.

'I don't know. She doesn't call in so often nowadays.' Rosie twisted her hands together. 'And Steve's changed. He's become quite secretive. Most of the time I haven't an idea what he's thinking.'

Paula glanced at her. 'He's grown up at last, Mum. There's nothing to worry about.'

When Steve disappeared on Saturday morning and missed the lunchtime meal, Rosie waited until he came back and then spoke her mind.

'You could make more effort, Steve. I don't think you've spoken more than a dozen words to Paula since she arrived.'

'I can't talk to her when she's not here. She's gone shopping, I gather. Alison told me.' He shrugged. 'Poor kid's plonked in front of the television again. Wonder she hasn't got square eyes, the amount of TV she watches.'

'Paula asked if she could leave Alison with me and I was happy to agree. She is my only grandchild.' Rosie paused. 'I'm taking her to the park later. I don't suppose . . .' She eyed Steve hopefully.

'I'm going out again. If you can be ready by two, I'll drop you off at the park gates. If not . . .' He picked up the newspaper.

Oh dear, where had family unity gone? Rosie scuttled off to collect wellingtons and coats.

Steve dropped his mother and niece outside the park and watched as they walked through the iron gates. Alison was hopping about cheerfully enough but he thought his mother's steps showed signs of weariness. He looked away, set his mouth into a straight line and drove away quickly.

He would *not* allow himself to feel guilty. True, he could have accompanied them, he had nowhere particularly to go, but why should he? The last thing he felt like doing was plodding about in a muddy play area, lifting Alison on and off swings and see-saws for a couple of hours. It had been his mother's idea to invite Paula and Alison for a visit. Well, she could entertain them.

He drove to the end of the road and turned into the main street. He was glad his sister's visit was to be a short one. Paula, he thought, was growing into a right little cow. She'd always been sharp-tongued but now she was so sarcastic, it was a wonder she didn't cut herself. Since her arrival, everything he said, everything he did, she had picked up on. She did her best to make him feel slow and stupid. Steve hunched his shoulders. What was happening to young women nowadays?

He realised he was passing the cricket ground, so he

drove into the car park, got out, locked his car and went for a stroll around the perimeter of the field. There was not a soul in sight.

The empty pitch, the rows of wooden seats and the leafless trees made the area forlorn and sad. His depression deepened. He shut his eyes and wished he could retreat into last summer.

The day he had scored eighty-nine runs in the match with the Ripon team, now that was a day worth remembering. He threw back his shoulders and clenched his hands.

Then he opened his eyes again. That was another thing about women, they didn't understand about sport. They said it was boring and men were childish to get worked up about such things. They had no idea. They had no idea what it felt like to hit a stroke cleanly, hear the smack of the ball on the willow, see it rocket into the blue sky and know you'd hit a boundary.

He sighed. Women didn't understand simple pleasures, they certainly didn't like their boyfriends and husbands talking about football or cricket. They complained that men didn't talk about *meaningful* things, and yet look what happened when he told Jill about the letter he'd received from Head Office about his corporate banking course.

'You're going to be stuck in Lancaster for six weeks? You said you'd be based in York.'

'No.' Steve had corrected her. 'I said it would *probably* be York. They told me in London that that the venue for the course would be somewhere in the middle of the north-east region. York was the obvious place.'

'So why did they decide on Lancaster?'

'I don't know.' Steve was beginning to feel irritated. 'I don't fix these things up. Perhaps accommodation was too expensive, or maybe they couldn't find a suitable venue. York's always swarming with students and tourists. Anyway, what's so wrong with Lancaster?'

'It's a lot further away. It won't be so easy for me to come and visit you.'

Modified by her words and her downcast expression, he had squeezed her hand. 'It's not that far. If you come on weekends, we could get about, see a bit of the countryside. Morecombe's not far away.'

She had pulled a face so he hurriedly continued. 'We could even drive into the Lake District.'

'No thanks. It never stops raining there.'

He had lost his temper then.

'Bloody hell, Jill, what is it with you? You pushed me into taking the damned course and now you're moaning about six weeks' separation. What *do* you want?'

'I want to know that you'll miss me. The way you've been lately . . .' Jill narrowed her eyes. 'I'm too bossy for you, am I? Well, God knows, you take a lot of pushing.'

They glared at each other and then she said, her voice rising, 'If you dislike me so much, perhaps we should break off our engagement.'

She wrenched off her engagement ring and held it out to him.

For a moment he had been sorely tempted, but you couldn't do that, could you? You couldn't wreck a long, loving relationship because you felt . . . unsettled. He had pacified her, kissed away her tears and replaced the ring on her finger.

It began to rain, heavily. Steve remembered his mother and Alison at the park. He turned round and hurried back to the car. He'd go and collect them and maybe take them to McDonald's for a treat. He'd been a bit mean with them.

On Sunday morning Paula went to see her grandmother. She went with Alison and her mother and then Rosie took

Alison off with her so Minna could have a real talk with her granddaughter.

They did talk, and during her visit Paula was chatty and witty and made Minna laugh. When Rosie returned with Alison and saw the two of them together, she smiled and whispered to her mother: 'You see. Paula's fine. You can stop worrying about her.'

And Minna had given her a swift, penetrating glance and nodded. When they said they had to go, she hugged Alison, gave Rosie a quick peck on the cheek but held Paula's slim body against her own for a long moment. She watched them leave and waved to them from her window.

And then, alone and with only the tick of her grandmother clock to comfort her, she admitted to herself that she was worried. Paula wasn't all right, she was all wrong, and Minna didn't know what to do about it.

The girl was unhappy and highly nervous. Her body was as tight and as stretched as a piano cord and she was as jumpy as a cat. Minna felt tired from just being with her. She thought of Rosemary's remark and marvelled. Rosemary was a good mother, how could she not see?

Minna sat in her chair and stared into space. Should she tell Rosemary that Paula was desperately unhappy? No, she thought not. It would do no good, merely spread the unhappiness.

Knowing something was no good unless one could help, and Minna knew from experience that when unhappiness went so deep, there was usually no help available.

She propped her chin on her hand and brooded. She knew about unhappiness. She had been so unhappy she wished to die and no one had been able to help, except . . . An amused fluting voice echoed in her memory. Cicily, the woman she had met at the races. Cicily Chesterton had helped her.

★ ★ ★

When her mother died Minna had been unhappy, but that had been a natural unhappiness that had faded with the course of time. And Betty, her personal maid, had been on hand to comfort her. But then her father had decided she should go to boarding school and his decision had made her wildly unhappy again.

She protested but Pieter had made up his mind and so, to boarding school she had gone. She hated the life. She had to wear woollen stockings for lacrosse, the food was horrid, and the teaching staff were lumpish plain women, all of them spinsters.

She bombarded her father with tear-stained letters and eventually, when she was five months past her fourteenth birthday, he allowed her to return home. He apologised for her misery with his usual charm.

'I didn't *want* you to go, sweetheart, but I thought it would be best for you.'

'It was a horrible place and I wanted to die.' There were tears in her eyes and her voice held conviction. 'I can only be happy with you, Papa. Please don't send me away again.'

He pulled her to him and hugged her. 'I won't,' he promised.

The following year was wonderful. Her father had emerged from mourning seemingly more determined than ever to live life to the full and, as he became the prince of festivities, Minna became his consort.

Perhaps a few of Pieter's older acquaintances disapproved. Perhaps they murmured behind their hands that she was too young for all that junketing, but if they did Minna never heard them. She was too busy enjoying herself.

Pieter never bothered with more schooling for her.

Minna was clever enough, he declared. Anyway, he couldn't abide too-clever women.

And so, at an early age, Minna did all the things a fashionable young lady did during the ninteen-twenties. She accompanied her father to the Derby, and race meetings at Goodwood and Ascot. Together, they watched the Eton-Harrow cricket match, an intensely social occasion held annually in Long Leave (mid-July). The match attracted thousands of spectators even though it was totally unintelligible to foreigners and people of a 'lower class'. It was unintelligible to Minna too, but she enjoyed seeing 'all those dinky little boys in stiff collars in the crowd'. Minna thought of herself as a young lady now.

A keen tennis player, she found that the All England Tennis Championships were very much to her taste. In the mid-twenties, Centre Court viewing was at a premium and even her father had to pull strings to obtain a seat for her.

In 1925, Minna saw Suzanne Lenglen win the women's title and immediately demanded her father buy her a dress modelled on the one worn by the champion.

'Made of drill or white linen, Papa, with short sleeves and fastened at the waist with a thin leather belt.'

After tennis there was Cowes Regatta at the end of July, where one might see the King in person or be invited to dine on one of the magnificent yachts. The Season wound down after Cowes but there was always the start of the grouse shooting season to look forward to.

Minna became known to the social set. Shc was liked but described as 'a bit of an oddity. Rather too poised for a child of her age but interesting.'

'Growing into a stunner,' was the opinion of the middle-aged men who were friendly with her father. They gazed wistfully after Minna as she tripped by, her slender legs in beige stockings twinkling beneath short flirty skirts, or when she stopped to smile at them, her huge dark eyes provocative beneath her stylish cloche hat.

And yet, in many ways, Minna was an innocent. She was wise in the ways of society but ignorant in the ways of the world. A child in a world of grown-ups with no friends of her own age. It was Betty, with her four years' seniority, who told her how babies were born.

Minna had not long returned from boarding school when she asked Betty to go to the chemist's shop for her. Red with embarrassment, she had given her some money. 'I've got the curse,' she whispered.

Matter-of-fact, Betty returned and handed Minna the wrapped packet.

Muttering thanks, she had grabbed it and held it behind her back. 'It's so horrible. I don't know why women have to suffer such things.'

Betty had shrugged. 'Fact of nature, ain't it? If we want to have kids we have to put up with the monthlies.'

'Kids? Oh, you mean babies. What have babies to do with it?'

Betty stared at her mistress. 'Don't you know?'

Minna shook her head. 'The matron at school said it was something to do with Eve and the apple. I hadn't a clue what she was on about.'

Betty sighed. She closed the bedroom door, sat Minna down and clearly and succinctly told her the facts of life.

Minna didn't believe her. 'It's horrible. I don't believe my mother and father ever did that. I know that animals . . .'

'I'm telling you, everyone does it. The King and Queen did, at least five times. That's the only way babies get born.'

Minna was silenced, then she said, 'Well, I won't.'

Betty stood up. 'You'll change your mind, I expect.' She

turned at the door, with a saucy swirl of her skirt. 'I've 'eard it can be quite nice, under the right circumstances.'

Betty was a good friend to Minna and Minna appreciated her, so she was highly delighted when the opportunity came to help the chirpy little Yorkshire girl. She knew Betty was an orphan.

'Me dad was killed in t'trenches in 1916 and me mum died three years later. I didn't miss me dad, he was a miserable old devil, but me mum was special.' Betty had wiped her eyes. 'She 'ad a bad chest, from working in t'mills. She knew she was dying so she tried to fix up for me and me brother to get some different work. She didn't want us working the looms. Her cousin 'ad a job in London, she got me taken on here. Tom, me brother, found a job at a local garage.'

In 1924 Betty's brother had moved up to London to be nearer his sister. She was thrilled. 'He's got a job as a taxi cab driver, ain't that grand? He says he'll give me a ride one day.'

Tom Langton was in lodgings and Minna never met him but from time to time Betty gave her titbits of information.

She showed Minna a large blue jumper she had knitted for him. 'To keep him warm in winter.'

But in the spring of 1926 Betty came to Minna with a woebegone face. Her brother had been sacked.

'But I thought he was getting on so well?' Minna patted Betty's heaving shoulders. 'What did he do?'

'Nothing really bad. He didn't pinch any money or anything like that.' Betty wiped her nose. 'But Tom's a bit of a hothead. He backed the miners' last strike. They're threatening strike action again and Tom handed out some leaflets when he was driving the cab. You know, "Not a penny off the pay, not a minute on the day." ' She looked at Minna's uncomprehending expression. 'They's what the the miners are demanding.'

'But Tom was doing his work?'

'Yes, but they still fired 'im.' Betty sniffed. 'And he'll never get another job without a reference.' The tears started rolling down her face again.

'Wait a minute, you say he's good with cars?'

Betty nodded. 'He's a wonder with 'em.'

'And if he's been a taxi driver, he'll know his way around London?'

'Yes.'

'Right.' Minna smiled. 'Tell him to come round here tomorrow night.'

'Round 'ere. Why?'

Minna laughed. 'My father sacked Randell last night. He was drunk. He nearly crashed the Rolls. Your Tom's not a drinker, is he?'

'Oh, no, miss. Never touches the stuff.'

'Good. Well, Papa will need a new driver, and fast. Looks like your brother might be just the kind of man he wants.'

Minna frowned. 'Only he mustn't start flashing strike leaflets around.'

'I'll make sure he doesn't.' Betty's eyes were shining. 'Oh, thank you, miss. Thank you.'

'He hasn't got the job yet,' warned Minna. 'But I can usually get Papa to see things my way.'

And so Betty's brother became a member of staff.

The General Strike of 1926 brought about a considerable reversal to Pieter Van Heerden's fortune. However, when the dust settled, he found he was still able to maintain his high standard of living. He kept his box at the Opera, his chauffeur-driven Rolls-Royce and his string of attractive lady escorts, but he came to Minna one morning and told her their home would have to be sold.

She looked at him in stunned silence.

'It makes sense, Minna.' He turned away from her accusing stare. 'And we're moving to a delightful little place near Richmond. Well, it's not little actually, but it's a damned sight smaller than this place. You'll love Richmond.' He looked at her pleadingly. 'There's the Park and it's a fashionable area. We'll be able to entertain . . .'

'I don't want to entertain. I want to stay here.' Minna burst into tears and rushed upstairs to her room. After a good cry, she sat up and telephoned Cicily Chesterton. Ever since they'd met at the races, Minna had considered Cicily her friend. The older woman was kind to her. She often took Minna out to tea and sometimes they went shopping together.

'Please, please, Cicily. Come round and persuade Papa not to sell.'

Cicily came round, listened to Minna's torrent of words and said she would speak to her father.

'But I can't promise anything, Minna. In fact,' she paused, 'I think he is wise to try and cut back on his expenses.'

'But our home isn't an expense.'

Cicily had shaken her elegant head and drifted downstairs. After washing her face, Minna crept down into the hall and listened unashamedly outside the door of her father's study. She could hear Cicily's clear voice very well.

'Do you really have to part with this house, Pieter? Poor Minna's heartbroken.'

'She thinks she is. She'll soon get over it.'

Minna gasped at her father's callous tone.

'I'm not so sure.' Cicily's voice was cool. 'Minna's led a strange life since you took her out of school. Racketing around the social scene with you may be exciting but it's hardly ideal for a young girl growing up. This house means a great deal to her and it will be a dreadful wrench if she has to leave. Are you sure you're doing the right thing?'

'Of course I'm not sure. I don't want to leave this house either, but I must. I need ready cash, and if I sell off any more shares the rumours will start. And you know what will happen then.'

There was a short silence then Cicily asked, 'Are things really so bad?'

'They've been better.' Minna heard her father sigh and then say, more jovially, 'But I'll bounce back. You know me.'

'I do, my dear.' Cicily's voice held affection. 'I've every faith in you. But, at the same time, you do such foolish things, Pieter.' She paused, and when she spoke again the warmth in her voice had disappeared.

'I saw Mildred Pearson two days ago. She was wearing a beautiful diamond brooch which she said was a gift from you.'

'Ah.' Her father sounded embarrassed. Minna pressed her ear against the door, straining to hear his reply.

'It's not as bad as it looks, Cicily. The brooch cost me nothing, payment for a bad debt, and I had to give Mildred something. She's been . . .'

'Kind to you. Yes, I've heard.' Cicily must have started to walk round the study. Minna could hear her heels clicking on the polished floor.

'That's another thing, Pieter. You have too many girlfriends. What impression does that give Minna?'

'She doesn't notice. She's just a child.'

'No, she isn't. She's growing up. Another few years and you'll be thinking of a possible marriage for her. Perhaps presentation at Court. You know what a stickler the

Queen is about morals, good behaviour. You'll need . . .'

'Well, marry me then.'

Minna's mouth fell open. Her head jerked away from the door and then swiftly returned.

'What?'

'Marry me, Cicily. You know that's what I want more than anything. If you marry me I won't need stupid little tarts to entertain me. Christ, I wouldn't look at another woman if I had you. And Minna's fond of you. Why not make both of us happy? Look, I'll even go down on my knees.'

Eyes wide, Minna pressed her knuckles against her mouth. She heard a scuffling sound and then Cicily's voice, taut with anger and something else.

'For God's sake, get up and don't be foolish. You know it would never work.'

'Why wouldn't it? Tell me!'

'Because . . . because . . .' Her voice faltered. 'I don't entirely trust you, my dear. You say you love me and I think you probably do, but there are other factors to consider.'

'Name them.'

'You're too reckless. I don't want to lose all my money.'

Minna heard her father's swift intake of breath.

'You don't think I'm after your money?'

'No, I know that you love me.' There was a wry note in Cicily's voice. 'But I think you are a little influenced by the thought of my wealth.'

Minna heard her father mutter a rude word and then Cicily's reply.

'No, hear me out, Pieter. If I was your wife, there might come a time in the future when you were tempted to "borrow" from me.'

Minna heard her father groan. 'How can you say that?

As if I would trick you into . . .'

'No, no. I don't say you would trick me, but you're a gambler, Pieter. You're prepared to risk all for a grand idea. I'm not like that. And, there's another reason for my refusal.' Cicily's voice softened. 'You want a son, don't you?'

There was silence and Minna strained to hear her father's reply. He would say no. He had her. Surely he had given up the idea of having any more children?

'You know I do.' His voice was low.

Minna rested her face against the panel of the door and expelled a long sigh.

'Yes, I thought you did.' Cicily hesitated and then said, 'And I don't, Pieter. I don't know why, but I have never wanted children.' There was a rustle of silk, as though she shrugged her shoulders. 'Perhaps I'm unnatural, but that's how I feel. I'm thirty-five years old. I don't like the risks involved. So you see, my dear, I think we should stay as we are, good friends and occasional lovers. If you want a new wife, you must look elsewhere.'

'But I love you, Cicily.'

The pain in her father's voice reached Minna and made her feel ashamed. She stepped away from the study door. She shouldn't be listening to this conversation. Besides, the thought of Cicily Chesterton and her father in bed together made her feel uncomfortable. She tiptoed across the hall and ran back upstairs, to her bedroom. When Cicily tapped on her door a few minutes later she didn't answer and after a moment Cicily went away.

A month later the house was sold and they moved to Richmond.

Chapter Sixteen

During the following weeks and months, Minna grieved for her beloved home but her pain was tempered by a definite change for the better in her lifestyle. Her father, perhaps stung by Cicily's criticism of him, began to introduce his daughter to a much younger set of people. He targeted the sons and daughters of his friends and business partners.

The first step was to invite them to accompany their parents to his house-warming party at Richmond. Always curious, they came. Then, when introductions had been made and tentative friendships formed, he set up other, more fascinating diversions. A fancy dress party for the youngsters at which guests must attend in circus costume, a tea-party at a London hotel where one must dress in school uniform and eat only muffins and meringues, a trip to Brooklands to see the car racing.

The youngsters agreed that Van Heerden was a card. The boys added that his daughter was a cracker.

Initially uncomfortable with youngsters of her own age, Minna relaxed when she sensed their approval of her. She began to take tea with girls her own age, she learned the pleasures of gossip. She accepted invitations to social evenings where sheepish young men, dressed in ridiculous Oxford Bags, rolled back expensive carpets so that couples could dance to the music of wind-up gramophones. She became a very good dancer.

After her growing years in the company of her father and his friends, most of the young men seemed stupid but it was flattering when they made eyes at her and even wrote poems to send to her. She treated her young swains with lofty indifference, and then realising that the more imperious she was with them, the more they adored her, she became insufferable. She broke appointments, made fun of them in front of friends, dropped them when she became bored.

When her father was busy in the City, she often had use of the Rolls. One day, when she was being particularly petulant with the two young men who were accompanying her to a tea dance, she became aware that Thomas, through his car mirror, was regarding her with some disapproval. She lost the thread of her conversation and sat back in her seat, discomfited.

Thomas was a strange young man. His looks and manners were nothing like his sister's. Betty was humorous and chatty, small and round like a little brown bird. Thomas was a tall, silent young man with an angular face and a stern expression. He never spoke until spoken to. Only once, just after he became Pieter's chauffeur, did he approach Minna.

He was waiting by the car for his master when Minna came out of the house. He straightened up and twisted his chauffeur's cap in his hands.

'I appreciate your kindness in helping Betty and me, Miss Minna. I'm a good driver and I won't let you or your pa down.'

'I'm sure you won't.' Minna had flashed him her best smile, the smile which made her admirers go weak at the knees. Thomas had merely replaced his hat on his head and turned back to the car.

Well, it didn't matter what the po-faced chauffeur thought of her. Minna looked away from Thomas's grim expression and turned her attention back to her slavish admirers.

Seamlessly, the pleasure-filled years slipped by. By the time Minna was seventeen, afternoon tea dances were old hat. She went to night-clubs instead and drank cocktails. Her favourite was the Manhattan, a mixture of Bourbon whiskey and dry vermouth.

By her eighteenth birthday she was one of the 'Bright Young Things', a group totally dedicated to the pursuit of pleasure and the banishment of boredom. Their favourite amusements were treasure hunts and hoaxes. Their practical jokes were carefully worked out and the treasure hunts ingenious, help with the clues coming from surprising quarters.

On one occasion, the Hovis bread factory on the Embankment baked hundreds of small, brown loaves with the next clue inside and another time the *Evening Standard* printed a special edition with the clue hidden inside the fake news.

Pieter, once again riding high with his finances, regarded Minna's exploits with indulgence. She was young and pretty and she was having a good time. Good luck to her. He too kept busy. He had a couple of racehorses in training, he backed a play in the West End, unfortunately it failed, and he always had a pretty woman on his arm.

Neither of them contemplated marriage. Minna thought she would never love anyone as much as she loved Papa, and Pieter was still vaguely in love with Cicily Chesterton. No, freedom to do what you wanted, that was the thing. Who wanted to settle down to the boredom of married life? Not the Van Heerdens. They wanted to live life to the full, and what a wonderful life they were living.

Father and daughter developed the custom of always meeting each other for a pre-dinner drink before they went their separate ways for the evening. That time was precious to Minna. They would mutually admire each other, Pieter handsome in his evening suit, Minna radiant in her fashionable skimpy dress which revealed long silken legs. They would chat and laugh, and before parting, would look at each other over a glass of champagne and exchange smiles of satisfaction.

And then, in the summer of 1931, their world collapsed. Britain was forced off the Gold Standard and the value of the pound plummeted.

Was it premonition that made Minna wake so early the day her world fell apart? Usually she slept late but that morning it was only a little after five when she got out of bed, put on her silk dressing gown and went downstairs.

This is ridiculous, she thought, as she walked down the staircase. Even the maids aren't up yet. Nevertheless, driven by some inner compulsion, she continued on her way. She walked across the hallway and down the corridor which led to her father's study.

He wouldn't be there, even Papa didn't work all night. Nevertheless, she tapped on the door. She waited. All was quiet. The tension in her throat relaxed a little. Of course he wasn't there, he was in bed, fast asleep. He had worked so hard during the last twenty-four hours. Since the big, black headlines had appeared in the newspapers he had been frantically busy. Minna had gone into his study last night, hoping he would join her for their usual hour together, but he had shaken his head and said, his voice brusque, 'No time, old girl. Have to sort this mess out.' He had looked up from his desk, his face white and tired-looking. 'Off you go and enjoy yourself. And don't worry your pretty head. I'll sort things out.'

Of course he would. Papa always sorted things out. Reassured, she had done as he asked.

But why did she have this sick feeling in the pit of her stomach? Minna opened the door.

At first, she thought he was asleep. He had his arms crossed on the desk and his head was pillowed on them. She could see his face which was peaceful and relaxed. She tiptoed over to him.

'Oh, Papa. You should have gone to bed.' She touched his hand and frowned. 'Papa?'

He was cold, too cold. Her eyes dilated. She forced herself to touch his face. He was icy. Then she noticed the queer smell. It was strange, sickly sweet. She put her hand over her mouth and gagged. 'Papa!' She screamed the word. He did not stir. He did not answer, and she realised he never would.

She screamed again and again and ran out of the study. One of the maids came hurrying through the connecting door which led to the servants' quarters.

'What is it, miss. What's happened?'

Minna gazed at her, wild-eyed. 'Go and fetch someone. Get the housekeeper. Tell her to ring for a doctor. There's been an accident.'

The maid blinked at her and then turned and ran. Minna staggered and nearly fell. She rested her hand against the wall to support herself. She couldn't think what to do. All she could remember was her father's face and that dreadful smell.

'Cicily,' she said aloud. 'Cicily will know what to do.' Trembling, her legs weak beneath her, she felt her way to the sitting room. She couldn't use the telephone in Papa's study. She couldn't go in there. In the sitting room, she raised the receiver, asked for Cicily's number.

'Yes.'

Thank God! Minna drew a quavering breath. 'Cicily, please come. It's Papa. I think he's killed himself.'

'Your father committed suicide by means of chloroform, Miss Van Heerden. If it's any consolation, he did not suffer.' The doctor, a thin, grey-haired man with a short wispy beard, coughed apologetically. It was his first suicide, he had met the deceased on a couple of social occasions and was at a loss to know how to handle the situation.

'I suggest you contact his solicitors immediately. They will . . .' His voice trailed away. 'They'll see to the arrangements.' He picked up his medical bag. 'And I shall have to contact the police.'

Cicily spoke, white-faced, her arm round Minna's shoulders. 'I can do that.'

He shook his head. 'Regulations must be followed, dear lady.' He glanced at the two stricken faces. 'If you like, I can prescribe something to settle your nerves?'

'No.' Cicily shook her head and then glanced at Minna. 'Unless . . .'

'I don't want anything.' She pressed her handkerchief to her lips.

'Good girl.' Cicily, after showing the doctor out, returned to her side and clasped her hand. 'Pills are not the answer, and we need to be clear-headed during the next couple of hours. There are things to do.'

Minna shuddered. 'I can't do anything, Cicily. Every time I close my eyes I think of him. His head on his arms.' She choked.

'Yes.' Cicily's face was drained of colour and there were dark circles around her eyes. She crossed to the drinks cabinet and poured out two brandies. She carried one to Minna.

'Drink this.'

Under protest, Minna did so.

Draining her own glass, Cicily spoke rapidly. 'I know how you're feeling. God knows, I loved the man myself, but we can't afford to give way to grief, Minna. The police will be here shortly. There will be questions to answer.'

'What sort of questions?'

'They'll want to know what drove your father to do what he did. They'll ask questions about his financial affairs.'

Minna clutched her glass. 'I don't know anything about Papa's business affairs. His accountants and the solicitors will tell them what they want to know. Papa had no business worries, his financial affairs were in order.'

'They *were*, Minna. I fear that is not the case now.'

Cicily walked around the room, nervous tension showed in her sharp voice and her quick steps. 'Your father had a wonderful way of making money, but he took risks. I warned him to be more prudent when the Stock Exchange slumped in 1929 but he wouldn't listen. The darned idiot!' Her face twisted with pain. 'He thought it would never happen to him, but it did, didn't it?' She swung on her heel and gazed out of the window and Minna watched her, a look of incomprehension on her face.

'Your father's accountants and solicitors will have to open his books for investigation. If what I fear has happened, his assets will be stripped to pay the creditors, even this house could go.' She turned towards Minna. 'Do you understand what I'm saying?'

'You mean, he's lost all his money? So that's why . . .?'

'It must be that. Your father loved life too much to throw it away for anything so trival as a woman or a loss of reputation.' Cicily came and knelt down beside Minna.

'I know this is hard for you, but I want you to go upstairs, take a case and fill it with anything you know to be of value which your father gave to you. Jewellery, of course, but any certificates of stock, or bonds your father may have given you. Will you do that, Minna?'

'Yes, I suppose so.' She got slowly to her feet. 'But most of my jewellery is in the bank and I can't think of anything that . . .'

Cicily gave her a little push. 'Anything you can think of,' she repeated. 'And then I'm going to take you to my house. The police, when they arrive, will want to talk to the staff. They can come and see you later. I'll tell the housekeeper what to say.'

Minna hesitated in the doorway. 'But we can't leave Papa alone, Cicily.'

Tears sprang to the older woman's eyes and ran down her cheeks. 'We won't leave him long, Minna. But right now, we can't do anything for him and I know your father would want me to look after you first.'

Cicily had read the situation correctly. Pieter Van Heerden left debts of over £100,000. When the news of his death broke, creditors besieged the company offices. It was ordered that his properties be sealed. Minna, helped by Cicily, managed to salvage a few things. Two of her favourite paintings, the grandmother clock that had been her mother's; all the rest of the furniture was impounded and then sold off.

Pieter's Italian paintings went and his Rolls-Royce. A former business associate bought his opulent desk with the gold and silver fittings. Even his clothes and his collection of walking sticks were auctioned.

Sheltering in Cicily's home, Minna wondered drearily where all her friends had gone for no one came to see her. Only a few of Papa's friends came to the funeral. Without Cicily, she thought, I wouldn't be able to stand it.

The worst moment in a terrible day was when she heard a former friend of her father's comment: 'Damned bad show. Didn't even shoot himself, yer know. Used chloroform.' The man shook his head. 'Only a foreigner would think of that. And he was in the trade originally, wasn't he? Worked for a firm of pill pushers, I hear.'

She heard his words and expected to feel anger, but all she felt was numb despair. When Cicily took her back to stay with her she went without a word. Cicily also arranged for Betty to come and look after her mistress. The rest of Pieter's staff were given notice.

Minna had burst into tears when Betty came into her room. The maid put her arms around her and rocked her into quietness.

'It's all right, miss. Things will get better.'

Instead, they got worse.

The Press picked up on the story of Pieter Van Heerden's suicide and reported the unravelling of his business empire with glee. It appeared some of his business dealings had been 'not quite legal'. It was suggested that, had he lived, he might have faced criminal charges.

Cicily, grim-faced, told Minna not to read the newspapers. 'When a man larger than life falls from grace there are always scavengers to pick over the bones.'

Minna bent her head. Cicely's own social life had suffered. She received few invitations nowadays.

Each day brought fresh revelations. And then, the last bombshell. Minna stared down at the newspaper with a puzzled frown. It reported that her father wasn't even Dutch, he was German.

Suicide Financier was a Hun! screamed the headlines, conveniently forgetting that Van Heerden had come to England years before the outbreak of the First World War. *Kraut Fleeced War Veterans of Their Savings.*

'I told you not to read such filth.' Cicily snatched the paper away from Minna and tore it up. 'They're Fleet Street vultures. They haven't a scrap of evidence.' But her eyes were heavy with tears and her face and figure showed signs of exhaustion.

Minna went to her bedroom, sat on the bed and wondered what she should do. She had been staying with Cicily for over six weeks and she thought it was time she moved on. Staying with her friend was ruining Cicily's life.

'I can't stay here permanently,' she confided to Betty. 'I'd be an embarrassment to Cicily. As it is, half her friends have stopped calling on her.'

'Fine friends,' Betty replied. 'Anyway, don't you be foolish, miss. You stay here with Miss Cicily as long as you can. At least you've a roof over your head and good food to eat.'

Her words reminded Minna of Tom's predicament. She asked Betty if her brother had managed to get another job.

'No. Word's got about he was working for your pa. Mud sticks, you know.' Betty whipped her hand over her mouth. 'Oh, I'm sorry, miss.'

Minna shook her head. 'It's all right, Betty. I know what people are saying.'

'Tom says he thinks him and me ought to go home, to Yorkshire. No one there knows about your pa. They don't care what 'appens in London. Tom reckons we'd get jobs if we went home.'

'Oh, Betty, don't go yet.' Minna clutched her arm. 'Don't leave me.'

'I won't go yet, miss. Not until you're on your feet again.'

But how was she to get on her feet? She was trapped in Cicily's house. On the rare occasions she went out, there was always someone who knew her. Someone would look uncomfortable and avert their eyes or, even worse, make a comment to a companion and smile.

So Minna began to go to places she had never been before. She walked down Oxford Street and thought the clothes displayed in the stores were cheap and tawdry. She took refuge from her thoughts by going to the cinema, sometimes she took Betty with her for company. On days she felt particularly restless she walked in the parks where sensible ladies in tweed suits, Jaeger jerseys and heavy shoes walked their dogs on leads. It was another world and one that did not suit her.

One day, as she re-entered Cicily's house, she heard her friend's voice. Cicily was speaking on the telephone and the door of the room she was in stood ajar. Minna couldn't help hearing what Cicily said.

'I know. I would love to visit America with you but I can't. You'll have to find someone else. Poor little Minna hasn't a friend in the world except me. How can I abandon her?'

Minna crept upstairs and summoned Betty to her. When she appeared she asked her, 'Has Thomas thought any more about returning to Yorkshire?'

Betty wiped her hands on her apron. 'Yes, he thinks he's going next month. It's all right though,' she eyed her mistress, 'I'll stay on with you for a bit longer.'

'That won't be necessary.' Minna swung round to stare out of the window. 'I shall accompany you and Tom to Yorkshire.'

'Eh?' Betty was struck dumb. She gaped at Minna.

'I should have thought of it before. Yorkshire's so far away. I can make a new start there.' Minna wheeled round to face Betty again. 'No one will recognise my name in the North. I can sell the jewellery I took from the house, that should keep us going until we all get a job.'

'A job?' Betty's face had turned bright red. 'I'm sorry, miss, but what sort of job could you do?'

'I don't know, I'll find something.' Minna dismissed Betty's forebodings with a wave of her hand. For the first time since her father's death she felt alive again. She was taking charge of her own destiny.

'But what will Miss Cicily say?'

'Cicily will try and dissuade me but, if I go, I think she will secretly be relieved.'

Betty pulled a face. 'Oh, miss, that's a dreadful thing to say. Miss Cicily's been like a mother to you.'

'Yes, but she isn't my mother, is she? And I can't expect to dump myself on her for ever. No, my mind is quite made up.' Minna went to her dressing table and took out a writing pad. 'Now, I must make plans. In the meantime, get hold of your brother and ask him to come and visit me.'

Thomas listened to her plans with a blank face and a downward gaze. When she finished, he said: 'You don't know what you're talking about, miss.'

The colour flared in her face. 'I know life in Halifax will be very different from life in London, but I have no choice in the matter. I must learn how to work for my keep. And I would rather do it in the company of friends than strangers. That is,' her voice faltered, 'you and Betty are my friends, are you not?'

'We are, miss.' Spots of red showed on his high cheekbones but he still kept his gaze on his boots. 'That's why I'm telling you, it wouldn't work.' At last, he returned her gaze.

'It's a hard life up North. You'd be much better staying here. If you don't want to live off Miss Cicily, then let *her* find you a job. She'd find you something easy, a companion to an old lady perhaps. You don't want to come with us to Halifax, there's nowt for you there.'

'I don't want to stay here. There's nothing but bad memories for me in London, I want a fresh start.' Her voice broke. She pulled a handkerchief from her sleeve and blew her nose. 'And I don't want to be a charity case. I want to stand on my own feet. But I'm scared and I thought that you and Betty . . .'

At her name, Betty, who had been seated next to Tom, also staring at her feet, looked up.

'It mightn't be such a bad idea, Tom. Miss Minna has some jewellery she can sell to tide her over for a little while. And she writes a lovely letter and speaks so nicely, perhaps she could get a job teaching little kids.'

'And pigs might fly!'

Minna stuck her jaw out and glared at him. 'I know you don't approve of me but you might remember that I helped you out once. Anyway, it doesn't matter what you think. I shall leave this place at the end of the month. And I'll get myself a job, with or without your help.'

'Oh, Tom.' Betty stared at her brother beseechingly.

A reluctant smile played round his lips. He shrugged his shoulders and stood up.

'Seems I'm outvoted.' He studied Minna's face. 'I still think it's a daft idea but if you're so set on it, you can come with us. Only, don't go moaning to me if things don't work out.'

'I won't.' A tide of pink enveloped her face and she stuck out her hand. 'Thank you, Thomas. I promise you won't regret your decision.'

He looked at her hand but did not shake it. 'I hope you're right, miss.' He turned for the door. 'Betty will tell you when the arrangements are made.'

'Thanks, and Thomas . . .'

He looked round. 'What?'

'You better stop calling me miss.'

He stared at her, a curious expression in his blue eyes. 'I'll remember that, miss.

Chapter Seventeen

In March, Rosie worked for two weeks on nights. Normally, she disliked night work. The hours dragged and when you went home in the morning you couldn't go to sleep even though you were tired because it was noisy outside and your body hadn't adjusted to the new scheme of things. However, this time she didn't mind.

She didn't mind anything at the moment because things were going right for her. Minna's health had improved, both her children seemed okay and she was enjoying the frequent chats she had with Mark Goodman during the hours she spent at Woldview. A friendship was definitely developing, she thought, because they always seemed to find plenty to talk about.

When she commenced night duty she realised that Mark was a person who had problems sleeping. During her first week, on checking her rounds in the early hours of the morning, she had been startled to find the Officer in Charge, dressed in sweater and slacks, ambling down one of the corridors towards her.

He apologised for startling her and explained.

'Sometimes, I have spells of insomnia. I won't take pills so I pass the time by taking a walk round the building, checking the security and maybe having a chat with the night staff or one or two of the old folk. They often sleep badly, as you know. Then, after a couple of hours, I go back to bed.'

'Don't you feel tired next day?'

He shrugged. 'Don't you?' He smiled when she hesitated. 'Look, I fancy a coffee. Shall I nip into the staff room and make us a cup?'

She looked dubious. 'Coffee won't help you sleep.'

'It will help you stay awake.'

She laughed. 'All right. Thanks.'

They sat together in the small office on the first floor and talked as they drank their coffee. It was a quiet night with no little red lights flashing to interrupt their conversation.

Mark sat in an easy chair, his curly hair haloed by the lamplight behind him, and told Rosie about his early life. He had gone to live in Canada when he was twenty-two, he said, and worked at a variety of jobs until he became a lumberjack two years later.

'The forests and rivers are so immense, Rosie. It's hard to describe how beautiful it is.' He sighed. 'The work was hard but I loved those years.'

'Why did you come back?'

Her question unsettled him. He frowned down at his hands and then said, 'My father and mother kept writing to me. I was an only child, they were getting old and frail. They wanted to see me, so I came back.'

'Are they still . . .?'

He anticipated her question. 'They're both dead now.'

There was a moment of silence and then, to her surprise, Rosie found herself telling Mark about *her* life. She mentioned Minna, making her awkwardness sound funny, and then she talked about her children, and at last she told him about Howard.

When she finished speaking she looked across at him and realised how intently he was regarding her. She was therefore surprised when he said: 'You've been lucky, haven't you?'

Her eyebrows drew together in a frown. 'I wouldn't say that.'

He shook his head. 'I'm sorry, that came out wrong. I mean, it's sad you lost your husband when he was a comparatively young man, but the time you had with him sounded so happy.' He paused. 'And you have his children.'

Rosie relaxed and nodded her head. 'Yes, I have.'

He sat back in his chair, apparently lost in thought, and she wondered if he regretted his single state, his lack of family. He must have had special relationships in his life, surely?

Then he stirred. 'It's strange, isn't it, sitting together at three in the morning and exchanging confidences? Tell me, what are you thinking of now?'

She blushed. 'I was thinking I should get back to my studying.'

'Ah, yes.' His gaze went to the books spread out on the desk. 'They look mighty serious. Not interested in light reading, eh?'

She grinned. 'Haven't the time.' She told him about her studies and experienced a warm feeling when she realised he was genuinely interested in what she was saying.

When she finished telling him of her ambitions, he leaned forward and clasped his hands around his knees. 'That's great, Rosie. If you're enjoying the course as much as you say you are, you'll pass your exams with flying colours. Enthusiasm, that's the thing. I remember when I started training . . .'

'Yes, how did that come about?' She was eager to know; from cutting down trees in Canada to caring for the elderly was a big step.

He smiled. 'I didn't particularly decide my career, it just sort of happened. I needed a job with prospects and I happened to see a recruitment advertisement in one of the newspapers.

'I wrote off for details and the rest followed. I enjoyed the training and now I enjoy my work.' He paused. 'Some people find that strange, I can't imagine why. Old folk can be so feisty, can't they?'

'Oh, yes.' Rosie thought of her conversation with Mrs Kingston.

'I know some senior citizens are rude or disagreeable, but that goes for any section of the community. On the whole I believe the old have a wonderful resilient quality which younger people often lack. And they retain a joy in life.' Mark laughed. 'Even if their teeth have fallen out and they don't hear so well.'

'Some of them.' Rosie thought of Minna.

Mark was warming to his subject. 'I spent a lot of time with my grandmother when I was young. She was a terrific person. I . . .'

A red light on the panel lit up and a buzzing noise was heard.

They both stood up.

'I'll have to tell you about her some other time.' He opened the door and stood back to allow Rosie to go through.

'Yes, please do. It's lovely to have someone to talk to during the dawn hours. Of course,' she grinned, 'I'll understand if you don't appear. It would be better if you could get a good night's sleep.'

'It would indeed.' Mark collected up the empty coffee cups and followed Rosie along the corridor.

The next night he did not come and Rosie worked at her books, but the following night he did. On three separate occasions during Rosie's spell of night duty they sat together in the first-floor office and chatted and drank coffee or tea. Nothing deep or meaningful was said but Rosie felt they were really getting to know each other and hoped Mark felt that, too.

But on her last night Rosie had no time to study or talk to Mark Goodman. An old gentleman, a retired army officer called Mr Allen, who had been given new medication by his doctor, woke up at two a.m. and imagined he was back in the North African campaign.

He got out of bed, dressed himself then appeared on the landing and bellowed: 'Out of your tents, you lazy slackers. Line up, it's time for drill.'

Rosie, hearing the commotion, arrived at a run and spent ten minutes trying to persuade him to return to his room but he would have none of it. Rommel, he told her earnestly, was just over the next hill.

As more and more testy and nervous residents appeared on the landing, Rosie knew she needed help. She pressed her alarm to summon another member of staff.

Mark Goodman appeared. This time, it seemed, he had been able to sleep for he was wearing slippers and a navy blue dressing-gown over black patterned pyjama bottoms. His chest, Rosie observed, was bare, and quite hairy.

He took a swift look round and groaned. 'Oh my God, what's happening? Is it a mutiny or the beginnings of a mass love-in?'

She smothered a smile and explained.

'Right.' He tightened the belt of his dressing-gown. 'Leave Mr Allen to me. You try and get the rest of them back to bed.' He shouldered his way towards Mr Allen.

'Captain Allen, do you remember me? I'm Major Goodman. I suggest we retire to your quarters where you can give me your report.'

He put his hand on Mr Allen's shoulder, opened the bedroom door and followed the old man into the room.

He came out again fifteen minutes later, just as Rosie had ushered the last nervous old lady back into her room.

'Phew! That was hard work.' Mark thrust his hands into the pockets of the dressing-gown. 'Never been in the army, so wasn't sure of my phraseology. Still, he's happy enough now. I managed to get him into bed by asking him to organise a patrol tomorrow morning to check the immediate vicinity for mines. If he's still rambling then I'll ask the staff to keep a close eye on him.'

'Poor Mr Allen.' Rosie explained about the new medication.

'Well, he'll probably settle down when he gets used to the new drugs. If not, I'll get in touch with his doctor.' Mark yawned and then apologised.

'No need for an apology. I'm sorry I had to disturb you, but I knew I needed help. Thank you for coming to my assistance so promptly.'

'Only doing my job.' He yawned again. 'Well, I'm going back to my bed. Buzz again if you need me.'

Perhaps it was his casual attire, or their easy chat, but to her horror, Rosie heard herself saying, 'Don't tempt me. I might just do that.'

A tide of colour swept her face when Mark paused and looked at her, one of his eyebrows raised questioningly.

'But only in the course of duty,' she added, a little shakily.

'But of course.' He laughed.

She watched the crinkles appear around his eyes and felt the familiar tremor inside her.

'By the way, Rosie?'

She made herself pay attention. 'Yes.'

'I'll run you home tomorrow morning. I have to be in town early.'

'Thank you.' She concealed a delighted smile. 'I'd better get back to the duty desk.'

'And I to my beauty sleep.' But still he lingered. 'You've two days off now and then you're back on days, is that right?'

She nodded.

He sighed. 'And Mrs Marshall is replacing you on night duty.'

'She's a good care assistant.'

'I know, but not the kind of person you can talk to in the middle of the night.'

The following morning, the weather was typical for March. There had been a hard frost but it was dispersing and the sky was bright blue and crowded with small white clouds. It was cold.

Rosie climbed into Mark's car, glad to see he had turned on the heater. They drove away from Woldview. The hedgerows were frosted with white and she wondered how her robin was faring. She mentioned him to Mark, who smiled.

'He'll be all right. Robins, like blackbirds, are survivors.' He glanced at her. 'You know, I think we resemble our respective pet birds. My dark colouring matches the blackbird who plagues me when I'm gardening and we both get irritated easily, and you certainly remind me of your robin.'

She turned in her seat to frown at him. 'Round Robin, do you mean? I'll have you know I've lost half a stone since Christmas.'

He shook his head. 'No, I didn't mean that. But you're a cheery sort of person, you move quickly, and I've noticed you put your head on one side when you're concentrating or doing some serious thinking.'

'Do I?' She was astonished he had noticed so much about her.

'Yes.'

Ahead of them, a minibus pulled out of a side lane and drove directly in front of them. The road was becoming busy with early-morning traffic. A blue Metro overtook them, shot past the minibus and scraped back into the lane moments before a lorry, travelling in the opposite direction, thundered by.

Mark scowled. 'Bloody idiots! There's patches of black ice on this road. You'd think they'd have the sense to be more careful.'

Rosie nodded but said nothing. She had noticed before that he was a cautious driver.

'You're quiet, Rosie.'

She bit back a yawn and explained. 'I'm tired.'

'Yes, of course. After two weeks on nights you must be longing for a couple of lazy days.'

'I am. When I get home, I shall have a lovely, leisurely bath and then fall into bed.'

He nodded. 'But when you've caught up on sleep, say tonight or tomorrow evening perhaps . . .' He paused.

She waited. 'Yes?'

'I wondered if we could go out somewhere? A meal perhaps, or a drink. Do you like jazz? There's a group performing at The Huntsman tomorrow night. They're good, I've seen them before.'

Happiness flooded through her. She squeezed her hands together. 'I'd like that,' she replied carefully. 'I don't know much about jazz, but I'm prepared to give it a try. You're a fan, are you?'

He smiled broadly. 'Yes. But traditional jazz. I'm not keen on the new . . .'

And then it happened.

A Datsun overtook them, travelling at break-neck speed. A minute later, the driver lost control, there was a screech of brakes and the car skewed across the road in front of them.

'Jesus.' Mark pulled on the wheel and his foot hit the brakes as he attempted to avoid the inevitable collision.

Rosie's breathing was shallow. She sat bolt upright, her hands clenched in her lap.

'Brace yourself.' Mark shouted.

She could see the frightened face of the man in the Datsun staring straight at her. There was a scrunching sound as the two cars came together. As their windscreen shattered a myriad of cracks appeared before Rosie's eyes. Her body slammed hard against the seat belt. She was conscious of a rolling movement, saw a patch of blue sky and then her head hit the side of the car and everything went black.

The bed was so hard. It wasn't her bed. She was flat on her back and something was stopping her from moving. Her head ached.

Rosie opened her eyes briefly but shut them again because the light was too bright. There were coloured sparks dancing around in the blackness beneath her eyelids. She gave a little groan. She felt awful.

'Rosie.'

It was Mark's voice. She squinted cautiously through half-opened lids. The dark shape of a man cut out some of the glaring light. She opened her eyes a little wider and saw Mark's face. There were purple bruises on his cheeks and a large sticking plaster across the left side of his forehead. He looked ghastly. She remembered the car crash.

'Mark.' She struggled to sit up but couldn't. She realised

she must be in hospital because there was a man in a white coat standing next to Mark, a doctor. She focused on her immediate surroundings. She was in a ward and it was a hospital sheet tucked tightly around her body that was imprisoning her.

She tried moving her arms but failed. It's like being a butterfly pinned on a specimen card, she thought crossly. She gave up the struggle and closed her eyes again. If her arms had been outside the sheet perhaps Mark would have taken her hand. She wanted that. She felt tears well up and forced them back. She said faintly, 'You look awful, Mark.'

'I'm fine.' His voice was strained. 'You've had us worried, Rosie.'

A pang of fear shot through her. She opened her eyes again. 'Why? What's wrong with me?'

'Nothing too drastic, Mrs Scott.' Another voice. The man standing next to Mark. The doctor.

'You've been unconscious for some time. Naturally, we were worried, but you're back with us now. We've tested certain reflexes and everything seems normal so you mustn't worry. You're concussed, that's all. No major injuries, no bones broken.'

'I've a terrible headache.' She shut her eyes again.

'Inevitable, I'm afraid. But no pain-killers yet. The nurse will be checking you out every few hours, testing your reactions to light etc. It's just a precaution.'

'Mmmm . . .' She was drifting into sleep. She was so tired. She forced herself to concentrate.

'Mark?'

'Yes.'

'How long will I be here?'

The doctor answered. 'Not long. Two, maybe three days, that's all.'

She made another effort to release her hand from the confines of the sheet and this time she succeeded. It waved about like a beached fish. She felt someone take hold of it. Someone with a strong, warm grasp. She was reassured. She opened her eyes and managed a smile.

'Mark, will you contact Steve?'

'Of course I will.'

'Tell him . . .'

'Don't worry. I'll see to things.'

'It's a pity . . .' Her head felt fuzzy, her voice trailed away.

He had to bend over to hear the rest of the sentence.

'. . . about our night out. The jazz club.'

He pressed her hand. 'Don't worry about it, Rosie. There'll be other nights.'

Rosie wanted to kill the nurse. Every time she got to sleep this devil in a checked blue and white uniform came into her room and made her wake up.

She flashed lights into Rosie's eyes and asked her to say how many fingers she was holding up, and on one occasion she stripped away the sheet and tapped with a little hammer on various parts of Rosie's anatomy. On her fourth or fifth visit, Rosie swore at her.

Next day, when she was feeling much better apart from the headache, she sent her apologies to the night nurse via another member of staff.

This nurse laughed. 'She'll think nothing of it, Mrs Scott. You'd be surprised what we get called sometimes.'

'I have a good idea.' Rosie lay back on her pillow and allowed herself to be washed. 'Some of the old people I look after have a colourful vocabulary.' The nurse went away and Rosie slept again. This time, she was left in peace.

When Steve came to see her in the afternoon, she was feeling much better. She smiled at her son and assured him she was fine.

'I might get out tomorrow,' she said, crossing her fingers.

'Well, don't come home until you're ready.'

He had brought a bunch of spring flowers and a magazine for her to read. He perched awkwardly on the end of the bed and stared at her anxiously.

'Are you really all right?'

'Stiff, and I'll have to wear this surgical collar for a while.' Rosie grimaced, and then smiled as she picked up the flowers.

'These are lovely, Steve. Thank you.' She looked up at his worried face. 'I'm actually very lucky. The doctor came to see me this morning and told me that if it hadn't been for Mark's excellent driving, both of us might have been seriously injured.'

Steve studied her face. 'He came round to the bank, you know, to tell me what had happened. He looked as thought *he* should have been in hospital. I'm surprised they didn't keep him in. He looked awful.'

'Yes.' Rosie was quiet, remembering Mark's appearance last night.

'He seems a nice chap?'

'He is. I do like him, Steve. I hope you and he are able to become better acquainted.' She smiled at the mixed emotions on her son's face.

'I haven't told Grandma.' Steve changed the subject. 'I didn't know what to do. Mr Goodman said you would only be in hospital for a couple of days and I didn't want to upset her and . . .' He moved his hands helplessly.

'You did the right thing, Steve. There's no point in distressing Minna. She won't expect me to visit until

Sunday, and I should be able to go and see her then. I'd rather she didn't know about the accident.' Rosie shifted position. 'What about Paula?'

'I rang them. Left a message with Dave. Haven't you heard from her?'

'No phone calls but perhaps she's written.' Rosie hastened to dispel Steve's frown. She felt better but didn't feel strong enough to face any upsets yet. She chose another topic of conversation.

'Have you received any more details about your course?'

'No.' He stared out through the window. 'They'll probably arrive next week.' He stood up. 'If you don't mind, Mum, I'd better get back to work. I'll come and see you tonight, shall I?'

'No, it's all right, love. I've had a message to say Karen Horton's coming to see me. You can ring in the morning to see if I can come home.'

Instead of flowers, Karen brought a bottle of Marks & Spencers champagne.

'Sorry it's not the genuine McCoy, but it's not bad. Better wait until you get home to drink it though.'

'Oh, Karen. How kind of you.' Rosie accepted her gift with pleasure. 'And I won't drink it just yet. I'll wait until there's something really good to celebrate.' She beamed at her friend. 'It seems ages since we saw each other.'

Karen pulled up a chair and sat down. 'I know. The residents keep asking me when you're coming back and I have to say I'm not sure. Mark Goodman seems hell-bent on keeping you at Woldview as long as possible and I gather you're happy about that?'

Rosie sat up straight in bed and knew that she was blushing. 'I've been wondering what to do, Karen. I miss you and the rest of the people at The Firs, but I do like working at Woldview. I suppose I should have come to talk to you about it, but after you agreed to extend my temporary transfer I thought I'd leave it a little longer.'

The corner of Karen Horton's mouth quirked upwards. 'Yes, I do understand your predicament. I've been hearing a few whispers, you know, and I can see that, despite the long journey to Woldview, there are several reasons why you should want to stay there.'

She watched the red rise in Rosie's cheeks and added, in a kindly voice, 'You don't have to feel guilty, Rosie. After all, it was I who put you there in the first place. And, yes, we worked well together, but that doesn't mean that things must forever stay the same. I liked having you on my staff, but no one is indispensable, you know.

'If Mark Goodman wants you added to his permanent staff and you want that too, then there's no problem. I'll sort it out.'

'Are you terribly busy?' Rosie's voice was humble.

'As always, but show me a Council home that isn't.' Karen Horton shrugged her shoulders. 'But the new Second Officer's good, the Cook hasn't thrown a tantrum since last month, and we've finally got the bathroom on the second floor into operation. Things are going well. Oh, and you might be interested to know that Mrs Kingston has decided she can live with her new room-mate.'

'I'm glad. I'd wondered about that.' Rosie smiled at her friend. 'How did you know I was in hospital?'

'Mark rang me last night.' Karen frowned. 'Poor man, he was so upset. I felt sorry for him.'

'Yes, he was dreadfully upset.' Rosie pleated the edge of her bed cover. 'Actually, I was surprised how badly he took it. After all, neither of us was badly hurt and apparently he coped magnificently when the crash actually happened. Why did he fall apart at the hospital?'

'Don't you know?' Karen sat forward on her chair. 'I gather you and he have become quite close friends so I thought he might have told you.'

'Told me what?'

Karen examined her fingernails. 'Oh, well, I suppose there's no harm in your knowing.' She took a deep breath. 'Mark was married for a short time when he was young. He lost his wife in a car crash.'

'Oh, no.'

'Oh, yes. He married his childhood sweetheart when he was twenty. A colleague of mine told me about it. He was on the panel when Mark was appointed to the job at Woldview. Apparently Mark didn't volunteer any information about it but during the interview, it came out.

'A panel member asked Mark why he hadn't stuck at a regular job during his mid-twenties. He had started promisingly enough on an engineering course at a London polytechnic but then he had just dropped out.

'Mark explained that his wife had been killed in an horrific car accident a year after their marriage. She was six months pregnant and the tragedy devastated him. He didn't care about anything any more.

'He dropped out of college and bummed around the country for six months and then, with help from his parents, he went over to Canada where he stayed for some considerable time.'

'Oh, Karen, how awful. Mark told me he had lived in Canada but he never said anything about being married.'

Karen sighed. 'It's all a long time ago now, but the man I talked to said Mark was very close-mouthed about the whole thing. He gave them the bare details and that was all. He did say, twice, that a drink-driver had been responsible for the accident but my friend thought Mark harboured certain feelings of guilt.'

Rosie shook her head. 'No wonder he was so affected by our crash.'

'You won't mention it?' Karen looked a little shame-faced. 'Perhaps I shouldn't have told you, but I get the idea that you and he are becoming close friends and I thought you should know.'

'That's all right. I won't breathe a word.' Rosie sighed. 'And, yes, we are friends, but nothing more than that.'

There was an awkward pause and then Karen enquired about the children. Rosie told her that Steve would soon be leaving to attend his banking course and after that, the rest of the visit passed in general conversation.

After her friend had left, Rosie lay back in her bed and tried to sort out her feelings. Mark had never breathed a word to her about his marriage but then, why should he? She swallowed a lump in her throat when she remembered how he had commented upon her luck in having Paula and Steve. The poor man, how lonely he must have been, how much he must have missed his young bride.

But so many years had gone by since she'd died. Did he still feel he must stay faithful to her memory? Surely not?

She shifted her position and sighed. Her love for Howard had been true and strong and she had grieved for him for years but now she felt no betrayal in wanting to love Mark. Life was for the living, everyone knew that. But if he felt differently . . .

She looked across at the bottle of champagne standing on her locker and felt a pang of loneliness. When Karen had given it to her she had thought of Mark. Now she wondered if she would ever have the opportunity of sharing it.

Chapter Eighteen

Steve was angry when he left the hospital. His bloody sister, after all Mum had done for her, couldn't be bothered to ring up and ask how she was. He ground his teeth together and gunned the car down a quiet street, thinking of what he would like to say to Paula. He spotted a telephone box at the end of the road and slammed on the brakes. His car screeched to a halt. He jumped out and, feeling in his pocket for change, went into the phone box and dialled Paula's number. She wouldn't be in, he thought, not at this time of the day. She was never bloody in.

She answered the phone. 'Hello, Paula Sheridan.'

Shocked at hearing her voice, Steve straightened up from his slouched posture and said: 'It's me, Steve.'

'Steve? My goodness, what have I done to deserve this honour? It's ages since we spoke.'

The amusement in her voice brought the anger roaring back.

'You little bitch!' he said through clenched teeth. 'Why do you think I'm ringing? You haven't contacted the hospital yet. Well, just in case you're interested, Mum's all right. They think she'll be allowed home tomorrow. So if, despite your busy lifestyle, you have a moment to spare, I suggest you get in touch with her.'

Giving her no time to reply, he slammed down the phone and went back to his car. He got in and sat for a moment, trying to calm down. As he did so, the satisfaction of speaking his mind to Paula was marred by a prickle of apprehension. I'm losing my temper too often, he thought, and although this time it was justified, often it isn't. He stared fixedly through the car window and wondered why.

Something hovered at the back of his mind but when he tried to catch hold of it, transform it into something he could make sense of, it escaped him. He yawned and rubbed his eyes. He should go back to the bank, but he didn't want to. The last thing he wanted to do was to be charming to customers or sit checking rows of figures on a computer screen.

Well, to hell with it. He wouldn't go back. He'd take the rest of the day off. He had an excuse. If Mum was being released from the hospital tomorrow, then he had things to do. The house could do with a tidy and there was shopping to buy. But he didn't want to do those things either.

He put the car in gear and headed out of town. He drove towards Market Weighton and then took the estate road at Londesborough Park which led to the Way. The Yorkshire Wolds Way was familiar to Steve. He often went up there to admire the view and refresh his spirits but today, looking over the Vale of York, he still felt depressed so drove on to the north of Wintringham and left the car to walk a little and stare out towards the North York Moors.

When he reached his usual viewing spot, he was disappointed. Overhead the feeble March sun had disappeared behind a mass of whitish cloud and the lack of colour from the sky made the moor a morose and brooding place. Steve looked in vain for the brilliant colours he remembered from previous visits, the splashes of purple, the vivid green of young bilberry plants. He also looked for signs of life, a family of rabbits, perhaps, or the heart-moving sight of a curlew or a hawk swinging through the sky. There was nothing.

Today, the moor was silent and empty and dressed for mourning in the russet browns of long-dead bracken and dark grey masses of outcrops of stone. Not even a moorjock was in sight, the hardy sheep that grazed the area.

Chilled, Steve retreated to the warmth and comfort of his car. He'd been an idiot to drive up here. What he needed was company and food. He realised he was hungry.

He drove back, but not to the empty house. He went into town, put the car into a car park and then walked until he came to one of the quaint streets which boasted a selection of restaurants and cafes for the use of the many summer visitors or locals requiring a quick and economical snack.

Steve headed towards the Copperfield Rooms, a family-run cafe he had frequented before. As he approached it, he was surprised to see Jill's mother push open the door and go inside. He hastened his step and followed her.

Evelyn Catley resembled Virginia Woolf when dressed in her everyday outdoor clothes. A flat pancake of a hat rested on her smoothly dressed hair, a brownish-green cape swirled around her lean figure and she wore sturdy, no-nonsense shoes. She looked, thought Steve, like a remnant from an earlier age.

He saw the young girl acting as waitress put her hand over her mouth to smother a grin as she watched Mrs Catley stand indecisively in the middle of the room, clutching an umbrella to her breast while searching for an unoccupied table. He understood the young woman's reaction but, for himself, he felt his spirits lighten. Evelyn Catley was a queer old stick but he liked her. Without a moment's hesitation, he went to stand by her side.

'Hello, this is a nice surprise. Shall we share a table? Look, there's one over there, in the alcove near the fireplace.'

She turned towards him. 'Oh, it's you, Stephen. Yes, that would be nice.' She gave him a vague, gentle smile and allowed him to escort her to the empty table. 'I thought at first there was nowhere to sit and I would have to leave. I was disappointed because they keep a wide range of teas here.'

She removed her pancake hat and gloves before sitting down. 'It's been some time since we spoke together. How are things? I hope your mother and sister are well?'

Of course, she knew nothing about the car crash. It was over a week since he had called for Jill at her home and then he had not seen her parents. He hadn't seen Jill herself for five days. She was visiting an old school friend of hers who had married and now lived in Coventry.

And she hadn't been in touch. No postcard, not even a phone call. A familiar feeling of frustration fluttered inside him. He nodded to the waitress, sat down and told Evelyn about his mother's mishap.

'Oh, Stephen. I'm so sorry.' She brushed away a wisp of mousy brown hair from her cheek. Her pale eyes looked concerned. 'But she's going to be all right?'

'Yes.' Steve waited until their order had been given and then continued, 'She hopes to be discharged from hospital tomorrow.'

'She must take it easy for a few days. She'll be suffering from shock.'

The waitress returned with their order. A pot of tea for two, a toasted teacake for Evelyn and a piled-up plate of sausages, beans, egg and chips for Stephen.

He picked up his knife and fork, plunged into the food

and decided he was feeling better. It was warm in the cafe, the food was good and his future mother-in-law was nice, if strange, company. And more importantly, Jill was due home on the seven o'clock train.

He swallowed half a sausage and thought about his fiancee, about her sweet mouth and the jokes they shared. He thought: Jill's so clear-cut about things. She'll help me get rid of my vague fears and fancies. He forgot that when he was actually with her, it was her assurance about everything that annoyed and irritated him.

'I'll pop round about eight, if that's all right?'

'Oh.' Evelyn paused in the act of milking her tea. She put down the milk jug and said carefully, 'Hasn't Jill been in touch with you?'

'No.'

'She won't be home just yet, Stephen. She rang this morning to say she was staying with Louise for another two days. I gather they've got tickets for a show.'

Rage swept through him, and he was disconcerted, knowing it was too intense a feeling for such a slight change of plan. He laid down his knife and fork and said, in a controlled voice, 'She never contacted me.'

Evelyn glanced at him curiously. 'Perhaps she couldn't get hold of you? You've been with your mother at the hospital. Jill probably rang the bank.'

'Yes, of course.' He felt a moment's shame. Maybe Jill was trying to contact him when he was driving around in a daze, being thoroughly wimpish and stupid. But he wasn't convinced. He'd been at work this morning, and surely if Jill rang her mother in the morning, she would have rung him at the same time? He sighed. The rage had dampened but it was still there.

He remembered their last date. It had started well enough, but by the end of the evening they were at their usual game, scoring points off each other, and had parted coldly, without a goodnight kiss. Jill was probably staying away to avoid seeing him.

He pushed his plate away, no longer hungry, and gulped down his tea.

'What's the matter, Stephen?'

He felt like bursting into tears. Evelyn was gazing at him with such a compassionate expression. He fought for composure, clasped his hands on the table in front of him and muttered: 'I don't know. That's the trouble.'

'Want to talk about it?' She poured out more tea. 'I'm a very discreet person.' She smiled faintly.

He shook his head. 'Thanks, but I don't think I can.'

'Why? Because it involves my daughter?' She took her gaze from his face and occupied herself with stirring her tea.

'Well, Jill's part of it, but it's more than that.' Steve struggled for the right words. 'I can't understand myself, so I don't think I could explain to anyone else what I'm feeling.'

'Oh, dear. You are in trouble.' Evelyn leaned over and lightly tapped his clenched fists with one long, slender finger. 'Well, let *me* tell you something. I like you, Stephen, I always have. When Jill first brought you to the house you must have been about fifteen, but I remember thinking, This young man has integrity. I was glad you were Jill's friend and I was delighted when you became engaged to my daughter. I thought, and I still think, that you would be good for her. Jill . . .' She paused. 'Jill is very much her father's daughter.'

'Oh, surely not?' Her remark roused Steve from his self-absorption.

Evelyn nodded. 'You won't see it, of course, not yet. But it is true.' She gazed around the cafe as if unwilling to meet his eyes. 'I realise you don't care for Terence, but he's not a bad man, Stephen, and he has kept his side of the bargain.'

She looked back at Steve and noted his puzzled expression. 'You must wonder why I married him?'

'Oh, no. I mean, it's not my business.'

She smiled and shook her head. 'Come now. You mustn't lie. Haven't I just said I believe in your integrity?'

'Well,' he blushed, 'you do seem very different from your husband.'

'Many couples are like that.' She saw his embarrassment and sought to dispel it. 'I'm not going to burden you with my family secrets, Stephen, but I should like to tell you a few things, because I think it has a bearing on how you're feeling now. Something's happened to you which has made a nonsense of everything you believed in previously, am I right?' She waited.

He stared at her. 'I suppose so.'

'Well,' she raised her shoulders in a shrug, 'it happens. It happened to me and it happens to most people during their lives, but it's how you *react*, that's what's important. Tell me, do you wish to break off your engagement to Jill?'

He gaped at her. 'Oh, no. At least . . .' He dropped his gaze and focused his eyes on the plateful of congealing food in front of him. 'Things aren't the same between us, but that's my fault. Jill hasn't changed.' He hesitated. 'I can't say any more.'

'Because she's my child?' An expression he couldn't read flickered over Evelyn's pale face. 'Don't worry. I'm quite impartial.'

She sighed. 'That's one of my worries, I'm always impartial. Still, I'm a good listener. Perhaps that's all you need. A good listener.'

He was tempted but he warned, 'I might shock you.'

She laughed. It was a light, girlish sound, surprising in view of the intensity of their conversation, but it had the effect of relaxing Steve. He even smiled when she said: 'I think I'd like to be shocked. My life is quite stultifying at times. It's my own fault, I know, but I . . .' She stopped, looked surprised at her own words, and then continued, 'But we're here to try and solve your problems today.' She sat back in her chair. 'Tell me.'

Slowly, agonisingly, he tried to explain. In a halting voice he spoke about his trip to London and his mixed emotions as he walked round the city. He spoke of his meeting with Liz and her conversation. He didn't say he had spent the night with her. He talked about the increasing tension between him and Jill and his general dissatisfaction with life in general. Finally, he mentioned his increasing anger and frustration.

During his outpourings, Evelyn never said a word. Her only movement was a shake of her head to discourage the waitress who approached their table to ask if they wanted anything further. When he finished speaking, Steve realised the cafe was less populated. Only one other table was occupied. All the shoppers were gone and dusk was pressing against the draped windows of the cafe.

He felt drained of emtion but more relaxed and was full of gratitude to Evelyn for listening to him. He glanced at her. What would she think?

She had turned away from him and was nodding to the waitress who was over by the till cashing up the day's takings. When the girl came over, Evelyn asked: 'What time do you close, my dear?'

'Not until six.' The waitress looked at Steve's untouched plate of food. 'Oh, dear. Was there something wrong?'

He shook his head.

'My companion recently suffered a tummy bug. When he started eating, he found he wasn't really hungry.' Evelyn smiled at the girl. 'If you're not closing, we'd love another pot of tea.'

The waitress nodded and went to fill their order and Evelyn looked and Steve and asked: 'Feel better now?'

'Yes, I do. It was good of you . . .'

She flapped her hand. 'But has it done any good? Have you a clearer idea why you're feeling so upset?'

He bit his lip. 'Not really. I've just changed, that's all.'

'Well, we must dig deeper then. It started with the trip to London, didn't it?'

'Yes, but honestly, I've taken up enough of your time.'

'I don't mind if you don't.'

She stared straight at him and he noticed her usually vague expression had completely disappeared. He remembered how sharply she had looked at him when he had commented on her tiger puzzle. Tigers! His thoughts jumped to Liz and he wondered how she was getting on with her life in India.

Evelyn was following her own thoughts. 'This girl you talked to, you say she was going to work in India on one of those Help the Third World schemes?'

'Yes.'

She frowned. 'Commendable, but surely you don't want to do anything like that?'

'No. But I'd like to be *like* Liz. She had a focus to her life.' Steve blushed. 'Does that sound pretentious?' Without waiting for a reply, he rushed on. 'You know, I never knew what a sheltered existence I led until I went to London. Everything has always been so neat and tidy.' He ran his fingers through his hair. 'I'm twenty-one and I can forecast exactly what my future holds. A job for life at the bank, marriage to Jill, a nice little house and then a couple of kids. It's not that I don't want those things, but it all sounds so *cosy*.'

'You slept with the girl in London, didn't you?'

A blush swept over his face but he answered honestly, 'Yes.'

'And you found her exciting, much more exciting than Jill.' It was a statement, not a question, and Evelyn's voice held a grim note.

Steve looked down at the tablecloth. 'It wasn't just that. To put it crudely, it wasn't just a quick lay.' His voice trembled. 'But, yes, it was exciting, and Liz and me, there was a bond between us. I don't suppose you believe me.' His voice trailed miserably away.

'Have you kept in touch?' Evelyn had not moved in her chair but it was as if she had physically and mentally removed herself from him.

'I warned you I might shock you.' In a frenzy of confusion, Steve gabbled out his words. 'I'm sorry, but you told me to tell the truth. And, no, I haven't written to Liz, although I want to. Like I said, it wasn't just sex with her, it was other things. She understood me.'

'And Jill doesn't.'

'No, not really. I tried once to explain my feelings but she looked at me as though I was mad.'

'What were you trying to tell her?' Evelyn had cupped her chin in her hands. She was watching him intently.

'In London . . .' He paused. 'There was a copper on the streets dealing with a prostitute. He looked younger than me. And by the station, there was an old man, a tramp, and I was too scared to go up to him and give him some money.' He made a face of disgust.

'And then, at St Hilary's, I met the "fat cats", totally absorbed in money deals, profit margins. They disgusted me.'

'Stephen, Stephen!' Evelyn Catley shook her head. 'I had no idea you were so naive. Surely you know the world we live in? I sympathise with your feelings, I really do, but you must learn to strike a balance. You mustn't see everything in black and white. Not all prostitutes walk the streets because they are hungry and not all bankers and businessmen are corrupt.'

'I know.' He flushed. 'I'm not a complete idiot, but it was the first time I've really looked around me and realised how much of life there is to know, to explore. And the one thing I do know is that I don't want to be a banker.' He frowned, struck by his own words. 'That's it! I'll get another job, maybe a job working with people.'

'For goodness' sake, calm down.' Evelyn raised her hands in the air. 'You're good at your job, you're doing well. What if you throw it all away and *don't* find the kind of job you want?' Seeing he wasn't listening to her, she raised her voice. 'At least go on the course in Lancaster. You worked so hard to get the place. And when you finish it, if you're still of the same mind, *then* consider the future.

'There are other people involved, you know.' She hesitated. 'What about your mother's hopes for you, and what about Jill?'

She saw the shadow of doubt in his eyes and, for the second time, leaned across and touched his hand. 'Poor Stephen, you've always considered other people, haven't you? That's why you're in such a turmoil now. I suppose it's something to do with your father dying when you were so young.' She patted his hand and then sat back.

'I'm not against your changing your life, if you feel that is what you must do. All I'm saying is, think very carefully. You'll have to carry the consequences forever.'

Her pale face flushed as she looked at him. 'When I was your age, I too was uncertain as to which way to go. I had two choices. I was clever and had a chance to go and work for a firm of accountants based in Chester, or I could marry a successful businessman whose aim was to become even more wealthy.'

She saw Steve look up questioningly and nodded. 'Terence wasn't in love with me but he had decided it was time to marry. He wanted a child, preferably a son. He had no time for courting a girl but he already knew me and felt I could help him with the business. I didn't know what to do. I didn't love Terence but he was, as my parents kept reminding me, a "catch". They also pointed out that I was a plain young woman. It might be my last chance to get a man.'

Evelyn shook her head when Steve opened his mouth to voice a lame denial. 'There's no need to lie, Stephen. I was, and am, a plain woman. I can't say the fact has ever bothered me.' She sighed. 'And so, I let my loving parents persuade me.

'They *were* loving, you know. They knew how hard life could be. And I have not been desperately unhappy. But there are times . . .' She turned and looked out of the cafe window. 'When I wonder what my life would have been if I had refused to listen to my parents, if I had been brave enough to take myself off to Chester.'

'If you had followed the tiger.'

'What?'

'The tiger in the jigsaw you were working on before Christmas.'

She shook her head. 'I'm sorry?'

'You must remember.' Steve had forgotten to be embarrassed. His voice was sharp, so important was it to him that she should understand. 'There was a jungle scene and I spotted an animal in the background, one you couldn't really see, and I mentioned it and you quoted some poetry.'

'I remember. It was the William Blake poem.' She looked at him with increased respect and said slowly, 'Yes, I think I see what you're getting at.' She screwed up her face. 'There's a Latin or Greek tag which translates as "Seize the moment". Is that what you mean?'

He nodded. 'Something like that. Liz,' he hesitated looking at Evelyn apologetically, 'the girl in London, she reminded me of that tiger.'

'She sounds a remarkable young woman.' Evelyn's voice was dry but not unfriendly. 'Quite different from Jill, I imagine?'

'She's not so pretty as Jill.'

'Yes, Jill is pretty, and she's poised and well-balanced and she knows what she wants from life.' Evelyn sighed and looked at her watch. 'Now I really must go.'

'Of course.' Steve sprang to his feet. 'I'm sorry I kept you so long.'

'I didn't mind a bit.' Evelyn approached the cash till and, ignoring Steve's protests, paid the bill. 'But you could run me home, please. It will save me walking to the taxi rank.'

In the car, they were quiet. But as they approached the Catley house, Evelyn stirred. She bent and retrieved her umbrella from the floor near her feet and asked, 'Have you told Jill any of this? Not about Liz, of course, but about your confusion over the future?'

'No, but I think I ought to.'

'Yes, that would be wise. You may find she's more sympathetic than you expect.'

'I hope so.' Steve swung the car round into the Catley drive. 'We've been together such a long time. Surely she'll understand?'

'I hope she does.' Evelyn climbed out and bent her head to say farewell. 'Thank you for trusting me, Stephen.'

He smiled up at her. 'No, I must thank you. I feel much happier now. Will you ask Jill to ring me as soon as she gets home?'

'Of course.' Evelyn seemed to want to say something else. She rested her gloved hand on the open door. 'If Jill doesn't see things your way, you mustn't feel too guilty. Some people go through periods of change, others stay the same. It's a fact of life.'

'I know that, but Jill and I have a good understanding. We'll sort this thing out.'

He smiled at her and then closed the door and turned the car round, out on to the road.

Evelyn Catley stood and watched him out of sight.

Chapter Nineteen

When Steve slammed down the phone, Paula stood for a moment and wondered what on earth was the matter with her brother. What was it he had said, something about Mum being in hospital? Her brow wrinkled and then her heart began to race. Had there been an accident? Had her mother suddenly become ill? And why was Steve so mad? And how was *she* supposed to know what had happened at home?

Shakily, she dialled her home telephone number and waited. There was no reply. Where had Steve been ringing from? Maybe he was at the bank but perhaps he was at the hospital? Oh, God, she didn't know either number. She swallowed hard, then dialled again. As she listened to the tone, a succession of lurid pictures flashed through her mind: Mum, lying in the road after being knocked down by a car or gasping with the pain of a heart attack. The knuckles of her hand whitened as she gripped the phone fiercely. Why didn't someone answer, and why did Steve assume she knew what had happened? She jumped when a voice said: 'Directory Enquiries. What town, please?'

She told them.

With brisk anonymity the voice said: 'One moment, please.'

A couple of minutes later she was connected to the

hospital and talking to the desk receptionist.

'Rosemary Scott? Yes, she's in Mountbatten Ward. Hold on, I'll put you though.'

The Ward Sister took the call. She listened to Paula's breathless enquiry and replied: 'Mrs Scott? She's coming along nicely. Might be discharged tomorrow, but we won't know for certain until after the doctor's rounds. What? Oh, I see . . . you've only just heard? Well, your mother was involved in a car accident. Fortunately, the gentleman driving the car in which your mother was travelling reacted quickly in a nasty situation. He managed to avoid an out-and-out crash with the car in front, but in doing so his own car skidded off the road and ended upside down.

'Mr Goodman, the driver, suffered minor cuts and bruises but Mrs Scott was knocked unconscious. The doctor who saw her decided she should stay in hospital for observation. She's feeling much better now. Whiplash injuries to her neck and still suffering from mild concussion, but she's going to be fine.

'No, sorry – you can't speak to her right now. She's down in the physiotherapy department. Yes, of course I'll give her your love. You'll ring again in the morning? I'll tell her.'

After hearing the news Paula felt better but still shaky. She made herself a cup of coffee, spilling milk on the work surface, and then sat down to drink it. Holding her hands round the cup for warmth, she thanked heaven she was on her own in the flat. Dave was at work and Alison out for a couple of hours with Tracey and her baby.

Her former flatmate Tracey Woodall, now Tracey Brewins, had re-entered Paula's life by accident. They had bumped into each other in a shopping mall and had brought their lives up to date over afternoon tea in one of the many cafes.

Tracey, Paula learned, had changed not only her name but her entire way of life. No more wild nights drinking pints for Tracey, she had better things to do. Two years ago she had married a man ten years older than herself. His name was George and he was a gas fitter, and the baby in the pushchair was her nine-month-old son, Bradley.

'We've got a house over Ancoats way, Paula. It's great. It has three bedrooms and a garden and everything. George's aunt lived there but she was getting on a bit and wanted to move into a flat so she let us have it cheap.'

Tracey had sighed. 'It's still a job keeping up with the mortgage payments. I was going to keep working, see, but this little monster came along.' She smiled and nodded at the sleeping baby. 'Anyway, I don't suppose I could land another job which would pay enough for a childminder. I've no skills.'

She paused. 'Remember how I said you were daft, starting night school when you shared with me? You were right all along. I'd love to be able to earn some cash but I can't. And here you are. You've got your little lass and you're temping at glamorous places like advertising agencies.'

'They're not all glamorous places, Tracey. I work damned hard.'

'Yeah, I suppose so.' She bent over the pushchair and straightened the sleeping Bradley's hat. 'And I'd have to leave him, wouldn't I? I don't fancy that. Still, there's times you get fed up of being stuck at home all day with no company.'

Paula changed the subject. She asked about Tracey's husband.

'He's a nice chap. Funny, I only started going out with George because he asked me when I had no one else in view. I thought I'd dump him when someone more glamorous turned up but he kind of grew on me.' Tracey laughed and popped a piece of toasted teacake in her mouth.

'He's a good worker and he thinks the world of Bradley. Not much in the looks department. He's going a bit thin on top, but he'll do for me.' She wiped a crumb off the side of her mouth. 'I guess I'm lucky.'

Paula nodded. Seeing the contentment on Tracey's plump face, she thought: Yes, you are lucky.

Before they parted company, the two young women exchanged telephone numbers.

'I could come over and see you one day when you're not working. We've a car. It's an old banger, but it goes all right.'

'I'd like that, Tracey, but give me a call first, won't you? I often take on work at short notice,' warned Paula.

Since that first, accidental meeting, Tracey had visited Paula twice and both women had enjoyed renewing their acquaintanceship. Both were now mothers and both were short of friends. Tracey had few youthful neighbours and Dave's increasing jealousy had caused Paula to drop the few friends she had made.

Tracey's buoyant personality cheered Paula up and made her more optimistic about her marriage. Hearing Tracey humorously recount a blazing row with George, who apparently had a quick temper, made Paula feel she was not the only one to encounter marital problems. However, if George had a quick temper, it seemed he was also quick to make up.

'He went out and bought me a pound box of chocolates when he cooled down, the devil.' Tracey dimpled. 'And he knows I'm trying to lose weight. But he says he likes having a good armful to cuddle.'

'What's an armful, Mummy?' Alison looked up from playing with Bradley. She was charmed by the little boy.

'Nothing, darling. Why don't you build Bradley a tower with your bricks?'

Alison obliged but Bradley was not in a co-operative mood. He picked up a brick, threw it across the room and howled.

'He's got a tooth coming.' Tracey had scooped up her son and tossed him up and down in her arms. 'We'll not be able to talk when he's in this mood, Paula. Tell you what, I've his stroller in the back of the car, I'll take the kids out for an hour, shall I? We'll go to the park for a bit and you can have a bit of peace.' She had given Paula a shrewd look. 'Have you been working a lot this week? You look whacked.'

'I've have been busy.' Paula omitted to reveal the true cause of her fatigue, the tension of wondering how Dave would behave from one hour to the next. 'It would be nice to have an hour on my own, Tracey. Are you sure?'

'Yep.' She had bundled the children into their coats and taken them off and shortly after they had left the flat, Steve had phoned.

Paula tried to remember his exact words but they escaped her. However, she remembered the bitterness in his voice and how definite he had been that she already knew what had happened. She was washing up her coffee cup when the truth struck her. Steve must have rung up and spoken to Dave, and Dave hadn't told her.

With careful hands she set the cup on the draining board. The simple explantion was that Dave had forgotten to tell her, but she didn't believe it. He wouldn't have forgotten such an important message. Eyes wide and blank, she stared into space. Dave had promised her he would never strike her again and he had kept his promise, but what was happening to their marriage now was almost as bad as the violence.

She was trying to live with his jealousy, but if it had come to the point where he deliberately kept the news of her mother's accident secret from her, to keep her at home, then something must be done. He must have some kind of treatment to sort himself out.

She thought about his enormous mood swings. One moment he would be tender with her and playful with Alison, the next minute he would become totally uncommunicative or shake with anger. He was always asking Paula who had telephoned her during the day and what post had been delivered.

His worst times were when she worked, he was better when she was home all day, but she had to work, not only for the money which they needed, but also to preserve her sanity. Nowadays, when she was on her own for very long, she became as jumpy as a kitten. That's why Tracey's visits had been such a Godsend, and now she kept things from him, innocent things, because she was never sure how he would react.

On the day she had bumped into Tracey, Dave had breezed in from work with a smile and a posy of flowers for her.

'Here you are, love. I know you like freesias.'

'Oh, they're lovely.' She had buried her face in the delicate blossoms, breathing in their perfume. 'Thank you.'

'It's a pleasure.' His green eyes were sparkling. 'Now, do I deserve a kiss?'

She had kissed him with fevour and they had ended up making love in the bathroom whilst Alison watched the children's programmes on TV. Then they had eaten and all was sweet normality until Paula had mentioned her meeting with Tracey.

'Tracey? That slut you shared with when we first met?'

Paula's heart sank. 'She wasn't a slut, Dave. She was untidy but . . .'

'She was. I remember you telling me you were always cleaning up after her and she was often drunk and argumentative.' He scowled. 'Why didn't you walk straight past her?'

'She wasn't all bad. She was fun sometimes, and good-hearted. Anyway, she's changed. She's married and has a little boy.'

'Sluts don't change.' Dave shouted the words. 'I'm surprised at you, Paula. I thought you were trying for a better sort of lifestyle. After all,' his lips thinned, 'my friends aren't considered good enough for you and yet you take up with a bitch like her?'

'She was never a bitch. She was generous enough to let me share with her when I came to Manchester . . .' Paula's voice trailed off when she saw Dave wasn't listening to her. He was on his feet now and there was a light in his eyes she dreaded to see. It was if he welcomed his rage with gratitude, she thought, as though giving vent to it eased his inner tension. She flinched as he swept his plate of food on to the floor.

'Well, don't see her again, do you hear? She's a bad influence and I don't want her near my daughter. Anyway, suppose you were with her and you happened to bump into some of your more *cultured* friends, you'd be in a fix then, wouldn't you?' His voice held a sneer.

She tried to block out the remainder of his tirade, which consisted of arrogant complaints and childish whining, and looked towards Alison. Her daughter had stopped eating. Her head was bent, her baby fine hair hung across her cheek. Paula couldn't see her face. She stood up and lifted Alison from her chair and carried her into the kitchen.

'Don't walk away when I'm talking to you.'

She stopped by the door. 'I'm going to give Alison her bath. It's getting late.'

She put Alison to bed, reading her two extra bedtime stories, and then she went straight to bed herself and lay flat and rigid as her thoughts circled relentlessly, like the Big Wheel at a fairground. How could he change so rapidly? Where was the man she had fallen in love with?

She remembered how loving he had been when he came home and when the tears came into her eyes, she forced them back. She heard sounds of water running and the clash of dishes. He was washing up. She gave a bitter smile. He would never apologise, but he would try and make amends by doing little jobs like that. Well, it wasn't enough.

Later, she heard the drone of the television set. About eleven o'clock he came into the bedroom and undressed. The mattress dipped and swayed as he slipped between the sheets. He whispered her name and she pretended to be asleep. He sighed and turned over and they lay back to back. She knew he lay awake for a long time and she knew, when his breathing deepened, when he finally slept. She wished she could sleep. She huddled beneath the double quilt and found the urge to cry had left her. Instead, she began to think.

There came a time, she thought, when you had to stop loving someone, otherwise you would be destroyed. She knew that for her, that time had come. She was too tired to think of a future without Dave but her newly found knowledge brought her some kind of relief. Her heavy eyes closed. Her last thought before sleeping was that Dave didn't know Tracey's address.

Two days after her release from hospital, Mark called on Rosie. She opened the door in answer to his ring and, at the look on her face, he laughed.

'Oh dear, do I look so terrible?'

She blushed. 'You look fine. It's me that's the wreck.'

He studied her face. 'You're pale and you look tired, but otherwise, you look fine. But if you're not up to having visitors yet, I'll come back in a couple of days.'

'Oh, don't go.' She put out her hand. 'It's lovely to see you, Mark. Please, come in.' She stepped back to allow him to enter.

He followed her as she led the way into the kitchen. 'I guess,' he remarked humorously, 'that neither of us would win a beauty contest right now.'

She turned her head, with some difficulty, and looked back at him. 'Apart from the plaster on your forehead, you look fine. No one would ever know you'd been involved in a car accident, but as for me . . .' She touched the neck collar around her throat, a self-conscious gesture. 'Wearing this thing, I imagine I resemble something out of a Frankenstein film?'

'Rubbish.' Mark shook his head. They were in the kitchen now and he glanced around, still talking. 'But even if that was true, Rosie, does it matter? Neither of us was seriously injured. Surely that's what counts?'

'You're right.' Rosie's face became serious. 'And our survival was due to you. I've not thanked you yet, have I?'

She saw from the frown gathering on his face that he wanted no thanks and so immediately adopted a lighter tone of voice. 'Don't mind sitting in the kitchen, I hope? The heating's not on, you see, and it's warm in here.'

She crossed to the oven and opened the door to check the contents. 'Also, I'm baking – a couple of apple pies.'

'You should be resting, not baking.' But Mark sniffed the air appreciatively. 'Lord, what a wonderful smell. I can't remember when I last smelled home baking; probably when I was about nine or ten and staying with my grandma.'

'Then you must stay and sample a slice. The pies are almost ready and I've a carton of cream in the fridge.'

'Apple pie *and* cream. My God! My mouth's watering already.'

She laughed. 'Sit down. Make yourself comfortable.'

He did so, and looked round the room. 'You've a nice big kitchen.'

'Yes, but it badly needs decorating.' Rosie carried the pastry board and rolling pin to the sink and turned on the hot tap. 'The whole house could do with a lick of paint but I never seem to get round to it.'

'I'm a dab hand at papering. Would you like me to give you a hand?'

Rosie paused, dishcloth in hand. 'That's good of you but,' she studied the bubbles in the sink rather than look at him, 'do you think that would be wise?'

He look perplexed. 'I don't know what you mean.'

'Well,' she scrubbed at the pastry board with unnecessary vigour, 'you already give me lifts into town and you know how people talk.'

His brow cleared and he laughed. 'Oh, I see. You think *people*, meaning the staff at Woldview, might put two and two together and come up with the figure five?'

She bent her head so he couldn't see her face. 'People like to gossip.'

'I know. I enjoy a good gossip, myself.' Mark stretched his long legs and and surveyed the tip of his boots. 'If it worries you, I can sneak the decorating stuff into the boot of my car after dark,' he grinned, 'and don a disguise when I visit your house.'

She turned towards him, grabbing a dishcloth and drying her hands. The colour had flared into her face. 'That's not funny.'

His face sobered. 'I'm sorry, Rosie. I'm a bit of a clown at times. Of course, you're right.' He was silent for a moment and then he said, 'What about that son of yours?'

'Steve keeps promising to give me a hand but he's especially busy at the moment, and he'll be working away in a couple of weeks' time.' Glad to change the subject, Rosie left the sink and began to wash down the kitchen table. 'The house will be quiet without him.' She sighed. 'I shall miss him.'

'Yes.' Mark's voice was quiet. 'It's always difficult, learning how to live on your own.'

'Oh, dear. I'm sorry, I should have thought.' Rosie's eyes widened.

'Thought what?' He looked at her, his expression enigmatic.

'Nothing, nothing at all.' Feverishly, she rubbed away at a stubborn segment of uncooked pastry. Conscious of the flush on her face, she murmured, 'I'm not used to people watching me work.'

His eyes did not blink. He said, 'You know about the crash, the other crash, don't you?'

She straightened up and faced him. 'Yes. I wasn't prying or anything, but . . .'

'Who told you?'

'Karen Horton.' Dropping the dishcloth, Rosie clasped her hands together. 'She came to see me in the hospital. I said I was worried about you.' Her voice faltered. 'I couldn't understand why you were *so* upset. You were in a terrible state at the hospital, and yet you knew neither of us was badly hurt. And you seemed to blame yourself for what happened which was ridiculous because you did all the right things.'

She paused. 'You even saved the life of that stupid man in the car in front of us. He could easily have been killed.

We were so close.' Her voice dwindled into silence.

Mark closed his eyes and then opened them again. His tense body relaxed. 'Yes, I suppose I did over-react after the accident. It brought it all back to me, you see.'

'I'm sorry.' Rosie sounded subdued. 'I didn't mean to revive bad memories. Karen will never mention the subject again, I'm sure.'

'Who told her?'

'A man at Head Office. One of the team who interviewed you.'

'I see.' Mark passed his hand over his chin and said tersely, 'So much for confidentiality.'

Rosie shook her head vigorously. 'Karen's good at keeping secrets, but she knew I was worrying. She realised how I felt about you so she told me *why* you were so upset.'

Realising she had given herself away, she gasped and swung round, presenting her back to him. Her face burned with embarrassment.

She heard his chair creak as he got up and then felt his hands rest lightly upon her shoulders. When she turned round again, she saw he was smiling.

'You don't look pale now, Rosie.'

She ducked her head. 'You don't *mind* me knowing, about the accident?'

His smile faded. 'No, not really. It was so long ago.' He paused. 'It's difficult to explain. I was so *angry* after the crash, Rosie. Looking back, I think I hung on to my anger because it choked down the pain and the sorrow. And that's why I kept on the move, I suppose. I was running away. I couldn't face what had happened.' He bowed his head. 'I'd known Jenny for ever. She was my friend as well as my wife and we'd been looking forward to the baby.'

He was silent and Rosie was silent, too. There was nothing she could say.

After a few seconds, Mark raised his head and attempted a smile but Rosie saw the shadow of sadness on his features. She put her hand on his arm and blurted out: 'Please, you don't have to tell me.'

'I want to.' He surprised her by leaning forward and dropping a swift kiss on her forehead. 'I want you to know that I eventually faced up to my loss and accepted it. I started living again, if you like. And then, a few more months down the line, I realised I wasn't the only person in the world who had suffered, and that, in some ways, I had actually been lucky.'

He saw her look of incomprehension and sighed. 'Jenny and I, we were so happy together. She was a crazy lady.' He shook his head. 'We did some wild things. Of course, we were very young.'

A brief smile came and went from his face. 'But I'm middle-aged now, Rosie. I think about the girl who died and the boy who grieved and I can cope with it. It's as if it happened to a different person.'

Rosie was still holding his arm. She gave it a little squeeze. Relief was unfurling inside her like a young leaf. Mark was no longer bound by the tragedy in his past and was confiding in her in a way which made her realise he trusted her completely. She wanted to tell him she was honoured by his confidences, but his thoughts had moved on.

'When that car in front of us skidded . . .' She felt the shiver that ran through him. 'I was petrified. It's happening again, I thought. And my reactions seemed so slow, and when the car went over and I saw you were unconscious, white and so still, I freaked out. Even at the hospital, when the doctor said you'd be all right, I didn't believe him. I'm jinxed, I thought. Something happens to everyone I care for. Oh, Rosie.' He closed his eyes. 'I couldn't bear the thought of you dying, too.'

She had no words. She simply raised her arms, put them around his neck and held him close. Her heart exulted.

She felt his body relax. His shoulders slumped and he rested his lips against her forehead.

After a long pause, he murmured, 'I did hear aright? That bit when you were talking to Karen – you said something about caring for me?'

'Yes.' She spoke softly.

'Well then.' He put his arms around her waist. 'You won't object if I kiss you?'

She turned her face upwards.

His lips were soft and his kiss gentle, but Rosie still felt her blood begin to race through her body. It had been so long, so long since a man had held her, so long since she had been desired and felt desire. The realisation that Mark wanted her filled her with joy, but then, when he pressed her closer to his body, her joy became tempered with anxiety.

He was so attractive. He had travelled widely. Surely he must have had love affairs with women much more attractive than she was. Her body tensed. Since Howard's death, she had been celibate and now she was no longer young. She had stretch marks, for God's sake. Should she pull back while she still had the chance?

She tried to imagine herself in bed, making love with Mark. She had thought about it before and enjoyed the thought but now the dream was becoming reality, her heart sank. It wouldn't work. She knew no tricks to tantalise and charm him. She was a middle-aged widow and his employee. It was ridiculous. What in God's name was she thinking of?

He must have felt her change of mood for he stopped kissing her. He moved away from her and studied her face.

'I'm sorry. Was I going too fast for you?'

She shook her head, blinking back tears.

'I don't want to frighten you off, Rosie. I know how much you loved your husband and I gather you've not done any serious dating since his death. If you'd rather, we'll keep our friendship platonic?'

'Oh, no.' She spoke rashly. 'I don't want that, it's just . . .' She couldn't explain. She wrinkled her brow in frustration and then suddenly, she realised she could smell burning.

'Oh, no.' She hurried towards the cooker and flung open the door. A cloud of smoke billowed out. She coughed.

'I'll see to them.' Mark had picked up the oven gloves. He hurried to her side and slid out the oven tray. The pastry tops of the pies were deep brown and the edges were singed black; the bubbling apple purée had overflowed and was spreading over the oven tray. Carefully, Mark placed the tray on the top of the cooker.

Rosie looked at them. 'They're ruined,' she said, her voice flat.

'No. They're a bit singed round the edges but they should be OK.' He threw the oven gloves over the back of a kitchen chair. 'Bit like us, really.'

Absurdly, tears stung her eyes. 'I wanted you to kiss me, Mark, but . . .' Her voice trailed into silence.

He came and put his arm around her. 'It's nothing to get upset about, Rosie. Actually our relationship has moved on quite a bit during the last quarter of an hour. Let's leave it at that for the moment.' He raised his head and sniffed the air. 'You know, those pies still smell good.'

'They're burnt. I'll have to throw them away.'

'Nonsense.' He stopped her moving away from him. 'If

we cut off the burned bits, they'll be fine. I'll do that and you get the cream out of the fridge. I'll not allow you to throw away something so good.'

He smiled at her.

She saw the familiar crinkles appear at the corners of his eyes and smiled back and went to do his bidding.

Chapter Twenty

In April, Steve went away to Lancaster, and Rosie found to her surprise that she hardly noticed his absence. There were pockets of strangeness, of course. In the morning when she woke, the absolute silence reminded her she was alone in the house, and when she dressed and went downstairs the continuing tidiness of her surroundings was a constant surprise. There were other small shocks, such as when she lifted the lid of the laundry basket and saw how few dirty clothes it contained and in the kitchen there was more space on the shelves.

Rosie smiled, remembering how often she had nagged Steve to throw away empty jars and food containers.

'How am I supposed to know when to buy more cornflakes when you keep putting the empty packet back in the cupboard?'

'Sorry, Mum.'

Steve would grin apologetically, but he never did get into the habit of throwing away discarded packaging.

She had been so apprehensive about his leaving. She would miss him so much and she had never, in her whole life, lived on her own. But now that she was the only occupant of the house, she found she was enjoying herself.

Sometimes, when she felt lazy, she would get up at her usual time, make toast and a pot of tea, set a tray and go back to bed to eat her breakfast and read the morning newspaper. She felt deliciously wicked on those mornings.

But she missed Steve, of course. She missed his affectionate banter, his occasional bear-hug and the way he would offer to run her to the shops. She even missed the sound of his music blaring out from his bedroom, but she remembered that the week before he had left home, there had been none of those things.

He had barely said two words to her. She had seen him in the morning and briefly at meal times. When he came home after leaving work he had gone straight to his bedroom and stayed there. She told herself it was natural. His life was about to change and he was nervous about going to Lancaster but she knew it was more than that. At last, she had plucked up courage, tapped on his bedroom door, gone in and asked him what was wrong.

He had flared up at her.

'Christ, Mum, will you leave me alone? I'm quiet. So what? Why must you always assume something is wrong? I'm studying, that's all.' He had gestured to the books lying on the floor beside his bed.

Rosie had muttered a lame apology and retreated, but she didn't believe Steve was studying. She had been into his room on a couple of occasions during the past seven days. She had changed his bed and hoovered and dusted and in doing so, she had noticed the page numbers in the open books never varied. He wasn't studying. And what was happening between Steve and his fiancee? Why did Jill never call at the house any more?

She had thought of ringing Jill. Once Steve had gone, she would ask the girl to meet her, she thought. Perhaps Jill could enlighten her as to what was troubling her son.

She had mentioned the idea to Mark but he had been dubious.

'Ring her by all means, Rosie, but don't start trying to pump her about Steve.'

'I wouldn't do that . . .' At his sceptical expression, she fell silent.

'You wouldn't be able to stop yourself, my dear.'

Mark had poured a little more wine into her glass. He had taken her out to dinner to celebrate the news that she could now abandon the detested neck collar and return to work.

'Whatever's bothering Steve, it's *his* problem, not yours, and he must sort it out. The only thing you can do is listen to him, if and when he decides to talk to you about it.'

She had frowned. 'But I'm his mother.'

'Yes. And Steve is no longer a child.' Mark replenished his own glass. 'Leave him to fight his own battles, Rosie.' He glanced at her unresponsive face. 'Forgive me for saying this, but it's my impression that too many mothers unknowingly foster a love-dependency relationship with their male children.'

'And what do you know about it?' Rosie scowled.

He shrugged his shoulders. 'Just my opinion.' He twisted the stem of his wine glass. 'Having had no family of my own, I suppose I shouldn't be offering my opinion, but you did ask for my advice.'

He was silent but when he saw that Rosie was disinclined to fill the silence, he went on: 'My mother never had the chance to "smother-love" me because we were so strapped for cash. She went out to work when I was a baby and my grandmother looked after me. Gran was a strong believer in fostering independence from an early age.'

He grinned. 'She was tough at times but she was a great lady.' He gave Rosie a sly look.

'Funny thing though, the relationship between a mother and her daughter appears to be quite different.' He reached out and touched Rosie's hand. 'Would you be worrying so much if it were Paula who was being so secretive and moody?'

Rosie sighed and rubbed her forehead and then she looked across at him, shaking her head.

'Paula's been secretive and awkward for years and of course I worry about her. I've spent many sleepless nights worrying about her but deep down, I know she's strong. Whatever happens Paula will cope.'

'And Steve's not strong?'

Rosie was momentarily flustered. 'Well, of course he is. At least, he will be, in time. He's younger than Paula, you know, and he's always lived at home.' Her voice faltered as she saw Mark's ironic expression. She looked down at her plate. 'All right, I take your point. Perhaps I'm being foolish.' She raised her head. 'I'll stop worrying.'

Mark regarded her, smilingly. 'Rosie, you'll always worry; you're that kind of person. You worry about your children, your mother and lots of other things. You love whole-heartedly but you take on too many responsibilties. You must allow your loved ones to make mistakes and then to put things right themselves.'

Rosie looked shocked. 'Some people need my help, Mark. My mother, for instance. I have to care for her.'

'To a certain extent.' He nodded. 'But from what you've told me about her, she still very capable in most respects.'

When she didn't answer him, he went on. 'And I know you worry about what the people at Woldview will think, when they find out we're seeing each other.'

Rosie sat up straight in her chair. 'I don't worry about that.'

'Of course you do.' He picked up his knife and fork and cut into his steak. 'Anyway, let's stop talking and eat, otherwise the meal will get cold.'

Rosie took her fork and prodded at her seafood salad. That wouldn't get cold, she thought resentfully. She was sticking to her low-calorie food. She had lost almost a stone in weight and was aiming to lose another eight pounds before the summer holidays.

She glanced across at Mark and felt a stab of antagonism. How come he knew such a lot about family life? He had never raised a family. But what really annoyed her was that he was right in saying she was worried about the risk of gossip at work. She stabbed at a piece of crabmeat and, putting it in her mouth, chewed gloomily.

She had never anticipated being a subject of gossip. And if it should start, it would be so unfair, because nothing had ever happened between Mark and herself. Since that day in her kitchen, when he had kissed her and she had reacted so stupidly, he had not touched her. Rosie swallowed the crabmeat and worked her way through a pile of prawns, cursing her stupid diffidence.

She wished she could relive that moment when Mark held her in his arms. Oh, she would behave so differently! But you didn't get second chances. And now even their friendship seemed threatened because he had begun to find flaws in her. He disapproved of her worrying nature. He disapproved of the way she had brought up her children.

She looked across the table at him, not realising her eyes held the hurt of a young child, and said in a small voice: 'Honestly, Mark, I don't worry about the staff. After all, there's nothing for them to gossip about.'

He smiled and put down his knife and fork. 'No, there isn't. But one day there might be.'

Two days after their conversation in the restaurant, Rosie boarded the bus for her first day back at work since the car accident. She felt apprehensive about returning. How much did her workmates know about the developing friendship between Mark and herself? How much did they surmise?

The heating system on the bus must have broken down. It was cold. She shivered, turned up the collar of her coat and thrust her gloved hands into her pockets. She tried to cheer herself up by remembering Mark's words to her in the restaurant after they had spoken about possible gossip.

'No, there isn't. But one day there might be.'

That must mean he was still interested in becoming more than friendly? The trouble was, she couldn't understand why he was attracted to her. But he was, he must be!

During her two weeks' sick leave, he had been a constant visitor to her house. He had taken her to the cinema one evening, they had spent a day visiting York, and finally they had gone to the restaurant where they had discussed Steve.

Rosie huddled further into her capacious coat. How she enjoyed being with him. Even the rare flashes of temper he aroused in her, exhilarated as well as alarmed her. For years her life had been a matter of duty and routine. Now she was feeling alive and involved in life again. *Her* life, not that of her children or Minna.

And it wasn't purely physical attraction, although that was the over-riding sensation she felt. She enjoyed Mark's company. She liked his sense of humour, the original things he occasionally came up with and his outlook on life. She felt she was becoming a more complete person by being with him.

Trying to be honest, she admitted it was because of Mark that she did not miss Steve's company. After years of being the children's mother and Minna's daughter it was wonderful being Rosie Scott. And the fact that Mark cared something for her was a terrific morale boost.

Sometimes, during the night, she worried as to what he saw in her. She was so ordinary. But as the days went by and he continued to seek her out, her fears subsided. His feelings for her must be genuine because it wasn't as if he was just using her for casual sex. That had not happened, not yet. She hugged that thought to her and began to feel warmer. When the bus halted at her stop she got off feeling suddenly, unaccountably, marvellously optimistic.

Mrs Cooke was the first member of staff to see her. She stared at her grimly. 'Nice to see you back, Mrs Scott. Hope you're fully recovered?'

'Yes, thanks. I . . .'

But Mrs Cooke's question was purely rhetorical. She interrupted Rosie, eager to impart the latest news.

'I suppose you've heard?' She stared at Rosie with gimlet eyes. 'Mr Goodman will have told you, no doubt. I hear you have become quite friendly with him, which I must say I find surprising.'

Rosie's mouth went dry. 'Mr Goodman was very good to me after I was released from hospital following the car crash.'

'Yes, well. That's understandable. He was driving the car, wasn't he?'

Rosie opened her mouth to defend Mark but Mrs Cooke brought the conversation round to her original line. 'You're a good care assistant, Mrs Scott. Surely you don't condone Mr Goodman's latest strange idea?'

'I'm sorry?' Rosie frowned. 'I don't know what you're talking about, Mrs Cooke.'

'He hasn't told you?' Her thin lips almost disappeared. 'Well, I don't intend talking about such goings on. Let someone else enlighten you. All I will say is that this place has deteriorated since *he* came. Mrs Webster would never have allowed such scandalous behaviour.'

Mrs Cooke turned and marched off, which was fortunate because she missed the tide of colour which swept over Rosie's face.

But she was perplexed. Mrs Cooke was obviously not referring to her friendship with Mark, so what was she ranting on about?

Once her complexion returned to normal, Rosie went in search of Barbara and clarification. The reception clerk listened to Rosie and then laughed delightedly. 'Didn't Mr Goodman tell you about it?' She looked at Rosie beneath lowered eyelashes. 'I gather he visited you regularly.'

She felt her spirits lighten. Barbara, at least, was not disapproving.

'No. Whenever I mentioned Woldview, he said everything was fine. So why *is* Mrs Cooke so upset?'

Barbara dimpled. 'Mr Goodman put Carrie Delmar and Maurice Thorne in a double room.'

Rosie considered. 'You mean . . .?'

'Yup.' The receptionist nodded her head vigorously. 'Two-thirds of the staff think it's a jolly good idea and one-third thinks it's disgusting.'

Rosie began to laugh. 'Oh dear.' A feeling of warmth and love for Mark flowered inside her. 'How like him.'

Carrie Delmar had moved into Woldview three months previously. She was a dainty little woman of seventy-nine years with snow white hair and cornflower blue eyes. She had struck up an immediate friendship with Maurice Thorne, a tall, thin, courteous gentleman who was eighty-one years old.

The staff had watched, and generally approved the courtship that followed. At least once a week Mr Thorne would take a taxi into town and return with a gift for Carrie, flowers or a book or magazine.

She would accept his gift with gracious good manners and then read to him, his sight was poor, or play draughts with him, and when the weather was fine they would stroll in the garden. They were always together.

As the weeks went by, the two old people became virtually inseparable and it was remarked how good they were for each other. Mr Thorne's spare figure straightened up and Mrs Delmar's already beautiful complexion flowered like that of a bride.

'Mr Thorne went to see Mr Goodman a couple of days after you'd had the crash,' Barbara told Rosie.

'I gather he said he and Carrie had no desire to marry because they both have children and it might cause difficuties with regard to their estates after they died, but they were desperate to be together, like a married couple.'

She giggled. 'Mr Goodman didn't tell me, but I was in the next room filing some papers and I could hear every word said. It was so sweet. Mr Thorne said he and Carrie wanted to be proper sweethearts and could Mr Goodman help them?'

She lowered her voice. 'Mr Goodman was lovely. He said he would be honoured to help and two days later he arranged for them to move into a vacant double room on the second floor. Oh, you should have seen them, Rosie. They were so excited. They decided which of their pieces of furniture to keep and Mr Goodman sent the things they didn't want to the saleroom for them.

'But when it got out a few members of staff thought the whole idea outrageous. Mrs Cooke got her head together with one or two of them and then went to see Mr Goodman. She told us she accused him of encouraging promiscuity between people too old and foolish to know any better, and in her opinion it was disgraceful. She said she was going to complain to County Office.

'When she came out of his office she was as red as a turkey cock. She wouldn't tell anyone what he had said to her but she said she was definitely taking things further.'

'And did she?'

Barbara shrugged. 'Don't think so. There's been no correspondence about the matter. She talked to all the staff but most of us sided with Mr Goodman.

'After all, why shouldn't the old couple share a bit of love and affection? A bit of cuddling never did anyone any harm.' She winked at Rosie and, leaning closer, whispered: 'Don't suppose Mr Thorne's capable of anything else except cuddling, but you never know. Love works wonders, doesn't it?

Rosie laughed and nodded. 'I guess it does.'

A week after her return to work, Mark took Rosie along to to The Huntsman to hear the jazz group he had mentioned to her just before the car crash. Apparently, the original gig had been so successful, the group been asked back.

'This time we'll get there,' he promised.

Rosie accepted his invitation with pleasure. During working hours they were careful to keep to their respective roles but it was good to know Mark intended seeing her in off-duty hours.

The Huntsman's public bar was large but on the night in question, it was packed with jazz enthusiasts. Rosie was fascinated by the different types of people who had turned up for the gig. Waiting for Mark, she watched long-haired students jostle with middle-aged men in checked sports jackets, and wraith-like girls with shaggy hairstyles and powdered pale cheeks exchanging comments with neatly dressed older women who looked like bank tellers or office workers.

She noticed that Mark, who was queuing for drinks at

the bar, was talking away to a skinny little man with pebble glasses and a 'wild child' girl with long bleached hair, wearing a mini skirt, patterned tights and clumsy boots.

Rosie also noticed how the girl watched his progress across the room when he said his goodbyes and brought the drinks over to their table.

'What a crush.' Mark handed Rosie her glass of wine. 'I knew *I* liked these guys but I didn't realise they'd become so popular with other people. The last time I travelled to see them perform, the place was only three-quarters full.' He sat down next to her. 'Do you mind it being so crowded?'

'No. I think it's exciting.' She moved up to allow him more room on the bench. 'Do you know many people here?'

'No one by name, although I recognise a few faces. The chap I was talking to at the bar knows his music. Interesting chap. Apparently he teaches physics at the local Poly. I'd like to meet him again.'

Mark liked people, Rosie reflected, and they liked him. She drank from her wine glass and smiled and nodded to the girl at the bar.

The musicians appeared, four casually dressed young men wearing coloured waistcoats and tattered jeans. They acknowledged the wave of applause and then began playing. Rosie listened and found herself utterly disenchanted by their strange music.

'What do you think?' Mark turned his head and grinned at her. He had to shout over the loud applause that greeted the end of the first session.

She saw the enthusiasm sparkling in his eyes and didn't want to disappoint him but neither did she want to lie. 'I'm not sure,' she said, nervously.

He nodded. 'That's okay. I know jazz isn't everyone's

choice. But stick with it, Rosie. It might just grow on you.'

And by the end of the evening, it had.

During the third and last session, the music and the mood of the audience changed. The numbers the group performed varied in the extreme. The last three pieces of music were quietly persuasive. The main theme held one tune but ripples and tremors of other melodies danced in and out of the original sound and the listeners became silent, attentive. Eyes closed and shoulders swayed as the audience surrendered themselves completely to the spell of the music. When the last chords faded away, Rosie opened her eyes and clapped until the palms of her hands hurt.

Mark took hold of her elbow as they jostled their way out of the pub.

'It got to you, didn't it?'

She nodded.

He slipped his arm around her shoulders. 'I'm glad.'

The night sky was dark and the air fresh and sweet. As they walked down the road, only the North Star and the slip of a new moon was visible in the blackness above them. They walked quietly towards a line of glowing car headlights. Mark had booked a taxi, as had many of the other jazz fans. Rosie knew he would never drive when he had been drinking. The crowd of people were dispersing in different directions on their way home. She could hear goodnights being called.

She looked up at Mark's profile, faintly illuminated in the light from the cabs they were approaching, and felt happy and serene. No matter what was going to happen in the future, she acknowledged she loved this man.

They reached their cab and Mark opened the door for her. She stepped into the back of the car and he followed her.

It was an old taxi-cab, the kind one saw in London

streets, with a glass door separating the customers from the driver. Mark pushed open the glass panel, gave Rosie's address to the driver, and then shut the panel again.

He sat back in his seat with a sigh of satisfaction. 'Wasn't it a great night?' He peered at her face in the dim light. 'You really did enjoy yourself, you're not just saying you did?'

She saw it mattered to him. 'I had a lovely time.' She took his hand and squeezed it. 'Thank you for taking me.'

He nodded. 'We can go again, some time.'

'I'd like that.' She released his hand. 'In fact, I wondered if you could let me borrow a few of your tapes? I'd like to listen to them, especially if you have any that sound like that last piece of music they played.'

'Sure I have. Listen.' He sat upright. 'When I get home, I'll sort some out for you and give them to you tomorrow.' He paused. 'After listening to jazz it always takes me time to cool down. It will give me something to do until I start to feel sleepy.'

'You and your weird sleeping habits.' Rosie sounded amused but when she spoke again, after a short pause, her voice had become quiet and thoughtful. 'You know, I don't feel sleepy, either. Maybe you shouldn't go back to Woldview tonight, Mark. Why don't you stay with me instead?'

She felt his body stiffen as he took in her meaning, and then, without a word, he pulled her to him and kissed her. The kiss lasted a long time.

When he did speak, his voice sounded breathy. 'Do you mean what I think you mean, Rosie?'

'Yes.'

She raised his hand to her mouth and kissed the back of it. 'Unless you'd rather sort out tapes?'

He laughed, and kissed her again.

Chapter Twenty-One

Although Rosie was the only occupant of the lift, she was not unduly alarmed when it suddenly jerked to a stop halfway between the fourth and fifth floor. Lift breakdowns were part of everyday life in Talbot Towers, along with empty beer cans rolling about in the corridors and graffiti on the walls. Waiting patiently for the lift to restart – it usually did – Rosie scanned the wall nearest to her for the latest additions to the biro art gallery.

Most of the drawings were simple, hearts transfixed with arrows and words like 'Mandy luvs Darren' written beneath them. Rosie thought it heartening that so many of the scribbles contained the word love, or 'luv', as the case may be. Unfortunately, there were plenty of the other kind.

The lift remained obstinately stuck so she put the bag containing groceries, Minna's groceries, on the floor and punched the restart button. Nothing happened. She wondered what to do next. She looked at her watch and frowned. Time was passing and she wanted to spend as much time as possible with her mother today.

Rosie was suffering pangs of remorse. She hadn't exactly neglected her mother, she'd never missed her regular weekly visit, but she had not of late popped in to see Minna unexpectedly, and it had been four days since she had telephoned her.

But I've been busy, she thought, and Mum would have contacted me if she had needed anything. And it wasn't as if she received a particularly warm welcome from Minna when she popped in on her without warning.

'I'm busy,' she would say, although Rosie had no idea what kept Minna busy.

Rosie hit the green restart button again and this time she kept her finger firmly on the winking light. She was getting tired of standing in the lift reading graffiti even if the messages spoke of love. Still nothing. She began to feel a little nervous and so to distract her thoughts she took Minna's shopping list from her coat pocket and checked she had bought everything. But reading about tins of soup and packets of rice was boring and with her mind not fully occupied, her thoughts inevitably drifted to Mark Goodman. She smiled. She couldn't stop smiling just lately, even her milkman had noticed.

'Eh, Mrs Scott, you're looking bonny today. What a treat it is, to see a happy face so early in the morning.' Les Taylor had winked as he handed over her milk and then stooped to collect the empty bottles from her doorstep. 'Won the pools, have you?'

She remembered she had laughed. 'No. Better than that.'

She'd walked through into the kitchen and thought about breakfast but remembering Mark, sleeping in her bed, had put the milk in the fridge and gone back to him, not to wake him up but to spoon herself against his back, feel his warmth against her own body and listen to his deep breathing.

All Rosie's doubts about starting a relationship with him had disappeared. They had faded like a dream the night he had first stayed with her, the night they had listened to the jazz group.

Alone in the lift, Rosie remembered.

When the front door had closed they had been in each other's arms and very soon after that, they had been in bed. Their haste to make love had made them clumsy. They had discarded their shoes first and then tripped over them on the way to the bedroom.

Just one coherent thought did Rosie remember. When Mark helped her to undress, she thought, Thank God my dress can slip down over my hips instead of me having to tug it over my head. And then she stopped worrying. It didn't matter that she was no longer young, because she could see by Mark's expression how much he wanted her, and she wanted him.

She'd felt a small shock of surprise when Mark stripped off and she saw just how hairy he was. If she had thought about it at all, she had thought she disliked the idea of hairy men, and Howard's body had been smooth.

But when Mark had pulled her to him she embraced him gladly. She put her hands on his chest, absorbing the texture of his skin and the feel of his heart beating, and when she did so, tiny tendrils of dark hair curled around her fingers, as if they were trying to stake a claim on her. She'd laughed, and rested her head against his chest, brushing her cheek against the feel of him.

Then they were together on her bed and Mark was kissing her bared breasts and the shock of pleasure that raced up her spine made her forget everything except the urgent need to consummate their passion.

Their first attempt at lovemaking was over too soon. It was inevitable, but they lay in each other's arms and talked a little. They reassured each other that everything was fine.

'I let you down, Rosie. I was too quick.'

'No, no. It was marvellous. I feel so relaxed and light

and floaty.' She pressed her lips against his.

He kissed her back and then his hand stroked her body. 'So . . . you've had enough? You want to sleep now?' His eyes held a mocking look.

'Well,' Rosie stretched like a cat. 'I might manage . . .'

There was a strangulated wheezing and then the lift began to move. Relinquishing her sweet memories, Rosie picked up the bag of shopping and waited for the lift to reach the seventh floor. She hurried along to her mother's flat but when she rang the bell there was no answer.

Rosie waited for a couple of minutes and then rang again. When she heard no signs of life her brow wrinkled. With fingers that had begun to shake a little, she dug in the bottom of her capacious shoulder bag for the spare key she always carried. She found it, unlocked the flat door and stepped inside.

'Mother?'

Total silence.

She hurried through to the sitting room. 'It's me, Rosemary.' She stopped short. 'Oh, Mum.'

Minna was lying on the sofa, her head resting on a cushion. She must have placed a blanket over her but it had slipped off her body and now lay in a crumpled heap on the floor. The room was cold and Rosie glazed in alarm at Minna's white face and shut eyes. Her mother looked like a corpse.

Dropping her shopping bag, Rosie hurried to her side. She fell on her knees and took hold of Minna's hand which felt icy cold. 'Oh, my poor love,' she murmured. 'What's happened to you?'

Minna moved her head a little and her eyes half opened. 'Betty, is that you?'

She wasn't dead. Relief surged through Rosie's body

and her training took over. She picked up the blanket, tucked it around her mother's body, turned on the fire and then went to phone the doctor.

Dr Markly had known Minna for years and he responded to Rosie's telephone call immediately. He came into the flat, nodded to Rosie and went to sit next to her mother. She did not appear to know that he was there. She was mumbling away to herself but at least she looked a little better. Rosie had sponged her face, tidied her hair and added a quilt to the blanket already tucked round her spare frame.

'Is it a stroke, do you think?' Rosie's voice was troubled. 'She doesn't seem in pain, although I haven't moved her of course. She's rambling, I'm afraid, and she doesn't know me.' Rosie's voice went up a notch. 'All she does is talk about someone called Betty.'

Dr Markly took Minna's temperature and tested her heartbeat. 'I'll need to investigate a bit before I can tell you what ails your mother, Mrs Scott. Her heart's strong.' He gave a faint smile. 'I think it's safe to say she's in no immediate danger.' He gave Rosie a keen look. 'Why don't you go and make a pot of tea?'

Rosie left him and went into the kitchen. She made the tea, she even put biscuits on a rose-patterned plate, mindful of Minna's view on entertaining, and then she waited anxiously outside the sitting-room door. After a short interval of time, the doctor opened it and gestured for her to come in.

She looked across at her mother and saw there was now a flush of colour in Minna's cheeks although her eyes remained closed and her lips still moved silently.

'Don't look so tragic, she's not dying.' The doctor snapped shut his medical case and sat down in a chair. He sighed. 'I really would like a cup of tea, please.'

Rosie jumped up and went to fetch the tea tray. Dr Markly drank two cups.

'Your mother's going to be all right, although I think she must go to hospital for a few days. I want a few tests carried out.'

'But what's the matter with her? She was all right when I visited last week.'

'She wasn't actually.' The doctor shook his head. 'There are several things wrong with your mother and some of them have been exacerbated by her headstrong behaviour.' Seeing Rosie's frown, he shook his head once more.

'I've tried to talk some sense into her, but you know your mother.'

'I thought she'd had a stroke.' Rosie hesitated. 'Or become suddenly senile. I know it happens.'

The doctor laughed, which Rosie found a little shocking.

'Senile, your mother? I doubt it very much.'

'But she didn't know me.' Rosie looked across at Minna. 'And she looks so frail.'

Dr Markly's face became serious once more. 'Yes, she's been neglecting herself and she'll need building up, but constitutionally she's strong.' He sat back in his chair and said abruptly, 'Did you know your mother suffers from osteoarthritis?

'No.' Rosie cluched the handle of her teacup. 'She never said anything to me about it.' She replaced the cup on the saucer and thought a moment. 'I've noticed her movements getting slower, but no other sign. I thought it was just old age creeping on.' Her shoulders slumped. 'I work with old people, I should have realised.'

The doctor studied her face.

'Not necessarily. Osteoarthritis is difficult to spot. You probably know that it tends to attack the sufferer's hands or feet, although it can hit other parts of the body. The affected limbs can look perfectly normal for most of the time, but when the disease flares up it's terribly painful for the patient.'

Dr Markly stood up and gently removed the quilt from the lower part of Minna's body.

Rosie caught her breath when she saw the red swollen feet and ankles of her mother.

'She's been having a great deal of pain for a long time.' Dr Markly replaced the quilt and sat down again. 'She's actually called on me for help, so you can imagine how bad it's been. Your mother is not, on the whole, kindly disposed towards the medical profession.'

He smiled when he saw Rosie blush.

'I've been trying different ways of helping her but she refuses to take her tablets on a regular basis. I sympathise with her to a certain extent.' The doctor pursed his mouth and tapped his fingertips together. 'The pills often bring about stomach upsets, but I've asked her to keep me informed as to her progress and told her we'd sort out some alternative treatment if necessary. Unfortunately, she never contacted me so I assumed the latest treatment was working.'

He sighed. 'I should have called, I suppose, but my partner's been off ill and I've taken over some of his workload.' He looked towards Minna. 'I assume your mother decided to stop taking the medication, suffered a great deal of pain and took rather too many ordinary painkillers. She probably stayed in bed a lot because it was difficult for her to move around and she therefore stopped eating properly.'

He shrugged. 'Constant, debilitating pain, little hot food, perhaps not enough liquids . . . it happens all the time with the elderly, I'm sorry to say.'

'I only visit her once a week.' Rosie pressed the palms

of her hands to her burning face.

The doctor coughed. 'You work full-time, don't you?'

'Yes, but that's no excuse.'

'And I presume you also keep in touch with your mother via the telephone?'

'Of course.'

'Then you have nothing with which to reproach yourself.' The doctor's gaze went to the bag of shopping on the floor.

'But I should have realized she was ill.' Rosie removed her hand from her face. 'Why didn't she tell me?'

Dr Markly gave her a compassionate look. 'Your mother cherishes her independence and privacy. She's patently a woman who wishes to deal with her problems in her own way.'

He stood up. 'Thank you for the tea but now we must get things moving. I'll ring for the ambulance so I'd like you pack a bag for your mother, please. The usual things, spare nightdress, toiletries, slippers. Oh, and will you try and find the pills I prescribed for her? I'd like to know how many of them she actually took.'

'Yes, of course.' Rosie stood up. 'I can go with her, in the ambulance?'

'Of course.'

Minna could hear voices but they were too far away for her to hear the words. Earlier, she had been conscious of someone sponging her face. The flannel had been soft and warm and she had smelt the fragrance of her favourite rose-scented soap; then she had slept. When she awoke she had felt more comfortable, less cold, and best of all, the nagging, burning pain in her feet had eased.

She tried to open her eyes because the voices were whispering again, tantalising her because she almost remembered who they belonged to. She wanted to open her eyes but her eyelids were too heavy, they wouldn't budge. She tried again and her right eye opened, just a crack. There was a woman sitting next to her, a woman dressed in something blue. Why, it's Betty, she thought. Betty always loved the colour blue.

She was moving and there was some kind of bright light above her. She was being taken somewhere. She would have felt frightened but she could still see the splash of blue. Concentrating very hard, she managed to raise her right hand. Someone took it and held it lightly but firmly in a warm grasp. Minna sighed with contentment. Betty would look after her. She drifted off to sleep again.

On her journey to the North, nineteen-year-old Minna discovered she had not completely lost her zest for life. True, there was still the odd hollow feeling inside her, somewhere just below her ribcage, but she no longer felt she was walking about three feet above the floor and when someone addressed her, she could make sense of what they said.

For weeks after Papa's death, voices had come to her as if from a long distance. It felt as though she was walking about with cotton wool stuffed in her ears. Indeed, for much of the time she had felt so odd, she had sometimes wondered if she had died. Perhaps she was a ghost and poor Papa and everyone else were trying to reach her? But that feeling had passed and she was back in the real world again.

She knew she would never be truly happy again but life had to go on. Papa had often used that very phrase, particularly when his stocks and shares had suffered a crisis.

'Never mind, Minna,' he had said. 'Life has to go on.

We'll sort things out, won't we, girl?'

She bit her lip and stared out of the train window. Somehow, Papa couldn't sort things out in the end but he'd expect her to try and she would.

She made herself think optimistically. The passing scenery, for instance, was actually quite impressive, almost as beautiful as Scotland. She said as much to her travelling companions.

'Aye, this part of Yorkshire's right bonny.'

She smiled to herself. She had noticed that Thomas's Yorkshire accent was becoming stronger the nearer they got to his childhood home. She asked: 'When will we arrive in Halifax?'

'Close on an hour, I reckon.'

He looked stiff and uncomfortable in his best suit but quite handsome. Pity he had such a long face. Minna pressed her lips together. He was still unhappy about her decision to join them.

She persevered.

Switching on a bright smile, she enthused, 'I can't wait to get there and for us to start our new life. Tell me when we're almost there, won't you?'

'Oh, I won't have to tell you, miss.' At last, he smiled but it was a queer smile, more like a grimace. 'You'll know we're nearly there. You'll notice the overcast sky and smell the smoke from the chimneys.'

She frowned and answered him in a sharp voice, 'I asked you not to call me miss.'

He stared at her and then looked down at his hands and Betty, her chubby figure shrinking turtle-like into her topcoat, answered for him.

'It's hard to break a habit, miss.'

Then, realising, she gave a little shriek and put a hand over her mouth.

Minna couldn't be cross with Betty. She laughed out loud and clapped her hands and after a moment, Betty began to laugh with her. Even Thomas's face split into a grin.

'Aye,' he said, when they had calmed down. 'It's hard but we must watch our words. We're going to look queer enough without us behaving like your servants and you being all high-and-mighty.' And again he gave Minna that strange, wary look of his, a look compounded of suspicion, doubt and – what Minna resented most of all – pity.

'I'm not high-and-mighty.' Her voice trailed away and she stared at him and it was left to Betty, who had no idea of the tension between her brother and her former mistress, to break the deadlock.

'We'll be all right as long as we stick to our story,' she said comfortably.

'Minna's our third cousin. She's lived down South all her life. We got in touch when we went to London to work. When she knew we were coming home, she decided to come with us because her mum and dad had died and she was all alone. That's simple.'

'Simple enough, but will it work?' Thomas looked across at Minna. 'I don't think so.'

'You don't think I can do it, do you?' Minna's cheeks grew hot as she challenged him. 'You think I'm a spoilt, selfish woman who can't look after herself and never will. You think I'll be a burden on you. But I won't. I can be strong when I have to be.' Her voice quavered on the last word and she looked away from him, then blinked and met his eyes again. 'If I don't make the grade, Thomas, then I'll leave, go back to London. Will that satisfy you?'

'I'm not doubting your courage, Minna.' His voice was low and this time he used her christian name easily. 'All I'm saying is that you come from a different world from us and it shows. It shows every time you speak, every time you move, even the way you hold up your head. Christ!' His voice became louder and he hit the palm of his hand with his fist, making both Minna and Betty jump. 'Can't you *see*? You don't belong with us. We're common clay, and you're . . .' He paused. 'You're fine bone china. We're no good together. I still think you should have stayed in London, where you belong.'

'No, no.' Minna shook her head vehemently. 'You're wrong. You're my friends. I think more of you and Betty than anyone else I know, except for Cicily, of course, and I don't fit into her life any more.'

'And you think you fit into our life?'

'I can, I will. Please, Thomas,' Minna clasped her hands together in mute appeal. 'You said I could be with you, please don't go back on your word. You're the only family I've got now.'

Thomas turned away from her anguished face and caught a blast of mute reproach from his sister's round blue eyes. He sighed and slumped back in his seat. 'All right, I won't mention it again, but don't say I didn't warn you.'

The train arrived in Halifax. Thomas stood up and manhandled the luggage on to the platform, then he helped the two women to alight. He picked up the two largest suitcases.

'Can you manage the rest?'

'Of course we can.'

Betty, with what to Minna seemed like effortless ease, picked up two smaller bags and a large parcel wrapped in brown paper and headed for the ticket barrier.

Minna took the remaining luggage, a cloth carpet bag, an umbrella and a gladstone bag. Hurrying after her friends, she winced when the gladstone bag banged against her shins and caused her to cockle over on her medium-heeled fashionable shoes. She saw that Thomas, looking over his shoulder, had seen her stumble and glared at him, defying him to smile.

His face did not change. He merely gave her a long look and continued on his way. Minna raised her chin defiantly and staggered after him.

Out of the station, and travelling on a bus to their destination, Minna's first sight of Halifax appalled her. She knew areas of London were crowded and dirty, but at least in London there were trees. Here, there were rows upon rows of terraced houses and cobbled streets. There were no gardens. And looming above the housing rose the tall thin chimneys of the mills belching out smoke. She remembered Thomas's comment on the train and realised he had not been trying to frighten her, he had been telling her the simple truth.

Before they had left London, Thomas had written to an old friend of his late mother and she had secured temporary accommodation for them. The boarding house was modest in the extreme, but it was clean and tidy. After a wash and brush-up and a meal, they all felt better.

Thomas went out to try and contact some of his former friends. He said it was important they find work as soon as possible. Minna and Betty went back to their shared bedroom to chat.

Through sheer force of habit Betty unpacked and laid out Minna's nightdress on the newest-looking bed and then put a wooden chair next to the scarred old wardrobe and stood on it to stow away the emptied suitcases.

'You should have let me do that, Betty. I'm taller than you.'

'Only an inch.' She grinned. 'Little titches, both of us. We should have left them for Tom.'

'No.' Minna's voice was curt. 'I don't want him to do me any favours.'

Betty's grin faded and she twisted her hands together. 'You mustn't mind Thomas, miss. He means well. He's a worrier, that's all, and he feels responsible for us. I've told him not to worry. "Miss Minna has a good head on her shoulders," I said. "She'll be all right." '

Minna looked into Betty's earnest, blushing face and felt a rush of love for her. They had known each other a long time and Betty had been maid, friend, sister and mother to her during the past years. Impulsively, she got up from the bed, went to Betty and hugged her.

'All right, Betty. I won't mind Tom, even when he's being sarcastic, although I wish he were more like his sister.'

Betty shook her head. 'We'll all shake down together, just you wait and see. Although,' she looked towards the beds, 'I must say, miss, it's going to seem awful strange, sleeping in the same room with you.'

'Well, I don't snore. Do you?' Minna put her head on one side.

Betty laughed nervously. 'I don't think so.'

'That's all right then.' Minna went and sat on her bed again. 'I suppose we should try and sleep. We're going job-hunting tomorrow, remember.'

'Yes.' Turning her back on Minna, Betty took off her dress, enveloped herself in an enormous calico nightgown and struggled to remove her underwear without showing any part of her anatomy.

Minna ripped off her clothes, pulled her silk nightgown over her head and leapt into bed. She groaned. 'Lord, this bed's hard.'

'Is it? Mine feels fine.' Betty had also got into bed. She yawned. 'Good night, miss.'

'Good night.' Minna switched off the lamp. In the darkness she said: 'Betty?'

'Umm . . .'

'Stop calling me miss.'

Six hours after being taken into hospital, Minna emerged from the cloudy regions of sleep and memories and opened her eyes fully. Seeing the other beds, she quickly realised she was in hospital and, raising her head from the pillow, she saw beyond the other patients, sitting in a chair by the window, her daughter.

Because Rosemary was staring out of the window, Minna had a few moments in which really to look at her daughter and the first thing that struck her was how changed Rosemary was, and how attractive.

Even the strained expression on her face could not hide the fact that she looked younger than she had done for years. The first thing that Minna realised was that her daughter had lost weight. Her features were more clearly defined and her figure looked trim and shapely. She must have bought new clothes because Minna didn't recollect the black slacks and deep blue blouse she was wearing. And her hair was glossy and shining with health.

Minna stared at her. My God, she thought, what has happened to her? Then she thought: She's got herself a man! Although her own experience had been limited, Minna knew the look of a woman fulfilled. And she'd never confided in her mother, the little minx!

Feeling aggrieved, Minna tried to turn over on her side, so she wasn't looking at Rosemary, but when she moved a sudden vicious stab of pain from her right ankle forced a grunt of pain out of her.

'Mother?' Rosemary's head turned. She jumped up and came to stand by Minna's bed. 'You're awake?'

'Obviously.' With great effort, she forced the pain lines from her face and stared up at her. 'And I'd like to know what I'm doing in hospital when I'm perfectly all right? Your doing, I presume?'

To her surprise, a huge smile spread across Rosemary's face. 'That's not strictly true, Mother. You were not all right, you were really ill, but you're definitely improving.'

The smile disconcerted Minna. She had expected Rosemary to blush, drop her head or fiddle with her fingers but she had done none of those things. She had smiled, and in that smile had been confidence and self-assurance and, if she was not mistaken, love.

Minna felt vulnerable, at a disadvantage. She must sit up, she thought, resume the old status quo, reassert her authority. She tried to lever herself up in the bed but pain caught hold of her again and she drew in a sharp breath.

'Let me help.'

Her daughter's arms encircled her, her warm rounded cheek pressed against Minna's old withered one, and she surrendered to Rosemary's care. When she was comfortably settled and had taken the pill with the glass of water which awaited her attention on the bedside cabinet, Rosemary told her what had happened.

'You've been rather foolish, Mother, but the doctors say they will be able to sort you out. You must stay in hospital for a while, though. Your condition must be stabilised and you need a good rest.'

She stopped speaking and looked solemn. Minna knew she expected a protest but hadn't the strength to make one.

She nodded and sighed. 'I suppose I knew something had to be done.' She rested her head against her piled-up pillows and looked at her daughter. 'But I don't want you to visit every day. You have enough to do. And when I leave here I shall go straight home, Rosemary. Please don't pressurise me to come and stay with you.'

She paused. 'And I don't want you to tell the children I'm in hospital. I don't want them to feel obliged to come trailing over here to visit.'

Rosemary shook her head ruefully. 'I'm glad you said that, Mother.' She sighed. 'The last time I rang Paula she told me she was terribly busy at the moment. And Steve . . .' She paused. 'Steve won't be home for quite some time.

'I was expecting him home this weekend. He had a few days off from the course but he rang and said he was going to visit an old school friend instead. He left a contact number in Lancaster but I don't even know where he's staying.'

Minna, more comfortable now, detected the hurt in Rosemary's voice. She reached out to her daughter and patted her hand. 'Never mind, dear. I'm sure you'll hear from him soon.'

Chapter Twenty-Two

When Steve saw the familar face of Andrew Fretwell beaming at him from the far side of the bar in The Crown, he was delighted. He waved back and the two young men pushed their way through the crowd of drinkers until they were side by side. Without embarrassment, they clapped each other on the back then ordered two more pints, collected them from the barman and went to sit down.

'I can't believe it.' Steve stared at his friend. 'Do you know, you've hardly changed at all.'

'I've got bigger.' Andy chuckled and drank from his glass. 'Thank God.'

Steve grinned sympathetically. He and Andy had started school on the same day. They had sat together at a double desk for over six months and become firm friends, despite being total opposites in looks and temperament.

Even as a five-year-old Steve had been steady and even-tempered. The teachers, soon realising his sterling qualities, appointed him class monitor. They relied upon the tall, quiet, fair-haired boy to collect the exercise books at the end of lessons and run errands for them. They even entrusted him with the classroom pets during the holidays. Many a white mouse, a rabbit or a guinea pig summered at Steve's home.

Andy, on the other hand, had been a saint or a devil. With the strong teachers, he had been the former. Possessing a quick intelligence and a keen brain, he worked well for the teachers he respected, but when taught by timid or mediocre members of staff, he had made their lives intolerable with his insolence and defiance.

Despite the dissimilarities between them, the two boys became firm friends. They remained friends until Andy's family moved away from the town shortly after Steve had celebrated his fourteenth birthday. His leaving had been a sad blow to Steve because he was still coming to terms with his father's death two years before.

Now, studying his old friend, he saw that physically, Andy had hardly changed at all. His dark hair was now clipped short and he was smartly dressed but his face looked the same, sharp-featured and lively and although he had 'got bigger' he was still below average height.

They talked and laughed and caught up on old times. Andy asked if Steve's mother had remarried. Steve said no, but his sister had married.

'Really?' Andy looked reflective. 'I had adolescent fantasies about Paula, you know.'

'So did a lot of people.' Steve shifted his feet and asked, 'Have you tied the knot yet?'

'Married? Good Lord, no.' Andy shook his head. 'What about you?'

'I'm engaged. But we haven't set a date for the wedding.' Steve looked away, avoiding Andy's gaze. 'I'm afraid we're having a bit of a bumpy patch at the moment. Jill came over to stay last weekend. I think we both hoped a change of scene would . . .' His voice faded away.

Tactfully, Andy changed the subject.

'So what are you doing in this neck of the woods?'

'I'm on a course.'

'What sort of course?'

Steve swirled the beer in the bottom of his glass. 'It's to do with my work.'

'Which is?'

'Banking.'

Andy whistled. 'Sounds impressive.' Then, seeing Steve's unresponsive face, he went to the bar for two more pints of beer. Back again he said, 'I bet you can't guess what I'm doing for a living?'

Steve roused himself. 'Something flash, no doubt?'

Andy grinned. 'O, ye of little faith. No, it's nothing flash. I worked for a car company for a while after leaving college but I didn't stay long. But I suppose that was flash compared to what I'm doing now.'

Steve's curiosity was aroused. Knowing Andy, he guessed his friend would be involved in active work so he mentioned engineering, building work and journalism, all to no avail. After a few more guesses, he gave up.

'I knew you wouldn't get it.' Andy smirked. 'I'm working at Greenwater Village.'

Steve was mystified. 'Sounds like a ski resort.'

Andy's smile vanished. 'Don't you know about it? You should. It's only forty-five miles away from Lancaster.'

'No. But I've only been here three weeks and I've had my nose to the grindstone. Us bankers do actually work for a living, you know.'

When Andy only half-smiled, Steve realised that he was really curious as to what his friend did to earn a living. He asked, 'What is it, then?'

'Greenwater Village? It's a place where handicapped people live.'

Steve stared. 'You mean, it's a school for the disabled and you're a teacher there?' He whistled. 'I would never have guessed that in a million years.'

A faint smile touched Andy's lips. 'As it happens, it's not strictly a school and I'm not exactly a teacher.'

'What does that mean?'

'It's difficult to explain.' Andy scratched his head. 'It's a proper village where teachers, co-workers and so-called handicapped people work together, as a team.'

Steve shook his head. 'I don't get it.'

Andy sighed. 'It's a place where people live and work. There's all ages there and all sorts of people. Many are physically or mentally handicapped and some need special teaching. Putting it generally, the more able-bodied help those less fortunate and the whole community tries to be self-supporting.'

Steve thought about what Andy had said. 'Sounds a good idea,' he said slowly. 'Is it some kind of new scheme the government have set up? I know they've been turfing people out of the orthodox mental hospitals.'

'No, no.' Andy shook his head vehemently. 'It's nothing at all to do with the government, and the scheme, as you call it, has been up and running for about fifty years.

'The guy who started the whole thing was an Austrian, I believe, but his original concept spread quickly and there's other places like Greenwater Village in this country and abroad. They do vary, of course, because they have to fit in with the places where they're situated but Greenwater's pretty rural.'

Andy's enthusiasm began to show through as he continued to explain. 'We've workshops – toy-making, textile weaving, metal work and basket making. We've a coffee bar in the village and a shop that supplies a whole lot of groceries and household things which is open to the public. We farm some land and run some animals.'

Suddenly, he went quiet and picked up his glass of beer.

'Sorry, I get a bit carried away sometimes. Mustn't bore you.'

'I'm not bored.'

Steve wanted to hear more. He thought his friend's enthusiasm was terrific and told him so.

'Go on, Andy. Tell me more about the place.'

He shrugged his shoulders. 'If you're that interested, why don't you come for a visit?'

'Could I?'

'Sure. It's a village, remember. We're not penned in or anything.'

Steve took a deep breath. 'Right, I will. When can I come?'

Andy blinked. 'Any time you like. Visitors are always welcome.' He looked at Steve thoughtfully. 'But why the interest? Not idle curiosity, I hope?'

Steve flushed. 'Is that what you think of me?'

'No, but I'm surprised you're so interested. Damn it all, Greenwater's a million years away from corporate banking.'

'Maybe that's why I want to visit the place.'

After closing time the two friends, now slightly inebriated, went back to Andy's hotel and finished a bottle of whisky he had there. Andy mentioned he was returning to the village next day. He had come to Lancaster for a business meeting.

'You're really just a businessman, then?' Steve felt unaccountably let down and his disappointment showed in his voice.

Andy looked at him with surprise.

'Among other things. One of my jobs is to go to the business communities and try and sell our products.' Seeing Steve's non-committal expression, Andy put his hands on his knees and leaned forward.

'It's not a *play* village, Steve. To survive we must be part of the real world, so we have to find buyers for the things we make. You'd be surprised how many people take bulk orders from our craft workshops. I visit shopkeepers and travel centres, and theatre people and musicians, too. Often they come and visit us, and they help us set up our own plays and shows.' Seeing a contrite expression appear on Steve's face, Andy relaxed back into his chair.

'I'm sorry.' Steve sighed. 'I shouldn't leap to conclusions when I don't know all the details. It's just that it sounded so terrific at your village and then you started talking about business.'

Andy shook his head. 'What's the matter with you? There's nothing wrong with good business.'

'I know, but that's all people seem to think about nowadays, turning a profit.'

Andy frowned and poured out more whisky. 'You sound pretty fed up. Want to talk?'

Accepting his refill, Steve found himself unburdening his worries. But only some of them. He didn't mention his difficulties with Jill but he touched on his ever growing dissatisfaction with his own life.

When he finished speaking, Andy had just emptied the remains of the bottle into their glasses. He picked up his own glass and admired the colour of the liquid.

'You've got yourself into quite a state, Steve. I sympathise, but walking away from a bad decision and making a change isn't such a big deal. I shouldn't brood so much. Just get on and do something about it, if you're not happy. Better now than when you're forty-five.' He sighed.

'You were a worrier at school, I recall.' Draining his glass he banged it down on the table. 'I think you *should* come and see the village. The people at Greenwater will stop you feeling sorry for yourself.'

★ ★ ★

A week later, lying in bed at the end of his first day at Greenwater Village, Steve found it impossible to think logically about his initial impressions of the place. Every time he closed his eyes and tried to do just that, a confused kaleidoscopic series of pictures flashed through his mind.

The group of kids about fourteen years old he'd spotted on his arrival at the village. He had expected frail, wan-looking youngsters, but these kids were playing rounders on the sports ground and shouting and laughing.

Then Andy had met him and shown him round. He had taken him into the bakery. Steve remembered the rows of granary and rye loaves set out to cool, the gorgeous smell, and Michael, the Down's Syndrome young man, proudly showing him his work.

There was the hilarious atmosphere in the workshop when a worker lost control of his potter's wheel, and the wine glass a dreadfully disabled man showed him, wonderfully engraved by him despite his handicaps.

Tired, Steve pressed his fingers to his closed eyelids, longing for sleep, but still the pictures came.

The startled lady visitor in the village shop who was paying for her purchase and the mentally handicapped seller who was so pleased at his sale that he rushed from behind the counter and hugged her. The woman had jumped and looked scared for a moment, and then she had laughed and hugged the young man back.

Walking with Andy through the patch of woodland and noticing how warmly everyone greeted him. The peace and quiet of the cowsheds where two middle-aged women were hand-milking the cows. The gentle animals raising their heads to stare at him and then lowering them again and affectionately butting their carers.

God! He sat up. He'd never be able to sleep. He took

hold of his pillow, banged it into a new shape and lay down again. Ten minutes later he was snoring.

On the second day of his visit, Steve bombarded Andy with questions.

Who lived in all the houses? Did any of the people work outside the village? With so many people suffering from so many handicaps, how did they get the treatment they needed?

Andy answered his questions patiently.

'Some handicapped people share a house. We've able-bodied house parents who look after the children and the adolescents. How many children they take depends on the type of disability. Yes, quite a few people go out to work.' Andy nodded to a young woman passing by.

'Janice catches a bus three times a week and works at a supermarket. She's doing well. I think she'll be leaving here soon and going back to live with her family. As to your last question.' He paused and shook his head. 'You still haven't grasped what we're about, Steve. Lots of people here don't *need* treatment. Okay, they're handicapped, but they've learned to live with the fact. They're getting on with their life and this village is their home.'

He shrugged. 'Oh, they know they wouldn't function too well in the outside world but here they do. They know that some people here are brighter than others, but that doesn't matter either. In Greenwater Village, the people who work in the laundry or pick the potatoes are considered just as important as the artists, like the man you met yesterday, the one who does the glass engraving.'

Steve digested Andy's words and then he looked at him with respect. He asked one last question. 'How did *you* get involved?'

Andy slowed his steps. They were skirting the boundary

to the sports field on their way to eat lunch. Silently, he drew Steve's attention to a group of youngsters who were attempting to play football.

They were playing with great enthusiasm but their movements were clumsy and more often than not they missed the ball completely when they attempted to kick it.

Andy smiled. 'After lunch, if they're still here, perhaps you could give them half an hour of your time, Steve? I recollect you were always good at sport when we were at school together.'

When Steve nodded, Andy answered his question.

'You wouldn't know, of course, but two years after we moved to Peterborough my brother Jonathan was born.' He glanced at Steve. 'When he was a couple of months old the doctors told my parents he was a Down's Syndrome baby. He had other problems, too. The doctor said he wouldn't last long but he made his fourth birthday, and then he died.' Andy's voice thickened. 'He was a good kid.'

He quickened his step. 'I got over it pretty quickly. Kids can be callous little sods, can't they? Mum and Dad grieved for a long time. I got fed up of their long faces eventually. But time passed and things got better. I never forgot Jon though.

'After school I went to technical college because I liked messing about with engines, but I had no strong ideas as to what I wanted to do with my life. I got my diploma and landed a job, and I thought I was okay but, one day, I read about this place.' He threw back his head and laughed. 'I was in the barber's waiting for a haircut and this magazine was on the chair next to me.

'When I left the shop I had the magazine in my jacket pocket. I just *knew* I had to find out more about Greenwater Village. I did, and here I am.'

They walked in silence for a moment and then Steve placed his hand on Andy's arm and said, 'Thanks for telling me.'

'No big deal.' Andy rubbed his hands. 'Now, what do you fancy for lunch?'

After a light meal, Steve returned to the sports field and coached the lads he had seen earlier. They would never make a first eleven, he thought, but after some practice he was surprised how much enjoyment he derived from seeing one of them thump the ball cleanly and send it soaring towards the goalposts.

Later, while drinking coffee in one of the staff rooms, he talked to staff who worked with brain-damaged and maladjusted children. When one young woman asked if he would like to sit in on her class, he accepted. The six children in the room behaved perfectly ordinarily for twenty minutes and then, suddenly, a child sitting at the rear of the room, a boy of about fourteen years old, went completely berserk.

Steve felt awkward and completely useless. He stood up and watched uncomfortably as the teacher went to the boy and with quiet words and competent movements subdued him and calmed him down.

At the same time, another woman came through from the next room, collected up the rest of the pupils who were showing signs of distress, and took them to join in her class.

When peace had been restored, and after the lesson, he sought out the two women and complimented them.

The one who had coped with the boy shrugged off his compliments.

'We're trained to deal with situations like that. Will's a good lad, really.' Seeing Steve's dubious expression, she explained, 'In his other schools Will was always heavily medicated. He was a handful, you see. When he was born he was starved of oxygen and now he's brain-damaged. We've cut down on the drugs, we think he deserves a better quality of life, but handling him without drugs is hard work.' She smiled. 'We'll get there in the end though.'

After dinner it was time for him to leave. He packed his bag and carried it out to his car. Then he turned to Andy, who was seeing him off, and shook his hand.

'Thanks for everything. It's been quite an . . .'

'Experience?' Andy laughed and finished his sentence for him. 'Hope you thought it was worth it.'

'Definitely.' Steve nodded his head vigorously. 'It's given me lots to think about.'

Andy raised his eyebrows. 'Hey, don't think too hard, Steve. Remember what I said.'

Steve gave him an affectionate punch on his shoulder. 'I won't.' He turned and opened the car door. 'We'll keep in touch?'

'You bet.' Andy watched as Steve drove away, then checked his watch and went back to work.

Like Andy, Paula was working long hours. In the offices of Harris, Templeton and Dean, most of the lights were out and the staff had gone home but she still had several letters to process. She didn't mind. In fact she relished the hours she spent working and when the offices were quiet it was easier to concentrate.

This was her second stint working for the advertising agency and when she had arrived, she had been given a much more important job. She wanted to do it to the best of her ability because she knew the company had rung up the temping agency and asked for her by name.

The fortunes of Harris, Templeton and Dean were

flourishing and a new accounts officer had been engaged. Paula's job was to act as his secretary/assistant for a month, after which time he would choose a permanent assistant from the young women training with the firm. Paula's boss was a tall, good-looking man called Les Beaver. He had a young face but rapidly greying hair which made his age hard to pinpoint. An intensely private individual, he was quiet, never mentioned his personal life but was good at his job and always courteous towards Paula.

She had worked for him for two weeks and wished fervently that she could stay for ever. She couldn't, of course. She was a temp and would remain one, but she decided that while she was with Harris, Templeton and Dean, she would make the most of it.

She took an interest in all the meetings she attended. She listened to the various views of the heads of department and began to realise what the respective posts required. She also realised what a fine negotiator Les Beaver had to be because he was the link man between the creative team and the customers.

Now, staring at the letter on the screen of her word-processor, she smiled appreciatively at the delicate way in which he attempted to persuade the customers, in this case a well-known manufacturer of garden furniture, that their ideas about the promotion of their products were unsound. She finished checking the letter, printed it out and wished she had someone with whom to share her newfound knowledge.

But there was no one. Tracey was a good friend and it had been marvellous the way she looked after Alison when the nursery had no room for her, but business talk bored her. And Dave . . . Paula shook her head. She could not talk about her work to Dave.

Although he was much better than he had been. He no longer baited her with sarcastic remarks or frightened her with his inexplicable mood changes, and he kept his hands to himself. He had, though, become terribly silent and withdrawn. It had been a long time since he had shown any interest in her sexually. Paula had begun to worry in case he was taking drugs.

Deep in thought, she had not realised that Les Beaver had entered the office. She jumped when he spoke to her.

'Still here? I thought you'd have been away an hour ago.'

'I wanted to finish the post before I left. And the Reddish report.' Paula waved to the pile of paper on the right hand side of her desk. 'The meeting's scheduled for ten a.m. tomorrow. Do you want to sign the letters?'

She handed them to him and noticed how tired he looked.

'Bad journey?'

He blew out his cheeks in a sigh. 'Pretty dreary. Road-works everywhere.'

'Oh, dear.' Paula knew her boss had been on the road all day attending meetings in different towns. 'But everything went okay?'

'Yes.' He was scanning through the letters. 'I'll sign these and then we can both go home.' He raised his head. 'Who's looking after your little girl? Alison, isn't it?'

Paula smiled. She liked him for remembering her daughter's name. 'She's fine. My husband's working late tonight too, so she's staying with a friend of mine.'

'I see.' Mr Beaver yawned widely then clapped his hand over his mouth and apologised. 'Sorry.'

Paula laughed. 'You're excused. I expect you're ready for home and a good cooked meal?'

He pulled a face. 'Not on, unfortunately. My partner's

away on business and won't be back until Friday'.

So he has a partner, thought Paula, but no children. She stood up and went to put on her coat.

He watched her and then said suddenly, 'I fancy a plateful of tagliatelle and a glass or two of wine. Care to join me?'

Surprised, she hesitated.

'There's a little place two streets away that's good.'

Still Paula delayed her answer. She liked Mr Beaver and she liked the way they worked together but she didn't want to foster any false ideas.

He must have interpreted her hesitation correctly. He smiled and said softly, 'By the way, my partner is called Adam Langly. We've been together five years. He's a surveyor.'

'Oh.' Paula blushed, and then seeing him smile, she smiled back. 'Thank you. I'd love to have supper with you. Italian food's my favourite.'

It was just after nine when she let herself into the flat. As the place was in darkness she assumed Dave was still at work. She slipped off her coat and then jumped when a voice said: 'So you've decided to come home?'

'Dave?' Her hand went out, feeling for the light switch. She found it and switched on the light. 'Why on earth are you sitting in the dark?' She crossed the room. 'And the fire's not on. You must be frozen.'

Crouching on her heels before the electric fire, she turned it on and then looked at her husband who was sitting in one of the two armchairs. Then her eyebrows drew together in a frown.

'Are you all right?'

He stared down at her without speaking. His face was white and she saw he was shivering.

She asked again: 'Are you all right?'

'I was, earlier.' His voice sounded odd, croaky.

She found herself beginning to worry. 'I'll make you a hot drink.'

As she began to stand up, he shot out his right arm and his hand encircled her wrist, trapping her.

She winced. 'You're hurting me, Dave.'

If anything, he increased the pressure. He leaned forward in the chair and thrust his face close to hers.

'Not as much as you've hurt me, Paula.'

She shook her head, bemused.

He tightened his grip even more.

'You can't deny it. I saw you.'

'Saw me where? What are you on about?'

'I saw you with him.'

Realisation dawned, and with it, fear.

'You saw me leaving the office with Mr Beaver?'

'Is that his name?'

'He's my boss, Dave.' She twisted her wrist, trying to break his hold on her.

He didn't even notice her futile attempt at escape.

'I got away from work early so I thought, I'll surprise Paula.' His face twisted into a parody of a grin. 'Alison's not here tonight so I'll take my wife out. It wasn't going to be anywhere posh, of course, not like that place your lover took you to.'

'He's my boss, Dave, that's all.' Paula tried to keep her voice from shaking. 'Let go of me, love. My wrist hurts.'

He didn't seem to hear her words. With his left hand he grabbed her chin and forced her face closer to his. 'I saw *everything*, Paula. I saw you laughing and talking in the restaurant. Enjoy your meal, did you?'

She flinched away from his white furious face. 'You're wrong, Dave. The man is my boss.'

'Better still.' Squeezing her chin, he shook her head from side to side. 'He'll have plenty of money. You like money, don't you?'

She gasped. 'Please listen. Mr Beaver . . . he's my boss . . . and he's not interested in me. He's not interested in any woman. He's gay.'

The sound of his laughter paralysed her. She became as limp and passive as a rabbit caught in the headlights of a car.

'That's priceless. Oh, my God, what an excuse. I should have known you'd come up with something good.'

He jerked up her chin and kissed her on her lips, thrusting his tongue into her mouth.

His action released her from her passivity. She jerked her head away and screamed.

'You bloody idiot! It's true.'

And then he hit her. He hit her for a long time. He hit her deliberately and rhythmically. She was his punchball. When he finally released her she slid away from him down on to the floor as limp and boneless as a rag doll.

He got up and stared at her, his face emotionless, and then he kicked her in the ribs. He left the room and the door of the flat slammed behind him.

Twenty minutes later she stirred, made little whimpering noises. Five minutes after that she dragged herself towards the telephone. On her second attempt she managed to tug at the cord and pull the receiver off the rest. It fell with a muffled thud on to the carpet. She reached for it and, spitting the blood from her mouth, called for an ambulance.

Chapter Twenty-Three

The flowers Rosie carried were wrapped in cellophane. The bouquet rustled gently as she walked down the hospital ward looking for Paula. She glanced at the third bed, the fourth, the fifth . . . and began to panic. Had she come to the wrong ward? Then a voice behind her whispered, 'Mum?'

She stopped, turned and stared.

'Oh, my God. Paula?' She had walked straight past her daughter.

The battered stranger, propped up high on pillows, attempted a smile.

Eyes wide, Rosie went over to the bed. She stared at Paula's black eyes, hugely swollen face and bulging split lips, and a dark sick hatred of her son-in-law contracted her stomach and made her feel nauseous. She couldn't even speak.

Paula held out her hand and said, thickly, through her damaged mouth, 'Don't, Mum. Don't look like that. I'm going to be okay. The doctor said so.'

Rosie fought down her shock and outrage and nodded. 'Of course you are.'

She laid the flowers on the counterpane, grasped Paula's hand and tried to smile, but close up she could see the stitching around the corner of her daughter's mouth and along her brow bone, and despite her self-control tears escaped from her eyes and rolled down her cheeks.

Paula looked away. 'Don't. You'll set me off and I don't want that. It hurts too much.'

'I'm sorry.' Rosie released Paula's hand and, lacking a handkerchief, mopped her face on her jacket sleeve. 'It's the shock.'

She sat down in the chair next to Paula's bed and tried to think of something cheering to say, but all her mind could hold was the fact that Dave had inflicted this terrible damage on her daughter.

So Paula spoke instead.

'The flowers are lovely. Thanks.'

Rosie realised that Paula's voice was slurred because she couldn't open her mouth properly, and as for the flowers, she wondered how her daughter could see them properly, because her eyes were merely slits in her terribly bruised face.

Rage towards Dave consumed her and, wise or not, she had to express it.

'How could he, the bastard? I could kill him. I would, if I could get my hands on him.' She shook her head. 'Why didn't you tell me, Paula? Why did you stay with him? You could have come home to me, long before it got to this state.' She gestured towards Paula's face.

'I'm your mother, surely you could have confided in me, asked for my help?' She paused. 'I knew *something* was wrong. Why do you think I kept ringing you? And yet you always said things were fine.'

Her torrent of words stopped when Paula turned her face away and whispered, 'It wasn't as simple as that, Mum.'

'It's simple to me.' Rosie wanted to express her anger, she wanted to rant and rave and verbally attack her son-in-law for his crime, but looking at Paula she knew now was not the time, so she gripped her hands together and willed herself to become calm. She must give all her attention to her daughter.

Paula looked so distant, so remote, Rosie felt suddenly frightened. Trying to bridge the gap that had, without explanation, suddenly yawned between them, she said in a quiet voice, 'The doctor who attended you gave me a few minutes. He said you'll be fine. There'll be no permanent scarring.'

'Yes, he's been to see me.' Paula rolled her head on the pillows and turned to face her mother again. 'My jaw's cracked so I won't be able to eat properly for a few days,' she tried to smile, 'not that I'm hungry. The stitches near my mouth will dissolve naturally and won't scar.' She put her hand to her head. 'This cut's deep. It might leave a permanent mark but he says it will be small. I've been lucky.'

'Humph . . .'

At her mother's exclamation, Paula's smile widened, so that she winced and put her fingers to her lips. 'I *have* been lucky, Mum. They deal with terrible injuries here every day. I was lucky to be kept in overnight.'

'Lucky! You mean, they could have *discharged* you, in the state you were in?'

'Shortage of beds, Mum.'

The outraged expression on Rosie's face turned into a thoughtful look. 'So it's possible they'll discharge you today?'

'Very probable. The doctor will be touring the ward just after two o'clock. I'll know then.'

'And if you are discharged, what are your plans?'

Paula looked down, studied her hands. 'You know that Tracey, my friend, had Alison with her?'

'Yes.'

'Well, I thought I'd go to her for a couple of days. She said I could.'

'That won't be necessary.' Rosie's voice was firm. 'You're coming home with me.'

'Oh, Mum. I don't know.'

'I'll see to everything. If you're discharged from hospital, I'll order a taxi. We'll go over to Tracey's house, pick up Alison, go to the railway station and go home.'

Smiling at her daughter, Rosie's heart smote her when she saw Paula's anxious face. 'No, maybe that was a stupid suggestion. I'm rushing you and it's obvious you won't feel like travelling today. I know, I'll sort out some overnight accommodation. After a good sleep you'll feel better. Tracey can keep Alison another night and then we'll all go home tomorrow.'

'I don't want to go home, Mum.'

The note of panic in Paula's voice stopped Rosie dead.

'Why ever not?'

'That's what he'll expect me to do. I'd be like a sitting duck. He'd wait a few days and then he'd come for me.'

Disconcerted, Rosie stared at her daughter. Paula had always been completely fearless.

'You're talking nonsense. Dave wouldn't dare come anywhere near you now.'

Paula shook her head vigorously, then winced. 'You don't know him like I do, Mum. I *know* he'll come.'

'Well then, just let him try.' Rosie's voice shook with the fury she felt. 'We'll be ready for him.' She wet her lips with her tongue. 'I'd cheerfully kill him myself.'

'You don't know what you're talking about.' Paula's voice was dull. 'You wouldn't be able to handle him.'

'Then I would get the police and they'd put him in prison.' Rosie sat up straight in her chair.

'It's not as easy as that. I don't think the police would be able to do very much.'

'Nonsense. That's their job, to apprehend villains.'

Paula pulled herself up higher on her pillows and clasped her hands around her knees.

She said quietly, 'I spoke to the hospital social worker this morning, Mum. She advised me against pressing charges against Dave. She said that domestic incidents,' she touched her mouth, 'that's what they call what happened to me, are becoming more and more common and that the police are reluctant to get involved.'

Seeing the look of disbelief on her mother's face, she went on: 'I know it's hard to understand, but it's true. Violence in the home is no big deal nowadays, particularly in the cities. The police get hundreds of calls about domestic violence but often, when they respond, they get nothing but abuse from the family involved.

'And if they do bring a charge against the man, the social worker says it rarely comes to court. Naturally the police get sick because of the work and effort that's wasted.'

'Why doesn't the case come to court?'

Paula shrugged. 'Because nine times out of ten the couple make up again.'

'But you wouldn't do that, surely?' Doubt surfaced in Rosie's voice.

'No.' Paula started to shake her head then changed her mind. 'Our marriage is over.' She stared into space for a moment and then roused herself. 'But I don't want the police involved.'

'Fair enough, but you're still coming home with me.'

Rosie refused to discuss the matter further. When Paula tried to pursue the subject her mother stood up and insisted she lie back on her pillows and rest.

'You look tired.' She arranged the covers around her

daughter. 'Anyway, we can't decide anything until the doctor has been to see you. But I really think you should come home, Paula. You're in no fit state to look after Alison and I'm sure you have no intention of going back to the flat. Let me look after you, at least for a few days until you feel stronger.'

She rested her hand against Paula's cheek. 'And stop worrying about Dave. Your brother will be back home next week, remember. He'll sort Dave out, should he dare to show his face.' Her eyes gleamed. 'Steve could floor him with one punch. And there's always Mark, of course.'

Paula, resting her head against the puffed-up pillows and surrendering herself to Rosie's ministrations, asked, 'Who's Mark?'

Rosie's busy hands paused. She smiled. 'Oh, I forgot. You don't know about Mark, do you? He's my boyfriend.'

Watching Paula's expression, Rosie gave a smile of satisfaction. As she had intended, she had diverted her daughter's thoughts from her own troubles, if only momentarily.

She picked up the flowers from the bed.

'I'll go and find a vase for these, and then I'll tell you all about him.'

When Steve was fifteen miles away from home, the rain eased off and the sun appeared. He slowed the car and wound down his side window to breathe in the fresh, sweet air. It was May and the hedgerows were full of frothy white blossom.

It was good to be going home. He glanced up at the blue sky and gave a smile of contentment. After months of doubt he was at peace with himself and the world, and it was as if the weather knew his mood and was collaborating.

Nevertheless, as he drew closer to home, his face became serious. Explaining his decision to Jill was going to be difficult. Her visit to Lancaster had been made before he had met Andy in the pub. Would she understand, and be able to share his plans for the future? He was not hopeful. But even more worrying than his relationship with his fiancee was this damnable thing with Paula and Dave.

He had been dumbfounded when his mother had phoned him and told him what had happened. He had thought his sister's marriage was a happy one, he had thought Dave was a decent sort of bloke. He couldn't imagine what had happened to turn his brother-in-law into a wife-beater who had put Paula in hospital.

He thought about Paula and Dave during the rest of his journey but he had still made no sense of anything when he arrived home. He parked the car and let himself into the house with a feeling of trepidation. He wondered who would be there to greet him.

His mother, her voice shaking with anger and outrage, had graphically described Paula's appearance to him and he wondered, with a lurch of his stomach, if she still carried the marks of Dave's attack on her. He wondered how to handle his first meeting with her. What could he possibly say?

His relationship with Paula had always been spiky. He couldn't suddenly smother her with kisses and assure her of his love. Neither could he see himself ranting and raving about what he would like to do to Dave.

He sighed and shut the front door behind him.

Immediately, two things cheered him up. One was a full frontal charge from his small niece and the other was the smell of steak cooking. He grinned and swept Alison up into his arms. He swung her round until she was dizzy and then set her down again, groaning.

'Oh dear, oh dear. My dainty little niece has got so big and fat, I can't throw her up into the air any more.'

Alison giggled and wrapped herself around his legs. 'I'm not *fat*. You are.'

He patted her head. 'You're probably right,' he agreed. 'I know I'm hungry.' He raised his head and sniffed the juicy aroma of the sizzling steak. Good old Mum, he thought. She's knows my favourite food.

The door to the kitchen opened and he looked up, expecting to see his mother, but it was Paula who came towards him.

She held out her hand. 'Welcome home, Steve.'

He studied her and felt absurdly like crying. Her face looked all right, she was no longer the bruised and battered woman his mother had described, but he could see she was badly damaged.

He saw it in the expression of her eyes, the hesitant, half-apologetic way in which she spoke, even in the defeated way she approached him. He remembered the last time he had seen her, full of quick movements, teasing him with half-mocking, half-funny quips at his expense, the way she glanced at him, challenging him to retaliate.

He looked at her and missed the confident tilt of her head, her impudent smile and the expression that said: Hey, look at me.

He coughed to hide his emotion and, looking down at Alison, said, 'Let go of my leg, young woman.'

When she refused, he produced a flat parcel from his jacket pocket and tossed it to her. It was wrapped up in gift paper emblazoned with pink and blue rabbits and she grasped it eagerly.

'Be a pet. Go and open it in the sitting room. Mummy and me want to talk.'

She whooped with delight, took the parcel and left them alone.

Steve looked again at Paula who had stopped a few feet short of him. He took one stride to stand before her and asked: 'How do you feel?'

A faint smile touched her lips. 'I'm feeling lots of things, Steve, but most of all I feel a failure.' She bent her head, avoiding his gaze. 'Your clever, bossy sister has finally got her comeuppance and I suppose you're entitled to think, Not before time.'

He cleared his throat and then, with careful tenderness, put his right hand under her chin and with his thumb and forefinger raised her face and studied her.

She had lost weight. Her cheeks were too thin. At first glance he'd thought her face unblemished, but then he saw the bluish tinge of fading bruises around her jaw and the yellowy stains beneath her eyes. His lips tightened. He brushed his fingers gently over the scar on her right temple and observed the fading signs of surgical repair to the corners of her mouth, and for the first time in his life, he felt murderous. Because, worse than the bruises and the scars, he saw the expression lurking at the back of her eyes.

He dropped his hand, and putting both arms around her slight frame, he hugged her to him. Then he rested his head on her hair and whispered, over and over again, 'It will be all right, Paula. It will be all right.' He felt her body relax against his.

The sound of the back door banging separated them. Feeling a little embarrassed, Steve squeezed Paula's hand and then went into the kitchen to greet his mother.

She was surprised he was so early.

'You must have made good time.' She put her hands on his shoulders and landed a smacking kiss on his cheek. 'I'm sorry I missed seeing you arrive. I'd popped out to the corner shop. I realised we had no English mustard in the house and I knew you'd want some to put on your steak.' She grinned at him. 'I'm doing your favourite meal.'

He laughed. 'I know. I can smell it.'

When he emerged from the kitchen, Paula was nowhere to be seen. Steve went outside and collected his luggage from the car. Going upstairs, he saw, with absolutely no resentment, that he was once again relegated to the small bedroom. He unpacked, went for a shower and then came downstairs again.

His mother had gone to town over his welcome. The large extending table in the sitting room had been opened up, Rosie's best tablecloth had been spread over it, her best dinner service had been laid out and the meal was perfect.

Pushing his empty plate away, Steve sighed. 'That was great, Mum. Thank you.'

'Apple pie and custard for seconds?'

He groaned and then nodded. Watching her collect the plates, she wouldn't let him help her on his first evening home, he thought how well she looked. He had expected her to be worn out, particularly when she told him about Minna being in hospital. He guessed she had been running backwards and forwards visiting her mother, as well as taking care of Paula. Suddenly he realised he hadn't enquired after his grandmother.

'She's much better. She went back to her flat two days ago. The new medication's worked wonders for her.' Carrying the stacked up plates, Rosie headed for the kitchen door. Alison followed closely behind her, clutching the gravy boat.

'Good job, really. We'd have been crowded out if she'd decided to come and stay with us. Still, I never thought she'd do that. Whatever her faults, your grandma's always been fiercely independent.

'Thank you, love.' Rosie smiled at Steve who had gone to open the door for her. She carried the plates through into the kitchen.

Returning to his seat, Steve saw his sister was staring into space. In an effort to distract her from her thoughts, he whispered: 'Mum seems cheerful.'

For the first time since his arrival, Paula smiled. 'Yes, she is, although it's not entirely due to your coming home.'

'Oh?' Steve wondered if Paula meant her comment to be provocative.

If it was, he thought, it's okay. If it helped her to recover, he could stand a few barbed remarks.

But with her next remark, he realised she had not been trying to provoke him for she said, 'Mum's got a serious boyfriend. Did you know?'

'Not really.' Steve considered. 'Before I went away, she was getting friendly with her boss. He's called Mark Goodman. Is that the guy?'

'Yes.' Paula's smile disappeared. 'You say he's Mum's boss.'

'Well, he's the Officer in Charge at Woldview, where she's working.'

'I didn't know that.' Absentmindedly, Paula chewed on a fingernail. Steve hadn't seen her do that for years.

'What's the problem?'

'I think I am.' She tried woefully to reconstruct her smile.

'What have you to do with Mum's friend?'

'Probably putting her in his bad books. You see, she hasn't been to work since I came home.'

'Why not? You're almost okay again. Is it because she's seeing to Gran as well as looking after you and Alison?'

'It's nothing to do with Gran and I can look after Alison myself.'

'So why isn't Mum at work?'

'Because I'm scared to be left alone.' Paula drew a deep breath. 'Pathetic, isn't it?'

Steve felt out of his depth.

'But you're safe here, Paula.'

'I'm not. Dave must know I'm here and one day soon he'll come to take me home again.'

Steve shook his head. 'That's rubbish. He wouldn't dare show his face here, after what he did to you. And if ever he does show up,' Steve doubled his fists, 'I'll show him what I think of him.'

'You can't be here all the time, Steve. Dave knows that. He'll wait, choose his moment.' Paula looked across the table at her brother, her eyes were enormous in her peaky white face. 'Can't you remember how he felt about me, Steve?' She stared down at the tablecloth. 'He's never going to let me go.'

He wanted to tell her to stop being ridiculous. If Dave came to the house, she could lock the door, ring someone up for help. They could see about getting some kind of court order to warn her husband off. She had to be sensible about this.

But he saw her hands, which were folded on the table, begin to shake and heard the panic in her voice and realised she was a long way from being cured. And so he spoke to her gently.

'Try not to worry. We'll work something out. Mum has to go back to work soon, but I'll sort out some flexi-time at the bank and some days you could take Alison and go and see Gran.'

'If Dave . . .' Paula stopped speaking when Rosie reappeared, carrying the pudding plates. She shot her brother a pleading, warning look which said 'Don't say anything', and he nodded his head.

After dinner, Steve helped his mother wash up while Paula put Alison to bed. He didn't say anything about Paula, but he did ask Rosie if she was still seeing Mark.

'Yes, when I can.' Rosie blushed as becomingly as her name. 'He's a nice man, Steve. Very understanding.' She looked up shyly at her son. 'You don't mind?'

'Mind, why should I mind?' Steve spread the drying cloth on the edge of the draining board.

'Well, you've fond memories of your dad, I know, and . . .'

He put his arm around her shoulders. 'I'm pleased for you, Mum. You've looked after other people so long, it's time you had a bit of happiness. But this business with Paula, it must make things difficult for you?'

'Yes. I've had to have leave from work. She's afraid of being on her own, you know.' She shrugged her shoulders. 'At least it's given me time to do some studying. I'm halfway through my course, and I'm getting good marks now.'

'Well done.' But Steve's voice was abstracted. He was thinking of his mother's private life, not her course work. He suddenly took hold of her elbows and swung her round to face him.

'Tell me, do you think Mark could take a few hours off on Sunday?'

'I suppose so. He is the boss.'

'Well, ring up and ask him. If he can, I'll take Paula and Alison off for the day to give you some free time. And it will do them good, too.'

'Oh, Steve, what a good idea. But are you sure? You've been away quite a long time. Won't you be meeting Jill?'

'No, it's okay. I'm seeing her tomorrow.'

'Well, if that's the case, I'll go and ring him now.' Rosie beamed at her son and went off to telephone.

Steve smiled. That was his mother sorted out. But it would take more than a day out to solve Paula's problems . . . and there was Jill. His smile faded. He ran his fingers through his hair, braced his shoulders and went back into the sitting room.

Chapter Twenty-Four

On Saturday morning, the weather was all that could be desired, but by afternoon rain showers began to blot out the blue of the sky. By four o'clock, only Steve's car remained at a popular viewing area, high on a hill overlooking a celebrated beauty spot. When he and Jill had arrived there the place had been crowded and they had found difficulty in parking. They had eventually squeezed into a space next to a station wagon owned by a couple wearing green wellingtons with three children in tow.

The family who owned the vehicle were sitting at one of the rustic tables provided by the council and having a picnic. Close by, a middle-aged couple strolled backwards and forwards, throwing a ball for their dog, a large and friendly labrador. There were two Frenchmen trying to make sense of their holiday guide and two elderly couples who remained firmly in their cars, enjoying the scenery but disdaining the fresh air.

When the storm clouds blew up, the people began to leave. First to go were the elderly couples. The Frenchmen drove away shortly afterwards and were quickly followed by the dog-owners. And finally, the family group called it a day. Packing up, the mother and father became short-tempered. They shouted to their children to hurry up and when the youngest child, a boy, clambered into the station wagon and trailed mud on the seats, his father slapped him hard on his legs.

Steve, in the middle of his own emotional upset, saw the incident and felt a wave of sympathy for the little boy who tried so valiantly to hold back tears. Steve watched as the father reversed his car out of its parking place and drove away. And then they were alone and in the almost tangible silence that followed, Jill began to cry.

Not knowing what to say, Steve merely slumped lower in his seat and watched the next wave of rain as it passed overhead and fell like fine curtains over the landscape, veiling the view before them. He felt wretched.

He asked: 'Shall I drive you home?'

She shook her head.

He waited for her to say something, but she didn't, so he found himself filling the heavy silence.

'I'm sorry if you feel I've let you down, but I had to tell you how I felt. And the truth is, I can't face the thought of spending the rest of my life working in a bank.' He glanced at her. 'I was hoping you'd understand.'

'I might have, but it's all the other things you've said.' Jill's voice was unsteady. 'This weird idea of yours about training to work with handicapped people – how long have you been thinking about that? And all this talk about being unsettled. Why did you wait so long to tell me?'

'It never seemed the right time.' Steve rubbed his hands over his face in a tired gesture. 'I didn't mean to be secretive, love, but I was in such a muddle.'

'You *should* have told me.' Jill's voice was bitter. 'I can't believe you, Steve. There was I, talking and planning for our marriage, our future, and you were busy with your secrets.'

'They weren't secrets.' Steve tried desperately to make

her understand. 'I couldn't make sense of my own feelings, Jill, so how could I explain to you?' He stared at her profile. She had stopped crying now and he noticed how firm her chin was.

'You're different from me. You're sure about what you want.' He raised his shoulders in a shrug. 'I'm sorry, but I can't be like that.'

'So it's *my* fault?' Red patches of anger flared in her cheeks.

'No, of course not.'

'It must be, if I'm so difficult to talk to.'

'Oh, Jill.' He shook his head.

'Don't look like that.' She glared at him. 'I've listened to you, now you can listen to me. If you think I'm going to marry a man who's proposing to give up a good job with prospects to look after ga-ga people for a lousy wage, you must be as thick as your prospective clients. It's just not on. I've always known you're not a "high-flyer", Steve.' Her eyes moistened. 'But I wasn't too bothered because I thought we loved each other and that we would have a good life together. You're bright, and honest, and we get on well, but this crazy idea . . .' She shook her head. 'I really worry about your sanity.'

He didn't know how to reply and so, miserably, he stared out of the window of the car.

Another sweep of rain was crossing the valley below them, obscuring the dry-stone walls and the grazing sheep and changing the landscape into a featureless, grey emptiness.

Jill said, 'You're not in love with me any more, are you?'

He looked back at her. 'I'm not sure.' And then, meeting her eyes, 'I don't think so.'

She sighed and closed her eyes and he, studying the face he knew so well, said softly: 'What about you?'

She opened her eyes and looked at him. 'How can I love you, Steve? I don't know you any more.'

They stared at each other until Jill bent her head and began tugging at her engagement ring.

He stopped her. 'No, please. I want you to keep it.'

'For old times' sake?'

He nodded, and reaching over took her hands in his. 'I'm sorry, Jill.'

She did not reply but neither did she pull her hands away from his grasp.

'We're not enemies, are we?'

She managed a wavery smile. 'No. But give it a little time, Steve.'

'I will.' He squeezed her hands and released them.

There was nothing more to say. He started the car and drove her home.

After she had gone, walking into the house without a backward glance, he sat for a moment feeling drained and tired. He had thought it might happen like this, that they would split up, and being honest, he had half-hoped that they would, but now he was free he experienced the bitter taste of failure. They had started out together so young and with such high hopes and now . . .

He sighed. Glancing in his mirror before driving off, he spotted Evelyn Catley strolling along in the rain in her shiny mackintosh. He hesitated, not really wanting to talk to her, but she saw him and waved a long thin hand. When she drew level with the car, he opened the door and said: 'Mrs Catley.'

'Stephen, so you're back. Aren't you coming into the house?'

'No. Not now.'

She hesitated. 'That's a pity. I wanted a word.'

He cleared his throat. 'It wouldn't be a good idea, I'm afraid.'

'Well then, I'll sit with you in your car for a moment, if I may?'

He moved back into his own seat and she got in next to him. She apologised for the rainwater dripping off her mac.

'I've been out for a walk. Ridiculous, isn't it, in this weather?' She smiled. 'When did you get back?'

'Yesterday.'

'And I presume you've been out with Jill all day?'

'Yes.'

She peered at him with her short-sighted eyes. 'Do I recognise a certain disinclination for conversation? If so, I'll leave.'

He flushed. 'No, no. I'm sorry. Please stay. I'm pleased to see you.'

'Good.' She settled herself more comfortably. 'Now tell me, I'm dying to know – did you find your tiger?'

Her words caused a tiny shock to his system. He had almost forgotten their conversation in the teashop. He turned and stared at her and then he said, slowly, 'Yes. I believe I did.'

A wide smile lit up her face. 'Oh, I'm *so* glad. I'd love to hear about it.'

He glanced towards the house. 'And I'll be pleased to tell you, but not today.'

Her smile vanished. 'Of course. I'm taking up your time.' She put her hand on the door handle.

He stopped her. 'It's nothing to do with you, Mrs Catley.' Steve struggled to find the right words. 'Jill and I have talked, properly talked, and . . .' He paused. 'We've decided to end our engagement.'

'Oh, dear.' Evelyn Catley's hand went to her mouth.

'Oh, I'm so sorry.' She gave him a concerned look. 'Are you sure, Stephen? Perhaps in time . . .?'

He shook his head. 'Our lives are heading in totally different directions. We both realise that.'

Evelyn studied his face. 'Perhaps it was inevitable. It's a great pity, though.'

'Yes.'

After a moment's silence Evelyn stirred. 'I should go to her. She'll be upset.' Her voice was quiet. She looked sad. 'I don't know what to say to her. I love my daughter and I think she loves me but conversation between us never reaches a deep level. She will look to her father for comfort. Terence is much more on Jill's wavelength.'

At the thought of Terence Catley's forthcoming delight at the news, Steve's face took on a grim cast.

Mrs Catley, seeing his change of expression, misinterpreted it. 'Now you mustn't take the whole blame yourself. It's always better to be honest with your partner. If something isn't going to work, it's better to find out now. And you know,' her voice became slower, more thoughtful, 'Jill's heart may be cracked but I don't honestly think it is broken.

'What I'm going to tell you sounds dreadfully like gossip, but under the circumstances I want you to know.' She took a deep breath.

'A short time after Jill visited you in Lancaster, she went to a Young Farmers' Ball with a man acquainted with Terence. He works for a firm of stockbrokers and the date was totally innocent. Miles Walker, that's his name, is an extremely proper young man. Apparently, he'd bought two tickets for the ball but the girl he intended taking was ill with the flu. He mentioned the fact to Terence and my husband suggested he ask Jill if she would accompany him.

'She took some persuading, but eventually she agreed to

go. I'm sure she enjoyed herself because I was just going up to bed when they returned. Jill was flushed and laughing and it was obvious she had made a strong impression on Miles.' Evelyn paused. 'He's a *solid* young man, and ambitious. Jill told me next day that he was full of plans for the future.' She sighed. 'He sounded very much like Terence when he was younger, that's probably why Jill liked him.'

She patted Steve's arm and then opened the car door. 'When things calm down, will you ring me? Perhaps we could meet one morning in that nice little cafe we used before and then you could tell me about your tiger hunt. Oh!' In the course of shutting the door behind her, she bent down for a final word. 'Did that girl in India ever write to you?'

'No.' Steve sat up straight.

'Well, perhaps now's the time to write to her? But, Stephen . . .' Evelyn lowered her voice. 'Take things as they come. Don't start anticipating the future.'

He actually laughed. 'No fear. I've learned not to do that.'

Evelyn smiled, closed the car door and went home.

Next day, Sunday, the weather was fine again and looked set to continue that way. At ten o'clock Mark drove up to Rosie's house, got out and went to ring her doorbell.

Rosie answered it.

'I'm ready.'

She was wearing a flowery summer skirt, a cream silk blouse and sandals. She had a cream cotton jacket draped around her shoulders. She picked up her bag and came out of the house, slamming the door behind her.

'Oh.' Mark looked disappointed.

'What's the matter?'

'I thought I might get to meet Paula, or to see Steve again?'

'Steve's still in bed.' Rosie went round to the other side of the car. 'And Paula, well, she's a bit shy about meeting you.' She got in.

Mark gave a philosophical shrug and slipped into his own seat. 'I'll have to put up with you, then.'

He laughed when he saw her brows crease and leaned across to her and squeezed her hand. 'You look very fetching, Mrs Scott.'

'So do you, Mr Goodman.'

On impulse, she kissed his cheek. 'You don't know how I've been looking forward to today.'

'I have an idea.' Driving away from the house, he asked: 'How are things going?'

'Not bad. Steve was rather quiet last night but he's a lot better company than he was before he went away. He'll be starting back at the bank tomorrow.'

'And Paula?'

Rosie sighed. 'Better, but still edgy. I noticed yesterday that she's written down the emergency number for the police and stuck it under the phone in the hall. She's absolutely positive Dave's going to turn up.'

'Poor kid.' Mark slowed down when the lights on a pedestrian crossing turned red.

'And your mum?'

She gave him a puzzled look. 'Why the third degree about my family?'

He glanced at her. 'Tell me.'

'She's doing all right. She snapped my head off during my last visit, so I suppose that means she's getting back to normal.'

'Good.' Mark drove on, picking up speed. 'Now we've been through the list, Rosie, can I ask you not to mention them again?'

She flushed. 'Why say that?'

'Because I've missed you, I haven't been alone with you for ages, and I don't want to share today with your family.' Mark's smile took away the sting in the words. 'I'm glad things are improving, but today's about us.'

There was a small, mutinous silence and then a look of remorse flooded Rosie's features. 'You're right, love. I've neglected you. *And* I've made things difficult at work, too. I'm starting back next week, I swear it. Paula must accept I can't stay by her side for ever.'

Mark sighed. 'I was talking about you and me, Rosie. I didn't mention the work situation, and you've already broken the rules. You mentioned Paula.' He shook his head. 'Deduct one point.' Then he glanced sideways and seeing the reluctant smile on her face, he grinned. 'Now stop apologising and tell me which direction to take.'

Rosie sat upright. 'I don't know. I thought you would decide where we were going.'

He slowed the car. 'You're the one who was born in Yorkshire.'

She chewed her lip, considering. 'We've been to York and you've visited the seaside places so perhaps we ought to go inland.' Her brow cleared. 'I know, we'll go to Coxwold village. It's a lovely run and I haven't been there for ages.' She sat back. 'You need to take the Helmsley road.'

He did so. 'Coxwold, did you say? I've never heard of it.'

'You'll like it. It's a very pretty village and Oliver Cromwell's buried there.'

'Is he? From what little I remember about history, I thought he was buried in Westminster Abbey?'

'He was, but when the Royalists came back to power they dug him up again, together with some other people, and they hung his body up at Tyburn.'

Mark's brow wrinkled. 'You never told me you were interested in history?'

'I am, quite, but I remember this story particularly because years ago we brought the children to Coxwold and we heard about it then.'

Mark negotiated a particularly tricky corner. 'Go on then.'

'Some time after that, a nobleman who had married one of Cromwell's daughters got permission to claim back the corpse. Unfortunately, his head was missing.'

Rosie laughed when she saw Mark pull a face. 'He'd been roughly treated, I'm afraid. Anyway, they dug around and found a headless corpse which they took back to Coxwold. They put him in a secret tomb in the Priory for safety but years later, when they raised the roof of the building, the tomb was found and now you can go and see it.' She glanced at Mark. 'Shall we?'

'What, go and see it?'

'Yes.'

'If you want to.'

'Oh, good. I'd like to see it again.'

He smiled across at her. 'Bloodthirsty woman.'

Rosie laughed. 'Possibly. But it will bring back memories. I remember Steve and Paula absolutely adored hearing all the gory details and Howard said it was a pity we couldn't find a place under the roof to keep my mother because . . .' She put her hand up to her mouth. 'That sounds absolutely awful, doesn't it?' She glanced at Mark. 'He was only joking, of course.'

Mark shrugged. 'Don't apologise. Sons-in-law often don't get on well with mothers-in-law. Mine wasn't too keen on me. Of course, after the accident . . .' His lips thinned.

'Minna didn't like Howard because she thought he wasn't good enough for me.' Rosie hurried into conversation to keep Mark's thoughts busy. 'Which was stupid because we had no particular position to keep up and we certainly had no family money. There's some mystery about her father, though. She has a photograph of him, he was very handsome. I thought I was in love with him when I was about five.' Rosie laughed. 'I suppose it was because she never told me anything about him.'

'So did your mother become reconciled to your marriage, when she saw you were happy?'

'Not really.' Rosie paused. 'A very complicated lady, my mother.'

'I'd like to meet her.'

'Really?' Rosie stared.

'Yes, she sounds quite a character.'

'She is.'

Rosie changed the subject. She stared out of the window and said, 'Isn't it a bonny day?'

Mark nodded his head.

They were making good time and were now deep in the North Yorkshire Moors National Park. As they chatted, they drove through delightful villages and passed old abbeys and imposing stately homes. Rosie pointed out Byland Abby and Ampleforth Abbey and suggested they stop for a look round on their way back.

They arrived in Coxwold in time for lunch. They parked the car and, getting out, walked down the main street which lay quiet and reflective in the warm sun.

'A good choice, don't you think?'

Mark, staring around him, nodded. 'It's beautiful.'

For a tiny village, the main street contained an amazing number of notable buildings. There was a magnificent church with an octagonal tower, an ancient manor house and an old grammar school dating from the early sixteen hundreds. The long wide street was gently sloping with wide, neatly trimmed grass verges and the well cared for houses built of the local yellow limestone.

At the top of the street, just beyond the church, was an intriguing old house surrounded by a beautiful garden. Mark stopped by the gate.

'Is this the final resting place of Oliver Cromwell?'

'Oh, no. He's at the other end of the village.'

'Well, someone important lived here. There's a sign.' Together they read the discreet notice board.

'Laurence Sterne! So there's two famous gentlemen buried in Coxwold.'

'Who was he?'

'More interesting than Oliver Cromwell, at least in my view.' Mark stepped back and studied the building and then looked back at the board. His face clouded over.

'Oh, we can't go in. What a pity.'

Replying to Rosie's questioning look, he explained.

'He wrote a book called *Tristram Shandy* which became famous. It was clever and funny and totally unlike any other book that had been written in those times.'

'Have you read it?'

'Yes.'

'You read a lot, don't you?'

'A fair bit.'

'I thought you did.' Rosie looked pensive. 'I've dipped into a few of the books in your flat.'

He squinted at her. 'Rosie Scott! You've only been in my flat twice and as far as I can remember, there was no free time for you to snoop about.'

She flushed and laughed. 'You were sleeping.'

'Was I?' He flung his arm around her shoulder. 'Let's go and find some lunch.'

They walked along the street and went into a charming pub called the Fauconberg Arms. They ordered tender York ham and chips. Mark went to the bar to buy them a drink. Rosie sat at a corner table and watched him.

God, she thought, I really love this man. But does he love me?

He liked being with her, he enjoyed talking and joking with her, and obviously they enjoyed each other in a sexual way, but was that enough? Was she clever enough for him? His books, for example. Some of them had seemed far beyond her understanding. Did things like that matter? She sighed.

He brought the drinks over. 'You're looking serious, Rosie. Everything all right?'

She smiled at him. 'Everything's fine.'

The ham was delicious as was the freshly made fruit flan smothered with cream that followed it. Mark paid the bill and they emerged into the golden sunlight of the afternoon.

'What now?'

Rosie grinned. 'Oliver Cromwell, or whoever the poor soul is.'

'Right.' He caught hold of her hand and swung it as they went into Newburgh Priory to see the remains of the Great Protector.

After leaving Coxwold they called in at the village of Kilburn and looked up at the famous White Horse carved out of the hillside above the village, then they drove back to the ruins of Byland Abbey.

They were the only visitors. They wandered about, talking little. They gazed up at the grey stone walls and listened to the birds singing, and then they walked a little way away from the ruins and behind an outcrop of granite. Mark pulled Rosie down to lie with him on the short, sweet-smelling grass.

He kissed her forehead and her throat and then he began to unfasten the buttons of her silk blouse. She lay unresisting. She felt the hot sun on her face and heard the buzzing of the gnats and it seemed the most natural thing in the world to open her arms and welcome the man she loved.

They made love, slowly, quietly, and when it was over, they were both quiet and reflective. They even drowsed a little. Half an hour later, Mark sat up and said, 'I suppose we'd better make a move.'

She shook her head. 'Just five more minutes.'

'Of course.' He laid back on one elbow and stared at her.

'That was wonderful, Rosie.'

She smiled.

He bent over her and kissed her cheek. 'You're quiet?'

'I'm thinking.'

'What are you thinking?'

'Honestly?'

'Of course.'

'Well.' She sat up and smoothed her hair. 'Among other things, I was wondering why you were attracted to me?'

His brows drew together in surprise. He thought for a moment and then said, 'The usual reasons, I suppose. You know, the birds and the bees stuff.'

'No, don't joke. I'm serious.'

'So am I.' He looked at her searchingly. 'But a question like that isn't so simple to answer.'

'Try. Please.'

He sighed. 'All right.' He thought for a moment. 'Remember the first time we met, in the garden?'

She nodded.

'I liked you straight away.' He paused. 'Your face was pink with cold and your hair was all over the place with the wind, and you looked . . .' He shrugged. 'Oh, I don't know . . . you were indignant about something.'

Rosie pushed her hair back from her face. 'The main gates were locked.'

'That's right.' Mark slapped his hand down on the grass. 'You were going on about how ridiculous it was, how difficult for visitors, and you looked rounded and feminine, but pugnacious, like a robin.'

Rosie laughed. 'You've compared me to a robin before.'

'Have I?' He grinned. 'Well, *you* thought I was a groundsman.'

'You looked like one.'

They both laughed.

'But I still don't know.' Rosie stopped and started again. 'Look, I'm being really honest now. And I am *not* fishing for compliments.' She took a deep breath. 'I'm a middle-aged mother of two grown-up children and I suppose I'm moderately attractive, but I know I'm nothing special.' She looked down. 'You're rather different. Surely you know that plenty of women would jump at the chance of going out with you?' Her shoulders went up in a shrug. 'So why did you pick me?'

Mark actually blushed. He scratched his head. 'Lord, Rosie, how am I expected to answer something like that?'

Still with an embarrassed look on his face, he turned away to look for a suitable blade of grass. Finding one, he picked it, bit down on it with his teeth and then turned to face her again.

'Ignoring your low estimation of yourself and your over-high estimation of my prowess with women,' he grimaced, 'I'll be honest, too. I find you attractive, I'm comfortable with you, and you're *extremely* good in bed.' His mouth quivered into a smile. 'I hope you don't find that offensive. Personally, and speaking for most men, that's a pretty important factor, you know.' His face became serious again. 'But it's more than that.

'Maybe it's a question of meeting at the right time. For years and years I held back from a steady relationship.' He shrugged. 'Yes, fifteen, ten years ago I dated a few nubile young blondes and we had a good time together, but it never became serious. But now I'm grown up, and I find I like the company of a proper woman.' He raised his eyebrows. 'Will that do?'

'Yes.' Rosie's face was a deep pink. 'Thanks.'

'My pleasure.' He stood up and, putting out his hands, helped her to her feet. 'But now, I fear, we must go home.'

Seeing the disappointment on her face, he explained.

'I have visitors this evening. A nice young couple who are forced to put the boy's mother into a home. They've come to look round. I want to see them personally because they're quite grief-stricken with guilt, although it's not their fault. You know how it is.'

'Yes.' Rosie put her arms around his neck and kissed him.

He smiled. 'Thank you. What was that for?'

'You're a nice chap, Mark Goodman.' She stepped back and looked at him critically. 'And this day out has done you good. You're as brown as a berry.'

He shook his head. 'Sorry, but I can't say the same for you.' He laughed as she put her hand up to her face. 'Your face is glowing like a beacon, Rosie, but I still love you.' He rested his finger on the tip of her nose. 'Sorry, but this is going to peel.'

'Oh, no.' She gave a mock frown. 'Why didn't you tell me?'

'I wasn't concentrating on your nose, love.' He took her hand. 'Race you back to the car.'

As they ran, laughing together, he added, 'Hope you haven't burnt anything else.'

Chapter Twenty-Five

Rosie went back to work on Wednesday and Paula and Alison were alone in the house. Both Rosie and Steve promised to telephone during the day, Rosie at eleven o'clock and Steve at three-thirty.

'You'll be all right, Paula, won't you?

She looked at their anxious faces and said, 'Of course.'

As soon as they left for work, she went into the sitting room and switched on the television set and then she tuned the radio in the kitchen to a popular music programme. She *would* be all right, but she couldn't bear total silence. She listened to the cheery voice of the radio's disc jockey and drank two cups of coffee, then she woke Alison and washed and dressed her.

She felt better when she was working, so she hoovered and dusted the downstairs rooms in the house and then prepared to tackle the pile of ironing. Most of the clothes belonged to Rosie and Steve, she and Alison had so few belongings with them.

Paula ironed the new vests and pants Rosie had bought for Alison in Woolworths and remembered that Steve was going to drive her through to Manchester at the weekend to pick up some of her stuff. Thinking of going back to the flat made her hand tremble so much she had to put down the iron.

Steve had impressed upon her that Dave would not be there. On his arrival home, her brother had firmly assumed the position of man of the house. He had rung the flat several times, when Paula was out with her mother, and when he had received no reply he had contacted the firm which employed Dave.

When he told Paula, she had flared up at him.

'You had no right to do that, Steve. I didn't ask you to. Why couldn't you leave things alone?'

'I did have the right.' His jaw had set stubbornly. 'I'm your brother.'

But his calls had been fruitless. The personnel manager of the messenger firm said that Dave hadn't been in for over a week.

'He hasn't contacted us at all. He's finished as far as we are concerned. Pity, really. He used to be good.'

Steve had persisted in his enquiry. 'But surely he'll come back, if only to collect his employment card?'

'I doubt it.' The man had paused. 'That young guy has problems. We've had a complaint about his attitude from a client, and a couple of weeks ago he was caught popping pills in the men's washroom. We can't have anything like that in our line of work.'

Steve had explained he was speaking on behalf of Dave's wife and left a telephone number for the man to contact them if he had any news.

Listening to her brother's account of the conversation, Paula felt sick. She didn't want to know about Dave's troubles at work, she didn't want to know whether or not he was taking drugs. She just wanted him to stay out of her life. Couldn't her family realise that?

Turning her face away, she had muttered something about feeling tired.

'I'll go for a rest, if that's OK?'

She had gone to bed and fallen asleep immediately. She was sleeping a lot lately, but one hour later she awoke and remembered, as she did so often, the expression on Dave's face just before he started hitting her.

And then she had curled her body up into a ball as she also remembered the pain of his blows and the sound of his fist, thudding into her flesh.

There was a silly little jingle playing on the radio. Paula held out her hands in front of her, watching them tremble, then she hurried upstairs and splashed her face with cold water. From the top shelf of the bathroom cabinet she took down the bottle of pills the doctor had prescribed for her. She tipped one of the tiny blue capsules into the palm of her left hand and then she paused.

She glanced in the mirror at her pale, haunted face and her lips tightened. She tipped the capsule back into the bottle which she replaced in the cabinet, and leaving the bathroom, she went into the bedroom she shared with Alison and smoothed moisturiser over her face and ran a comb through her hair. As she replaced the comb back on the dressing table she heard the phone ringing.

Her breath caught in her throat, but a look at the alarm clock by the bed reassured her. It was eleven-thirty, the call would be from her mother. She ran downstairs.

After a brief chat, Rosie rang off and Paula called to Alison: 'Come here, pet. We're going out.'

Alison was pleased. She skipped up and down and chattered non-stop as they made their way to the small local park. Paula smiled and answered her many questions. She only glanced behind her once.

At the park she sat on a bench next to another young woman and watched Alison play with a tiny boy of about a year old. He reminded Paula of Tracey's little lad and she thought, with a touch of guilt, that she must ring Tracey, who had proved such a good friend.

The young woman sitting on the bench was chatty. She was a single mum, she told Paula.

'The bastard wanted me to have an abortion so I told him where to go. I lived at home for a bit but the Council's just given me a flat. We manage all right, don't we, Jimmy?' She looked across at the toddler.

Paula felt envious. She wished she was a single mum with a place of her own, but she would want to work, she had always paid her own way.

She wondered if she would ever go back to the temping agency. The manageress had contacted her last week. When the phone had rung, her mother had answered.

Rosie, signalling to Paula, had spoken to Mrs Kirby for five minutes, explaining the situation, and then had handed the phone to Paula. Mrs Kirby, sounding somewhat subdued by the information Rosie had given her, asked about Paula's present state of health. She listened to Paula's reply, offered her commiserations, and then spoke of Harris, Templeton and Dean.

'Mr Beaver rang me personally. Your sudden disappearance worried him, as it did me. I was unable to give him any information, of course.' Traces of disapproval still lingered in Mrs Kirby's voice and Paula murmured her apologies.

'I kept ringing your home number but no one answered the phone. I offered Mr Beaver another temp but he declined, said he would sort something out for himself.' Mrs Kirby had sighed. 'I think we've lost that particular contact.'

Again, Paula apologised, and somewhat molified, Mrs Kirby, remembering perhaps that Paula was one of her best employees, continued.

'Then, when I checked your file again, I saw I had your

mother's telephone number.' She waited.

'I know I should have been in touch, but I'm afraid I haven't been able to make plans.' The quick tears sprang to Paula's eyes. She blinked, hating her own weakness.

'I hope you're feeling better now?' Mrs Kirby's query contained a note of genuine concern. Paula's numerous apologies had sweetened her.

She answered cautiously, 'I'm improving.'

'When you feel well enough to return to work, please let me know.' Her employer was back to her businesslike self again. 'The agency's extremely busy.' She paused. 'If you like, I could give Mr Beaver a ring? I know you enjoyed working for him.'

'Oh, no.' Forgetting her employer couldn't see her, Paula shook her head. 'I would be too embarrassed to go back.'

'I wouldn't tell him the truth.' Mrs Kirby sounded surprised. 'We could say you were struck down with a particularly nasty virus.'

'I can't think of coming back yet, Mrs Kirby, but thank you for ringing. I'll be in touch.'

Paula had put the phone down and Mrs Kirby had not rung back.

'Mummy, look.' Alison came running up, clutching a leaf with a ladybird clinging to it.

'Isn't it pretty?' Paula adjusted the hairslide in Alison's fine, wispy locks. At least *she's* happy, she thought. She looked away from her daughter's face and then froze. Across from the bench, close by the park gates, a man was standing. He was too far away for her to see his face but he was of slim build and had fair hair.

'Well, I'm off.' The young woman next to Paula stood up and called to her little boy.

Panic rose in Paula's chest when she gazed around and saw there was no one else in sight.

'I'll walk with you.' She grabbed Alison's hand.

'If you like.' The woman looked surprised.

As they approached the gates Paula's tension grew until she could hardly breathe. She kept her eyes fixed on the gravel path and then, when they were almost at the exit, she looked up. It wasn't Dave. The breath fluttered out of her lungs in a wheeze and her legs went weak.

'Are you all right?' Both the woman and the young man looked at her curiously, then the young man looked away as a young woman and a little girl came down one of the side paths.

'I've found it.' The young woman waved a bedraggled teddy bear in the air.

'You're as white as a sheet.' The girl who had shared the bench with Paula frowned.

'Yes, yes. I'm fine.' Somehow, Paula kept on walking. At the kerb she waved goodbye to the young woman who ran for an approaching bus. Then she and Alison were on their own. Paula rested her back against the wall which rang round the park and shut her eyes. When she opened them again, Alison was staring up at her, an anxious expression on her little face. Paula smiled at her and glanced at her watch.

It was still early. She didn't fancy going back to the empty house. She took hold of Alison and held up her hand to stop another bus which was passing, one which went by the road where her grandmother lived.

Minna was delighted to see them. 'You've brought Alison, too.' She patted the little girl's face.

Paula, following Minna into the sitting room, looked around and thought how everything remained the same.

The pictures on the wall, Grandmother's sewing box, the dainty ornaments on the mantelpiece; the familiarity was comforting. Even Minna's voice, telling Alison to take her shoes off and not to kick the legs of the chairs, was welcome.

Paula smiled. 'Have you anything here she could play with? She'll be occupied then.'

'I know that.' Minna went to her sewing box and opened the lid. She took out an old-fashioned toffee tin, handed it to Alison and gestured to her to sit on the rug by the fire.

'This is my button-box, Alison. You may play with the contents but don't put any of the buttons into your mouth.'

Alison's eyes grew wide. She tried to prise the lid off the box but failed and Paula sank on to her knees by the side of her daughter and did it for her.

'I remember this. I remember the tiny pearl buttons and these big gold ones.' She pushed her hand into the mass of buttons and found one.

'Look, Alison, there's a picture of a lady in a long dress on this one.' She pounced on another. 'And here's a soldier with a sword, wearing a bearskin hat.'

She smiled up at Minna. 'I *loved* playing with the buttons.'

'I remember.' Her voice was dry. She frowned at her granddaughter. 'You're looking peaky.'

Paula lowered her head and sorted out more buttons. 'I'm not so bad. I'm beginng to feel better.'

'Have you decided what you're going to do?'

'No. Not yet.'

'You're not going back to that man, I hope?'

'No.' Paula spoke quickly. 'I don't want to see him ever again.'

'Good.' At last, Minna smiled. 'I knew I could rely on your common sense.'

Paula blushed and changed the subject. 'How are *you*, Grandma?'

'Fine.' Minna dismissed the question with a wave of her hand. 'But I would like a cup of tea, Paula, and I think I'll let you make it this once. I've just finished clearing out some cupboards and I'm a little tired.'

Paula's brow creased. Minna never allowed anyone to make the tea unless she was feeling ill. She surrendered the button box to her daughter and stood up.

'Yes, of course I'll see to it.'

Before she left the room, surreptitiously, she studied her grandmother. She saw that her back was as straight as ever and her eyes were bright and sharp, but her face was gaunt and there were lines of pain etched around her mouth.

Rosie had said Minna was greatly improved but Paula doubted it. She went towards the kitchen, saying cheerfully, 'I promise I won't break any of your precious cups.'

She took special care in arranging the tea things on the tray, knowing that Minna appreciated daintiness, and gained her reward when she carried it through and saw her grandmother's approving nod.

'You were always deft with your fingers, Paula, unlike your mother.'

She took the proffered teacup and saucer carefully, and Paula, noticing her poor swollen fingers, turned away and handed Alison a cup of orange squash, only half-full. Her daughter looked up and beamed and then went back to arranging the buttons in patterns on the hearthrug.

'She won't spill it, Gran. I've taught her to be careful.' Paula sat down and took her own cup of tea.

Minna asked Alison if she wanted a biscuit. Alison nodded and took one. Minna said the old gentleman living next door to her had died and she hoped his flat would be taken by a 'decent' person. Paula said she hoped so, too, and then Minna, obviously deciding that was enough small talk, said: 'Have you seen this man your mother's acquired?'

Paula, unaware that Minna knew anything about Mark Goodman, jumped.

'Er. No, I haven't.'

Minna's face was a picture of disappointment. 'Oh, dear. I was relying on you to tell me about him. You've been home for two weeks, Paula. Why haven't you met him?'

When she did not reply, Minna put her cup and saucer back on the teatray with the suspicion of a bang.

'Do you think there's something peculiar about him?'

Paula blinked. 'Of course not. Why should there be?'

'Well, she's keeping him a secret, isn't she? She's not mentioned him to me, you haven't seen him yet, Stephen came to see me after his trip to Lancaster and never said anything. Perhaps he's an undesirable character?' Minna frowned.

A bubble of amusement rose somewhere inside Paula and she relished the sensation. It had been a long time since she had felt like laughing. She couldn't, of course, Minna would be offended. She said, carefully, 'Really, it's none of our business, Grandma. Mum will tell us when she's ready.'

'She won't tell me. No one tells me anything nowadays,' Minna catalogued her complaints. 'Stephen was upset about something before he went away but he never said anything, and when I spoke to your mother about him she said he was fine.' A spiteful note entered the old lady's voice. 'She hadn't even noticed because she was too wrapped up in her mysterious gentleman friend. As for you.' She stared at Paula accusingly. 'You were in hospital before *I* heard what had been going on.'

'Grandmother.' Paula spoke sharply and nodded towards Alison, who was now lying flat on her tummy, trying to pile up the buttons into columns.

'She's not interested.' Minna dismissed the child with a wave of her hand and turned her attention back to Paula's concerns.

'Has your husband tried to contact you?'

She bit her lip. 'No.'

'What do you intend doing about the flat, and about money, to help bring Alison up?'

'I can manage. I'd rather look after her on my own.' Paula lowered her voice. 'I don't think contact with Dave would be good for her.'

'Good.' Minna sat back in her chair with a sigh of satisfaction.

'In my opinion,' she said, conversationally, 'most women are better off on their own. Men are nothing but a liability.'

Paula was silent, remembering fleetingly the first two years of her marriage; but the contrast between past and present was too painful so she redirected her thoughts.

'Mum and Dad were married a long time. They were happy.'

'Well, yes.' Minna sniffed. 'But I think that was because Rosemary was always so placid and accommodating. She agreed with Howard's every suggestion. It's difficult to fall out with a woman like that.' She stared into space. 'But when a woman is strong enough to demand an equal partnership, things go badly wrong.'

Paula studied her grandmother's face. 'Are you saying that your marriage was unhappy?'

Minna did not immediately reply and Paula blushed to the roots of her hair. What on earth made her ask that?

'Our marriage was a *good* marriage.' Minna fixed her

gaze on Paula's face with the intensity of a brooding eagle. 'We kept our marriage vows, and brought up our only child in a Christian household. Mind you, Rosemary was a quiet, solemn child.' She shook her head. 'I often wondered if she was happy. Perhaps if we'd had other children, she might have been more outgoing.'

'Alison's an only child and she's happy enough.' Minna's remark had touched a raw nerve and Paula's voice was defensive. 'She goes to nursery school and has lots of playmates.'

Minna didn't hear her. Her thoughts were far away and she continued as though Paula had not spoken.

'It's a pity the family line has been so thin. Papa would have found it most disappointing.' She sighed. 'He wanted sons, but I was an only child and so was your mother. Now, if I had had sons . . .'

Realising her grandmother had not been criticising her, Paula relaxed and said a little cheekily, 'I can't imagine you surrounded by a clutch of children, Grandma.'

Minna came back to the present and sighed. 'No, neither can I.'

She sat more upright in her chair and asked Paula to pour her another cup of tea. Accepting it, she shook her head. 'To tell you the truth, I found one child rather a burden. How can one understand what goes on in their little heads?' She sipped her tea. 'To be honest, a large family would have driven me insane.'

Spontaneously, they both laughed and Paula felt an added warmth when Minna, reaching forward to pat her knee, added: 'Babies have no appeal for me but I do enjoy the company of my grown-up granddaughter.'

There was a wail as Alison demanded their attention. The button box had lost its appeal. Minna found the little girl a sheet of paper and a pencil and sat with her as she drew a house with cotton wool clouds emerging from the chimney and Paula cleared away the tea things and washed up. Then it was time to leave.

'Steve said he would ring me, Grandma, so I'd better be at home to take the call.'

'Of course.' Minna saw them to the door. 'It's been lovely seeing you, but it is time for my rest.'

Paula looked at her anxiously. 'You will take care of yourself?'

'I always do.'

The two women embraced.

Alone again, and relishing the peace, one small child took up so much space, Minna went back to stare at the photograph of Thomas and the youthful Rosemary. Her conversation with Paula had reminded her of times gone by and not all the memories were unpleasant. She picked up the photograph frame and studied the two faces. They stared back at her, both wearing the same expression: dogged, patient, awaiting approval.

She sighed sharply and replaced the photograph frame with a slight bang. What a pity Rosemary hadn't inherited her looks.

But Paula had. With difficulty, Minna knelt and opened the bottom drawer of the sideboard. She took out an extremely old photograph album, levered herself to her feet and went to sit down. She opened the album. A sepia-coloured photograph which had come adrift from its mounting slid down from the first page and fell into her lap. It was the very one she was seeking. She picked it up and studied it.

Herself at the age of twenty-one looked back at her. The young Minna stared defiantly at the long-forgotten photographer and the world in general. Her chin was up. Her hands were not, as was usual, demurely clasped in her lap. She was standing before a stylised backcloth, one foot slightly forward and one hand resting on her hip. Her dark hair clung in close waves to her rounded cheeks and her gaze dominated the portrait. Her face was pale and her dress severe, with no trimmings. With no distractions, her beauty was overpowering.

Minna felt a throb of satisfaction. She knew she had been right. Despite the changing fashions in dress and hair-style, the woman in the photograph could have been Paula. With a gentle finger, Minna touched the face of her young self. When she was gone, the genes of herself and her father would remain.

Minna knew herself and had no illusions about the affection she felt towards her granddaughter. She knew her love for Paula was precisely *because* of the resemblance between them, and she had always hoped passionately that Paula would have a good life. The kind of life that had been denied to her. But now, Paula was sharing more than looks with her, for she too had married the wrong man. What's more, she had married a man who had beaten her. At least Thomas had never done that. Although . . .

Closing off that particular door in her memory, Minna flipped over the pages of the album. Many more of the photographs had come loose during the passage of the years. The gum behind the mounts must have dried up for the pictures lay awry across the black pages of the album and the the small gold and silver corner mounts that had restrained them were scattered about like a flock of little birds.

Two days after their marriage, Thomas had taken her to a grand estate and they had walked through the woods and along the edges of the moors where the grouse were bred. He had pointed out a bright-eyed, prettily coloured young bird hiding amongst the heather.

'That'll be one of the youngsters Billy released a couple of days ago.'

Billy Hawley was the estate's gamekeeper and a friend of Tom's.

'Grand-looking, isn't he?' Thomas had made soft cooing sounds and the bird had cocked its head on one side and listened. 'Beats me what pleasure your London friends find in coming North to slaughter hundreds of them.'

Actually, standing so close to the young bird, Minna agreed with his view, but she would not admit to it.

'They're bred especially for the sport, aren't they? If people didn't shoot, they'd never have a life at all and your friend would be out of a job.'

'Aye, I suppose you're right.' Thomas had glanced at her from beneath lowered lids. 'You usually are.'

Minna flipped over two pages. Thomas's photograph had remained firmly attached to the centre of *his* page. She looked at the picture. In size and content, it was the twin to hers.

Trust Tom's photograph not be become dislodged, she thought. Was there ever a man who clung so firmly to his convictions?

She sighed. When she had taken their photographs and stuck them in the album, Betty had protested.

'You and Tom should be on following pages. You're married now. You belong together.'

Minna had laughed. 'Well, you're the one who brought us together. We both love you, so your photograph can be in the middle.'

She turned back one page. There was Betty, smiling for

the two of them, her hair set in rigid waves, wearing her new blue dress that highlighted her bust. Dear, dear Betty. She looked so happy.

It was Betty's idea to go and have their pictures taken professionally. They couldn't afford the usual trimmings for a wedding. They were married in church but there had been no wedding photographs and no flowers. Minna had carried a prayer book. There had been no organ music and few guests and certainly no reception. But for the wedding, the three of them had splurged on new clothes.

Minna went back to Tom's portrait.

He had been photographed wearing his new suit, and most uncomfortable he looked in it. The high collar looked as though it was strangling him. His haircut was incredibly short, a way of saving money, and his expression was serious to the point of being dour. The suit had been cheap and it showed.

Minna shrugged. Her late husband had never tried to be stylish.

She was about to turn the page when something stopped her, she wasn't sure what. Nevertheless, she studied Tom's photograph again.

He was standing in front of the same sylvan backcloth before which she had posed. His feet, in sturdy shoes, were planted side by side and the photographer had made him grasp the edge of his jacket with one hand while the other arm dangled limply by his side. Minna looked at his hands.

They were nicely shaped and, in so much as a working man could care for them, she remembered how he had cared for his. After work, or after gardening, he used some special cream to remove stains and always kept his nails clean and clipped short.

His body was strong and his arms and legs muscular. In the photograph, because his suit was made of cheap material and had been cut meanly, his leg muscles could be seen, straining against the material of the trouser legs.

With a rush of memory, Minna recalled the first time she had seen Thomas without his clothes and also remembered the feelings his naked body had aroused in her. Even after all these years, she remembered. She banged the album shut and threw it down upon the floor. Then she wrapped her arms about herself and shivered.

'What a waste it was,' she whispered. 'What a terrible waste.'

Chapter Twenty-Six

Hateful Halifax. Minna hated everything about it. The cold, the freezing rain, the draughts that sneaked into rooms through ill-fitting window-frames. She hated the noise. The factory whistles in the morning summoning the weary back to work, the shouts and screams of dirty unattended children playing in the gutters; the children themselves with their running noses and apathetic faces speaking, when they spoke at all, words she could barely comprehend.

Surely there must be somewhere pleasant? Surely, somewhere there were streets with grass verges, trees and well-dressed people conversing intelligently?

One day she was unwise enough to mention the thought to Thomas.

He had looked at her with scorn on his face.

'Of course there are. You don't think the mill owners live in places like this, do you?' He had shaken his head. 'But the swanky bits of Halifax are further out of the town, and there'd be no point your going anywhere near. You're part of the labour force now, Minna.' His smile was sardonic. 'If you want intelligent conversation, I can take you into the Labour Club. I'm a member.'

She had walked away from him. She didn't want to listen to men in cloth caps going on about wage demands and shorter working hours. She wanted to be with other young women. She wanted to giggle about the latest scandal, talk about books and clothes. She wanted to escape.

She thought, more than once, about writing to Cicily Chesterton but her pride stopped her. Then one morning, taking a rest from job-hunting, she went into the reading room at the municipal library and leafed through the London papers.

A small picture on the Society page caught her eye. It was a picture of Cicily with another woman. Minna read the text beneath. It said that Cicily and her cousin, Amy Tyrell, were leaving for an extended holiday in America. They would not be back in London until the spring.

She had closed the newspaper and sighed. Her last chance of escape had been denied her. And yet, in her heart, she knew she would not have gone to Cicily, even if the opportunity had presented itself. She was not a quitter.

She looked at the workers coming home in the evening, so tired and defeated-looking, and swore she would not become like them. Every morning she brushed her hair until it shone, put on her still-good coat, touched her lips with lip salve bought from Woolworths, and went out looking for work.

They had been in Halifax four months. During the first three weeks they had fared well. Thomas had been the first to find work. He had contacted old friends, followed their advice, and a few days after their arrival, had been taken on at a garage. Even in a depression there were those who made money, and running a car was a way of telling everyone that you had succeeded.

The wage offered was poor, but as his employer said: 'Thoo's lucky to be offered a job, lad.'

Then Betty was offered a job. Her employer was the pregnant landlady of a large boarding-house.

'Joe, my man, says I should have some help. It's our first kid, you see, and I'm forty years old. Joe's hoping for a lad but I don't care. Can you start right away? Once baby's born, I hope to keep you on, at least for a couple of months. Does that suit?'

Betty had smiled her good-natured smile. 'That's fine, Mrs Prince. It'll tide me over and things might buck up soon.'

'And pigs might fly!'

Minna was less fortunate. Thomas told her to concentrate her efforts on shops and offices.

'The mills and factories won't employ you. You've no experience. Anyway,' he had glanced briefly at her slight figure, 'you'd never manage the work, but you'd look good serving in one of the better class dress shops, and you say you're good at figure work.'

Minna discovered that better class shops were few and far between. They had been forced out of business by the recession. She turned her attention elsewhere. She tramped round dozens of establishments asking if they needed a bookkeeper or accounts clerk. Only two places granted her an interview.

'We were thinking of increasing staff.' The sharply dressed young man picked his teeth with a toothpick and studied Minna's appearance with interest. 'Fallen on hard times, have we?'

When she flushed and did not answer, he grinned.

'We must be the only company in this town to have increased our business.' He chuckled. 'We're a loan company, see?'

'Oh.' Minna nodded and tried to look enthusiastic.

The young man fingered his chin. 'Yes, you'd look good in the front office, collecting the money. Add a bit of class, you would.'

Hope stirred within her.

'You're good at figure work, you say?'

'Oh, yes.'

'And typewriting?'

Her face fell. 'Well, no. I don't have that skill, but I'm sure I could learn.'

The young man's smile disappeared. 'You're wasting my time, missie. I need a typist. Do you think our customers like repaying their loans? We send out hundreds of letters a week.'

With bad grace, he had hustled her out of his office.

The man who finally offered her a job ran a wholesale tobacco business. His office was a dingy little room at the back of a huge warehouse. The paint was peeling off the wall and there was no form of heating.

'Heat's no good for tobacco,' Mr Burnhill informed Minna. 'It dries out too much.'

Mr Burnhill sat behind a desk littered with scraps of paper. He overflowed his creaky swivel chair. Wisps of hair were plastered over his bald dome and his eyes looked piggy in his suet-like face. He asked Minna to write something down for him and then studied the sheet of paper.

'Aye, you'll do. You've a good hand and you can number, you say?'

Minna nodded.

'I need someone to sort out this paperwork.' His podgy hand gestured at the mess of papers on his desk. 'You can work out a filing system for me. I haven't the time, you see.' He leered at her. 'Too busy, wheeling and dealing.'

Minna hesitated. 'I can't type.'

'That's a good thing.' He roared with laughter. 'I haven't a bloody typewriter.' He heaved himself out of his chair and offered his hand. 'See you on Monday.'

She touched his fingertips and then pulled away, resisting the urge to wipe her hand on her skirt.

'Yes. Thank you'

She left the office feeling miserable but, as she walked home, her spirits rose. Mr Burnhill was unattractive but he had given her a job and she told herself she could handle him. With a bit of luck he would be out most of the time. She gave a little skip. She was going to earn money.

On their arrival in Halifax they had stayed three days in the boarding-house and then moved into lodgings. A widow woman, a former friend of Betty's mother, had rented them the upstairs three rooms of her house and the use of her kitchen. She had even given them a few necessary utensils, a pan, mugs and three knives and forks.

Minna had been living in the real world long enough to know they had been lucky. Their living room possessed a good-sized window. There was a sideboard with a fine aspidistra standing on top of it and room inside for their pots and pans. On one wall hung an engraving of the Stag at Bay.

Betty, admiring the picture, suggested that Minna put up her own two paintings.

'Oh, no. I don't think so.'

'They'd be safe, you know. People round here don't have much, but they're honest.'

Minna had hesitated and, strangely enough, Thomas had come to her rescue.

'Let her be, Betty. When she finds a place good enough for 'em, she'll have them out of that box of hers.'

Minna wondered if he was being sarcastic but when she looked at his face she saw only sympathy. It flustered her.

There was a folding table and three hard chairs and one

easy chair in the living room. The other two rooms were bedrooms.

'You two girls share the biggest room, I'll have the coffin.' Thomas grimaced. His title for his room was apt.

The privy, of course, was down the yard.

They settled in and for just over a month their life was secure. Then things went wrong.

Betty's employer went into labour and suffered a still-birth. Three days later she dismissed Betty.

'Nothing personal.' Her eyes burned in her white face. 'Don't need help now. With only Joe to see to, I can manage.' Her face had twisted with pain. 'Everywhere you look there's unwanted kids. Not fair, is it?'

Betty, tears in her eyes, agreed.

Three weeks later Thomas had his wages cut.

'He's dropped my money by fifty per cent, the bastard! He says if I don't like it, I can leave.'

'Oh, Tom.' Betty's face turned bright red with shock and embarrassment. She hated Thomas to swear. 'Has the work dropped off? Is that why?'

'Has it hell! We're busier than ever. He's just working the system. He knows there's been more lay-offs in the works. He knows I can't leave.'

Tom's shoulders had drooped.

Betty went to make a cup of tea. She brought it to him and said, 'Never mind, Minna's still working.'

A week later, Minna came home and told them she had walked out of her job.

They looked at her in appalled silence.

'I had to. I'm sorry. I just had to!' She burst into tears and rushed into the bedroom. Later, she told Betty why she had left.

'It was Mr Burnhill, Betty. I couldn't stand any more.'

She recited the usual, sorry tale.

'He started on the first day. Crowding me, breathing down my neck, sliding his hand around my waist, trying to touch me higher up.' She shuddered. 'And he's so gross, Betty, and his hands are always damp, like wet fish, and his breath's bad.

'I thought I could cope. I learned to keep away from him. I always tried to stand at the other side of the desk, silly things like that, but he just got worse. He seemed to think I was having a game with him.'

She took a deep breath. 'But I still would have stuck it out, I would, except that . . .'

She started to shiver and Betty moved closer to her and slipped her arm around Minna's shoulders.

'What happened?'

'I'd taken some sales dockets into the warehouse.' Minna whispered the words. 'I thought I was safe because he had gone out on business but he'd come back early.

'He was at the back of the warehouse, checking a new delivery of cigars. He sneaked up behind me and grabbed at me. I twisted out of his grasp and said something, I don't remember what, something jokey, I think. But he didn't appreciate it. He grabbed me again. Look.'

She pushed up her sleeves and showed Betty the bruises.

'I began to feel scared. His big, fat face came close to me and he started to say what he wanted to do to me. He said I was a tease and I needed a lesson.'

Tears began to roll down her cheeks. 'It was awful, Betty. He put his hand up my skirt and he fumbled with my underwear and I was terrified. I couldn't move, but then I thought how horrible he was and I knew I had to fight back.

'I got one hand free and I clawed at his face and then I brought my knee up . . .'

She covered her face with her hands.

'You did right, Minna.' Betty's voice was concerned. 'Don't feel ashamed.'

'Ashamed!' Minna revealed her face. 'I enjoyed it, Betty. I wanted to stamp the fat pig to a pulp. He let go of me and doubled over and I grabbed a wooden crate of cigarettes and threw it at him. It hit him and he staggered back and I ran.'

Betty stared at her. 'Do you think he was badly hurt?'

'I don't know. I hope so. That crate was heavy.'

Betty frowned. 'What about Tom? Shall I tell him what happened?'

'Oh, no.'

'I'll have to tell him something. He'll know something serious must have happened to make you leave.' Betty nodded her head. 'I think I must tell him.'

'If you must.' Minna shrugged. 'He won't go and see Burnhill, will he?'

'Oh, no. He knows there's nothing we can do.'

Betty went to tell her brother and for the rest of the day Minna avoided meeting him. She kept wondering how he had reacted to the news and felt shy at the thought of facing him. But next morning, when she saw him, it was almost an anticlimax, for he behaved as though nothing had happened. Minna felt oddly disappointed.

Thomas was supposed to be a man of principle. Didn't he *care* that she had been assaulted? If it had happened to Betty, she thought, he would have gone to Burnhill and roughed him up.

But then she looked closer at Thomas and saw the look of strain around his eyes and the tenseness of his form and realised that Betty's remark had been true. Burnhill was a businessman, he had money. There was nothing Thomas could do. Fury enveloped her. That pig of a man had won.

He would employ some other young girl and the same thing would happen to her.

Thomas asked, without looking at her, whether she wanted a cup of tea. She said yes and forced a smile when he handed it to her. She resolved to try and forget the incident. She had escaped unharmed. What she had to do now was find another job.

But there were no jobs, and apart from the pittance Thomas brought home every Friday, there was no money. A week later, without telling her friends, Minna chose a piece of the jewellery she had smuggled from her father's house after his death and took it to a pawn shop. The owner offered her five pounds.

'That's ridiculous. It's worth more than fifty.'

The man shrugged. 'That's part of the problem. It's too good for round here. I doubt I can shift it. You can try somewhere else.'

She took the money. She was hungry. On the way home, she shopped. She had learned what to buy. Cereals, bread, potatoes, margarine and tea – cheap carbohydrates that filled empty stomachs. She walked past a butcher's shop and her mouth watered when she remembered the fillet steak and lamb chops she had eaten so thoughtlessly and carelessly in her former life.

They were no longer living in their original lodgings. They now rented two rooms in a dilapidated three-storeyed house in the poorest district of Halifax. The house was split into numerous small units. Betty and Minna shared a lumpy double bed in one room and Tom slept on the floor in the living room.

The house contained a communal kitchen on the ground floor and the only washing facilities were housed in a room built on to the rear of the property. Here were two sinks, cold water taps only, a copper for boiling clothes, a mangle and an antiquated boiler fed by pennies. The room was cold and damp and the enamal bath was chipped and ugly.

Three weeks after moving in, Minna decided to brave the bath. She had been walking the streets for three hours looking for work. Her feet were aching and she knew her clothes smelt fusty. It was autumn now but the day was unseasonably warm. She was on her way home and had just heard a church clock strike three.

Between three and five the bath house was deserted. Those people who had jobs were working. Those who hadn't were out looking for work or caring for children, or simply lying on their beds and drowning their sorrows in cheap gin, or sleeping. They needed to sleep when it was quiet.

With up to thirty-five people living in the house the noise was never-ending. Babies screamed for attention, couples fought, and there was constant banging on doors and abusive language from neighbours who craved peace. Sometimes, Minna wrapped her hands round her head and swore that all she required from life was a little peace and her own room.

The conditions in which they were living affected them all but Minna suffered the most, and it showed. Her patience was short and her tongue sharp. Because Thomas was often quiet and moody, she goaded him. She tried to provoke arguments. She relished an argument. It made the blood run more swiftly through her veins and dispelled that awful feeling of apathy which affected so many of their neighbours.

When she was in one of her moods, Thomas usually ignored her but every now and again he would retaliate. He became sarcastic, referring to Minna as 'your ladyship' and mentioning her lack of any worthwhile skills. When he did so, Betty became more upset than Minna.

She would anxiously try to patch things up between them and then suffered their united wrath.

Since their move, Minna had contented herself with strip-down washes. She had looked at the bath and decided it was not for her, but today she ached for the feel of warm water on her body. She entered the house, climbed the uncarpcted stairs to their rooms on the second floor, and let herself in. The blessed silence in the house, perhaps because of the hot weather, was duplicated in the rooms. Minna shut her eyes and savoured the peace.

Of course, Betty had told her that morning that she was going out. She had found two hours' work, ironing for a woman who took care of three old ladies. Thomas was at work, he was never home before seven-thirty.

The idea of having a bath became more appealing. She checked her purse for change. Yes, she had coppers for the boiler. With a feeling akin to excitment she went through her meagre possessions looking for a piece of scented soap she had secreted. She found it and placed it with her face flannel and a threadbare but clean towel.

She hesitated, wondering what to do about her clothes. There were no niceties in the bath house, no mirror, no chair upon which to lay your clothes, and the stone-flagged floor was always running wet. Minna took off her clothing, put her coat back on and thrust her feet into her outdoor shoes. She picked up her bathing things and went downstairs.

The unusually warm day must have made the inhabitants of the house sleepy. Even the babies were quiet. Outside the bath house door, Minna listened. Not a sound. She pushed at the wood. The door stuck for a moment and then opened. She went in and the door swung shut behind her.

Thomas was bending over the bath. Steam was rising in

the air but not enough to mask his naked figure. Staring, Minna saw his width of his shoulders and the way his back tapered down towards his buttocks. She saw his bottom was small and well-shaped and noticed how white was his skin. And as she noticed all this, her mouth opened in shock and surprise and a strangled squeak emerged from her.

Thomas swung round. 'Christ! What are you doing in here?' There was horror on his face. Shielding his manhood with one hand, he reached up and grabbed a towel from a length of cord suspended above the bath and held it in front of him. 'How did you get in? The door's locked.'

Minna shook her head. The towel Thomas was clutching was small, totally inadequate. She was so nervous she knew she was going to laugh and knew she mustn't.

She looked away, back at the door through which she had just passed. The fastening was primitive, just an iron hook that dropped into a ring driven into the wall. The plaster around the ring had crumbled and the ring was hanging loose, at the end of the hook.

'I'm sorry.' Her voice shook. She let go of her coat and raised both hands to her mouth. She must not laugh. 'I wanted a bath. I thought no one would be here.' Her brow creased. 'Why *are* you here?'

'I've a couple of hours free. I have to work tonight.' His voice was no more than a whisper, and his expression was odd. She realised *he* was staring at her.

Belatedly, she realised why. She had released her grasp on her coat and the top half had fallen open revealing her bare breasts. She blushed violently and, grabbing at the material, she covered herself.

'Don't do that.' Thomas's voice was gentle. 'I'd never hurt you, Minna, but please, let me see.'

A funny feeling started inside her, a feeling of quivering

excitement. She released the hold on her coat.

He looked at her and then said quietly, almost reflectively, 'You're so beautiful. I knew you would be.'

The tremor inside her intensified. She drew in her breath. Tom's hands had dropped to his side. He was no longer furtively shielding himself. Minna studied his muscular, well-proportioned body and saw the expression on his face and knew he desired her.

Heat throbbed through her body like a giant pulse and she gasped, wondered what was happening to her. Whatever it was, she welcomed it. She felt carelessly, recklessly alive.

Without even thinking, she stood up straight and flung open her coat. Thomas had called her beautiful. She knew that she was. She watched his face change, she saw the the look of desire flare in his eyes and, seeing it, exhilaration flooded her. Staid Thomas was a man after all, a passionate man. She could make him her slave.

She studied his body again and took a step forward.

He put out his hand, palm outwards. 'Don't, Minna. Don't come any closer.'

His resistance infuriated her, added to the fire now burning inside her. He had called her beautiful. Surely he wanted her? Surely he wanted to share with her in experiencing this strange mystical experience she had read about in books but had never personally experienced? It was time for her to experience it. Did she have to wait until she was old and ugly before a man claimed her? And Thomas was beautiful. She wanted him.

She studied his face and then brought up her own hand and brushed it against her naked breast. A tremor rang through her. Oh, this was exciting, being naked in front of a man.

Still watching him, she took another step forward, and

then another. He watched her, unspeaking, but she saw evidence of his rising passion. She stood in front of him and touched his chest. His skin was without blemish and his chest was broad and manly. He was so different from the spoiled young men who had courted her in London. She smiled, remembering them, and her hand dropped and touched the place the towel had hidden.

He drew in a harsh breath. 'No. This is madness.'

He was so big. Were all men like this?

He began to shake. He stepped back and looked wildly around the room. 'Suppose someone comes?'

'They won't.' She spoke with utter conviction. 'No one will come.' She put her hands upon his shoulders and her small firm breasts brushed against his chest.

His breath was exhaled in a groan and he caught hold of her and pulled her against him.

She could hear his heart beating. He was so tall and strong, he could have crushed her, but she knew he would not hurt her. His hands caressed her gently and his mouth was tender. She sighed and felt the bones in her body dissolve. She knew he was containing his power and his strength and she luxuriated in his caresses like a cat before a fire. She arched her back as he kissed her neck and then gasped as his head moved lower. She trembled as his mouth travelled over her breasts and his tongue circled the erotic zones of her darkened taut nipples.

She fought to stay in control of her emotions. He mustn't become my master, she thought, but her body betrayed her when he sank on his knees before her and pressed his face against her stomach and stroked her thighs. She threw back her head and moaned. Her hands, resting on his shoulders, clenched and she whispered, 'You're beautiful, too.'

'Am I?' His voice was muffled.

She nodded. Every nerve-end in her body was crying out for satisfaction. She bent forward slightly and raked her nails lightly over his back. When he groaned, deep in his throat, she smiled. If he was doing wondrous things to her body, she was affecting him the same way.

When he touched the dark silky hair that covered her femininity, she almost gave way. Almost, but not quite. She opened her eyes and looked around her. She was going to participate in the final mystery, but not here, not in this place.

She eased herself away from him and, bending, whispered in his ear.

'What?' His eyes were blind, his ears deaf.

She said again, 'We can go upstairs, Thomas.'

He blinked like a sleep walker. 'How can we?'

'We'll be alone. Betty won't be back until five.'

'But . . .' His hands loosened their grip. There was confusion in his eyes.

She cupped his face and kissed him. Their first kiss. She said, 'It will be better upstairs.'

The beginnings of a frown darkened his face. 'Minna, I can't . . .' He tried to find the the right words. 'I don't know. I need you now.'

'And I want you.' She kissed him again. 'But I want it to be good and we can't even lie down in this place.' She ran her hands over his shoulders; his body felt tense and unyielding. 'Upstairs, we have the bed.'

'You don't understand.' There was anger in his voice. 'Men are different from women. They can't always . . .'

'Oh, they can.' She whispered in his ear. 'I'll make you.'

Abruptly, he released her. 'You like your comfort, don't you, Minna?' He sighed and moved away from her. He stood up. 'Perhaps it's for the best. We're mad, both of us. This should never have happened.'

Doubt hit her like a shower of cold water. She had spoilt it. She had spoilt everything. Shivering, she wrapped her coat around her and handed Thomas his clothes. He turned his back on her as he dressed.

They moved towards the door in silence but as he opened it, Minna's despair lightened for, as she walked past him, her arm brushed against his and she distinctly heard his breath catch.

Instantly, she caught hold of his hand and, raising it to her mouth, she kissed it.

'When we get upstairs, I'll show you, my love. It will be wonderful, I promise you.'

And it was.

Chapter Twenty-Seven

If it had ended there, they would both have escaped the half-life of an unhappy marriage. They could even have remained friends.

Looking back over a gap of more than fifty years, Minna acknowledged that she bore the heaviest burden of guilt. But she had been foolish rather than wicked. Her first experience of sexual passion had overwhelmed her. She had never guessed that it could be so wonderful. Her life at that time was miserable, sex was an escape and Thomas the means of effecting that escape. She seduced him at every possible opportunity.

But opportunities were rare in such a noisy, seething house. Minna, remembering the difficulties, pursed together her wrinkled lips. How many times did they manage it? Five times? Six? Maybe the difficulties, the dangers, added to the intensity of their coupling? She remembered the nights she had lain beside the gently snoring Betty and fretted away the hours devising a way to be with him. And he became as avid for their meetings as she. His initial reservations about their behaviour had melted in the heat of their passion and, of course, he told her that he loved her.

Minna never said she loved him. She thought little of love. Thomas was just Thomas, a kind but normally rather boring man who was Betty's brother: but stripped of his clothes he was physically beautiful and, by some strange alchemy, his touch could drive her wild. After a long, dark time, she was happy again.

But the gods were cruel.

Minna was old now and she knew her years were numbered, but unlike most old people she found no comfort in religion. There was no fatherly smiling gentleman waiting to welcome her into his heaven.

If there were gods, she thought, they were the old gods, beloved by the Romans. They looked down at the puny mortals below them and manipulated their lives for their own amusement.

She sighed. More likely there were no gods at all, just an impersonal natural law which saw that you paid for your pleasures. *Who pays the piper?* She shook her head. *The one who called the tune*. Perhaps that was fair. Without realising, she rubbed the aching joints of her fingers. She had paid and so had Thomas, which was unfair because, without her prompting, he would not have sinned.

When her monthly bleeding was late Minna was unconcerned. She was always irregular. But the days went by and nothing happened and doubt began to nag at her. Six weeks late was a long time. It couldn't be a baby? She didn't even like babies. Babies happened to other women, not her.

Nevertheless, she bought half a bottle of gin and drank it sitting in boiling hot water in that repulsive bath. Nothing happened. She didn't feel pregnant. Her breasts remained small and didn't bother her. She was not sick in the mornings. Nevertheless, she was scared. She had always confided in Betty, but not this time. She told Thomas instead.

His face paled. He slipped his arm around her and held her close. 'I'm sorry, Minna. This shouldn't have happened. It's all my fault.'

Even in her misery, she felt a flash of irritation. 'I was there, too.'

He didn't hear her. He was turning the problem over and over in his mind.

'We must get married.'

She stiffened. 'There's other ways. I've heard women talking. You can take something.'

He held her away from him and, for the first time, she felt frightened of him.

'Don't even think of it. You could end up dead, do you know that? And what about the child? It's mine as well as yours. No.' He sighed. 'We must marry, and as quickly as possible.'

She bit her lip. 'It's early days, Thomas. Something might happen, naturally, I mean. We could wait a little longer.'

'No, we can't. Round here, even an eight-month child's a scandal. I don't want my child hearing gossip when he's growing up.'

He's even decided the sex, she thought bitterly.

'A church wedding, but a quiet one.' Thomas pulled at his lip. 'If only we had more money. We can't afford flowers or even a small reception.' Lost in thought, he didn't notice Minna's silence. 'Betty will be so surprised, but delighted, I'm sure.' He glanced at Minna. 'We'd better not mention about the baby, not yet. There's no need to shock her. We'll just tell her we're in love and have decided to marry. That bit's true.' Thomas kissed her cheek.

'Everything will work out, Minna. I'll find a better job. We'll move from this place and our baby will want for nothing. I promise you, we'll be happy.'

Minna closed her eyes and sighed.

Oh, simple, simple man.

They married. In church, Minna was docile, her face impassive. Thomas looked anxious and proud. Betty's face showed unalloyed pleasure. They had a meal in a cafe, a rare treat, and then went home again. As night approached, Betty, with an arch expression, took herself off to a neighbour's house. Before she went, Thomas, his face as red as a turkey cock, muttered something about buying a truckle bed for her the following day.

Alone at last, Minna's depression lifted a little. At least there was something good about this ridiculous fiasco. She went into the bedroom and put on her prettiest nightgown and she waited.

Thomas came into the room twenty minutes later. He seemed surprised to see that she was still awake.

'It's been a tiring day for you.'

She frowned. 'It's our wedding night, Thomas.'

He undressed quickly and slipped into bed. She ran her hands over his naked chest. 'Umm. I'm glad you don't wear a nightshirt, Thomas.' She laughed and bit his shoulder, a gentle bite.

He lay still.

She raised herself on one elbow. 'What's the matter?'

'Things have changed now, my love.' His voice was gentle.

'Of course they have. We're married now. We can do whatever we want without feeling guilty.'

'But you're having a child.' He paused. 'Perhaps we should stop being so wild.'

A chill enveloped her. She said, through her teeth, 'That's nonsense. Lovemaking will not hurt the baby.'

'It might. We can't be sure. Anyway, you're my wife

now. It puts a different complexion on things.'

She considered his words and then rage burned through her. 'You mean, I can behave like a whore when I'm single but now that I'm married to you, I must be prim and proper?'

'Oh, Minna.' He shook his head. 'You're always so dramatic. I think you *are* tired. It's been an unusual day and in your condition,' he passed his hand over her stomach, 'it's only to be expected. Try and sleep.' He turned over on his side, his back to her.

She wanted to kill him. God in heaven, if she had possessed the means of doing it, she would have killed him.

Betty, virginal Betty, instructed her in the ways of maternity.

'You must rest every day but you must also have some exercise. Don't lift anything heavy or climb steps. Eat a piece of dry toast in the morning, it will stave off sickness, and if you get heartburn,' here she had smiled, 'it means the baby will have curly hair.'

Minna gritted her teeth and nodded. She never felt the slightest bit sick, without or without toast. She had no heartburn; in fact, she had no symptoms whatsoever. Betty said she had read that a pregnant woman's breasts became sore and tingly. Minna's didn't. They didn't even increase in size. She did feel tired though, and lethargic. She hadn't even finished the little coat Betty insisted she should knit.

Four months after the wedding Thomas told her she must go and see a doctor.

She protested. 'There's nothing wrong with me. It would be a waste of money, Thomas. The other women round here don't go and see a doctor unless they think something is badly wrong.'

'They're stronger than you, Minna. You're a lady, remember. You're used to a better class of life.'

He was right there. Their financial situation had not improved. They hadn't eaten meat for two weeks.

'You're looking very peaky and I'm sure you should have started to put on weight. Look at your stomach, it's as flat as a pancake. Don't worry about the money. I worked over-time last week.'

Still protesting, she went. Betty accompanied her. Sitting in the doctor's waiting room, surrounded by coughing, dirty-faced children and wan, exhausted-looking mothers, Minna thought she knew what was wrong with her, but she couldn't tell Thomas.

How could she tell her husband that there was no joy in her life? The only thing she and Thomas had shared was an exciting love-life and now that had ceased. Oh, he was kind and even loving at times, but he treated her as if she was made of glass. He's more concerned with this wretched baby, she thought. At the moment, I'm just a container for something he wants. A tear slid down her face. There was nothing, absolutely nothing to look forward to.

'Don't get upset, Minna.' Betty's voice was soothing. 'The doctor will see that you and the baby are all right.'

Betty waited outside when Minna went in to see the doctor. She leafed through a magazine to stop herself worrying. When Minna rushed out, she dropped the magazine and jumped to her feet.

'What is it?'

At the sound of her voice and seeing the expression on Minna's face, the rest of the people in the room looked up. Even a grizzling baby stopped crying.

Without a word, Minna rushed past her and out into the street.

Betty hurried after her. 'What's the matter? Oh no.' Her hand flew to her mouth. 'There's something wrong with the baby?'

Minna had propped herself up against the brick outside wall of the surgery. At Betty's words she started laughing hysterically.

Betty, gentle Betty, slapped her face. '*Stop* that. Stop that at once. Tell me what he said.'

Minna choked and stopped laughing. Eyes wild, she whispered, 'There *is* no baby, there never was.' She stared into Betty's uncomprehending face. 'I'm not pregnant. The doctor said that inadequate food, a poor diet, often stops women bleeding. He's seen several cases.' She closed her eyes. 'Oh God, Betty. I needn't have got married. It was all a ghastly mistake.'

Betty was still finding it hard to understand. She patted Minna's shoulder and said, 'I'm so sorry, Minna. And Thomas! Poor Thomas, he'll be so disappointed.'

Minna threw back her head and started laughing again.

With her own hands shaking with shock, Betty took her home and put her to bed.

Flat on her back, staring upwards at the cracked, stained ceiling, Minna brooded. She would never get out of this house. She would spend her whole life there married to Thomas.

I didn't want marriage. I don't love him. Sometimes I don't even like him. He doesn't know how to laugh. He's like an old, old man. I loved the way he made me feel, but he doesn't do that any more. He thought it might hurt the baby.

She started laughing again, burying her head in the pillow to muffle the sound. There was no baby to hurt. I'm glad about that. But I'm trapped now. We've nothing to talk about. He makes a noise when he drinks soup. Papa would turn in his grave if he knew . . . Oh, Papa. She broke into noisy sobs.

Betty came in and sat on the side of the bed. She put her arms around Minna and nursed her like a child.

'Don't take it so hard, Minna. You've got me and Thomas. He'll be heartbroken, you know, but he loves you so much, and I do, too. Try and be strong, for our sakes. We'll all take care of each other.' Her cheek, pressed against Minna's, was also wet with tears.

Snuggled against Betty's billowy breast, she was transported back to her childhood. How often had Betty comforted her? She felt, which was rare for her, a surge of pure love for her friend. She gulped, sat up and moped her face with the sheet.

'I'll try, Betty. I'll try.'

Thomas took the news hard. He had spent all his spare time carving a wooden cradle for the child and when he heard the news he picked it up and carried it outside. He took it round to the back of the house, where there was a patch of waste land, and there he made a fire and burnt it.

When he came indoors again, Betty chided him. 'That was silly, Thomas. There'll be a baby one day.'

'Will there?' He had given Minna an unfriendly glance.

She had bowed her head in acceptance. Thomas knew, more than Betty, Minna's true feelings.

It was ten long years before he held his child and when Rosemary was born, Betty was not there to welcome her.

Betty. Bending over slowly and carefully, Minna picked up the photograph album she had thrown to the floor and, opening it, looked again at her sister-in-law's photograph. What a wife Betty would have made, loving, kind, accepting – but she had been too busy keeping her brother's marriage alive.

Not understanding the reason, but becoming conscious of the emnity between the two people she loved most in the world, Betty had striven to mend their marriage. At every opportunity, she had praised one to the other. She praised Minna's ability to make thc best of their poor home, she praised her exquisite needlework – during the first two years of their marriage, Minna had worked from home, labouring over hand-stitched quilts and bedspreads. She also reminded Thomas he had the prettiest wife in the neighbourhood.

When she was with Minna she cited Thomas's many admirable qualities. Unlike many of the men who lived in the house he neither smoked nor drank. He handed over almost every penny he earned, he worked hard and he was not a womaniser.

Because she cared for Betty, Minna closed her lips on all the negative qualities of her husband. She found him dull, he had no humour, no wit, and the only thing he cared for was the talk at the Labour Club. Worst of all, he no longer approached her sexually.

Staring down at the picture of Betty, the old Minna felt sorrow for all three of them. What a mess they had made of things. And yet, with the wisdom of age, she saw how easily it had happened.

She sighed. Thomas had slowly come to realise that she had never loved him. In crude terms, she had used him as a stud. That's why she had been so distraught when she thought she was having a baby. She had not wanted his child, she had not wanted him. But he had decided to make the best of it. After all, he would have had his child. When even the promised baby had proved to be a myth, he had given up. Hurt and disappointed, he had withdrawn himself from her.

And she? She had become a disappointed, nagging shrew.

Minna tapped the page softly.

If their tragedy had been played out in modern days she would have left Thomas, but in the thirties it just wasn't done. And Betty would not have countenanced it. Betty believed marriage was for ever. Betty thought that if they could climb out of the pit of poverty everything would be all right. And she had devised her own plan. She would help them. She would improve their prospects for a happier marriage by finding a way to make more money.

She went out and got a job. In a laundry, she told them. She worked long hours and insisted on contributing most of her money towards household expenses. After two years she said she had become supervisor. Her money was much better now.

They moved to a much better class of lodgings.

Thomas's working life also improved. Another garage owner poached him away from his original employer. This man paid fair wages. With Minna's contribution from her part-time sewing job they actually began to save. They moved again and then, three years later, they rented a small terraced house. It was bliss. The walls were thick, they could not hear their next-door neighbours. There was a garden for Thomas and, at last, Minna put up her two Italian paintings.

Betty kept getting bad coughs and colds. She suffered from congestion of the chest but she was rarely away from work. Minna was now working at a shop that sold wool and sewing materials. She was allowed to put some of her needlework in the window and the tablecloths and the embroidered runners sold well. Minna told Betty she should go out more with friends from work, enjoy herself a little. Betty nodded and smiled.

One evening Thomas, who had become a great reader, raised his head from a copy of *The Hound of the Baskervilles* and said Betty must go to and see a doctor.

'You've coughed all night, Betty. You must really get yourself sorted out.'

She always did what her brother asked. She came back from her visit a little quieter than usual but composed.

'It's a family weakness, apparently. He's given me some medicine.'

Thankful she had obtained proper advice, neither Thomas nor Minna noticed that the cough remained. She had had it so long, it had become part of her.

Thomas saw an advertisement in the local paper. Dean Clough's was advertising for a mechanic to service their machines. Dean Clough's was a large textile company, specialising in making carpets. Thomas applied and was given the job.

In the late thirties, after great deliberation, he decided they could afford to buy their rented house and the day the contract was signed, Minna told them she was pregnant.

Betty was overjoyed. 'I told you. I *knew* it would happen one day.' She hugged Minna. 'You see, things have a way of righting themselves.'

Minna had nodded. She couldn't tell Betty that her baby had been conceived in an act of mutual despair and conflict.

When telling her about the chance to buy the house, Thomas had been almost totally negative. He agreed the price was fair but he was worried about the mortgage payments. He was terrified of falling into debt.

'We've managed in rented property up to now. My family never owned their own house.'

'But it's a wonderful opportunity, Thomas. We'd be mad not to take advantage of it.'

Thomas had shaken his head. Minna's temper had simmered. Finally, it had boiled over.

'For God's sake, see sense. We'll never get this chance again. Property prices are bound to rise. We can't possibly lose.'

'Ah, well.' Stung by the barely concealed contempt in her voice, Thomas retaliated. 'You'll know all about it. Your dad thought he knew about buying and selling, and look what happened to him.'

'Why, you . . .' Minna swung her fist at him.

He caught her hand and stopped her hitting him. They looked at each other and then he had her down on the floor and was pulling her skirt up. And Rosemary had been conceived.

That had been their last chance. If only they could have talked afterwards. His act had been almost that of rape but it had brought Minna alive again. But they didn't talk. Spent and shaken by the passion, she had smiled at him and he hadn't noticed. Confused and ashamed, he had stumbled to his feet and was adjusting his clothing.

'I'm sorry. That was a terrible thing to do. Forgive me.'

He had hurried from the room and she had been left with the taste of ashes in her mouth.

Five months after that, Betty died. She was in her early-forties. She collapsed at work, was brought home and died three weeks later. Both Thomas and Minna were inconsolable, and their grief was mixed with guilt when they learned of her secret.

Betty had lied to them. For the past eight years she had worked, not at a laundry, but in a woollen mill. She had worked at the looms.

'She was a grafter.' One of her workmates called in on them to offer her condolences. 'Ever so quick with her fingers. She always made top bonus.'

'She did it for us.' Thomas's voice was harsh. Seated at the table, he raked his fingers through his hair, a savage gesture. 'I should have realised. You don't earn the money she was bringing home washing clothes.'

For once, Minna spoke softly. 'She must have *enjoyed* it, Thomas. I know that, years ago, we needed her money to survive, but she could have left the mill a few years ago. But she stayed on.'

She paused. 'Betty didn't have many friends. Perhaps she enjoyed the companionship at work.'

'You have no idea, have you?' Her husband's voice was as cold as ice. 'How can you? You've never really worked in this part of the world. You've played at office work. You earn a few coppers stitching your pretty cloths and you think you know about work.'

He banged his hand on the table, making her jump. 'There's no companionship in the mills. There's no cosy chats. There's hundreds of machines filling the air with a fearful racket. You're deafened by the noise. You need one hundred per cent concentration on your looms because, even if one thread breaks, everything snarls up and you have to fix it. You lose *money*. That's what you work for, Minna. Money! And all the time there's particles of dust and fluff floating about in the air. They enter your nose and your mouth and make you choke.'

He swung round and faced the window.

'That's why Mam never wanted us to work in the mills. It killed her and now it's killed Betty, and all you can talk about is companionship.'

He had looked at her with hate in his eyes.

★ ★ ★

It had happened years ago, but it was as if it were yesterday. Minna's hands shook as she replaced the photograph album in the drawer.

The months between Betty's death and Rosemary's birth had been terrible. Remembering the awful tension that had existed between herself and Thomas, Minna thought it was no wonder her child had been born with a such a self-effacing nature, and yet Rosie's birth had been the catalyst in their marriage.

From the moment Thomas laid eyes upon his daughter, his attitude had changed. He would never regain his original feelings for Minna but she had blessed him with a priceless gift and because of that, he softened towards her.

Slowly, painfully, they had reconstructed their life together and, as the years passed, they developed a peculiar kind of understanding. It was never love, they were so totally different from each other, but as they grew older, they became closer and when Thomas died, Minna was surprised how much she missed him. Of course, she never let her loneliness show.

What her daughter thought of her parents' marriage Minna had no idea but she guessed that, because Rosemary was so like Betty, she knew they did not love each other.

All that twaddle she had told Paula, about Rosemary being lonely because she was an only child, was untrue. Rosemary had been unhappy because she sensed the lack of love in her home.

Rosemary. In the act of putting a cardigan over her shoulders – her journey into the past had made her feel cold – Minna paused. She wanted so much to see Rosemary's new man-friend. It was not just curiosity, although that was a part of it. She hoped, with all her heart, that this new man would be good for Rosemary.

Howard had been a good man and a good husband but he had been solid and too much like Thomas for Minna fully to appreciate him. Let Rosemary's new companion have some lightness about him, she thought. Let them have fun together, before it's too late. Let him teach her how to laugh.

Chapter Twenty-Eight

'We're doing what?'

'Going for a trip in a helicopter.'

'You're joking!'

Rosie's face was a study in consternation.

'No.' Mark glanced in his car mirror as they approached a crossroads. He turned left.

'I'm not going in a helicopter, Mark.'

'Why not? It's perfectly safe.'

'I'd die of fright. I haven't even been in a plane, remember?'

'Oh, it'll be fun, Rosie. We'll have a bird's eye view of the countryside.' He glanced at her. 'It's only a fifteen-minute jaunt. We'll be at your mother's in plenty of time for tea.'

She was quiet.

They had just left a village fête. Rosie had enjoyed that. She and Mark had wandered round the exhibits of prize vegetables and flowers, they had watched the jump-off of the pony class and eaten strawberries and cream in the refreshment tent. The month was June and the weather perfect.

Beneath an azure sky the coloured bunting strung round the exhibition ground had sparkled in the sunlight. The beautiful weather had attracted the crowds and the air was layered with many sounds. The soft mooing of cattle sounded beneath the shrill voices of children trying their hand at the hoopla stall. There was barking of dogs and the occasional roar of laughter from the beer tent.

Just after two o'clock a fitful breeze had sprung up, welcome because it kept the temperature at a pleasant level. Rosie, gazing upwards at the flag snapping above the marquee, had been sorry when Mark said they must leave.

'Already?'

He reminded her, 'Your mum's expecting us for tea.'

'Yes, I suppose you're right.'

They had got into the car and driven away.

Rosie was a little apprehensive about taking Mark to see her mother. She had delayed the moment as long as possible but Minna had nagged at her until she had agreed. And Mark had promised to humour the old lady.

But his rush to get away hadn't been to accommodate Minna. He had been planning a helicopter ride. She wished he had mentioned it before.

Sensing her unease, he said: 'It had to be today, Rosie, because the people organizing the trips are moving on tomorrow. I've never been in a helicoper and I'd like to give it a go. If you're really nervous, then of course you needn't come with me, but I think it would be nice if both of us did it.' He smiled. 'It would be something to tell your mother.'

'She'd certainly be surprised.' Rosie grinned faintly. 'My mother considers me a dull person. She much prefers Paula.'

Mark took his hand off the wheel long enough to squeeze her hand.

'That's sad. She obviously doesn't know the real you.'

Rosie smiled at his compliment and replied honestly. 'I was dull, I suppose. I've never done anything out of the ordinary. I've never rebelled, never left home, never . . .' She paused.

'Had an affair.' Mark glanced sidewards at her. 'Have I corrupted you?'

She laughed. 'If you have, I've enjoyed it.'

'So have I.'

They continued their journey.

Rosie sat and thought of all the things she did now. Once a month she went out with four of her women friends from the course. She had recently supervised a weekend trip for four of the residents at Woldview on a painting holiday. She had enjoyed that. With Mark, she had gone to another jazz evening, and every Friday she now took Alison to the swimming pool. Three years ago, she thought, I wouldn't have dared show myself in a swim suit.

She was distracted from her thoughts by Mark's voice.

'So have you decided what to do, about the helicopter?'

'I'm coming up with you.'

Falcon Helicopters was a Scottish-based company, said the notice outside the cordoned off area. They were travelling around providing pleasure trips for adventurous people and promoting the range of their services.

'There you are.' Mark glanced at Rosie. 'You're adventurous.'

She smiled, nervously.

'Business Charter, Aerial Photography, Surveys, Weddings . . .' Mark, reading from the notice board, paused. 'Weddings?' He smiled. 'Hey, that's an idea. Fancy dropping off a helicopter outside the church.'

Rosie, wrapping her short jacket around the upper part of her body, nodded. In a more normal situation, Mark's talking about weddings would have engaged her total concentration but this was no normal situation.

They were up on the high moors now. There were no buildings to shelter in and the gentle breeze blowing at the fête had been transformed into a wild and blustery wind. There was a knot of people awaiting their turn in the helicopter and she and Mark were at the front of the queue. She shivered.

The frantic fluttering of the red plastic markers intensified as the tiny object in the sky dropped lower and became a small white helicoper with red markings.

'You said it didn't go very high,' she murmured.

Mark looked at her. 'If you're really scared, Rosie, you don't have to go.'

The helicopter's rotary blades whirred loudly as the machine hovered, then set down on the short turf. Rosie watched the two orange-clad attendants rush over to open the doors. A young couple climbed out. They were smiling broad smiles. They were followed by a little boy of about seven years. He, too, was smiling.

Rosie gritted her teeth. 'I'm going.'

'Keep the seat belt fastened throughout the flight. I repeat, definitely no smoking. When you come back, don't go *anywhere* near the rear of the helicoper. Walk away from the helicopter from the front.'

The young woman who belted Rosie into her seat was a model of efficiency.

Next thing she'll be saying: 'Have a nice day.' Rosie knew that fear was making her bitchy. She gulped and pressed her knees together in an effort to stop them shaking.

Mark, sitting next to her, took her hand and held it tightly. His eyes were shining. He said something. She craned her neck to hear his words.

'We have lift-off, Rosie.'

★ ★ ★

It was wonderful. They really did have a bird's eye view, and they were up and away so quickly. There was a moment of nervousness as the helicopter rose from the ground, soared up into the air and banked sharply to the left, and then it was magical.

They stared out of their respective windows and shouted to each other, pointing out things of interest. They looked down at the wild moor and then exclaimed as they passed over a village. The houses below were doll's houses, the cars parked outside them smaller than the ones Steve had played with when he was small.

Then there followed a fascinating panorama of changing scenes. They saw the glint of a lake surrounded by woods, they followed a winding river and studied the lay-out of a famous stately home as they flew overhead. Finally, the pilot took them to the coast.

As the helicoper flew over Scarborough, it reduced height and Rosie gasped as they circled above the ancient Norman castle towering above impressive cliffs. The weather was so perfect they had a fantastic view. They could see the curve of the North and South Bays, the long sweeps of sand and the blue sparkling sea, white-capped where it reached the shore.

Rosie jumped and then laughed when seagulls took off from their perches on the cliffs and swooped in the air, screaming defiance.

Alas, it was over too quickly. The helicopter turned and headed back. Before they realised it, they were back on the ground.

They climbed out and hurried away from the noise of the machine. Rosie realised she and Mark were smiling as widely as the previous passengers. When they reached a quiet spot, she hugged him.

'That was wonderful.'

He nodded. Arms linked, they looked back to see the next passengers climb aboard.

'I'm glad you came up with me.'

'So am I.' Rosie grinned. 'I feel quite exhilarated. Certainly strong enough to introduce you to my mother.'

He ate sandwiches, two scones and a piece of fruit cake. Minna was pleased. There was nothing worse than taking the trouble to lay on a meal and then your guest not eating anything. Not that she had done much. Paula had done the real work. She had left Alison with Steve for a couple of hours and had come over to the flat to help.

Paula, thought Minna, had become more sensitive since her troubles. Without need for words she had whisked round the flat, putting away things that lived on high shelves, washing the kitchen floor and polishing the furniture. All things Minna could no longer manage. She had set out the tea, using the best cloth, and pinned her grandmother's small ruby brooch to the bodice of her navy blue dress.

Minna had thanked her and patted her hand. Paula had blushed, smiled, and hurried away to do something else. She was a good girl, but Minna knew her activity was not just to help her grandmother. Paula thought, if she kept busy, Minna would not be able to enquire as to her well-being, ask her if she had made any plans for the future.

Minna knew that Paula was improved, but not yet totally cured. She understood. The traumatic experience endured by her granddaughter would have taxed the strongest constitution. Nevertheless . . . Minna sighed, she had expected more of Paula. She had expected her to be strong.

If only the girl would confide in someone. *She* had tried,

God knows, but her granddaughter had been unresponsive to her gentle probing. Indeed, she had flashed her grandmother a warning look, a look Minna knew only too well for she had used it herself on many occasions.

Admitting defeat, Minna had asked about Mark Goodman instead, and Paula, glad of the change of subject, told her.

'I like him and I think he's good for Mum. She's a different person when she's with him. She laughs and chatters. I felt a bit awkward the first time we met. Well, obviously, Mum must have told him about Dave, but he never mentioned him. We just talked about general stuff.

'He's interested in Mum's studying, which I think is nice. I gather he's lent her some of his books. And he's got her interested in jazz!' Paula laughed. 'Can you believe it? Mum, listening to jazz! He and Steve seem to be OK together and Alison likes him, too.'

'Quite a universal charmer?' Minna frowned. 'Charm's very well, but men who possess it are usually unreliable.' She glanced towards her father's photograph and her face softened. 'Still, I'm glad to hear they get on so well. It's just that Rosemary's innocent in many ways. It would be easy to take advantage of her.'

Paula's eyebrows rose. 'I'm not so sure. She's changed a lot during the past year. Anyway.' She shrugged. 'Mum has no money so he can't be after that and she's a widow with two grown-up children, so he can't steal her virginity.'

'Paula!' Minna's voice was stern but her mouth twitched.

'Well, it's true.' Paula gave her grandmother a challenging look.

'Life's a lot different from how it was in your day, Grandma. I'm glad to see her happy. She's had enough grief in her life, losing Dad.'

Secretly, Minna agreed. She was also flattered her

granddaughter felt she could speak so honestly to her and she was delighted to see a spark of the old Paula. However, she didn't admit it.

'And what if he breaks her heart and then leaves her?'

'We all take that risk.' Avoiding Minna's eyes, Paula stepped back from the table and studied it. 'Will that do?'

Minna checked. 'Yes, it's lovely. Thank you, my dear.'

Paula came over to her grandmother, bent over and put her cool cheek against hers.

'I'd better go. They'll be here soon and this is your tea party.'

'Must you go?'

As she moved away, Minna clutched at her arm.

She suddenly realised she was nervous. She couldn't imagine what Rosie's new manfriend would be like. What would happen to her if their relationship became serious? What if this Mark Goodman didn't like her? What if he took Rosemary away from her? If her daughter had to choose, whom would she choose?

Minna closed her eyes. She knew the answer to that one. She would choose Mark and who could blame her? She let go of Paula's arm.

'No, I didn't mean that. Off you go.'

She saw the surprise in Paula's face and smiled. 'I'm all right, just a touch of nerves. I don't see many strangers nowadays.'

Paula bent again to kiss her. 'It will go well, Grandma, I promise you. You'll like him.' She went to the door and waved goodbye to Minna before leaving the room.

Minna straightened her back and lifted her chin. Whether she liked him or not was immaterial. He was Rosemary's friend and nothing to do with her. She would not try and influence her daughter but, her eyes glinted, she would not make allowances for this man. He was charming, was he? Well, he needn't try and charm her.

Paula had been right about one thing. Crumbling her cucumber sandwich on her plate, Minna looked at and listened to Rosemary. Her child was positively sparkling. She had never seen her so lively. And this tale she was telling, about a trip in a a helicopter . . . Rosemary, flying about in a helicopter! Minna felt a pang of envy.

With a feeling akin to despair, she heard herself playing her old tricks, cutting short her daughter's conversation and making a sour comment to her companion.

'It sounds a somewhat foolhardy exercise. Do you often take part in foolhardy tricks, Mr Goodman?'

'I used to, when I was young.' He smiled at her.

He was good-looking. *Too* good-looking. He would never stay with Rosemary. He would be up and away when he got bored and her daughter would be left heart-broken. Minna scowled.

Unperturbed, he continued. 'But now I'm older, I'm more sensible. And a trip in a helicopter isn't foolhardy, you know.' He paused. 'The Royal Family use them all the time.'

Touché. She allowed herself to smile. 'Well, I'm glad you both enjoyed the experience. Do have another scone.'

'Thank you.' He took one.

'I gather from the few things Rosemary has said that you are a widower and have been on your own for a long time?'

Mouth full of scone, he nodded.

'And you met my daughter at work.' Ignoring Rosemary's frown, Minna ploughed on. 'In fact, you are Rosemary's employer?'

He swallowed and replied. 'No. The County Council employs both of us.'

'Ah, yes.' Minna dismissed the Council with a wave of her hand. 'But you're the head of the establishment and Rosemary is merely a care assistant.' She raised her eyebrows. 'Doesn't that make it rather difficult with the staff?'

'There were a few whispers when we first started going out together, but not now. At work we keep strictly to our jobs. As for care assistants, they're important members of staff.' Mark smiled across at Rosie whose face portrayed embarrassed anguish.

'And if Rosemary continues to do well with her course, she should have no problem in being awarded a diploma in Care for the Elderly in September. With that qualification, she could apply for a higher post.'

'Indeed.' Minna pondered over his reply. 'So *if* Rosemary gains a diploma, she'll move somewhere else to work. You won't be seeing so much of each other?'

'Mother, please stop interrogating Mark. This is supposed to be a pleasant tea party.' Face burning, Rosie jumped to her feet. 'If we're all finished, I'll clear away.'

She snatched up the milk jug and sugar bowl and marched out of the room and into the kitchen.

Minna stared after her in surprise. She'd never experienced such spirit in her daughter. Her next words to Mark were milder and slightly apologetic.

'I'm sorry if my questioning appears rude, but Rosemary's my only child.'

'I know.' He stood up. 'Will you excuse me for a moment?' When she nodded, he followed Rosie into the kitchen.

'Are you all right?'

'She *has* to spoil things.' Rosie put the sugar bowl into a cupboard and slammed shut the door. 'I think she's jealous.'

'Very probably.' Mark imprisoned her hands in his. 'She's crippled with arthritis, isn't she?'

'Yes.' Rosie laid her head on his shoulder. 'I dread the day she can't manage on her own. You see what's she's like? I can't bear the thought of her living with me but it's going to come to that.'

'Not necessarily.' Mark stroked her hair. 'Anyway, now's not the time to sort out problems. Your mother's gone to a lot of trouble to put on such a super tea. Let's humour her, shall we?'

Rosie sniffed and then nodded. Hand in hand, they went back into the sitting room.

'I've persuaded Rosie not to clear away yet.' Mark reached for another scone. 'I have a huge appetite, I'm afraid. Do you mind my helping myself?'

'Please do.' Minna spoke quietly. She watched Rosemary sit down and take a piece of cake.

Mark enquired, 'Did you bake these yourself?'

'Alas, no.' Minna held up her hands. 'I can't bake any more. The scones are shop-bought.'

'You must tell me which shop.'

'I know the one. I'll show you.' Rosie entered the conversation.

They ate and talked until they had all had enough food and then Rosie brought a tray and started clearing away for the second time. Mark offered to help.

'No, no. You talk to Mother.' She gave him a sideways glance as she went through to the kitchen.

'It was a lovely tea, thank you.' Mark sat back in his chair.

'I'm glad you enjoyed it.'

Minna's face was pale and she looked tired. Mark set out to entertain her. He spoke about some of the funny things that happened at Woldview and she smiled faintly. Then, hearing the clatter of pots being washed and knowing that Rosie was occupied in the kitchen, he said, quietly, 'You needn't worry, you know. I won't hurt Rosie. I think a lot about her. And I have no intention of coming between the two of you.'

Minna stiffened and her voice, when she replied, was stronger. 'The thought never entered my head.'

'Good.' A smile flitted across his face. 'That's that out of the way. I'm glad we've finally met. I've heard a lot about you and I was curious.'

'Not too many good things, I fear.' Her voice was dry.

'Both good and bad.' He shrugged. 'I work with the elderly all the time and I know they are no different from any other people. There are the wise and the foolish, the ones who play on their old age and expect everything to be done for them. Then there are the ones like you, with an independent spirit.'

He paused, and then when she remained silent, continued, 'I admire them. Of course such people are often dogmatic. They think they can tell others how to run their life, which is wrong. Everyone deserves their independence.'

The door opened and Rosie came into the room. Mark swiftly changed the subject. 'I see you collect stamps. May I look at them?'

Minna nodded. She watched him stand up, cross to the sideboard and pick up her stamp album. She stared at the back of his head.

Mark Goodman was different from what she had expected. She needed to think about him. She turned her attention to Rosemary.

'Paula hasn't made any plans yet?'

'No.' Rosie sighed. 'I wish she would. I don't mind her staying with me but she's in a sort of limbo. She can't make any decisions about anything.'

'No news from Dave?'

'Thankfully not. I should think he will leave her alone now.'

Rosie paused. 'You know about Steve?'

'Yes. Paula told me. He's broken his engagement.' Minna sniffed. 'He was too young to get engaged. It was ridiculous. Everyone knows boys take longer to mature than girls. No man should get married before the age of twenty-five.'

'My marriage was happy.' Mark had sat down again, the album on his lap. 'I was very young.'

'Yes, well . . .' Minna's voice softened. 'Through misfortune, you and your wife were not allowed much time together. In the general run of things, husband and wife outgrow each other within five years and bore each other to death.'

Mark held up the stamp album to hide his face and murmured to Rosie: 'Marriage is obviously a lethal condition.'

She shot him a warning look.

Paula arrived home five minutes before Steve had to leave. Although it was Sunday, he had agreed to work for three hours at the bank.

She apologised for being late. 'Sorry, but Gran needed a bit of reassuring. She's fidgety about meeting Mark.'

Steve, stuffing papers into his briefcase, smiled.

'If anyone's fidgety, I reckon it should be Mum. But it will be okay. Mark's a laid-back individual. He'll defuse any tension.'

'You like him, don't you?'

'Yes. He's good with Mum. I'm glad they've got together. When you go back to Manchester and I leave, she'll need someone.'

Disregarding the bit about her returning to Manchester,

Paula asked, 'Is the bank shifting you then?'

'No.'

She tried to see the expression on his face but he avoided her, turning away to put his jacket on.

'So why should you leave?'

'I can't live at home forever, Paula.' He started for the door. 'Alison's gone upstairs. She said she was going to draw you a picture.'

Paula sighed. 'I hope she doesn't get crayon all over the sheets.'

'She won't. See you.' A bang of the door and Steve was gone.

Paula went and put the safety chain on the front door. She wasn't frightened about being on her own now but it didn't do to take chances. She went upstairs and looked in on her daughter. Alison shooed her away.

'My picture's not finished.'

'All right. Call me when it is.'

She went back downstairs and into the kitchen to make herself a coffee. She had just switched on the kettle when the doorbell rang. Without thinking too much about anything, she went and opened the door.

Dave was on the doorstep. When she pulled back in alarm, he thrust his hand into the small space between the door and the chain.

'Let me in, Paula. We have to talk.'

'No.' She tried to shut the door but his hand prevented her. Her eyes dilated with fear.

'Go away, please.'

He shook his head. 'I'm not going away. I have to talk to you.'

Paula felt hysteria rising inside her. She wanted to scream, but if she did, Alison would hear and would come downstairs.

Instead she whispered: 'Go away. Please go away.'

'Five minutes, Paula. You can spare me five minutes, can't you? I'm your husband.'

Fury roared through her and her eyes narrowed. 'You don't deserve five seconds, you bastard. I'll tell you what you deserve. You deserve a jail sentence. Now go away before I call the police, and don't ever come here again.'

Like a child, his face crumpled. 'You're right. I know you're right. I can't apologise for what I did to you. But it was because I loved you, Paula. The thought of you with someone else drove me crazy.'

'I wasn't with anyone.' She had gained control of her breathing again. The knowledge that he couldn't get hold of her calmed her. She took stock of his unkempt appearance. Dave looked in a bad way. He was thin and pale. His uncut hair straggled over his collar and his clothes were dirty. Unwillingly, she asked, 'What's happened to you?'

He shrugged.

'Lost my job, the landlord repossessed the flat. I owe him money. I've been living rough. I don't care. I don't care about anything since you left me.'

'You surely don't expect me to come back to you?'

'No.' He looked down and shuffled his feet. 'But we need to talk.'

She shook her head. 'There's nothing left to talk about.'

'There's Alison. She's my daughter.' His voice sounded petulant. 'I want to see her.'

He was lying, she knew it. His interest in Alison had always been spasmodic. He was just using his daughter to get to her. She hardened her heart.

'You can't see her. I'll not have her upset.'

He rubbed his dirty hand across his eyes. 'I wouldn't upset her. Oh, Paula, please let me come in. I can't cope with life without you.'

His voice was so blurry and the look in his eyes so strange she wondered if he was on drugs. The man who had talked to Steve about him had said he was on drugs.

She shook her head. 'There's no point, Dave. We're through.' She pushed to close the door.

He slammed his fist on the door panel. 'Shut this door and I'll kill myself, Paula. I swear it. If I can't have you, there's nothing worth living for.'

'Go ahead. I won't stop you.' She finally managed to slam shut the door. She dropped the latch, sat on the bottom of the stairs and listened. There wasn't a sound. After a couple of minutes, she went upstairs and into the front bedroom and peeped out through the curtains. Dave was walking away from the house. She gave a sign of relief.

The next moment she heard Alison's voice from the back bedroom. 'Come in now, Mummy. It's finished.'

When her mother and brother came home, Paula told them of Dave's visit. Steve swore under his breath.

'If I'd been there . . .'

'I handled it,' Paula reassured him. 'I'm glad he came, Steve. I've been so afraid of him because I'd built him into some kind of monster but when I saw him again, I realised he was pathetic. I'm not afraid of him anymore. If he comes back, I can deal with him.' She had stretched her arms out wide and smiled.

Her brother had looked at her suspiciously.

'You're not softening towards him? You won't . . . ?'

'Never.' She moved and flung her arm around her mother's shoulder. 'I'm free. It's all over.'

But there was one last act to play.

In the early hours of the next morning a policeman knocked on the door of the house.

'Does a Mrs Paula Meridith live here?'

'Yes.' Steve had opened the door wider.

'Could we speak to her please?'

'Yes.' Steve moved back and allowed the policeman to enter.

Dave had taken a drugs overdose.

Steve drove Paula to the hospital. 'Shall I come up with you?'

'Better not.'

She had taken the lift up to the third floor. Dave was in a bed in the corner of the room. He looked dreadful but she had been told he was out of danger. She drew up a chair and sat down next to him.

He looked at her. 'You came.'

She nodded.

'I warned you. I meant what I said. I can't live without you, Paula. If you don't come back to live with me, I'll do it again.'

She studied his face and then she leaned towards him and said in a soft but clear voice: 'Blackmail won't work, Dave. Nothing will. Our marriage is over. I'll never come back to you. I'm going to make a new life for myself and Alison. You must do what you think fit. Threatening to kill yourself won't change my mind. You must do what you like, it's your life. But I will not be made to feel responsible for you. I'm sorry . . .' For a moment, her voice trembled but then it steadied again.

'I'm sorry it's ended this way, but it *has* ended. I hope I never see you again.'

She stood up and walked away from him. She didn't look back.

Chapter Twenty-Nine

The journey home was conducted in silence. Steve glanced at his sister once or twice but said nothing. They arrived at the house. Steve switched off the car engine and Paula got out and looked towards the front door. Rosie was already on the step, she must have heard the noise of the car. She was wearing her dressing-gown. When Paula walked towards her, Rosie took hold of her daughter's hands and squeezed them.

'He's not . . .'

'Dead? No.'

'Come into the room, I've left the fire on.'

Following her mother, Paula saw the anxious glance pass between Steve and Rosie and drew in a short breath of nervous exasperation but later, when presented with a mug of tea and her mother's concerned face, she smiled and felt her tension begin to relax. The sometimes insidious family ties could be extraordinarily comforting. She sipped at her tea and then put her head against the back of the chair and sighed.

'Can you bear to tell us?'

'Of course.' Paula took another sip of tea and then recited the things she and Dave had said to each other.

She ended, 'I said I wouldn't let him blackmail me. Whatever he did or did not do in the future was nothing to do with me. I would not be involved.' Paula's voice tailed off. She looked across at her mother.

'Was I right to say that, Mum?'

Rosie hesitated. 'What else *could* you say? If he knows that you'll come running back whenever he's in trouble of some sort or other, he'll keep you dancing to his tune for ever. You'll never be free of him.

'But Paula,' her voice became hushed, 'what if he *does* kill himself? How would you feel then?'

There was an ominous silence.

Steve replied, his voice loud in the quiet room. 'She'll be too sensible to feel guilty. Won't you, sis?'

Paula thought about the night she and Dave had met. She thought how his quick smile and green eyes had affected her. She thought about their first motor-bike ride through the dark countryside and the first time they had made love. She thought about the laughter and the silly jokes they had shared, and her eyes filled with tears.

Dave and she had been young together but now their youth had flown. She was strong enough to become an adult but Dave . . . She sighed and rubbed her hand over her face.

'Yes, Steve. I'm too sensible to feel guilty but I'll never stop feeling sorry . . . for both of us.'

Next morning, when Steve and her mother had left for work, Paula decided it was time she considered her future. Her mother, she knew, would tell her to stay just as long as she wished but she didn't wish. Her mother's house and her company had been a refuge to her but now it was time to get out into the world again.

Accordingly, she settled Alison down with a new box of paints, a sketchbook and a bag of sweets, and told her to play quietly. She collected her address book from the bedroom, sat by the telephone and wondered where to start. Finally, she took a deep breath and picked up the phone.

That night, she waited until Steve announced he was going out and then she sat down with her mother and told her the news.

'I'm going back to Manchester, Mum.'

Rosie took the news calmly.

'I knew that's what you would do, once you had sorted yourself out.' She sighed. 'I shall miss you.'

'We'll come back and visit.'

'When are you thinking of leaving?'

'In a few days.'

'So soon? But where will you stay?'

'I've had a word with Tracey. She said we can stay with them for a while. It won't be for long. I'll look for permanent accommodation as soon as we get back. Perhaps I could arrange to share a flat with someone.'

Rosie looked worried. 'Have you thought things through properly, Paula? You haven't any money to speak of and even if you get a job, there's still Alison's welfare to consider.'

'Tracey said she'd be happy to look after Alison for me. She's at home with her little boy, Alison loves playing with him. I'll pay Tracey what I can afford for child-minding and some money towards our keep.'

'But you haven't a job, yet. Has the temping agency . . . ?'

Paula interrupted her. 'I have, actually, or I will have in a couple of weeks.' She explained. 'Do you remember me telling you I'd written to Mr Beaver, the man I worked for at the advertising agency?'

'Yes. You said you wanted to apologise to him.' Rosie sighed. 'I can't see why you felt the need.'

'He's a nice guy, Mum, and I let him down.'

'What nonsense. You were in hospital.'

'Only for a day. And when I came home with you, I never got in touch with him. I couldn't face telling him the lurid details.'

'But now you have.'

'Yes. Mrs Kirby told him I'd had a virus. I thought he deserved the truth. I didn't expect a reply but he wrote back to me. He said he was sorry to hear about my troubles but he didn't labour the point. He also said that if I needed a reference for another job he would be pleased to give me one. So,' Paula took a deep breath, 'this morning I rang him.'

'And he's given you a reference?'

'Better than that.' Paula smiled. 'I told him I was returning to Manchester and we chatted. He said his PA – that's personal assistant – is good but she's seven months pregnant and she'll be taking maternity leave soon.

'Officially, she's due back in December but Mr Beaver says she's uncertain about what to do. Her husband has a good job, they've no cash problems and she says she might decide to become a full-time mother.'

'Good for her.' Rosie spoke decisively.

Paula frowned and continued with her tale.

'Also, the company's presently advertising for another audio typist. He's sure I'd get the job if I applied. I know the work, you see. Once I'm a permanent employee, and *if* his assistant decides not to come back, then I could apply for her job. Oh, Mum,' Paula's eyes gleamed, 'wouldn't that be terrific?'

'If it works out that way. There's a lot of ifs and buts. What if you don't get the job?'

'I have a good chance. I've already worked for Mr Beaver. We got on well together. He complimented me on how quickly I tuned into his way of thinking.'

Rosie's eyes sharpened. 'Is he interested in you? It sounds as though he is.'

Paula laughed. 'Of course not. Don't you remember me telling you that he's gay? Anyway,' her face became serious, 'I've had enough of men for the moment. I want to concentrate on building a career for myself, and Mr Beaver would be the ideal employer.'

Rosie rubbed her chin. 'Oh yes, I forgot. I can't remember half the things you told me at the hospital, I was so upset. But if the PA job does come up, he may not be the only one to interview you. What if you don't get it?'

'Then I'll still be working as an audio typist. He's virtually guaranteed that.' Paula's mouth set into a straight line. 'But I don't intend staying an audio typist. If I don't get to work for Mr Beaver, I'll set about getting more qualifications and then I'll try again, somewhere else.'

Rosie began laughing and Paula looked at her suspiciously. 'What's so funny? I'll do it, you know.'

'I'm sure you will. I was just thinking, what a family we are. There's Steve travelling to Lancaster and passing exams to gain advancement at the bank, me and my diploma course, and now you.'

Paula grinned. 'Yes, you're right.' She paused. 'Where do we get our motivation from?'

'I would guess it's from Minna's family. My father wasn't ambitious and Howard, bless him, was content with his station in life. But Minna told me her father started off with nothing but worked hard and made a fortune.'

Rosie shook her head. 'I don't know what happened to all his money, perhaps he lost it again.' She sighed. 'I wish I knew more about my mother's earlier life. It's so frustrating. Every so often she'll drop little titbits of information and then she clams up again. I know she enjoyed a wealthy lifestyle when she was young.'

'Yes. Steve mentioned it. Gran told him she lived in London when she was a girl and she went to cocktail parties and things like that. He didn't know whether to believe her.'

'Oh, yes. She'd be telling the truth.'

Rosie changed the subject. 'This place will be quiet when you've gone. I've got used to having you and Alison around.'

'I'll keep in touch.'

A smile twitched at the corners of Rosie's mouth. 'I've heard that before.'

'I mean it this time.' Paula rested her hand on her mother's arm. 'You've been good to me. I appreciate it.'

Rosie's eyes moistened 'That's what mums are for.'

'Anyway, you have Mark to console you.' Paula grinned. 'I'm sure he can take your mind off absent children.'

Rosie blushed and laughed.

At the same time Paula was talking with her mother, Steve was in a pub confessing his future plans to Mark Goodman.

'I'll have to tell Mum soon, I've put it off too long already, and I wondered if you could give me some pointers?'

Mark scrutinised the ingenuous expression on Steve's face.

'Come on, Steve. I've only known your mother since Christmas and you've known her all your life. You don't need advice from me.'

'I do, and I know you can help. If you tell her it's a good idea, then I think she'll accept my change of plan more readily. After all, you two seem to get on so well.' He glanced shyly down at his pint of beer.

The pub was a small local one, frequented by men in their twenties. A burst of laughter came from a group of youngsters at the bar and Mark looked from them back to Steve, his expression nonplussed.

'I've no kids. I'm not a family man, so don't take my words as gospel but I suggest you keep it simple. Get her on her own, sit her down and tell her what you've told me.'

When Steve remained silent, he continued, 'I can't see that it's such a big deal. Plenty of young people decide to pack in their jobs and take off round the world, hitch-hiking or similar, but you're not doing that, are you? You've decided a bank job is not for you and so you're going to train for something you've decided will suit you better.'

'But it's such a change of direction. She'll think I've gone mad.' Head lowered, Steve picked gloomily at his fingernails. 'It wouldn't be so bad in normal circumstances, but since Christmas, our lives have been totally abnormal. Gran's been ill, Mum's tied up with her studies, I've split up with Jill and then there was that awful business with Paula.' He looked across at Mark. 'You know the stress that caused Mum.'

'Yes, she was terribly upset.' Mark was quiet for a moment. Then he said, 'But hopefully things should settle now. Paula's faced up to her fears and her husband's been sent packing, hasn't he?'

Steve looked up. 'Mum's told you about that?'

'Yes. She looked tired this morning when she came in to work so I whipped her away to my flat and made her a coffee. I encouraged her to talk and she told me about the police coming to the house and about Dave's suicide attempt. She also told me how Paula dealt with the problem.'

Mark paused and smiled admiringly. 'Your sister's got a lot of bottle.'

'Yes.' Steve sounded gloomy. 'Maybe she should have been born the boy.'

Mark's forehead creased. 'What does that mean?'

Steve picked up his glass and drained it. 'Oh, I don't know. It's just sometimes, I wish I was more like my sister. She doesn't worry about things. She doesn't struggle to reach decisions. She just dives straight in and sorts everything out.'

'You've done the same. You given in your notice at the bank, you've split up with your fiancee because you knew it wasn't working, and you've decided to train for a job working with handicapped people.' Mark's eyebrows went up. 'Making all those decisions seems pretty decisive to me.'

Steve shifted in his seat. 'Yes, but I can't move on as easily as Paula. I keep going over those decisions, worrying if I've done right. I can't seem to let things rest. I mean, what about Mum? I've delayed telling her because I wonder how she's going to take my news. I don't want to disappoint her but I bet I will, and she's had enough on her plate lately. And this business with Jill, was I right about that? We've been together since we were fifteen, you know. Maybe we should have stuck together for a bit longer?'

He looked up and saw Mark's thoughtful gaze fixed upon him and his voice took on a tinge of defiance. 'I bet you're thinking, What a wimp! Here's this chap, twenty-one years old and he can't make up his mind about anything.' A tinge of red spread across his cheekbones. 'Mum told me you were in Canada at my age, working as a lumberjack.'

'You mum got it wrong.'

Mark did not shout, but his voice sounded around the small bar like a whiplash. The lads at the bar, walking past their table to play the fruit machine in the corner, looked at him with surprise. He saw them and moderated his tone. He leaned closer to Steve.

'When I was twenty-one, your age, I was married to my childhood sweetheart. Unlike you and Jill, we were wonderfully happy and the more so because she had recently become pregnant.' He sighed and rubbed his forehead. 'I was like you then. I was happy, but I also worried a lot. I worried as to whether we should have delayed having a family, could we manage financially, would I make a good father? I wanted the best for my family.'

He paused. 'Then one day a drunk driver came out of nowhere and ran into our old car and it was all over. I was the only one to survive. I had no one to worry about.'

He stared down into his glass. 'So, by the time I was twenty-two, I had no family. Well, to be precise, I had a mother and father, but we had never been close. My grandmother brought me up but she died shortly after my marriage. So I had no ties. I was young, and free, and bloody miserable.'

He fixed his gaze on Steve's face and his eyes burned. '*Never* be ashamed of caring about other people's feelings, Steve. Consideration, love, compassion, they're not things that weaken a man, they're part of his strength.'

Mark picked up his glass and downed the beer in one draught. Then he looked back at Steve.

'I've met plenty of the other kind, I can tell you. Big, strong, hard men. Don't make them your role models, for God's sake.' He closed his eyes briefly, opened them and apologised. 'Sorry, I got a bit carried away. Lecture's over.'

'No.' Steve nodded his head vigorously. 'No, I'm glad. I think you're right. I agree with you.' He looked at Mark respectfully. 'And I'll do what you suggest. I'll tell Mum like I told you.'

Mark nodded.

Steve moved his glass around. 'Can I ask you something else?'

Mark groaned and then laughed when he saw Steve's face cloud over.

'Okay. Go ahead.'

'You and Mum, is it serious between you?'

Mark hesitated. 'That's not an easy question. To be honest, I'm not quite sure. It's early days, you know.'

'You've been seeing her since January.' Steve's forehead creased. 'I think it's serious as far as Mum's concerned.'

'It's not your place to say, is it?'

Mark, seeing Steve's embarrassed face, relented. 'Things are never cut and dried, you know that, Steve. Your mother's changed, even in the short time I've known her. Changed for the better, I hasten to add. She finding out things about herself, good things.

'She's discovering a new way of life and there are lot more experiences ahead of her. I don't feel that now is the time for her to be making commitments about the future.' He shrugged. 'Later on, who knows? Right now, we're just enjoying ourselves.'

'I'm not so sure.' Steve's voice was abstracted. 'She's always happy when she's meeting you. When I go away, she's going to be on her own a lot. I was sort of hoping she might get settled down.'

Mark's eyebrows shot up but his voice, when he spoke, was humorous.

'Hey, when I preached caring and loving, I didn't mention family interference. Your mother's capable of sorting out her life. You leave her to get on with it. You just take care of yourself.'

He waited a moment and when Steve was silent, he stood up and picked up the empty glasses. 'Another one before we go?'

Steve looked up at him, frowning and then he sighed and smiled.

'Yes. Thanks.'

Mark bought the drinks and brought them back to their table, putting them down carefully.

Steve looked up at him. 'Sorry, I spoke out of turn.'

'Yes, you did, but we'll forget it, shall we?' Mark picked up his glass. 'Want to stand up?'

Looking curious, Steve did so.

'Right. Going back to *your* life, you're quite sure you're doing the right thing. You have no doubts about that?'

Steve's face cleared. 'Yes, I'm sure I'm doing the right thing and, no, I have no doubts.'

'That's the important thing.' Mark paused. 'Well, for my money, I reckon you've made a good choice and I'm sure you'll make a success of your new career. Here's to you.' He raised his glass.

The colour ran into Steve's face as he too picked up his glass.

'Thanks.'

They smiled at each other and drank.

After Paula's departure to Manchester, Rosie increased her visits to her mother. She called at the flat at least twice a week. It was sometimes difficult. The thought of September examinations loomed up and there were so many books to read and so many papers to write but Rosie knew Minna needed extra attention. Paula had mentioned she thought her grandmother was failing in health and Rosie felt from her own observations that this was so.

Accordingly, she tried her best to make her visits pleasant. She took little treats, a strawberry tart from her mother's favourite bakery, or a tape of Minna's favourite orchestral music, and tried to think of good things to tell her. Paula was a favourite subject of conversation between them.

'She's still living with her friend, flats are so expensive, but at least she has a job.'

'Typists don't earn much money. Why didn't she go back to that temping agency?'

'There are better prospects where she is now.' Rosie decided to take a risk. She told Minna about Paula's hopes for the future. 'If she becomes Mr Beaver's PA she'll earn good money and there'll be chances of added responsibility in the future.'

'Well, I wish the child luck.' Minna folded her hands in her lap and brooded. 'She deserves it. When I think of that dreadful husband of hers.'

'Don't think about him, Mother. Paula has put the past behind her, we must too.'

'He's left her alone, I hope?'

'Yes.'

'She'll be all right then.' Minna nodded her head. 'Paula's strong. She can survive without a man hanging round her.' She darted a glance at Rosie's face. 'But what about you?'

'Me?' Rosie jumped. 'We weren't talking about me.'

'We are now.' Minna sniffed. 'How are things progressing with Mark Goodman?'

Rosie moved uneasily in her seat. 'Oh, we're fine.'

'You're happy?'

'Of course.' Rosie's voice was defensive.

'Has he mentioned marriage?'

'Please, Mother.' The colour flared in Rosie's face. 'That's our business, not yours. People don't rush into marriage nowadays. They take their time and hopefully make fewer mistakes.'

'What do you mean, mistakes? Are you changing your mind about him?'

'No. But not all relationships have to end in marriage. Some people prefer a more flexible arrangement.'

Minna gave her daughter a disbelieving look. 'You're not some people, Rosemary. You're the marrying kind. He's dragging his feet, is he?'

Rosie stood up. 'I'm going if you don't change the subject, Mother. You have no right . . .'

'You *have* slept with him?'

Bereft of words, Rosie stared at her.

Minna sighed. 'Don't go silly on me, Rosemary. I may be old but I'm not out of the Ark. I hope you are sleeping together. He's an attractive man. If you haven't been to bed with him, something must be wrong with you.'

Rosie's cheeks were scarlet.

Minna sniffed. 'Oh, all right. You don't have to answer if you don't want to. We'll change the subject. How is Steve getting on?'

Rosie breathed hard and then said, in a subdued voice, 'He's happy. I know that from the scribbled notes he sends and his phone calls. I wasn't pleased when he told me his plans but I think now that he's done the right thing.

'He rang me last night. He's settled in and gets on well with the other students. They all went to help out at a special adolescent unit last weekend. He said he got a football game going with some of the mentally handicapped boys and everyone had a whale of a time.'

'Um.' Minna shook her head. 'It seems a strange way for an able-bodied young man to earn his living.'

'I know. I thought the same, but he was so determined to do it, and it's his life. Oh, he was asking if any letters for him had come from India. I asked who on earth did he know in India and he went all mysterious on me. I'm beginning to think I don't know my son as well as I thought I did.'

Minna sighed. 'There've been a lot of changes this year, Rosemary.'

'Yes, there have.'

Minna studied her hands. 'And there may be more before the year's out.'

'Oh?' Rosie lookd at her mother questioningly.

A slight tremor sounded in Minna's voice. 'I think we must discuss my future, such as it is.'

'Of course.' Rosie sat very still. 'If you want to.'

Minna smiled faintly. 'It's a matter of necessity, my dear.' She took a deep breath. 'I think you know that I am finding it increasingly difficult to look after myself, even with all your help.'

'Oh, Mother.' A worried look flitted across Rosie's face. 'I thought as much. Why did you turn down my suggestion of getting you more help?'

'It's no good patching a worn blanket, Rosemary. No, I've decided. I must give up this flat and go into a home.'

'Mother!'

'It's the only solution. I can't manage on my own any more and I will not come and live with you. And don't look like that. You know as well as I do that it just would not work.'

'No, Mother.' Distress sounded in Rosie's voice. 'I don't know that. We'd manage. If you had your own room and we sorted out various house rules . . .'

'You're deluding yourself, child.' Minna sounded irritated. 'If I lived with you, both our lives would be hell. I would try and dominate you.' She sucked her mouth in. 'You see, I know my faults, and you might slip back into your old, timid self.

'On the other hand, you might be more assertive – you are now, you know – and then we would fight all the time. Either way, our life together would become impossible and exhausting.' Minna shook her head. 'You know I'm right.'

'You're not.' Rosie's voice was determined. 'We have our differences, but we care for each other.'

'Of course we do.' Minna stared at her. 'But that has nothing to do with it.' She shook her head. 'We dance to different tunes, my dear. Our affection for each other will remain intact as long as we lead separate lives. Now, I don't want to hear anything more about it today, but,' she fixed Rosie with a firm look, 'I want you to start making enquiries. But not at Woldview, if you please.'

'Why not?' Rosie blinked. 'Mark runs the place very well.'

'Oh, use your commonsense. I don't want to live in a home where either of you are working. I would feel like a child in a class taught by one of her parents. No, find me a comfortable place that serves good food, and Rosemary . . .' For the first time, stress was apparent in the old lady's voice. 'I don't want to be where half the residents are ga-ga. You know what I mean. Those poor old souls who sit staring into space all day. Can you try and find a place where there are some *intelligent* residents? People who still take an interest in the world and enjoy a little conversation?' Minna looked anxiously at her daughter.

'*Are* there people like me in any of the homes you know?'

Rosie hesitated, then she went over to her mother and put her arms about her. 'Of course there are, Mother.'

She rested her face against Minna's face and her mother let her keep it there.

Chapter Thirty

Rosie did most of her thinking when she was in the bath. Perhaps it was something to do with relaxing in the warm water or maybe it was the steamy atmosphere – whatever, it worked for her. So, returning home from her visit to Minna, she tipped half a bottle of bath essence into a tubful of hot water, lowered herself gingerly into it, lay back and thought.

Ten minutes later she reluctantly concluded her mother was right, they would find it impossible to live together. Besides, if Minna had made up her mind to go and live in a home then nothing in the world would make her change her decision. That left the problem of finding the right home. Rosie compiled a list in her mind and found she was rejecting every one. She sighed, and scooping up a handful of bubbles, blew them away from her, up in the air. So easy to advise other people, so hard when the aged relative under discussion belonged to you.

Of course, her mother might be able to afford a private nursing home. Rosie grimaced. She would have to ask Minna about her financial situation, not an easy subject. And a private home would need equally careful vetting. Rosie frowned and added more hot water to her bath.

By the time she stepped out of the water, she resembled a boiled lobster. She looked down at herself, sighed and reached for the bath towel. At least she had reached one decision, she would go and talk to Karen Horton.

Karen heard her out and looked pensive.

'I presume you're looking for a single room?'

'Lord, yes. Minna would rather die than share with anyone.'

'Then that lets me out.' Karen opened the file in front of her, studied it and then scribbled down names on a sheet of paper. She handed the paper to Rosie.

'There are presently vacancies at these three homes. Why not make appointments and take your mother round to view?'

Three days later, pressed into service by Rosie, Mark collected the two women and drove them round to inspect the homes named on the list.

Minna liked none of them. The first home looked like 'a prison'. At the second stop, the Officer in Charge, a young woman with a wild, frizzy haircut, was described in her hearing as 'a stand-in for Mr Rochester's mad wife', and at the third, Minna simply tightened her mouth and shook her head.

'They've all been officially approved as being up to a high standard, Mother. They're checked regularly and the personnel have to fulfil stringent requirements.'

Minna sniffed. 'So do the staff at Broadmoor.' She gave Rosie an imperious look. 'Don't upset yourself. If there's nowhere decent for me at the moment, I'll wait until there is.'

Rosie nodded but she knew Minna's time in the flat was running out. Her mother's movements were becoming increasingly restricted. She required help in dressing now. When Mark dropped them at the flat, she helped Minna out of her outdoor clothes and then once again urged her mother to come and stay with her.

'Only for a little while.'

Minna pretended not to hear.

Then they discussed the possibility of finding her a place in a private nursing home.

When Minna revealed her financial situation, Rosie was shocked.

'I thought you drew money from a trust fund?'

'Oh no. That was closed when I moved here. The house in Halifax didn't sell for much, you know, and there were all the moving expenses.'

Minna gave one of her customary sniffs. 'Your father never thought we'd need to save for our old age. He was a Labour man through and through. He was so thrilled when the health service came into being in 1947. He believed the government's talk about adequate pensions for all. He thought that a person paying towards the state pension all his life would be looked after in his old age. Your father was a naive man.'

'But he must have left some savings. He never spent much.'

Minna refused to answer and Rosie, after a quick look at her face, dropped the subject. She remembered that during her childhood there had been spasmodic rows between her parents about money. Her father had been a great one for helping out lame ducks and Minna believed charity began at home. Mostly, Minna had her own way, but not in matters of conscience.

Rosie, born just before the war started, had little memory of the conflict but as she grew she learned a little of her father's role from Minna's occasional snide comments.

'Your father was turned down as a fighting man. I gather he had rheumatic fever as a baby and it left him with a slight heart murmur. He seemed as strong as a horse to me, but the doctors wouldn't pass him as fit. My goodness, that hurt his pride. That's why he became an air-raid warden. I think he felt the need for a uniform. All the other men in the street were in the Forces, you see.'

Rosie remembered she had listened to her mother but drawn her own conclusions. An air-raid warden . . . she frowned as a few, faint memories resurfaced. Didn't her father come home black-faced and exhausted some nights, after a bad raid? And didn't he sometimes bring someone home with him?

There'd been one night . . . yes, there must have been some heavy bombing because her mother had taken refuge with her underneath the heavy oak table in the kitchen . . . when Dad brought an old lady home with him. Rosie remembered, she couldn't stop crying. And another time it had been a young couple with a baby girl. They had been bombed out of their home and Dad had insisted they stay the night. They had left the following morning, but knowing her father, Rosie felt sure they had not left empty-handed.

But the war had ended and her father had worked for long years after that. And it wasn't as if the family had spent a lot of money. Rosie remembered what a treat it was when her father gave her money to meet her friends at the milk bar or slipped her ten shillings to buy a record by Dickie Valentine or Donald Peers. No, they hadn't spent much because they had never had much to spend. Her father had worked hard all his life but his job had been poorly paid and without prospects of advancement.

Poor Dad.

Poor Rosie. Her problems were piling up. Before she realised it, July had come and gone, her course-work was behind schedule, and in September she had examinations to face. Her tutor impressed upon her the necessity of keeping up to date.

'I know studying has to be fitted in between one hundred and one other things but this is a crucial time for you. We've masses of work to get through and if you slip behind any further, you'll fail the course.'

Rosie did her best to catch up. She tried to work a couple of hours every night but it was difficult with the additional help Minna required and the uncertainty as to her future. She saw Mark every day at work but spent less and less of her free time with him.

During the second week in August, Steve telephoned her and asked her to travel down to spend a weekend with him.

'It's a specially arranged Open Weekend, Mum. An opportunity for familes to come and see what we're doing here. You'll meet the teachers and instructors, and on Saturday you'll get to know some of the teenagers we're working with. They're being bussed over from the Special School for a rehearsal. They're putting on a show for their end of term and we're organising it with them. You will come, won't you?'

She said she would, and despite not being able to afford the time, she found she was looking forward to her visit. Unfortunately, on the Thursday morning of the week of her visit, Mark suggested they go away for the weekend.

'I've switched the lists around, Rosie, so we can both be off together.' He smiled and hugged her shoulders. They had bumped into each other on the top floor of Woldview and there was no one else in sight.

'What do you say? It will give us a chance to catch up with each other. You're always so busy. I'm beginning to forget what you look like. I've got details of a super little place in the Peak District.'

He was asking her, but he had already anticipated her answer.

Rosie sighed and shook her head. 'Oh, Mark. I would love to say yes, but I can't. I wish you'd mentioned it earlier.'

She began to explain the reason for her refusal but he didn't give her a chance.

He scowled and stepped away from her. 'I'm sorry you need so much prior notice. I know how busy you are. I suppose I can't expect you to spend the whole of your spare time with me.'

She frowned. 'What spare time?' The loudness of her voice surprised both of them. 'I have no spare time, Mark, and I'd love to come with you but I've promised Steve I'd visit him.' She explained the situation.

Mark apologised. They smiled at each other and kissed before separating to go about their duties, but somehow a shadow seemed to have appeared over their previously sunny relationship.

Rosie tried not to think about it. She hadn't time. She left work, went home and wrote an essay on dealing with bereavement. The next day she caught a train and went to visit Steve.

It was a lovely weekend, Rosie was glad she had gone, and on their last evening together, she and Steve found time to have a heart-to-heart talk.

'I did worry whether you were doing the right thing, Steve, but not any more.' Rosie smiled at him fondly. 'You're terrific with the kids, you tell me that your banking experience will come in handy and I can see you're happy.' Her smile grew wider. 'Of course, the letter I brought through for you, the one from India, might have something to do with your high spirits?'

She continued, only half-joking. 'You're not thinking of

throwing another blinder, are you? You're not planning to go to India?'

'No, Mum.' He laughed. 'And yes, I'm happy. Only sometimes,' his face grew serious, 'I think of Jill and I feel guilty.' He paused. 'Do you ever see her?'

'Yes. I saw her only last week. She waved to me but didn't come over; she was on the other side of the road and the traffic was heavy.'

'Are you sure that was the reason?'

'Yes.' Rosie answered firmly. 'Jill looked fine and you certainly don't need to worry about her. As a matter of fact, I had coffee with her mother just over a week ago. I was surprised when she phoned and invited me round. As you know, we've rarely met, even though you went out with Jill for so long.' Rosie paused. 'Evelyn Catley's a strange woman, isn't she?'

Steve smiled. 'She's better for knowing.'

'Yes, you're right. She certainly made me welcome. She gave me coffee and told me that Jill had got herself a new boyfriend, a man called Miles Walker. She was most insistent I tell you about him. I wasn't certain. I didn't want you to be upset.'

Rosie looked into Steve's face and seeing his look of pleasure, added, a little sharply, 'It seems Mrs Catley understands you better than I do.'

'Of course she doesn't.' Steve laughed. 'But I spoke to her once, about some of the difficulties Jill and I were experiencing, and I suppose she just wanted me to know that Jill was okay.'

'I see.'

But she didn't see. Steve had never discussed his problems with her.

With an understanding beyond his years, Steve placed his hand lightly over his mother's hand. 'Sometimes, it's easier to talk to people who are less involved, Mum. When you love someone, you don't want to worry them.'

She nodded and smiled and then she withdrew her hand and rifled in her handbag. 'She asked me to give you a message. I wrote it down in the back of my diary.'

She produced the diary, turned to the back, squinted at her writing and then read: 'Ask Steve to try and watch BBC 1 at six-thirty on the twenty-fourth of this month.' She replaced the diary in her bag. 'She wouldn't tell me any more.'

Steve made a note of the date. 'Very mysterious. Didn't she give a clue?'

'Only something that didn't make sense.' Rosie screwed up her face.

'She said, "Amazing where tigers lead you." '

Rosie travelled home on Sunday afternoon and on Sunday evening she went over to her mother's flat. They discussed which items of furniture Minna would dispose of when she moved and Rosie said she would enquire which auction rooms had a good reputation.

Before she left, she helped her mother to take a bath. It was a hard situation for both of them, Minna because she valued her privacy and felt humiliated at her daughter's ministrations and Rosie because she knew exactly what her mother was feeling.

She helped Minna into her dressing-gown and then went to make them both a mug of hot chocolate. When she came back into the bedroom she found Minna already in bed.

'Thank you.' Minna accepted her drink and stood it on a cork mat on her bedside table. She said, unexpectedly, 'You're a good girl, Rosie.'

Rosie!

Her cheeks flushing pink, Rosie clutched at her mug and mumbled, 'Not so young, mother.'

'That's true.' Minna looked thoughtful. 'I keep forgetting.' She patted the side of her bed. 'Can you spare a few minutes to talk?'

Rosie was tired. It had been a long day. Nevertheless, she sat down. She could never remember her mother calling her Rosie before. It had to be worth a few minutes of her time.

She watched Minna take a sip from her mug and she noticed how thin, almost transparent were her hands. She averted her eyes and swallowed some hot chocolate before saying, 'Try not to worry about moving. I'll find something suitable for you.'

'I know you will.' Minna laughed softly to herself. When Rosie looked up, surprised, Minna explained. 'You've chocolate all round your mouth. When you were a little girl, you could never drink cocoa without it ending up all over your face.'

Rosie half-smiled. 'Yes. I seem to remember you getting cross about it.'

'Did I? Oh, Rosemary, is that how you remember me, always cross?'

Rosie blinked at the pain in her mother's voice. She looked at Minna and saw she was genuinely distressed.

'No, of course not.' She put down her drink and moved closer to Minna. She caught hold of her hand. 'I was always very proud of you. I boasted to the children at school about how beautiful you were.'

'Did you, really?' Her mother's eyes widened and colour bloomed in her face.

'Of course I did.'

Minna sighed. 'Oh dear, if only I had the time to make amends.' She patted Rosie's hand and then pulled away from her. She sat up higher in bed.

'It's time you knew a little more about your history, Rosemary. I've kept you in the dark too long.' She hesitated. 'Of course, you'll understand I can't tell you absolutely everything, but it's only fair that you know something about your family. For instance,' her voice wavered for a moment and then became strong, 'you'll be surprised to learn that your father was once your grandfather's chauffeur . . .'

On Monday, Barbara grabbed her as Rosie went into work. She took her into the staff washroom for a chat.

'Have you fallen out with Mr Goodman?'

'No.'

Barbara pursed her lips. 'I don't believe you. He's been in a bad mood all weekend.' She paused. 'I'd thought, seeing how you were both down on the board for weekend leave, you might be going away for a break?'

'I have been.' Rosie told her about Steve.

'Well, I'm glad your son's getting on so well.' Barbara studied Rosie's face. 'But I wish you'd have a chat with Mark. Something's upsetting him and I have to work for him. Can't you make him more amenable?'

Rosie smiled. 'I don't have that power.'

'Don't you believe it!'

Rosie laughed and then asked, 'Where is Mark now?'

'At County Hall, attending a meeting. He'll be back about three.'

'I'll probably see him then.'

Rosie went to attend to her duties but throughout the morning Barbara's words stayed with her. Thinking about them, she realised her relationship with Mark *was* changing.

Initally, he had been the leader, and the teacher, but

that was no longer true. During the last few months, she had become more assertive. She no longer blindly accepted that Mark's opinions were always correct, and when she disagreed with him, she told him so. But surely he was too big a man to allow that to ruffle him? He had encouraged her in her search for self-confidence.

Pehaps he was just feeling neglected? Rosie's mouth curved into a smile. Well, she could do something about that.

During her lunch break she asked a colleague who was going into town to give her a lift. She went into the local bookshop and bought a book that she had seen in the window during an earlier visit. It was a heavy tome, billed as the definitive guide to the history of jazz. She had been meaning to buy it for Mark's coming birthday but decided she would give it to him today. She caught the bus back to Woldview and put the book in her locker.

She worked until four-thirty and then she collected the book and went up to the office and asked Barbara if Mark was back.

'Yes, he came back from County Hall and worked for an hour and then he suddenly threw his pen down and went out. My guess is he's in the garden.'

'Thanks.'

Rosie went outside. She found Mark, as she expected, working near the lawn where the sundial stood. He was clearing debris from the shrubbery.

'Hey.' She smiled at him.

'Hey, yourself.' He smiled back.

He looked tired, she thought, but good-natured enough. She walked up to him and kissed him lightly on his lips, keeping her left arm behind her.

'I gather you've been growling at Barbara.' She raised

her eyebrows. 'Was County Hall too much for you or is it something else?'

He shrugged. 'Nothing specific. But on a day like this, I'd rather be out here than attending meetings.'

She looked around her. 'I can see why.'

He nodded.

Mark had worked hard throughout the summer. The area was still untidy, but with a mountain of rubbish removed, the shrubbery was attractive in a wild way. The borders around the lawn had been cleaned of choking weeds and dead wood and were now colourful with low-growing shrubs which spilled patches of pink, blue and green on to the turf. Behind them, hydrangea bushes bent low under their loaded flower heads of pink, blue and white, and behind them was a buddleia bush with deep pink flowers to attract the butterflies, and a rich mass of lighter pink blooms on a shrub which Mark had earlier told Rosie was called Tamarisk Pentandra.

'Delicate-looking shrub,' he had said. 'But one of the toughest you can buy.'

As they stood quietly, admiring the garden, a blackbird alighted on Mark's garden fork.

Rosie whispered, 'Is that your blackbird?'

'I don't know. Let's see if he shouts at me.'

A moment later, the bird flirted his tail and chattered and they both laughed.

'Oh, I miss being able to come out here and work with you.' Rosie spoke impulsively.

'Yes, well.' Mark scuffed the ground with his foot. 'You have so much to do at the moment.'

'I know.'

He looked at her. 'Any luck with finding somewhere for your mother?'

She shook her head.

'I'm sorry.' He paused. 'It must be difficult trying to study.'

'It is, rather.'

'Are you regretting you took it on?'

'No. I'm still determined to pass.' Rosie paused. 'Your help has made a lot of difference. In fact, I've bought you a thank you present.' She produced the book she had been hiding behind her. 'This is for you.'

Looking surprised, Mark took the book and studied the cover. His face lit up. 'This is fantastic, Rosie. Thank you.'

'It's a pleasure.' She paused. 'You haven't already got it?'

'No.' He turned it over and read the blurb on the back.

'Good.' She looked around. 'Have you lots of things to do?'

'Are you joking?' He listed them. 'Some plants need staking and tying, the chrysanthemums behind the hedge need to have the tops pinched out, the . . .'

'Stop.' She held up her hand. 'I've got one hour to spare. Shall I help you in the garden?' She paused. 'Or is there something else you would rather do?'

He stared, smiled, and caught hold of her hand. 'The latter, please.'

'Okay.'

Hand in hand, they walked back to the house.

A week later, Karen Horton asked Rosie to come and see her.

When Rosie did so, Karen said without preamble, 'It's about your mother. For the first time in ages my waiting list has disappeared. I still can't believe it.' She stared at Rosie and explained.

'First of all, two residents died last week. It was sad, of course, but Mr Peacock was ninety-nine years old and never came out of his room and Miss Tennett was ninety-four with a cantankerous nature so the rest of the residents were not too upset. Two days later I heard that Mrs Mountjoy was leaving to go and live with her younger sister. Then three days ago the doctor told me he was transferring Ada Adams to hospital and she won't be coming back.

'So, according to regulations, I notified the administrative people I had vacancies. I expected them to forward details of people waiting for a place but they said they only had two people for me.'

Karen refilled her coffee cup. 'It's something to do with the extra private nursing homes that have opened in this area. Anyway, I realised that not only did I have vacancies, I had a single room. Now, I'd promised Mrs Kingston so I went and told her the news, and guess what she said?'

Rosie shook her head and crossed her fingers. A single room!

'She said she didn't want it. She's perfectly happy sharing with Mrs Thorne. Can you believe that woman? After all the fuss she made.'

Rosie, leaning forward in her seat, asked: 'So the single room's still vacant?'

'Yes. Would your mother like it, do you think?'

Rosie closed her eyes and breathed a sigh of relief.

'I'll make sure she does.'

She fixed up an appointment to bring Minna for a look round and literally skipped to the bus stop.

Minna agreed to move into the single room. She was no fool and knew from her daughter's glowing descriptions in the past that Karen Horton had the welfare of her residents at heart. On viewing, she grumbled of course. The room was smaller than she'd imagined. The view was nothing, and how could she possibly decide which pieces of furniture to take with her?

Rosie knew there was really no contest. Mark helped transport Minna's favourite things to The Firs. He positioned her grandmother clock opposite the door, placed her sewing box near her easy chair and hung her two paintings on the wall facing the bed. The photographs were placed on the dressing-table.

As they prepared to leave, Minna thanked him somewhat brusquely. She saw them go without emotion but outside, getting into his car, Rosie cried.

'It doesn't seem right, Mark. How can I leave her here?'

He gave her his handkerchief to blow her nose on, waiting a moment before saying: 'It's her decision, Rosie, and it's the right one. You know that.' He smiled. 'Don't worry too much. Your mother will soon have things running to her satisfaction.'

Chapter Thirty-One

During the next ten days, Rosie went to visit her mother whenever she could. Minna continued to grumble but less forcibly and Rosie felt more optimistic about her settling in at The Firs. However, on one occasion when she had left work early and had slipped in to spend an hour with Minna, Karen Horton pounced on her as she was leaving.

'Rosie, a word please. It's about your mother . . .'

Rosie's expression was rueful. 'What's she done?'

Karen ticked off each episode on her fingers.

'She upset Mr Taylor by telling him he couldn't smoke. He *was* in the smoking room at the time. She tried to get the menu changed.' Karen rolled her eyes. 'Cook loved that. She told three residents in the television lounge that they were half-witted because they watched game shows.' Karen paused. 'Is that enough?'

Rosie hung her head. 'I'm sorry. I'll try and talk to her but I don't know if it will do any good.'

'No, don't bother.' Karen sighed and shrugged her shoulders. 'We both know new residents often behave aggressively; it's a defence mechanism, a wish to get a place in the pecking order. We'll let things ride for a few more days.' She sighed again. 'I'm just waiting to see what happens when Minna comes up against Mrs Kingston. Talk about the clash of the Titans.'

Rosie's laugh was somewhat strained.

She had spent an hour with Minna who had been in a gracious mood. They talked about the children and Minna mentioned she had received a cheque from the salerooms.

'I was pleasantly surprised, Rosemary.'

She told Rosie she had been for a stroll in the gardens earlier and had spoken with a gentleman who, as a young man, had worked for a stockbroking firm in London.

'I mentioned Papa's interest in stocks and shares but I didn't elaborate, of course.'

'Of course.' Rosie's voice was sympathetically noncommittal. She now knew something about her grandfather's life, including the way he had left it.

'And you, Rosemary, how are you?' Minna studied her daughter's face. 'You look a little tired.'

'I'm fine, studying hard, of course. It won't be long before my exams.'

'I suppose not.' Minna looked at her wristwatch. 'Well, thank you for calling but I won't mind if you go home now. Dinner will be served at six thirty, you see, and I want to change my dress. The food will not be brilliant,' she pulled a face, 'but one must try and keep up one's standards.'

Rosie stood up. 'Are you sure, Mother? I could stay a little longer, if you like?'

'No, off you go.' She watched Rosie move towards the door and then she said, 'I've already had one visitor today.'

Rosie stopped. 'Oh, who?'

'Mark Goodman called in this morning.'

'I didn't know.'

Minna gave Rosie a sharp look. 'I don't suppose he tells you everything.'

Rosie flushed.

'He brought me a bottle of sherry, which was very nice,

and told me about taking a group of people from Woldview for a holiday in the Lake District.'

'Yes, they're going in August.'

'Are you going?'

'No. I'll be preparing for my exams.'

Minna pursed her lips. 'Mark seemed rather quiet, not at all like his usual self. Don't get too involved in your studying, Rosemary. A man doesn't like to be neglected.'

'We can't all go to the Lake District, Mother. Someone has to look after the residents still at Woldview.'

Rosemary dropped a cool kiss on Minna's cheek and departed.

As she let herself into the house, she heard the telephone ringing. She answered and it was Steve.

'Don't forget to switch on the TV, Mum.'

'Sorry?'

'The TV. It's the twenty-fourth. Remember Mrs Catley's mysterious message?'

'Oh, yes.' Rosie had forgotten. She looked across at the wall clock. There were ten minutes to go. 'What side did she say?'

'BBC 1.'

'Right. Thanks for the reminder.' She paused. 'I've just come back from seeing your grandmother.'

'How is she?'

'Fine. How are you?'

'I'm great. Loving every minute. Oh, and there was another letter from India this morning, from Liz.'

The girl in India, Rosie wondered if she would ever get to meet her.

'She's received your letter with your change of address then?'

'Yep, and, believe it or not, Paula's written to me. She

sounds good, Mum. I think she's going to be all right.'

Rosie, in a heartfelt tone of voice, replied, 'I do hope so, Steve.'

He laughed. 'We've had our bad luck, Mum. Things are going to be better for us in the future.'

Rosie smiled to herself. 'Go and switch on the programme. I'll speak to you later.'

She put the phone down, kicked off her shoes and went into the kitchen to switch on the kettle, then she returned to the sitting room and turned on the television. As she did so, she thought about Minna's comment about Mark. It was true, he had become much quieter over the last couple of months. Rosie, remembering the happy-go-lucky man who had taken her to Coxwold for the day, sighed and then turned her attention to the TV screen, for there, sitting next to the presenter of the show, was Evelyn Catley.

The presenter was speaking to her: 'How did you feel when you heard the news, Mrs Catley, or may I call you Eve?'

'You may, although it would rather defeat the purpose as my christian name is Evelyn.'

Mrs Catley's voice was low but perfectly audible. Wearing a midi dress of navy-blue silk, a white scarf draped around her shoulders, she looked smart but still slightly dishevelled, the way she always did.

Rosie gasped, and without taking her eyes off the screen, she sank into the nearest chair. She smiled as the presenter turned to face the camera and commented, a little nervously:

'Apparently this talented lady possesses a sense of humour.' He coughed, and then said, 'In the fifteen-year history of the Vincent McKenny Poetry Competition, no woman has ever been awarded this prize. This year, Mrs Catley, a hitherto unknown poet, has confounded all the predictions and has been judged the winner by our distinguished and knowledgeable panel of experts. She wins this magnificant trophy . . .' a pause as a large silver trophy was carried in and placed on a table '. . . the acclaim of the judges . . .' a fleeting camera angle of three men and one woman seated behind a flower-bedecked table '. . . and a cheque for eight thousand pounds.'

For the second time, Rosie gasped.

'Before you're presented with your trophy and,' again the presenter flashed his practised smile, 'your cheque of course, would you like to say a few words to the viewers?'

For the first time, Evelyn Catley showed signs of nervousness. She bent her head and plucked at her silk skirt before replying.

Rosie found she was holding her breath, willing her to do well.

After a minute, Evelyn looked up. 'Obviously, I would like to thank the panel of judges. I was deeply honoured.' She paused, raising her hands palm-upwards in a graceful and unstudied gesture. 'I'm a quiet person, not used to displaying my feelings.'

She paused again. 'Only in my poetry do I betray what I think, how I feel and,' her voice became stronger, 'it appears that the learned people who judged the competition found the ideas expressed worth while.'

There was a camera cut, showing all four members of the panel nodding vigorously.

'I thank them for their understanding and appreciation.' Evelyn's lips trembled into a smile. 'And now I have been told there's a suggestion that a collection of my poetry may be published. At first, I must admit, I was alarmed. My poetry is me, and I am a very private person, but after discussion with the interested publisher,' her smile grew wider, 'I confess I find the prospect of publication exhilarating.'

She straightened her already straight back and stared into the camera. 'I therefore take this opportunity to thank someone else.' She paused. 'I've written poetry for over fifteen years only to hide my poems away in a drawer. I never thought they were of any literary value, you see. Then one day, during a conversation with a young man, a friend of mine, he said something to me and his words stayed in my mind.

'When I read about this competition I remembered his words and I decided to take a chance. I picked out my three favourite poems and entered them in the competition and the rest you know.'

'That's very interesting, Mrs Catley.' The presenter's expression suggested the reverse. He hurried on to his next question. 'Tell me, have you any idea what you are going to do with the prize money?' His expansive smile reappeared. 'From our research we understand you are interested in jigsaw puzzles.' He paused. 'You'll need to find a rather more expensive hobby now?'

'You're quite right.'

Evelyn edged slightly along the couch, away from him. 'In five days' time I'm flying off to Peru for a holiday.' She looked at him, straight-faced. 'I've always been inordinately interested in the history and mythology of the Incas.'

Rosie wrapped her arms around her body and laughed out loud at the announcer's expression. She watched Evelyn being presented with her trophy and cheque by a distinguished-looking gentleman in a dress suit and then she switched off the television.

As she prepared her meal, she found herself remembering Evelyn's words and smiling again. As she had mentioned to Steve, she had found Mrs Catley a strange woman, but also, and not mentioned to Steve, she had felt sorry for her. She had seemed a lonely and forlorn lady. And yet now, thanks to Steve – the young man Evelyn mentioned *must* have been him – she had the chance to change her life. In the act of sliding sausages on to her plate, Rosie chuckled again. She wondered what Mr Catley thought of his wife's forthcoming trip to Peru.

In Manchester, Paula had also watched Mrs Catley's television appearance. She had called at Tracey's house to pick up Alison, and Tracey had asked her to stay for tea. They had eaten their meal and Tracey, refusing Paula's offer to wash up, had gone through to the kitchen. Paula had flicked through the evening paper and then turned on the television and there was Evelyn Catley. Paula watched for a moment and then called out to Tracey.

'Come and see. There's a woman on the box I know. She's the mother of Steve's ex-girlfriend.'

'Really.' Tracey, a great TV fan, rushed out of the kitchen and into the lounge, falling over her son who was crawling around on the carpet.

'Oh, darling.' She dropped on to her knees and picked up Bradley's plump little body. 'Did Mummy hurt you?'

Bradley, red faced, struggled to break free.

'Do you think I've hurt him, Paula?'

Paula gave him a brief glance. 'No. He wants to get to Alison.'

Tracey released her child and he crawled rapidly towards Alison's pile of Lego bricks. Reaching them, he swiped them with his hand and Alison shouted at him.

'Go away, I don't like you any more.'

Paula reached out and turned up the volume control. 'She's won a poetry prize.' She whistled. 'Eight thousand pounds.'

The two young women looked at each other.

'What a waste of money.' Tracey looked glum. 'They should give big money like that to people who are young and need it. I bet she hasn't a mortgage to pay. She looks high class.'

Paula frowned. She watched the screen for a few more minutes and then switched the set off. 'I don't agree. If her poetry was the best, then it's fair she got the money.'

'How do you know which poems are best? Who reads them, anyway?'

Paula, who enjoyed reading poetry occasionally, changed the subject. She appreciated Tracey's good qualities; she was sweet-natured and kind. She was a good child-minder for Alison but in other ways she was a bit limited.

She said, 'You should have let me wash up, Tracey. That's the least I could do after you prepared tea.'

'Think nothing of it. Anyway, it's finished now.' Tracey sank into an easy chair. 'Just you being in here with the kids is a bonus and anyway, I enjoy your company. George is at work so much I hardly see him. The kids are all right, but you can't have a proper conversation with them.'

'You do wonders with them.' Paula was sincere. She didn't know what she would have done without Tracey's help. 'I couldn't look after toddlers all day. I haven't the patience.'

'Well, it wouldn't do for us to all be alike.' Tracey fidgeted with her fingers. 'Paula, can I ask you something?'

'Yes, of course.'

'I thought, I mean . . .' Tracey ran her tongue over her lips. 'Have you heard anything about that job you're after, that promotion?'

'Not yet.' A frown creased Paula's forehead. Was Tracey wanting more money for child-minding fees? If she did, it was going to be hard to raise the cash.

'I won't find out until the beginning of December. That's the time the woman who worked for Mr Beaver is supposed to come back to work. Still, I'm hoping and at least the job I'm doing now is permanent. Why do you ask? If you need more money . . .'

'Oh, no. It's not that.'

Tracey was now biting her thumbnail.

Paula's frown deepened. 'Then what is it?'

'I've something to tell you.' Tracey sat up in her chair. 'I wasn't going to mention it, but I think I should.'

Paula waited, but instead of telling her whatever it was, Tracey asked her another question.

'Now that things have simmered down, Paula, how do you feel about Dave?'

Paula scowled. 'In what way?'

'Well, have you forgiven him?' Tracey's face had turned red. 'Would you take him back if he asked you?'

'Good grief, Tracey, what a question.' Paula shook her head. 'Don't you know me better than that? Of course I wouldn't. As soon as I can, I'm going to get a divorce and I'll be happy if I never see him again.'

'You really mean that. You don't miss him at all.'

Paula drew a deep breath and when she replied her voice was quieter.

'Sometimes, when I remember the happy times I feel sad but,' she shook her head, 'I know I've got to move on. Dave has no place in my life any more.'

Tracey smiled. 'That's all right then, I can tell you.' Seeing the impatience of Paula's face, she rushed on. 'I saw Dave yesterday, when I was in town.'

Paula tensed. 'Where did you see him?'

'Just off the main shopping centre.'

'How did he look?'

In the corner of the room, Bradley and Alison were amiably building Lego bricks. Alison had not looked up at the sound of her father's name.

Tracey considered. 'Well, he looked a bit scruffy. He had his hair in a ponytail, it looks as though it could do with a wash. He had his leather jacket on, you know the one.'

Paula nodded.

'He was going into a pub. The thing was, he wasn't on his own.'

She looked across at Paula.

'Go on.'

'He was talking to a girl, he had his arm around her shoulders.' Tracey paused. 'She had a look of you, Paula. She was young and slim and had dark hair but it was long.'

Paula sighed and sat forward in her chair. She covered her face with her hands. Tracey watched her anxiously. 'Did I do right, to tell you?'

'Oh, yes.' Paula uncovered her face and managed a smile. 'I'm glad you did. You see, I've been worrying about him. The last time we spoke . . .' She stopped talking and brushed her hand over her mouth.

'So you don't mind him having a girlfriend?'

'No, except . . . you say the girl looked young?'

'Yes, about eighteen I would say.'

Paula sighed. 'Poor kid.'

Towards the end of August, Mark took his group of residents off for their holiday in the Lake District.

Rosie saw them off. 'I hope you have good weather.' Under the bustle surrounding the departure, she squeezed Mark's hand. 'Wish I could come with you.'

'There'll be plenty for you to do here. I'll send you a postcard.'

He touched her cheek and then turned to board the coach. She waved goodbye and then went back into the house feeling let down. Was she imagining it or was Mark withdrawing from her in some indefinable way? He still behaved caringly towards her, they still made love, although not so often, but he rarely joked or laughed and she had the feeling something was worrying him.

If only he would confide in her, but he wouldn't. When she tried to draw him out, ask what was bothering him, he simply shrugged and told her she had an overactive imagination. If she persisted in her efforts to make him face the changes in himself he grew testy and accused her of looking for problems where none existed. She didn't know what to do.

During a conversation with Barbara, the young woman confirmed Rosie's suspicions.

'Mark's getting ever so difficult to work with. He's got some bee in his bonnet but I don't know what. I wish he'd sort himself out.'

Rosie wished the same. Nagging away in her mind was the old, familiar worry. Had he got tired of her? Was he frightened of getting too involved? She swore to herself that when her exams were over she would tackle him. She would make him reveal his true feelings.

One blustery day in late September, Rosie got ready for her visit to Woldview. It was her day off, but she had something special to tell Mark. The weather forecast had mentioned heavy showers so she prepared for bad weather and wore her raincoat and winter boots.

September seemed too early to go into boots but the weather was so uncertain. Autumn had come early and already the leaves were deserting the trees. Just before she left the house, she checked her handbag. Yes, it was there, the brown envelope containing the precious slip of pink paper.

Only one other person had seen the paper. She had shown it to Minna last night. Ariving at The Firs, she had found her mother's room empty. After a wander around, a member of staff had suggested she try Mrs Kingston's room. Her mother was there, drinking sherry and listening to music by Mozart, played on Mrs Thorne's new CD player. She had looked a little annoyed at her daughter's appearance.

'It's rather late for a visit, Rosemary.'

When Rosie told her the reason for her visit, Minna's attitude changed. She insisted she examine the evidence of her daughter's success. She read the pink slip and then showed it to her two companions.

'See how well she's done! Look at her marks! Rosemary works full-time, you know, and she comes to see me regularly. She studied dreadfully hard.'

She had smiled at Rosie and Mrs Thorne and Mrs Kingston had smiled with her.

Rosie's eyes had stung with tears. At last, her mother was proud of her. That in itself made all her hard work worth while. And today, she was going to tell Mark about her success. She glanced at the clock and went to catch her bus.

Feeling a little embarrassed about her sentimentality, she decided to enter the grounds of Woldview following the path she had taken on her first visit there. She pushed open the blue-painted door and walked through the patch of woodland, smiling at the red and yellow leaves swirling around in the fitful wind

Earlier, Mark had mentioned he wanted to garden at the weekend and Rosie hoped she would find him near the sundial but when she reached the lawn, the place was deserted. She stood for a moment, disappointed.

She turned and walked towards the house but then, after a few yards, she stopped. She could hear rustling sounds and then a soft curse.

'Mark?' she called. There was no reply so she stepped off the path and walked through the rough grass towards an oak thicket which stood near a large holly bush. She knew that behind the thicket Mark had established a propagating bed where he was tending old-fashioned roses and attempting to establish some new species.

He was there, kneeling beside a straggling rose bush which still bore deep-red blooms. A pair of secateurs lay on the soil beside him and he was sucking at the back of his right hand.

Rosie stopped. 'Oh dear, has the bush fought back?'

He scrambled to his feet. 'You could say so. Perhaps it felt I was over-doing the pruning.'

She went up to him. 'Let me see.' She took hold of his hand and looked at the scratch. 'Not too deep. You'll live.'

'Glad to hear it.' He put his head on one side and studied her face. 'You're not supposed to be here today.'

'I know, but I couldn't wait until tomorrow.' A smile split her face.

'You've got your results?' His smile was as wide as hers. 'It's good news?'

She nodded.

'That's wonderful.' He threw his arms around her and kissed her.

She blushed.

'What were your marks?'

'Eighty-two per cent.' She opened her bag and produced the slip of paper.

He took it from her and read it. 'That's amazing. I'm

proud of you.' He handed back the slip. 'Who have you told?'

'My mother, and now you. I'll phone the kids tonight.'

He looked at her. 'I hope Minna was suitably impressed.'

'Yes, she was.'

'Good.' He studied her face. 'I know it's early days, but have you made any plans?'

'Sorry?' She came down to earth with a bump.

'You can apply for a better job now, and the sooner the better.' He paused. 'You can't stay on as a care assistant, Rosie. That would be a waste.'

She frowned. 'I know, but there's no rush.'

'I'm not so sure. You know how long it takes to process job applications. If the other students on your course have done well, they'll be looking round for advancement. You'd better make enquiries and if there's nothing suitable around here, then you should consider trying further afield.'

His words hit her like a physical blow. She stared at him in amazement and then she shivered, realising it was starting to rain. Glancing upwards, she saw the sky had clouded over, was now a grey, leaden colour.

Mark had looked up, too. 'Here it comes. We'd better get indoors.'

Ignoring his comment, she asked, 'Do you want me to move away, Mark?'

'Of course I don't.' There was still light enough for her to see the colour run up into his face. 'I'll miss you like hell, but we both knew it would come to this. And now you've passed with such high marks, the sky's the limit. A year, eighteen months as a second officer then you could try for a first officer's job, end up with your own place.'

She thrust her hands into her pockets. 'I was planning a

slightly less dramatic change. I was hoping for a second officer's job somewhere within the local authority. That way, we could stay in regular contact. And to help things along,' she forced a smile, 'I'd decided to take driving lessons. As a second officer, I could afford to run a car.'

The rain had developed into a downpour. Mark picked up his secateurs.

'We're getting soaked. Let's find some shelter.'

A hidden blackbird let out a sudden piercing chirp from the depths of the holly bush and Mark glanced that way and nodded. 'Over there. It's better than nothing.' He led the way and Rosie followed.

Sheltering beneath the glossy green leaves she decided now was the time to speak honestly.

'This is probably horribly embarrassing for you, but I must know.' She drew in a breath. 'Do you love me?'

She saw him start and she laid her hand on his arm, stopping his reply until she had finished what she had to say.

'I love you.' She gave a wry smile. 'And as you've probably guessed, I'm really the marrying kind. However,' she shrugged, 'if that's not on the cards, then I'd settle for a steady relationship. But Mark,' her voice quivered and she stopped for a moment, biting her lip, 'there has to be a commitment, and after what you've just said, I'm not sure that there is.'

She looked up at the falling rain. 'I know you won't admit it, but during the last couple of months, you've changed and I don't know why. Perhaps you felt things were getting too heavy between us and you didn't know how to tell me?' She shook her head. 'So now's the time for honesty. Do you love me or don't you?'

In the silence that followed her words, the soft sound of the falling rain intensified. Rosie clenched her hands so hard her nails bit into the soft flesh of her palms.

Then Mark spoke. 'Of course I love you, Rosie.'

'You *do*?'

He nodded. His intent expression conveyed the seriousness of the words he was saying.

'I wasn't sure how you felt. I didn't want you to feel any pressure to stay with me. You've worked so hard, Rosie. You deserve success and now you have a chance to carve out a career for yourself. And you've changed so much. You had so little confidence when we met, you were almost timid, but now look at you. I think you could have anything you want.'

'I want you.'

Without realising, she had turned to him and grasped the front of his jacket with both hands. 'Yes, I've changed, and it was you that showed me how to change. And I want a better job, I want lots of things. But most of all, I want you.' She tilted her head and looked into his face.

His hands came up and covered hers.

'Are you *sure*, Rosie? Remember, I've been your first manfriend after a long time on your own. Perhaps you should wait, see if—'

She interrupted him. 'You said I could have anything I wanted. Well, I want us to be married. Will you marry me?'

She watched his lips begin to smile, she watched the smile reach his eyes and when the skin around the corner of his eyes began to crinkle she opened her eyes very wide to stop her tears falling.

She looked up at the sky. The rain was easing and patches of blue were breaking up the grey. She blinked. A watery sun was attempting to escape from behind a cloud.

Just before Mark kissed her she saw the raindrops clinging to the wavy edges of the holly leaves above them fragment into the colours of the rainbow. They glittered like lit chandeliers in the pale rays of the sun.

The S[illegible]
Stranger

FRANCESCA WEISMAN

PENGUIN BOOKS

PART ONE

I

It must be night.

The thought struck him oddly, less like a simple observation than like the gradual unravelling of a crossword clue. Oblongs of reflected light skittered across a darkened ceiling; the sky beyond the glass was of the deepest, richest navy. There was a nip to the air that slid in beneath the raised sash, too sharp to be anything but a post-suppertime chill. These notions came to him jaggedly, painfully. His head ached as the disparate pieces threatened to become whole.

At least there was no open wound, that much seemed certain. His fingers worried the thin skin at the back of his skull, nails parting hair with a frightened curiosity. Nothing wet, nothing torn: just a tenderness and bruising. He sat back and exhaled with exertion and relief, still not quite recalling what had brought him to this moment.

Slowly and sorely his body unfolded itself. He was alone in the big room that stretched the length of the house. To the front, terracotta paving skirted an occasionally wild lawn, shielded from the street by privet and seasonal laburnum. Beyond the French windows, the back garden spread generously, an ordered chaos of silhouettes against the late spring night sky. There was the sundial, the hanging bird feeder, the no-longer-used children's swing. Damp fingers of lilac grazed an ageing garden bench.

His gaze skimmed the lawn like a searchlight, and his heart gave a little jolt. There was something bizarre, disconnected, horribly like a severed limb. Only after several seconds of staring did it reveal itself as a Wellington boot. Yes, yes, he told himself: Frieda, his Labrador, often made free with such things, discarding them randomly and without respect. Yet he had to strain to make sense even of a sight so ordinary, as though the simplest of additions had acquired the mystery of long division.

Well, perhaps it was inevitable – this jumpiness, uncertainty. After all, for God's sake, he had been attacked. It was coming back to him now – the unexpected, grotesque thrill of it. His neck and his arms were stiff, his backside and flanks tender: he could imagine the bruises, blooming and florid, spreading beneath his skin.

Now he thought about it, he could reconjure some of his footsteps from earlier – it must have been a few hours back, though he was still fuzzily guessing. He had been walking Frieda across the heath, following one of their usual routes over the hill favoured by kite fliers and then skirting the outer edge of the copse. It was time for supper – or later – for families with young children: whole swathes of the heath were quiet and unpeopled. His assailant had leapt upon him from behind, so his weight had been flung forward, first on to his palms and knees, and then – more pressingly – on to his stomach. One of his hands was grazed at the edge of the loose-stoned path, but the rest of his body met only with damp grass and earth. His lungs shrank, compressed and tortured, his windpipe gurgled and his brain throbbed. His attacker ground away on top of him as though in some ghastly, misguided sexual fervour, and Frieda's panicked barking faded to a watery, distant echo.

Then it had stopped. He was unsure if he had blacked out, and if so, for how long, but when he came to properly, all was peace, and he was more or less whole.

Now what? He should telephone the police, he supposed. He moved towards the hallway where the telephone perched on an antique occasional table. Already, in anticipation, he could hear in his head the click of the receiver lifting from its cradle, the growl of the dial tone, and the clearing of his throat.

Police, please, he would say. *My name's Callum Scott. 14 Pilgrim's Row. I need to report an incident.* But what after that?

He was reluctant to admit it, perhaps even to himself, but a career's worth making a killing out of humiliating the police did, after all, make it difficult to seek their help. Callum Scott QC (at only thirty-nine) had made the most handsome of livings from championing the underdog, cross-examining agents of the establishment and making them look like fools. He recoiled – even if slightly – at the thought of some young local constable, sitting wide-eyed on his Chesterfield and silently smirking at his misfortune.

Too bloody right, they'd probably want to say. *How does it feel now the boot's on the other foot?*

But something besides that bothered him, hovering at the corner of his brain. For if he summoned the police now, whatever could he tell them? He couldn't give even the vaguest description of his assailant. There had been the footsteps, the snap at his skull and the body blows, and a sharply malevolent hiss. No passer-by had helped him up, and he doubted there were witnesses. There had been no obvious attempt to rob him: at any rate, he'd lost nothing. As Frieda's canine anxiety had panted into exhaustion, he'd scrambled his way upwards and managed to get home. On arriving back, the fatigue and the pain had sent him immediately to sleep, but after this gradual awakening, he began to feel almost lucky.

Looking back on it, even then, it had all started to strike him as curious. The many long years in the justice profession had made him intimate with crooked impulse. This attack had a disorder to it which didn't make sense. Even the most desperate, drug-crazed robber usually acted after some logic, spotting the Rolex, the briefcase or handbag, the hint of a wallet bulking a pocket. But he had been walking Frieda casually, dressed down in jeans and a shirt, jangling only keys and loose change, and the attacker hadn't so much as patted him down.

You did get mindless violence as well, of course: he'd recently finished a case where the hapless victim ended up dying from a seemingly motiveless stab wound. But then, you see, there was a horrible pattern to it: the trigger of a misplaced, eyeballing glance, perceived as haughtiness or disrespect. Yet he hadn't even seen this thug, much less exchanged words or glances.

On reflection, it was unlikely to be a sexual pervert, despite the closeness, beneath fabric, of human skin on skin. The sexual offender usually craves some bonding with his victim, the twisted illusion of willingness and intimacy. None of that without eye contact, without even a hint of what lay beneath. And why had his assailant stopped without really, truly hurting him?

His head was beginning to ache again, perhaps with the expanding and unwelcome mystery. He had to take a deep breath and steady himself. He reached for the receiver.

For a second, the telephone – a heavy, black, Victorian antique – smudged and blurred beneath his eyes. He thought he was seeing a giant beetle, and then a vast, dark, runny dog turd. The threat of nausea gurgled at the base of his throat and he placed a flat palm against the wall as his body rocked forward. Then the telephone was again a telephone and his shaking fingers clutched the handset.

Tremblingly, he grappled with the old-fashioned, circular dial.

'Police, please,' he said, unaccountably annoyed at the tinny, mechanical operator. He was miserably irritated at how long it took him to get through. When he did, he could hear the scepticism mounting almost immediately: *Who's it calling this time? Is it really an emergency?*

'Yes, hello. My name's Callum Scott Q – I mean Callum Scott. I'd like to report an incident. I've just been attacked.'

'Right you are, sir,' said the voice, serious now. 'Can I ask where you are now?'

'I'm at home, at my house. I'm calling from my home.'

'And this attacker broke in?'

'No, it happened on the heath. I live nearby. I walked home.'

'And how long ago was this, sir?'

'I don't know – several hours – one, two. Look, I haven't worked it out. I'm a little . . . disconnected.'

'I see, sir. Any injuries?'

'I'm in some pain, but I'll be fine.'

The other's scepticism was returning. 'Did the attacker rob you, take anything?'

'No, I've got everything.'

'And can you give us some description, sir?'

'No, I didn't see him. He came from behind.'

'Right now, sir. If you give me your address I'll get someone round to do a full report. But it might not be straight away. Would you prefer tonight or tomorrow morning?'

Annoyance crept into Callum's voice. 'Tonight, it should be, don't you think? I have just been assaulted, after all. I'm lucky it wasn't much more serious.'

He reeled off his address, and then immediately started to feel dizzy.

When he came to for the second time, he heard a heavy breathing and a nearby tapping. It was Frieda panting at his feet and the mantel clock ticking. The accidental sprawling of his limbs suggested he'd half collapsed on to the sofa. But the aching in his head was milder and he didn't think he'd been out long.

Callum decided that hot, sweet tea and biscuits might be of benefit; he considered the energy and composure necessary to make it to the kitchen. He straightened himself on the sofa and stared at the room ahead of him. The house was so vast, so many-chambered, that if one were in a vulnerable condition getting about could seem quite daunting.

People thought he was mad, he knew, staying here alone now that Shona and the kids had left. But he had fallen in love with this place long ago, it was a shining example of his success. He adored the vivid tangle of its gardens, and its nearness to the heath, and the secrets of its interior, every quirk and every crevice.

In the early days, despite the shortage of time and the abundance of money, he had elected insistently to do much of the decorating himself. Many had been the time when, halfway up a ladder, he had turned to see Shona, head cocked, regarding him quizzically as she shielded a waiting mug of tea. *You don't love me at all*, she would joke, not always with whole-hearted levity. *You've got a secret mistress. You're having a tryst with this old house.*

And he really did love the place. Partly he stayed because of course one day they'd all be back: Shona and the kids descending with cheerfully noisy disorganization. But all that stripping and replastering had added intimacy to affection, so he knew the landscape of this mansion as one might a lover's body: its variety of textures, its unexpected dips and curves.

All of which was just as well, really, because, despite the instinctive familiarity, as he thought of the kitchen and the kettle and the teapot the whole room appeared bizarrely skewed.

Callum straightened up on his feet and paused for breath like an athlete. Surely nothing could have been moved. Yet why weren't things where they should be? And what was that long, threatening object, leaning at a sinister angle in the corner, a menacing, offensive item where his cricket bat should have been? Had there been a burglary while he slept: a break-in as well as a battering? Was he the sudden victim of a conspiracy of malice and violence?

He managed to stop himself from swaying forward

and then there was a clicking, a lightening in his brain. He was looking at his cricket bat after all and everything was as it should be.

He sighed and shook his head and pressed a palm against his brow. The headache pulsed beneath his skin, now blunter and now sharper. He was beginning to understand a little more about the victims of crimes, those on the raw end of acts he'd so often defended. How even the simplest of scares could shake your mind and body.

Callum continued on his way to the kitchen, fortified by the prospect of oatmeal biscuits. Passing one of the many splendid sideboards, he ran his fingers over the surface, fingering the sturdy photograph frames, the reassurance of images of those he'd loved. It didn't matter that they were gone – some absences are merely temporary. They were like benign ghosts, vigilant spirits, forever looking out for him.

This was his favourite – the four of them together: Shona holding Saffron, a bundle of baby limbs and blankets; Rudy jumping at her elbow, yapping like an eager puppy. He had stood behind with a father's circling embrace.

He raised the picture up, as though its closeness could comfort him, but as the figures approached a chill shivered along his forearms. No longer could he see familiar faces that he could trace with his eyes shut, but a mess of curves and angles, mixed-up features a-jumble. He was staring at the silhouette of an amoeba, with multiple, straggling pseudopodia. His family disappeared within the photo frame. It was like losing them a second time.

Callum dropped the picture abruptly as his world swam in greenish darkness. The heavy frame hit the sideboard, knocking a chip into the varnish. He forced himself to grope for it, to make the crooked puzzle straight again. He leaned it up against the wall and fixed his eyes on a band of light in the top left corner, the halo of Shona's red hair, lit up from behind.

Your type, then, friends had said, all sly winks when they'd first met her. *Always go for the same sort, don't you?* And he didn't really mind hearing it, because he knew it was true. Pale skin and auburn tresses, thin faces, broad, sharp bones. He liked them pretty, obviously, but not in that peroxide, smoky-eyed, lads' mag way. People thought he was harking back to his Irish roots, perhaps to his mother, but in fact there was another prototype, also from his childhood. Nothing unusual in that, it must be the same with all men. Look at Humbert Humbert, smitten with love-lust as a prepubescent and then trying to relive it till well past his sell-by date. At least he, Callum Scott, was keeping it legal.

Callum kept staring at the halo, like a sailor fixed on the horizon. Surely if he concentrated long enough, the disordered features would settle. The seconds ticked by and he heard his breath rasping. He wiped his hand across his brow and streaked it with slivers of sweat. And then the vision was disturbed by three sharp knocks through the dark house. They jolted him from the stillness of his reveries and triggered a volley of Frieda's barking.

He thought, *Who on earth . . . ?* and then *Police*, and then (crazily), *You're quick/Whatever kept you?* He shook his head at the paradox while the caller rapped again, the knocks sharper now, impatient at his shuffling.

'Down, Frieda,' murmured Callum, emerging into the hallway. 'I'm coming, for God's sake, I'm coming. Have some patience, won't you?' He thought of the unhelpful, automatic voice he'd spoken to earlier; wondered if the police might have heard of him or recognized his name. Reaching for the handle of the front door, he somehow expected hostility. So he was surprised to see, there on the doorstep, two men with wide, worried, serious eyes.

'Evening, sir. Callum Scott, sir?' One of them flashed an ID card in a battered leather wallet. 'I'm DC Fletcher, Holborn CID, and this is Pete Williams, my colleague. May we come in?'

'Of course,' said Callum, standing aside rather shakily. 'I'd rather lost track of the time.' His watch revealed it was well past midnight.

'On your way to bed, were you, sir?' asked DC Fletcher, looking around and rubbing his hands, as though this were November instead of late May. The two men were about his age, and wearing jeans and waist-length jackets. Their unfamiliar features blurred and sharpened in the dimness, but from their postures they looked awkward, like guests without an invitation. For the first time Callum registered his house was in darkness.

'I – no –' he started to say. 'Look, won't you come this way?' He led them into the long living room, flicking on a standard lamp, and then a sidelight. Electricity lent the place the warmth of normality. Just as he'd pictured earlier, they sat on the Chesterfield.

'Sorry to hear about the attack, sir,' said DC Fletcher. 'The one you reported earlier. You all OK now, then? Don't need to see a doctor?'

Callum knew he should, with a head wound, but said he'd be fine to answer a few questions. He offered them tea, praying they'd say yes, so he could finally make himself some, but then, when they accepted, he realized he couldn't make it to the kitchen.

'Don't worry, sir,' said Pete Williams, steadying Callum back in his chair. 'You tell me where the things are and I'll go and get it.' A flush of shame warmed Callum's cheeks as he uttered some cursory instructions. It was a pity, because the tea came back weak, and the officer brought digestives instead of the oatmeal. But it would have sounded far too foolish if he'd said, *D'you mind bringing the other sort?*

Still, there they all were, with their cups of tea in the nice china, the officers all solicitous and polite and the night outside mild and fragrant. Pete

Williams got out a notebook, like the ones Callum had often seen photocopied among case papers, but DC Fletcher had a huge clipboard, so unwieldy it was a wonder he produced it from seemingly nowhere.

'Now then, sir, Mr Scott,' said DC Fletcher. 'Obviously we need to ask you a few questions. This attack earlier. Tell us everything you remember.'

As soon as Callum began his account, the whole thing started to seem vague and trivial. He almost wanted to apologize, to tell the officers he shouldn't have bothered them, it was all so insignificant, surely they must have more important tasks.

But his skin was prickling coldly, because their faces had become more serious. They kept nodding, and saying, Uh-huh, and was he sure he couldn't remember any more details? It was like going to the GP for some antibiotics and being shunted off suddenly for a brain scan.

When he could think of no more to add to what seemed a pitifully thin memory, he watched DC Fletcher sit back with his clipboard perched on crossed legs.

'The thing is, sir, we are taking this matter seriously. There's something else, you see, of which I think you should be aware. Three days ago, another man was the victim of a seemingly motiveless attack. Near to where you were, on the heath, sir, and also walking his dog. Only difference, sir, this man ended up dead. Pathologist's report suggests the killing was deliberate. His family and friends have no idea why anyone would be after him. But there are very similar hallmarks. Not wishing to be alarmist, sir, but you may have escaped a serial killer. And with so little clue as to motive so far, there's no knowing what he might do next.'

DC Fletcher folded his arms, let the news seep through the night.

Pete Williams said, 'Now, sir, one more time. Anything else at all?'

As they were leaving, they asked him to change his clothes so they could take his shirt, slacks and shoes away for analysis. They even took Frieda's dog lead. He bid them farewell in his dressing gown. Just as well, he thought, as by now he was too exhausted to undress.

If earlier he had felt disconnected, now things were infinitely more sinister. And the house itself mocked and threatened him, in its shifting, shadowy emptiness. A serial killer without logic, who had let him get away. Had he been targeted? Would the attacker return to finish the job?

Every creak of the floorboards jolted him; the breeze at the window pane made him freeze. The very homestead that he loved had suddenly turned against him, like a cherished, trusted lover revealing the colours of betrayal. Falling asleep beneath fresh linen, the evening came back to him in snatched dreams. He heard muffled footsteps, felt the blows again, the strained panting at the back of his neck. Sometimes he heard his name in one poisonous, hissed syllable: *Cal.* But he was shattered, and beyond telling if it was real or imagined.

2

When she breathes in, the air is sweet and heavy. The hallway is thick with the scent of cut flowers. Mainly lilies, but also roses, carnations, and many other blooms her mother can't even name. Every sideboard and table is heavy beneath bouquets, and now they've run out of vases they've started using old bottles and jam-jars.

It's the outsiders who've brought them all, or *goyim* as Rosie's mother says. Jewish people don't deal with death like that: flowers are for births, weddings and bar mitzvahs. At the cemetery, they put big pebbles on the gravestones. Stone on stone, all sombre, none of this sweet-smelling colour. It could be nice, but not with all the doors closed and curtains drawn. It's not as if you feel like you're in one of Kew Gardens' hothouses. More like a closed-up, too-small sweet shop, with bright sticks of rock and barley sugar; not the delicious kind but the nasty sort with a smell that almost makes you sick.

Rosie stays on the landing and leans against the banister. She's still too small to peer over the top, so she squints through the gaps instead. It's weird how if you can see better, you can sometimes hear better too. She's got a view right down to the front door, and to the door into the living room – that one's slightly ajar, though it should probably be closed. Sing-song voices bubble through the narrow gap and up the stairs.

Father died last week and they buried him almost immediately. Rosie saw a BBC TV drama once where the grandpapa of the family died, and they kept him in the front room for ages so people could sit and cry and make grand speeches. Nothing like that happened here, which rather disappointed her, but 'that sort of practice', said her mother, 'is not for people like us'.

Now that Father's coffin is in the earth, the house is prepared for a week-long ceremony of mourning. 'Sitting shiva', Rosie's mother calls it, and has explained that *shiva* is the Hebrew word for seven, the number of days they will mourn. The word makes Rosie feel cold, although it is nearly high summer: it makes her want to go and sit in a corner, hugging her knees, which is a little bit the way she felt in the hospital when she realized Father was dead.

Every day since the burial Mother wakes early and does her make-up. She pouts and preens in front of a little hand-held mirror. The bigger mirrors, on the walls and dressing tables, have been hidden away, shielded by dark cloth. Rosie's mother wears her russet-brown hair in a straight-fringed, shiny bob, and she puts on pale-pink, frosty lipstick and lashings of dark mascara. 'The old-style look,' she says to Rosie, when she catches her peeping, 'from when I met your dad and the city was still swinging.'

With her make-up on Rosie's mother goes to sit on a low chair in the living room. It's far too near the ground for her, like a child's stool, and her long legs poke out and upwards in a bony, almost-triangle. From morning until dusk visitors stream in and out. The floaty notes of the doorbell keep on echoing through the hall. There are huge plates of crustless, triangular sandwiches and endless glasses of fruit juice and cups of tea. Though the shivery death feeling is everywhere, the chattering, munching guests look as if they're at a party.

Of course, Rosie's mother cries every morning before doing her make-up, and every night, when she takes it off, you can hear her bawling again. Rosie hates the juddering, halting sobs which make her teary herself. But mostly, when she thinks about it, she feels fuzzy bewilderment.

Father only went into hospital a few days before he died. He was sitting on the sofa, watching telly, when he started to get a bad stomach-ache. 'Heartburn' her parents called it, though Rosie hadn't understood until then how a person's heart really could burn, all the way into nothingness. He went green and started to breathe funnily, and Rosie's mother's face turned ashen. She picked Rosie up and bundled her into the study, closing the door with a thump behind her. With her head pressed against the wood panelling, Rosie heard her mother call an ambulance.

Next day Mother went to visit at the hospital, so nervous and absent-minded she forgot to wear lipstick. But she came back with a wobbly smile and said everything would be all right, and even sat down with Rosie at supper and let them have fish and chips together. The following afternoon Rosie went visiting too: she was walked out of school at lunchtime into the glorious June sunshine. She liked the hospital almost immediately, with its mazy corridors and high ceilings, and the friendly doctors and nurses all smiled and made a fuss of her. Father looked strange at first, propped up against the iron bedstead with bits of plastic tube coming out of him, but he laughed out loud when he saw her and kissed her as vigorously as ever. Then he kissed her mother, unusually sloppily, who blushed and drew away and said they'd both be back tomorrow.

The following day, when they arrived, the nurses started wrinkling their foreheads, and Rosie saw at once that her father's bed was empty.

It struck Rosie then that her mother had also disappeared, and she ran out and stood alone in one of the shiny, high-ceilinged corridors. She wondered briefly if she'd been abandoned, or if she'd see either of her parents again. She tried howling, but quietened when she caught the edge of her mother's whisper. There was another voice, also female, which she guessed must be one of the nurses.

Following the trail of half-familiar sound, Rosie inched down the corridor. Nearing the source of the whispers, she slid through a narrowly opened door. This was a private room off the main ward, with an enormous picture window. The room was flooded with pale-gold sunshine, and she had to shield her eyes. Neither her mother nor the nurse noticed Rosie, and she had time to stare and wonder at the high metal trolley which bore the supine body of her father. He was very flat and very still, and the skin on his face quite smooth. She guessed he must be having the most wonderful dream: he had none of the furrows in his brow he sometimes got when her mother shouted and rattled. The nurse had her arm round Rosie's mother and they were staring through the window. Rosie managed to climb up on a little chair and stretch to touch her father's cheek. It was pleasantly warm, and she was just about to wake him, when her mother turned and gasped and dropped her handbag on the floor.

'Rosie! You wicked thing. Get down from there this instant.'

She picked her daughter off the chair with one brisk, rough, gruff movement and Rosie's ribs jarred so hard this time she really did start to cry. She knew too well the sharp lash of her mother's tongue in this mood, the icy edge of her anger and the impatient rasp of her nails. It would have been an awful lot worse if the nurse hadn't been there.

'Calm down, Mrs Verner. You must both be terribly upset. Don't take it out on Rosie. She only wants to say goodbye.'

And so it gradually dawned on Rosie that that was what they were doing.

Now Rosie is learning there are many places she is not welcome. She tiptoes from room to room, careful not to crack the smooth silence of her mother's grief. If she peers round the door when her mother's doing her make-up, she'll be waved away or merely ignored. If she gets too close, and hiccups or sneezes, she might be picked up and banged down outside.

All the good things about summer, Rosie's favourite time of year, have been put in abeyance while the ceremony of death unwinds. Although it is Wimbledon time, it is 'simply not appropriate' for her to watch the tennis. Last summer she sat for hours listening to the *thwack-thwack* of the ball against catgut, while her father sat watching beside her and tried to explain the rules. They both had a bit of a penchant for Chris Evert, with her pretty blonde bunches, who according to her father was set to win again a second time.

Now the television room is out of bounds, and filled with the coats of guests. Trapped between her bedroom and the landing, Rosie dreams of hosing the garden. She knows from listening to the grown-ups that it's one of the hottest summers ever: the broad, back lawn is scorched yellow, and thick black fissures criss-cross the earth. There are lush tulips and red-hot pokers impossibly bright against the sky, but in this heat it can only be hours before they wither and die. Yet when Rosie grabbed a yellow watering can and started to sprinkle them liberally, her mother caught up with her briskly and said, 'You mustn't do that.' There was something about a water shortage, and it not being a job for girls.

Yesterday, for the first time, Rosie slipped into the big room. All the visitors were talking and eating, and there was such jostling and humming of voices that it was a while before anyone noticed her. Then Mrs Goulding from up the road spotted her with a trill of surprise, and other grown-ups shook their heads as though she shouldn't be there. Rosie marched towards the table determined to obtain a smoked-salmon bridge roll. Numerous pairs of eyes swivelled and followed her on her quest.

She reached her hand over the edge of the table and towards a dish in the middle. Her elbow caught the corner of the snowy white tablecloth, and she stumbled backwards, disconnected, causing two dishes to go flying. Their booty of sandwiches and vol-au-vents scattered across the parquet flooring. A jug of grape juice wobbled and toppled, and a purplish stain seeped through the tablecloth.

Like a tornado, from behind, Rosie's mother emerged and scooped her up. Firmly, she removed the hard-won bridge roll from her grasp.

'That's enough now, you'd better go and play outside.'

Rosie guessed from the mask of strain pulling at her mother's cheeks, that were it not for the onlookers she'd have been banished to her room. Her flailing arms managed to grab a stray vol-au-vent from the table, and with swift deliberation she threw it at her mother's blouse.

'Ooh, you little devil child, you –' But people like Mrs Goulding were saying things like, 'Ah, leave her be', and lots of visitors were shaking their heads with sorrowful, downturned mouths. Rosie got off lightly: she was allowed to escape into the garden, but later she was sent to bed early with only toast for supper.

Today is the sixth day of mourning and Rosie has spent most of the time in her room. Her mother has ordered her to stay here until she has learned to behave. It's another sweltering morning, and the cracks in the lawn are getting bigger. Butterflies perch and flutter on the broad sill of the window. Once, Rosie managed to ensnare and kill one, crushing and flattening its wings in a book. Although both her parents told her repeatedly not to kill anything, everyone seemed to tread on insects, and even her father killed a few spiders. As for the butterfly, it's not as if she spoiled it: its lovely coloured wings will stay beautiful for ever.

The bedroom looks over the garden, and Rosie can see guests with plates and glasses. If they dart a look up towards her she makes sure to duck and hide. Sunlight spools down through the rosebushes and heats the crazy-paved terrace. She can imagine how the stone will feel by teatime, sealing up a burning warmth. She longs to run outside, but doesn't want to be spotted.

Rosie contemplates her escape with practised gravity, for she is used to doing things secretly, like a hidden thing. Father loved her dearly, he couldn't possibly have loved her any more, but he was always a little too breathless to run for too long amongst the trees and shrubs. Mother has never wanted to do that sort of thing anyway. So Rosie has learnt to play alone, unseen, untroubling. She knows how to move about as carefully as a soldier, avoiding the enemy, letting the old house offer camouflage. Of the mansion's thousand chambers not one is a toy-strewn nursery. But Rosie can make up her own games and she doesn't need a playroom.

Then something catches her ear which makes her stand straight in her sandals: arresting, in this house, because of its rarity. It is the sound of other children. Climbing on to the pink-cushioned window seat, she can see clean over the ledge. There is a woman about her mother's age, with the flimsiest of shawls over her bare shoulders; two boys are with her, probably her sons. One's a lot older than Rosie, say twelve or thirteen; the other a little younger, but still older than she is.

The air is quite still and there isn't a breeze, but the woman's shawl flutters as she bends her white arms. She's got a ball in one of her hands, which she tosses in the air. It hits her palm with a slapping noise, a little like the *thwack* of the tennis players.

Now and again, she throws it to one of the boys. The older one catches it and loops it back in a weak arc. With the younger one, she pitches lower, almost rolling the ball along the ground, and he stops its path with a bat and shunts it skeltering back.

'Good, William. Well done, Cal.' The woman's shawl spreads and preens, like the wings of Rosie's murdered butterfly. For reasons Rosie cannot name, she sounds constantly on the verge of laughter. The words dip and rise like waves, more like singing than speaking. She pitches the ball to the younger boy, who punts it back with extra strength. Her voice peels into congratulations and Rosie, too, claps spontaneously.

The sound floats down to the garden and the boy looks upwards, questioningly. She sees two near-black brows beneath a dark, curling fringe, but is too far away to see the colour of his eyes. She ducks instinctively, blushing, although unsure if she's been seen. And then she resolves to go down into the garden.

Minutes pass. Still fearful of being spotted, Rosie contemplates slinking out. It is out of the question to use the French windows in the big room, so she decides upon the little side door in the vestibule beyond the kitchen. 'Ye olde servants' entrance', her mother sometimes calls it; and though they do not have servants, and never have, Rosie knows some have lived here once. She imagines their ghosts coming out at night and doing dusting.

With great care, she ventures beyond the landing. She skips down two sets of stairs, but resists the temptation to jump. Down in the hallway, the door to the big room whips open, a blast of voices gusts out, but no one has spotted her. She edges across the hall and through the kitchen and into the vestibule beyond.

Now Rosie can make her way down the sidepath to the garden: a place that's never on show, littered by dustbins and old watering cans. Finally she reaches the terrace and peers out over the lawn. The boy with the dark brows is no longer there, though his brother is still playing: he has picked up the bat and is dragging a furrow across the scorched grass. The woman with the sing-song voice has her face turned towards the house. Someone calls out, 'Colleen, over here, there's someone I'd like you to meet', and then her whole body turns and she meanders towards the French windows. She holds a hand out behind her as though trailing fingers in water.

'William, come on. We're going back inside for just a minute.'

Rosie feels a stab of disappointment at missing the boy with the dark brows, but still the open air and the freedom are much too good to waste. Avoiding the open lawn, she continues along the side-path, shielded from view by clumps of golden rod and lavender. The further back she goes, the wilder the shrubs grow; there are untamed roses which need pruning, Michaelmas daisies and stinging nettles.

The crazy paving gives way to split-up stone slabs and loose earth. Right at the back is the copse her father called 'our secret forest'.

Here, finally, she can escape the relentless sun. Light sifts through the jagged branches and speckles the earth pale and black. Rosie skirts her favourite hiding place and comes upon the animal cemetery. This is a secret not even her father shared.

Some of the graves hold only dead insects, and everybody kills those anyway. She places them in matchboxes and buries the cardboard deep and hidden. Little secret signs remind her of where she placed the graves. She killed a bluebottle out of tenacity, and a pigeon out of kindness, because it had a broken wing and leg. She knew she was doing the right thing as she twisted its fragile-boned neck. The grave is marked with a feather, but she won't unearth the body.

She cannot explain why the company of dead creatures brings such comfort. Perhaps it is the secrecy of it, and the obvious transgression, in a world where she is forever watched and almost always reprimanded. Perhaps, in death, she's taking these creatures to a better place, like where they say her father's gone now that he's no longer 'with us'. If that's right, it must be OK to kill even a healthy animal.

Emboldened by this thought, Rosie considers her next prey. Perhaps, to mark the occasion, she should kill a real animal: not an insect, or a bird, but a thing with warm blood and four legs. A sort of a tribute to her father. It makes her queasy, but seems right.

Squatting by the pigeon grave, Rosie wonders what to add to her ghostly menagerie. There's a spitting noise to her left, and as she turns, her stomach lurches. It is a savage feral cat with yellowing fangs and a tigrish coat. She has seen the cat before. It's as if there's some sort of signal.

Rosie edges nearer, the cat yowls and spits. She coos and makes mewing noises, the beast arches and bares its teeth. She ignores the smell of her own fear and grasps at a heavy branch. Dirt is gathering beneath her nails and sweat collects in her armpits. Perhaps if she stuns the creature the process will be less bloody. She is dry-mouthed with dread, as she raises the branch to shoulder height, and then, heaving, brings it down towards the fierce feline's skull.

There is not so much a crack as a vast, magnified rustling, as the cat battles the woody tangle, all claws and teeth splayed. Blood rushes to Rosie's cheeks as she tries to back away, but she, too, is trapped by the weight of crooked branches. Her foot slides on a clod of earth and she tumbles on to her backside: the cat leaps straight for her face, narrowly missing, but catching her forearm. Rosie watches the liquid, vermilion beads bubble over her white skin: she is petrified with horror as the cat takes aim again. An ancient prayer nudges to the front of her brain, and she screws up her eyes, convinced the stray is about to claw her heart out.

‘Well, well, little girl, this is a bit of a to do, isn’t it?’

All of a sudden, Rosie’s whole body becomes lighter: the ground and branches fall away, and strong arms pull her clear. The voice speaks again, but she doesn’t make out words. Her feet kick out in mid-air, but large hands keep her still. With the fear of the cat lifted, she realizes how much the scratch is hurting. She turns to see who it is, who has lifted her out of danger, but her body is crushed awkwardly and she has to strain to twist her neck. She knows it’s a man’s voice, and there are little wisps of hair on the hands. Maybe she’d recognize him, but she can’t tell without a proper look. The man’s skin smells funny, sharp and stale at the same time. His big fingers can almost circle right round her waist. He presses one palm against her stomach, and her insides gurgle like a radiator. The other hand slides beneath her backside; his fingers wriggle and tickle her thighs. She squirms, wanting to break free, but the man just holds her tighter.

‘What’s your name, little girl?’

‘Rosie,’ she whispers, still unable to see his face.

‘Well, Rosie, that’s a pretty name. D’you feel better now that horrible big cat has gone?’ But the threat of the savage stray is receding in the face of this new intrusion, closer and more uncomfortable.

‘Can I go inside now?’ pleads Rosie, her elbows digging into her captor.

‘Yes, of course you can. In a little while. But first I think we should play a game.’

'I don't want to play a game.'

'But you'll enjoy it once we've started. And it's a way of saying thank you to me for rescuing you. I know what we'll play. What about blind man's buff?'

The man puts Rosie down, lowering his weight behind her. From somewhere he produces a cloth, all the while keeping one hand round her. He ties the blindfold tight, so the bridge of her nose feels like it's swelling. The cloth smells musty and sweaty. She doesn't want to turn, but he makes her, till she's dizzy and breathless, and she can feel her skirt fluttering out and his fingers on her bare legs. She is terrified and sick with the thought of where the fingers might go if she stops, so all she can do is carry on turning, turning, turning . . .

'Hello,' says the second new voice to enter the secret forest. 'What's this game? Can I play?'

The game – if that is what it is – stops more abruptly than it began. Either Rosie stops turning or the man stops turning her. In any case, she is standing still, arms out like propellers. The blindfold is lifted, and she blinks into the dappled light. The boy with the dark brows stares with a friendly curiosity. The man walks off quickly on to the lawn: she still hasn't seen his face.

'Hello,' says the boy again. 'Your friend's gone. Is the game over?'

'He's not my friend,' says Rosie, thinking, *And it wasn't a game.* She moves her fingers out stiffly and smoothes the creases of her skirt, the way she's seen grown-up women do, with pursed lips and rigid shoulders. Her heart is beating loudly and the skin on her bare legs tingles, but there's no pain or discomfort except for the cat's scratch. Part of her feels jolted, trembly; the other rather important, as though she's escaped storybook danger.

The dark-browed boy bows his head and moves a little nearer. A long, golden pole of sunshine pierces the branches. Rosie's eyes and brain go fuzzy and her stomach tilts, as though moving too far upwards in her small body. Then the boy smiles and she finds herself smiling back.

'I saw you before,' she offers, 'playing ball on the lawn.'

'Do you live here?'

'Yes.' She raises her chin proudly. Her stomach returns to its proper place, and the trembly feeling calms. Up close, she notices, the boy's eyes are hazelish-brown, though in the shade they look darker.

'My mum likes your house. She keeps saying she wishes we could have somewhere like here.'

'It's too big now there's only two of us,' sniffs Rosie. 'Mum says we'll have to move.'

'I'm going to buy a big house like this when I'm rich and grown-up.'

'I'm six,' says Rosie. 'How old are you?'

'Nine, but nearly ten. Much older than you.'

Rosie moves to a clump of grass just beneath the shade of the willow tree. Comfortably clear of the animal graves, she gestures to the boy to sit down.

They sit with their backs towards the slim tree trunk, hugging their knees in front of them. Beyond the curtain of the willow leaves, Rosie glimpses the sing-song voiced woman.

'Is that your mother there?'

'Yes.'

'When she talks it sounds like singing.'

'That's because she's Irish.'

Rosie wrinkles her nose with interest. 'People say my mum looks Irish. But she's not, she's Jewish.'

The boy nods knowledgeably while on the other side of the willow more guests emerge on to the lawn. Rosie wonders if one is the blindfold man, but it's impossible to tell. The boy looks seriously at her arm. 'Did you get that just now? Doesn't it hurt?'

She nods silently, half-gagging at the memory of the cat.

'Don't you think you should go in?'

'Can't, my mum'll spot me. I'm not supposed to be out here.'

'How did you get out then?'

'I sneaked out the side entrance.'

'Well, let's go back that way then. Come on, I'll help you hide.'

Rosie pauses, appraises him.

'OK?' he says.

'OK.' And then she realizes, suddenly, the scratches have stopped hurting. They stand together, dusting the earth from the backs of their knees. 'My name's Rosie,' she declares. 'What are you called?'

'Callum,' says the boy, and darts his eyes away, shyly. Her eyelids batten down and, for an instant, the world beneath them shows up in negative. She places an imprint of his face there, to carry with her, into the future.

3

The sun's first rays stirred Callum, for he had slept with the curtains open. Shona had liked it this way too, during the warmer parts of year: keeping the windows open and drapes parted to let the light and air breeze through. He found it pleasant to feel the first fingers of the day's warmth on his skin, and could sleep quite comfortably until it was time for the alarm. Today, though, he shuddered awake from a heavy sludge of dreams, the details of which escaped him as soon as he opened his eyes.

Yesterday's headache had mercifully calmed. Callum stretched his limbs beneath the linen and flexed each toe individually, as though to check, post-trauma, every one was still there. Despite the earliness of the hour, and last night's misadventure, he felt remarkably rested. Thinking of the day ahead, he determined to take it easy: he had no commitments in court, and could do paperwork at home. He'd just finished a case out of town, and hadn't been into Chambers for a week, but one more day could do no harm. With no need to rise promptly, he could afford a few hours' extra slumber. For a time he could not measure he lay there staring at the ceiling, then tried a page or two of his bedside thriller to coax him back to sleep. But the book had some bad passages, which simply bored him, while the better ones frankly unsettled. He set it aside and, instead, found himself sliding in and out of day-dreams, until downstairs the letterbox rattled and he realized that someone was knocking.

Callum slid out of bed and shrugged himself into a dressing gown. In unslippered feet, he trod into the corridor. Tentatively, he made his way towards the stairs. Upright and mobile, his body felt frailer than before. On the lower landing he stumbled stiffly, and had to flap the air to steady himself. With shallow, uneven breaths he looked towards the front door. The knocking had ceased, but he could hear someone shuffling, and through the frosted, stained-glass panel, he saw the shape of a stranger.

Callum sloped forwards and snapped the door open. He saw a tall man, with honeyed hair, his face hidden, turned streetwards. Callum's chest cavity tightened and he feared, once more, he'd lose his balance. He drew breath as the face turned towards him. 'What are you doing here? What do you want?'

Callum could scarcely believe the man's audacity. This was James, a one-time acquaintance, with whom he'd worked and been friendly, before the friendship turned treacherous. James had always been coarse, street-smart, with a warmly expressive temper, but even Callum's most cynical self had been shocked when he'd run off with Shona. Now his lower jaw worked with the suggestion of anger.

'What do you want?' Callum repeated.

'I'm sorry if I disturbed you.' The voice was young, diffident, almost afraid. 'This wouldn't fit through the letterbox, and you have to sign for it anyway.' The honey-haired man turned to face Callum full on, revealing a wide, acne-pitted brow with an absence of wrinkles. There were two jagged front teeth and an earring Callum had never seen before. He took the parcel from the postman and recognized his mother's handwriting. She'd been on holiday recently and was no doubt sending her usual gift.

'I beg your pardon,' muttered Callum, as he took the proffered clipboard and scribbled his signature. 'Excuse me if I was abrupt. I thought you were someone else.'

'No worries, sir,' said the boy, beating a hasty retreat down the driveway.

Callum closed the door and took the parcel, but he had no appetite for opening it. His skin was flushing hot and cold as he made his way towards the bathroom. He leaned over the basin to splash cold water on his face. His reflection stared back at him, estranged, drawn and haunted. The mass of his dark hair seemed to float off into nothingness; his haggard cheekbones slanted off at impossible angles. Only his eyes reassured him, like a mirror-image acknowledging the original. They were full of loss and fear. He lurched forward, and was sick.

By ten o'clock, after fitfully dozing, Callum realized he was far from his usual self. Perhaps more than one day's rest might be in order. His clerks, who ordered his diary, monitored his caseload, and either charmed or fended off solicitors (whichever was necessary), would no doubt be wondering what he was doing today. He shuffled to the hallway to telephone Chambers.

'Guy, Callum here.'

'Callum, good morning. How are you, sir?' It was a patter that often amused Callum, the vogueish use of his first name, this pretence at equality, tripped up by reminders of the old master-servant relationship. Mind you, he reflected, the way things were in Chambers, it wasn't always easy to tell who was serving who. Nominally, the barristers ran things, each one his own boss: delicately unravelling the pink ribbons from their briefs, whispering urbanely with solicitors, sipping tea with crooked clients. But it was the clerks who took in the cases, kept their eyes on the coffers, and who sometimes knew more of the underside of things than they would ever disclose. Callum occasionally felt artificial dispensing 'casual' orders. So few knew him, he thought, as he sat in his suburban palace: they could not guess how hard-won the grandeur was, how rough-hewn he was underneath. He cleared his throat.

'Guy – I've been – I'm afraid I'm not feeling too well.'

'Sorry to hear that. Nothing too serious, I hope?'

'No, don't worry, Guy. Be a long time yet before

you see the back of me.' Both paused for a few seconds for a spate of shallow, social laughter. 'But I wonder if you might just make sure my diary's kept clear for the rest of the week. I think I might take some time out, spend a few days at home.'

'Right you are, no probs.'

Guy politely masked what Callum could guess was near-incredulity; in close to seven years he'd barely even taken an afternoon off sick. And since Shona's desertion, there weren't even days off to be with the family.

'If any of my solicitors call, find out if it's really urgent. I'll take anything on the Lansdowne case, but apart from that I don't want to be disturbed.'

'Of course.'

'And, Guy, is Anthony in Chambers? I'd like a word.'

'He's tied up at the moment – sorting out something from this morning. Shall I get him to call you when he's free?'

'Thank you, Guy, yes.'

'Hope you feel better soon, sir.'

Callum forgot to feed Frieda until she began to whine pitifully, and he kept looking at the place on the Chesterfield where the two policemen had sat. When the telephone rang, his whole body jolted, though he knew with near certainty that it had to be Anthony.

'Cal, old boy. How are you? Guy said you were out of sorts.'

Callum was almost never out of sorts and there was just a hint of triumphalism in Anthony's voice.

'Not so bad, Tony,' he replied, resenting having his frailty emphasized, and knowing how much the diminutive would irritate Anthony. Not only did Anthony detest any short form of his first name, but he preferred to introduce himself as Anthony Portman and – where possible – QC.

'Look here, don't you know I'm Anthony Portman QC,' Callum had once heard him scold a rather bemused looking traffic warden. Callum had stood a few yards away as Anthony's thin features turned a sharp, angry pink, and wondered why he stayed such firm friends with this rather bumptious barrister. Yet common experience bound the two – Oxford, bar school, their professional growing years, not to mention a family connection stretching back into childhood. Anthony was, after all, dependable.

Callum said, 'Thanks for calling back so soon.'

'Not like you to be off-colour, Cal. What's up?'

'Anthony, I'm not off-colour exactly. It's a little more complicated than that.'

'Oh?'

Somewhere outside a crow squawked; it seemed to Callum the quiet then thickened. He found himself lowering his voice, as though to retreat from invisible listeners.

'The thing is, Anthony, yesterday I was attacked.'

'Good God!' If Callum had wanted to make an impression (which, he told himself, he hadn't) he had clearly succeeded. There were several ensuing seconds of uncomfortable silence.

'Well,' stuttered Anthony, at once flustered, effeminate, 'I didn't expect to hear that. I hope you're all right.'

'Yes, yes, I'm fine,' Callum hissed with resentment. He ignored the skewed self-image which slanted accusingly through the windowpane; the way the room contracted and expanded like an open, beating heart. 'But that,' he added slowly, 'isn't the point.'

'Well, do get to the point, old boy, you're starting to worry me.'

'I was attacked on the heath. Don't worry, they didn't take anything. Of course I told the police. But do you know what they said?'

'For God's sake, Callum, no. Just come out and tell me. You're being very mysterious. This isn't *Book at Bedtime*.'

'They said someone else had been killed in the same place a few days earlier. They took my clothes and things for forensics. They're looking for links.'

There were seconds of hush, and then Anthony cleared his throat. He spoke as though regretting it, but he had to make an announcement. 'Well,' he said eventually, 'it never rains but it pours.'

Callum had wanted to appear nonchalant, but fear fizzed up on his tongue. He said, 'What do you mean?' and the other sounded instantly sorry.

'Nothing, old boy. There's no need to get worked up.'

'Has something else happened?'

'Look, it's probably nothing. I shouldn't have mentioned it.'

'But you have. So what is it?'

There was an uncomfortable pause.

'Well, there was a break-in at Chambers. Last week while you were away. I didn't want to worry you with it. I've just been speaking to the police. Thing is, someone made off with your desktop.'

'That's *all* that was taken?'

'That's all. Nothing else.'

Callum thought, *All my work. Confidential information.* And then: *That's it. Proof. Someone is after me.* This time he could not put up a pretence at being macho. 'Jesus,' he breathed, and then again – helplessly – 'Jesus.'

'Look, I wish I hadn't mentioned it now. These things are always happening. God knows we represent the thieving buggers often enough. It's probably just an unhappy coincidence. Your machine was nearest the door.'

Then why did you mention it, thought Callum, *and sound so bloody self-satisfied to boot?* But out loud he said, 'Anthony, there's something I want you to do for me?'

There was a wary pause. 'Yes?'

'I know you've got friends in the CPS – I want you to call the North London branch. Ask if they know anything about the heath killing. I want to know if there're any leads.'

'For God's sake, Callum. What business have you been in all this time? This is the CPS we're talking about. Swiftness is not their watchword, and neither is openness.'

'No, Anthony, I know. But remember I've been attacked. I'm not looking for miracles. Just do what you can.'

'All right, Callum, I'll humour you. But I think you're being paranoid. You'd be better off seeing a doctor rather than playing detective. You are all right, aren't you?'

'Of course – I've not been hurt – it's just that I can't really . . .' The sentence trailed into uncertainty. What did Callum want to say? *Can't see* was far too dramatic, not to say inaccurate. The morning-lit room spread before him, with a perfect, bland clarity. *Can't focus*, perhaps, but that wasn't quite right either. He could count five fingers held in front of him without a split second's faltering. 'My eyes,' he murmured, softly, but too quiet for Anthony to hear. And then 'can't really concentrate' was the phrase's lame conclusion. 'Just a few headaches, that's all. Nothing too serious.'

'Well, make sure it isn't. And don't start going on any wild goose chases.'

Magazines were scattered over the low coffee table in the waiting room. They were all women's things, about food, fashion and babies: the funkier, glossier offerings frosted with a cruel, imperious glamour.

On the chair opposite, a tired woman struggled to control her toddler; it coughed, and gnawed her fingers, sputtering mimicked obscenities. She shushed her wayward offspring and darted an apologetic glance at Callum. He smiled, and crossed his arms; waved the apology away. Why, he wondered, when health was so universal a concern, did places like this feel so oppressively female?

He had rung this morning for an appointment, unable to keep shrugging off the headaches. The receptionist had been terse with him, saying they were full and he'd have to wait. He'd had to resort to that old-school-tie business, saying *Tell Dr Armitage it's Callum Scott.* Pulling rank, pulling strings: something he'd sworn he'd never do, at least not in those distant days of youthful rebellion. Perhaps this was his punishment, to be stranded, trapped here, amongst the smells and the chaos of alien women and children.

He had walked here across the heath, resolving to take the usual route, obeying the old axiom of getting back on the bike immediately after falling off. But his legs had carried him tentatively, as though understanding their owner's frailty. At the edge of the copse, his heart had beat a little sharper; even now, here in this waiting room, each remembered rustle made him start.

'Mr Scott,' said a flat-voiced nurse, 'Dr Armitage will see you now.' Callum rose from his chair and followed her into the surgery.

As soon as Peter Armitage said, 'Callum, what a surprise,' Callum got the sinking feeling that he shouldn't have come. Being a patient, begging assistance, was unwelcome and foreign. 'I had a blow to the head,' he started to say, 'nothing really, I don't want to trouble you unduly', and then he looked at Peter Armitage and realized his face had entirely vanished. He saw a nobbly cloud just above the hairline, an uneven sphere, and two dark, watery discs. Callum drew a hand across his brow. 'I don't know what's wrong.' Then he looked straight at the watery discs and Peter Armitage's face came back.

After an extended, perplexed consultation, it became clear the doctor did not know what was wrong either.

'I'm going to refer you to a specialist,' he said. 'A neurologist. This is clearly a vision thing.' He sounded like some political sloganeer. 'Now, if you wait outside for a minute, I'll get my nurse to bring you a prescription. You'll need a good supply of painkillers, and for heaven's sake get some rest.'

Callum went back to the waiting room. At least he could still read. He picked up the local paper. POLICE STILL IN HUNT FOR GRISLY HEATH KILLER. The bold, blocked print headline was easy to decipher, and then he read on, and his spine snapped stiff and straight.

'Police refuse to confirm whether the suspected heath murderer has struck again. Investigating officer, DC Fletcher, warned all locals to be vigilant, but when asked if there was a possibility there could be a serial killer on the loose he said this was something he could neither confirm nor deny. He said another resident of the neighbourhood had been attacked, but it was unclear at this stage if the incidents were linked.'

Callum couldn't read any further – he was starting to feel sick. He reached out for the paper, wanting to pocket the article, secrete it. He could take it home and study it in more detail at his leisure. But at that moment the toddler dived at him, sliding the leaves of newsprint aside and spilling a small flask of synthetic-smelling fruit drink. The child's eyes were huge and menacing, his mouth a fleshy, gruesome leer. Callum shrank gulping into a corner, wondering what on earth he was looking at.

'Dean, don't do that! How often do I have to tell you to behave!'

The mother dissolved into apologies, and Callum darted to safety. The article he had been reading was absorbed by the stain.

'Mr Scott, your prescription,' sang the nasal-voiced nurse. Callum rose from his seat, took it and walked out of the surgery.

Callum took the bus back home. The sky had clouded over: there was going to be a late spring storm. The light that poured through the windows was an eerie, yellowish grey. Callum smelt the air through the open back door, the hint of distant damp, and listened out for thunder. Instead – could he be mistaken? – there was the *flap-flap* of the letterbox.

He moved out into the hallway, his eyes alert for post or junk mail. The doormat and surrounding parquet were as pristine as he'd left them. Then the *flap-flap* came again, and now another sound beyond that: someone jangling money, or jewellery, or the fumbling for keys. He was so quick to anxiety, he almost looked through the spyhole. But then he didn't need to, for it started to make sense.

There she was on the doorstep, the yellow-grey storm light surrounding her. Her hand delved inside her handbag, buried up to the wrist; her weight was slanted on to her back foot, as though she were about to push the door. He couldn't really *see* her: her face was a pale, near-blinding blank, but its strangeness no longer shocked him, because this time he'd prepared for it. He concentrated instead on the shining russet halo, letting the rest fall into place as the seconds ticked by. Finally, 'Shona,' he said, 'whatever are you doing?'

It was so long-lost, so forgotten, this once familiar proximity, that he didn't think to stand aside and let her into the hallway. The first spats of rain had fallen before she said, 'Callum, can I come in?'

Her voice rasped in her throat and she sniffled heavily, before withdrawing a tissue from the bag she'd been fumbling in.

'You sound bad,' he observed. 'Your voice is really husky.'

'Summer flu.' She sneezed loudly, and pushed past into the hallway. He closed the door behind her then followed through into the living room.

'Do you need me to get you something?'

She sneezed again and her shoulders shuddered. 'Don't you worry, this is nothing. I came to see how you were.'

'Oh, I'm bearing –' Callum started, and then paused, mid-sentence, stiffening. 'What do you mean, you came to see how I am?'

Shona coughed, twice. 'I – I phoned your clerks, you weren't there. They said something was wrong. I thought I'd come to see you – nothing's ever wrong with you.'

Callum experienced a thrill both of pleasure and alarm. This was so unlike Shona. 'How nice of you to show such concern.'

'Not a bit of it.' She was defiant, as she stuffed her tissue up her shirtsleeve. 'The past is the past. Of course I care if you're all right.'

Callum thought of Guy and Freddy – their boundless discretion, his endless exhortations to them not to tell callers anything about him. Even if the caller was his estranged wife. His shoulder blades tingled. But this was Shona, for God's sake, who'd borne his two beautiful children. He remembered their warm mornings in bed during the months her stomach had swelled, their laughter low and conspiratorial as tiny kicks stippled her skin. She leaned forward now, slowly, and her thin fingers cupped his cheek.

‘Callum, you’re not yourself. Let’s sit and have a cup of tea.’

Shona had always been an expert at such delicacies. She knew the optimum strength of brew and, of course, his preferred biscuits.

‘How,’ Callum asked softly, ‘are my darling children?’

‘They’re just grand, Callum.’

‘It’s been so long, Shona.’

‘You know we’ll sort things out. Those children know you’re still their father.’

As though that blunt, incontrovertible truth were supposed to bring him comfort. That trick of awarding somcone something that was already theirs anyway, pretending generosity when you were the thief in the first place.

‘Thanks a bloody lot,’ said Callum, the resentment starting to warm inside him. ‘I didn’t need you to remind me of that.’

‘Don’t get bitter about it, Callum. It’s been hard for me too.’

‘Yes, but you’re with the children all the time. I have to stay away from them and be patient just because of the unpredictable temper of your so-called bloody boyfriend.’

He saw her shoulders rise and stiffen.

‘You know it’s not that simple.’

‘But it’s true, isn’t it? James gets angry when I take them because he’s jealous and insecure and somehow when I see the children I’m also getting back in touch with you. And instead of telling him where to get off you just go all wishy-washy and ask me to tread carefully and back off for a while. Well, I'm telling you this, Shona. I know what court battles are like from the inside, how grubby and grimy and unpleasant it all gets, and that's why I don't want to put Rudy and Saffron through any of that if we can possibly help it. But much more of this and I'm getting perilously close.'

She lowered her eyebrows. 'It will get better again. And I wouldn't throw out criticisms so lightly, if I were you. I might care to remind you, there are some respects in which you yourself are lacking.'

Both sat back then, abruptly, as though silenced by their own hostility. A burst of thunder clapped somewhere easterly: the storm was rolling in from Highgate. Shona's cup and saucer rattled in her grasp.

'Anyway, after whatever . . . happened to you. Things aren't so bad, are they? I mean you are all right, aren't you?'

She didn't ask for more details and he didn't volunteer them. It was one thing to accept tea from her, another to admit that his whole world had gone haywire, that even as he watched her, the image blurred and cheated. And anyway, why such capricious, sporadic kindness? He felt resentful once again.

'I'm getting some headaches, Shona. But I'm going to be fine. Though our good doctor Peter says I need to rest. I'm afraid I can't sit and chat for long.'

His voice had come out sharper than he'd intended. She rose, and through his half-blindness he pictured her looking upset, her features collapsing and then reassembling into so many patterns he could recognize. She smoothed her skirt, babbled social niceties, her voice quick and light, the Irish lilt ironed out. As she walked away from him down the hallway, he concentrated on things that still made sense: her hair swaying down her shoulder blades, the delicious curve of her hips.

'Well, have a good rest, Callum. Glad to see you're still with us, anyway. Do as the doctor says – it's bound to be for the best.'

'Yes, sir,' he replied, and saluted, but this time with softer humour.

Shona stood on the open step, and fumbled in her bag again. 'Bye for now, and do give my best regards to Simon.'

Callum had been leaning on the door-jamb for a casual, seductive farewell. Now he stiffened, and stood up, and felt the tingle on his skin again. 'Simon?'

'Yes, he's always been so helpful, and terribly concerned about you.'

But Simon had left Chambers months ago, and hadn't been there since before his split with Shona.

She stood with her hand behind her, on the door-knob, waiting to escape into the storm. There was another clap of thunder, and the rain's rhythm thick-ened. She touched his face for a goodbye kiss, holding him closer, but her nails scratched his skin and there was a desperate catch to her voice.

'Look after yourself, Callum. And for God's sake, be careful.'

4

'Right, that's it,' says Rosie, and slides the last, emptied drawer clear. She speaks out loud and with purpose, even though alone in the room, but keeps her voice lowered in case any passer-by thinks she's loony. In the earlier stages of tidying up she could distract herself with music, but now the tapes and the machine have been packed away too. The room looks so spartan it's enough to make you weep.

Puffed out, she sits back on the narrow, stripped bed. Everything smells of citrus and antiseptic. It is past four o'clock, and already pitch-black outside. Some of the chapel bells have begun to peel.

It is the end of Michaelmas term in Rosie's final year at Oxford. Already she has sent home a few bulky items for the Christmas holidays, leaving only essentials to last a couple of nights. This evening she will leave her things at the Porter's Lodge while she says goodbye to some friends, and return to collect them when she finally departs. She will probably take the coach rather than the train. Time is running out. She chinks the door closed behind her.

Out on the streets the sound of Sunday bells is louder. A coolish evening drizzle has started to spit down. Mist rises from the black river as Rosie strides across the bridge. She huddles down into her overcoat, sheltering behind its upturned collar. The evening dark thickens and sounds of the night make her flinch. It's a jitteriness that's been increasing because of the work she's been doing – sharpening her self-understanding: no pain, no gain. But she shrugs herself into boldness and holds her head high.

By the time she gets to Radcliffe Square she's almost slithering across the cobbles. Architraved windows of pale yellow light her way like Christmas candles. From inside one of the chapels a high and frail-voiced choir is practising. Rosie turns out into Broad Street, with its welcome hint of civilization. She bursts gratefully into the warmth of the appointed café.

Felicity looks up and grins from an oversized breakfast bowl of coffee.

'Finally, she's here.' She points significantly at her watch face in mock disapproval. Annie, sitting opposite, flaps the smoke from in front of her. She shoots a couple of raised eyebrows at Rosie, who scrapes back a squeaking chair.

'Girls,' declares Rosie, shaking out her damp hair, 'I pray you, don't mock me. I'm cold and wet through.'

'I don't know about you,' declares Felicity, brightly, 'but I'm starving. More coffee for me and a plate of toasted teacakes. Same for you, Annie? Oh, and what was it we agreed about last one here gets the orders in?'

Annie and Felicity each give the merest twitch of laughter, as Felicity slumps back in her chair, shoulders rounded, legs slightly parted. She slides a dog-eared, page-curled paperback across the table's stained surface, then bends its spine, fans its pages like a magician shuffling a deck of cards. 'Look,' she says to Annie, 'what I wanted to point out to you.'

Rosie notices that the book is *New French Feminisms*, and that Felicity wants to talk about something French and feminist by Julia Kristeva. But Annie doesn't seem to be terribly absorbed. Her fingers are spread in front of her and she's studying her nails intently, as though looking for ragged bits that might spoil the outline. Rosie rises with a sigh and makes her way to the counter.

Suddenly, there is an unexpected flurry of activity. Noise and movement barrel inwards, as sudden as a gust of cold wind. All around, the baritones of male voices are laughing, shouting, singing. There are insolent jokes, and the calling of names, and Rosie is jostled from behind.

'Ow!' she cries out crossly, interrupted while ordering the teacakes. She turns around, but the culprit has disappeared into the male maelstrom. The intruders scrape two tables together and crowd around them clumsily. Antonio, from behind the counter, sends Rosie a sympathetic wink.

'Sit down, lovely,' he lilts. 'I bring the things to your table.'

Rosie turns and walks back towards her table, and

then stops. Something catches her eye and she gives a yelp of remembrance. One palm spreads itself over her breast and her breath escapes in a gasp. Then she feels ridiculous, a C-grade actress hamming it up. Some of the intruders look at her, but one profile has turned away. She proceeds to her seat self-consciously, her blood hot beneath her skin.

Back at the table, Annie gives her a squeeze of comfort. 'You all right?'

Rosie wants to say, *Don't, please, not in public*, and then in the far corner the profile turns slightly. The quickened beat of her heart is both thrilling and unpleasant.

'I thought I saw – I was reminded –'

Felicity looks at Rosie, follows her strained gaze across the room. 'Leave it, Ro,' she says firmly.

'But I could have sworn –'

'Don't. You know it's all that stuff you've been working through recently, reliving your childhood and making yourself vulnerable. Don't let it get to you.'

'I suppose you're right.'

Rosie feels her lips turning down at the corners. She's never said too much about the memories of her father's garden: the games that were no fun, that she'd never wanted to play anyway. At first, she had assumed that it would be a one-off, like a scary, too-fast car drive from which you thankfully emerged unscathed. It would be a relief but also a thrill to recall your grand escape. But then there'd been the other times, not only in the big, old garden, but in the newer, smaller semi that they'd moved to several miles away. There were plain, sliding garden doors instead of the old, ornate French windows, and a small oblong of lawn little bigger than a patio. But her mother still took pleasure in having summer guests *al fresco*, and there were still shadows behind tall shrubs, the occasional alcove out of earshot. The games continued – painful, stealthy – until Rosie was almost eleven.

Felicity cradles her cup and swivels her eyes across the café. The intruders, she observes, are probably rugger buggers of some variety. They start up a dim swell of song, to the occasional beat of fists on table. It's odd that they've chosen to come in here rather than decamp to the pub, but though Antonio looks like he might confront them, he simply breaks into a weak smile. It is ninth week, after all, and this is a slow Sunday evening.

Rosie's food arrives, but when she bites into the teacake, the crisp, clear sweetness she was expecting is heavy and doughy.

'You'd never guess,' Felicity is saying, 'that we used to hold women's meetings in here.' She gives a disdainful jerk of the head towards the macho invaders, but Rosie's seen something again and her stomach is turning somersaults. She shoves back her chair abruptly.

'I'm not feeling too good. I need to get outside, have a walk. Perhaps go back to college. Get a breath of fresh air.'

Annie's forehead creases. 'But you've already checked out. And it's wet and freezing outside. And, anyway, what about supper at mine – like we agreed – before you go.'

'Come on,' agrees Felicity, 'we can go now.' Her tone is firmer, motherly, as though she half-expects such outbursts. 'If you're not feeling too good you can have a lie-down at Annie's place.'

But Rosie's brain throbs, and the room swims with memories.

'Look, no. I have to get some air. I'm sure the JCR'll still be open. I'm not sure if I feel like supper. I'll call you at the house.'

Outside the rain has stopped, and she gulps cold, fresh air gratefully. The chill has sharpened, and her breath is lacy in front of her. She forges towards St Giles – the wrong way, but she needs to stretch her legs. Shadows thicken on the old stone as she takes a left into Turl Street. It is then that the footsteps start up their click-clack behind her. With term over, the town is quieter, and this little side-street almost empty. *Click-clack*, *click-clack*, the footsteps come closer.

It's too early to get really frightened, but the café has made her jumpy. *Click-clack*, the footsteps grow nearer, and she is sweating in the cold night. She senses someone coming up behind her and thinks, *Oh God, this can't be happening.*

And then a voice calls out in the darkness, and one memory is submerged by another.

'There you go,' he says to her. 'That should do the trick.'

Rosie takes the glass from him and sips, the gin warming her blood. 'Do you more good than any bloody hot chocolate, that will,' he says, and she has to agree. She lets her muscles relax against the warm, worn pub upholstery. He knocks back a mouthful of Guinness, gulping it with slight strain. Such complete laddishness does not come naturally, which makes her smile.

'I saw you looking over in the café back there,' he says. 'I thought you realized – that you recognized me too. I was grinning back like a fool and I couldn't work out if you were responding.'

'No – I – I mean there was something else. I made a mistake, you'll have to forgive me.' Rosie splutters the last of her sentence into the gin glass. She cannot believe she is sitting here with Callum, her childhood playmate, who only moments earlier was struggling to get her attention. But when she looks up, he is smiling at her quizzically, and has edged a little closer along the cushioned banquette.

'It's you who should be forgiving me. How could I have acted like that? Running after a lone woman in a dark, empty street. Duh!' He slaps his brow. 'But seriously, Rosie, you've not changed. It must be what? Nine, ten years?'

Actually, it's longer – more like twelve years, going on thirteen. Her mother used to embarrass her by calling them 'sweethearts' within earshot. Still, for almost two years he used to come round at regular intervals, and they'd play in the garden and climb trees and chase butterflies. Once they went on a trip to the zoo, under the supervision of his mother – who was much kinder than Rosie's, less sharp and more subtle. She had that sing-song Irish brogue, which sometimes surfaces in Callum, though his accent is mostly ironed out, and at times sounds downright plummy.

'That lovely old house of yours,' he muses. 'Your mother doesn't still live in it, does she?'

'No!' Rosie snorts. 'It was way too big, even when my dad was alive. She wanted to get rid of it almost as soon as he was gone, but it took two years or something like that because of all the legal wranglings. We wouldn't have stayed in it much after you and I last saw each other.' And then she lowers her eyes, uneasy at her words' intimacy, as though they really had once been sweethearts, instead of occasional playmates. She is grateful for the distraction of the door flying open, heralding a freezing draft and a fresh influx of punters.

'Tony! Portman, you old bugger!' cries out Callum, pulling away from her. He gives a friendly wave across the pub, and Rosie recognizes a handful of the macho invaders from the café earlier. A tall, beak-faced young man comes towards them, with a thin-lipped smile at Callum.

'We were wondering where you'd got to. Apparently, we shouldn't have worried.'

'Keep your mouth clean, Portman, and just get us another round.'

Portman frowns, fiddling in his pockets for coins. He accepts the tenner offered by Callum and heads off towards the bar. Rosie watches the back of his head being swallowed by the crowd, and for a second the old queasiness comes over her again. Then Callum's thigh brushes hers – accidentally? on purpose? – and his soft-voiced but arch apology brings her back to the moment.

Portman returns with the drinks and they chink glasses and say cheers. Rosie tells her companions she is in her final year doing PPP, and has stayed up in ninth week to get some extra revision done. Both Callum and his friend Portman did law at Christ Church, went down four years ago and are now junior barristers in London. They're in Oxford for the weekend, on some all-male, sports-orientated reunion; painting the town red, taking rooms at the Randolph. All three enact the ritual of mentioning lots of names they think the others might know, but it's relatively fruitless and the fun quickly dries up.

'Blimey, Christ Church,' says Rosie. 'Aren't you the posh one?'

'Not just Christ Church,' says Portman. 'But top law scholar to boot. And you should see how he's turned out. The young toast of Middle Temple.'

Callum waves the flattery aside, but Portman keeps on repeating himself. His words are punctuated by breathy hiccups, and he's slurring his sentences.

Either he's had a few too many, or he can't carry his liquor.

'Yes,' he drawls. 'Callum Scott. Great white hope of the legal world, anointed prince of the Old Bailey. Not to mention his good looks and his way with the ladies. Cal, we mere mortals can but sit and salute you.'

Portman lifts his drink but the glass tilts and some of the clear liquid falls in glistening drops on Rosie's coat.

'Steady on.' Callum's smiling, but his cheeks are flushed pink. He turns to Rosie. 'I'm so sorry. Let me see if I can get a cloth.'

'No, no. Don't be silly.' She's feeling embarrassed too now. 'It's nothing – really.'

Rosie does her best to look nonchalant but Portman's behaviour is disconcerting. He's swaying even while sitting down, his moist, glittering gaze mainly on Callum. Rosie wipes her coat with an old tissue. Portman drains his glass and wipes his mouth.

'Well, it's back to the Randolph, then.' He looks across at Callum. 'Coming?'

Callum leans back against the banquette, arms spread wide, ankle crossed over his knee. 'I thought I'd just stay a little longer.' For the first time he looks awkward.

'What, one more round then?' Portman sounds confused.

'No . . . I mean, you go on. I'll see you there later.' A note of exasperation creeps into Callum's voice, and then Portman finally gets the point, and starts to button his jacket. At the chimney breast, an open fire sputters. Portman's brows are drawn down. He stands and bids them goodbye.

Then it comes to Rosie – the sickness of recognition – as Portman quarter-turns for the door. His oblique profile, then his back view, and his hands worrying his pockets. This was what set her off in the café, what sparked the tinges of nausea. All logic and common sense tell her she has to be wrong, but as she sits back against the banquette, her heart thumps against her ribs.

'Whew,' breathes Callum, cartoonishly. 'Thank goodness he's gone.' He spreads his arms wider. 'Now . . . how about just one more?'

The evening deepens over Oxford. Rosie has stopped counting how many, precisely, is constituted by 'just one more'. Her head swims with alcohol and her brain has turned to fuzzy felt. Besides, she's hardly eaten: her stomach clonks like thawing plumbing.

'Shit!' She sits up suddenly, almost spitting. 'Shit! Shit! Shit!'

'What is it?' says Callum, looking alarmed, but still quizzical.

'Felicity and Annie. I was supposed to phone them. We were going to have supper together. And I've completely lost track of time. I've got to get back to London.'

Callum arches his eyebrows. 'Surely not tonight?'

'Yes, *yes*. All my things are packed and waiting at the Porter's Lodge. But there'll still be coaches from Gloucester Green. I'd best make a move.'

'Well, I think you're crazy,' says Callum. 'You could stay just one more night and then go back tomorrow, first thing.'

'But my room's all locked now,' wails Rosie. 'I've nowhere to stay.'

She doesn't say that she could stay with Annie, because that would lessen the drama. But the surge of panic is real: perhaps it's the drink, or the strange memories. Callum calms her down, and they agree to check out the coaches at Gloucester Green. If she's missed the last one back to London, there's bound to be somewhere she can stay.

'If the worst comes to the worst,' he says, 'you can always come back to the Randolph with me.'

Rosie keeps her mouth shut as they walk down the damp street. If there were any light to see by, she thinks it would show every bit of skin blushing. The rain has returned and the chill in the air is now biting. Her teeth chatter audibly and he reaches an arm round her shoulder.

'God, Rosie, you're freezing. I can feel your bones shaking.'

His arm feels big and warm, almost bear-like, reminding her of the difference in their sizes. She'd like to inch in close to him, but her body's stiff and clumsy. Her step so jars against his that he releases his semi-hug, and they hobble up to Gloucester Green to the rhythm of her shivering.

It turns out Rosie hasn't missed the last coach, but there's only one more in twenty-five minutes. Apparently nearer to London it's snowing badly, and there're some problems on the roads so they're operating a reduced service.

'My things! They're back at College!' Rosie claps her gloved hands. 'But if I hurry there and back I might just about make it.'

'This is insane,' murmurs Callum. 'Just one night. Why break your neck?'

She turns to him fiercely. 'Look, it's been a really lovely evening. But I know you've got things to do. You don't have to escort me.'

'Nonsense. I can't just leave you like this.' He steers her firmly by the elbow. 'Now, let's go and get your luggage. Take it one step at a time.'

The rain thickens steadily as they walk back over the river. The quiet, echoing night is rich with promise and menace. Damp hair sticks on their foreheads; droplets course down their cheeks. Rosie slides on a patch of black ice, and Callum has to swerve to catch her.

'Careful,' he whispers, drawing her upwards and inwards. He steadies her on her feet till she's standing straight-backed again. His face is so close, she thinks he's going to kiss her, but once he's sure she's all right they simply carry on walking. They arrive back at the lodge with ten minutes before the last coach leaves.

'We could give it a go,' she says desperately. 'You never know when you might be lucky. And if I miss the coach,' she babbles, 'there's always the train.'

'Ridiculous,' Callum snorts, curling his lips. 'If there're problems on the roads, who can guess at the railways. Rosie, this is crazy. Just give it up for the night. Come back and stay in my room.' He grins. 'I promise to be gentlemanly.'

Part of her wants to say, yes, and let him hold her tired body. Despite the chill in the air, a warmth is swelling in her stomach. His lips glisten with icy rain which she'd like to lick away. But it wouldn't be good form, to act too much like she wants him. And he's long since left university, he's more or less a grown-up. She can't apply the rules of some drunken student party.

Eventually, Rosie concedes wearily, if she must stay with him she must. But first, she will try Annie, see if she could crash out at her place. She rattles a coin into a payphone, but the line buzzes and no one answers.

'They'll probably never talk to you again,' says Callum, 'after you've stood them up this evening.'

'There's a B&B on St Giles, not too far from the Randolph. I know it's a little late in the day, but I could try it as a last resort.'

'OK,' he says, impatient now. 'But let's just get going, shall we?'

For the umpteenth time, it seems, they step out into the night.

For their last walk that evening, Callum does not hide what's on his mind. His thigh constantly brushes hers and he keeps his arm on her shoulders, but as they're both carrying her bags, closer contact is difficult.

'Crazy night it's been,' she murmurs, rewinding incidents in her head.

He says, 'I think *you're* a little crazy,' but she doesn't see his face. They're nearly at the Randolph, and she can see he's about to turn off. But 'the B&B' she reminds him, and he groans, puffing out his cheeks.

They step into a narrow slice of terraced building, sandwiched between an old pub and a greasy spoon. There's something distinctly seedy about its too-brightly lit lobby. Somebody like a night porter sits behind a high, dark desk. He raises his eyebrows at Rosie when she asks if there's a room.

At first, the night porter looks doubtfully at his watch. She thinks he'll turn her down, and Callum's already preparing to leave. But she feels dutybound to plead, though she half wants to fail. The night porter stirs and belches softly. There is a room going, after all.

They heave her bags up the narrow stairs, Callum swearing softly after her. The room is small, with a sliver of a single bed wedged into a corner, and a horrible, Formica-covered, seventies-style wardrobe. There's a nice view out over St Giles, but it's hardly the Randolph. Callum puts her bags down and they stand awkwardly opposite one another.

‘Thank you so much,’ she says thinly. ‘For helping. For everything.’

‘Yes, well, nice to bump into you, Rosie. Amazing coincidence.’ His arms flop at his sides as though he’s suddenly younger. Panic surges within her, that the night’s promise can slip away like this. She wants to rewind, change everything. She takes two small, weak steps towards him.

‘Thanks again.’ She puts her hand beneath his hairline at the nape of his neck, feels the cold, wet skin exposed there. She has to tiptoe slightly to kiss, pretending an innocent farewell. But this close and he has gone sly again, kissing her back with hungry warmth. Both their lips are chapped and frozen, but his tongue and breath are hot. He runs his fingers through her hair and nuzzles the space between neck and shoulder. He holds her for so long she thinks he’s going to ask to stay here with her, but when he draws away he just licks his lips and smiles.

‘Back to London then tomorrow?’ She nods. ‘A group of us are going back, around twelvish. I don’t suppose you’d like to join us? We could meet up for brunch beforehand, or do something later, once we get there.’

Rosie’s jaw drops, stupidly. Her words stick under her tongue, like a scratched record. ‘Tomorrow – I can’t. I have to see someone in London. I mean . . .’ It has all come out wrong, and he is stepping away from her.

'That's OK. Don't worry. If you've got other plans.'

'I mean, it's not that I don't want to. It's just tomorrow's inconvenient.' But she can't tell him what she's really doing, the true reason she can't make it. Another time, she wants to say, and to thrust her telephone number upon him. But it's been one knockback too many, and the warmth is draining from his face.

He touches her cheek lightly as he closes the door behind him, and she leans her weight against it, her breath rasping in her chest. Her whole body aches with desire and regret.

5

'Visual agnosia,' said Dr Lieberman. 'A neurological disorder.' He spoke in a slow eastern European accent, which Callum could not quite place.

Callum sat in the consulting room, with its close bookshelves and tall windows. Fatigue was pounding at his temples after a long and sleepless night. Yesterday, he'd sat up for endless, angst-ridden hours, surfing the internet until first light had made his head ache. He'd progressed from the comparatively modest Online Medical Dictionary, to the more specialist Eyecare Homepage, and as his fingers moved shakily across the keyboard his enquiries grew forever more challenging. Eventually, almost too tired to read, he had switched his machine off and tried desperately to reassure himself.

Now here he was, in this room, with this doctor, staring ahead through the Regency sash window. He could see the curving, stuccoed terrace, and the park beyond that. He heard the doctor's guttural accent but felt curiously at a distance.

Agnosia – the word was horrible: heavy and vulgar and ugly. The hardness of the *g,* the clumsiness of the *n,* and a senseless combination of vowel sounds leading off into nothingness. Some illnesses –

athlete's foot, tennis elbow – could sound almost dashing by association; this one sounded repellent, making him think of scabs, pus and dribble. Though it entailed none of the above, the diagnosis had overwhelmed him.

'It's a condition,' said Dr Lieberman, 'which results from some kind of brain damage. It could be from a serious illness, or the trauma following an accident. Neurological disorders are some of the most mysterious in medical science. A diagnosis of this kind is really quite esoteric.'

'Dr Lieberman,' said Callum, 'there are just two things I want to know. One, what is wrong with me? Two, how do you cure it?'

Dr Lieberman had a bushy grey moustache which waggled actively as he spoke. The moustache was quite dominant, it was all Callum could really see of him. He sloped back in his chair and pressed his fingers together. He breathed deeply, as though to the rhythm of a mantra. When he spoke, it was with the sloth of one addressing a child.

'What you are suffering from is a dislocation between your vision and your understanding. As purely physical organs, your eyes are still functioning as normal. But the messages your eyes are sending to your brain are becoming confused. So, for example, your eyes may present your brain with an image of a familiar object, but your brain will fail to translate it into what it really is. Hence, occasionally it may seem to you that you cannot recognize things or people.'

Callum leaned forward in his chair. 'I can't believe you are right. This condition comes and goes. Mostly I see things quite normally.'

Dr Lieberman's moustache wriggled furiously on his upper lip. 'Yes, yes, that's quite in order. As I said, it's not as though your entire visual capacity has been destroyed. It may be that certain images – perhaps some household objects – present you with problems, whereas others present you with none. As though only fragments of your visual memory bank have been affected. So on occasion your vision will seem completely normal.

'Alternatively, there may be times when your visual messaging service breaks down entirely, but your brain's own common sense fills in the gaps for you. So, for example, your dog – yes? He is here with you outside?'

'She,' corrected Callum, unable to curb a hint of petulance.

'Well,' continued the doctor, 'at times you may not be able to see her. But your brain is aware you are looking at her, so it *tells* you you can see her. Sometimes,' he lowered his voice conspiratorially, 'your brain fills in the gaps erroneously. So if you *think* you should be looking at something, you may see something that isn't there.'

'You mean to say,' asked Callum quietly, 'I might actually be hallucinating?'

'In a way, yes. Although simple confusion is more likely. You may get one thing mixed up with another, especially where there is a similarity. You may also find some images present you with more difficulties than others.'

Callum wondered what images might be presenting him with most difficulties. He recalled the photographs on the sideboard; Shona's visit; his own reflection. *Faces*, he said to himself, *I'm having trouble with faces.*

Dr Lieberman was chatting away about how rare these sorts of cases were. So few of them had been documented that it was difficult to give a thorough diagnosis. But what was not difficult, Callum thought, was to detect the excitement in the doctor's voice. Now and again he clapped his hands girlishly: he was nothing short of happy.

Callum listened in surly silence, then took a deep breath.

'Excuse me, Dr Lieberman. This is all very interesting, but I really must interrupt. What I want to know is: where do we go from here? What's the prognosis? How will I be cured?'

For the first time in the consultation, the little doctor looked stunned. Having risen from his chair, he had been pacing the room as he spoke. Now he stood still as a statue. Callum concentrated on the doctor's eyes – he was quite positive he could see them – and, if he was not mistaken, they had widened in surprise.

'*Cure?*' murmured the doctor, as though this were an entirely new concept. 'Of course I'll be referring you for brain scans, just to be more precise about things. But in neurology – neuropsychology – we do not necessarily have cures.'

'But there must be something you can do for me, some sort of treatment, some medication. I should have thought, with modern advances . . .' Callum's voice trailed off, bleakly.

'I can give you medication for your headaches, and as you've had this trauma you should certainly rest. And of course there is therapy, talking, getting to understand your condition.'

Callum descended the stairs biting his bottom lip. *Brain damage*, the doctor had said. It was scarcely believable. The receptionist smiled at him, and lowered her lashes shyly. Perhaps she found him handsome; he knew that many women did. A natural flirt himself, this time he did not smile back. He was wondering how quickly he might be able to get a second opinion.

Outside, the sun was absurdly bright, an ill-match for his grim mood. It made no sense that a group of teenage girls sat lounging in the park opposite, brown bare arms chopping the air, their words cut up by laughter. Callum reached inside his pocket. He retrieved his mobile, dialled quickly, blindly.

'Hello, Mother? It's me, can you hear me?'

There was a split second's time lapse and then he heard her brisk, rhythmic voice.

'Callum, is that you? Darling, I can hardly hear you.'

'I'm calling you from the mobile. Perhaps the signal's not too good.'

'You're at court, I take it. Tell me, Callum, did you get my present?'

'No – I mean, yes. About the present. It was lovely.' He had been going to tell her the truth, but found himself bridling in the face of her morning optimism. There would be another time. Besides, another doctor might give him better news. 'How was your holiday, Mother?'

'Grand, Callum, just wonderful. But you sound a little down. Is everything all right?'

'Oh, it's just . . . the children, that's all. I know you're still pally with Shona and I wanted to have a chat about making a really concerted effort to see Rudy and Saffron again, that's all.'

'Not before time. Look, why don't we chat about this later? It's just you keep on breaking up and at times I can barely hear you.'

Callum bid her goodbye and headed for the railings to untether Frieda. A boy of about five was whispering to her and stroking her, while his mother stood a few paces back, smiling on indulgently. Frieda whined softly as Callum crouched to release her. He smiled at the strangers, as though any friend of Frieda's had to be a friend of his.

As he untied her and ruffled her fur, he muttered, 'There, there, girl, I'm here.' And then he thought back on the consultation and wondered: could he really tell if this were Frieda? He knew it had to be, of course, but if someone had spirited her away and replaced her with a similar-sized golden Labrador, would he definitely know the difference? But Frieda's wet nose nudged his shins, her tail wagged with a furious joy. *Of course* he would know Frieda. They walked towards the park together.

Later, driving into Chambers, he thought once more of Dr Lieberman. Despite what the specialist had said, here he was, against the odds, smoothly easing the nose of his car through the tightest grid of streets. Really, he was fine, he told himself, there were only the occasional lapses. His shoulders kept jolting and his throat was unusually dry, but he wasn't afraid – simply getting reacclimatized. He parked outside Chambers and clunked the driver's door shut. Through the little window that overlooked the courtyard he saw Guy hunched over the telephone.

Callum stepped across the threshold of what was carefully called the 'welcoming area'. The receptionist was perched behind a high, bleached pine counter, sitting on a stool so tall it appeared that if she moved, she'd surely topple. With its pale greys and oatmeals and the sheets of light from the long windows, the room was designed to be modern and unthreatening. Yet as the carpet spread before him, broad and long, its edges blurring, Callum had to catch his breath, to watch himself lest he stumble. He shook his head, spoke softly.

'Hello, Marie.'

The slim-backed receptionist swivelled towards him and paused, and for a heart-fluttering moment he thought he'd made a mistake. His tongue curled against the roof of his mouth and blood gathered in his cheeks.

But she said, 'Hello, Mr Scott, good to see you,' and though her words were without warmth, his shoulders slackened with relief. He made his way towards the clerk's room.

This was the hub of Chambers, where every telephone call meant business. Clients were sweet-talked, favours called in and granted, cases allocated and fees agreed. Guy was in there with two juniors. Callum caught snatches of their usual banter, cajoling stressed-out solicitors. He went and stood just by Guy's shoulder, imagining the other's surprised pleasure on seeing him. And then Guy turned, his eyebrows raised, his voice a high-pitched, halting stutter.

'Good lord, Callum. Gave me a shock, sir. Shouldn't you be at home resting? Good to see you, sir, anyway. Feeling a little better?'

'Much better thanks. Just getting a few headaches. But I'll be right as rain in no time. Just thought I'd come in to pick up any updates on my casework.' He cast a glance at his pigeon hole, which was conspicuously empty. 'Nothing for me in over a week then? No messages from my solicitors? What about the Lansdowne case? There's surely something in on that?'

Lansdowne was a gangster at the centre of a multi-handed scam involving fanaticism, guns and murder.

Once a budding drug lord, he had recently undergone a conversion to Islam at a controversial London mosque and his ardour had taken on an altogether more spiritual dimension. He was due to stand trial, alongside select cohorts, as the prime player in a web of nefarious conspiracies. Amongst friends, he frequently substituted Samir for his birth name of Jason. Now, in the undertow of fear that ran constantly through the capital, it was suspected Lansdowne might be linked to fundamentalist underground cells.

It was a case that had been earmarked personally for Callum from the start: he had acted for the less notorious younger brother, and was on particularly good terms with his instructing solicitor. Even under current circumstances, convalescing at home, Callum expected to be kept in touch with anything relating to the matter. Yet looking at Guy now, he knew he'd touched a raw nerve. Neurological disorder or not, he could see his clerk blushing.

Guy started scratching the back of his neck. 'Yes, the Lansdowne case. I think you'd better have a word with Anthony about that.'

'Anthony? Is he here?'

'I think you'll find him in his room.'

Callum sniffed. In fact he and Anthony shared an office: it was broad and high and light, and usually looked beautiful. But when Callum stood in the doorway, he saw only a disarray of cardboard boxes. Many of the shelves behind his desk had been emptied, whereas those behind Anthony's were ostentatiously full.

As for Anthony himself, one had to stare for seconds before spotting him, rather like an ornithologist peering beyond the flora's camouflage. At last his head popped up from between boxes on the floor. His body contorted in a crouch, he looked distinctly bestial.

'Good God, old boy,' he cried out. 'You gave me quite a fright. I didn't think I'd see you here.'

'Perhaps you've been too busy spring cleaning?' offered Callum, though the steely irony he'd aimed for came out tight and uncertain. 'You've certainly done a nice job of tidying up my files. You might want to tell me what the fuck's going on.'

'Ah.' Anthony rose, puffing and dusting off his hands and knees. He looked around and grabbed a swivel chair, which he pulled up close and sat in. 'Anyway, Cal, tell me. How're things? Feeling better?'

'There was very little wrong with me in the first place. Though it is gratifying that you're so concerned about my health that you've completely forgotten my question.'

Callum set his jaw but this further attempt at intimidating his colleague resulted only in the other man wiping sweat from his upper lip.

'Gosh, I'm thirsty. Must be getting a bit out of shape in my old age.'

'Well, far be it from me to detain you unduly. Just

tell me the latest on the Landsdowne case. Guy said to ask you about it.'

'Ah, yes,' said Anthony, helplessly. 'That. Yes, I really should have spoken to you about that earlier.'

'Spoken to me about what, exactly.'

'The Lansdowne case. The client's family . . . there was a bit of a problem, but it's been sorted.'

'So it's all settled now, then?'

'Yes . . . but . . . ah . . . there were one or two complications. I'm afraid the client wasn't happy with you. I've taken over the case.'

Callum, too, found a swivel chair and sat down in it heavily. It creaked rudely at the impact of his weight falling backwards. His vision blurred, he felt he were being hit all over again. 'This . . . has . . . to . . . be . . . a . . . mistake.' His words came out singly.

'Members of the family started ringing in stroppily to speak to you last week. Something was bothering them. I suppose they got all arsey because you just weren't at their beck and call.'

Callum stood so quickly, his chair fell over, and he nearly followed suit. 'But it's been just over a week, for fuck's sake. And someone could have called me at home. And, anyway, even the Lansdowne clan should know that QCs can't be on hand all the time. Why didn't the solicitors keep them at bay for a few days?' He felt as he had back in his dark living room, when everything familiar had turned strange. But something fresh, a searing anger, was scalding him from the inside. He stared without pleasure at

Anthony's thin lips. 'And how come you're on the case now? How can all this happen, just like that?'

'Cal, don't take it personally. The solicitors were beside themselves – huge case, media interest, client who wants everything done yesterday. And they wanted to keep it in Chambers – sort it as quickly as possible.'

'And you just happened to be available. How convenient is that?'

'You were out of sorts, Callum. And there were all those setbacks – like your computer going. You sounded distressed when I spoke to you – I thought you might even be grateful.'

'Grateful!' Callum spat the word, literally foaming at the mouth now. 'Has the world gone crazy? I'm off for just one week, and supposed *friends* are already writing my obituary. Christ, I was attacked, it was unfortunate, but people take more time off with the bloody flu.'

'But you did seem rather off key when I spoke to you over the telephone.'

'Because I wanted some answers to a few questions?'

'You were a little . . . obsessive.'

Callum breasted the other man at the doorway. 'Get out of my way.'

Anthony stood watching him; a helpless, skinny outline of a man. 'Callum, don't be like this. I'm your friend, I'm only trying to help.'

'Some friend, eh, Anthony.'

'And I did as you asked me to.'

'What's that then?' Callum stilled, and was looking at him expectantly.

'Made enquiries of the CPS. About the killing on the heath. Actually someone rang me earlier. Apparently they've made an arrest. Young man named Tyrone Freedman. A DC Fletcher is dealing with it. I don't know any more though.'

Callum thought furiously, but the name Tyrone Freedman meant nothing to him. He raised his chin, and nodded, but this was no moment to say thank you. He strode out of the office without another word to Anthony. Back in the clerks' room Guy was sitting alone.

'All right, sir?' Guy sounded as though he wished he were somewhere else.

'As well as can be expected.' Callum stood opposite his senior clerk, whose neck was shrinking into his shoulders. 'I thought I told you to call me at home if there was anything on Lansdowne.'

'Sir, I'm sorry about that. It got taken out of my hands. In the end Anthony said he'd do all the explaining.'

'That family were among my best clients. There is something very wrong about this.'

'Like I said, I am sorry, sir. Is there anything I can do for you?'

Callum clicked his tongue bitterly. 'Right now, I think not.' But before the door, he paused. 'Guy, one thing.'

‘Sir?’

‘While I was away, did my wife call?’

‘Not to my knowledge, sir.’

‘One of the others didn’t speak to her?’

‘Not as far as I know.’

‘You would remember if she had?’

‘Of course, sir. And I’d tell you.’

Callum nodded, heading outwards, saying he didn’t know when he’d be back.

*

He heard a slamming, and a barking, and a rustling of branches. There was warm breath at his neck and a voice speaking, but no words. The outlined boughs of the copse bled into the horizon. He wanted to twist, to face his attacker, but something tugged at his windpipe.

Callum turned over in his sleep, ignoring the nightmare. The warm spring breeze soothed him. Then he jolted awake.

At the open casement window, the light curtains billowed fatly. The night wind hissed inwards. One of the casements had unlatched itself and banged its frame repeatedly. Callum leapt from his bed, fearing shattering glass. He pulled the window shut firmly with an unwieldy creak. The wind was up outside; perhaps there would be another storm. He stood still for a minute, listening to the house in the darkness.

Somewhere above the gables groaned; the old pipes belched and whispered. And then he heard something else – like windchimes or distant, breaking glass. He held his breath for some seconds, listening out for what might come next. There was nothing more than the rumbling innards of the old house itself.

Callum flicked on the bedside lamp and lightly rubbed his gummy eyes. It was chilly now, just standing there in his bare feet and pyjamas: the plumped up pillows and rucked duvet beckoned him back to his bed. But the fractured dream and the waking had alerted him to his full bladder. He stepped out of the bedroom and made his way down the corridor.

Up until the attack, the night had never frightened Callum. But now he slid down the passage like a blind man, his palms and fingers groping the walls. It wasn't the shadows that made him fearful, nor indeed the dark itself: rather what might greet him if he could really see, if he dared to turn the light on. So he stood in the blackened bathroom listening to the hiss and release of his urine, and when he was finished he was no longer sleepy. Unexpectedly, he realized he was hungry and thirsty. A visit to the kitchen would do him good, he reasoned; the visceral reality of food and drink might chase away any demons. Already happier with this thought he wandered out to the staircase. He had reached the first landing before he heard it again.

This time it was like rattling, like a cough in a child's chest. Callum stood on the stair with one foot raised, still listening. Though his world was thick with phantoms, there was no clear hint of an intruder: nothing as sharp as a misplaced footstep or a stranger's stifled sneeze. His lungs gulped air vigorously, but he tried to breathe quietly. Splintered floorboards pricked his naked soles as he trod towards the kitchen.

When he reached out for the light switch, he saw his fingers were trembling. But moonlight flooded through the windows and revealed no foreign silhouette. He took a breath and flicked the switch: there was no hidden, crouched assassin. He blinked into the brightness and then he saw the broken glass.

At that stage, he would recall, he did not yet feel really frightened. The miracle of electricity had robbed the house of its chill. The glass was an old tumbler he'd been drinking from earlier, which must have slid off the counter: any manner of innocuous forces could have knocked it from its perch. As he squatted to clear the fragments he was most concerned for his bare feet.

And it was then he smelt the smell: a rotten odour which sickened him. How was it, he marvelled, that he had missed it up till now: had his senses grown so dislocated that only one worked at a time? It didn't matter, he smelt it now, and the air thickened and choked him. It was like an abattoir, an uncleaned kennel and bad meat all rolled into one. His mind whirred furiously, reaching for some explanation, and he gagged on the back of his hand. But this was something he knew he was right about: this was blood and flesh and guts. Here, in his own kitchen, he inhaled the stink of slaughter.

He straightened from his crouching position, his hand still over his mouth. Blindly he stepped over the glass fragments, feeling the prick and tear and warm, smeared blood. But there was blood besides his own, a dirty trail of brownish crimson. He followed it round into the alcove towards the space where Frieda slept. There he saw her lying open-mouthed, the filthy liquid pooling round her head. Her skull and neck were all disjointed, and a slice of flesh gaped through her fur. Callum stepped towards her desperately, the muck gathering at his feet. His throat constricted as in a nightmare: he wanted to scream, but merely whimpered. He knelt beside her golden head and looked into her stilled and cold brown eyes. Her slackened jaw and tongue were motionless. There was just the foul after-stench of death.

6

Even in the dull, blue-white November light, Rosie falls for Paris all over again. She is here to see Annie, who now works as an inter-continental financial adviser, only Annie is on her way back from Frankfurt, so they are to meet this afternoon. Rosie could have waited, postponed her flight to allow for Annie's schedule, but instead she has chosen to have one night and one morning here by herself.

For a fraction of London prices she booked herself a small but pretty room in a hotel near St Lazare. It has modest French windows and a curlicued, wrought-iron balcony, opening out on to a line of identical windows overlooking a narrow, ordered street.

This morning, she strolled across Pigalle – its neon signs unlit and dirty by daylight – and sloped her way up the cobbles towards Montmartre. Then she looked at her watch, unfolded her map, and started to worry she was lost and late. *Je peux vous aider, Madamoiselle?* offered more than one passing Parisian, but she flattened the map against the breeze and managed to sort herself out.

Now she sits in a huge, high-glass lobby waiting to be picked up for lunch. The building is a glittering tower not far from the Banque de France. The cold, marbled floor makes noises echo like in a swimming pool; it looks as if there isn't a speck of dust within a mile. Although she is dressed with what this morning seemed like stylish casualness, watching the immaculate, uniformed receptionists, she feels scruffy and unfinished.

One of the girls, with china doll make-up, gives her a sharp glance. Rosie looks pointedly at her watch as though this is proof she has a right to be there. She'd like to read, but the paperback in her rucksack is all dog-eared, and furrowing it free from all her other baggage runs the risk of spilling sandwich crumbs. Fortunately, a familiar English voice comes to her rescue.

'Hello, Rosie.'

She jolts. 'Blimey, you startled me.'

Annie grins broadly. 'Nice to see you, too.'

They tread across the vast atrium, Rosie ducking a giant palm frond. Annie says something quick and incomprehensible to one of the receptionists, and steps through the glass doors into the grid of streets beyond. She strides determinedly away from her workplace into the maze of the second *arondissement*, turning into a side-street and pushing open a door.

Inside a man with a knee-length white apron is wiping a counter surface. The two look at each other with recognition and they speak briefly in too fast French. Annie guides Rosie to a dark corner table where she sits and struggles out of her coat.

'Well, so this is it, eh? The financial high-life. What's it like then, international banking?'

Annie is dressed in a light-grey wool suit and court shoes, with the kind of heels that click so loudly passers-by turn round and stare. She looks old, thinks Rosie, 'but in a good way', as Felicity would say. Not aged and wrinkled but sophisticated and grown up. Her make-up is impeccable. Rosie starts to feel childish.

Annie gestures almost imperceptibly to a waiter who wafts over and hands them menus. 'Oh, it has its moments. Plenty of stuffed suits, as you'd expect. But living in Paris is lovely.'

They scan the menus, order salads, clink bottles of Stella. Annie leans sideways. 'So how're things with you?'

'Oh, you know, nothing earth-shattering. Just staying at my mother's at the minute doing a bit of temping, this and that.'

'Well, after your stunning degree result, I suppose you deserve a rest. D'you know what you want to do . . . in the longer term?'

Rosie nibbles a stem of rocket. 'I did do particularly well in my psychology paper. I thought I might find out about Clinical Psychology courses.'

'And then become . . . ?'

'A psychiatrist. Or maybe a psychotherapist. Imagine making loads of money out of all those wacky patients.'

Annie frowns. 'Yeah, well, you know what they

say. You have to be in therapy before dispensing it, and it helps if you're a bit nutty yourself.'

'So which of those credentials *don't* I have?'

The waiter clears the plates and brings them coffee. He flicks crumbs mistakenly on to Annie's pristine lap, who raises her eyebrows and almost smiles, as though signalling *Pas de problème.*

'You seem to have really struck lucky,' says Rosie. 'You look fabulous, you're here in this wonderful city, you speak great French. It's all here for you, Annie. What an adventure.'

Annie looks surprised, very nearly cross.

'It's just my job, Rosie. I guess we all have to fall into the real world some time. I don't think Felicity approves.'

'Oh?'

'She's still doing her editing job on that magazine – I think she reckons I'm a sell-out. But, you know, I had to get a life.'

Rosie leans forwards, puts her face close to her friend's. 'Hey, there's more to being a strong woman than cutting your hair short and reading Camille Paglia.'

'Yeah.' Annie manages a nonchalant smile. 'And talking of strong women, Rosie, how's your love life?'

'Nada,' Rosie replies briskly, her front teeth gnawing on a sugar cube.

'I find that hard to believe.'

'Well, you know, I worked pretty hard for finals.

And now you've got this job and all, but I'm still finding my feet.'

'So there's been no one at all?'

'Oh, not since . . . no, no one.'

Annie puckers her lips. 'You're not still obsessing over that guy – that one-nighter. Whatsisname – Collum?'

'Actually his name's Callum, and he wasn't even a one-nighter. And, no, I'm not obsessing about him. So wrong on all three counts.'

'Please, Rosie. Don't do this to yourself.'

'I'm not doing anything. And it's not your business.'

She has been through this a thousand times, with Annie, with Felicity

'You know you've got to forget about him. He was just after a hot night's sex; when he didn't get it he pissed off.'

'Not completely true.' They have been over this ground before. 'It's not as if I'd just met him. We had a whole special, shared history. We'd known each other since childhood.' *We climbed trees in the secret forest, he was my childhood soulmate come back to me.*

'If he was really that interested, he'd have asked to see you again.'

'He did – he wanted us to meet up – it was me who pushed him away.' *He cared enough to run after me in a dark street.*

'But he could have asked for your number – there was nothing to stop him ringing.'

'It was awkward – I rebuffed him – he'd only just met me.'

'Aha! So you admit it! What happened to your special, shared history?'

Rosie sits back. 'I was crazy then. You know I really acted weirdly.'

Annie looks at her watch, signals over to the waiter. '*L'addition, s'il vous plaît.*' She turns to Rosie. 'Look, I think you're wrong about this bloke. He's just a smooth-talking, sexy chancer, probably a womanizing prick. Months later, you're still thinking about him, and he's probably on a different girl each night. But if you're really so stuck on him, if you think he's your kindred soul, just look him up in London. You're bound to find him. At least you'll know then.'

*

First off, Rosie flips open the telephone directory. It's a blow to realize she doesn't even know if he's listed: if he lives alone or with his parents, what his father's initial is. And it doesn't exactly help that his surname is Scott – there are reams of 'C. Scotts', ranged like anonymous soldiers.

But fate hands her a surprise gift, like a sign that it's meant to be. 'Scott, Callum, barrister – 6, The Courtyard.' And, of course, there's a number. She feels a tingle of excitement.

In the end, though, she decides she won't ring after all. The telephone creates distance, but it's also somehow creepier. All those black-and-white suspense movies with callers who don't talk, only breathe. If he sees her there, smiling, he's bound to be reassured. Besides, it'll look casual, as though she was – you know – *just passing*.

After thinking about it carefully, she makes Thursday the allotted day. It's a good day, near the weekend and with a hint of festivity, but not like Friday, when things deaden, and you can never find anybody. The roads around Chambers are so tiny and impenetrable, she worries a little that she won't be able to find The Courtyard. But after scanning an A–Z, she thinks she's worked out a route.

It's that part of the year when everyone starts to think about Christmas shopping. No one at the temp agency is surprised she wants the day off. On the Strand, she buys presents for Annie and Felicity, and decides the neat, cuboid paper bags go rather well with her outfit. Tinselled shop fronts reflect the light with a hard, winking glitter: impossible to tell how she looks as she stops to check her hair. Then she finds the mouth of the lane which leads away down to Chambers.

Her heart starts to beat faster, she stares for ages at the street sign. She heaves a breath and takes the turning; the air is brittle with first frost. She finds 6, The Courtyard, and steps through the doorway. Her fingers start to thaw painfully. She thinks she shouldn't have come.

Callum's name is painted on to a board at the foot of a staircase; a line-drawn hand, etched on to wood, exhorts 'Reception, this way, please.' She makes her way into the clerks' room, her breath comes fast and hard. But no one's even noticed her. A blond boy, fresh-faced as a teenager, is speaking rapidly on the telephone. She steps towards him; clears her throat.

'Excuse me – sorry – I'm just –'

'Hold on, madam, be with you in a sec.' He places a hand over the receiver. 'Yes, sorry, how can I help you?'

'I'm looking for Callum Scott.'

Her heart jolts like a cannon. Amazingly, no one else seems to notice the earth swaying.

'Yes, Callum. I'll just check for you. Is he expecting you?'

'No –'

'Callum – is he in Chambers?' The boy's question floats into the room. Someone calls back over the buzz, 'Yeah, he should be in his room.'

Rosie flexes her freezing toes. Her knotted stomach tells her this is a mistake. But then the blond boy smiles at someone behind her.

'Someone looking for me, Simon?'

'Callum, we were wondering where you were. This lady's here to see you.'

'I –' Rosie turns to him stuttering, wishing she'd never been this brave. But then she sees that he's smiling.

'Why, Rosie, what a pleasure.'

'I was passing. At least, shopping. I mean I'm back in London now, you know.' The sentence collapses hopelessly. She waves her neat little bag at him, as though this were some kind of alibi.

'Rosie, bad timing, I'm afraid.' He talks quickly, like everyone here. 'I'd love to spend some time with you, but I'm seeing clients at five thirty.' Before she can feel disappointment, he glances at his watch. 'But we could go for a swift coffee. If that's OK with how you're fixed . . .'

They sit at a cramped table; she licks cappuccino froth off her spoon. It's amazing how she can't shrug off this pretence at being casual. 'I live in North London, and I was Christmas shopping, and I thought, you know . . .' He is grinning, but a little absently, either unfazed or just uninterested. This is all coming out wrong. She puts down the coffee spoon.

'Actually, after that night in Oxford, I really regretted not keeping in touch. And then, back in London, I decided to look you up, but it took a while to pluck up the courage.'

Callum is now smiling properly, giving her his full attention. 'Rosie, I'm so glad you tracked me down. That night in Oxford was weird.'

'That was really my fault. I'm sorry.'

'Well, you know, even as a six year old, you always were a little quirky.'

'You remember what I was like as a six year old?'

'Of course, all those times we played together. You and your secret forest, you chasing butterflies.'

'Wow! You remember all *that*.'

Callum taps his skull, knowingly. 'Formative years, lawyer's memory for detail. And don't forget you were the first woman in my life. Apart, of course, from my mother.'

So she was right! And she can laugh in the face of cynics like Annie. Callum feels it too: they do have a special, shared history. Of course, he doesn't know everything that happened in her father's garden – not the stealthy, sordid meetings that make her skin itch at the memory. No one knows about that, really – even Annie and Felicity just a little bit, and that's only after a particular discussion they had at a College women's group. There was the time – and it was only once – when she was nine, alone with her mother, but the words didn't come out right, and her mother grew impatient. *Do hurry up, Rosie, I haven't got all day. Now what was it you wanted to tell me that you seemed to think was so important?* Rosie had been working out sentences with a horrible embarrassment, but now the pink of shame in her cheeks became a deep flush of hurt and anger. She closed her lips into a pout and ran up to her room in silence.

Yet even that sad reminder can't dampen her spirits this afternoon. This is all going much better than she could ever have dared hope. She doesn't have to get round to explaining that the last time they met she was in therapy; that she was going through a bad patch and couldn't come to London with him because she had a particularly important meeting with her analyst. He doesn't seem to notice – or care – when she says she doesn't have a proper job, so there's none of that strained self-justification – the hint of grander, long-term plans. The conversation flows so easily, it's all too soon the hour slips by.

They walk together back down Fleet Street, their footsteps crisp against the pavement. He stops at the top of the narrow lane that tails away into his lawyer's world.

'So, Rosie. Nice seeing you. We ought to do this again some time.'

She fishes in her bag and retrieves a recruitment consultant's card. On the stiff, blank white back of it, she inks out her number.

'There. Now you've no excuse.' She slides the card into his pocket. He stands still, smiling down at her.

'Not that I need one.'

For several days she wanders in a giddy fug of anticipation. She eats little, sings to herself, and takes on nothing from the temp agency. Her mother regards her with brows creased in a silent concern, but though she sometimes opens her mouth and looks worried, no maternal enquiries follow.

Then, just as the giddiness is turning desperate because there's no sign of him calling, he rings while she's in the bath and leaves a brief, neutral message. She rings back at once, against her better instincts.

'Hello, it's me. Rosie. Just returning your call.'

‘Ah, yes, it’s Callum here.’

She laughs. ‘Yes, I know. It’s me calling you, remember?’

The conversation is short. There’s a Christmas fair at Lincoln’s Inn, all proceeds to go to charity. Would she like to come along?

‘There’ll be a makeshift ice rink and stuff going on outside. So remember to dress warmly.’

‘I’ll kit myself out like an Eskimo.’

‘Well, there’s no need to go overboard. Don’t wear too many clothes.’

When the conversation is over, she finds herself laughing like a fool.

On the day itself, despite warning, she wears a shortish skirt and tights. She hopes it doesn’t look too blatant, but can’t resist the silhouette. She waits for Callum in the clerks’ room and when he sees her they kiss formally. He glances briefly at her legs and murmurs something, but she doesn’t hear what. He puts his arm round her shoulders and they step together out of Chambers.

On the way up the lane, they pass a young man who looks familiar.

‘Anthony. How was the Bailey? You going to this fair thing?’

‘I’ve got some advices to get done. If I can I’ll come along later.’

Anthony’s narrow eyes slide over Callum, then Rosie. His gaze is slow and questioning. Rosie shivers slightly.

'Anthony,' says Callum brightly, as though he's only just remembered something, 'let me introduce you to Rosie. I think I've mentioned her to you.'

The other man nods. 'Yes, I remember. We met briefly last year in Oxford.' His long fingers curl round Rosie's in a weak but formal handshake. His skin is cold and dry. He doesn't look her in the eye.

'Nice to meet you again, Anthony.'

Callum slaps his friend's back. 'Maybe see you later.'

Rosie hugs her coat tighter. A knife-edged gust cuts through her. They quicken their step, to keep from freezing.

'Your friend Anthony,' she ventures, 'the way he looked at me. I don't think he likes me very much.'

Callum's fingers squeeze her shoulder. 'Don't you worry, that's his way. People find him a little difficult, but he's all right underneath.'

'You don't find him a little creepy? I remember him from that night in Oxford. He got really pissed and he was going on and on about how fabulous you were, only it was like he was jealous, a bit mad, and it all got a little weird.'

'Oh God.' Callum rolls his eyes. 'You have to get used to it. Anthony has his own complexes and he doesn't always carry his drink too well. But don't take it personally. Deep down, his heart's in the right place.' He touches her face gently and she coils her fingers round his hand.

'Right. Well, that's OK then.'

'As a matter of fact, do you know I really know him because of you?'

'How d'you mean?'

'Some relative of Anthony's was friendly with your parents. My mother met them round at your place and years later I met Anthony. I knew it was your parents who made the introductions because my mother talked about that house.'

'Blimey,' breathes Rosie. 'It really is a small world.'

'So you see, indirectly, you introduced me and Anthony.'

'Lucky me, then.' The wind shudders. 'And lucky you, too.'

It's still early when they arrive at Lincoln's Inn, but the place is already filling up. Bits of lawn and courtyard are covered over, but it's not much of a shield against the cold. A framework of floodlights tinges the air milky-blue. Callum and Rosie buy raffle tickets, and have a go on the ice rink. She falls over almost at once, scrabbling helplessly for the railings. But Callum skates fearlessly, and takes her by the hand and leads her.

'See, it's easy . . . just relax . . . let your body balance by swaying . . . don't pick your feet up, just glide.'

Afterwards, they join the queue for mince pies and mulled wine. Every now and again Callum bumps into someone he recognizes. When he introduces Rosie, there are one or two arched eyebrows, but mostly she's greeted with friendly indifference.

Men in black emerging from nowhere herald the start of the stage show. They start assembling a building-block stage and lining up rows of chairs. Some of the revellers have brought children: this is clearly a family affair. Callum takes Rosie's hand firmly and steers them both towards the back.

Their chairs are just beneath a gap in the canopied ceiling, and in the direct line of an unwelcoming draught. Callum pulls her into his body, till she's more or less on his lap, takes off his greatcoat and swaddles them both beneath it. 'New variation on babes in a manger,' she giggles, but secretly she cannot believe that anyone's actually arranged an outdoor show in such arctic conditions.

'That better now?' whispers Callum, his voice turning sly. Rosie registers the change in tenor as she lets him press closer. Far away, on the stage, there's some sort of spoof on Red Riding Hood. Callum's hand rubs her thigh, then slides up beneath her skirt. There is a shock of warmth against her belly, as the flat of his palm finds its way beneath her clothing. Red Riding Hood bats her childish eyelids, and Rosie feels her underclothes peeled downwards. The wolf says something to Red Riding Hood, the audience ripples with laughter. Callum gives a low, appreciative chuckle, and slides his fingers inside her.

Abruptly, Rosie swivels to face him with alarm. A small voice tells her to deter him, maybe even give him a slap. But his fingers are moving faster, so that her breath's quick and shallow. Although the air is like ice, a surge of warm blood heats her skin.

'OK?' whispers Callum, his face now nuzzling her breasts. She notices several shirt buttons loosened, though she hasn't spotted when or how. He pulls the coat tighter around them, to make a curiously innocent tableau, like two freezing children sheltering from the elements.

'Behind you!' yells the audience, and there's a brief, suspenseful silence.

Rosie gives a stifled yelp and one or two faces frown at her. Callum laughs, his fingers thrusting deeper, and pulls her mouth against his shoulder.

She comes swiftly and generously, her mind emptying, the stage a blur. She is dimly aware of her body throbbing beneath the coat, her skirt rucked up, one breast bared, the laced edge of her bra snagged. Callum rearranges his coat over her, and she sits there outwardly respectable, but inwardly she is marvelling that she could behave in such a manner. He must think her so cheap now, to let herself go like that. But he simply shifts her on his lap, so she can feel him stiff beneath her.

'Wow,' he whispers warmly. 'Rosie, you're amazing.'

After that, they are inseparable. London hurtles towards Christmas, the store fronts trumpeting their bargains. Rosie has invited Callum to supper at her place and is giddy with nerves at the prospect. The only thing she can cook well is risotto, and she doubts her ability to impress. But her mother is spending the evening at the theatre, and the thought of the private flat entices.

Callum arrives early, leaving her no margin for error. But the timetable for cooking does not appear to concern him. He's holding a tinselly, festive bag which he produces with a flourish. 'For you,' he crows, and she unwraps a bottle of the latest designer perfume.

Rosie laughs, surprise and gratitude peeling out of her, even slight embarrassment. She hopes the evening won't go downhill from now on. She rolls her sleeves up and heads kitchenwards. 'Now it's my turn to treat you.'

It's an extravagant claim, given the price of the perfume and her rather limited skills as a chef, but if the exchange is an uneven one, it doesn't seem to bother Callum. He catches Rosie from behind, and dabs perfume on the back of her neck. There's a second's shock of cold, light liquid. Callum pulls her backward. 'Wow, you smell great.'

He presses her back against his stomach, slides his hand beneath her sweater. She has no option but to abandon the first stages of slicing peppers. His palms press her ribcage, trace the groove between her breasts. His warm mouth is by her ear, his breathing loud and arrhythmic.

Then a key turns in the lock, and there are soft, rapid footsteps. Rosie feels her skin flush, like some caught-out, sinning schoolgirl. She prizes herself free, wheels round, faces the doorway.

'Mother,' she stutters, 'I thought you were at the theatre.'

Sarah Verner stretches her gloved fingers, her lips curled in a dry smile.

'I was. I forgot the tickets. Don't worry, I won't be long.' She stands still for just a second and extends a hand towards Callum. 'Rosie seems a little too preoccupied to introduce me. I'm Sarah, her mother.'

Callum smiles a quizzical smile, his hand outstretched for one long second.

'Mrs Verner – Sarah. Callum Scott. We've met before. Rosie and I knew each other as children.'

He smiles his best smile. Sarah says, 'Ah yes, I remember,' and Rosie moans inwardly, just momentarily, wondering what her mother might say next. But then they shake hands quickly, firmly, and Sarah withdraws rapidly, turns her back and smoothes her collar, finds her wallet, heads outwards. At the door she coughs loudly, as though comically signalling her exit.

'Good looking woman, your mother,' says Callum.

'Don't you go getting ideas now.'

He laughs softly, pulls her closer, nuzzles her shoulder in reassurance.

They go their separate ways for Christmas, but meet up first to say goodbye. He gives her a necklace, and a card laced with innuendo. He won't be back in town till January, but can't wait to see her then.

And once into the new year, their appetites grow stronger still. He takes her for Indian meals and

Italian, and they grow dizzy with red wine. They skip work for movie matinees, sitting at the back like lovestruck teenagers. Sometimes, when he's at court, she finds him and whisks him off to lunch: they buy sandwiches at a favourite Greek café and he tells her tales of the underworld which make her shudder. He meets her mother properly and they remember each other from his childhood. They walk on Sundays through St James's Park, wondering what it will be like in summer.

One day she arrives at Chambers to pick up Callum for supper, as they've agreed. Simon grins at her as usual, but then remembers he has a message for her.

'Callum said to tell you, something's come up, he's working later than expected. He still wants to see you, but says if you could just hang on.'

She feels a flutter of uncertainty, but then there's an intervening voice.

'Cal's held up in conference, but he says he won't be too long.'

Rosie turns to see Anthony standing there, his broad, thin lips pursed. She beats back the familiar goose bumps and forces a rictus-like smile.

'Hi, Anthony. You OK? Don't worry, I'll wait.'

Anthony steps towards her. She sees one hand tremble slightly.

'Look, Cal said he'd be a while, but suggested we go across to the Queen's Arms. He'll meet us there when he's finished.'

'It's OK. I don't mind –' Rosie shifts in her seat,

putting extra space between them. But Anthony looks down his nose at her with alarming intensity. 'Cal did say I should look after you.'

Simon gives a chuckle. 'Don't worry, he don't bite.'

She keeps up the false grin. 'OK then. Let's go for it.'

As they hurry together up the lonely narrow lane, Rosie breathes on her fingers, wishing someone would join them. Luckily, the Queen's Arms is crowded; they can barely find a seat. She'd prefer to stand at the bar, but Anthony finds them a table. Behind it is a threadbare two-seater, of an unfetching brownish red.

'Save our seats,' says Anthony. 'I'll be back with the drinks.'

Rosie sits strumming her fingers, already looking at her watch. But if Callum's working late he might not be here for ages. The drinks come back, and so does Anthony. She cranes her neck: no sign of Callum.

Anthony drinks Guinness and eats crisps loudly, making crumbs. Perched stiffly on the sofa's edge, he rarely looks her in the face. He asks what she does for a living; she says she's temping, but wants to be a psychologist.

'Ah, yes,' says Anthony. 'Callum mentioned.' He sniffs.

Rosie twists her hair between her fingers; the pub is getting loud and smokier. The air is warm and dry and heavy, weighing down upon her eyelids. Every now and then she thinks she's seen Callum, pushing through the crowds towards her. But if she sits up straight and looks properly, it turns out not to be him.

'I don't think he's coming.' Rosie can't disguise her misery. 'Well, I suppose he must have his reasons. Perhaps I should go, I'll call him later.'

Anthony's face tightens. 'We've just got here. At least one more drink.'

She agrees, partly feeling bludgeoned, partly because the thought of missing Callum by a hair's breadth is unbearable. She drinks a second gin and tonic, her body sinking back into the sofa cushions, her skirt riding high on her thighs. Anthony's eyes glisten. She wants to pull the skirt straight but fears the gesture might seem coquettish. She clears her throat significantly, but finds there's nothing to say.

'You know,' says Anthony, 'you mustn't be too upset. If Callum doesn't show, I mean. That's just his way.'

The first real tinge of panic tightens in Rosie's chest. 'What d'you mean, that's his way?'

'Just what I say. He's a lovely guy, everyone's crazy about him. But not one to be trusted.'

Now Rosie really wishes she hadn't stayed. She leans forward, looking for her bag, but Anthony's torso blocks her way. He taps his nose, illogically, affecting an air of knowing, but it seems out of place and he can't quite pull it off. 'Good old Callum and his haphazard ways, eh? No need to get too upset though. Let's have a go at enjoying ourselves anyway.'

To her horror, he settles in close on the sofa beside her. His thigh rubs against hers, he stares at the exposed length of stocking. His fingers spread on the dull, unvarnished table in front of them, and then slowly, deliberately, he settles his hand on her knee.

For a few seconds, Rosie is paralysed with disbelief. Then she snaps her back straight and throws his hand off her. Her heart is jarring uncomfortably. Anthony, off balance, sways sideways in his seat, and as his hand flaps to steady himself he knocks over his Guinness. Frothy, dark liquid flows over wood, on to carpet. Several people at the bar turn to see what is happening.

'Get off me. What the hell d'you think you're doing?'

'What am *I* doing? What are *you* doing?' Anthony is fairly hissing. 'Please keep your voice down. I won't have you making a scene.'

'A scene? You've just indecently assaulted me.'

'Oh, don't come the innocent with me.' Now his voice is really nasty. 'I wasn't born yesterday. I know all about you.'

Despite the light and the crowds, and the warmth and the noise, Rosie realizes she is frightened. Anthony's eyes glitter venomously.

'I don't know what you're talking about.'

'Of course you do. I've heard all about you. I know all those stories.'

'What stories? What are you talking about? What's Callum been saying to you?'

He gives a tinny laugh. 'Still she goes on pretending. Dear girl, you must know I'm not talking just about Callum.'

Rosie stands up, grabs her bag, mumbling crazily to herself.

'You're a good actress, Rosie. But I know your little secrets.'

It's too much, she feels as if she's stumbled into some ghastly parallel universe. She has no idea what Anthony means, but his reptile's gaze terrifies her. It no longer matters where Callum is; if and why he's stood her up. All she knows is she has to get home: away from here, away from Anthony. She looks frantically for her coat, finds it bundled on to the floor. Then she puts the wrong arm in the wrong sleeve, tripping on her way out. By the time she's reached the door, several punters are staring at her. *More water, love!* shouts one. She buttons her coat, pushes the door.

But out in the street, Anthony's still at her shoulder.

'Calm down, don't overreact. Stay and have another drink.'

'You must be joking.' She practically spits at him, and turns on her heel towards the tube station.

'I'm sorry I've upset you,' he says drily. 'I thought we could have a nice evening. But do take my advice, Rosie, and be careful of Callum.'

This really is going too far. She turns on him. 'You

dare to speak to me like that. Taking me for a drink, trying to feel me up in public. Just who d'you think you are?'

'For God's sake, woman, it was a misunderstanding. There's no need to get so heated. At least I'm not the one leading you up the garden path.'

The air stills; she stops and stares at him. 'Who's leading who up the garden path?'

He smiles and pauses significantly, like he knows her world is about to split apart. 'Rosie, why don't you just come back to reality? Surely by now Callum must have told you about Shona?'

7

'Oh dear,' said DC Fletcher, and then again, for want of anything more vividly expressive, 'Oh dear.' Callum looked across the soiled tiles at the detective in his kitchen. The storm had broken the hot spell and the summer light was grey and shallow. Sad and shaken in his slippers, he felt horribly exposed.

He had hardly slept, but lain awake in a disbelieving stupor. Early in the morning, he'd called the officers, failing to dress before they arrived. The ramshackle mansion, untidy and disordered for days, seemed more haunted house than suburban palace. And no kitchen could look attractive dominated by the carcass of a dead Labrador. Callum had noticed a couple of the younger men's twisted mouths as they entered. Homicide was glamorous and scary; this – what was it? besticide? – had an edge of black comedy.

'Less *Crimewatch* than *Animal Hospital*,' he had overheard one officer snigger. If they detected he'd been weeping they'd think him farcical, or pathetic.

But DC Fletcher looked round the kitchen methodically, picking up glasses, opening cupboards. He checked door handles and window latches.

'No sign of a forced entry, Mr Scott.'

From the front his face was indistinct, almost pudding-like. Callum found it easier to register an impression when the man turned, in profile. He noted the prominent, near Anthony-esque nose, the fulsome lips, the shallow eyesockets. From the side he looked quite Roman, almost distinguished. But in reality he was coarse, he concluded. Somewhat pedestrian.

'I take it you'll treat this with appropriate gravity, Detective. Given what's happened so far. Someone's clearly out to get me. This was no ordinary burglary.'

DC Fletcher puffed out his cheeks as though catching his breath. 'We take everything seriously, as you know, sir. In fact, we have made some progress in connection with the heath incidents.'

Callum remembered Anthony's tip-off. 'And what's the latest on that?'

The detective paused, and Callum thought the swarthy skin turned slightly pink. The younger officers continued whispering and dusting for fingerprints. DC Fletcher jerked his head sideways and the two older men went out into the hallway.

'We've arrested and are investigating a young man named Tyrone Freedman. It looks as though we've got enough to charge him.'

Callum shook his head at the floor; his feet looked pitifully white and blue-veined. 'Detective, someone else is after me. You must have the wrong man.'

This time, from whichever angle, you could see DC Fletcher's mouth hardening. 'We have evidence,

Mr Scott. Fibres found on the dead man's clothes match fibres taken from a jacket we found at Freedman's house. If the two attacks were linked, as we think, then it looks like the same man was after you.'

'Circumstantial,' reasoned Callum. It was like being back in court. 'The jacket may, indeed, be guilty. But how can you prove it was Freedman who was wearing it?'

DC Fletcher nodded, and drew breath. 'Freedman declined to provide an alibi for either occasion. Enquiries of our own lead us to believe that his whereabouts during both incidents are unaccounted for. And we have witness statements which suggest he may well match the descriptions of Mr Squires's killer.'

'And you're holding an ID parade?'

'We will be looking to do that soonest.'

Callum paused, working hard to speak without sounding as though he were pestering. 'The burglary at my Chambers. Have there been any fingerprints matching up from that case?'

DC Fletcher chewed his lip. 'No, sir. Nothing on that.'

'And the murder of my Labrador. What d'you intend doing about that?' The detective breathed heavily as though suffering from heartburn. 'Detective. It is clear that someone is after me. I was attacked on the heath, my computer was stolen from work, and my Labrador, a dear, cherished companion

– please don't smirk – has been viciously slaughtered. Tyrone Freedman was in your custody last night, he couldn't have broken in here. Unless he's not acting alone, you're charging the wrong man.'

DC Fletcher's breath had grown so strained it was verging on wheezing.

'Mr Scott, I know you're concerned, and this is your line of work. But please don't try and tell me how to do my job. We have evidence to suggest Freedman may be guilty of the attacks on you and Mr Squires. There are no links to the burglary you mentioned, and you yourself know how commonplace that sort of thing is. And –'

'My dog was killed too. Is that so very commonplace?'

'My officers, as you well know, are in your kitchen pursuing the investigation even as we speak. But we cannot look at this as a significant crime without some sort of evidence. As I said, there is no sign of a break-in. Mr Scott, does anyone else have access to your house?'

'Only my wife and children, and my mother.'

'Would you like us to talk to them?'

'No, of course not,' Callum almost spat. 'I mean that would be ridiculous.'

'In that case, Mr Scott, perhaps you'd better just let us continue with our investigation.'

'Yes, very well, Detective.' He smiled thinly, kept his teeth closed. 'Thank you for your help.'

Before they left, the two younger officers helped

drag Frieda's body into the garden. No, Callum confirmed, he didn't need help in dispensing of her. He would bury her later, discreetly: he wouldn't discuss that in front of them. The kitchen looked bare and uninviting, the floor tiles still stained and sordid. Even with the windows flung open to let in the newly cooled air, there was still a lingering stench which reminded him of last night.

He had wanted to make breakfast, but could not bear to stay in the kitchen. Instead, empty-stomached, he retired to the living room. Exasperation swelled against his hollow, hungry insides. DC Fletcher was well-intentioned, but plodding, his investigation was going nowhere. Callum was sure he'd never catch a stealthy thief or subtle killer. Maverick-like, Callum wondered if he might have to help himself. His empty stomach fizzed and bubbled, as though warning him of something. And then he sat up brusquely, rubbing his forehead.

Somewhere in the recesses of his memory, the name Tyrone Freedman was starting to mean something.

Callum hurried out for a walk. He didn't go directly to the heath, but meandered impractically, without purpose, for the walking was chiefly to clarify his thoughts. His path zig-zagged the hilly side-streets past the antiquarian bookshop, where locals stood on the pavements and rummaged through musty, open boxes. A greying stringbean of a man stood reading intently, sniffing loudly. To Callum, the noise was almost deafening: he headed out to open ground.

As he reached the heath's edge, rain started to fall again in fat splats. The previously sun-dried, cracked dirt-path had begun to moisten and blacken. He hurried on, though lovers and schoolchildren were now fleeing the benches. A clutch of swans flapped and squawked on the dark-watered pond.

In the past, Callum hadn't had much time for this sort of wandering: he'd had to squeeze in summer afternoon walks, preferably accompanied by the children. Now, as he stared out across the black water, the copses and pathways emptied leaving only the hardiest adventurers. Those that remained were solitary hikers, save for one or two mothers determined to give their offspring exercise.

Callum found himself dispirited that he should find himself amongst this number. The damp weight of his clothes grew heavy against his skin. From behind there came a scream, and his body twisted suddenly: he thought someone might be in trouble, perhaps he could help them. But there was just a young boy, tripping over a rotting log, then picking himself up and running – towards his mother, out of the rain.

It was a late afternoon towards the end of the week when Callum made his way into Chambers: the daylit hours this time of year still stretched mellow and generous. As he approached The Courtyard, most barristers were filtering out the other way, a preponderance of black-and-white clad men and women, making for nearby pubs and winebars. Many were heading for the pleasure barges, where they would take their drinks gazing out upon the river. Callum nodded at several familiar faces, though he spotted no one he knew well. He wondered how efficiently the rumour-mill had been turning; or if his changed world was marked upon his skin.

From outside, he could see already that the clerks' room was almost empty. It was past seven, and with the sky so blue, Guy had clearly gone home early. He hesitated on the threshold, wondering if he could slip inside unnoticed. In fact he was spotted, but only by Freddy. He recognized from behind the boy's thin frame with its unmannish shoulders: when Freddy turned, his blank, unformed expression was as usual.

'Evening, sir.' The boy's voice was brittle with uncertainty. 'We've not seen you around for a few days. Guy was just saying he wasn't sure when you'd be coming back, you hadn't phoned in.'

None of the floors above creaked with industrious footsteps; Callum couldn't hear the whir of hard drives or the tapping of keyboards in other rooms. A girl carrying a clutch of mugs floated towards the sink at the end of the corridor; as she drew nearer, Callum couldn't place her, but noted a babyish Cupid's bow mouth. Apart from that, the place seemed empty.

'I'm not here for long, Freddy,' said Callum, trying to sound casual. 'There's just some paperwork I need to check upstairs.' The junior clerk just wrung his fingers, willing the conversation to end.

'Guy's not around,' he said redundantly. 'Shall I let him know you stopped by when I see him?'

'No need,' said Callum quickly. 'I'll have to phone him myself at some point. Things to discuss. Leave it till then, eh?' He half-turned in the doorway. 'Oh and Freddy, is Anthony about?'

'No, sir,' replied the boy, his skinny fingers still weaving. 'He's off with most of the other crime team. Drinks party up at Red Lion Street. Sean Hargreaves made up as a judge.'

'Ah yes,' said Callum, trying to sound casual, 'of course. Unfortunately, I can't make it. I have to be somewhere else. Well, anyway, I won't be long.'

He stepped forward to climb the stairs, regretting his impulse to pretend. But it was too uncomfortable to consider why no invitation had reached him. Out of the corner of his eye, he saw Freddy reach for his jacket; the girl with the Cupid's bow hovered, as though waiting to be asked something.

The staircase echoed emptily as Callum made his way up to the first landing. The room he had shared with Anthony now looked more bereft than ever. He felt a stab of misery and anger, like a victim of wrongful eviction. The surface of his desk was free of friendly, familiar clutter, and many bundles of papers had been cleared and stacked away neatly into boxes. A hard, clean shaft of light pierced the long pane of window. Callum reached for one of the boxes ranged on the shelf behind Anthony's desk. It slid from its niche releasing a thin film of dirt; dust motes careened in the sunlight, papers splattered to the floor.

'Shit,' he breathed, too loudly. Down the stairwell floated voices of two junior female colleages: amiable Lindsay and the more brittle Cassandra. Lindsay was a friend, a family lawyer who spent just enough time away from work with her young children to avoid intimidating her male colleagues and arousing resentment. Cassandra, on the other hand, was a criminal specialist and lone female, just approaching the age where her status aroused suspicion rather than desire. Besides which, all too frequently, at a relatively early hour, one could sidle up close to her and smell her damp, toxic breath.

'Yes, I know,' Lindsay was saying, 'it's an absolutely dreadful ruling.'

'Anyway,' rejoined Cassandra, 'Sean was never my cup of tea.'

Their voices clashed and clucked in a female confusion. Down on all fours to retrieve the papers, Callum shrank as they drew nearer.

'Do have a lovely evening, anyway,' said Cassandra, with her usual edge of sourness. 'Tell me all tomorrow, darling.'

They were right outside the landing now, at the door beside the ladies' room. Callum hid behind the desk in an almost canine crouch. Dust was tickling his nostrils; he stifled a sneeze into a hiccup. Lindsay made her farewells and her footsteps faded down the stairwell; the door to the Ladies clunked shut, and a key turned in the lock. There was a clatter and rush of small, sharp objects falling. Through the embarrassingly thin walls he could hear Cassandra moan and curse.

He imagined her in there, spilling all her make-up, her eyes and her breath already fuzzy with drink. He raised himself from his crouch; she'd be a few minutes. He rearranged the scattered pages, straightening them like a deck of cards.

'Regina v Ford' read the indictment; it wasn't what he was looking for. He slid free another cardboard box, but that wasn't the right one either. Next door, the toilet flushed, and Cassandra coughed loudly. Another box slid loose, the cardboard dangerously close to splitting.

Now Callum recognized Anthony's conspicuously neat handwriting: 'R v Lansdowne and others'. It was the case which circumstances – and Anthony – had so cruelly snatched away from him. Despite a renewed stab of regret, he was close to finding what he was looking for. But the papers were many and voluminous, at least fifteen full boxes. He didn't want long statements or exhibits, he was simply looking for a witness list. Anthony, for all his fastidiousness, hadn't placed the boxes in any order; he had to pull three or four of them free before finding what he sought. He found the indictment and the witness list just as there came the echo of Cassandra belching. He read rapidly, his brain throbbing, but found no sign of Tyrone Freedman. And then he turned to the index of unused material.

His pulse quickening, Callum scanned three pages of names, page numbers and sub-headings. Letters and numbers stretched and shrank, but he narrowed his eyes and breathed deeply. At the heart of the case against Lansdowne was the allegation that he'd murdered a fellow gang leader, possibly one less religiously inclined than himself. His victim was no friend of the police, but there were other reasons for wanting Lansdowne. It was hoped that, if promised with lenience, Lansdowne could offer significant information about other converts at his mosque. Freedman was a crony, who might know something of his friend's movements.

And right towards the end of the material, there it was, just as Callum had suspected. Tyrone Freedman had given a statement. Callum was sweating with anticipation but the proof, when examined, was somewhat bland and unexciting. Freedman had simply spoken to Lansdowne on the day of one of the murders, confirmed he was heading to the West End. It seemed of little consequence – Freedman was Lansdowne's friend, not a traitor. Callum slotted the box back into place on the shelf.

Next door, the taps turned, there was a rush of water, the room was quiet. The key turned again in the lock and Cassandra stumbled out on to the landing. Callum held his breath as she paused at the top of the stairs, but just as he thought she would walk away, she looked over her shoulders.

He watched her head turn, and managed to fix his eyes on the straight nose and strong jaw. Her profile threatened to dissolve, but then she looked directly at him, and he was able to focus fully on her sad, moistened eyes.

'Callum, darling, you slipped in like a ghost. Don't you know you won't find Anthony? He's gone up to Sean's do.'

'It's all right, Cassandra. I just came here to check some papers.' Her tights were snagged beneath the left knee, revealing a ladder of pale flesh. 'Aren't you on your way out?'

The skin plumped at her neckline, milk-white splotched with red and pink. Her upper body leaned towards him; then she paused, and retreated.

'Lovely to see you, darling. I hope you'll be back with us soon. Anthony will be so sorry he missed you.'

The air turned sour in her wake as she clunked her way out.

*

Temporarily, he had become insomniac, or at least had started to sleep fitfully. So when the doorbell roused him from his slumbers at first he thought it was morning. He was still rubbing his eyes childishly as he shuffled into the hall, flicking the stickiness away and reassembling the day's jigsaw. Almost in a dream, it came to him that he was fully clothed; that the air was middle-of the-day hot; that he'd been on the sofa, not the bed. But that he'd dozed off after lunch was the least interesting of his discoveries.

This time, he knew to expect her, because she had moved to the side of the threshold. The femaleness of her silhouette was outlined through a column of opaque, coloured glass. He saw her in profile, blackened and ghosted, one distorted hand tucking her hair behind her ear.

When he opened the door she was turned away from him, her nails fidgeting at her neck. She'd had her hair cut, it stopped above her shoulder; the capricious auburn tint of it winked and altered in the sunlight. She held herself high, her spine straight; her neck extended. He felt a small, palpitating thrill that she should compose herself just for him.

When she spun round and looked at him, her face was the usual unmeasured blank canvas. But he concentrated on her hair and on the wide gash of mouth. She stared at him in protracted silence.

He said, 'So, you're back.'

Something must have been troubling her, because many moments passed before she could speak properly. They remained standing there, not quite moving, though he thought he noticed her edge forward, as though to make her way into the house which had once been her home. He squinted over her shoulder into the pale-yellow daylight. There was a chirrup of childish voices and light footsteps clipped the pavement. At the bottom of the drive, a dark-haired boy hovered into view.

Callum's mouth widened, then exploded into a smile.

'Rudy!' He could barely restrain himself from squealing. He looked out towards the street, and then back at her, delightedly. 'Shona . . . You've . . . It's wonderful. You've brought the children with you.'

She continued to stare, saying nothing, although he heard her draw breath. Then she shook her head slowly. The boy he'd mistaken for Rudy trailed over on to the far pavement, accompanied by yells from a harassed young mother. Callum slapped his brow, already damp with disappointment.

'Excuse me. I got a little overexcited.'

Now, finally, she spoke, and her voice came out hoarsely. 'Callum, Callum.' She sounded as though she were close to dismay, or despair. There were several moments more quiet, and then she added, with some bathos, 'I just wanted to know how you were.' She stretched out her hand to touch his cheek; her sharp nails grazed his stubble. He laced his fingers round hers, lowering her hand, and stepping backwards. The weight of his body pulled her into the house with him.

He walked ahead of her down the hallway and led her into the living room. He saw her white hands run over things, travelling the edges of bits of furniture. It was as though she'd stepped into his world with him, half-blind, needing reassurance. When she sat, it was as though she were immeasurably far away from him. She started a sentence but her voice trailed away in a nervous, girlish sigh.

He cleared his throat, paused deliberately, and then thought: best come right out with it.

'Shona, someone's killed Frieda.'

Her voice came out in a whine, the distress thickly audible.

'I – I don't understand. What are you saying to me?'

'I'm saying, Shona, that someone's after me, to the extent of killing my dog. They broke in the other night. She was dead in the morning.'

She had shrunk into the corner of the sofa, her head bent forward, her face hidden. She barely raised her eyes to speak to him. She appeared more upset by all this than he was.

'Callum – what's happening to you?'

He couldn't quite tell if she was about to cry, or if she'd already begun. Certainly her voice was still lower and huskier than usual – still rough, he imagined, with the last of summer flu. He wanted to draw near her, to embrace her, but without prelude the move seemed as coarse as an assault on a stranger.

'Would you . . . would you like tea?' He wasn't wearing a watch, and was out of vision of all wall-clocks. The segment of day he'd been awake through had completely slipped through his memory. He half-hoped Shona would say, Yes, and take herself into the kitchen. But she just sat, breathing heavily, and said, 'No. No tea. Thank you.'

A sheet of sun sliced through the window; once more the temperature was rising. In the path of its light, she became a sharp mosaic of colour: the helmet of hair brightened, the skin impossibly white. He noticed she was wearing a dress of shot green silk, gathered in beneath the bust, clinging loosely to waist and hips. It could have been designed for a much younger woman, but she wore it without self-consciousness. It shifted like liquid when she moved. The back of Callum's throat went dry.

'Shona, things are getting bad for me. I don't quite know what is happening, but I really want to see the children.'

'The children. Of course.' Her head was still bent so it was as if she were murmuring through gauze.

'I mean you will try and arrange it, won't you?'

'Oh, Callum – this is difficult –'

'I know, I know, but talk to James. I won't mention you came to see me . . .'

She raised her head and sniffed loudly. 'No, you *mustn't*.'

'I understand,' he said, softening.

'Let's not talk about it just now.'

She sat upright, her body stretching, and he saw

the dark patch of damp on her dress. Realizing her tears had flowed so freely made him bold enough to go nearer. He moved on to the sofa where she was sitting and spread his arm along the back of it. Without touching, he sensed her tensing.

'Shona, what's wrong? Why are you crying?'

'Everything.' Her fingers waved haphazardly, without precision. From her small bag she produced a handkerchief and started dabbing her eyes with it. 'All this. Your state. You and me.'

This time he let his arm slide forward so that one hand cupped her shoulder. She was bonier, more brittle, than he remembered, or perhaps it was the quiet rattle of her sobbing. Her skin had acquired a graininess, a texture he didn't recognize: in the time they'd been apart, the whole feel and form of her had altered. He pulled her closer, waiting, watching, listening for resistance. At first everything about her felt wooden, as though she held herself stiff, calculating the moment she might break away. But when he murmured 'don't shut me out', and folded her body into him, she was soft and limp as a rag doll. He kissed the top of her bright head and she placed her ear against his chest.

'Pounding like a drum,' he said, smiling, one finger searching out the crevice between breast and rib. Then he glided his hand up the smooth stretch of her neck, trying to tilt her chin upwards, though she turned away like a shy child.

'God, I've missed you.' He had thought the words

would come out velvety, but his voice was hoarse and broken. This time she turned her mouth towards him and let him kiss her full on. She tasted dry, sweet and sour, at once strange and familiar. 'It's been so long . . .'

Now she was facing him, her body curled into his. She took his skull beneath her palms, and tightened her grip. He felt opened up and vulnerable, the skin and bone as thin as rice paper. Blood pulsed and thickened behind his temples; she said, 'Close your eyes,' and he obeyed.

She let him kiss her neck and then her breasts, while her hands skinned the shirt from his bare back. Her fingers were strangely cold for this warm day, with nails sharp enough to tear the skin. She wriggled out of her dress and he prized it loose, on to the floor, where it nestled, concertina'd, like a discarded lizard skin. For a moment he opened his eyes and looked at it, mesmerized, the fluid light and dark of it shimmering as he began to rock beneath her. Then she turned his face towards her and drew her fingertips down over his eyes.

He made love to her warmly, but gently, trapped beneath the blackness of his eyelids. After so long an absence, she had the shape of a stranger. The scent of her body was different – perhaps spicier – as though the smell of her new life could be detected on her skin. His fingers walked the length of her spine, told him how she'd aged or altered. He could tell she was self-conscious, trying to mask her quickened breathing. But he liked it like this, this blend of nearness and distance, each touch explosive, exploratory, like unpeeling a fresh skin. As he shuddered towards climax, her nails dug in beneath his shoulder blades, and cold, clean pain cut through him, so he could not stop from crying out.

For moments afterwards, Callum lay there drowsy, a thousand other moments like this playing and replaying in his brain. He opened his eyes slowly, just in time to see her wipe the blood from beneath her nails.

'Vicious lady,' he whispered, laughing.

She didn't laugh back, or even speak. With a compact, feline efficiency, she she was gathering her underclothes, reinserting her earrings and tidying her hair. Callum looked across the floor to the glittering cocoon of her dress.

'I wish you wouldn't go so soon.'

'Have to.'

She drew her knees up to her chin, as though embarrassed at her nakedness. 'Have to get dressed now. Close your eyes.'

'Shona –'

'I mean it.'

She put her fingers against his eyesockets, the pressure so close and tight that his lids battened down involuntarily. Then he lay there, unseeing, as she took the few, soundless steps across the floor. The light beneath his lids bled from orange to purple to black as she bent and unbent in the path of the sun. When he opened his eyes she was fully dressed with her back to him.

'Goodbye,' he called out, as she retreated into the hallway. She raised her hand, her fingers rippling in a wave, but she didn't say anything.

After she'd gone, he saw she'd left her handkerchief. He picked it up, inhaled its perfume, but it wasn't one he recognized.

*

Callum sat in the front waiting area of Holborn police station. The glass panel walls gave out on to a cubic terrace of grey paving slabs. He felt embarrassed to be here, hoped he wouldn't see any solicitors he knew. But it was better to talk in person than be constantly fobbed off on the telephone.

'Mr Scott,' said DC Fletcher, appearing through a near invisible door. Almost cheerfully, he strode up to Callum, and the two men shook hands. The officer patted Callum's forearm, as though in congratulation, or perhaps commiseration, and then turned and led Callum into the hinterland of the station.

Up a staircase they climbed, and through several twisting corridors. Everything was of the same dull grey as the paving slabs outside. Eventually they reached a small square office, dominated by tall filing cabinets and an overcrowded desk. DC Fletcher offered Callum tea, which Callum declined, so the policeman refilled his own heavy mug.

'Good of you to see me like this, Detective.'

'Not at all, Mr Scott. What have you got for me this time?'

Both men sat and DC Fletcher folded his surprisingly slender fingers.

'I think I know something about Tyrone Freedman.'

There was a dull clunk as the policeman put down his heavy chipped mug. His back straightened, just perceptibly. His fingers inched towards his notepad.

'Yes?'

'He was involved, albeit loosely, in a case I was previously instructed on. He was interviewed for the prosecution, but his statement was of no particular assistance so it simply remains among the unused material. The interesting thing is, that for no reason at all, I was asked to give up the case.'

'Ah, well,' said DC Fletcher. He steepled his fingers. There were frown lines between his eyebrows and it was clear he was concentrating. There was none of the impatience he'd exhibited previously, in Callum's kitchen. 'And would you mind telling me, Mr Scott, what the name of that case is?'

Callum paused, and his mouth filled with bitter saliva. 'Does the case of Jason Lansdowne and others mean anything to you?'

'Ah, yes,' said DC Fletcher, and Callum knew the name had struck home. Every policeman in London would know about this case. The latest news on it was that a clutch of homes belonging to some young men in South London had been searched on the suspicion that their occupants harboured ricin. Nothing was proven, but Callum knew it was suspected these were Lansdowne's gang. DC Fletcher nodded, interested. 'A client you'd fallen out with?'

'That's the odd part,' rejoined Callum. 'There was no falling out. I'm sure there's some other reason why I've been sacked, which at present remains a mystery. But there is something else that's been troubling me, and I wondered if you could enlighten me?'

'How's that?' The policeman sipped on his insipid grey-brown tea.

'What could possibly be the link between Freedman and Christopher Squires?'

DC Fletcher coughed, his voice definitely quavered. 'Surprisingly, Mr Scott, I have been giving that some thought. You say the link with Mr Squires. That's assuming there *is* a link.'

'I don't follow.' Callum frowned. The detective's coughing had got louder.

'Mr Squires was murdered on the heath, walking his golden Labrador. He was a forty-year-old local, and a regular along that route, at that hour'

'Yes, I know that. But where does that take us?'

'Freedman and Lansdowne are linked to you, Mr Scott, but there's no suggestion at all at this time of any connection to Mr Squires. What if Mr Squires's killing was carried out according to a description, but something went wrong? I'm looking at a case of mistaken identity. Mr Squires's murder may have been one big fiasco.'

Callum drew breath at exactly the same moment as the other man. Both exhaled, raggedly.

'It was you that they wanted.'

8

'Why didn't you tell me?'

She is blinded with tears, her fingers curled inwards like a baby's. She hurls herself at his chest, and the air inside him gulps and hisses, and she knows what it must feel like to want to beat someone unconscious. Knock the living daylights out. Punch them to death.

They haven't spoken for days – how many, she has lost count. At first, she stayed in her room, muffling her sobs like a teenager, hoping her mother wouldn't look in and ask what on earth was wrong. Sarah Verner appeared helpless, untutored for such a crisis.

Then she thought he would telephone, pretend that nothing was the matter. She'd respond to him casually, her voice cold and hard as stainless steel. *What is it?* he would ask, and she'd give a haughty, glassy laugh. *Oh, Callum, you are a cad.* Or: *I'm afraid your cover's blown, honey.*

But he hasn't phoned, he doesn't care, and her polished cruelty is left unaired. She wishes she could forget him – ball up his memory and bin it – but there is a constant heat within her, a rage and grief like spitting fat. No matter how hard she tries, she cannot seem to turn it off.

And so she's been reduced to this. Calling him herself, participating in the charade of sounding ludicrously normal, mumbling when he said how sorry he was, but how busy he'd been but really he'd missed her and could he see her tonight? She'd swallowed her anger, saving it for when she could see him, until she found herself tripping and cursing her way down the Strand, her insides swaying like a see-saw. She collided with a woman carrying a baby and a bag of fruit, sent green apples flying as the woman shouted hoarsely: *Bitch, lunatic, what the fuck d'you think you're doing?* She stifled the urge to swear back; clamped her jaw tight and stormed onwards.

On her arrival, Simon had looked at her with arched eyebrows.

'Callum said you'd be dropping by, but I think he thought it would be a little later. Shall I tell him you're on your way up?'

'Is he with someone?'

'No.'

'Then there's no need. I'll surprise him.'

Surprise isn't exactly what she has in mind. More like a cold-fingered shock, like mercury flooding your veins. The stomach-lurching nausea that comes with the most unwelcome of news. Hell hath no fury. *Callum, how could you do this to me?*

He is alone when she comes upon him, sitting at his desk reading. He looks up at the sound of footsteps, and is abashed when he sees her – there is no mistaking the altered shadow that descends across his features. He stands slowly, steps towards her, perhaps unsure of which mask to put on: shy pleasure, slight surprise, minor professional irritation. She knows she is already crying, moisture pricking the rims of her eyes. He moves closer, his face a blank, 'Rosie, how great to see –'

She steps back, beyond arm's length. 'Don't you touch me. Why didn't you tell me?' The words and tears cascade, not at all how she had planned it.

'Rosie, what are you talking about?'

'Don't pretend you don't know.'

She launches herself against him, and he handcuffs her wrists with his fingers, so she is left struggling like a madwoman. But he won't confess or apologize. Footsteps pass in the corridor, briefly halt, quickly continue. She is dimly aware of Anthony's outline hovering ghost-like in the doorway; Callum glances backwards, momentarily, and then Rosie looks and Anthony has gone. Callum stills her wrists with a movement so forceful her skin reddens and throbs. He goes over to the door, shuts it.

'Rosie, we have to talk.'

Her heart pounds with rage and fear.

'So you *know* why I'm angry.' Her lungs are constricting, each breath more of an effort. 'The game's over, Callum. Anthony told me about your engagement. You don't have to lie any more. Just tell me if it's true.'

Callum sits back down at his desk, and there's a

lull, a ghastly quiet. He shakes his head and mutters under his breath; she catches the word 'Bastard'.

'What did you say? Who's a bastard? Anthony? For blowing your lying fucking cover? For putting me out of my misery?'

'Look, Rosie, it wasn't his place to tell you anything about me. Yes, there are things you should know. But I needed time to explain.'

The blood beats behind her temples; she is not sure she can control her voice.

'He – he told me to avoid you. That you're already engaged. What's to explain about that – unless it's not really true?' The sound of her heart thudding fills the void left by his silence. 'So it is true then, Callum. You don't deny it?'

'Rosie, it's not the way it looks –'

She picks up her bag, wipes the back of her hand across her eyes. A carousel of sound and feeling whirls and clashes in her brain. There's no way of remaining dignified in the face of such hurt and humiliation. She turns away from him, rapid and unseeing, so that her knuckles scrape the sharp edge of a desk and begin to pulse white and purple. It doesn't matter. Any extra pain is irrelevant now.

'I guess that's it, then. Better go now.'

She pulls the door to with too much fury, so it almost crashes into her face. Someone's standing there – maybe more than one person – probably Chambers gossips eavesdropping. She doesn't care to look who. She makes a dash for the stairwell, taking the last three steps in one bound; her foot twists under her ankle and pain shoots all the way up to her thigh. But it doesn't stop her movement. Outside the door, she's as good as sprinting.

Halfway up the narrow lane, she becomes aware that someone's following. She doesn't turn to see who it is, but hears Callum cry out.

'Rosie, *please*. This is all wrong.'

She accelerates, widens the gap between them. She knows he's still chasing her because in the course of the short pursuit she grows to recognize his breathing and the stuttering of his footsteps. Now and again he wheezes, 'Rosie, please stop.' But she gets to the tube before him and disappears into the crowds.

Rosie sees the answering machine winking as soon as she slides open the front door. At the same moment, the telephone rings. She doesn't pick up.

'Rosie, it's me. I lost you at the underground. If you're there, please come to the phone.'

She erases the message. The evening slips into night.

It doesn't matter now what the morning might bring. Her skull spins with a constant headache of loss and disappointment. The temp agency rings; she tells them she's unwell for the duration. Postgraduate brochures slide through the letterbox, thud on to the carpet. She can't muster any interest. Sarah Verner tiptoes round the flat, knowing not to question her daughter too searchingly. One evening, as if by accident, they collide in the hallway. Rosie hovers by the answering machine, her fingers stretched towards the 'play' button. The two women stand looking at each other, curiously off balance. They circle uncertainly like beasts vying over prey who don't really want to oust each other. Rosie's skin is sallow, her hair unwashed for days now. She notices her mother's sunken eyes only as an afterthought.

'Rosie? Is . . . is everything all right?'

It is unfamiliar territory, this reaching out, offering solace. Rosie finds her tongue is knotted inside her bottom lip.

'Fine, Mother, just fine. I was just wondering if Annie had called. And by the way, are *you* OK? You look a little tired.'

Rosie's mother nods vigorously, as though pleased by the question, and Rosie retreats towards the bedroom, her stomach rumbling miserably.

Sometimes, in her head, she hears Felicity upbraiding her. *He's just a man – what d'you expect?* She should have known, after being so modern, so forward. Callum just thought she was easy, took his chances when he saw them. That's what you get if you're a woman. So little ever really changes.

Then, on a grim Tuesday, when she's barely out of bed, her face still smeared with broken sleep, the front doorbell rings. She's alone in the flat and she shambles to answer it, stumbling like a pensioner, mind and body dislocated. Her hair is unbrushed, wild and spiky from the pillow. Her skin hasn't yet woken up. It's the last thing she's expecting.

'Rosie, please let me in.'

Callum stands there, his eyes hollow. He doesn't look much better than she does. He puts a hand pre-emptively on the door, as though expecting her to slam it. 'Just let me talk to you.'

His words fall into the bottomless gap between them, and she steps backwards, not speaking. Silently she turns and leads him into the kitchen.

'Are you alone?'

She nods, but apart from that, offers nothing. She doesn't invite him to sit down, so they both stand there, awkwardly. It's odd because part of her is wondering how he could possibly dare to descend on her like this; part wants it all to be a mistake, that he loves her after all; part simply wants to wash her hair. In the end, it's this last and most basic impulse which wins out, especially as Callum glances her over and says, 'You look like shit.'

'Yeah, well, thanks for that. I wasn't exactly expecting company.'

He is about to answer, then thinks better of it. 'Look,' she says, suddenly uncomfortable, thinking how blissful a shower would be, 'I've barely got up. Let me go and get sorted. Help yourself to some coffee.'

Bad feeling is momentarily submerged by the urge to get clean. In the bathroom, the mirror quickly steams up with the rush of hot water. Incredible that he has seen her like this, every last bit of armour peeled away. But then it's not like she had any choice. She opens her mouth to the shower water, the jets pummelling her skin and skull. Her hair curls damply at her neck. She throws on a towelling robe.

'Considerable improvement,' says Callum, as she rejoins him in the kitchen.

'Not that anyone asked you.'

She is cross, but can't help noticing the overwhelming fresh coffee smell. It's hard to stop her stomach rumbling. Callum, looking absurdly at home, has already lined up two coffee cups and is gently rocking the cafetière.

'You do want some, don't you?'

'Yes, but –'

Don't bother making yourself comfortable, are the next words she's envisaging. Or: *Just because you make a good cup of coffee doesn't mean you're welcome here.* But neither sentence ever gets out, because Callum is there on the chair next to her, pulling her close, leaning in.

'Don't. Don't say anything, Rosie. Please let me explain.'

He gets the coffee and pours her some, then sits straighter. As if he's preparing a speech. Typical barrister.

'What Anthony said to you – I know it's unforgivable – but things aren't what they seem.'

'Oh?'

'I am engaged, it's true – well have been, anyway. She's like – a family friend. People my mother knew back in Ireland.'

'Right.' Any resolve Rosie has to remain dry and nonchalant is quickly dissolving. Callum's intimate liaisons, a family network that excludes her – what sort of apology is it; does she really need to hear all this? She pulls her robe a little tighter.

'The thing is, we were really more like friends than lovers. Yes, I'm fond of her. Perhaps even there's some love there. But when I met you, things were different. It was like I'd been waiting for you. I was going to break off the engagement, but it's complicated, I hadn't got round to –'

'Stop!' Rosie holds her hand upright, surprised at the command in her own voice. 'Listen, Callum, I personally haven't had this kind of shit from any previous boyfriend, but millions of other women out there have. If you think I'm going to fall for this rubbish you must have a pretty low opinion of me. It's the old story, isn't it: you had a woman and you want me to believe you were going to leave her.'

She starts to get up, abandoning the coffee, but he grabs her hand and stops her, his grip tight enough to bruise.

'No. Wait! I know that's what it sounds like, but it's not what you think.' His voice is so sharp it is arresting; she looks into his eyes and sees his pupils black, dilated. There's no way of untangling these battling threads of hurt, hope and disappointment. She sits back down, reluctantly.

'What is it, Callum? What is it that makes you so different?'

'Rosie – that night in Oxford, I felt a special bond between us. What we shared in childhood all came back. I know you felt it too. And then you acted so weirdly, pushed me away. I thought, best not get involved. I got engaged during the next year.' She can't help wincing as he says it. 'It was all very recent. But – but then you turned up again. And, Rosie, I realized something. I'd just been looking for you.'

She stares at him, shaking her head, not understanding. Now he's rummaging in his pockets like an excited schoolboy. Impossible not to smile a little as he unloads the motley booty: keys, a crumpled shopping list, a defunct biro, a dry-cleaning chit. Now he's finally found his wallet, his fingers clamp round it triumphantly. She's reminded of her hassled self, flustering for loose change at the checkout queue.

Callum opens the wallet and delves behind the rainbow of credit cards. Clearly tense with anticipation, he extracts a folded photograph. He spreads it straight on the table, slides it towards her.

'There, me and my fiancée. Now tell me, what d'you see?'

Rosie doesn't know what to make of this. If she didn't feel so burned by it all, she'd be tempted to laugh. She's never been in love like this, or hurt like this, and now her cheating beau is sitting opposite her, pleading for forgiveness for two-timing her by showing her a picture of his fiancée.

'Callum, this is –'

'Stop, Rosie. Look. I want you to tell me if you see it.'

'You're crazy, I swear it.' But she looks down all the same. The picture looks ordinary enough, the background a bright summer garden. Both Callum and his girlfriend appear to shine with youth and confidence. Their smiles are wide and white and Callum's dark hair thick and lustrous. The girl is pretty, as you'd expect: red hair, white skin, green eyes. True, she and Callum are smiling more with fondness than with passion; there is no leaning in towards each other, no casual brushing of shoulders. Less intimacy than comfortableness. But what does that prove?

'Now, d'you see?' says Callum, like a magician who's pulled off some wild party trick. Rosie looks at him askance, wondering what on earth she's missed: when did the flashbulbs explode, the jack leap from his box? But Callum's enthusiasm is undimmed, his words slippery, urgent. 'You don't see it, Rosie, but look again. She looks like you, doesn't she?'

Rosie is so startled by this assertion that at first her muscles freeze. Then she hunches down over the picture in unashamed scrutiny. Certainly it's obvious that there are superficial likenesses, but now she starts to see beyond the simple jigsaw of colouring, to the broad-boned skull beneath the skin, the full but slightly crooked mouth. The girl is taller and more voluptuous than she is – but, yes, there is a strong resemblance. Or is she simply seeing things through Callum's eyes, moulded by his manic persuasion?

'Callum, I – I don't know. What d'you want me to say? Yes, she looks like me. Or I look like her. Perhaps we're both just your type.'

'*You're* my type, Rosie. You were the first, after all. It's like I've only just realized it. I've always been looking for you.'

Rosie breathes out slowly, aware of her lungs deflating. 'Callum, don't do the extravagant romantic. You should know that won't wash with me.' Although her heart beats uncomfortably and she thinks she must be blushing. She picks up the picture. 'What's her name, your fiancée?'

'Shona.'

'She's pretty.'

'Yes, she is.' He looks at his fingernails. 'Rosie, I know you think I'm a bastard. But I've made a horrible mistake. I'm telling Shona it's over.' Rosie reaches for her coffee, but a mouthful dribbles on to her white robe. As the stain seeps into the towelling, she feels clumsy and unseemly. Callum, gnawing his fingers distractedly, clearly hasn't noticed. 'Rosie, there's no slick or original way of saying this. But I'm begging you to listen. Please give me another chance.'

*

Rosie sits at the tiny, Formica-topped table. A muffled voice from above blares words she cannot make out

– first in English, then French, then a hard, guttural German. The microphoned sound is so smudged it's a wonder anyone understands anything. For the umpteenth time, she unzips her bag, checking everything is there: keys, wallet, passport, a neat mini-dictionary. A pleasant nervousness knots and unknots in her stomach.

At least she didn't yield immediately. Give her that much credit. She made him wait for her, plead with her, until she was sure. It was difficult, especially when he was putting so much effort into it. Telephoning her, sending cards and flowers, booking fancy restaurants and paying. And, yes, he's assured her that it's all off with Shona. Even now, she's not sure if she believes him just because she wants to. A wish so hard, so all-consuming that it keeps her awake at night. But she's turned wary of him, still raw. Their relationship's become almost chaste.

It's taken until spring for her to agree to this trip. *Don't do it, Ro,* said Felicity, *this guy sounds like bad news.* And Annie snorted: *He just likes the thrill of the chase.* But she hasn't had a break in the sun for almost two years; her bones ache for some warmth. Callum's arranged a place in Ithaca, where the spring heat will just be simmering. He's booked them a villa, the plan is to have a few days alone there, and then some of his friends will fly out to join them.

Rosie balked at that idea at first, then she felt herself slowly warming to it. Going on holiday with Callum, being acknowledged publicly by his friends: what better validation could there be, what firmer proof that he'd moved on? If she turned him down, played hard to get, he'd surely think her churlish and finally give up. There'd be only herself to blame.

Now she sees him in the middle distance, split away from the crowds, emerging from the newsagent's with a full plastic carrier bag. He sits down opposite and starts to rifle through his purchases.

'Look. I got you a few things.'

Mineral water, newspapers, a bar of chocolate; even a glossy, girly magazine. A host of trivial accessories for the flight, but just as she'd have chosen them. She is constantly floored by the thoughtfulness of these near-hidden, minor gestures, as though he knows exactly what she's missing, and wants to make sure it's all OK. She breaks off a square of chocolate.

'I'm terrified of flying you know. Don't be surprised if I dissolve into tears like a baby.'

'Don't worry,' grins Callum. 'It's quite a short flight. And I'll be there all the way.'

'Well, you really don't have much choice.'

'Don't push your luck.' He clasps her hand beneath the table and squeezes it. The disembodied voice from above says their flight is ready for boarding.

Barring Rosie wobbling once or twice, dangerously close to the brink of vomiting, they touch down on Greek tarmac after a trouble-free flight. A coach parcels them off to a strip of coastline where they catch the ferry to Ithaca. Although it's still only April, the sun is high and sharp in the sky. Everything is bright, clear, defined: as though all England were a dulled living room with lowered blinds and half-spent bulbs, and here someone's taken away the curtains or flooded the place with full, fresh wattage. The splashed deck of the ferry lurches but Rosie no longer feels sick. Salt spray freshens her tongue and she puts her face to the wind.

The villa Callum's booked perches on the slope of a pine forest. It's a box-like angular affair of terra-cotta-washed sandstone, wrought iron balconies and shutters painted a dark bottle-green. Inside, the high ceilings, ceramic floor tiles and spare furniture produce a peculiar blend of sparseness and grandeur. There's a courtyard with gaudy splashes of geranium and bougainvillea and a glittering rectangle of swimming pool that winks in the sun.

'What d'you think?' asks Callum. Rosie puts down her bags and turns away from him, runs delightedly through the corridors. She ascends the cool, stone, winding staircase with its curling, burnished banister; flings open the doors into bedrooms, discovers a hidden, marbled bathroom. Her footsteps and laughter rebound off walls and ceilings.

'I love it! I just love it!'

'I take it you're happy with my choice, then?' Callum joins her at the top of the stairs and rests his chin on her shoulders. 'Of course, one thing about arriving early, we can choose which room we want.'

Predictably, they choose the largest of the double rooms, with its own en suite bathroom and a huge iron-framed bed. It's already been prepared for them, with freshly starched white linen. Best of all, the space occupies a corner of the villa, so there are two balconies with French windows, one facing south, the other east. The southern terrace overlooks the courtyard, where the strongest afternoon heat collects. The eastern one is Rosie's favourite, it will catch the flimsier rays at sunrise; its view sneaks glimpses of the edge of the pine forest, and the cove and sea beyond.

After unpacking, they run through the house like children. They put light shirts and trousers over swimming things and find the path that leads down to the beach. Although they can see it from the balcony, at ground level it's almost hidden. The prickly branches are so low in places they have to bend to keep from being scratched. The earth kicks up a dry, red dust. There's a clean and distant smell of lemons. Rosie's sandal hits a boulder and she skids, nearly toppling over. Callum catches her before she's fallen, or gets her backside pink and dusty.

'This remind you of anything?' he asks, with a conspiratorial smile. And she doesn't answer, but smiles also, because this transports her back in time too.

They reach a clearing and the path dips and then

there it is: the sea. The smooth turquoise water froths against the pale-grey shingle. There are a few out-of-season idle surfboards, and a hardy, distant bather, but apart from that the beach is empty. Not exactly a tourist trap, and too early in the year for the heat to have gathered.

'Almost like our own private beach,' says Callum. 'We can do exactly as we want.'

Before Rosie can blink, he's peeling off his shirt and trousers, kicking off his leather sandals and wading in towards the shallows. She watches as the water gathers to his thighs, then his waist, then he flips himself forwards and is lost beneath its quiet surface. When he comes back up his mouth is sprouting foam jets like a whale, his hair glistens black and flat against his scalp and he's coming back to get her.

'Come on in, it's paradise.'

She squeals like a rodent as he scrambles towards her, knowing her aversion to cold. But he's stripping her almost brutally, and pulling her back in with him. The water hits her like a shock, like a sharp slap or a knife.

'Bastard! Too cold, too cold!'

He pushes her under, and when she splutters up she sees that he is laughing. She chucks the spume into his face and makes her way back to the shore. 'Too cold! Let's go back.' She's shivering so hard she can hardly get the words out. He holds her close and rubs her body, making sure the blood flows free again.

Then he gives her a warm, wet, briny kiss and she can almost crunch the grains of salt.

Over the next few days, they learn what it is like to wake to the sound of water raking shingle, to fling open the shutters and inhale fresh pine spliced with eucalyptus. For breakfast, they eat bread and Greek olives on the east balcony, and take turns to pad down to the kitchen for fresh coffee. They get to know the local village; the cheapest restaurants, the finest cheese shops. Rosie discovers that during a quite specific slice of afternoon, there's a corner of the courtyard which brews the heat up like an oven. If she lies in the right place for the right time, she gets hot enough to swim. Climbing out of the pool, she settles back down on the warm stone, and sees the outline of her body picked out by tiny jewels of water. Then Callum's weight and shadow are over her, his tongue carving a path between the droplets, his breath hot between her breasts, over her belly, on the slope of skin between her hip bones. Her limbs shiver but her skin warms. She snakes her fingers through his dark hair and slackens her thighs to let him in.

For that precious sliver of time, Rosie collects memories like photographs. She will remember their late morning love-making, sliding in and out of conversation, seeing Callum sit straight and oddly curious, tracing the pattern of her nakedness. The suppers at their local taverna, the air warm with cooking fish, and his detectable annoyance when one of the waiters flirts with her. The way she looks up from her plate and catches him head on one side, watching her. The way he remembers things from their childhood, and details from that night in Oxford. A book she's mentioned she enjoyed; a day she looked particularly miserable. How even when she was eight, and he was already in the senior school, he looked at her one day during playtime and noticed her body slightly changing. Things about herself that even she has forgotten.

All these things Rosie stores in her private album of memories. As well as the way they fall into bed at night, too tired even to make love, and then she wakes up in darkness, her breath stifled, because he's holding her so tight. Despite the discomfort, she doesn't want to lift his heavy arm. And then she moves, and he moves with her, making sure she keeps close, as though even in his dreams he doesn't want to let her wander.

'I wish,' says Rosie, 'that it could always be like this. Not that I don't want to be with your friends, but it's such bliss just us together.' They are sitting on the southern balcony, her with orange juice, Callum with beer. The afternoon sun dips over the crests of pine trees. A van is about to deposit a gaggle of Callum's friends.

'It'll be fun, Rosie. Different, but enjoyable. People are bringing people so I won't know everyone either.'

Rodney, an old schoolmate, is going to be coming

with his new girlfriend; and there'll be Sarah and Jessica, a lesbian couple Callum knows through work. Rosie can't help smiling to herself. Felicity would approve. And Anthony's coming, too, bringing someone unknown. Rosie tries not to prickle when the subject is raised.

'He just makes me uncomfortable. You should be wary, too, after the way he treated me. And he tried to sabotage us.'

'Who can blame him for being jealous?' Callum grins boyishly, generously. 'Look, he's an old friend. It was a misunderstanding.'

'Who's he bringing with him, anyway? Some new girlfriend?' The thought of Anthony with a lady friend seems oddly implausible.

'I don't know. I think it's a friend. Or cousin. We'll soon find out.'

As though on cue, there's the sound of an engine pulling up beyond the courtyard. 'Troops arrive!' exclaims Callum, quite obviously excited. He bounds down the winding stairs and Rosie follows more slowly. Out on the road outside, the van is disgorging its cargo: an assortment of holdalls and suitcases, followed by the human passengers.

From where she stands in the shadows, Rosie sees Sarah and Jessica, two girls with bright freckles, who look more like sisters than lovers. There's a broad, chestnut-haired bloke who must clearly be Rodney, and the pretty, frail, blonde girl with him – that must be his new woman. Rosie feels her spine stiffen, knowing who is to appear next.

Anthony climbs down from the van, sweat glistening on his forehead. He looks absurdly English and old-fashioned, wearing what look as though they're cricketing slacks. He wipes a line of perspiration from the top of one sharp cheekbone, and then turns, beckoning to his guest to alight and stand there with him.

Rosie waits, tense with anticipation, partly in case Anthony sees her lurking there; partly wondering who on earth he's brought with him as a guest. Guessing the sort of woman who'd be his girlfriend is quite intriguing. But the feet and then legs that emerge are quite masculine. Anthony stands by his companion – perhaps his cousin, as Callum said – and the two grow bright and dark in the shifting path of light.

The companion turns towards the house, and looks in Rosie's direction. His gaze burns through the shadows. Rosie stands there rooted, closes her eyes, tries to blink away the vision. Then she turns and rushes for the staircase, because she knows she's going to be sick.

9

The afternoon light was glaring and Callum found it hard to open his eyes fully, and what with that and a slight headache he didn't notice things immediately. He went to the newsagent's for bread and milk and came back swinging a plastic carrier bag, which accessorized his jeans and shirt and made him feel like a scruffy student. 'We could,' DC Fletcher had said, eyes down, fiddling with his nails, 'find you another address. Where you could lie low. Incognito.' And then, when Callum had failed to respond, 'Just for now. In fact, I'd advise it.'

Callum had thanked the policeman, but declined the offer. It was enough that his attacker had wreaked such havoc already: the last thing he wanted was to be driven from his cherished home. In any case, bit by bit all trace of grandeur was being stripped away from him. It was like going back in time only without the resurgent, youthful energy.

Head down, he reached his front drive, where he dropped his newspaper and bent to retrieve it. There was a soft quiet broken only by the distant revving of engines, the fluting of birdsong and the slighter sounds of suburbia. And something else – nearer: the clunk of wood on wood, a beating and a squeaking to the rhythm of the breeze. Callum stayed crouched on the drive trying to work out what it was. When he looked up, the sun caught his eyes, and he saw only a whitened, heated blur. He stood slowly and approached the house, noticing the clunking growing louder. A jagged edge of fierce brightness picked out the stained glass around the doorway, and it was then that he noticed the front door was open.

Callum knew at once this was not his own absent-mindedness. His eyes might have taken to mocking him, but his mind was still meticulous. Besides, he'd not been too long gone, and could remember leaving earlier, thinking it felt warmer outside than in, chinking the key inside the lock. He could feel the edge of metal now, jangling inside his front pocket. He stepped across the threshold trying not to make a sound.

Because the hall was windowless it was like stepping into darkness. The contrast with clear daylight made it seem murky and surreal. Callum strained to see signs of disturbance – a displaced rug or crooked umbrella, but everything was as usual, bar the rudely gaping door. And then a sound came from the back of the house – floating forwards from the kitchen. The clink of metal on china; the rush of water into the sink. There was the lightest of footsteps: the sense of someone moving swiftly.

The sweat had gathered on Callum's brow and part of him wanted to turn and flee. He had his mobile phone with him: he could call someone from outside. But the breezy ordinariness of this person's noises made him want to press onwards. From the lightness of the sound, he would guess it was a woman.

He put down the bag and newspaper, and both rustled in the quiet, but whoever it was in the kitchen just kept on going about their business. Then he stood flat against the wall, like a skulking gangster in a movie, and through the rectangle of brightness he could see right through into the garden. A tall woman with strong shoulders stood by the sink, her back to him. When she turned to the side he couldn't quite catch her profile for the lines of her face appeared to stretch, then collapse. But he knew the dark mass of hair that snaked and coiled at her neck, the long, white hands, now slightly knotty, and the pose of grave intent. His chest muscles relaxed and he wanted to laugh out loud.

'Mother!' he said. 'What on earth are you doing?'

She turned, with a dramatic little yelp, and placed a hand across her chest. 'Jesus, Callum. D'you have to sneak up on me like that? You scared me out of my wits.'

'I could say the same for you, Mother. Creeping into my kitchen like a burglar. It could have been absolutely anyone. D'you know you left the front door open?'

He went to kiss her on the cheek, and saw she was filling a small watering can. 'I was just going out into the front to water a few of your plants. Especially the hydrangeas and potted shrubs – they're as dry as dust in this hot weather. Callum, d'you have to neglect things so?'

She carried the watering can through the hallway with the same straight-backed briskness she'd had in her youth. This time, coming back in, she made sure the door was firmly closed.

Callum laughed, despite himself. 'Fortunately, you haven't quite frightened me to death. At least I'm still alive to tell you how great it is to see you.' He spread his arms to embrace her but to his surprise his mother stepped up to him, and cupped his face with both her hands.

'Callum, you always try to be so strong. But I know what's been happening. You've been brief with me on the telephone, and that time I spoke to you, I knew something was wrong. I phoned Chambers, and asked when you'd be back from court, and they told me you were ill. I thought, if he hasn't told me, he must have his reasons. And then I was shopping and I bumped into Shona, of all people, and she said, *Colleen, haven't you heard?* She told me there'd been some kind of accident. And then that snippet in the paper – I've been half-worried to death.'

He put one hand over hers. 'Mother, I'm so sorry. I would never have wanted you to find out like this – I should have told you earlier. I just didn't want to worry you.'

She placed a hand across his brow as though to

check for childish fever. 'You don't think I'm worried this way? Now tell me, what's been going on?'

They both drew up chairs and he was reminded of his schooldays when he'd rush home and they'd settle down together and he'd regale her with his triumphs. This time the narrative was slightly less glorious.

'You're right, Mother,' he admitted. 'I have been odd with you on the phone. There are things I've wanted to discuss, but I just couldn't bring myself to tell you. The truth is, as you may realize now from the papers, a short while ago, I was attacked on the heath. No, please' – he gripped her fingers – 'honestly, it's not that bad. Whoever it was didn't take anything, and I wasn't hurt, not really. There're just one or two small things.' He loosened his grip round her fingers, but she took his back into her own.

'But, Callum, they told me you were ill. What exactly is the matter?'

'There's nothing to worry about, Mother. Though we do need to talk about this. I need to find out if anything runs in the family.' Her eyebrows shot towards her hairline, and he softened his voice immediately. 'It's just a small thing. A little trouble with my eyes.'

'You mean to say you can't see properly?' Her voice rose in consternation.

'I can see, I can get around, but there are occasional headaches. And, it's difficult to explain, but I do tend to get confused.'

'You've seen a doctor? A specialist?'

'He said it was the result of a head injury and there was nothing they could do.' The words sounded thin and sad. 'But he can't be right, of course. He wants to refer me for brain scans, but there's another avenue I'm looking at. There's someone else, another specialist, I've read about him on the internet. At the moment, he's involved in some research project at London University, and there's a long waiting list to see him, but he might be free by the end of summer. I'll be there, at the head of the queue. I know I'm going to get better.'

His mother stood, rubbing the heels of her palms against her skirt. She tilted his face up towards hers, so they were staring, eye to eye. He took in the fine grain of her skin and the bold set of her jaw.

'Yes, Callum, you will get better, if that's what's meant to be. Or you will get better in your own time, in your own way. But if you end up less than perfect there's no shame in that. It's all right to fall short, to feel weak some of the time.'

He looked at her silently.

'What I don't like to see is you shambling around this big old house alone, cutting yourself off from the outside world as though you're tied to the past. It's been years now since Shona's gone, not weeks or even months. Are you sure you're still happy here?'

'Mother, we've been through this before. You know how I love the place.'

Callum set his jaw sullenly. *Move on*, Colleen would say to him. *With your money you'd have no trouble finding somewhere nice. One of those trendy loft apartments made of pale wood, glass and chrome, or a Regency town house, if you've set your heart on something bigger. A place to start afresh. Empty of memories.*

But what she didn't understand was that what he wanted were the memories. The wide sweep of lit-up bay that had welcomed his and Shona's party guests; the country-pine and flagstoned kitchen where Shona had quietly stacked the breakfast plates. The steps of the paved terrace that led out on to the grass, where Rudy learnt to leap – laughing, squealing – on to the soft, bright stretch of lawn.

Colleen shook her head and moved her mouth, as though muttering soundlessly. It was a habit she'd had for as long as he could remember: momentarily withdrawing, working something out inwardly. She sat back, folded her arms, gazed about her as though searching for something: stood briefly, walked to the dresser, began to study a photograph.

'The children,' she said softly, turning the photograph in her hands. 'You said you wanted to speak to me about seeing them again.'

Callum went and stood by her, looking over her shoulder at the picture. It had been taken years ago at a garden party, when he'd had a sense of his own resilience which now appeared to him ludicrous. He'd been working on a case with both Anthony and James – Anthony as a fellow defence barrister,

James as a street-smart enquiry agent, tracking down recalcitrant witnesses. In the photograph, Callum's mouth was wide with laughter, as he supported Rudy between his knees. Anthony and James grinned together with faux male camaraderie, while Shona stood slightly apart, her weight slanted over one hip.

'I hate that picture,' said Callum. 'I don't know why I keep it there – I suppose it's just so nice of me and Rudy.'

'You know,' said his mother, 'I never did like James. Good at his job, yes, but there was always something coarse about him. As though he spent too much time among the lowlife and it rubbed off on him too keenly. All that time, pretending to be your friend, and then running off with Shona.'

Callum opened his mouth, then closed it, considering. 'Well, yes. And no. I mean Shona's always going on about him being unpredictable, and how insecure he gets, but sometimes I do wonder. I mean I do think he's bothered because we've never got divorced, but a part of me suspects . . . Well, Shona does have a tendency to dramatize. It has crossed my mind once or twice that maybe she's the one who's making things difficult.'

Colleen looked at him, her lips curled. 'That sounds to me like you're up for a challenge. If that's what you think, there's only one way to find out.'

Callum nodded, also smiling now. 'I'm just going to have to go and see the children myself, aren't I?

I can't wait all my life for someone else's permission. For heaven's sake, I am their father.'

She clapped her hands together. 'That's more like the Callum I know.'

'Well, that's who I'm going to be again. No minor attack or little illness is going to get me down. Reckon I'll go back into Chambers as well, sort things out properly with Guy.'

She pressed his fingers between her palms as though in silent encouragement, and he thought how tall and unstooped she was, how handsome her bone structure. Of all the women in his life she was by far the most loyal. He wanted desperately to protect her, to stop anything from harming her; but so often, of the two of them, it was she who seemed the stronger.

The telephone rang and their fingers disentangled. Callum walked into the hallway and picked up the receiver.

'Yes? Yes, it is . . . Ah, good afternoon to you.'

He could hear his mother moving crockery quietly and softening her tread. Too subtle to hover at his shoulder, she'd be bound to listen anxiously while appearing to remain nonchalant.

'I see . . . Yes; that doesn't entirely surprise me . . . Yes, well, I'd do the same in that position. It's the obvious next step to take.'

He gave a few more acquiescent murmurings and the conversation petered to its close. 'Well, goodbye and thanks for ringing. Thanks for letting me know.'

'Who was that?' asked his mother, who was already getting out the lunch things.

'That was DC Fletcher, the officer investigating my case. We speak from time to time. He keeps me informed of developments.'

'Oh? And what . . . developments . . . have there been this time?'

'There's a man who's been charged with the heath murder, the one they think attacked me too. He's been remanded in custody. They put him on an ID parade.'

'And?'

Callum paused, but he knew he was going to have to tell the truth. 'He wasn't picked out. They think his lawyers'll go for bail.'

After the discussion with his mother, it seemed the natural thing to head into Chambers to tidy up loose ends with Guy.

In the clerks' room he saw Freddy, and they greeted each other without a flicker. The skinny youth appeared relaxed, never on the verge of recalling anything embarrassing about the last visit. Guy, relieved of the burden of breaking the bad news about Lansdowne, was clearly more at ease. They chatted about Callum's caseload, and it transpired that despite the alarming sparsity of papers on his office shelves, no clients except Lansdowne had expressed dissatisfaction. Everyone was waiting for his return, wishing him better. As soon as he felt ready, he could pick up where he'd left off.

'What about the burglary?' asked Callum. 'The theft of my computer. Any more news on that?'

Guy shook his head, but Callum laughed. 'Oh, well, thank God for back up disks, eh?' Perhaps, he reflected, as he meandered down the corridor to the Gents, a random computer illiterate had stolen his desktop, who'd never prize out its confidential information. He stood in the passage opposite the conference room, because the bathroom had an engaged sign; and then the door opened and a man came out, and everything started to go wrong again.

He didn't recognize him instantly, after all they'd only met a few times. And then there were the prosecution photographs, though they could be grossly distorting. In this light, away from windows, and his eyes not what they used to be, if they hadn't been standing quite so close he might not have made the connection. The man had white teeth and black skin and was wearing plentiful, spicy aftershave; he had on a sharp suit that clearly wasn't a barrister's. He was youthful and clean and well-kept, and quite obviously monied, but nevertheless something indefinable told Callum he was a client.

And then, the thing was, the man recognized him. He looked round where he stood, and smiled a healthy but forced smile.

'Hello, Mr Scott. How you been keeping?'

Callum blinked and his brain ticked as the jigsaw fell together. Now he recalled and understood. He was looking at Jason Lansdowne.

'Mr Lansdowne ... Jason. This is a surprise.' It was, in more ways than one. 'Aren't you meant to be in custody?'

Lansdowne looked at his shoes and smiled rather charmingly.

'I'm sorry – I didn't mean –' Callum tried to rephrase his sentence.

'That's all right, Mr Scott. I understand what you mean. Truth is, they've reduced the charges. So now I'm out on bail. Looks like my case is going well now. Here for a con with Mr Portman.'

'Yes,' said Callum. 'I see.'

It was difficult to be offended by anything about this young man; he'd always smell fresh, listen carefully, remember to say thank you. He was of a particular class of criminal recognized by all defence lawyers: they scrubbed up well, they learned their lines, they never let you see their seamy side. Indeed, if you were one of their crew, they might move heaven and earth for you. Sometimes there could grow up a strange but genuine affection.

As far as Lansdowne was concerned, Callum had been part of his crew. Then he'd been pushed out inexplicably. That sour knowledge hung between them. It was Lansdowne who broached it first.

'Mr Scott, about my case. I know you was meant to be my brief. I just want you to know, about the switch, please don't take it the wrong way.'

'That's all right, Jason,' said Callum, trying hard to be polite.

'I mean you done a good job for my brother, in the past and that. I just don't want this to be personal. I mean, it wasn't all down to me.'

The man turned away from him to go into the conference room, but Callum, against his better judgment, caught and held him by the forearm.

'Jason, I don't follow. Did someone else tell you to sack me? If it wasn't down to you, then who?'

Lansdowne grinned rather mirthlessly and shook his head slowly. He lifted Callum's arm away, lightly. A hint of patois sneaked into his accent.

'Nah, nah, Mr Scott. It ain't that easy, you know. There's things I can't talk about. Trust me, you better off not knowing.'

There was just that trace of Lansdowne's other side, the part that was bloody and dishonest. And the part that would swaggeringly enjoy getting the better of anyone.

'What is it, Jason? What am I better off not knowing?'

Lansdowne slouched against the wall. His feet were splayed and pelvis slanted in a pose of almost sexual arrogance.

'Mr Scott,' he advised, 'people like you, you're good with words and bits of paper. But there's things you should stay out of. Like you deal with murders all the time, but you ain't seen no dead bodies.'

Callum was unsure what Lansdowne was getting at, although the boastful, bravura tone was not unusual with cons like him when they wanted to show who was boss. In fact, the man was wrong. Callum *had* seen a dead body. If he thought back long and hard enough, he could still see the skewed neck bones and the skin drained of vital colour. But it was a little piece of personal history that he'd long been silent over. It was many years ago now and nothing to do with his career.

He had the urge to put Lansdowne in his place, but recognized that would get him nowhere. He started to say, 'If you'd just tell me –' but then the door to the conference room opened.

'Jason.' Anthony stood there, glowering. 'I was rather wondering where you'd got to. If you'd like to go back in, perhaps we can resume our conference.'

Lansdowne slipped smiling through the door but Anthony stayed in the corridor. 'Callum, good to see you around.' His voice was a little too loud.

At that moment in time, Callum had no wish to confront his friend, and he started on an automatic spiel about coming in to sort his work out. But Anthony leaned in and lowered his voice to a whisper.

'Don't get clever with me, Callum. I know what you've been up to. Cassandra caught you snooping the other day and I know you were looking at my papers. Not that it matters – but this case is mine now. Highly irregular, don't you think, to accost ex-clients outside conference?'

Callum leant away from Anthony and straightened his tie. Without saying anything, he turned and walked away down the corridor.

*

Since their separation, Shona had moved steadily northward, to the outskirts of a suburbia that was barely London any more. Callum thought of it as a limbo land that was neither town nor country. A place mapped only by the outer pages of the largest A–Zs.

Callum travelled to the end of the tube line and stepped out into the open. He walked the slope of the station approach and looked to hail himself a minicab. A rank of secondhand Fords and Volvos with white 'Taxi' signs sat waiting. Nothing so metropolitan as a London black cab.

The back seat of the taxi was a beige leather that the sun had warmed. Callum rolled up his shirtsleeves and wound down the window. The sound of the streets was a soft, subdued hum. Everywhere on the high road were strolling mothers with babies, and clutches of middle-aged women in the throes of heated gossip. Jason Lansdowne would have stood out like a sore thumb if you dumped him here. Although the air was clear and quiet, Callum found it oddly stifling.

The taxi gathered speed as it drove into widening streets. Eventually it pulled up in a sun-dappled avenue full of mansions half hidden at the end of long driveways. Ornamental security gates were common here, as was varying mock-historic architecture. Monochrome mock-Tudor follies stood alongside red-brick neo-Georgiana. It was one of these latter edifices which now housed Callum's family.

Callum walked carefully up the drive, trying to recall the last time he'd been here. The front lawn was freshly clipped and seemed to sparkle with newness. He didn't like to breathe too hard or scuff his toe along the pathway. He was careful to wipe his shoes as he arrived on the front porch.

Several times, on the way here, he had thought how reckless to arrive unannounced. He could not even be sure that anyone would be in. But it was a weekday afternoon and the school day would be finished. And at least by coming here unplanned he could not be deterred, or avoided.

He took a breath, and with one tentative finger pressed the doorbell. The first few feathered chimes of 'Ding Dong Bell' rang out. Callum waited on the doorstep wondering what he'd say to Shona. He'd be unthreatening and conciliatory, not as though he were intruding. Better not murmur too softly, or lean too close, or breathe the scent off her skin; above all better not hark back to that last slice of fleeting intimacy. He had to watch his step here in unwelcome, alien country.

But the light patter down the hallway told him it wasn't Shona coming. There was a high boyish voice – 'Can I open it? Can I?', and a lower, gruffer, male voice saying, 'Careful, now, careful.' The wide door swung open and there stood Rudy and James.

Any ambivalence or awkwardness Callum had felt on making this journey was washed away by the sight of his seven-year-old son. Rudy stared up at him, with his own dark curls and searching eyes. He shouted 'Daddy!' and jumped up into his father's arms.

A warmth flared up inside Callum, tickling his skin and his ribs. He briefly nuzzled his son's hair, which smelt of a childish, milky soapiness. He could detect, too, the scent of the slightly soiled summer shirt, the boyish sweat, mud and grass. He pulled his son a little closer. Through the thin cotton shirt he could feel Rudy's bones and sinews. The boy wriggled away from him and Callum ruffled his hair.

'Looking well, young man. Just came by to see how you're doing.'

Rudy started squealing something about football, and about playing in the garden. Callum straightened his back and readjusted his gaze. James was standing further in, in an alcove off the hallway, beneath a wall-mounted cuckoo clock that Callum had always found ridiculous. James was several years younger than him, with fair hair and muscled shoulders. Now they eyed each other with a wariness, an almost bestial mistrust, that Callum came across only rarely in good-looking, rival men.

'Callum, we're not expecting you. You've no arrangement to see the children.'

His voice was measured, neither warm nor cold, without modulation, except for the occasional hint of defiance. Callum spoke slowly, breathing moderately, determined to control the anger which had started to bubble inside him.

'Is Shona in?'

'She's not here. She's taken Saffron to a kiddies' party. I'm looking after Rudy.'

'Right. Well.' In an odd way, he was relieved. Shona's absence seemed less complicated, removing the spike of lover's jealousy. 'Well, it was really the kids I came to see.'

James nodded as the cuckoo clock chimed the quarter hour above him. Callum noticed he was holding a dishcloth: an oddly female accessory.

'I suppose you'd better come in.'

As soon as he'd stepped across the threshold Rudy restarted yelling. 'Daddy, Daddy, are we going outside? Are we going to play football?'

'Well, I'm not sure about that. I don't know how long I'll be staying.' He glanced over at James. 'Why don't you run out in the garden, while I have a little chat here?'

Rudy did as he was told and the two men stood there, awkwardly.

'Look,' said James, 'I understand how you want to see the kids. But I'm not sure it's a good idea just descending unannounced. I mean, obviously Rudy and Saffron adore you, but random visits could get them overexcited. These things need to be planned.'

Callum opened his mouth, prepared to respond, to stand his ground, to announce to all who might listen that no one could stop him seeing his children. But then he stopped. Despite the unpleasantness of seeing someone else taking his place, he was momentarily floored by the other man's reason. Could the unthinkable be true, that Shona exaggerated James's obstinacy, and that in fact, without her, a calmer logic descended? Was it simply feminine caprice that brought out the men's rivalry?

'Stay for now,' suggested James. 'And we can arrange something another time.'

Callum went out on to the lawn where his son was toying with a football. Rudy showed off his skills eagerly, glowing with unashamed pride, and it didn't take long to make his father quite breathless. Afterwards they went in together, and Callum gave him one last hug.

'You'd better go and do your homework now. It won't be long till we meet again.' The skin on his son's cheek was absurdly soft beneath his fingers. He swallowed as Rudy ran upstairs, and then James walked him down the path. The two men stayed self-conscious, about a foot apart, as though to touch each other's skin might cause burns or minor injuries.

'Well then, I suppose we'll be seeing you. I'll have a word with Shona.'

A car meandered by and honked, and James turned his head and waved. A smile lit up his handsome features for the first time that afternoon. Callum followed his gaze and saw the flash of a woman – a column of russet brown and green which fizzed and flared before his eyes. The sun shone on to her dress, which glittered like a second skin.

'Shona,' he started to say, and then stopped short, embarrassed. James looked at him, curiously.

'Something wrong with your eyesight? That's one of our neighbours.'

'It – it's just the green dress. I thought Shona – had one like it.' He was wrong of course: the hair was too dark for Shona anyway. But he had started to falter, remembering the detail of their last meeting, of her grainy skin on his, of the need to keep it secret. Yet when he looked back at James, there was no glower of suspicion, just an arrogant smirk, a hint of someone self-satisfied.

'Shona doesn't have a green dress. She's hardly got anything green. She stopped wearing the colour ages ago, got fed up with all the clichéd, Irishy comments.' He was poised to go back into the house, but paused as though he'd scored a point, smiling with a quiet triumph. 'How well d'you think you know your wife?'

10

Rosie stands on the eastern balcony and stares out towards the pine forest. She can see the beginning of the sea path clearly, curving and tunnelling down to the beach. If she leans to the right, she can glimpse also the corner of the courtyard, already starting to bake on this unseasonally hot day. Sarah and Jessica are down there now, their high-pitched squealing floating up to her. There is the slapping sound of cream being slathered on to skin; male laughter – probably Rodney's – and the splash of a dive into the pool. All that, and then in here, the iron bed and fresh white linen. She feels a pull inside her chest.

But there's no choice; it has to be done: she shrugs and heads for the landing. Her heart thuds a little harder in the stairwell, a vulnerable place to be caught alone. Once she's down on the ground floor she can see out through the French windows, and also smell the coffee and the warm bread that the others had for breakfast. Anthony is talking to Callum but there's no sign of Claude, his companion. Rosie straightens her shirt and steps into the sunshine.

Sarah and Jessica have planted sun-loungers in the hottest, brightest corner. Both have taken off their bikini tops to expose small breasts and pointed nipples. The skin on show is fair and freckled, exuding the thick, sweet smell of suntan lotion. They've joined their sun-loungers together and their bodies snake towards each other, in a brazen show of intimacy that Rosie finds oddly disturbing. It's not, she tells herself, that they're both women, but that it's just so . . . *public.* Would she dare to paw and nuzzle Callum so boldly, in front of all the others? For a moment the scene plays before her, and her heart twists with desire – and an afterbeat of sadness, at having to let it go.

She presses on to the other side of the pool, where Callum and Anthony are talking. Callum's shoulder muscles are slightly stiff – you can see the knots beneath the skin. Water drips down from his hair forming dark stains on the paving stones, his whole body awash with droplets which reflect the sun like sequins. He's disagreeing over something with Anthony, engaged in a mini-argument. Anthony's voice is lowered, his words hidden from all but Callum. Rodney crashes into the pool and swims over to flirt with the lesbians. His girlfriend, Fiona, sits reading in a shady spot. There's still no sign of Claude.

Then Anthony glances her over Callum's shoulder and immediately breaks off what he's saying. He walks away towards the shady spot to sit down by Fiona. Apart from Rosie, who's got long shorts on, he's the only one who's dressed: Fiona has on a pink sarong and all the others are in swimming things.

Rosie starts to feel uncomfortable, knobbly-kneed and baggy like a schoolboy. Then Callum turns and waves at her, his wet arm spraying water. Before she can reach him where he's standing he's dived back into the pool, and is splashing about and laughing at her from the water.

'Rosie. It's so fabulous in here! Get your clothes off and jump in.'

'It looks great, Callum, but I can't. Not just now. I have to talk to you.'

She fears she sounds like a damp squib, stiff and formal and maiden-auntish, standing there in her long shorts while the others splay bare, glistening thighs. Callum disappears beneath the blue surface, before bubbling up just by the pool's edge. Then he hauls himself out on to the paving stones, accompanied by an arc of moisture. Jessica shakes her thighs ostentatiously, like she's bothered by the droplets. Callum's trunks cling to his groin and his torso heaves with gulps of breath. Despite themselves, Sarah and Jessica stare in unashamed scrutiny. Rosie quells a stab of jealously.

'Darling, there's something I have to tell you.'

'What is it, Ro? Aren't you feeling any better?' Everyone knows that she was sick; she pretended some fish they'd bought from the village had disagreed with her. Callum reaches for a towel and comes to stand up close, in front of her. She can almost feel the droplets springing off him, and her own skin turning watery. It's half-arousing, half-distracting, because there are other things on her mind.

'Actually, I'm not feeling so great. I think I'm really coming down with something.' He puts his hand above her waistband and starts rubbing her stomach. 'Also I spoke to my mother this morning; I called her from the village. Something's happened at home, she didn't sound too good either.' Callum makes as though to hold her, to rub in a little sympathy, but she steps slightly away from him, because she wants to get this over with. 'I'm really sorry, Callum, but I'm going to have to go home early.'

'No, not really?' He pulls away from her, startled. 'Honestly, is it that bad?'

'Don't worry about me. It's just better this way.' She smiles at him thinly, hoping to come up with a better lie later. 'Better let's talk when we're alone.' She nods vaguely at the others.

His brow is furrowed with concern, a disappointment which at other times might have pleased her. Except just now she's burning up because the whole thing's so unfair. 'Well, how soon exactly d'you have to go?'

'I popped into the travel shop this morning. I can get a flight tomorrow evening. It'll cost that bit extra, but it's no big deal.'

'Jesus, Rosie, you really have to go? And we're having such a fabulous time.'

She winds an arm around his wet waist. 'It's been

the best week of my life. I'm sorry to spoil it. But let's enjoy every last minute.'

Rosie runs down to where the forest's edge meets the mouth of the pathway. She bends to clear her way into the tunnel of branches, but she's going so quickly, it's almost like a dive. She's been running fast, and her heart's beating; out in this quiet she hears it clearly. There's just her breathing, and in the near distance, the light lapping of waves.

She makes for the clearing, before the path dips towards the beach. Sifted through pine branches, the sun makes a leopardskin of the earth. She sits down against a large boulder, regardless of the pink dirt. Her last afternoon on the island, and she's spending most of it alone.

Callum and the others have jumped in the jeep for a drive. They're headed a couple of miles up the coast to explore some locally renowned diving school. Callum's been boasting about the various certificates he's got, and of his knowledge of marine biology, also daring the others to meet his challenge of diving when the waters are still spring-cold. The lesbians went all girly and dewy-eyed listening to him, saying how they wanted to try it too; and of course Rodney couldn't be out-machoed, had to rise to the challenge.

Callum turned raised, questioning eyebrows towards her, but Rosie said she didn't mind. *No, no, go. I'll be fine. Besides, I need the time to pack.* Anyway, he's promised to be back early enough to drive her to the ferry, and they can say their goodbyes in private, away from all the others here. Last night, long after the others slept, they stayed awake with the French doors open, and the bedsheets thrown back. Well into the early hours when it was not quite dark and not quite light they formed shadow shapes against the white walls, arched apart, then colliding. She started as hard as she could to see clearly in the dimness, taking in Callum's outline, measuring his body's every crevice. She knows the swivel of his shoulders, the flicker of his curious fingers. Now the skin on her thighs is sore and tender; she can still feel his rawness against her. Going home early isn't so bad – it has its advantages, after all.

Nevertheless, part of her still wonders if she's doing the right thing. She hasn't explained properly to Callum – that'll have to wait till London – and her stomach goes a little colder when she thinks that he might doubt her. She could stay, and tell him now, but that would cause too much of a scene, especially with Anthony and Claude hovering, ever-ready to contradict her. What Anthony already knows – or believes he knows – she doesn't like to think.

Ignoring it is out of the question. Too frightening – what might happen next? The situation seems so nightmarish, she half-wonders if she's right, but then she thinks it through again, and it all makes sense. She's sure.

Claude – Anthony's cousin, and his senior by six

years, but the likeness so remarkable that almost everybody comments on it. That would account for the lurching memories that swam through her on first seeing Anthony. And didn't Callum say a cousin of Anthony's had known her mother? Right age, right connection – there's no question the jigsaw fits.

Rosie draws her knees up to her chin, sits the way she used to sit in childhood. It was all right earlier, standing there as they bundled into the jeep, carrying their packets of biscuits and plastic bottles of mineral water and the foldaway map. The others scrambling into the sun-warmed seats while Callum stood by the roadside, and they gazed fondly at each other and exchanged sentimental pleasantries.

—Take care, I've heard it's dangerous under those waves.

—Take care, I've heard packing suitcases can at times be quite hazardous.

—Don't forget to come back.

—Don't you dare leave without me.

But later, when she heard the clank of the courtyard gate and someone coming back too early, she didn't have to look to know the arrival wasn't Callum. She gazed over the balcony and saw a tall, willowy figure, striding lazily past the swimming pool and up inside the house. Even now, she doesn't know if Claude came back alone. Has Anthony returned with him? – it's difficult to imagine him in a wetsuit. What about Fiona? Unlike Rodney and the lesbians, she evinced no enthusiasm for diving.

Something dry and coarse and light scratches against the bare skin of Rosie's ankle. She looks down and catches a gecko, slithering its way across the path. Its tail disappears in a small spray of pink dust. Earlier, she'd heard a body clanking about in the kitchen, and then the power-jet of water as someone turned on one of the showers. And then she left – plonked the newly packed holdall on the bed, passport and tickets lined up beside it, and thought she'd escape out here, outside, until the rest of them came back. She ran as though someone were following her, that's why her lungs feel so painful. But probably no one was. Probably she's imagining it. It'll all be OK. She'll just stay here a while longer, surely soon the jeep will return. Callum will want to come back earlyish anyway, to be sure of spending some time with her. The remainder of the packing can be done in just a second.

Her legs are starting to cramp from being bent beneath her chin, and her back is sore from the boulder. She gets up and wanders round the clearing. At the far end where the trees arch up and outwards she can see the sea and sky. From this angle the dip to the beach looks more dramatic than it is – like those trick photos of people appearing to be clinging for life on to a cliff's edge. Still, you have to be quite careful not to slip at the path's end: if you stumbled, and missed your way, you'd have quite a nasty fall.

The sun shines down on to the water, splitting into a thousand diamonds on its surface. The different shades of blue and green are more than picture-postcard perfect. It's such a beautiful day Rosie considers walking down to the sea's edge. But it's safer here – more hidden – and she'll hear the others returning: the jeep's engine growling as it pulls up outside the courtyard.

Rosie finds the gecko again – or perhaps another one – and bends to make friends with it. She wanders around, sits, stands, sits again. There's a snapping of twigs and she turns round with a jolt. Her breathing, calmed now after running, goes shallow again. Nobody's there, and she guesses it must be another unseen forest creature. There's another flash of lizard's tail and she coos out to unnamed fauna. Then a further snapping of twigs – nearer now, and heavier. Rosie stiffens as Claude comes into view at the entrance to the clearing.

'Well, well, Rosie. Fancy finding you here.'

He's obviously just come down from the house, and his hair is freshly showered, slicked black against his scalp, his beak-like nose even more prominent. Same nose as Anthony's, but worse still, if that's possible. She nods towards him in acknowledgment, but doesn't say a word.

Claude enters the clearing and sits against the boulder where she was sitting previously.

'I'm sorry you're leaving so soon. Before I've had a chance to speak to you.' Her heart is beating loudly now; if she spoke her voice would be all wobbly. She's desperate to ask if Fiona or Anthony came back with him, but that would give away her fear. She stares at him mutely, from beneath lowered eyelashes.

'Quite the little hideout you've got here,' he says, standing up, gazing about him. As if he's looking round her flat, or she's a child showing off a tree-house. 'Ah, Rosie, Rosie. You were always one for secret places, those games you loved to play.'

And it's then his voice turns sinister, because she knows that he's remembering. The childhood forest in the garden, the adult games of blind man's buff. They played it once, then twice, then over again, except Rosie never wanted to join in. He never wanted to let her see his face, but now she looks up and catches his eye. She knows he knows she knows. It's like this dirty bond between them.

Claude sits against a tree trunk nearer her. A pine needle pricks his flesh, and he swears softly, exasperated. Rosie smiles at this, in spite of herself: a little prick for a little prick. He mistakes it for camaraderie, and, encouraged, moves still closer.

'You know when Callum first started seeing you – as a grown-up, I mean – Anthony told me about you. Said he fancied you like mad, and it seemed a waste not to do anything about it. Anthony's not a bad chap, you understand, but everyone knew Callum was stringing you along.'

At this, Rosie's teeth clench, and she can no longer remain silent. The mention of Callum is too much.

'What is it you told Anthony?'

'Only the truth, Rosie. There's no need to fret. I knew at once what he meant when he talked about you. I said I knew you slightly. That you were a girl to be reckoned with. One who knew her own appetites.'

Now Rosie cannot contain herself. She gets up, stumbling slightly. 'You bastard. You don't know me at all. I was . . . I was a *child*, for God's sake. Did you tell Anthony that?'

Claude laughs cruelly, but also deludedly. She realizes he might believe his own lies. 'I said I'd known you when we were both a little younger. Who needs to be exact? Anyway, it's true, isn't it? Aren't I right?' He stands, edges towards her. 'Come on, Rosie, don't deny it. Anthony told me the way Callum talks about you, and you should see the way he winks when your face is turned the other way. And I heard you both last night – don't forget my bedroom's next to yours.' He's close enough now to place his fingers round her forearm. 'What's the matter, Rosie? There's no need to be ashamed.'

'Get away from me, you creep.' She steps backwards, away from him. 'And don't speak about Callum like that. That's not how it is between us.'

'Oh-ho. Come on, Rosie, you're a modern woman. Why be coy?' He snatches again at her forearm, but she whips it away from him. A bracelet of purple imprints shows where his fingers pressed her skin. He bends his face towards hers, so near she can smell his breath. It's a strong, synthetic mint; she pictures him shaving, brushing his teeth. Her stomach turns to think how he's prepared himself. She takes another step backwards.

'Don't come any nearer. Don't lay a hand on me.'

'Come on, Rosie. I know you like teasing, but isn't it time to stop playing games?'

She steps sideways along the path, and he steps with her, in her shadow. They move shambling together in an awkward, crab-like shimmy. Her heel hits the sharp edge of a rock and pain shoots up her leg. Together, they shift to the edge of the clearing, the postcard of blue so close it's like they could touch it.

'Just don't try anything, Claude.' She is shocked to hear herself using his name. 'You lay as much as a finger on me and I'm telling Callum, Anthony, everyone. I'm telling them everything.'

'Oh no, you don't.' Now he's near her again, and his fingers are grasping her shoulder. The bone swells beneath his grip, as though fit to burst through the skin. 'You wouldn't do that. Why tell them now after so long? You know they'd never believe you. And just think what I'd tell them. And besides' – now his smile is really nasty and she smells the stale breath beneath the minty one – 'besides, after all, it's me who's telling the truth.'

Rosie prizes his hand away from her but her lungs have swollen in her chest cavity. It's a wonder she can keep breathing. They reach the edge of the clearing, and the sun glancing off water blinds her.

There's a giddiness behind her eyes, the dusty path begins to see-saw. And then she hears it. The sound she'd been hoping for, listening for. An engine slowing at the roadside, a blend of voices, a happy chatter.

'That's it.' Her voice rasps, barely stronger than a whisper. 'That's them – the others. They're back.' She looks defiantly into Claude's eyes. 'Now, see what I'll dare tell them.'

She leaps back into the clearing, away from Claude, and from the shallow cliff's edge. But he's behind, grabbing her arm, bending it, twisting it into her back. He pulls her close in towards him, less than inches from his face. She can see the dark pin-pricks of stubble and the red veins in the whites of his eyes.

'No, you don't. Not so fast.'

'Let go of me. You're hurting me.'

He keeps one hand behind her back, places the other between her shoulder blades. The fingers creep slowly upwards till they're almost curled around her neck. Their two sets of footsteps halt and stutter between boulders. His fingers press tighter, she feels her windpipe constricting. To one side of them, the sky-sea view glitters, tips and sways. Fragments of earth and dirt and gravel spit out from beneath their sandals. The whole of Rosie's head fills up with a harsh funnelling sound, and then she realizes it's her own breath, hoarse and strained as an asthmatic's.

Tears are pouring down her cheeks, not from fear

or memory, but from pain. The fingers at her throat grow tighter. Her brain slips inside her skull, her eyeballs bulge inside their sockets. She tries to free the hand behind her back, but he twists it harder, and more tears well up. The ground on every side is spinning: a blurred kaleidoscope of nightmare.

Then she stops seeing, hearing, understanding, remembering. It's like her head's pushed under water. She can't hold her breath much longer. The two of them – a grotesque, four-legged beast – stumble once more together, and then she wrenches her hand free and catches his wrist. He tries to hold her down, but she bends her lips towards his skin, swallows down the rising sickness, bares her teeth and bites the flesh.

And then it's a blur, a strobe-lit chaos of fear, relief and agony. The tang of blood is on her tongue, between her teeth, in her saliva. She scrambles back through the clearing to where the path reaches the road. The sea spins away behind her, and the pine branches recede. She thinks she hears a babble of voices, the sound of laughter from the villa. It will be seconds – perhaps minutes – before her breathing and her senses return to normal. Cries echo through the trees behind her, but she hears only the call of gulls.

*

Rosie sits by the telephone, counts the days off on the calendar. Callum would surely ring her from the village, find out if she's arrived safely. Joke about how the diving's going, tell her how he misses her. When he doesn't she thinks perhaps the village phonebox went kaput. He couldn't get a phonecard, or the right change. He's simply waiting till he sees her.

Mornings blend into afternoons, then evenings into nights. A brown envelope slips through the letterbox, an offer of the place she wanted on a clinical psychology course.

'This calls for a celebration,' says Rosie's mother, on discovering the news. She walks towards the kitchen with rapid efficiency. Rosie bites down on her thumbnail watching her mother's quick, light gait. Sarah appears at the kitchen door with a bottle and long-stemmed glasses, gesturing to her daughter to come and join her at the table.

'Do have some, Ro. It's such marvellous news. Think what an exciting career might lie ahead of you.'

Rosie looks over at her mother's thin shoulders. Everything seems to be an effort for Sarah, as though all that aloofness in early motherhood has left a vast hole in her vocabulary. She's had no practice at light merriment or gentle congratulation. Rosie goes over, takes a glass, sips reluctantly. Her eyes slide over the calendar. Callum should be back today.

The telephone rings, but it's always someone else. There's one time the caller pauses, with a hint of a word stuck in the throat, and her heart leaps, she's sure it's him, she could even recognize his breathing.

But the caller bangs down the receiver: the started word is never finished. Just some wrong number, after all. The daylit hours expand into the long, light, late spring evenings.

Family problems, she'd told Callum. She'd have to leave the villa early. She'd never really explained. He didn't like to intrude – it was obvious, that was it. He was waiting for her call, for her to give the all clear.

Rosie waits till her mother's out, and pads up and down the hallway. Her heart jars against her ribs. She lifts the receiver and dials.

Nobody answers – the phone rings, clicks on to the answermachine. She has a perilous split second to steady her voice. She thinks of Anthony and Claude by the poolside, exchanging soft, malicious whispers. But never mind, no need to panic. Callum would never take any notice.

'Hi, Callum, it's me. Thought you must be back by now. Hope you had a safe journey, and the rest of the holiday went well. Everything's fine here. Can't wait to see you. Lots of love.'

It's been an anti-climax, not getting him, but also something of a relief. And now he's bound to call her back. She takes a walk, tries to distract herself. When she returns the phone is ringing.

'Hello –' she's breathless, it's obvious; but she'll pretend she's been out running. More glamorous than pining nervously, or being too unfit to dash upstairs. 'Hi there, I've been wondering –' and then the smile is rubbed out from her voice.

'Rosie, it's me,' interrupts Annie. 'Haven't spoken to you in ages. Just called to see how your trip was. You haven't rung me for aeons.'

'Oh, yeah, hi.' Rosie hates herself for sounding so disappointed. 'I'm sorry – it's just things have been . . . how are you anyway?'

There must be an obvious downward note in her voice, because Annie asks if all is OK. She tells her yes, everything's great, she's been accepted on that psychology course. The holiday was fabulous – and then she invents a reason to hang up.

Callum doesn't return her call. She waits a decent interval – three days – and then leaves a further, terser message. Maybe his answermachine's broken, and he didn't get the first message. Maybe something's happened to him. She wonders crazily if she should call the airline, check the flight. Has he come back safely, did he come back at all? But no, this is lunacy: she's starting to behave like a madwoman. There's been no plane crash reported in the news, and if something had happened, someone would have told her. She thinks of the big bed and fresh white linen, Callum's warm hands tickling her spine. She knows she's worrying unduly, things are bound to become clear soon. She must learn to relax.

But they don't, and she can't, and Callum's eerie silence persists. Nervous as a schoolgirl, she decides to telephone Chambers. Again she waits till her mother's out, and paces for minutes before dialling.

'Six, The Courtyard,' says Simon's voice, sounding harassed but chirpy.

'Hi, Simon, it's Rosie. Just trying to reach Callum.' The forced jollity is painful. She swallows as she waits for his response.

'Oh, hi there, Rosie. How are you? I'll just see if he's about.' He sounds disconcerted to hear from her – but no, she must be imagining it. Getting paranoid for no reason. Why on earth would Simon be like that? She's left on hold for endless seconds, and then he's back on the line. 'Uh – Rosie, he's not here at the minute. Shall I tell him you called?' Rosie breathes into the silence, unable to find words. 'Sorry . . . Rosie . . . You still there?'

'Yes, Simon, beg your pardon. Callum's not there. He is . . . OK, isn't he?' She mustn't give away too much, betray the fact she's been neglected.

Simon laughs, slightly effeminately. 'Yes, he's fine. He's just busy. I'll make sure he gets your message and he'll call you when he's free.' He hangs up before she even has time to say thank you.

But Callum doesn't call back – by now she'd be surprised if he did. She tries to convince herself Simon may not have passed on her message. But things no longer add up. It's as she'd feared. There's something wrong.

After she'd left, what might Callum have found out about Claude? Does he, by now, know more than she'd bargained for? But if it were something really serious, wouldn't he ask her about it? He's a brilliant lawyer, for God's sake: he knows there are two sides to every story.

The notion comes to her – so painful, it's almost unthinkable – that he was playing with her, never serious; he's taken his fill and moved on. But how can it be? The way he chased her, begged her, pleaded with her. He broke off his previous engagement! He was jealous even of a Greek waiter; they slept curled in each other's arms. How could all of that mean nothing?

Rosie has lost the ability to function properly. She finds herself incapable of regulating the temperature in the shower, and winces sharply as the water jets from freezing to scalding. She smashes one of the headlights on her mother's car trying to ease out of a parking space. She gets a job through the temping agency, but is given the sack after just one day: her fingers skewed all over the keyboard spray doggerel up on to the screen.

Her mother looks worried. She must have noticed Callum's absence, but she's not saying anything. Rosie comes upon her sitting at the little desk in the hallway, and Sarah looks up hurriedly, her forehead creased deeply. She's holding a brown window envelope that looks unremittingly boring, as though it could never bear the kind of letter that comes from someone you want to hear from.

'Rosie, do tell me what's wrong.'

'Nothing, Mother. Nothing.' Rosie hovers, then walks away, her body exhausted, her mind unravelling.

She has had her fill of this pining, frazzled uncertainty. She must take matters into her own hands: she must confront Callum, face to face. She's been in denial about the island, trying to bury the painful memory of Claude and the clearing, but now she itches to tell Callum her side, before he thinks it's something else. Or perhaps he already does. Her stomach lightens unpleasantly. But it's going to be all right: once he sees her standing there, in front of him – is reminded of her skin against his, her tongue against his teeth – once all that happens, how can things not go back to normal? Of course, it is intolerable to think of turning up to Chambers unannounced, being told to wait or even turned away. She cannot risk more rejection. There must be an alternative.

So she decides to go to Chambers and wait for him, but watching from outside until he comes. She knows the path he takes when he's leaving, the direction he turns to walk up the lane, which way he heads towards the tube station. She will find him and catch up with him, and they'll sort it all out. If she doesn't see him one day, she'll try the next day, and the next day. It doesn't matter how long. She has all the time it takes.

There's a drizzle over the Strand as she turns down the narrow lane. It's warm, light summer rain, but still enough for an umbrella. Of course, she hasn't brought one. Her hair starts to curl with damp. She takes up her place of watch at the entrance to The

Courtyard, where she can just about see the doorway to No. 6. She starts to circle on the spot, the air cools, she hugs her shoulders. Can she really be doing this – becoming a manic, lovelorn spy? She has to squint sometimes to see properly; half-thinks she should have brought binoculars. Raindrops gather on her cheeks, making nonsense of her make-up. She stamps her feet to shake off cramp. It gets a little later, a little colder.

Her heart does somersaults when Simon comes out, and she has to dive into the shadows. When she re-emerges to her lookout, she's fearful of seeing someone else, and worries she's missed Callum, but she'll give it a little longer. Everyone passing now has umbrellas. There are dark, moist stains on her light jacket. Some strangers look at her distastefully, as though she's dishevelled as a tramp; others crease their brows and peer at her, as though wondering what she's up to. Even in her own mind, she's beginning to feel quite sinister. A passing, warm-faced man in pinstripes asks her kindly if she's lost.

She's starting to shiver, and sneeze a little, and she guesses she looks quite deranged, and she's about to give up when she hears approaching footsteps. She straightens up where she's standing and sees someone coming out of No. 6. The steps are dulled on the damp paving stones. It's Callum, and he's not alone.

Never, up till now, has Rosie truly known what it means to hold your heart in your mouth. Her whole chest cavity has hollowed, emptied, while her mouth is full of pulsing, unsaid thoughts. If she opened her lips now they'd belch out all over the courtyard. But how can she accost Callum when he's with someone? How will she get to say what she wants?

She moves closer, sees his companion: a tall, curvy girl with red hair. They walk together amicably rather than intimately, a slight distance between them. It's the girl from the photograph – his ex-fiancée: Shona! Blood floods into Rosie's cheeks, she forgets her carefully rehearsed speeches. The memory of the forest fades, alongside the dull pink dust and poolside whispers. Suddenly there's fresher danger, a clearer reason why Callum's blanked her. Her throbbing brain still won't believe it, but if she doesn't ask, she'll never know. Her entire ribcage is rattling. Callum and the girl draw closer. Rosie steps out from the shadows.

'Callum –' Her voice is small, soft and shrunken by the rain. The girl turns, looks at her questioningly: without warmth, without enmity. Callum nods at her briefly, says something too quiet and hurried to be audible. He exchanges words with the other girl – who can tell what they're saying. *Who's that?* perhaps she's asking; maybe he tells her, *No one special.* The two move on, untroubled, quickening their pace against the rain. Rosie stands frozen, unsure if she's blinded by raindrops or by her tears.

11

Callum fell into sleep fitfully, the open window still rattling. There was so much that was troubling him, but he thought a pattern was emerging. Memories of the past few weeks clashed, and he slid into dreaming. Later, he would think he understood the meaning of the dream, and the reason for dreaming it then. At the time, it swam over him, a blend of nightmare and remembrance.

In the dream, it is hot, the air dry and sunlight hard. He is standing somewhere high, and he can almost reach and touch the sky. He is both indoors and outdoors; just behind him is a tall window. He stands on its ledge, or on a balcony; part of a bright, pink-orange villa.

Before him a green forest stretches, the trees' crowns lush and high and shiny. Sun floods down on to the branches and the whole surface moves like liquid. Beyond the sea of green is a sea of turquoise, the water calm and still as glass. He stares out at it and smiles. A swell of pleasure licks his skin.

Then sharp, strange sounds disturb the silence; a harsh cracking, like sticks or bones, and the sound of breathing so hard it is like an oncoming hurricane. Dark, winged creatures flap out from the depths of the forest, filling the sky with their shrill, desperate squalling.

And there is another creature, too: a human being, a girl. Her face is white as a ghost's with a moist, scarlet stain for a mouth. She's breathing hard, and brings with her the gathering sound of the storm. Somehow she reaches the villa, and joins him where he's standing. She kisses him, caresses him, every inch of her skin against his. He's warm and trembling at the touch of her, then cold and clammy as she vanishes.

Then he's alone again, except he's not alone, there are hundreds of them. Shadow figures, with eyes to the ground, who walk along beside him. He never sees their faces, but he knows they come from everywhere: from his workplace, from his childhood, from his past and from his present. They are in the forest, it's getting darker: some of them shine torches. It's like a search party, and there's the occasional high scream of a siren. People are afraid, but excited: they're looking for something, someone. It's like watching a scary movie and being in it at the same time.

Callum stands at the forest's edge and shines his torchbeam on the water. He's on a cliff, both sheer and shallow, miles high yet he can jump it. He calls out to the searchers, he's telling them he's found something; a crowd swarms in behind him and a hundred eyes turn to look.

Callum crouches and stretches his fingers towards a disjointed man's body. The face is turned to the ground, eating earth, dark hair plastered to the skull. His long-nailed fingers splay, claw-like, as though grasping for something. His legs are bent, grotesquely crooked, one foot turned right round on the ankle. The skin is cold, the pulse silent. Callum turns the body round.

An indrawn breath of horror sweeps through the searchers above. The face stares up at all of them, with its flinty, beady eyes. One torn eyelid is lowered, a gash of filth snakes from the temple. The teeth are bared, sharp and canine, and the cracked lips smeared with blood. The nose is beaked, long and pointed, the whole skull skewed on the neck. Then the broken skull lifts and the body twitches . . .

Callum woke with a jolt as the dream became a waking memory. He remembered the harsh angles of Anthony's face, for once softened into sadness. Claude was dead, they'd had to tell him, and now everyone would do what they could to help. Then there was the exhausted, dusty day that followed the vivid night search, the secluded beach retreat suddenly swarming with local policemen. One detective, in particular, exuded a slow-grinding mistrust; he had a silver-specked moustache and a habit of licking his lips loudly.

Yes, it had been a suspicious way to die, he'd muttered, when pressed by Anthony. It seemed unlikely that anyone would be so careless as to fall where the cliff dropped off so suddenly. There were bite marks on the dead man's arm, suggestive of a struggle. The detective gave a smoker's wheeze. Had anyone seen anything?

Callum had had no choice then, he'd had to admit what he'd seen from the balcony. Rosie running breathless out of the forest, just before he'd driven her to the ferry. They had waited, at the very least, for her to be contacted and questioned, but extraordinarily, the court said there was no need.

Accidental death, was the verdict. Despite the detective's suspicions, the coroner pronounced it all too easy to slip at that point in the cliff's edge. The drop looked mild but it was sheer. It was a tragedy waiting to happen. The breaks in spine and skull were overwhelmingly consistent with slow, scrabbling slippage – there was no single, clear snap to suggest the impact of being pushed. The bite marks were shallow – perhaps an animal's – and led to no set conclusion, and there were no clear indications that the dead man had been struggling. What Callum had witnessed was vague and circumstantial. The cost of tracing a witness abroad could not, in this case, be justified.

Callum shivered as a fresh gust invaded the bedroom. The bedsprings squealed angrily, but the house around him was empty.

PART TWO

12

It is a child's hidden treasure chest; a trove of trinkets; a box of memories. Rosie runs her fingers over the outer edge of the marquetry, here rough with the grain of wood, here shiny and smooth. The lid comes away with effort, as though time has gummed it closed. Inside, the few items seem impossibly precious. A cat's tooth; a locket; a crumbling photograph of her father. A key she's hoarded since childhood to the old house's garden gate. A beaded bracelet that her mother gave her and a long since unread love letter.

Rosie has come home. On arriving at the airport, she had hailed herself a taxi, and then sat glued to the window, staring, as London and its suburbs rolled past. Not that she hadn't travelled this route frequently, but for so many years it had been as a sporadic visitor, based abroad. This time there is something more permanent, though she doesn't know how long she'll be staying. She simply knows she has no immediate plans to go away again.

The taxi had taken a corner too fast and suddenly, beyond the windscreen, the wide slope of the high street slid away towards the skyline. Rosie took in the big bookshop with its doors thrown open to the pavement; the cluster of tables outside the restaurant, diners spilling over the edge of the kerb. Away to her left, little lanes of high Victorian houses, punctuated by plane trees, wound down towards the heath.

She is back in the neighbourhood where she grew up. Nearby is the house where she was living as a child, and not far from that, the flat her mother moved to later.

Rosie can remember the time when, still in her twenties and living with her mother, she first discovered that Sarah was suffering from cancer. Sarah would sit at the kitchen table, opening dull but ominous brown envelopes, rubbing her shoulders as though cold, coughing a lot. It was only later Rosie discovered that the letters were from the hospital. It was a rib-jarring, chilling shock to see that strong, beautiful woman ailing. But the danger was averted; Sarah was treated, the cancer receded. Life was allowed to reassume normality.

Then Rosie left. She qualified as a clinical psychologist, did some research in Paris, then secured a fellowship at the university in New York. Her work was much admired. Only rarely did it occur to her that she was alone.

Her first meeting with Michael is etched with clarity in Rosie's memory. She saw him sitting across the way from her in the faculty cafeteria, the sun's rays playing in his rich hair as he toyed absently with a sugar bowl. She had carried her lunch towards him, wondering if she had the boldness to sit down opposite and start a casual conversation. But in fact she had promptly slipped, spaghetti napolitana spattering everywhere. The good-looking stranger would surely be repulsed, she had guessed, or at least cross, at best unimpressed. Instead he had come over grinning, offering to help. In a moment they were balling up napkins and mopping up puddles of ketchup.

Michael had never quite quickened Rosie's heartbeat enough to make her breathless, but he was handsome and clever and generous and gentle. She can recall waking at midnight, and watching him sleep, her insides suffused with warmth and softness; but never jolting in a cold sweat from broken dreams, with a stabbing longing in her heart. Perhaps that wild yearning only happens when you're younger. Perhaps, no matter when it happens, it can only happen once.

Still, they were good together, and at any rate, after Toby was born, she believed she had never been happier. Despite the absence of marriage papers or joint accounts the bonds were strong. Michael was a soft-fingered, loving father, never afraid of broken sleep or soiled nappies, and they'd lived in a downtown Manhattan apartment, which was just big enough for their small family. It had windows that lured in and captured the sun, making whole chunks of the day quite literally golden. The nights were much rowdier than in London, as the pavements of Greenwich village hummed, but Rosie liked to fall asleep to the jarring rhythms of late-night revellers. She loved waking early in the summertime to hear the street already moving; having a bagel breakfast in the nearby diner just two doors down from the distinctly camp magic shop. When the weather was mild, they spent long hours chasing Toby round Washington Square. In winter, their lips got chapped in the snows in Central Park.

As for Rosie's work, it was reviewed in professional journals with grave enthusiasm. She was starting up a private practice, in a carpeted study with smooth dark shelves. A group of interesting neurotics were lining up to receive her wisdom. How was it possible that she could feel anything but blessed?

They stayed like that, in their crazily perfect, liberal quasi-family, for more than three years until it started to go wrong. There were no rows, no infidelities, just a slowly diverging forked road. Even if Michael was out working late and she'd been at home alone for hours, she felt none of the old thrill arranging salad and bread and wine and cut flowers. Then there'd be these phone calls from colleagues, and sometimes students, and she'd have long involved conversations, and Michael would always ask the same old question – with drawn down brows – 'Who on earth was that?' And they argued over Toby – endlessly, pointlessly. Whether the baseball boots Rosie bought were too tight for his growing feet; if Michael had let him breakfast on a cereal that was too sugary.

Then Rosie got the phone call, the news slicing

through her belly. Way back on the other side of the ocean, her mother's cancer had returned.

As soon as the illness had progressed past a certain point, Rosie knew she was going to leave. It was like following news of the run-up towards a war and reaching the point of no return. No chance to avoid or retreat now, just the painful advance into uncharted territory. Michael was sympathetic – he could not take lightly the prospective death of a parent – but still he looked askance at her when she said she was flying out.

'What, right now? Is it really that bad? What about your lecture tour? You've been working so hard for it.'

She'd shrugged, it all meant so little. 'I'm going to do San Francisco next as planned. An old promise I can't get out of. But then I've a flight back to England on Thursday.'

'How long will you be gone for?'

'I don't know, I just can't say.'

'Well, you must have some idea.'

'Cancer doesn't operate according to organized timelines, as you Americans would say.'

'I'm sorry,' he had whispered, and stepped closer to touch her cheek. Even now she still regrets the way she turned her face slightly away from him. 'I understand it could be weeks, or even months' – he'd struggled to soften his voice – 'you just can't predict these things.'

It was early spring, but the dullness of the moment hung with a dreadful heaviness between them.

'What will you do about work, about your practice, the professorship?'

'I don't know,' she had said again, waving a dishcloth disjointedly. 'The university are giving me a term's sabbatical, that shouldn't be a problem, and my private patients'll just have to have their anxieties cured by someone else. After that . . .' she shrugged helplessly. Michael knotted his jaw.

Eventually he had said it. 'I can't believe you're leaving us.'

The back of Rosie's throat constricts every time she recalls this sentence. Easy enough to respond to the 'leaving me' bit, all the usual clichés do it: 'it won't be for ever', 'we both need some space', 'things haven't been right in a long time'. But Toby. He's only three. It's another story entirely. The pain of his absence is there now, permanently, in the centre of her chest cavity: it's like a separate, beating heart, underpinning every deed and feeling.

'I have to go,' she had said simply, the tears already starting to prickle. 'I can't not go, you understand that, and there's no way I can take him with me. He's got his friends here, all your family, the whole school thing – it's all arranged and familiar. Over there – who knows? – it could all just be chaos.'

'He's gonna miss you, Ro. We both will, but Toby in particular. It'll be like hell.'

They both made vague murmurings about seeing

how things worked out in the long term; how it would all gradually fall into place; how they would wait to see how it panned out. As if this whole thing were a parting of an altogether more trivial nature. Neither would ask the unaskable, for to be too clear would be too painful. They already had enough to cry about. No need to wonder if she'd come back at all.

This time round, London is a total revelation. Rosie's been back and forth over the Atlantic on countless occasions on work assignments and for pleasure, but there was always that reminder she was just flitting through, bridling against her fear of flying, working through her hectic schedule. Now, because she doesn't quite know where she'll go next, it's a little as though she's been plonked slap bang into the middle of her old world.

At the airport, she had looked for signs that the travel industry was suffering, that the atmosphere of war and terrorism were taking their ghostly toll. In truth, she wasn't sure that she spotted any difference, though she told herself if she looked hard enough the changing spirit of things was palpable. Less bustling queues in the newsagent's; more empty seats in the coffee shop. The quietness of it suited somehow, in keeping with her own mood.

Then, in the cab ride back, a strange thing started to happen. She wound down the window and let the air touch her face. She smelt the sharp, green scent of burgeoning spring, and fresh clipped privet and trimmed front lawns. There was a small flutter in Rosie's ribcage and inescapable waves of guilt. But she couldn't ignore it: could it be that she felt happy?

Even the dank sobriety of her mother's flat could not – at first – serve to dampen her spirits, though the air smelt so thick it was as though no one had opened the windows for years. Rosie dusted down surfaces and threw out old clumps of rotting flowers while her mother reclined, coughing, on a chaise longue in the corner. Privately, Rosie was shocked at how advanced her mother's illness was. Her cheekbones were sharp and her skin had grown papery. They didn't talk in great detail, though Sarah kept saying *thank you*. Rosie, for her part, kept her news brief and simple.

She didn't, for instance, reveal that she didn't know if she was going back. That she had begun to seriously doubt that her affection for Michael had ever been enough. That even though she was thousands of miles away from her unique and precious three year old, she was feeling a shocking spring in her step which made her feel young and restless.

Instead, she answered Sarah's questions vaguely, with breezy flaps of her hand. Michael was doing well and Toby was beautiful and bright and healthy. Their relationship remained fluid, but then she knew her mother had always found it bizarre, and Rosie made sure it came across as no more bewildering now. She showed her photographs of the three of them with Michael looking dashing and Toby heart-melting. The apartment in Manhattan provided a simple, stylish backdrop. She had with her a copy of her latest hardback and some glowing reviews from Sunday supplements. It was a carefully constructed, authentic picture of quiet fulfilment and success.

In the last fortnight of Sarah Verner's life, Annie and Felicity came visiting. In the intervening years, Annie had written and called regularly, but Rosie had lost touch with Felicity, and was curious at their reunion. When her two old friends called in she leapt to welcome them into the flat, and then the three stood still and quiet as they gazed at each other intently. From her chaise longue in the corner Sarah looked on silently.

'Wow,' said Rosie, 'look at you two. You look fabulous.'

It wasn't entirely true. Annie remained beautiful, a slender, slightly subdued stiletto of a woman, whose engagement ring announced that she would soon be embarking on her second marriage. But though she continued to fly high in the world of international finance, she secretly longed for a cottage and children, which she now feared she might be unable to have.

Felicity, these days a senior editor at an all-female publishing house, had long since jettisoned her gaudy earrings and smoothed the spikes in her hair. Though her tongue was still sharp, her eyes were duller, her cheeks sunken. When offered tea and biscuits she accepted with disconcerting enthusiasm.

Rosie kissed them, took their jackets, and said, 'I'm so glad you came. It's amazing us being together again, three ageing musketeers.'

She had thought they might reminisce on their days of rebellion, but the visitors were engrossed with the photographs of Toby.

'He's gorgeous,' sang Annie. 'Rosie, aren't you the lucky one.'

Over on the chaise longue, Rosie saw Sarah smile. Perhaps, under the circumstances, this was the best she could give her mother: the sort of things most dearly needed, in order to pass away in peace.

*

Now Rosie sits closing and reopening the box of memories. Spring twilight falls outside, and the windows turn to slate-grey oblongs. The flat is calm, almost silent; shadows spread across the floor. The chaise longue where her mother lay smells of death, but also peace.

Rosie thinks of Toby, running, laughing and gurgling somewhere on the other side of the ocean; and of Michael – is he missing her? Does he lie awake at night? But also of something lighter, something lither, like a ghost whispering in the shadows.

The last time Rosie lived with her mother she was in her early twenties. She was driven by dreams, and determination, but also by a sharp longing; she can remember a search which never ended, which as good as drove her to distraction.

As though re-enacting long-lost gestures, she finds

herself reaching for the telephone directory. The evening breeze hisses softly. Her fingers flick through the heavy pages. Her mind is full of old pictures. The grandmother clock's tick is loud against the quiet. A sudden clank of plumbing is enough to make her jump.

She feels embarrassed doing this, as though hidden watchers are sneering at her. What would anyone think if they could read what she's thinking? But she's too far gone to care, her curiosity sharpens like appetite.

Rosie's forefinger skims its way slowly down the page. She steels herself against disappointment, for the odds are against finding him. But it turns out not to matter, for she manages to find him anyway. Even the telephone directory still calls him 'barrister' and, yes, the address is still 6, The Courtyard. The number's the same as all those years ago, though she doubts she's got the gumption to ring it.

But she carries on staring, as the box of memories sits beside her. Below the business address is the personal one, his private place, his own home. Maybe he's there now, looking out as she is at the evening. Probably surrounded by family and all the trinkets of success. It is impossible to imagine him wondering hungrily about the past.

Memories jumble and then Rosie's throat goes dry. Because she is no longer dreaming, but reading digits in front of her. A collection of characters that spell an address, but also a key to a house. Someone's private, personal living space. She could find her way there.

But this is impossible, it can't be so – her eyes – this light – they must be playing tricks on her. Rosie looks again at the page, but there is no need for reading glasses. It is just as she had thought. Is this just coincidence?

14 Pilgrim's Row. Her heartbeat is sharp, but steady. She remembers the broad hallway, so often shrouded in shadow, and the light that spilled in spinning rainbows through the stained-glass panelled door. The impossibly grand staircase was a long, exciting climb, especially if you were hiding from parents or playful ghosts. Upstairs, the maze of corridors turned and twisted round endless corners, and innumerable oak doors led off to guest bedrooms and studies. But best of all, there was the garden – the lawn and tangled, dark-green copse; and her own room with its window seat, her private, secret viewing place.

Rosie's insides are light as she sits back on her haunches. Something pulls deep within her, the past vivid as blood. Outside it is dark, and she should really turn the light on, but instead she sits there in the dim room and again picks up the box of memories. One by one she takes out and touches the items she has hoarded, presses them into her palm, squeezing tighter, feeling the texture. Everything has its story, leading forwards, or backwards. The cat's tooth and the locket; the old key and the love letter.

It is an afternoon not long afterwards that Rosie leaves to make her journey. The light is clear and there is no need to take an A–Z. Her footsteps carry her instinctively, almost without effort. But she is tired, she hasn't slept properly, and even her dreams have started to exhaust her. Yet there's a different sort of energy now – she could make this journey with her eyes shut. The road curves round and the pavement dips and the walk gets easier because it's downhill.

Later, retracing her steps, she's invigorated. She opens the door to her mother's flat and goes back into the half-dark. She will not sleep tonight, she knows that: the waking dreams will start to flood in. Her heart's beating fast and a light sweat coats her skin: for the last stretch of the way home she could not help it, she's been running.

It won't be the last time she makes this journey, she can't leave this business unfinished. Rosie sits staring at the street below, listening to the echoing bustle from around the corner; her breathing is tight around her heart, and she cannot believe what she has done.

13

The clock on the kitchen wall ticked on towards two. Callum sat at the table looking at his half-emptied teacup. The house had been empty of children for far too long. But now, Rudy and Saffron would be arriving any minute: they'd be bound to ask where their old toy box was, and he was not sure he could remember. He could always distract them with the garden if those looming clouds failed to gather. And he'd stacked up on biscuits and chocolate bars – he hoped Shona wouldn't scold him. Would she deliver the kids herself, he wondered, or would it be James instead? Perhaps they'd come together like a new and perfect family. Callum grew restless, started to pace, occasionally worrying they wouldn't come at all.

It was almost exactly two and already he was wondering what might have happened. Even when the children had been tiny Shona had remained alarmingly precise. If she thought she couldn't make an appointment she'd never let it go without a call. Now he was perched on the sofa, listening with keenness for the sound of an engine. If the visit failed to materialize the afternoon would become an endurance test.

And then he heard the sound of approaching footsteps. He sat up, his shoulders tense: what expression should he wear? But there were too few footsteps coming closer, and no cacophonous children's chatter. The tension in his shoulder blades hardened. He was expecting no one else.

Callum went and stood in the hallway and watched the silhouette of the approaching visitor. It loomed larger and nearer, the outline bleeding into a blur. Although he had been thinking of favourite children's games, he could no longer shut out his nightmare. The little pine forest and the beach, and the secluded, heat-baked villa. The figure on the other side of the door was female – that much he could make out. One slim arm was in mid-air, poised to rap at the door, but before she could knock, he was there, and he had opened it. She said nothing, did not introduce herself, and the stillness gathered between them.

'I suppose,' he said finally, 'you'd better come in.'

They sat opposite each other in the living room, Callum in the armchair with her on the sofa. Those features which he could make out seemed acute and overdrawn: the thin frame, the nervous posture, the auburn hair against white skin. His blood warmed when he thought of how they'd last sat here together – her green dress and sharp nails, and the cool, bare lines of her body. She sat there not speaking, and his mouth and throat grew dry.

'I can't believe it,' Callum ventured at last. 'You ought to be ashamed of yourself. It's incredible, what you've done.'

There was no way of making sense of the set of her mouth or forehead, and he found all he could see was what he knew had once been there. Even when she spoke, her voice was subdued.

'I'm so sorry about it all, Callum. I didn't mean for it all to happen this way.'

'How can you live with yourself, doing what you've done?'

And she said, 'What, Callum, done what?' and he realized his hands were shaking.

'Don't act the innocent with me, Rosie. You came here the other day, I realize that now. You pretended to be someone else.'

There was a short silence and he looked away from her but he supposed she was staring. Her voice was loud and hard.

'I'm not entirely proud of what happened last time between us, Callum, with how I acted. But you have to take responsibility for yourself as well. How could I have possibly known the way I would find you?'

'But you let me believe –'

'You thought what you thought, Callum. I didn't plant any ideas in your head. I came to find you after so long, and it was all impossibly strange – I couldn't believe what was happening. But I didn't plan anything, and I didn't force anything – now are you going to tell me you regret it all?'

Callum sat back. He could hear her true voice now, and he wondered how he had ever mistaken her for a flu-ridden Shona. Yet he was struck all over again by how much similarity there was, the white and green of skin and eyes, the insistent, reprimanding lilt.

You thought what you thought – it was like some pop song's refrain. But was it possible – it was unthinkable – could he, and all of them, have been wrong? He moistened his lips against his tongue

'What are you doing here, anyway?'

For a moment, she didn't answer, and the sun was too bright through the window, and as he narrowed his eyes her shape was blurred as though he were staring at her through liquid. Long ago, when they had holidayed together, he had held her body in his arms, weightless in salt water, the parting waves as clear as glass. But the joy of that vacation had descended into chaos, as they'd struggled to come to terms with Claude's stomach-lurching death. For days, weeks beforehand, Anthony had been warning him about her, and the sordid hidden past he could have learnt only from Claude. Drunk with youth and lust, Callum had refused to listen, and then Rosie had fled the island and it all made horrible sense.

'It's been a long time, Callum.' The lines of her body flickered. He had never asked her, of course, that was what nagged at him. At first, in the insanity and obsessed conviction of shock and grief, talking to her had been unthinkable, corroboration unnecessary.

Then he'd grown uncertain, lifting the telephone, dialling her number, but it had felt like a betrayal, he'd clammed up guiltily, dropped the receiver. And then, with indecent swiftness, London life resumed its pace; Shona unexpectedly resurfaced, and her slower passions were like a balm to him. As he'd regained his composure horror had turned to mere irrelevance, and though the past remained uncertain it had become easiest to ignore it.

'Things have moved on for both of us.' Rosie was still talking. 'I've been living abroad. Now I'm back I came to find you.' He stayed watching her, quietly. 'Something weird has happened to you, Callum, and I don't know what it is. Obviously something's wrong with your eyes – I'm sorry if you've had some sort of illness. But after all that's happened between us, don't you think I'm the one who should be asking questions?'

He said nothing and she stood up, her pelvis tilted forward slightly. The slant of her body was like a young mother's, supporting a baby's weight with the slope of her torso. 'This isn't much of a reunion, is it?' she said, flatly.

He could ask her now, outright, but he'd never know if she'd be straight with him. And then again, the more he thought about it, there were other reasons to be wary. He hadn't thought – but then you never knew – could they have been female footsteps on the heath? Was it possible, after all, that a woman's voice had hissed his name?

'Perhaps,' he said softly, 'you're right. There's stuff we need to talk about.'

And so here they were, the two of them walking together towards the kitchen – strangely enough, Rosie taking the lead. She sat at the antique pine table – she looked indecently at home here – and she picked up the biscuit jar, with the animal-shaped biscuits he'd bought for the children.

'These are American, you know.' She held the jar in her hand, turning it so that it caught the light. 'Michael used to get these for Toby, although I told him not to, I didn't want Toby's teeth spoiled.'

It didn't seem to occur to her to explain who Michael and Toby were. But he didn't care much either, because he ought to have been opening the jar himself now, slicing up sandwiches, pouring glasses of juice and milk. He should tell her to go, she was just being a nuisance, but then the nightmare came back to him and a sharp, dark curiosity.

'You've been abroad, you say?' He hoped she wouldn't notice the calculated tone, the deliberate, careful enquiry. 'How long for? When did you come back?'

'My mother's died,' she said bluntly. 'Her cancer finally got the better of her. We've just had the funeral. I've only been back a couple of weeks.'

For just a second, then, he was sorry and then he wanted to ask her something else but as he opened his mouth the doorbell rang.

'Must get that.' His heart leapt with joyous relief.

He thought he would see Shona, but instead there was James, looking stern and polite, flanked on each side by the children.

'Here they are, the little blighters. Sorry we're so late, you know, traffic.' Callum ushered all three into the living room and they sat down together in a neat little line. Then he rushed back into the kitchen, feeling the mildest twitch of panic. Rosie was still there, leaning against the counter, by the coffee pot and the biscuit jar. She started to speak, but he interrupted her:

'Rosie, I think you'd better go now.'

*

Callum drank his nightcap alone, and reviewed the day with satisfaction. Rudy and Saffron had clearly enjoyed themselves, despite the initial trauma of discovering Frieda's absence.

'Where's she gone? She's not here!' Rudy had yelled in consternation, and of course Callum had softened the blow, had crafted a gentle, careful story. Frieda had suddenly become ill, he'd said, and the vet had been kind to her, and now she was sleeping for ever, and it was better for everyone. Saffron looked blank, and then spent several minutes bawling, but Callum smiled at the way his son tried to stiffen his trembling jaw.

Once they had done enough emotional recuperation, they played football in the garden and ate animal biscuits. Rudy continued to grow sinewy, and to kick a football with élan, while Saffron sat on the lawn's edges, clucking, occasionally flapping at the flower beds. They had apples they'd brought from home, but Callum said they didn't have to eat them all. And then who should telephone but Lydia, reminding him that Chambers were holding their annual picnic. All children invited. Was he going to attend?

At first he was going to refuse – but then he thought, why not? The children were with him, why not show them off? They bundled into a taxi and made their way to a meadow in Richmond, and when they arrived were greeted with wreathes of smiles. The female contingent made a particular fuss of them, and ensured that all delicacies came their way first.

'They are adorable,' pronounced Lydia, cradling Saffron like a newborn, 'and they clearly love you, Callum. You must be so proud.'

Even Anthony, usually rather awkward when faced with childish boisterousness, made a determined effort to be laddish, discussing football with Rudy and sharing his food with him. Callum had sat back and felt the sun strong on his face. On afternoons like this you had to believe something was right with the world.

When it was time for the children to go home, both James and Shona had come to collect them. It was odd seeing them stand there together in the hallway, like an ill-at-ease visiting couple coming to pay their respects. All three adults stood about stiffly, acutely aware of the need to remain civil. Callum found himself dreaming of speaking coaxingly to Shona, but Shona looked uncomfortable, overly conscious of being looked at. It was James who injected a note of formal politeness.

'Rudy and Saffron, remember to say thank you. And wash your hands before we go.'

Callum bristled at the strict paternal tone – as though he had been rendered an outsider, become an extra, second father. He wanted to butt in, but then Saffron emerged from the bathroom, wailing with tiredness and tummy ache, and Shona drew down her eyebrows.

'What have you been doing with them all afternoon, Callum? Not giving them grease and sugar and too much junk food?'

'Come on, Shona, it's their day out,' said James wearily. 'A few biscuits won't kill them.'

At least on parting Shona had agreed, with remarkable swiftness, that they could come again next Sunday, and furnished him with details of Rudy's sports day. There was so much to look forward to. He had almost forgotten Rosie.

Callum shook his head and raised his glass, and then he flinched with quick surprise. There was a noise beyond the shrubbery. He hurried over to the window. Then the telephone rang, drawing him back into the hallway. He lifted the receiver and uttered his name tentatively.

'Yes, I know it's you – who the bloody else would

it be? What I want to know is, what in God's name did you get up to this afternoon?'

The words stung, so sudden and accusatory that it took him several seconds to recognize the voice.

'Nice of you to call, Shona. What on earth are you talking about?'

'The children have been up all night bellyaching and running in and out of the bathroom. James and I haven't had a moment's peace and I've never seen Saffron like this. I always warn you against spoiling them, Callum, but this time you've surpassed yourself.'

Callum stiffened with resentment, and against this blanket of discomfort the nearby clanking in the garden quite failed to register.

'The children had a lovely time, Shona. I did no more than give them a bit of a treat, as any father would.'

'Well, I wish you'd tell me exactly what kind of treat, Callum. Rudy's thrown up – you know he's got the constitution of an ox – and as for poor Saffron, she's positively green.'

'Shona, it's not as if I've poisoned them. I'm sorry they're out of sorts but children do get tummy upsets.'

'Well, thank you for your concern, I'm sure it's wonderful to be so cavalier. But you're not the one cleaning up sick and wiping toddlers' bottoms. Much more of this and I'll be calling out the emergency doctor. So tell me, Callum, what did they eat round at your place?'

'Just a few of their favourite biscuits, Shona. And

then I took them on a picnic organized by Chambers.'

The silence crackled with her reprimand, and then she exploded. 'Well, no wonder, Callum. Didn't you watch them? God knows what they've been stuffing down. They've probably overdosed on champagne and foie gras.'

'Listen, I'm sure it's going to be fine, but do let me know if . . .' Her words were submerged by the background swell of screaming children, and Shona huffed, 'Got to go now' and crashed down the receiver. Callum sat back down with his nightcap and with knotted jaw resumed his sipping. The whisky coated his tongue sourly, warmed the back of his throat. It was only when he swallowed that he thought he heard coughing.

The length of his spine tensed. Surely it must be just the wind, and yet the air outside was still. He set aside the whisky glass and stood up, swaying slightly. Through the darkened French windows he saw nothing but the swing.

There was no sound, he told himself, it was just his paranoia: or a summer barbecue, after dinner beers from next door's back garden. He turned back to gather his drink up, but midway through the gesture froze.

There, by the swing, just emerging from the willow – that was more than shadows dancing. Had his crazy eyes tricked him? A pair of skinny arms jerked outwards like a blackened marionette. He began to feel dizzy and knocked over the whisky glass. He opened the French windows and stepped slowly into the open. Beyond the trees, the shadow of the marionette moved again.

'Oi – you!' Callum cried, his toes groping the dark pathway. The grass had not been cut and the soil was thick and sticky.

Somewhere – anywhere – a neighbour switched a light off, and a scantily lit patch of lawn was thrown into near blackness. Callum lost sight of the figure but still heard recurring coughing. He wondered for a second if it made more sense to retreat.

The intruder coughed again and Callum turned aside. The sound was coming from a different direction – was the figure now behind him? He swivelled his head to see if he could make out the silhouette. At that moment he felt a sharp blow to his skull.

He thought it couldn't be happening again, that he would once more become a victim, but this time he was prepared, and managed to steady himself. He smelt someone's breath at his neck – dry, and faintly sweet – and a long-fingered hand hovered just by his cheek.

The hand grappled towards Callum's throat, but he fought it away. The fingers felt thin, and the attached wrist was slender – Callum slid his own hand round it, and yanked forward the arm. The cough came again, higher, now a squeal of pain, and Callum and the intruder fell together towards the light.

'Gotcha!' grunted Callum, his vocal chords

straining. The other's body squirmed against his like a wriggling, kicking child. He tugged it towards the window, where he could at last see his attacker's face.

14

She sees him next in the bookshop.

She has just had her hair cut in the salon down the high street, and now she sits in an easy chair at one of the small round tables. In front of her is a scattering of volumes left by other casual readers. Time was when bookshops were full of closely stacked, dusty shelves, and the narrow aisles between them drenched in slightly sinister mustiness. Now it's all armchairs and espressos – yet one more import from America. Rosie's heart gives a leap when she thinks she sees one of her own books – to think that here, in a now alien city, some stranger might be reading it. But this is a gaudy tome about the ethics of the dating game – pop psychology that just so happens to have a similar cover. She smiles and shrugs her shoulders, both amused and disappointed.

He is sitting at one of the tables, on the opposite side of the shop. His face is hidden, turned away in the direction of the cash register, and she can see the back of his head between the labels 'True crime' and 'Reference'. She does not recognize him yet, and stares at his neck and shoulders absently.

Last night she made a telephone call to America and spoke to Toby, and now her mind has floated back to the days before she and Michael parted. They'd been living together in the apartment in Manhattan, but although they shared a bed, they remained separate between its covers. They would sleep with their spines straight and their faces turned outwards and if their limbs brushed each other, they flinched like strangers on the subway. If it happened that Toby woke them, they rose with sleepwalkers' weariness. They prepared breakfast, showered, dressed, without saying anything.

Once Michael had left the apartment at four o'clock in the morning, after a particularly fractious interchange over whether to use a certain babysitter. Rosie had left her alone in the apartment, and returned to find her smoking in the hallway, while Toby merrily set about trying to dismantle a block of kitchen knives.

'Don't you *care* who you leave in charge of our son?' yelled Michael, sitting up against the headboard. 'He could have seriously injured himself, and meanwhile she could've burned the house down.'

Rosie looked at his usually calm face, now florid with anger. 'Of course I care. But I have a life and a career too, you know. I needed to get out and it's just unfortunate Vivian behaved like that. If you're so bothered about it, why don't you put some effort into finding us a sitter for once?'

'*Unfortunate* you say! Would you show the same equanimity if Toby ended up in Casualty?'

'Oh, for fuck's sake, Michael, don't overdo it.

You're the one who smokes anyway – you're always popping out for a quick fag when you're alone with Toby.'

'At least,' said Michael coldly, though he was near hysterical with fury, 'I don't put my son at risk. I'm fit to be his father.'

Then Rosie snapped. 'You think you're so perfect. But we can manage without you. So why don't you just fuck off?'

And Michael, to her intense dismay and consternation, had bounded out of bed and dared her to live up to the challenge. He had fastened jeans over slim hips, slung a shirt over his back. It had been raining, but he had left still, the door banging behind him, and she heard his footsteps on the sidewalk softened as though he were walking on grass. When Toby stole into her bedroom she had to blink her eyes dry.

'I heard a noise. Where's Daddy?'

'He's had to go out unexpectedly. He'll be back soon. Go back to sleep.'

And Michael was back soon – if coming back after two hours of wandering the sodden, night-time streets of Greenwich village counted as soon. His hair was slicked on to his forehead and a saturated pack of cigarettes poked from his breast pocket, the cardboard decimated by the rain.

'Rosie. We have to sort this. I haven't got any energy left for fighting.'

Now, many weeks later, she has been reminded

of that night. Toby's words on the telephone were a strange repetitive echo. Only this time she was the wanderer, the one whose actions were in question.

'Mummy, are you coming back soon?'

She didn't know what to tell him – could provide only inadequate clichés – 'Whatever happens, I'll be there for you.' 'You know I'll always love you.'

She sets aside the book on dating, an intolerable lump forming in her throat. In front of her she imagines scenes from her past life, now the old apartment, now Toby's schoolyard. The man with his back to her is just one more anonymous stranger, until he turns and she sees his profile, and his dark hair curling at his neck.

He turns his head further and she sees him toss aside a book he's just been reading. There is a needle of curiosity – by no means for the first time – as to whether, quite by accident, he might be reading something by her. But she suspects that it's not so, he's on the wrong side of the bookshop. There's a stiffness to his posture as though he thinks he's being watched.

He's looking over at her, and she has the ridiculous urge to duck and hide. He's staring hard, like a lost man regaining his focus. A weak, almost apologetic smile starts to form across her lips, and then she changes her mind and remains stony-faced. Perhaps he hasn't seen her: perhaps he won't recognize her – perhaps, in these circumstances, she can simply fade into the background.

Rosie looks on as this man with whom she was once so intimate appears to struggle against impulse, not knowing what to do next. He makes as if to get up – then stays seated, thinking better of it; gathers his breath for speech, but appears to change his mind.

Rosie's skin prickles. She looks back down at the dating book and thinks she'll pretend to be reading. If he manages to read the title he'll really get the wrong idea. Eyes down, still pretending, she scans the rest of the table top, and her fingers inch towards a rather more respectable guide to Eastern meditation. She finds herself very nearly interested, and is about to start reading for real, when someone just above her clears his throat and she looks up.

Callum has come right over. At first she's almost angry. But when she looks into his eyes there's a slow sadness, a diffidence. Words are rumbling in his throat, but they take a while to stutter outwards.

'Rosie. I'm sorry. I owe you an apology.'

And she's so surprised, she forgets to really register what he's saying: to question – as later she will, endlessly – exactly what he is apologizing for.

Rosie sits in her office and looks out over the front lawn. Through a knotted arc of cherry tree branches, she can see the narrow pavement. It's an extraordinary stroke of luck that, so soon after her arrival, under such circumstances, she's secured this post. The practice is on the first floor of a converted Georgian house, just a stone's throw from her mother's flat, and the streets she knew so well as a child.

She looks down at her next appointment card: 'Dorothy Squires'. She can't help wondering if it's a joke. How could anyone called Dorothy be so stupid as to take such a married name? Perhaps it's someone's stage name. Rosie's tongue curls in her mouth.

Tomorrow. Five o'clock. Callum said he'd come to the seminar. It's not exactly a rendezvous, and she can't be sure he'll turn up, but when he raised an eyebrow and considered it, she felt a frisson of excitement. She still doesn't quite understand why he approached her in the bookshop, and the half-told story about his accident is almost too pathetic. She has a sense that he wants something, but if it's her, then she's flattered.

There's a knock on the door from Clarissa, her secretary. *Ra-ta-ta-tat*, like a knock in a pantomime. A slick head pokes inwards. 'Your three-thirty's here.' Rosie swivels back to her desk. 'Be with you in just a few moments.'

Rosie always finds out something about her clients from a brief telephone interview. So she knows Dorothy Squires is just a little older than she is, and a professional woman, who's had some recent trauma. Something to do with her husband. She'd been crying on the phone. The sobs had turned to hiccups and she'd become quite hysterical, so Rosie spoke to her gently, and decided not to probe. There'd been some soothing and cooing, as though she were pacifying a baby.

Now she stands, paces, and wonders to herself – as she still does, even now – whether she'll be any good at this. She presses the intercom. 'Clarissa. Can you send Mrs Squires in?'

The door opens narrowly, and a woman slips through. She is not tall, but holds herself upright, and her clothes hang well on her body. Everything about her is expensive, from the sandals to the French manicure, so it comes as a surprise when Rosie looks into her face. Pale and free of foundation, the small, neat features look naked. They should be glossed and finished, like the clothes and the nails, but instead they're creased and crumpled, as though there's a protective layer missing. There are grooves around the eyes, the face much older than the body.

'Come and sit down, Mrs Squires. Dorothy.' Rosie bites her bottom lip, and then she sees the woman's hands are shaking. She puts out her own hand slowly, places cool fingers in the woman's palm.

'Sit down, Mrs Squires. Take your time. It's all right.'

Mrs Squires is still shaking as she sits on the sofa. Rosie hands her a tissue and waits for the sobbing to subside. When it does, she speaks softly.

'So. What do you want to tell me?'

Dorothy Squires speaks in staccato.

'I just needed to talk to someone. I don't know if I can go on like this.'

Rosie nods gently.

'It's my husband. It's so difficult. You know . . . since he's gone.'

'You mean he left?'

The woman pulls herself out of her hunched position and stares straight at Rosie. Her eyes are flint-like fragments amongst the crumples of her skin.

'Not left. He's dead. To be exact, he was murdered.'

Rosie breathes in sharply, hoping the shock isn't obvious. The woman in front of her may need no help in finding herself. She's not looking for her inner child. Her husband's been murdered.

'How did it happen?'

'He was attacked. On the heath. A meaningless act of thuggery. The police thought they'd found the man, but now it's looking less sure.'

'That's awful. That would be really difficult for anyone to deal with. You really mustn't blame yourself for feeling . . . well . . . traumatized.'

Dorothy Squires looks across at Rosie fiercely.

'I *don't* blame myself. I blame the contemptible hoodlum who did it.'

'Of course. Tell me how you think therapy could help you.'

'The worst of it is,' continues Dorothy Squires, 'it was all some mistake. They wanted someone else.'

'Oh?'

'Another man was attacked. A near neighbour – we know him vaguely. Some hot shot QC – it's been in the papers. Except he survived, and my husband was killed.'

Rosie twists in her seat.

'A barrister was also attacked? And you think he was the intended victim?'

'I don't know. Perhaps.' The other woman is angry. 'I don't really care.'

Rosie flusters, and says, Of course, thinking back to what Callum has told her. About his accident and having a small misadventure on the heath. Then she looks at Mrs Squire's angry face and thinks, she's not doing her job very well. She thinks: if she's going to be good at this, she needs to be a lot more careful.

The seminar is entitled 'Psychotherapy or psychobabble?' It's being held in a cool, grand conference hall in one of the university buildings in Bloomsbury. There's to be a discussion and a panel of speakers, consisting of Rosie and three academics – all much more distinguished than she is. She ought to feel honoured. She goes out into the atrium. A shaft of sunlight slants through the large, arched, frosted window.

The seminar has been advertised mainly among students and academics, relying largely on the semi-celebrity status of Professor Miller, one of the panellists. He's one of those therapists with an advice column and slots on morning TV. 'Done well for himself, hasn't he?' Clarissa had muttered, impressed.

'Just think, Rosie, in a couple of years you could do all that.'

It's a quarter of an hour before the scheduled starting time, and a mixed bag of audience members are crowded at one end of the hall. Rosie's done talks like this before, and always this is that nervous, butterflies-in-the-stomach time when you're half afraid no one will turn up, and half-afraid they will. But this time, this early, the listeners are waiting.

Rosie looks out across the hall. She stares past a group of laughing women, probably on some book club outing, at an ageing Casanova with a ridiculously young girlfriend. Then her throat starts to clog up, and she clears it too loudly; several people glance at her meaningfully, as though expecting some announcement.

Callum turns. He stares right at her, staring at him. He raises his eyebrows, starts a shrug which never finishes: an oddly familiar gesture which has mutated slightly over the years. It's that look of spotting someone across a crowded room, like saying, *Hey, I'm glad you made it* or *You're the reason why I'm here.*

Rosie takes a step forward and then Professor Miller is at her shoulder. Conference organizers fluster round them and usher them on to the platform.

After the talk, she stands by the refreshment table. Someone from radio comes up to her and asks to take a few details. The book club women are smiling at her. And there is a quiet voice just behind her.

'You were very good. Clearly in adult life you've found your calling.'

Rosie turns to face him.

'In adult life. I like that. As though you remember me only as a child.'

'Well –' His voice tails off and he looks at his shoes.

'You came,' she says simply. 'I'm surprised. And I'm glad.'

'I – I wanted to see you again.'

She smiles, tries not to look too pleased.

'Shall we go somewhere quieter and have a quick coffee?'

He nods at her offer, though his posture is guarded. They pick up cups and small plates and go off into a side room. The loud but civilized hum of the crowd recedes.

'I liked your talk,' says Callum. 'All that stuff about progress and the past. I listened carefully.'

'And you learned something?'

'There's always stuff to learn.' He pauses, as though wondering whether to elaborate. 'Not that I agreed with everything you said.'

'So tell me what you thought. You know I've always liked a good argument.'

'Well,' he replies, talking carefully now, like a lawyer, 'I'm not sure it's true, what you said about drawing lines. Like shutting out things which have happened, and pretending they don't exist. Some things need to be remembered, need to come out in the open.'

She narrows her gaze, catching her breath beneath her diaphragm. His dark eyes and the slope of his shoulders have barely changed from all those years ago. She thinks of standing in the rain on the Strand, watching him walk away from her, and her whole body cries out to know why exactly he did it. But it's a question that makes her nervous, she must psyche herself up to ask it: that, and wait until she's strong enough to hear whatever might be his answer.

'I'm always glad if anyone finds my talks thought-provoking,' she says instead, affecting casual social chit-chat, 'even if they don't agree –'

He cuts in before she's finished. 'I told you, I think you're completely wrong.' Her body jerks away from him. There's a low insistence to his voice which is anything but friendly.

'Can you be a bit more specific?'

'It's all very well moving on, but supposing someone's done something wrong. Perhaps they have to face up to it, maybe even pay for it.'

Now she thinks she knows where he's coming from. About time, too: the topic's long overdue. But she won't make this any easier for him: he's broached the subject, let him wrestle it. He moistens his lips, as though to say something, then breathes, appearing to change tack.

'So . . . you made a name for yourself in America?'

She nods.

'How long were you there for?'

'Oh, years. I mean I've lived there for most of the last decade, though I was also in Paris for a bit. I was in San Francisco for a short while but mostly in New York. I did my postgraduate thesis here and then went abroad for my first fellowship.'

'And you've got . . . you know, family now?'

'Did I settle down, you mean? Marry and have kids?' Her voice is curt. 'I have a long-term partner and a son but we're . . . taking time out.'

It's the first time they've done the conventional catching up thing. Every meeting up till now has had some other agenda. But Callum is determined, as though on some lawyer's mission. She nods briefly, fixes his stare, as the questions keep coming.

'And you've been back . . . how long? You were telling me vaguely last time.'

'Just under a month ago. That was when I flew back. I was on the first leg of a lecture tour, but I cut it short.'

'So you got here the last week of May?'

'Yes, right at the end.' She tries a laugh, to sound casual, but it sounds wrong, because no one's joking.

Callum steps a little nearer, widening and narrowing his eyes. Perhaps he's trying to detect something that cross-examination can't uncover. She holds her hands behind her back, interweaves her fingers tightly. She can feel the ridges of her knuckles, imagines the skin stretched thin and colourless. This close, and she can almost smell his hair.

'Rosie, you know there's still so much I need to talk to you about. But not here, not now. Will you meet me again?'

Rosie scribbles her number on the back of a piece of paper, and when Callum hands her a card, she slides it away, somewhere safe. Callum gets up and walks away without looking over his shoulder. She wonders what he really wants to talk about, and how long she can keep this act up.

15

DC Fletcher was already there when Callum got back. There were no sirens or flashing lights and none of that luminous yellow cordon tape, but the police vehicle was a marked one and the detective may as well have been in uniform. Not much point in him being undercover, Callum thought a little bitterly. You could tell that types like him were coppers from over a mile off. For almost the first time he could remember, Callum felt socially embarrassed. Attracting all the wrong sort of attention. What would the neighbours say?

His footsteps grew heavier as he walked up the driveway. The officer was ahead of him, his hands deep in his pockets: his head was angled forward, as though he still wished to be unseen.

'Ah, Mr Scott, sir. Excellent. I've been waiting for you.' Something about his features lightened, but it could not be called a smile. 'I just thought I'd call round, sir. Little bit more to discuss.'

Callum nodded curtly and the two men went inside. As though summoned from nowhere, two younger officers appeared and followed them. They had the sort of bland, rounded features that made it difficult to remember them: they might have been there at Frieda's death, but Callum wasn't sure, and cared less. He led DC Fletcher through to the kitchen.

The detective eyed the coffee pot and made a few shuffling movements and then – with just discernible disappointment – spoke.

'We're here to see if we can find out any more. About the attack two nights ago. Any further evidence.'

Callum might have laughed, had not the notion of amusement almost left him altogether.

'What further evidence are you looking for, exactly? I caught the intruder myself, red-handed, so to speak. You identified him face to face. What else is it you need?'

Callum had seen his attacker with the lights on, and he was more boy than man, with a honeyed complexion and curling lashes like a girl's. When he had telephoned the police, the youth crumpled up into resignation, like a child caught doing a prank who knows his punishment awaits.

'Mr Freedman,' DC Fletcher had said, when he came to arrest him. His eyebrows lifted only slightly. 'Or perhaps I should say Tyrone. After all, we're hardly strangers these days. And now it seems we meet again.'

They took him away, hands cuffed behind his back, tight enough for Callum to see the caramel skin chaffing red.

'We'll be keeping your man under lock and key tonight,' DC Fletcher had said. 'He'll be in court tomorrow. I doubt there'll be any chance of bail this time.'

Now it was daylight again and the detective's shirt smelt of sweat. The fingers of the junior officers crept like insects' legs over the furniture. Callum spoke without clearing his throat and his words came out thickly.

'What more do you hope to achieve by combing my house for clues?'

'Mr Scott, don't forget this is a serious investigation. An attempt was made on your life, and another man is dead. We're still trying to find out why this happened, why Freedman would want to do this. So if you'd be so good as to let us continue with our job. We'll be looking for signs Freedman – or someone else – may have been inside without you noticing, and please would you make a note yourself if you observe anything – however small – missing.'

Callum tilted back in his chair, neither acceding nor refusing. Tired as he was, he could still remember his first attacker. Tyrone Freedman's boyish form was not the one that had near-crushed him. He had no hope the afternoon would bring any fresh discovery.

Most of the sun had gone, but the day's heat had been gathering. It had poured through the long windows of Callum's office in Chambers, collecting in the woody grain of desk and floorboards. Callum lifted a plastic bottle and took a swig of mineral water.

Thankfully, Anthony was out and he had the room to himself. He sat with one elbow on the table, his chin cupped in his fingers. From downstairs he could hear the banter that floated up from the clerk's room, like a song without words, only its rhythm detectable. It was tempting to go down, to grab a slice of that laughter, but he had set himself a task and was determined to complete it. Only a few minutes earlier, Cassandra had poked her head in, and with her usual moist-eyed smile she gave a high-pitched, girlish giggle.

'Still here, then?' she simpered – rather insultingly, Callum thought, as though his high-flying, hard working days were something of the past. He'd smiled back at her without speaking, as her body tilted against the door jamb. But in fact, more importantly, he didn't want her to know that she was right: he had no cases to keep him here, he could have been drinking gin on one of the pleasure barges. But something convinced him that if he persisted he would find what he was looking for.

That morning, Tyrone Freedman had appeared in court and lost his bail. He was now on remand for both murder and burglary. Freedman had been a witness in the case of Jason Lansdowne, and the amiable Lansdowne had sacked Callum for no reason. Callum was grimly certain he could fathom the connection.

A low flying wasp buzzed in through the open

window. Its arythmic hum merged with the tapping of his fingers. The downstairs laughter was diminishing, sounding very far away. Carefully, Callum reached into his desk drawer. Inside was a CD, which he slotted into his computer. The disk was slippery in his fingers: it was not something he ought to have had. He had seen it on Anthony's desk, and snatched it when the room was empty. He knew it to contain all the key information on the Lansdowne case. Guilty as a thief, he resolved he would copy it and then comb each fact, each detail, till the puzzle unfurled itself.

The wasp buzzed at Callum's shoulder; the computer keys clicked. The cursor skipped feverishly between words. Click-click went the keyboard. Callum waited for some breakthrough. But after many minutes searching, he removed the CD none the wiser. He concealed it beneath a pile of papers and shrugged his shoulders. The noise in the building had subsided and his armpits were growing stickier. He rested both elbows on the table and stared outside, unenlightened.

When he had just taken silk, flushed with his own success, Callum had gone through a phase of almost superhuman organization. Perhaps he had been swollen with the vision of even greater things to come; perhaps it was simply that Shona had left, and he was looking for ways to distract himself. At any rate, he'd placed on to his computer names and facts from a whole raft of cases. Despite the theft of the machine, he still had all his back-up disks. At the click of a button, he could call up a whole potted history of his career.

Now he lowered his eyebrows and chewed his back teeth. His fingers spread tentatively over the keyboard as he considered his next move. He slid one of his old disks into the machine. 'Freedman, Tyrone', he tapped in, the rhythm cautious, and then instructed the computer to carry out its search. Perhaps there was a link he'd forgotten, or could not know about.

The computer paused, churned and searched as Callum's body tilted backwards. An on-screen icon of a magnifying glass began its blind circling.

'Found,' the little instruction box told him eventually. 'File – Jason Lansdowne. Open – yes/no?'

But now Callum himself was circling as dizzily as the magnifying glass. This was the file he'd just been through, which had offered apparently nothing. He pursed his lips, funnelling air out between his cupped fingers. Then tapped in 'Lansdowne, Jason', and instructed the computer to search again

Callum sat back once more as the machine's engine churned. The wasp lowered its nose towards him and he flapped it away.

'Found', the computer responded, and dutifully scrolled up names of files. Callum's eye slid down the screen and he sat up with a jolt.

The first of the files was predictably 'Lansdowne, Jason', and Callum ignored the computer's request as to whether to open it. But there was a second file, under a different name, and it was one Callum recognized. The screen grew fuzzy in front of him. He searched his brain for a connection.

'East, Jamal,' he read, and his own brain was now like a computer, calling up a segment of the past he'd rather have forgotten. A gang of teenage hoodlums, and a killing terrible enough to make headlines. A summer night and a young student walking home romancing his girlfriend, thrown to a drowned death below a bridge over the Thames. The whole gang got hauled into the dock but it had been East who'd been the ringleader, his head thrown back like a colt's and his eyes narrowed in hatred. Callum couldn't remember Lansdowne having anything to do with the case – perhaps he'd been a minor defence witness who'd never been used – but he remembered East all right. He'd been Callum's client.

Anthony had represented the second-in-command: the lieutenant, as the prosecution put it, to East's malignant captain. When all five co-defendants went down, East had pledged revenge and vindication. Incarcerated for life, he'd refused to communicate further, save for a terse request to change counsel, and a semi-literate outpouring of scorn.

Where was he now? The boy would now be a man, but he'd have many days yet to slug out in the libraries and exercise yards of some prison. Likely as not he'd continue his career from inside prison walls. The armpits of Callum's shirt were soaking but the sweat on his skin had cooled. Footsteps skipped down the corridor and Anthony appeared at the doorway. He looked across the room at Callum and lifted an eyebrow.

'Cal. Didn't expect to see you. Still here so late?'

'You're the second person who's said that today. Why is everyone surprised to see me working so hard? Don't I have a career any more?'

Anthony strode across the room, and Callum stiffened with the memory of their recent confrontation, and the knowledge of Anthony's hidden, stolen disk at his elbow. He lowered forward to hide it, then cursed himself for being so obvious.

But Anthony simply picked up a satchel, and turned indifferently towards him.

'See you anon, then. Don't work too late, will you?'

Callum sat there, staring outwards, as the fierce heat around him softened.

*

He had anticipated his mother's appearance because she had telephoned to say she was coming, but the manner of her arrival was nonetheless unexpected. As soon as he opened the door he was reminded of childhood holidays, when she'd marched ahead of him and his brother up the pathway of seaside guesthouses, unbowed despite the burden of a family's worth of holdalls.

Today, she carried only one small, neat suitcase, but

her back was slightly stooped as she placed it down beside her. She kissed him briefly before speaking, and he wondered if this were deliberate, that she did not wish to embarrass him with any puzzle of recognition. She must have understood he would know her by her skin's smell, and he kissed her back with tenderness, noticing how she smelt a little papery.

'You look well,' she said firmly, drawing back and pushing past him. He angled his body towards the holdall, but she grabbed it defiantly. 'No need to stand on ceremony. I'll see myself in.'

No sooner had he stepped aside than she had swept up the staircase, her long skirt swishing after her like the train of some royal. He heard the banging of a door and the rapid unzipping of a holdall. When he joined her upstairs she was rearranging the guest bedroom, opening the windows and clucking at traces of dust.

'What sort of place is this to put me up in, Callum? Feels like you haven't aired it in years, and in this stifling heat too.'

He folded his arms and smiled.

'Nice to see you, too, Mother. But it would help if you had let me know exactly when you were coming.'

Now she was opening the wardrobe and straightening the clanging hangers. Industrious as a housekeeper, she muttered something monosyllabic, as though she had only half-heard him, and was too busy to make small talk.

'You know,' he persisted, 'it's not that I'm not delighted, but still, all the same, it's a bit of a surprise . . .'

'You seemed a little down, not yourself by any means, when I last saw you. I thought you could do with cheering up, alone here in this big house, and you know what with my own flat being quite small and that horrible square of yellowing lawn that calls itself a garden. Now that the summer's here, and all this heat, I fancied somewhere really pretty to sit outside.'

She had long disapproved of this house, and she was pursing her lips and looking ahead of her, so Callum knew, without asking, that she had to be hiding something. He thought: she thinks I'm losing it, and she doesn't want to let on. Either that or she's worried because she knows something I don't.

He watched her long-fingered hands as they stacked up old trinkets.

'Is that all I get for a welcome then? My own son staring off into space. You're not going to send me home, are you?'

He leaned forward and encircled her shoulders, and they went wordlessly downstairs.

At the kitchen table, she buttered bread cut into triangles, and he started to talk to her about the children and how he'd taken them on the Chambers picnic. Then the telephone rang and he scraped back his chair and stood. Heading out into the hallway, he saw her brow creased up in worry.

'Yes?'

'Callum.'

At once he became suspicious. This was Shona's voice, hard-edged, with a kind of accusation. She didn't have to explain herself – it was there in two simple syllables. He remembered the way she'd spoken to him before they'd come to parting, those final weeks of painful questioning, their marriage flailing like a sick dog. She'd accused him of working too hard, even of loving someone else. Once, when he'd returned late, he'd found her up, rigid and wakeful. *Callum*, was all she'd said, but the word was cold as stone. In a second he'd understood that some kind of era was passing.

Now he replied, 'Shona,' and wondered if this was what it had come to: he and his wife greeting each other with no more than each other's names. But at the same time he was thinking: this is beginning to make sense. His mother and Shona were near neighbours, Rudy and Saffron had kept them amicable. Perhaps the two women had spoken and his mother knew what was coming.

'Callum, I have some bad news, I'm afraid. It's the children – they've been ill.'

He breathed in so sharply his heart hurt. 'Tell me.'

'It was the stomach upsets I phoned you about. They carried on. We did have to call out the emergency doctor as I feared.'

His voice grew sticky in his throat. 'They're . . . they're all right, though? They're better, aren't they?'

The receiver was slippery against his palm. In the doorway his mother hovered, as silent as a shadow.

'Yes, Callum, they're OK. Rudy got better the next day. But Saffron was very ill. She had go to hospital for tests.'

'Hospital? Good God, Shona, why didn't you tell me?'

'I was angry with you, Callum. Especially after what the doctors said.'

'I don't understand.'

'Callum. This is going to be difficult. The children had something that was contaminated. It looked as though either they'd eaten something rotten or else . . . they'd been poisoned.'

It was as if the words had been made material and had fallen like lead weights upon his ear drums.

'Shona . . . I . . . could you . . . I don't think I quite understand.'

'Yes, Callum. You did hear me right. They'd eaten or drunk something. Not enough' – her voice caught – 'to kill them. But enough to make them pretty sick. And, Callum, from the tests and the timing of it, it looked like this happened when they were with you.'

'Shona – you're not saying – you can't possibly think I would do anything to harm the children. There's been some terrible mix-up.'

She sounded infinitely weary. 'I don't know what to think any more. Probably not, no. I mean, I know you don't really want them hurt, not in your right mind.'

'What's that supposed to mean?'

'Callum, I know you haven't been yourself lately. And I know that you may have been a little – irresponsible with the children. You might not be careful enough about what they eat, and who knows what they had at that picnic?'

'Shona.' He lowered his voice to a hiss. 'This is nothing to do with the picnic. You know I always give the children the very best care. There is much more to this than meets the eye. Someone is out to hurt me. This poisoning might have been deliberate. It might have been meant for me.'

'Maybe, but even if it's true, it means the children might be at risk with you. I'm sorry – I never wanted it this way. But, for the moment, you'll have to stop seeing them.'

Before he could respond, she had replaced the receiver, and he was left standing there stupidly, talking to emptiness like an idiot. When he looked toward the staircase, he saw his mother still hovering. She opened her mouth as if to say something, but he pushed past her and hurried out.

16

She lifts the receiver and dials, starting to count up to twenty. She has reached 'eight' when the ringing stops, and someone picks up.

'Yes?' It is a woman's voice. Rosie crashes down the receiver. She doesn't wait to register if the voice is old or young; if it is rough-hewn or soft-centred; if she can specify its accent. The wind worries the shrubbery, its rustle stealthy as a thief's.

Rosie has sat by herself all evening, gathering courage to do this. It doesn't matter that she feels let down: she is growing used to anticlimax. In front of her is her book of cuttings; snippets snatched from various newspapers. She's finding out so much more, leaving no stone unturned. Sometimes it feels mad, a wilful return to youth's obsession. But this is something she couldn't have foreseen, and now she's not sure what she's planning.

*

Rosie is starting to store things up in her memory bank the way she did fourteen years ago. There are periods in life always destined to remain vivid. People remember everyday details from the time of their first teenage crush, the kind of clothes and make up they were wearing; the sort of thing they had for breakfast.

It feels like that today. Rosie thinks she will remember the whole stretch of the morning – waking early, at six, and briefly imagining Toby crying. Her muscles stiffen – she must go to him; check that his sheets are dry. Then she realizes she's just dreaming, and doesn't have to wake yet. She falls asleep again, relaxed, both relieved and disappointed.

She wakes again at nine and breakfasts on coffee and fruit. They're going through a hot spell and the air feels thick, blunting appetite. Then she puts on light clothes and takes the short walk to her practice.

This morning, there's mostly paperwork to do, and answering a few telephone calls, including one from Professor Miller. He wants her to join him on some radio panel: she almost agrees, but says she'll think about it. Not long ago, the offer would have seemed like gold dust. Now she's preoccupied. There's more to life than mere ambition.

There is only one client coming for analysis this morning, and that's Dorothy Squires. Rosie's surprised she's come back: this somehow seems the wrong place for her. The woman needs grief counselling more than therapy and her rage has made her unresponsive. But anyway, she's back, which makes Rosie think all this is destined. As though her whole world is unravelling, full of half-revealed connections.

Mrs Squires arrives on time and is smart again in beige linen. Her nails are filed sharp and painted a hard matt scarlet, but her face is looking softer, as though she's had a good night's sleep. Perhaps she's discovered some fabulous new moisturizer – she looks like the kind of woman to buy expensive cosmetics.

During their session, she talks incessantly about her husband. Mornings without him stretch out endlessly, and she's come to dread each night. She talks of pulling back the bedsheets, her limbs trembling with loneliness. It is the error of his murder that makes her bitter to distraction.

Rosie listens, transfixed, but finds the narrative oddly empty. She has no sense of what life was like for this sad woman and her ghost husband. Did they have children? How did they spend their anniversaries? She only sees a grieving widow, and feels this twisted, hidden link to her.

When Dorothy Squires leaves the building, Rosie goes to the window and looks down at her. She walks straight-backed but slowly, turning right out of the front door, making her way to the corner, turning right again at the crescent. The high nearly-noon sun throws a sharp-angled shadow. The woman disappears into the crescent, and Rosie has the urge to follow her. She wants to shadow her, discover which front path she might walk up, what the façade of her house looks like, what happens behind her front door.

Outside, papers shuffle, the phone rings, Clarissa answers. Rosie hears her firm voice.

'Yes, she is about this morning. I'll see if she's free.'

Rosie remains where she's standing, stills the impulse to flee. She clears her throat; wonders who's calling; steals a glance in the mirror. Her reflection stares back at her, the eyes shadowy, wary, watchful.

'Rosie?' His voice dovetails upwards, uncertain. She doesn't answer, because she cannot believe he's calling her, but perhaps he takes her silence for indifference, or lack of recognition. 'It's me,' he says, sounding almost apologetic. 'Callum.'

Her mouth is dry. 'I know. I mean, yes. I mean, nice to hear from you.'

Callum speaks haltingly. This is not the arrogant, golden boy of their youth. But it's still more than she'd ever hoped for when he asks her if she'd like to meet him at his home. He hasn't put in this much effort since turning up unannounced fourteen years ago on her mother's doorstep. Heart-warming, really. It makes everything so much easier.

She comes upon him by surprise. He's a figure moving slowly, his shadow following across the lawn. There's an incongruous domesticity to the way he bends to prune the rosebushes, handling secateurs hesitantly, diffident forearms scissoring. Burnt grass crunches underfoot. A fallen limb of rosebush snaps. Callum jerks his head upwards; he sees her; his face freezes.

'How . . . I didn't hear . . . did my mother let you in?'

Rosie smiles lightly. 'I didn't even know she was here. I came round the side, I saw the gate was open. I caught a glimpse of you from a distance, gardening. Not something I ever thought I'd see.'

He gives a weak laugh, and bends to deposit the secateurs. His shirt is soaked, the sleeves rolled up, though you can still see it's an expensive cotton. As though this isn't something he does regularly, and doesn't have the requisite scruffy gear. The shirt sticks sweatily to his back, clinging in the dip between his shoulder blades.

'Well, let's go inside and sit down, shall we?'

The flowers and shrubs are vivid in the rich summer light. The thick green weeds in the copse take her back inescapably to childhood. Not even the games of blind man's buff, shattering the peace of the secret forest, can hijack her affection, taint the fondness of her memories. In the great house she'd sit wide-eyed while her father read to her from encyclopedias; the garden was a wilderness of adventure, where once a dark-browed boy had rescued her.

'Why not let's stay out here? You know how I love this place.'

He darts a guarded look, uncertain, then seeming to understand.

'Of course. You also know this garden so well.'

'And you came back,' she says simply. 'You bought

the house where we played as children.' The words are so strange and so heavy that she has to breathe rather than speak them. And Callum's wide-eyed – he opens his mouth – but then he looks away, thinks better of it.

'It's a real gem of a place. Quite a coincidence to find it on the market when we were looking in this area. Anyway, like you say, let's stay alfresco.' His hand flaps vaguely, evasively. 'Sit anywhere that looks clean enough.'

Rosie bites her lip, steps away, then takes one of the garden chairs beside a summer trestle table. He goes and fetches barley water, as though they were children again. Both their glasses are drained before they've said anything.

Callum fiddles with his damp shirt, folds one cuff up and down. Rosie bends forward, adjusts a shoe-strap, and then lifts up the secateurs. The blades gleam sharp against the sunlight. She saws the air, absently.

'Careful with those. One false move could be lethal.'

She stares for a few long, hard seconds, then sets down the implement. He slumps, tense shoulders slackening. 'It's good of you to come.'

'Cut the crap, Callum. We might not have seen each other for years, but I used to know you pretty well, remember? When you called this morning, you sounded quite desperate. I want to know why you're burning up to see me.'

'You're getting to sound quite American in your old age.'

'You haven't answered my question.'

His head's inclined towards the shadow, so she can't tell if she's made him blush.

'I just wanted to see you again. We didn't get a chance to speak at your talk.'

'You seemed to want to see me pretty quick. I wonder what made it so urgent.'

There's a smile, but it's hollow. 'Is it a crime to be eager? You could always have said no.'

'Doggedness of that sort was never exactly your style, Callum.'

'Rosie, you know that's not true. I've always tried hard when I've wanted something.'

They're sitting bantering, but neither laughs. Callum's stare is too purposeful to pass muster as levity, as though he's focussing hard before taking a photograph. He certainly wants something, she's just not sure it's her. He tenses as she leans forward, alert, on guard.

'This heat is making me thirsty, Callum. Another glass of something wouldn't go amiss.'

'Of course. Rude of me not to offer. Perhaps we should go in after all, get some shade?'

And they retreat into the house through the open French windows. Losing the white, outdoor glare is like plunging into darkness. Somewhere else in this house someone turns taps on, bangs a door. The clink of the domestic slowly recedes into silence.

Rosie sits on the sofa and Callum arrives with two more glasses. Both start speaking, then trail off. Rosie asks if, since the accident, he's starting to feel better; he says he'll soon be right as rain, though his words see-saw weakly.

'Your children? How are they? You were about to spend some time with them last time I was round here.'

He swallows barley water too quickly; she sees his Adam's apple bobbing.

'Thanks for asking, Rosie. They're just fine.'

Then he clears his throat, but still doesn't say anything. It's as though they both have these questions on their mind, but neither wants to be first to ask. She watches him silently, crossing and uncrossing her legs. Therapist's rules, always let your subject speak. His glass shakes when he puts it down, a drop of barley water spilling.

She can tell he's concentrating, still working out exactly what he wants to say to her, but he's also distracted, looking at the plane of her thigh as it disappears beneath her skirt. She rocks forward in her chair, her pelvis tilted, her shoulders back. Again Callum swallows; his shirt is still damp.

'It must have been strange for you coming back so suddenly, after so long away. Especially in the middle of that busy lecture tour – when was it? – forgive me if I've forgotten.'

Rosie's mouth widens, but she knows it doesn't look as though she's smiling.

'I was in San Francisco before flying home. The university, faculty of human sciences. Title of my lecture, "Mind over Matter". I give you these details in case you wish to double check.'

She gives her most brazen, I dare-you-to stare, but her insides are weak. He gives a strained chuckle.

'Don't be silly. I'm just interested, that's all.'

She raises her eyebrows. 'You're acting pretty weirdly, Callum. Anything you'd like to share with me?'

Rosie leans forward again, this time taking his gaze with her. He stares at the outline of her breasts as she bends to scratch an ankle; she looks up, catches his eye, and her heart twists with nostalgia. He glances sideways too quickly, and she knows he knows she's seen it. She wants to give a knowing smile, but the muscles round her mouth aren't working right. An insistence in his questioning is making her uncomfortable.

'Anyway,' he says, carefully, as though words were foreign objects. 'I'm glad, after all, you made the effort to look me up. That you found me, in the end.'

'Admittedly, I could so nearly not have.' She catches him staring again, and does her best to look offended.

'You always were the ingenious, persistent type, Rosie. Tracing me at work, ringing my clerks, finding me at home.'

He fixes her eyes and she stares back, trying to read his expression. With one nail he rubs his wrist, as though worrying an itch. She speaks slowly, with what she hopes is a calm, strong authority.

'I did make an effort to find you, Callum. But don't flatter yourself too much. Let's not overdo it. I never telephoned your clerks – not this time round.'

Callum furrows his forehead, his jaw drops perceptibly.

'But you said – about Simon –' and then he stops, clamps his jaw shut. 'No of course not. I've misremembered things.'

'You're quite confused, aren't you?'

She stands up and goes over to him. It's difficult to recall him so floundering. She reaches down, runs her fingers down the side of one cheek. He shudders, looks away from her. She turns his face back towards her.

'I never did understand you, Callum. Even all those years ago, when there were moments we felt like soulmates, you'd do something or say something and then I'd think I hardly knew you.'

She lowers her face and she can feel his whole body inch towards her, malleable as a child, instinctive as an animal. She steps away again, suspicious, but this time Callum holds her close, brings her body in towards him, his fingers tight around her wrist.

'You're wrong, Rosie. It was the other way around. It was me who always wondered about you. There was so much I didn't know about.'

His mouth moves against her ear, her blood pulses beneath his grip. There are footsteps in the hallway, a door is closing, someone's leaving. Rosie doesn't ask who it is. A thicker quiet descends around them.

She understands they're now alone. She hears his rapid, irregular breathing. His loosening fingers tickle her forearms, his brows drawn down in concentration.

'This is so weird, Rosie. You've not changed, you've barely aged.'

Now his voice has altered, its hard purposefulness softened. He sounds surprised, as though this is not what he'd been planning at all. She tries to look at him levelly.

'What are you doing, exactly?'

The words were supposed to be arch, but her voice comes out a jumpy whisper. One of his hands has found the small of her back. He draws breath softly. She looks at him and shivers.

'You haven't answered me, Callum. What's going on here, suddenly?'

He shrugs, as though beaten by circumstances he hadn't foreseen. 'I just can't get it out of my head, Rosie, the way we used to be together. You were always so sure of what you wanted, not like the other girls.'

His fingers edge towards her shoulder blades – she catches them, holds them, stops them. They turn white beneath her grip. She holds his gaze steady.

'Callum, let's not be flip about this. Are you sure this is what you want? After what happened all those years ago?'

She looks right into his eyes and this time he doesn't look away from her and then it's like a veil has lifted from his features and there's an expression she doesn't recognize. Though his eyes are still level, they are wide and hard, the whites showing. Pure fear transforms his face. Then his lips curl at the edges.

'What happened all those years ago. You can remind me about that later.' He raises one hand to her face and gathers her body in towards him.

17

It felt to Callum like a lifetime since he'd been here. He parked his car at a meter and walked the familiar stretch of road. There was the edge of a playing field and the red-bricked hospital façade. The glare of the sun hurt his eyeballs as it glanced off passing windscreens. He loosened his tie and slung his jacket over one shoulder. His neck shrank into his collar as though he were trying to hide his face.

In just a few moments, he had arrived at the prison gates. Beyond the broad, grimy archway the dark-grey walls rose up forbiddingly. The stark prison yard was an unrelenting concrete; in this weather, even looking at it was enough to make you sweat.

Callum hurried through the open door into a small, bare square of waiting room. Sundry lawyers formed an irregular queue leading up to a smeared glass cubby hole, behind which a nonplussed officer sat checking visitors' booking forms. Callum knew the routine only too well. A metal door would slide open at the push of a button, and those visiting would step through to a concealed, imprisoned hinterland. Clothes and briefcases would be x-rayed, sometimes sniffer dogs would check groins. Then they'd be ushered along a corridor to the sterile cubicles for legal visits.

But today, as if by magic, Callum was to make his way through a different door. He bit his lip and bent his head as he followed the arrow towards Social Visits. He left behind the legal men and women in their sober, uncomfortable suits and took his place behind a teenage girl with blonde crimped hair and denim micro skirt. A man beside her – boyfriend? Brother? – turned and glaringly asked if Callum had a pen on him. A cropped-headed jailer regarded him skew-whiff.

'You sure you're in the right line, sir?'

Callum nodded, shuffled his feet, held his bottom lip between his teeth. A cocktail of noxious odours floated up inside his nostrils. He restrained his crumpling features, disguising his disgust. He kept his breath shallow and his eyes glued to his shoes.

'Cal, old boy. What are you doing here?'

Callum looked up and saw a mouth smiling, wide thin lips and one capped tooth. It was the last thing he wanted, to bump into an acquaintance. He pieced together watery eyes, paper-dry skin, and a thatch of grey hair. Edward Bloomfield, once of Chambers and a friend of Anthony's. Callum raised an eyebrow and nodded lightly.

'Edward.'

Bloomfield's wide lips formed a slightly snarling oval.

'Long time no see, Cal. Are you sure you haven't

joined the wrong queue, or are you deserting your profession for the wilder life?'

The girl with crimped hair was moving forward and showing a visiting order. Callum moved up behind her and tapped the side of his nose.

'Long story, Edward.' He hoped he sounded casual. 'We'll catch up another time.' One of the great doors slid open and he disappeared behind it.

Now he was ushered up a wide staircase and made to wait at another door. Jailers patted down visitors, shaking their heads at cigarette packets. The rubber-floored corridor smelt of meths and stale urine. Beneath his damp shirt, Callum's heart thumped. He clutched the visiting order in his pocket. His plan suddenly seemed shaky.

Another jailer opened the door and the visitors started to file through. A wall of sound escaped outwards, like the roar of the sea. Women and infants screeched and yowled as they were reunited with their menfolk. The vast hall was filled with long, straight lines of low tables. Cast-away cigarette butts littered a dirty brown carpet.

On either side of the tables, visitors and inmates leaned inwards. There were even one or two toddlers crawling across the grubby floor. Callum took his place at the end of one line with a couple of empty chairs beside him. He was glad for the meagre hint of privacy.

At the end of the room was an officer behind a desk on a podium. He stepped up to Callum questioningly, and Callum handed him the piece of paper. The officer skimmed it, and nodded.

'Right you are. I'll go and get him.'

Callum sat back and waited. His palms were slick with nervous sweat. The minutes passed and he wondered if perhaps his visit had been refused. It had been a reckless plan anyway, he should have known it would come to this. He fixed his gaze on a particularly vile stain on the carpet, and then a voice above him spoke. Once it had been an adolescent's uneven whine; now it was lower and more gravelly, but still with the same sneering complaint. He didn't look up immediately.

'You,' said the voice. 'I shoulda known it.'

Callum lifted his eyes. All he could see was hazy in the dirtied, filtered sunlight, but he knew the boy-man he was looking at was the same old Jamal East. He thought back to when he'd defended him, a time when he'd believed with heartbreaking naïvety in his own resilience and good fortune. Shona and he had been together; he'd still considered James a friend and someone on whom he could depend to help with cases; and his rivalry with Anthony had seemed a benign, schoolboys' contest. Indeed, he could even remember the whole group of them out drinking, at the end of East's trial, just after the verdict had come in. Partly it was a celebration, because of the press coverage, and the relief of finishing; partly commiseration, because, of course, they'd lost.

'You couldn't have done any better. You were brilliant.' Shona had done her best to comfort him.

Callum and Anthony had stared at each other, party to their own shared, hidden knowledge.

'This was a nasty one,' Callum had said. 'That East's a real piece of work. Now that I've lost, he'll probably haunt me for ever. Friends, we could be witnessing the beginning of our own *Cape Fear*.'

It had been a joke, but even then, that sinister possibility hovered. Now, thinking back on it, Callum shivered at his prescience. He tore his gaze from the carpet and faced the inmate head on.

'Mr East. I'm glad that you came.'

East returned his stare with lips pouting as if ready to spit. His agitated features danced out of focus, but Callum saw his skin was thinner. He'd always had these popping eyes, fixed in a kind of hungry disgust.

East sat down and got up immediately, as though his skin had touched hot metal. Callum thought he would flounce off on realizing the deceit. But East stayed, though the saliva was gathering on his tongue.

'Man, watcha doing here? I thought someone was coming here to help me with my appeal. Didn't I tell you I never wanted to see you again?'

'I am here to help you. Some new information has come up, which combined with fresh and recent case law could assist you with your case. I felt so bad about what happened all those years ago, I wanted to make it up to you.'

'So why d'you write to me pretending to be someone else?'

'If I'd said who I was, do you think you'd have let me visit?'

East sat back down on his chair and spreadeagled his thighs. His knees poked at jagged angles through the baggy tracksuit bottoms. Even with diffident eyes, it was easy to see his face. The eyes like angled almonds, the razor cheekbones, the cruel clown's mouth. His breath hissed out through equine nostrils. He chewed his teeth as though drawing on an invisible cigarette.

'I don't believe you,' he said at last.

Words stuck on Callum's tongue, blocked his throat like a curled fist. 'You wouldn't be here,' continued East, 'just to help me, Mr Scott. I ain't so stupid. Not unless you wanted something.'

Callum sat back slowly. 'And what might *I* want from *you*?'

East grinned wide and vulpine. 'I dunno. You tell me.'

Callum squinted into the light, trying to read the other's gestures. Like trying to second-guess a lover, searching for hidden signs of betrayal.

'You're right,' he said slowly. 'I do want something from you. I do know how to help you, but I think you could also help me. Certain things have been happening around me lately. I think you might know what I'm talking about. I have this strange feeling you could shed a little light on things.'

East laughed – a shallow, mirthless volley. 'You taken to talking in riddles, Mr Scott? What's wrong – you afraid the police might be listening.'

'No, Mr East. Nobody's listening.' He leaned forward. 'Mr East. Last week a young gentleman called Tyrone Freedman was caught hiding in the shadows in my back garden. I have the strongest of feelings he wasn't there to inspect the flowers. This young man, as it happens, is remanded in custody on charges of murder and attempted murder. I'd like to find out a little more about him, and I have reason to believe that you could help me.'

'Mr Scott, sir. Ain't the police helping you with your enquiries? 'Coz I thought you was friends with them even though you call yourself a defence lawyer.'

'I'm not asking the police. I'm asking you.'

'Then you got the wrong man. I don't know shit about Tyrone Freedman. Now what's this information you got for me, or are you just wasting my time?'

'Think carefully, Jamal. I think you do know Mr Freedman.' Callum leaned in towards the other man till he could see his neck embossed with veins. 'I think you know plenty about Mr Freedman, and I think you could probably tell me a few things about his little night-time garden adventure. Only perhaps you don't feel quite ready to talk about it. So let me make it easier for you. If you talk to me a little, I promise you won't regret it. I could help you see the big blue great outdoors a lot sooner than you might think. Otherwise, things could get difficult. Even for you, it could get a lot harder. I think you understand me.'

East made as if to laugh, but his mouth stayed straight and stubborn. He was a lifer, but he had been only fifteen when sentenced. He had his tariff to serve, and there was always the question of parole. In the best-case scenario, he could be released while still a young man. But there was plenty in his past that could keep him in for much longer. If Callum chose to play mean, there were always secrets he could tell.

'Don't joke on me, Mr Scott. You ain't got the balls to play dirty.'

'Don't underestimate me. What use is my career if my life is in danger?'

'OK, Mr Scott.' The youth arched his back. 'I'll level with you. I am acquainted with Tyrone Freedman. And let's just say I ain't too surprised he was hiding out in your garden. But you ain't gonna find much on me, no matter how hard you start digging.'

Warm blood coursed in Callum's cheeks. 'So you do know something about all this.'

'I ain't said nothing, Mr Scott. Don't you go jumping to conclusions. Just because something happens to you, don't mean it's me behind it. Take it from me, I ain't your only enemy.'

There was a heartbeat of silence. 'What do you mean by that?'

'Just what I say, Mr Scott. Now, how about my appeal?'

'No, Jamal, not yet. First you tell me what you know.'

'No deal, Mr Scott. You think I'm that stupid?'

Callum opened his mouth, but the boy's skinny legs were straightening. East nodded at the podium, signalling he was ready to return to the wing. Callum slid him a business card.

'Why not drop me a line? Like I said, if you can tell me anything, I'll make it worth your while.'

East turned to look at him as he was led away by the officer. 'Thanks for your visit, Mr Scott. Don't go doing anything stupid.'

The house was empty when Callum got back. He stood in the hallway and looked for a note, cocked his head on one side and listened for signs of life. The air remained still. He ran his fingers through his hair.

Callum had booked a favourite restaurant and he and his mother were to treat themselves. He had more or less expected she'd be here, but perhaps she had gone out to the hairdresser's. There was still a rich, afternoon light, so he decided to go for a walk. He stepped out on to the driveway and left the quiet house behind him.

He reached the outskirts of the heath, and then took the path that led to the copse, pausing to sit on a favourite bench overlooking one of the ponds. A pebble from behind hit the black liquid surface, and the water skimmed and rippled with someone's reflection. Callum jerked, twisted round, suspecting someone was watching him. The long wild grasses rustled but after all he was alone.

Returning home for a second time he rattled his keys free and called out casually.

'Mother, I'm home. Down here.'

The cadence of his voice floated up the stairs, unanswered. His shirt was sticky on his back and he went to fetch a glass of water. The tap fizzed into action, and he rinsed a glass and gulped thirstily. There was a clanking and a clattering that was more than just the pipes clearing. His mother must be showering, that was why she hadn't answered. He placed the emptied glass on the draining board and wiped his cold, wet mouth with his hand.

Callum took the stairs two at a time and saw the door of his mother's room ajar. He would surprise her unawares, he thought: already he was considering some witticism. But as he stepped up to the door a gust of wind blew it open and he saw, within a second, that the room beyond was empty. The curtains fluttered inwards like the loose gymslips of schoolgirls. It was odd that she'd gone out without closing the windows. He heard a drip in the next door shower room, and found the mirror misted and damp. He tightened the shower tap, went into his bedroom.

Callum sat down upon the bed, rose, wandered back down the staircase. By now he was feeling disconsolate. He recalled how, not two years ago, he'd bought his mother a new mobile phone – a neat, slinky silver one – and pressed it pleadingly into her palm. She'd stubbornly refused to fathom its wizardry and had eventually given it back, remaining defiantly untraceable. Callum's fingers curled inwards. He meandered into the kitchen, ran a troubled hand over the dresser.

A lick of realization came over him slowly. He wondered how he had failed to notice it earlier. He was staring into emptiness, at a corner of the dresser. There, where the surface spread bare, there should have been a picture. The photograph of his family had been taken.

But perhaps he was wrong; perhaps the picture had fallen and his mother had placed it somewhere safe, perhaps she'd taken it away to clean it, neatness freak that she was. Callum shifted where he stood and looked sidelong at his watch. It was not yet five o'clock.

He climbed the stairs once again, pulling off his shirt as he did so, went to shower, then stepped back out into a thickening heat. He was glad of the water still sprinkled on his skin. He sprawled out on his bed, took a deep breath and slept.

It was an explosion of noise which woke him, like the sound of something shattering. Despite the warmth, his teeth chattered and his body jerked upright. But even as the sleep slid away from his eyes, he was unsure if what he'd heard was real or imagined. The bedclothes were damp for he had fallen asleep without towelling himself. He shook himself awake and pulled on underpants and a dressing gown.

At once his eyes slid over to the alarm clock at his bedside. Past six o clock. They would have to be leaving soon. He went out on to the landing. 'Mother?' he called out, but he could already see from where he was standing that her bedroom was still empty. He took the stairs downwards at a trot, but there was no one on the ground floor. It was so very unlike her to be late, or forget to ring him.

Perhaps, he thought, she had telephoned, to explain the delay. He checked the answering machine. No messages. But perhaps she was yet to call. She could easily have gone into town, and got stuck on the tube. You never knew with public transport. She could still make it, just about.

Callum went back to his wardrobe to find his preferred white cotton shirt. It was nowhere to be seen and in a moment he remembered that his mother had just washed it and it would still be hanging out to dry.

He followed the maze of the corridor round two corners to the utility room, which gave off a synthetic sweet pine scent that he could smell from yards away. The shirt might be still damp, and it was not one you could tumble dry, and he was feeling sulky all over again, when something took his mind off laundry. A sound again, somewhere above him, like a heavy object falling, at first muffled, as though by wool, and then sharper and more disjointed. Callum stood still in the passageway. He realized he was shivering.

Protectively, he pulled his dressing gown tighter. The clattering feathered into quiet, and he stood listening to his breathing. The noise was coming from above him. No trapped rodent could scratch this viciously. And then there came another sound. Soft and rhythmic, like someone knocking.

Callum rolled his eyes upwards. A thin crack of light, three sides of a rectangle, outlined the trap-door which led up into the loft. He breathed in, puffed out his cheeks. His wrists were fragile, unsteady. He went to open the trap door.

The stepladder unfolded itself and Callum placed a foot on the lowest rung. He flinched as the bare sole of his foot hit cold metal. Everything vibrated. He started to feel dizzy.

Within a few seconds he could see into the attic. He took in the insulation round the water tank and an old bicycle he'd stored up there and an ancient suitcase of Shona's he'd never thrown away. They were like details in a picture too familiar to register. But his heart twisted as he saw floorboards stained dark and sticky.

There was no noise any more. The knocking had stopped. Callum held his breath, stopped his senses, wanting no longer to see, hear or smell. His legs had turned so weak he thought he would tumble down-wards. But he made himself climb till he could peer above the final rung.

Evening sun glanced through the skylight, and he saw the shadow of a hand moving. He fell forwards, hitting the floor, his blood mixing with the fresh stain.

PART THREE

18

He has never seen her like this before. It is the shock, and his weakness, which throws him so dizzily off balance. Tendrils of blood from his nostril dribble into the crevice between nose and mouth. His stomach churns. His eyes blur.

He steadies himself on to all fours like a beast, like a crawling baby. Her body is limp, a stream of spittle wetting the cloth which has gagged her mouth. Another piece of material – hideously misplaced, misused bandana – squeezes her temples, acting as a blindfold. Her breathing is barely detectable beneath the loose linen dress. Like the last life slipping out of her, or the remnants of a terrible fear.

Callum rocks back on to his haunches, progressing from crawl to crouch. His breath sticks somewhere beneath his breastbone; he's not sure he'll manage to speak. Wordlessly, he spreads his fingers. He lifts each of the cloths from her face, terrified at what he might uncover. The face beneath is bruised, lumpen, one eye half-closed like a boxer's. He presses one nail against the edge of a cheekbone, tracing inwards, like a lover.

'Oh dear God. Mother.'

The words, when they do come, slide out like a

frog's croak, echoed by her reply, which is a phlegmatic, halting moan. But she can't put together words. There is just the expression of pain. He can see round one wrist the skin is an angry bandage of scarlet.

'Mother. What's happened? Who did this to you?'

She can't answer him: he knows that at once. He can see the purplish, swollen tongue, the cracked and incompetent lips. He lifts what must have been the blindfold from the weeping raw skin above the brow bone, peeling it away like a wound's dressing, wishing he could be tender as a nurse.

'Oh Lord. Oh God.'

His brain can't produce a proper sentence, his voice breaks and blurs to a sob. He needs a telephone right now, so that he can call the emergency services from where he's sitting. But there isn't, and he can't. He quavers at the thought of lugging himself back down the stepladder, let alone somehow manoeuvring his mother so she remains more or less unbroken.

Grindingly, he stands up. The sloping eaves are too low for him to raise himself to his full height. He moves in a shambling sort of limp till he is standing behind her. He does not know how to move her. Some kind of red alert flashes in his brain – the injured should be left alone, untouched by all but experts. Let them remain at least in part unshattered.

He nudges his body towards the stepladder; his mother moans behind him. She stretches out her hand, her fingers yearning towards his ankle. A youngster hauling its parent back; role reversal in one ghastly, perverted moment. Callum twists his gaze backwards, sees cobwebs, hears something like gnawing. He steps back once again, bending his face towards her.

'It's all right, Mother, I'm not going to leave you.'

Once, as a child, he did life-saving lessons. He wasn't an outstanding swimmer, but he was competent and stylish – after all, he'd been good at almost everything, more or less. He thinks of those classes, leaning backwards in the water, supporting someone else's weight, pulling them gently but firmly shoreward. Could he apply any of the rescuing principles now – pull his mother's weight backwards, let them ride the currents together? He eyes the stepladder despairingly.

'Don't worry. It'll be all right.'

Somehow, he hunkers down, sliding his arms beneath her. Together they slither sideways, like some mythic eight-limbed beast. He arrives at the square of open trap door, reaches backwards with his feet.

'It's fine. It'll be OK.'

He has no notion if she hears him. For a second, some scent – embarrassingly dry and foul – rises up off her skin into his face. For some reason it conjures with it any number of other aromas – the grimy corridors of the prison, the stench of Frieda's rotting carcass. The scented candles of Angelo's, the close-up tang of Rosie's skin. Sweet and sour, fresh and stale. His vision blurs. He clears his throat

It's as though his mother keeps shrinking, held like a rag doll against his body. One of his arms is round her waist as he moves shaking down the stepladder. The short distance between floor and ceiling has become a sheer and endless cliff drop.

'Where's the bastard did this to you?'

His muttering is fierce, his anger frothing into little bubbles at his lips. His mother grunts – a cough or a choke; as though in response, as though in protest. He snaps his jaw shut, guiltily. Perhaps his speculation has upset her.

Minutes and seconds extend into a time he cannot measure. It's as though they remain for hours on each rung of the ladder, his mother growing heavier with each passing moment. Her breathing turns to a wheeze. Callum's shoulder blades ache. As if carrying someone this way defies every sinew's instinct.

The ladder jolts. He thinks of bones jarring beneath the skin. More spittle dribbles out around his mother's lips. Her mouth widens, then closes again. The spittle is pink, blood tinged. If only he could remember some of the first aid he once learnt.

'Don't worry. Be there soon. It'll all be all right.'

There is a kind of whining from her in response. The floor is suddenly nearer. He stubs the air backwards with his toe, misses the last step and stumbles. The landing floor is hard. The soft mass of his mother covers him. For a moment he is plunged into a heavy purple blindness. She gives that horrid, haunting whine again, as though calling out from hell. He turns his face, gasping for breath. In every inch of him there's pain.

*

Rosie breathes in. Yet again, the telephone at the end of the line remains unanswered.

She is in front of her bedroom mirror, putting on her make-up. There are shadows beneath her eyes. She covers them with a light foundation. She glosses her lips, pouts till the colour is neat, applies a thin coating of mascara, fluttering her lashes dry. Perhaps it is disturbing to be paying attention to such small vanities. But, after all, appearances matter. She straightens her back, buttons her shirt.

It was cold this morning, almost autumnal, such is the quixotic nature of the English summer. Shoes then, rather than sandals. No, the sandals look better, setting off her ankles, making her legs look longer. Do women never grow past caring about such adolescent details?

There was a place where he bit her, when they were last making love. She still carries the needle-like tooth imprints on the slope between neck and shoulder. It is brazen and obvious in a thin-strapped summer top. She will have to dress to conceal it, like being a schoolgirl again.

He is deeply unhappy but perhaps she can still save him. Perhaps it is not too late.

She opens the front door and sets off.

Callum's toe catches on the hallway rug and he nearly falls on to his face. These last two days his body has disobeyed him at every moment. 'You'll have to take it easy, sir,' the young doctor at Casualty had said. Callum had ground his teeth. What did such a naïve youth like that know?

He is afraid he will take too long to recover his balance, so that although the telephone is ringing, he will be too late to get the call. The hospital, of course. That's the call he both dreads and expects. And hopes for in a way, in case they're calling with good news. Except somehow it never works that way. You never get roused at midnight to hear everything's all right.

He reaches the occasional table, and the bleep still rages on. He lifts the receiver, speaks as though into an abyss.

'Yes?'

'Cal, dear boy, it's Edward.' Callum's mind registers blankness. 'Edward Bloomfield, you remember. We met the other day. At one of Her Majesty's more salubrious establishments.'

Callum's incomprehension comes out as silence, but Edward Bloomfield keeps on talking.

'Callum, I don't want to speak out of turn, but after bumping into you the other day, I was chatting with Anthony and saying how nice it had been to see you after so long, and how we should catch up, and, well, Anthony told me the dreadful news. About what happened to your mother. I just wanted to say, we're all thinking of you at Chambers. We're with you and we're praying for you.'

The voice is going on for ever, but why is Edward Bloomfield ringing? Not as if they're the best of friends. Callum seems to remember he's a churchgoer. It's a little disconcerting that Anthony's spreading the bad news with such alacrity. Callum murmurs 'thank you' absently. God, what about the children in all this? How will he explain to them about their grandmother?

The conversation with Edward Bloomfield feels like it's lasted a year. But there's a shadow advancing up the driveway, its outline bleeding beyond the glass.

'Thank you, Edward. I have to go now.'

'I understand, old boy. The very best.'

Bloomfield's voice is achingly benign. The shadow moves. The doorbell rings.

Already it's hotter than she expected. Rosie's clothes feel too heavy. She wonders if she'll sweat. The sandals were the right choice, though, and her toenails varnished a bright, bloodied scarlet.

She thinks of his skin against hers, his warm lips and his prying tongue. He opens the door. His face is a canvas of grief and terror.

They sit together in the kitchen – like long ago, like just recently. He knows there are still things he has to ask her, but right now he can't find the energy. All he knows is he wants to sleep, wants all this to fade like a nightmare.

The telephone rings again, he stands, moves out of the room. He feels no need to excuse himself. He leaves her sitting there, silently. He lifts the receiver, but says nothing. Someone speaks, far away. Words coming from the end of an immeasurably dark tunnel.

He stands stock still. The receiver slides from his fingers, swings at the end of its coiled flex. The hallway sways in front of him. The floor lurches closer.

Rosie's there, suddenly, beside him, her eyes wide and questioning.

'Callum, what is it?'

'My mother . . . she's taken . . . I don't think she's going to make it.'

He doesn't even remember whether he's told Rosie about his mother anyway. Why should he make sense? His world has lost all logic.

'I suppose you'd better leave. Yes, you'd better be going.'

She shakes her head. 'But I can't leave you alone like this.'

He squints at her features, wanting to draw close, wanting to pull away. For a second, all he can remember is the way she last felt in his arms, and he wants to cry out to her: *Yes, yes, please stay with me.* But outside, a car brakes hard, the screeching waking him from such madness. And his heart sinks, because he recalls the things he's yet to ask her.

19

There is a knock on the door which rouses her.

For a moment he had reminded her of their long ago island holiday, the tide scudding over shingle lulling them to sleep. A memory of one afternoon came back to her, as vivid as midsummer.

She was lying supine on hard ground where the wrong blend of sun and shade had scorched the soil rusty and stripped the grass from the earth. Branches criss-crossed overhead beneath a kaleidoscope of blue. If she stared long and hard enough it looked as though pieces of sky were moving.

Callum was nearby, sitting close, but not close enough to touch her. To do that, he had to lean inwards, to run a fingernail along her forearm, or push the hair back from her forehead. Every so often, the feel of him startled her, as though she were in a dreamworld so powerful she had forgotten her surroundings. Sometimes, on coming outside, they would bring books and sit reading; occasionally Callum bought English newspapers in the village and did crosswords. Today they had taken nothing. They were not reading, not speaking. Even to kiss or laugh might spoil the quiet moment.

Rosie was thinking you could only feel this peaceful

after getting really tired. Tired by crying, tired by doubting, tired by wondering whether you were loved. You imagined the very worst, and then you discovered – quite miraculously – that you had been wrong all along and you were wanted after all. Suddenly your heart skipped, you could last for hours on air and water. You thought every clichéd chorus of every love song could have been written just for you.

She was thinking: this is not the kind of emotion that can ever repeat itself. No matter how young it came to you, you could never forget it. It was so strong it made you lonely, obliterating all senses. But if something, someone, made it go wrong, what sort of madness might that cause?

*

Callum twists his head so suddenly the muscles in his neck hurt. He is as startled as Rosie is by the knocking, surprised enough to shudder slightly. He leaves her sitting in the kitchen, for all the world as though she's bewildered, and he no longer really knows if he wants her to stay or leave.

In the hallway, he stands still, grinds his toes into the thick rug. Then he stretches out his hand and pulls the front door towards him.

'Good afternoon, Mr Scott. Sorry to butt in at a time like this, when I know you must be worried about your mother.'

Nothing fits together, because there is Anthony on the doorstep, but why is he calling him Mr Scott, and why is his voice coming out all peculiar? Anthony won't look at Callum directly, so all Callum can really see is his nose, and staring at the sharp slope of it Callum realizes his own anger. Why is Anthony intruding just now? And telling strangers like Edward Bloomfield about his personal trauma?

'Look here,' says Callum, and then the man on the doorstep speaks again. 'DC Fletcher,' he breathes. 'For a moment I mistook you.'

'No need to apologize,' says the policeman, rearranging the hair on his forehead. 'I hope you don't mind if I ask you a few questions.'

Callum shakes his head.

'Detective, this is really the wrong time. I can't give you a statement right now. I have to go to the hospital.'

'Then – when?'

'I don't know. How can I know?'

'Well, I do hope everything's OK, sir. But don't forget, this is important.'

'Yes, thank you, Detective. I'll be in touch.'

'No, I will. Goodbye, sir.'

Callum bundles the policeman out like an unwanted parcel. A small hand is on his wrist.

'Callum, is everything all right?'

He looks down at Rosie. 'Yes, no – how could it be?'

She shrugs up at him.

'Look, Rosie. I have to go. I can't finish our conversation.'

'Is it to do with that man who just called? Was he

a policeman?' Her voice has gone strangely infantile. The thin skin at her throat pulses.

'No. I mean, he was a policeman, but it's not because of that. I have to go to the hospital.'

'Of course. To see your mother.'

He still can't quite remember how much he explained to her, but she waits patiently as he rushes through the house, collecting his keys, wallet and jacket. For a moment, patting his pockets, ticking off items on a mental itinerary, it's as if he's getting himself together for some mildly pleasant excursion.

'You shouldn't drive,' says Rosie. 'D'you want me to take you?'

'No. Thank you. There's a cab office on the high street. I've an account with them. They'll sort me out.'

She is standing there, unmoving, like a permanent fixture.

'Shall I stay? I can be here when you get back. I can help with things, look after you a bit.' And she says it for a second time. 'You really shouldn't be alone.'

Callum shakes his head quickly. His heart thuds unexpectedly.

'Thank you for offering, but, really, not just now.' She smiles weakly and he feels guilty. 'Look, we'd better be out of here.'

'Oh, I – er – look. Sorry to hold you up. Could I just use your bathroom?'

'Yeah, sure, it's upstairs – I mean, you know where

it is.' He looks at his watch, resenting the precious minutes he'll have to wait for her. But only a fool would leave her alone here, with all that remains uncertain. And then he thinks again of the call from the hospital, imagines his mother, prone and pallid. Callum realizes that at this moment, he no longer cares. 'Look, I really must go. You can let yourself out, round the back.'

She gives a laugh that's more of a whimper, embarrassed by all these formalities. He walks away from her, twisting backwards as he opens the front door.

'I'll call you, Rosie.'

She is still standing there, unmoving, like a too-shy little girl, lurking quietly in the shadows, listening intently behind doorways.

Rosie goes down the wide staircase, taking each step slowly. Extraordinary, after all this time, to be alone in this house again. Amazing that Callum should have left her here, when he's so full of mistrust. But he's clearly not thinking straight. He's got other things on his mind.

She's about to step outside when she remembers two things. First, she promised Callum that she'd go out the back way. Second, she left her handbag and all of her things in the kitchen.

She goes back, sits down, places her elbows on the table. There's a comb and some lipstick and a small mirror she brought with her. She may as well look respectable before facing the outside world.

Her fingers shuffle the flotsam that floats around in her handbag. There are some old credit card slips, a parking ticket, one of her schedules from the summer's lecture tour. She places them on the table, still rummaging for the make-up. Odd to be doing this, for all the world as though she were at home here.

And here is something she did not expect to find. It is a photograph, the scene years old, although the memory is raw. She and Callum stand together, the background an island forest. The nostalgia is so strong it pulls her muscles rigid.

Rosie blinks. There is something deeply illicit about this picture; it is as though she were sitting here stealing a glimpse of pornography. And then she starts, interrupted. There is a footfall on the gravel.

Rosie stows away the photograph, her fingers trembling, inefficient. It can't be Callum, back so soon. Surely he didn't forget something. Whatever would he think – or do – if he found her still here, like this?

The footfall echoes again, and there's a ring at the doorbell. It isn't him, then. He hasn't forgotten his keys – she saw him herself, placing them carefully in his pocket. Perhaps it's that policeman come back on the off chance, because he's remembered one more, really important question. Like in all those crime dramas on the telly. Goose pimples prick her forearms.

Rosie's hands and fingers flail at her possessions

on the table. She wants to sweep the surface clean, but her mind and body can't coordinate and far too much flotsam remains on the table top. Her limbs are ungainly as she hurries for the back door. Her feet clatter on the paved terrace and down the narrow side alley. Whoever the mystery visitor is, he or she hasn't quite given up yet. She can hear them still knocking and pressing the doorbell, huffing into cupped hands and stamping quick, anxious feet.

Rosie slides behind a loquat tree and her heel cracks on a loose paving stone. Her weight falls forward and she gasps; there's an arpeggio of clitter-clatter. The visitor must have heard her; footsteps come back out on to the drive. She makes for the end of the pathway.

'Oi, you. Who's there?'

The voice is harsh, high-pitched, imperious. A male voice, but not masculine. Rosie's mouth fills with saliva. Even with the cracked heel, she starts to run.

'You, come back here. Don't think I haven't seen you.'

The voice crescendoes behind her, but she's back out on the pavement.

'Is that who I think it is? Come back here at once.'

She takes off her sandals, so carefully chosen. Barefoot and bloodied, in a moment she's fairly flying.

20

The hospital corridor stinks. It's strange, because it's not the filth that smells, it's the cleanliness. Dettol and detergent and newly scrubbed glass and plastic. It goes straight up Callum's nostrils, gives him an unexpected high. He's giddy with hunger and tiredness and nervousness. Clear glass panels in the walls ripple like water.

'Ah, Mr Scott.' There's a voice which clearly recognizes him. Some consultant he's already forgotten whose face is a film of wavering angles. He has no idea where he should be going. A hand extends towards him. There's a blue room with chunky sofas and the air smells sweet like dry dead roses.

Callum's ears go full, as though he's swimming underwater. The consultant's mouth lifts, so it looks like he must be smiling, but at the same time his brow is furrowed, and his eyes drawn close together. The planes of his cheeks and his chin slope together all wrong. His tongue is swollen and scarlet, the teeth like great uneven slabs of chalk.

Callum is mesmerized by the movement of tongue against teeth, how the tip of the bright-red motile muscle points and pokes, tuts and hisses. He is wondering why this consultant doesn't fork out for some cosmetic dentistry. His mind spins, he thinks back to a documentary he watched about plastic surgery. He hears the words 'irreparable damage' but can't fathom their relevance.

The consultant's teeth swim towards Callum and his tongue grows very large.

'Mr Scott, are you all right? Is there anything you want to ask me?'

Callum hears a strange rattling at the edge of his skull.

'Is my mother all right today? Can I go and see her now?'

'Mr Scott.' The consultant comes embarrassingly close. His voice cracks with kindness. 'I don't think you're quite yourself. Can I fetch one of the nurses to sit with you?'

Callum can smell some sort of aftershave on the other man's skin.

'I really . . .' he stumbles upwards, his hand gropes the air for balance. The aftershave is overpowering, almost blocking Callum's airways. The blue carpet see-saws like the horizon viewed from a boat in choppy waters.

Rosie phones home.

She doesn't want to speak to anyone, apart from Toby; doesn't want to answer any difficult questions, just wants to tell her son she loves him.

'Hello?' Michael answers quickly, and she recognizes the edginess in his voice, as though Toby's playing up and he hasn't had a decent night's sleep in weeks. She can just see him leaning on the fridge door, skinny ribs straining through his T-shirt, scowling as he surveys the measly contents of the kitchen.

'Can I speak to Toby, please?'

'You've rung to speak to my son. Who shall I say is calling?'

'Come on. Cut the crap, Michael. You know it's me.'

'And who would "me" be? Apart from someone who rings to speak to Toby and can't even bring herself to say hello. Full marks, Rosie. Thanks once again.'

'Give me a break, Michael. I didn't call up to have an argument. I just want to speak to my son.'

'Oh. Ho. *Your* son. The one you haven't seen in . . . how many weeks is it now? Or should that be months? Remind me, please, I seem to have lost count.'

'Michael, I didn't ask for this. I came over here at the beginning of the summer because my mother was very ill. She's dead now, in case you'd forgotten.'

She knows Michael's expression, or can fathom it just from listening to his voice, to the rhythm of his breathing. He's biting his back teeth, his lips distended like a wolf's. He's sucking his cheeks hollow. His body looks like a wound-up spring.

'Yes, Rosie. But she didn't die yesterday, did she?'

'That's not very fair, is it?'

'And you leaving your son on the other side of

the world without a clue as to when you'll be back – that's fair, is it?'

'Who says I'm leaving my son?'

'So when're you coming back?'

Rosie says nothing. She thinks of the heath, of the old house, of the box of memories and trinkets. There is unfinished business. She has no words for Michael.

'Look. Please. Can I just speak to Toby?'

Michael draws breath. Even now, without words, without seeing his face, with thousands of miles between them, she can read his mood exactly.

'So. You're not coming back. What use is a phone call to Toby, if he's never going to see you again?'

She thinks about parrying, can't find the energy.

'And maybe you might think about whether it's a good idea to phone Toby at all. You'll only get him starting asking questions and he'll get all upset again.'

'Just one word, Michael, please.'

'No, Rosie. You can't speak to him now anyway. He's still at daycare.'

'All right then, Michael. Just tell him I love him, OK?'

'This is not the time to come over all sentimental, Rosie. You always were a fucking lousy mother. Whatever it is you left us for, I hope it's worth it.'

Michael slams down the receiver. Rosie recoils, shaking. She bites into the white flesh of an apple. It comes away blood-streaked from her gums.

*

The house is terrifying. Loneliness has never felt like this. Not even after Shona left, or in the aftermath of the heath attack.

Callum's hurting all over, his body sore and stiff and empty. He wishes someone else were here to run him a bath, put fresh sheets on the bed. He finds the bottom of the staircase and collapses on to the lowest step. His head is bowed, his shoulders slumped, but his throat's too dry for sobbing.

He phoned his elder brother, Will, from the hospital. Will went back to Ireland years ago, to take things slowly, unremarkably. The two haven't been close since childhood. Will may have been the elder brother, but he was always the second in command. And then, in his quietness, he became almost subversive.

'Never did play the game, like you, little brother,' Will would say, with a distinctly double edge to his voice. When Callum called him from the hospital he was shocked, even desperate, but still Callum could hear the absurdly cheerful background chirping of children. He'll be flying over from Ireland. Perhaps he can sort out the funeral.

Shona can wait – not like she's got such a heart anyway. But the children – how will he tell them? His head lolls forward. His eyes close.

Daylight filters on to the carpet, coloured by stained glass. Callum can barely open his eyes. He reaches for the ringing telephone.

'Callum. It's me. How are you? How was the hospital?'

His whole body tenses.

'Not so good, Rosie. Bad news, I'm afraid.'

Seconds pass. Neither speaks. He can hear Rosie breathing.

'Oh God, I'm so sorry.' Her voice is a whisper. 'But I really do know how it feels.' Her breath is strained. Almost asthmatic.

'I'm sorry, Rosie. I have to go. I can't talk now.'

'Don't, Callum. Don't shut me out. Remember this has just happened to me. We're both orphans now.'

He sighs, his muscles frozen, too stagnant even to hang up.

'Can I – should I come round and see you perhaps? Maybe you need some company.'

He waits, hears his heart beat.

'I don't want anyone round here just now.'

It's not true, he craves company, even silent shadowy figures, just to move about mundanely, wiping surfaces, lifting coffee cups. And an image of Rosie strikes him – her arched back and bright, green dress – that warms his blood for just a moment, surprising and disturbing him.

But he can't say yes, though part of him wants to. He can't trust anyone. Certainly not her.

The kitchen looks like a bombsite. He can't remember how it got like this. Perhaps he doesn't see things properly these days – the bowl sitting on the draining board, the saucepan waiting to be rinsed. Maybe he does things without even realizing – he's tipped a whole load of stuff over the kitchen table and can't for the life of him recall when or why.

Callum slows his breath, as though there might be someone listening. There's a bit of washing up that's been waiting a little too long, and the window pane is smeared and he couldn't say when it was last cleaned. But these things alone are not, in fact, what's bothering him. It's the table, covered in bits of card and paper and God knows what. As though someone's taken a wastepaper basket and emptied it all over the place. Disorientated as he is, he can't have been that careless. He thinks again, is sure of it. Someone else has been here.

Callum sits at the table, steadies his hands and his nerves. If this rubbish is of any significance, there's certainly no obvious logic to it. But perhaps he should be more thoughtful, start looking for clues. The back of his neck prickles. But nothing makes much sense.

There's a corner of an envelope with a half-torn off postmark, a crumpled business card of some doctor, a shopping list nearly in fragments. He lifts the paper and peers at it with forensic attention. Something about it smells fresh. The person who's been here was a woman.

Callum's brow furrows – tense, then relaxed again. He sits back in his chair and lets his shoulders drop. A huge guffaw rumbles outwards, through his belly, throat, mouth and nose. Of course a woman's been here. Rosie, when she stayed here after him.

Now Callum regards the fragments with a renewed curiosity. He wonders who the recipient of the letter was; who the business card belongs to. Does that perfume fill her whole handbag, could he smell it on her skin?

And then he sees something else – a thicker shinier piece of paper. It's folded over, but more neatly. He picks it up and spreads it flat. Two thinner scraps of paper escape and float away like leaves – a receipt for some cosmetics and a chit for a hotel room. But this pamphlet – it's a schedule from the lecture tour Rosie was telling him about. He scans it with interest, noting the dates and venues for readings. May 18th – San Francisco. And the hotel chit's for the same date – The Plaza, San Francisco.

A small frisson courses down his spine. *May 18 – San Francisco*. The hotel chit covers that week. Rosie was telling the truth. He cannot say for sure if she's cottoned on to his suspicions, but no matter what his questioning, she's got a genuine defence. At the time he was attacked, she was miles away, across the ocean.

For a moment Callum stops, ever the lawyer, wonders whether to place full reliance on this evidence. Has she planted it to mislead him, could it be a double bluff?

But surely not – there was no way she could have planned this haphazard scene. And her own mother's illness – the conspiracy couldn't possibly extend to that. Besides – he's smiling now – the way she keeps things, then forgets them. It's so very much like Rosie. He feels a little skip behind his heart.

So she's been telling him the truth – she was on another continent when he was attacked! This spiral of violence is nothing to do with her – perhaps she really can be trusted. Certainly, he'll have to come right out with it, and ask her finally about the island, but when he thinks about it, after all, has he ever known anything for certain? It was always Anthony who'd had it in for her, who'd been so determined to believe she was a killer, and in the madness following Claude's death, they'd all resolved to cut ties with Rosie. But isn't it true that grief brings with it insanity? You'd never want the freshly bereaved on your jury. It's been absurd – for all these years, they've assumed her guilt and never spoken to her.

Callum runs into the hallway, an odd stirring in his stomach. He dials hurriedly, clumsily, getting the wrong number first time round.

'Rosie? It's me again.' She sounds confused and pleased to hear him. 'What you were saying earlier. About you coming over. Well, I've been thinking about it. What I said. I've changed my mind.'

21

It's the oddest feeling; Callum doesn't quite know where to look. He fixes his eyes on Rosie's white fingers. They're ridiculously small; you can forget how fragile a woman she is, and then you measure her against the rest of the world and realize how much bigger everyone else is. He doesn't look her straight in the face as he offers 'let me get that'.

She releases her fingers and puts the case down. He lifts it up for her, lugs it over the threshold.

'Blimey, this is heavy. Have you brought the contents of your entire wardrobe?'

She turns aside, speaks through half-closed lips.

'That's all my work stuff. Didn't you notice – it's the smaller case.' He's not sure if she's made a joke. She looks the tiniest bit uncomfortable. 'I came because you wanted me to, Callum. You can use someone around right now. It needn't be too long.'

There's an edge of defiance about her, like some hurt that's never quite left her. In that second he wants to touch her, but the moment's not quite right. His whole body softens with the sense of apology.

Rosie sits on the bed in the guest room. Not the room Callum's mother had; that would just be too weird. The air in there smells thick and stale, as though remembering her dying body. But here, in this small, almost L-shaped room, at the corner of the house with the pretty corniced alcove. It's not the room she really knows, but it has what she likes most, a luscious view of the garden.

You forget, with such huge houses, you can go for hours without bumping into someone. Since arriving as Callum's house guest, it's as if she's hardly seen him. She thought he was getting friendly, then he seemed to pull away again. Now she can hear him clattering about doing something domestic downstairs. It feels a little as though they're children, hiding out in a strange mansion.

Rosie bends towards her suitcase, which she's slid under the bed. There are a few clothes in there which she hasn't yet taken out, they remain packed and folded, and she's uncertain what she'll do with them. The green dress is among them. She shudders at the memory of it. But she won't unpack it. It would be so wrong to shake it out and place it on a hanger. Like wanting to second-guess fate, only to set it spinning out of control.

Beside the suitcase, there's her smaller bag. In it she's got her work files, plus a few things a little more personal. That one she'll keep well hidden, pushed back behind her sandals. Not that Callum would pry – he's too self-involved to be drawn to others' secrets. But after what he's been through, you never could tell.

Here he comes now – she hears his footsteps on

the staircase. He pauses on the landing, a loose floorboard heaves beneath his tread. She can sense him hovering, pulling away and then approaching again. Rosie zips up the work briefcase and places it neatly out of view. She tries to strike a pose that suggests she's preoccupied, one leg tucked beneath her buttock, an open notebook on her knee. The crescendo of footsteps starts again. Callum materializes in the doorway.

'Rosie.'

He's half-turned away from her, so she can't see him full face. But the slant of his features is of someone avoiding something. From his slumped, lumpen posture, she fears something unpleasant.

'Thanks so much for putting me up in here.' She smiles at him lightly. 'It's a really lovely room, this. How are you anyway? You don't want to talk this morning?' No mention of the green dress, rustling archly in the case beneath the bed. Or the stretch of empty corridor that runs between their separate bedrooms.

'Will's arriving tomorrow.' Callum's looking at the floorboards. 'From Ireland. Hopefully he'll help sort things.'

She nods. 'I remember him.'

'And also later . . . Rosie, this is awkward. Shona'll be here with her man. And she'll be bringing the kids. I haven't told them yet. It's going to be hellish.'

She tries to be sensible. 'That's tough. Just take it slowly.'

'Look. I don't quite know how to say this, but

when they come, I'd prefer it . . . I mean I think it would be better if they didn't know you were here. I mean they're going to be very confused. Perhaps if you went out, just for a little while.'

The heat rises in Rosie's cheeks, but she bites her tongue.

'Of course, I understand. I was thinking of going out just now.' She turns her face away from him, blinking out into the garden.

*

Callum opens the door slowly. He already misses Rosie. How is it possible to get used to someone so quickly? He's not really concentrating so he gets a slight shock.

'Cal, old boy,' says Anthony. 'I was just passing. I hope you don't mind. I had to call to see if you were all right.' He leans forward and softens his voice with the conspiracy of the grief-stricken. He places a hand on Callum's shoulder. 'Dear boy, we're all so sorry.'

Callum brushes the hand away as though flicking away dust. This time, there's no mistaking his colleague: the high voice grates loud and familiar. Anthony, oblivious to his discomfort, strides inwards.

'I won't outstay my welcome, Cal. Just wanted to make sure you're looking after yourself. Eating and sleeping OK. Can I get you something now?'

Anthony moves into the kitchen with an unaccustomed bustle. Callum winces but says nothing.

'Well, you're not looking too bad, all things considered. I know it's a terrible cliché, but life must go on, eh?' Anthony's pupils are darting all over the place. It's not clear if he's embarrassed or if this is his usual social gaucherie. His clattering quietens for a second and he clears his throat portentously. He's facing out towards the window and now he turns his head back slowly.

'Actually, Callum, I don't want you to get the wrong idea about this. Of course we're all thinking of you. But that's not the only reason I've come.'

'Oh? Surely not more of my clients defecting to you?'

'Ha. Very good.' Anthony gives a false laugh. 'But seriously, Cal. I called round the other day. Someone was in your house. I saw them running away.'

Callum shakes his head slowly, realizing just how tired he is. 'You were here the other day? What are you talking about – you saw some burglar?'

'Well, I don't know what they were up to, but it all looked pretty suspicious. I thought you should know about it. The thing is, Cal, we know this person.'

'Anthony, what are you talking about?'

'Cal, this isn't easy. But I'm pretty sure I'm right. The person running away was your old pal, Rosie Verner.'

Callum swings back in his chair. Flares of anger prick his cheeks.

'You've got this wrong, Anthony. Rosie and I are back in touch. Whatever you thought you saw, I can assure you you're mistaken.'

Anthony's arched eyebrows climb halfway up his forehead. 'Have you taken leave of your senses? Have you forgotten what Rosie did all those years ago?'

'Nothing was ever proven. The court's verdict was accidental death.'

Anthony's voice rises hysterically. 'But that court was a shambles. You said so yourself at the time, repeatedly. Rosie should never have got away with it.'

'I know that's what I said at the time, but looking back on it, I'm not so sure. We were all so upset by Claude's death, it was as though we were caught up in some crazy nightmare. You were so convinced it was all Rosie's fault it seemed profane to disagree, and what I'd seen from the balcony – it all fitted, I couldn't forget it. But now, all these years later, I can't believe we never gave her a chance.'

'There was no point in asking Rosie anything. We agreed on that. She'd only have lied and tried to poison things further.'

'We never tried,' says Callum quietly, 'so we'll never really know.'

Anthony struggles vainly to control his trembling vocal cords. 'Callum, you're not thinking straight. Never mind what the court said, we know what happened on that island. And now Rosie's back, and she's acting suspiciously again. I'm telling you I saw her in your house, running away. She was coming down the side-path. She clearly wanted to remain hidden.'

'Look, there is a perfectly innocent explanation for why Rosie was coming down the sidepath, but I don't have the energy or the inclination to explain to you now. And why exactly are you so keen to dump her in it anyway? Oh, and more to the point, perhaps you can tell me why you were spying on my house in the first place.'

'I came only as a well-wisher at a time of profound grief.'

'Well, that's odd, because, as I recall, when you called round my mother wasn't dead yet.'

Anthony recoils like a faulty jack-in-the-box. 'Do keep things in perspective. We all knew about the accident already.'

'Well, I thank you for your good wishes, but perhaps you'd like to go now. You can use the front entrance.'

Anthony's face changes, his features even more angular.

'You be careful, Callum. Don't let your feelings blind you. That woman, she's no good, she's got rottenness in her bones.'

Anthony holds his palms out like a preacher in a pulpit. Callum turns his face aside. He lets the other see himself out.

*

Rosie's feet sink into the soft soil beneath the grass. She's not wearing walking shoes, just the sandals, but there's no time to regret the mud. Once, when they were lovers, Callum asked her how many men she'd had. She equivocated, feigned the sophisticate, said she'd even dated a married man. It was only later she realized that, like all men, he'd prefer an innocent.

Perhaps he still sees her like that, forthright and unseemly, slightly soiled. For here she is, even now, invited in and then turfed out. She closes her eyes, conjures his features, but she can't see beneath the skin. She hugs her cardigan tighter, bends her head against the drizzle.

It's almost dark. The long summer is on its last legs, dusk a little earlier each day. Callum's walking over the familiar heath to forget the afternoon. Anthony prying and poking, surprised, sulky Rosie, but most of all the pale, bewildered shock of the children.

Listening to news of her grandmother's death, Saffron screwed up her face and bellowed, but it was Rudy whose dark eyes became hollow and dismayed. He clamped his lips tight in defiant, tearless silence, and when Callum tried to touch him he turned his face and ran away. He hid himself somewhere in the house and they almost didn't find him until James scoured the whole place and found him cowering in a wardrobe.

'We'd better take them home,' said Shona, as soft as she'd sounded when he'd first met her. 'Let's speak again later. You look shattered, Callum. I know this is difficult, but just try to relax. Take a walk. Have a bath. Then go to bed.'

It was vintage Shona: her soothing counselling, intimate and conspiratorial. For a moment it was as though there were just the two of them, him scarred and wretched, her the comforter. For that second James looked ousted, a redundant third party, out of place. The walk to the heath was perhaps unusual therapy but only the fresh air has made him feel sane again.

Now, on his return, the hall is shrouded in shadow. He doesn't know if Rosie's back – perhaps she's flounced off for good. She was right to feel put out. It'd be nice to have her here, to share his supper.

Callum flicks the hall light on, but no one stirs or calls down to him. He flings his jacket over the banisters.

At the top of the stairs he turns right into the bathroom. The boiler cranks into life as he turns on the hot water; heat thickens the air and steam mists up the windows. Rosie's left a small glass bottle on the side of the bath; he tips a droplet into the water and his lungs fill up with lavender. He loosens his shirt, pulling it down across his bare back; walks across the landing to undress in his bedroom. He slides out of his shoes and rustles his trousers to the floor. He relaxes his muscles and lies back on the bed.

'Fuck!' Callum's voice comes out so sharp he barely recognizes it. At first there is shock, and then his upper back flares with pain. His spine shudders with resistance and there's the hot, wet release of blood.

His fingers search for the wound's source and come back dirty scarlet.

Callum snaps his body straight and squints down at the bedspread. There, staring up at him, is the photograph that went missing. The surface glass is splintered into protruding, jagged triangles, the frame is smeared with something foul. Callum brings the picture closer. He stares for seconds at each figure and then he has to catch his breath. His own face has been torn out and replaced by a blood stain.

Callum flings aside the photograph and stands up to get dressed again. He pulls the wardrobe door open. Twisted hangers collide. A mess of torn shirts greets him, some literally shredded. He wrinkles his nostrils at the smell of fresh filth.

Scrambling back into his worn clothes, he runs barefoot on to the landing. Downstairs, he hears the telephone, but does not go to answer it. He ignores the running bathwater and the cold against his bare skin. There's a sound that might be a key turning, but no sign of anyone entering.

Down the short stretch of corridor, the door to Rosie's room is ajar. He says her name hoarsely but the room is neat and empty. Callum goes over to the bed and his bare foot hits something hard. He winces, recoils and looks down at his bruised toe.

There's a bag and a case rustling under the bed. The suitcase is partly open and he glimpses several pairs of knickers; the smaller one is sharper, harder, the one he'd laughed at for being so heavy. He crouches down to open it, recalling Anthony's grim warning.

Nothing here, after all, no more than Rosie herself said. Just stacks of ringbinders, sheaves of paper and notebooks. But there's an appalling, illicit pleasure at peeling back Rosie's privacy. He lifts out a ringbinder and starts to leaf through it.

The first page is blank, and he thinks this file's not been used yet, and then he turns another page which feels thicker, uneven. It's been soaked through with glue: Rosie uses this as a scrapbook. She's lined up a whole range of pictures and news cuttings. Some from local press, some national, some original, some photocopies. Callum gulps down cold air, he reads haltingly, out loud. *Heath attacker strikes twice. Police seek help with Squires killer.*

Callum pauses, shakes his head, at the memories of a summer's killing. Page after page turns over more of this gaudy obsession. Then he heaves the whole case out and flings it open violently. He opens file after file, but everything else is innocuous. The turning of papers makes a sharp, deafening flapping. He searches desperately for some reason for Rosie's twisted souvenirs. And then just as he's about to stop, he comes across the box.

It's small, wooden and pretty, subtly coloured and carved. For some reason it's obvious that this is a woman's thing. It's full of mementoes, telling a tale of girlish hoarding – little pieces of jewellery, beribboned papers that must be love letters. But that isn't all. There's also a small key.

Callum picks up the key and rolls it around in his palm. It is blackened and dulled, so you can tell that it's old. But what's important to Callum is that this key is so familiar. To be more exact, it's the key to his garden.

He falls back on to his haunches. This is something Rosie's kept from childhood. So easy to forget that she also once lived here. He'd never even considered whether anyone had ever changed the locks. She could slip in through the back and sneak around undetected.

Callum bites down on his thumbnail, searches for that old, dependable intellect. The lecture tour, the hotel chit – were they part of some deception? He tries to imagine he's back in court, where he could always think on his feet. Somewhere down the corridor, bath water is overflowing and elsewhere, downstairs, there's the chink of a key. Callum doesn't hear, or if he does, he doesn't care. He slaps a palm against his forehead. How could he be so stupid?

All the clues Rosie left had told him she had been away – not just on the day of the heath attack, but for the whole of that week. She'd told him she'd come over to see her sick mother. But how could he have forgotten? The very day after the attack, when he'd come back from the doctor's surgery – she'd visited him then. At the time he'd thought it was Shona, but even then he'd felt uneasy. The visitor had talked of speaking to Simon who'd left his Chambers years ago: it was a concocted story to wrong-foot him, told by someone hiding something. Yet Shona had no need to deceive him. It must have been Rosie: finding him near-blind, cheating his eyes but betraying herself still. And if she was lying about that she could be lying about anything.

Callum rises to his feet slowly, forehead creased in concentration. And then he hears the bath still running, and light footsteps coming closer.

22

Rosie crosses the threshold and the smell of the lavender hits her. It's the smell of her own bathroom when she's escaping, relaxing. But at the same time there's too much of it, a suffocating sweetness. Somewhere in the middle distance there's the rush of white noise, like an untuned TV or a miniature waterfall. There are no downstairs lights on, but Callum's jacket's slung over the banisters. She leaves her handbag on the side shelf, places the jacket on a hanger. She makes sure the sleeves don't crease. Her fingers shake, just perceptibly.

Halfway up the stairs she calls out to him – 'Callum'. The white noise is nearer. She's starting to recognize it. Callum doesn't call back to her, yet she knows that he's there. The passageway is warm, and the air spliced with that lavender, and there's also a scent lingering that she knows from his skin. Like he's been walking around without clothes on. The bathroom door is ajar, she prods it lightly with her fingertips. The air starts to smell musty and water's pooling on the floorboards.

'Callum?'

She bends to turns the taps off. In here, the smell overwhelms. Water slides in through her sandals.

The thick, damp air curls her hair. He's here but something's happened. Why else forget a running bath? She turns and heads for his bedroom.

'Callum?'

The door is closed and there's no answer to her knock. But there's a cough from down the corridor and the sputter of pages turning. It's coming from her guest bedroom. Her heart begins to sink.

The closer she treads, the heavier her skull feels. The cough comes again and the sound of Callum's throat clearing. Now she can see the bedroom door open.

'Callum?'

His back is turned towards her, his body slumped at the edge of the bed. His unbuttoned shirt has slipped down from his shoulders. She digs her nails into her palms. All around him are her cuttings.

'Callum?'

On this fifth, final calling, he turns his head slowly. His eyes are thin slits of anger. Her skin turns hot and prickly. It should never have been this way. His jaw is so tense he can't speak. The smell of lavender lingers like some lost, remembered danger.

She speaks to him softly.

'I suppose you've found out then?'

He can't see her. His vision, skewed and weeping, is literally blurred now. Moisture slicks over his eyes. He's almost crying real tears. He doesn't know if it's fear, or grief or regret.

Rosie expands and contracts, glowing scarlet, draining bloodless. Her features clash and jumble – the wide-set eyes, the burnished hair. She's tiny, but not so tiny, from certain angles she's elongated. She's an approaching female ghost, now like Rosie, now like Shona. He tries to listen to her voice, but each word's a flat, discordant note. He stands up as she treads closer and he can see how sharp her nails are.

'What's all this about, Rosie? Were you really so bitter?'

'Not bitter.' Her voice is soft. 'Just mindful. I don't forget.'

'*You* don't forget.'

'Callum. I loved you. We were young, but I really did. You were there, and then you weren't. I tried to reach you, but I couldn't. And you never explained. But, yes, I've always kept your letters, and now each little detail matters.'

'But the attack – these newspaper cuttings.' His voice trembles with indignation. 'Have you turned into some mad obsessive or were you always like that?'

'Callum, don't say it that way.'

Her features slide and swim in front of him as she comes a little nearer. One hand is raised towards his cheek, the long and shiny fingers glinting. He catches her wrist and pulls her inwards. With the pad of his thumb he can feel her pulse. Sweat glistens on her upper lip and her breast rises and falls.

'You know you won't get away with this.'

The flesh above her collarbone quivers.

'I'm not trying to get away with anything.'

'You thought I wouldn't find out.'

'I thought, in the end, it wouldn't matter.'

There is quiet between them, except for the beat of their breathing. Hot water gurgles in the pipes as though a brook were running through the room. Warmth rises off her skin. He stretches one arm out tentatively, snaps it into the small of her back. He jerks her slight weight in towards him. She judders like a doll.

'Bitch! You fucking bitch!'

'Callum. What the –'

Her skull swings back on her neck, perspective twists and squashes her features. She gives a strange, strangled grunt as though her airways no longer work. With his other hand he encircles her, his fingers roaming like a groper's. They travel the slide of her pelvis, the slope from breast to waist to hip, hunt in the folds of her clothing, dig deep into her pockets. The soft pad of one finger is pricked by something sharp. Callum yelps, makes a fist round it, dragging it outwards.

'Callum, what are you doing?'

He turns the metal nail file in his palm, holds it close up in front of her.

'What's this? One of your weapons? Neat, this one, nice and small.' He jolts the file forward, the sharp tip of it touching the corner of her brow bone. Her eyes squeeze shut, instinctively. She gives a small, high scream.

'It's a nail file, for God's sake. I use it for – guess what? – filing nails. Callum, would you mind telling me what this is about?'

He presses the sharp tip closer, till it draws a tiny thread of blood. One eye looks elongated, distorted by the bloodline.

'God, Rosie. You're an evil one. Still trying to play the innocent.'

'Callum, please.' Her voice is small – he's finally succeeded in scaring her. 'You're clearly upset. Can't we talk about this?' She's got it all worked out.

He leans slightly away from her, so they're no longer skin to skin, but he's still got both arms round her, and he looks down at her fiercely.

'What's to talk about, Rosie? You've come back and destroyed my life. You've taken away what I love most, and you've shattered my existence. What we had was so long ago – how could anyone still be so bitter?'

Her mouth moves and her body writhes, but he holds her still and close and silent.

'You see, at first I was suspicious of you, but then I started to believe you were my friend. And then I found your pervy scrapbook, and your charming box of souvenirs. And I've had a little while to think about it, and it's all starting to make sense.'

'No!' The word spurts out of her like a gas jet. 'Surely you don't think – Callum, I'd never do anything to hurt you.'

'You are so, so sick. How else d'you explain that scrapbook?'

'Callum, I can see now what you're thinking, but this isn't what it seems.' Her voice is quieter; she fights for breath. 'Try and see things from my point of view. I came back here, after so long, and I'd never stopped loving you. By an amazing coincidence I found you were living in my old house. I came round that time to visit you, and it felt like stepping into another world. You couldn't even see me, but still I felt something between us. Then it turned out one of my patients was the widow of Christopher Squires. I found out about the murder and it was as though fate were sending me all these links to you. I started looking up old newspapers, trying to find out what had happened, and that's when I started the scrapbook. I can see how it makes me look like some mad obsessive old harridan, but things around me were surreal. Can't you imagine how it felt for me?'

'Very good, Rosie. But not quite good enough. I've also found your old key – the one to the garden gate. You kept it all these years. You're the only one who could sneak in like that – you or someone else you gave it to.'

'Callum – it's what you said. It's nothing more than a souvenir. You know how I love this house. It's all that's left of my childhood. When I found out you lived here now, I could hardly believe it. It sent shivers down my spine. But I never broke in here.'

'It's too late for all this, Rosie. I've really got your

number. The weekend my children visited – you were here just before them. That weekend they were poisoned. You had the chance to tamper in the kitchen. Do you really expect me to believe that all this is mere coincidence?'

Words tumble out of him, each one slipping into the next. His heart beats so hard it's as though he's been running too fast. Rosie pulls a little closer, looks up at him, imploringly.

'Please, Callum. Stop this madness. This is a crazy conspiracy theory. You're clearly not well. But we can sort this out.'

He shakes his head at her and snorts. He almost wants to spit. 'Not how you planned this, is it? But I don't think I'm the mad one here. All these years I've been your dupe. Even after what happened on the island, I still gave you the benefit of the doubt.'

His hands move up from her waist, till they border her breasts, then he brings them slightly inwards, his palms on her collarbone. She gives a thin, stifled gasp and he thinks she can't breathe. Her head lolls from side to side and a film of tears fills her eyes. For a moment he thinks he's killed her and, alarmed, he pulls back; not like this, not so soon, this is not how it must be. Salt water trickles down her cheeks.

'It's a bit late for crying now, isn't it? You killed Claude Portman all those years ago. Left his corpse on the island beach. You didn't show much regret then.'

Rosie's lips make a loop like a flaccid rubber band.

She makes another strange sound, like you might hear from someone drowning. He presses his palms down harder. Her jaw tenses as if some puppeteer were pulling her strings tighter.

'Oh . . . dear God . . . is that really what you thought?'

'And even when confronted with it, you don't have the grace to admit it.'

Flecks of spit leap from his tongue, land like glitter on her cheeks. Her voice is so hoarse he can hardly hear what she says.

'Claude Portman was a bastard. He abused me as a child – right here, in this garden. You of all people should understand. But I didn't kill him.'

'That's funny, because his dead body was found on the beach. Something happened to him in the forest – I saw you running out of there with my own eyes. And then you disappeared. Yet another coincidence?'

'We had an argument in the forest. He attacked me and I pushed him. I ran away without looking back. If he fell it was an accident. I'd been planning to leave the island anyway. I never even knew he was dead.'

She's crying properly now, her voice coming out in sodden, staccato sobs. Her eyes are beaded with water, rimmed by swollen, salty red.

'You're giving this a really good go, Rosie. But I'm sorry, it doesn't work any more. I know all about you from Anthony. He told me all those years ago.'

'For God's sake, forget Anthony. You know he's always hated me. I think it's because of Claude, who poisoned him against me for his own reasons. But, Callum, you have to listen. This is not how it seems.'

He bends closer, so close he could slide his tongue along her cheekbone. The skin beneath his fingers is turning purple with the pressure. There's still a skinny line of blood from where he cut her with the nail file, but all the teardrops make the blood run so her face looks warped and stained.

'Jesus, Rosie. You killed Claude, you killed my mother, you killed Christopher Squires, and you want to kill me. You knew what I did for a living and you hunted down people who hate me to help you in your quest. And you can't even admit it.' Anger spreads over his skin, as hot and thick as scalding tar. Not only does he fail to see properly: he cannot hear, or feel, or think. His forearms, wrists and fingers tense and stretch all by themselves. Beneath their wild grip, Rosie's malleable as wax.

She stops breathing, she stops crying, her body goes very still. A sheet of silence slides between them. He pulls her face right up to his. He thinks perhaps, if he looks close enough, his vision might come right again – but he's wrong, he still can't see her, she's just a puzzle of crooked lines. She did this to him. He may never see properly again. He balls one hand into a fist.

There's an odd, sudden splitting noise as though his hand had moved independently, and he sees his closed fingers knock hard against her cheekbone. Her skull rolls sideways from the impact. He sees her jaw drop. A rivulet of spittle dribbles out from her mouth. He's never hit a woman. His heart races noisily.

Rosie gives a low groan. She tries to raise a hand to shield herself. He cuffs both wrists with his fingers. Then he pulls her in once more, so he can smell her sweet skin. Breath and adrenalin course together through his body. He flings her, hard, away from him, her body splaying against the wall. It's like she's a wooden puppet, with all the joints bending. He can almost hear her bones rattle. Her face sinks into her shoulder.

He lifts his hand again, then stops. She can do him no more harm now. A tiny part of him softens, just wishes it weren't true.

'I just don't understand why you did it. Surely you're not that twisted. I just can't believe . . . if you could only say sorry.'

Her face is still turned away from him and he thinks perhaps she can't move it, but her chin trembles upwards and she stares out under swollen eyelids.

'You said yourself there were other people involved in this – someone you found in your garden. I know nothing about them. And the week you were attacked – I was still in America. Callum, I can prove it.'

'Liar! Your proof counts for nothing – I've already worked it out.' He pulls back his open palm, brings it down with a full, fat slap. 'You see, at first it didn't make sense. But then I remembered. That first visit you paid me, just the day after it happened. I thought it was Shona, but even then she sounded different. Said she had a cold. Won't you stop at anything? And she said she'd spoken to my clerk, but she got his name wrong, she said Simon. Simon left years ago. Does he ring any bells with you, Rosie?' Her face spins once again. 'You see, you're clever, but not that clever. No doubt you'd find a way to reach my clients. You know plenty about my career. I don't think there're any limits to your deceit.'

She cowers back up at him. Strands of her hair are caked in blood. They scratch her skin like sharp splinters. Who knew pain like this existed? It runs in faultlines across her brain, like the sharp pulse of electricity. Her skull is brittle as an eggshell. She doesn't dare to move her head.

Callum's somewhere above her, like a skyscraper that might tumble. She can still smell his salty smell. Her tongue is thick and rubbery. She wants to say something, but her throat is raw and sticky. The taste of blood comes from somewhere. She doesn't know where the words are.

Callum's chest heaves. He's not speaking, not moving. She moves her lips, slides her tongue between the ridges of her teeth. She thinks she can still form words, just.

'Please, Callum, stop. I can't take any more. You'll kill me.'

His bare feet move slowly. Maybe he's going to

kick her. She doesn't look at his face. She can hardly see any more, anyway.

'Why shouldn't I?'

Because of Toby, she could say. *Because there's the sweetest three-year-old boy somewhere on the other side of the Atlantic who one day wants to see his mummy again. Because it's not worth it, you'll make yourself a murderer, you'll ruin your life even more. Because you're Callum, and I loved you once, and you're not supposed to act this way.* She tries to lift her face, to look at him, but the pain spins and crackles and smothers her. There's a low noise that rises slowly, and then she realizes he's speaking.

'There's one thing I want from you, Rosie. I want to hear you say sorry.'

She doesn't really understand him. Perhaps he'll kill her anyway. But she can't fight any more. Her words are all whispers.

'Oh, God. I'm sorry.'

And then – then, she doesn't know what. Her eyelids close and she's in blackness. She feels a blow across her crown and the darkness fizzes mauve and scarlet. Rough hands slide into her armpits and her body is hauled upwards. Her skeleton jangles at every joint. She squeezes her eyelids tighter.

She can smell Callum's breath, if she could put her fingers out she'd touch him. She can still remember – just about – his body beside her, between cool sheets. She tries to conjure pine and citrus, but there's just fading lavender, filth and blood. He's heaving, lifting, shifting her body like a sack of toxic rubbish. There might be humiliation, were it not submerged by so much pain. She feels a drop, an uneven sliding, as her body bumps away from him. Her stomach's wheeling up above her. She cradles her breasts, protects her heart.

The bumpy descent stops. Her eyes are still closed. She senses Callum still beside her, then he moves her again. There's the sound of a door opening, and a blast of cold, wet air. Arrows of light rain sting her skin. The ground is soft, the earth clammy.

The door thuds, a car passes, she can no longer smell Callum. She doesn't want to see anything – she can't open her eyes anyway. Exhaustion creeps over her like a sodden, rotten blanket. It's way too cold for late summer. Every sound is far away.

That might be someone passing – it could be Callum returning. Or they could be the footsteps of a stranger. Or the dustman, come to bag her up.

23

Nothing makes much sense, but it doesn't matter anyway. Callum's eyes are really hurting now and the house is full of ghosts. Phantoms of the dead, but also of the living. His mother smiling down at him, calmly cutting bread. A brazen youth hunched in the bushes. A small pale girl with wide green eyes.

There is a perfect symmetry to it all, and surely now anything is possible. So artfully did Rosie plan this, so obsessive was her drive, that she managed to track down and touch the lives of East and Lansdowne and Freedman. Tap into the underworld which fed him, but which could turn and bite at any moment. There's no limit to her scheming. She's made a lifetime's passion out of it. *Hell hath no fury* doesn't even begin to describe it.

He must have really hurt her. But she's probably not dead yet. Probably she'll recover. Somewhere, in the recesses of his lawyer's mind, he knows the force he used was disproportionate. But then – what the woman's done to him. Whoever on this earth would blame him?

Now he must telephone the police, it's the last piece of the puzzle. He won't go and move her, or try and hurt her any more. Just leave her where she is. She's too broken to get back to him. Let chaos linger just a short while. The evidence must tell its story.

Callum walks into the hallway. It feels as chilly as a morgue. Summer's really ebbing away now: the long, balmy days will recede. The months will scamper toward winter, with its drab skies and slow, dull evenings. And then that'll be another year gone, with so much starkly sad reflection. Wondering where another slice of life went, denying those extra few grey hairs.

But this season's changed everything. His fingers stray towards the telephone, but he finds he can't dial just yet. Behind his tired eyes, memories jostle. He'd never really forgotten Rosie.

Of course he'd pretended. Shona had known all along there was something about this house – some magnetic pull, some link beyond tall windows or old fireplaces. She'd known about Rosie, but only as an irregular, youthful fling. Then she found out from Anthony about the childhood friendship and the house.

'I've always known it Callum. You love this house more than you love me, and now I know why.'

The discovery came surprisingly late in their marriage, and it'd been almost over by then anyway. But then he came home late one evening, and saw her sitting at the kitchen table, with her arms folded like a schoolteacher and her lips pursed with odd primness. There was a sour shadow in her eyes as though she'd suffered one last betrayal. He told her his love for Rosie was long lost, but he could still recall her shape, her sound, her smell. It had never been entirely possible to blot out that island memory.

As he lifts his right hand to dial, his fingers are still trembling. After all these years as a defence barrister, making the call goes against the grain. But then this isn't just shopping someone. He's very nearly been murdered. And Rosie's not like Tyrone Freedman – some misunderstood, neglected youth. She's had privilege, she's had chances. She acted out of choice, or madness, or both – an evil too vast to be captured by words.

His fingers clamp the receiver, but still Callum hesitates. Should he try DC Fletcher, or simply dial 999? But he might not get DC Fletcher, and time is of the essence. He extends his index finger, a door rattles closed behind him. He holds his breath and counts to three, twists his head over his shoulder.

Pain cracks at his skull and the floorboards lunge up at him.

Rosie opens her eyes. The agony sharpens, subsides again. She can hear her breathing, her heartbeat. It is a surprise to be alive.

She had thought she was imagining things, but here she is, and this is real. The light rain coats her skin like a layer of damp clothing. She stumbles to her feet. There is so little time left. The garden gate is unlocked, it swings open easily. She grasps the handle, lurching forward, like a lost swimmer scrambling ashore.

*

Not for the first time that day, Callum is crying. Great circular, salty teardrops, that fall and splatter on the floorboards. One of them hits his foot, as though he's walking in the rain. *Walking barefoot in the rain* – the cliché comes to him and he laughs. His shoulders shudder slightly.

'What's so funny?'

A disembodied voice rumbles at him as though from very far away. Another blow cracks at his cheek. Pain tingles down to his jaw. The skin on the back of his legs smarts raw, a reminder of his assailant dragging him up the stairs. His hands are tied behind his back, his ankles bound, like an errant slave. His attacker's flesh, inches away, smells hot and frightened, like his own. But there's also the smell of cold rain, flooding inwards like autumn. And something else, slick like petrol, smooth and oily with intent.

'Nothing to say to me?' says the voice. 'Like: *How could you do it?* Or *I can't believe it's you*. Or perhaps: *I knew it all along*.'

Callum's head is hurting. His hand still aches from the fight earlier. He's thinking of the schedule in Rosie's handbag. A woman visiting, the day after his accident. The voice doesn't want to let him dream on. It wants him to live the moment. Feel the heat, eat the shit. Thick fingers wrap around his jawline.

'Look at me, Callum. Look at me.'

Callum's eyes are like a bloodstained lens, but he doesn't need them any more. He knows the voice and smell, even the fingers. He opens his throat, but his voice is quiet.

'Fuck off, James.'

'Funny,' says James. 'You don't sound too surprised.'

'Should I be?'

'You tell me. I thought you had other prime suspects.'

James's face is like a jigsaw that's been put together all wrong, but that baring of woolfish teeth is probably his version of a smile. Callum jiggles his wrists in their makeshift cord cuffs.

'You're not going to ask me then? How this all fits together?'

James's breath fills Callum's nostrils. Callum turns his face away. He doesn't need to ask why. It's all too ghastly, too obvious. He's seen the fits of raging impulse, the background stare of simmering jealousy. Knows the chillingly smooth proficiency, the determination to track human prey. Callum inhales wheezily.

'No. I'm not surprised.'

James lifts Callum's crushed hand, presses it in his own. Their fingers interlace.

'I didn't think you would be. You must have known – after all – that Shona kept on thinking about coming back to you. She wouldn't say so outright, of course, but I knew her so well, you see. The way she'd fidget with her fingernails after she'd dropped the children off to visit you, or when she was telling off the children she'd crow, *Whatever would your daddy say?* And the way she spoke to you today, like she'd never really left you. The thought of her leaving me – I just couldn't ever let it happen.'

Two of Callum's vertebrae snap together. The strange oily smell is thicker, nearer.

'You're such an easy man to destroy, Callum. A man in your line of work has so many enemies. I wanted to get me a few helpers, which was why I stole your computer, and of course I knew about all your cases, from all those years spent tracing witnesses for you.'

'Yes, of course,' says Callum, dully. He concentrates on the shirt that James is wearing. It's of a loud and lurid check, the colours flickering and oozing like stains. There's aftershave on James's skin that overlays the smell of sweat.

'Obviously I knew about Jamal East. We did that case together, remember? I remembered you representing him, and I knew that he would hate you.'

For the first time, perhaps, Callum really is surprised. 'But Jamal East's trial was years ago. You and Shona weren't even . . .'

'Do you think my love for Shona just happened overnight? Do you think when you've loved someone for years, wanted them and watched them while someone steals them from you, that you don't store up each tiny, relevant detail?'

Callum breathes softly. His mother was right all along. James did his job so well because he brought a grim obsession to it, getting right inside the minds of the brutes he followed because he was not so different from them himself.

'So. You found East. Who put you on to Freedman – no doubt you paid them. And of course Jason Lansdowne couldn't possibly instruct me any more. Quite a little gang you had there, working against me.'

'I don't think it's wise to belittle us like that.' James, still holding Callum's fingers, bends them backwards from the palm. 'After all, we made quite an impression on you, didn't we? Pity about Tyrone, turned out not to be so bright. Killed the wrong person on the heath. Then got caught in your garden. At least he was willing, though. You'd be surprised how difficult it is to get people to kill to order, even if it is for handsome wages. Of course I found you on the heath myself, but your dog barked and there was someone coming. Had to leave it for another day.'

'And my mother, and the children, for God's sake. That was all down to you.'

'The children just got a tummy ache. I knew they'd get over it. The important thing was, Shona blamed you. But it's a real pity about your mother. She brought it upon herself, of course. Always looking down her nose at me, and being so chummy with Shona. Not only did her death hurt you, but it was pretty useful to get rid of her.'

Shona, thinks Callum, had suspected all along. That's why she'd visited him that day – she'd never phoned his clerks – but she'd suspected James of something, and was there to check up on Callum, to warn him. *Look after yourself, Callum. And for God's sake be careful.* But James must have been reassuring. He had recast himself as a peacemaker, suddenly turning reasonable over the children. Somehow Shona's suspicion – and her concern for Callum – had faded.

James blows on his fingertips. The oily smell is getting closer. There are stars in front of Callum's eyes as though he's walked into a cartoon. From an almost invisible pocket, James extracts a slim cigar. The other hand produces a lighter. It's like he's performing in a magic show.

'I'm right in saying, aren't I, that you've never been one to smoke. Under the circumstances, though, I don't suppose you'd mind . . . ?'

It's much colder now, and Callum's bones shake, there's a wet patch on the crotch of his trousers. The sickness rises in his gullet and his eyes fill up with salt.

Dirt gathers beneath Rosie's nails as though she were a bare-handed rock climber. The skin on her finger-tips is ragged and oozing. Pain doubles her over, so that sometimes she walks, sometimes crawls. The house pulses with light and shade. She smells the smell of petrol.

She hears the voices from upstairs, but knows she

cannot make it upwards. Callum's crying out in pain, his pleas bleeding through the air to her. The other man's voice is hard and flat, his words cut up by slaps and crunches. Once, she hears his footsteps, the same steps she heard in the garden. A figure stomps out in the corridor, the floorboards bowing, creaking rhythmically. She hears a door slam, water flushing, a fizzing tap, then more stomping. The man goes back across the corridor. She ducks instinctively for cover. She had thought, after what happened, that by now she would be past fear. But blood courses in her cheeks, reminding her she wants to live.

She reaches for the telephone on the antique occasional table. The signal's dead, just like in a movie. She knows she doesn't have to do this. She views the door, the drive, the pavement – the outside world that beckons, welcomes. Upstairs, the voices harden. There's more indeterminate thrashing. She makes it back up to her feet and searches desperately around her.

There, sitting neatly on the side shelf, she sees something she'd forgotten. Her handbag is waiting for her, exactly where she'd placed it earlier. She rummages through its contents, trying to control her errant reflexes. There are her keys, her phone, her wallet – her passport back to her old life. The battery's still running on her mobile.

She lengthens her spine, just like in yoga classes, and clears the clogged phlegm from her throat.

Callum opens his eyes. The heat crackles like folding paper. The skin on his face itches and burns, and he imagines pink-white roasting to a blood-red. His back hurts. If he moves just an inch it's like he's spread out on pin heads. His fingers scrape the sharp stones. He's lying on gravel.

A gloved hand strokes his cheek. His skull moves, but just barely. The hand steadies his jaw bone. The clumpy fingers are gentle. Someone swathes him with a blanket, the fabric laid down slowly, softly. It strikes his skin like flint on sandpaper. He lets out a little wince.

'All right, sir?'

There's a voice above him, but he's not sure where the accompanying face is. The cry of sirens fills the air. Staccato bursts of blue and white light flash and fade against his eyelids.

'You're going to be fine, sir. It's a real escape you had. Someone up there's on your side, sir. Lucky we got here so quickly.'

Somewhere else, across the gravel, the small stones slip and slide and spit. Someone's struggling vainly. He hears James's voice.

'Oi, get off me! You've got this all wrong.'

And there's someone else, a voice he recognizes.

'Mr Steadman, I'll be the judge of that. You may care to exercise your right to silence.'

It's DC Fletcher, he thinks he knows the slightly stooped, diffident posture. And he can see his hair and the contour of his features. Or is he just imagining this clarity?

'Lie back,' says the paramedic. 'Let's get you into the ambulance. Once we've got you to the hospital, you'll be right as rain in no time.'

In his swathed, prone position, Callum feels as good as shackled. But his mind's roving freely, and it doesn't yet make sense.

'How come I'm here? How come you saved me?'

'Someone called the Emergency Services. Wouldn't leave their name. Must have seen the smoke. Be thankful for good neighbours.'

'But the house is burning badly. You must have got here really quickly.'

James shouts and writhes as DC Fletcher cuffs and uncuffs him, reluctantly handing him over – just for now – to the paramedics. Surely he'd have tried to escape as soon as he set the house alight. Whoever made that phone call must have done it before the fire started.

Callum's lungs fill up with air and his teeth and tongue spread wide.

'Rosie,' he cries out, but her name is lost among the mayhem.

*

Rosie's managed to find her car. She'd never have thought she could still run. Thank God she's parked up in front of a thick hedgerow, away from the direct view of wide, uncurtained windows. Her upper body lurches forward and she retches violently. A thorny branch tears her face as she straightens herself again.

Luckily, it's not too far to drive home. She thinks

she can make it. She squeezes into the driver's seat and examines herself in the rearview mirror. Ghastly, really. Quite hideous. But then again, after an application of concealer and mascara, no more ghastly than many a woman recovering after the night before. OK, it's the wrong time of day for a hangover. But considering what she's been through, she doesn't actually look too bad.

She turns the key in the ignition. The engine growls into life. But then she slumps forward on to the dashboard. Perhaps this driving thing's not such a good idea, after all. She slithers back out on to the road.

Rosie hugs her jacket tighter, tries to hide the rips and stains on her dress. And the last thing she wants is to slip inside her sandals. She keeps her arms folded primly hoping maybe she'll look normal. Nearer to the main road it's not too hard to hail a taxi. A cab pulls up – the driver looks at her as though assessing a bad smell, but after giving her the once over, he decides to let her in.

'Elm Grove? But that's just near here, you could walk it. I'll have to do a minimum charge.'

She thinks that might be against the law, but it hardly matters right now.

'I'll pay triple if necessary. Just get me home, please.'

The cab driver doubles back, weaves away from the high street. The road curves back to where she's run from, winding sharply round the heath. Plumes of ash grey fill the sky. The call of sirens deafens. Rounding the corner, the vehicle stalls; the driver puckers his lips and whistles.

'Blimey, someone's been careless about where they threw the fag ends.'

Rosie manages a smile. The taxi driver cranes his neck.

'Looks like I might have to do a detour then, love. Don't mind, do you? Little journey but it could take longer than we thought.' He pauses, restarts the engine. 'Pity, innit? Lovely old houses.'

The taxi turns and pulls away from the blazing, crackling house. Rosie can't resist it. 'I grew up here,' she says. 'Actually I know someone who still lives here. Right nearby, just where those flames are.'

'Really?' The driver wheels round, impressed, as though she's said she's related to some celebrity. 'D'you want to drive round? Maybe take a closer look.'

Already, at the bottom of the hill, the lime police cordons stretch like bunting. Queues of motorists and pedestrians are beginning to gather.

Rosie sits back in her seat, makes sure her jacket still covers her dress. Her pulse is racing like an athlete's, but the acute pain in her body is already subsiding. The cab screeches downhill, and then swerves right, just yards from the police cordon, and she sees the outline of a figure, tall, dark-haired and hesitant.

Everything's all right, she thinks, *he's not been hurt in the fire. He'll look over and catch sight of me, run to thank me, say how wrong he was.*

But the outline's shifting – she's wrong, it's not him, it's only the shape of a stranger.

'Just drive on,' she says. She keeps her eyes on the road ahead.

NOWHERE'S CHILD

By Francesca Weisman

Penguin £6.99

On a deserted London street late one evening in 1980, a beautiful young woman is brutally murdered. When Detective Smallbone is called to the scene he's surprised to discover that he recognizes the victim: she's a model, a rising star.

Yet his investigation proves fruitless. The killer left no clues, her past is a blank and no one seems to know who she really was. But just as the pressure on Smallbone is at its height, the case takes a surprising turn . . .

Away from the crimes of the city, a young autistic boy called Kit is living alone with his mother. For Kit the world is unfriendly and strange, but he knows that as he grows up he must somehow find his place in it . . .

Many years later, Kit comes to London, trying to make sense of himself and searching for some answers. His quest leads him to an ageing Detective Smallbone – and the case of a murdered model in 1980 . . .

Read on for a taster . . .

NOWHERE'S CHILD

[illegible] Williams

[illegible]

[illegible] beautiful [illegible] which [illegible] [illegible] [illegible] supposed to answer that [illegible]

[illegible]

[illegible]

[illegible]

[illegible]

PROLOGUE

She disappeared hours ago.

You've been here so long, humped and stooped behind the refuse, you might almost have forgotten why you came. The sick-sweet stink of the place swells inside you, and your hooked knees and shoulder blades strain against cramp.

The discomfort is so great, the watching through squinting eyes and the waiting, that you're almost ready to give up, abandon the whole idea. Who, after all, could ever have guessed it would come to this? And then, just as you unfold your elbows and steady your sore, bent thighs, there is the sound of a door creaking open then closing again.

She sways into view at the edge of the pavement.

Wine has blunted her senses, made her stupidly bold. She must have heard your footsteps, and the rustling rubbish as you straightened, but she's blasé and untouchable, snorting out tendrils of smoke. Still, your footsteps keep up with her, break her rhythm, draw level. They do not quite match hers. She turns back again.

Freezes.

For a second, she thinks of running, makes an amateur lunge for it. Her torso jerks forward, but your wild arms bring her close. She steps backward, begging.

– Please. God, please. No.

You step closer, bringing her into your body like a lover.

Your palms press tight upon her collarbone and the blood starts to drain. The surface of her throat purples and her nostrils funnel air with a high, peculiar whistling.

– Please. No. I'm sorry.

She's down on the ground now, her legs kicking out gracelessly. Film glazes her dulled eyes. Her lips slacken fatly, like unfashioned plasticine. A stream of bile smears her chin, a liquid filth stains her underskirt.

– Oh, God. Please. I haven't said anything.

Her pleas fail to soften you as you bring out the small knife. The blade works beautifully, like an extension of your fingers, not like rigid steel at all but strong and agile as a snake. You carve through the soft, shallow flesh and her sad, thin legs spasm. The blade travels downward, chasing the trail of the breastbone, slicing the rise of flesh either side, still stirred by faint breaths. Blood crimsons the blouse where it strains over her nipples.

Now back up for the last lap: past the dead pout of her lips, following the jut of cheekbone and brow bone, skirting nostril, then eye. The open mouth belches a warm, putrid gas. The blade zig-zags the eyelid, scoops lightly at the jelly.

One whimper, one final twitch beneath the pelvis. And then it's over. She's gone, face turned down on the pavement. A dustbin lid tumbles and clatters, the corpse merges with its surroundings; the indeterminate rotting stink, the oily film in the gutter. She's become a messy meal for feral cats, a curiosity for pigeons.

A curtain stirs, is drawn again: a distant car stereo crescendos, then fades.

And then the quiet street is empty. No one the wiser.

I

1984

Kit lived with his mother in the small quiet house which nestled at the apex where the road curved round. Its brittle windows shone like shrewd eyes in the sunshine. Whilst playing in the garden he'd sometimes peer inward and watch his mother's shadow move in the low-ceilinged hallway.

He didn't begin his search in earnest until he was past twenty, but his sixth sense started working well before then.

Kit developed a habit of watching his mother, of monitoring her progress from rarely more than seven paces. He marked the curve of her neck as she bent to wash the dishes, the plunge of her fingers into the thick, soapy water. He followed the pattern of veins on the back of her hands as she crouched to lace his shoes, or tucked his shirt into his waistband. Often he'd wake early and listen for her footsteps: for the gurgle of the shower and her sweet, throaty singing. She loved to listen to the radio and sing along with it, and once he caught her unexpectedly in her pyjamas skipping round the room.

When she realized he was spying she came to an abrupt halt, but then carried on, only more softly now, scooping him up in her arms so that he travelled the room giddily with her. He reached out with small, four-year-old fingers and touched the softness of her skin.

On a cold autumn morning he woke well before breakfast. His stomach howled as noisily as the bathroom pipes in winter and his mouth watered with the wish for butter melting into toast. Weak, dappled light strained on the other side of the curtains, and on the tiny L-shaped landing the floorboards creaked twice.

In unslippered feet, Kit slid from the bed. He wandered half-blind through a pattern of shadow. Opening the bedroom door was like lifting a veil of secrecy. From down the narrow stairs, which had in those days seemed endless, he heard half-muffled grunts followed by a few beats of silence, then a sing-song goodbye and the clink of the front gate. Without understanding, he felt exposed to vague danger. He held his breath and retreated, not quite closing the door. And, like a creature from cartoons he'd seen, he peered through the crack.

His mother came bounding up the stairs in a long, flowing robe. Her cheeks were flushed pinkly as though she'd been walking through air-frost. As her bare feet hit the landing, she let her long robe fall open. Her pale body startled him: the strange pointiness of the breasts with their blatant, rosy nipples; the shallow dip of her belly towards a triangular shock of hair. She trailed a heavy, sweetish smell, like the flower beds in summer. Kit dived for the bedclothes as his room door flew open.

Shocked by his own trespass, his breath quickened to hiccoughs. His mother drew near to the bed and pulled down the blankets. Her face hovered above his: sharp-nosed and upside down, the inverted cheeks strange and squashy, the brows heavy and knitted. He wished he could say sorry, but only the hiccoughs came out.

'What's this, little man? Have I caught you spying on me?'

He thought of a nursery rhyme book with a boy whose thumbs had been cut off with giant scissors. Her nail was sharp on his cheek and her breath hot and stale. The finger hovered and pressed, ready to scratch or perhaps pinch him.

'Do you know what happens to nosy children? Who comes and gets them?'

Kit tried to squirm down to the dark cocoon beneath the blankets. His hiccoughs were high and rough now, hurting his chest. But then his mother's hand loosened and her heavy brow lightened. Her face broke into a smile and she gave a long, loud laugh. He didn't understand, but suddenly his breathing grew easy. He let her crowd in and cradle him in the crook of her shoulder.

Although men often stopped to stare at her in the street, Kit's mother appeared to lead a solitary existence. In the small neighbourhood where they lived at the edge of the suburb she kept herself to herself and there were things she would not do. She did not stop for long chats with the fruit seller when she went to buy apples, or drink cups of tea in the café with the other women who had pushchairs.

Once Kit went with his mother to a restaurant a long way from the neighbourhood. He asked her where they were, and she vaguely explained 'town', but didn't add anything further and appeared somewhat distracted. None of the women here had pushchairs and some wore long coats and tight gloves. The two or three children present had soft voices and clean faces. One tall woman walked past and gave such a sour look that Kit wondered if her food had been rotten and she had pains in her stomach.

'Support the workers against Tory privatization, love?' asked a young man who had just breezed in off the streets, wearing a hairy black jacket and clanking a large plastic jar. The tall woman's face crumpled so Kit knew her stomach must now be in agony, and Kit's mother raised her eyebrows, and then laughed softly and slipped the young man a coin.

'The other half, eh?' he said, and blushed just detectably, and carried on staring at her. Kit thought his mother looked pleased, but her smile faded to a far-off lost look, and she quickly gathered their coats to leave.

Kit learnt of buses and trains which led to Town, away from the clusters of slow shops and orange bricked houses, far from the park with its low trees and beds of trimmed shrubs. But it was to prove a very long time before he went there again himself.

Now and again his mother took a bus into Town alone, and left him for the afternoon with a sitter called Miss Dickenson. Miss Dickenson had pink skin and white, wispy hair; there were a few whiskers on her chin and she had poor hearing. He asked Miss Dickenson where his mother was, but she didn't say much apart from a casual, hand-waving reference to shopping.

'Can I go too?'

Miss Dickenson sucked her teeth (which might have been false) and adjusted her glasses which were made of pink plastic.

'You'd better ask your mother. Are you allowed to eat Mars Bars?'

'Will I get punished?'

'Ah, not just this once.'

His mother scolded him if she caught him with sweet, sticky traces, but it was worth it for the lingering after-taste of chocolate in his mouth. He would always worry, though, that if he had the chocolate then by some quirk of fate he would be deprived of the soft toys or Matchbox cars his mother would come home with. Then again, sometimes she'd come empty-armed and he'd wonder why she'd bothered to go shopping at all.

Once, in the living room, he asked if she would take him. She turned her face to the window and started fiddling with her hair. When she turned back to him, her skin was all reddened, and she lifted him, and kissed him.

'Maybe. When you're older.'

Kit never looked much at his reflection until just after he started nursery school. The boys in the playground were the ones who made him do it. Two of them, Danny and Robby, as he sat apart watching them. Their games were raucous and bloody-kneed, their shins covered in grazes. He preferred to watch the pigeons and the sunlight in the trees, but they pulled him to his feet and gurgled with laughter. One of them spat at him.

'Stinky Kit. Kit stinks!'

They circled their eyes with their fingers, and gurgled harder and nastier. Miss Jones came and scolded them, and shook her head sadly.

'Children. *Children!*'

She took Kit inside and he was allowed to go home early.

Later, he stood staring at the mirror in the bathroom. His eyes stared back, wide and clear: one green and one blue. If he lowered his lids and squinted, his vision would blur, and his face became a mess of features in strange, terrified disorder. They were as senseless as the letters on the flashcards or the fearsome snickers of schoolchildren.

From the kitchen, up the stairway, came the sound of rushing water, roaring in and washing over him as he stood drowning in the moment. Half-blind, he hit the mirror, yearning to straighten his reflection.

'Kit,' called his mother, 'are you ready to come down?'

His eyes widened; the vision sharpened: he was normal once more. So what if one of his eyes was a different colour to the other?

His mother had the clearest eyes, he could stare at them all day.

Thanks as ever to Faith Evans, to Beverley Cousins, and to my mother and sister for their interest and encouragement while I was writing this.